IN THE NIGHT OF TIME

IN THE
NIGHT

TIME

ANTONIO MUÑOZ MOLINA

TRANSLATED FROM THE SPANISH BY
EDITH GROSSMAN

HOUGHTON MIFFLIN HARCOURT

BOSTON • NEW YORK   2013

For information about permission to reproduce selections from this book,
write to Permissions, Houghton Mifflin Harcourt Publishing Company,
215 Park Avenue South, New York, New York 10003.

www.hmhbooks.com

Library of Congress Cataloging-in-Publication Data is available.
ISBN 978-0-547-54784-8

Book design by Chrissy Kurpeski
Typeset in Minion

Printed in the United States of America
DOC 10 9 8 7 6 5 4 3 2 1

For Elvira

What I am now I owe to you.
— *Ford Madox Ford, The Good Soldier*

In the events in Spain I see an insult, a revolt against intelligence, non-rationality and uncivil primitivism unleashed to such an extent that the foundations of my own rationality are shaken. In this conflict, my judgment should lead me to rejection, to turning my back on everything reason condemns. I cannot. My affliction as a Spaniard dominates everything. This voluntary servitude will be with me forever, and I can never be an exile. I feel all things Spanish as my own, and even the most odious must be endured, like a painful malady. But that does not prevent me from understanding the disease that we are dying of, or more precisely, the disease we have already died of; because everything we might say now about the past sounds like something from another world.

— *Manuel Azaña*

Can it be true that our country is shattered, life suspended, everything unresolved?

— *Pedro Salinas*

IN THE NIGHT OF TIME

1

Surrounded by the confusion in Pennsylvania Station, Ignacio Abel stopped when he heard someone call his name. I see him first at a distance in the rush-hour crowd, a male figure identical to all the others, as in a photograph of the time, dwarfed by the immense scale of the architecture: light topcoats, raincoats, hats; women's hats, the brims at a slant and small feathers on the sides; the red visored caps of porters and railroad employees; faces blurred in the distance; coats open, the coattails flying backward because of an energetic pace; human currents that intersect but never collide, each man and woman a figure similar to the rest and yet endowed with an identity as undeniable as the unique trajectory each follows to a specific destination — directional arrows, blackboards displaying the names of places and the hours of departure and arrival, metal stairs that resound and tremble beneath a gallop of footsteps, clocks hanging from iron arches or crowning the large vertical calendars that are visible from across the station. It was necessary to know it all precisely: the letters and numbers bright red like the caps of station porters that day in late October 1936. On the illuminated sphere of each of the clocks, hanging like captive globes high above the heads of the crowd, it is ten minutes to four. At that moment Ignacio Abel moves through the lobby of the station, through the great expanse of marble, high iron arches, and dirty glass vaults filtering a golden light where all the dust floats alongside the clamor of voices and footsteps.

I saw him with increasing clarity, emerging out of nowhere, almost a figment of my imagination, holding his suitcase, tired after dashing up the staircase at the entrance, through the oblique shadows of the marble columns, and into that enormous space where he might not find his way in time. I distinguished him from the others, with whom he almost merges, a dark suit, an identical raincoat, a hat, clothes perhaps too formal for this city and this time of year, European clothes, like the suitcase he carries, solid and expensive, its leather worn after so much traveling, covered by hotel and steamship-company stickers, the remains of chalk marks and customs stamps, a suitcase that weighs a great deal for his hand, aching from gripping the handle so hard. With the precision of a police report and a dream, I discover the actual details. I see them rise in front of me and crystallize at the very moment Ignacio Abel stops in the powerful currents of the crowd and turns, as if he had heard his name: someone must have seen him and shouted his name in order to be heard over the clamor, amplified by the marble walls and iron vaults, the resounding confusion of footsteps, voices, trains, the vibration of the floor, the metallic echoes of the loudspeaker announcements, the shouts of newsboys yelling the afternoon news. I feel through his mind just as I feel through his pockets or the inside of his suitcase. Ignacio Abel looks at the front pages of newspapers expecting and fearing to see a headline in which the word "Spain" appears, the word "war," the word "Madrid." And he looks at the face of every woman of a specific age and height, foolishly hoping that chance will allow him to see his lost lover, Judith Biely. In the lobbies and on the platforms of train stations, in the sheds of port installations, on the sidewalks of Paris and New York, for the past few weeks he has crossed entire forests of unknown faces that continue to multiply in his imagination when sleep begins to weigh down his eyes. Faces and voices, names, phrases in English that he hears at random and that remain hanging in air like streamers. *I told you we were late but you never listen to me and now we're gonna miss that goddam train.* The voice also seemed to be speaking to him, so hesitant in his practical decisions, so awkward with people, holding his suitcase, in his worn European suit, vaguely funereal, like the suit of his friend Professor Rossman when he first appeared in Madrid. In his overstuffed wallet Ignacio Abel carries a picture of Judith Biely and another of his children, Lita and Miguel, smiling on a Sunday morning a few months earlier — the two broken halves of his life, once incompatible, both lost now. He knows if you look at photographs too many times they no longer invoke a presence. The faces let go of their singularity, just as an article of intimate clothing treasured by a lover soon loses the intensely desirable scent of the one who wore it. In the police-file photos in Madrid the faces of the dead, the murdered, have been so severely disfigured that not even their closest relatives can identify them. What will his children see now if they look through the family albums, so carefully catalogued by their mother, for the face they have not seen for the past three months and don't know if they will see again, the one no longer identical to the face they remember? The father who fled, they will be told, the deserter, the one who chose to go to the other side, to take a train one Sunday afternoon and pretend nothing had happened, that he would return calmly to their summer house the following Saturday (though if he had stayed, it's very likely he'd be dead now). I see him, tall, foreign, thin by comparison with his passport photo, taken only at the beginning of June and yet at another time, before the bloody, deluded summer in Madrid and the beginning of the journey that perhaps will end in a few hours; his movements are hesitant, frightened among all those people who know their exact destinations and advance toward him with an unyielding energy, a powerful determination of husky shoulders, raised chins, flexible knees. He has heard an improbable voice speak his name, but as soon as he turns he knows no one called him, and yet he looks with that same automatic hope, seeing only the irritated faces of people now delayed, enormous men with light eyes and inflamed faces, chewing on cigars. *Don't you have eyes in your head, you moron?* In the hostility of strangers, eyes never play a part. In Madrid right now, looking away from a stare is one of the new strategies for survival.

You better not seem afraid or you'll automatically become suspect. The voice actually heard or only imagined in a kind of acoustical mirage has produced in him the response of a man about to fall asleep who thinks he has tripped on a step and either wakes startled or sinks back into sleep. But he knows he has heard his name with absolute clarity, not shouted by someone who wants to attract his attention in the noisy crowd but softly, almost a murmur, Ignacio, Ignacio Abel, a familiar voice he can't identify but is on the verge of recognizing. He doesn't even know whether it's the voice of a man or a woman, the voice of someone dead or alive. On the other side of his locked door in Madrid, he heard a voice repeating his name in a hoarse, pleading tone. There he stood in silence, holding his breath, not moving in the dark, not opening the door.

In recent months you can no longer be sure about certain things, can't know whether a friend, seen a few days or only hours ago, is still alive. Once death and life had clearer, more precise boundaries. You send letters and postcards and don't know whether they'll reach their destination, and if they do, whether the one who should have received them is alive or still at that address. You dial the telephone and there's no answer, or the voice at the other end belongs to a stranger. You pick up the receiver to speak with someone or get information and the line is dead. You turn on the faucet and water may not come out. The customary, automatic actions are canceled by uncertainty. Ordinary streets in Madrid abruptly end in a barricade or a trench or a heap of rubble left by an exploded bomb. On the sidewalk, turning a corner, you can see in the first light of day a rigid body pushed against a building that served as a blank wall for a firing squad the night before, the half-closed eyes, the yellowed face, the upper lip contracted into a smile that reveals teeth, the top of the head blown off by a shot fired from a few inches away. The phone rings in the middle of the night and you're afraid to pick up the receiver. You hear the elevator motor or the doorbell in your sleep and can't tell whether it's a real threat or only a nightmare. So far from Madrid yet Ignacio Abel still thinks of those fearful nights and months of insomnia, fearful nights in the pres-

4

ent tense. Distance doesn't cancel the verbal tense of fear. In the hotel room where he has spent four nights, the deafening noise of enemy planes woke him; he opened his eyes and it was the rattle of an elevated train. The voices continue to reach him: who has called his name just now, as I saw him standing motionless in his open raincoat, holding his suitcase, wearing the anxious expression of someone who looks at clocks and signs afraid he'll miss a train; what absent voice imposed itself above the uproar of real life, calling him, Ignacio, Ignacio Abel, urging him to run faster or to stop and turn around and go back?

Now I see him much more clearly, isolated in that instant of immobility, encircled by sudden gestures, hostile looks, the rush of the crowd, tired after working in offices, hurrying to catch trains, driven by obligations and trapped by the spider webs of relationships he lacks, like a vagrant or a lunatic, though in his pocket he carries a valid passport and in his hands the train ticket and his suitcase, the battered yet still distinguished suitcase I can almost see as if through Ignacio Abel's weary, avid eyes. I see the hand clutching the leather handle, feel the excessive tension of his grip, the pain in his joints from repeating this action for over two weeks, when the same figure of a tall, middle-aged man, now lost in the crowd, walked alone at night along a street in Madrid where the streetlights were out or broken or painted blue and the only light filtered through the closed shutters of a few windows. The same figure, cut out of the photograph of Pennsylvania Station and inserted in a Madrid street, Calle Alfonso XII perhaps (the name was changed and for a time it was called Niceto Alcalá-Zamora; now it has been changed again and is called Reforma Agraria), or walking past Retiro Park fifteen or twenty days earlier on his way to the train station, staying close to the walls, his suitcase banging against the corners as he tries to disappear into the shadows. In the silence of a curfew, an approaching car can mean only danger, even if all your documents are in order. He would have to know the exact departure date, but he hasn't kept count of the number of days he's been traveling, and time moves away very quickly in the past. A city in the dark, besieged by fear, shaken by the sound of battle, the engines of planes that approach but are still no more than an echo of distant misfortune. He looks at one of the clocks hanging from the iron arches and calculates that for several hours it has been night in Madrid, as the minute hand advances with an identical spasm in all the illuminated spheres, jumping from eight to seven, a stroke of time like an urgent heartbeat, the step one takes into the void on falling asleep: seven minutes to four; the train he's supposed to catch leaves at four and he has no idea where to go, which of the paths intersecting in the crowd like currents on the ocean's surface is the one that will carry him to his destination. As in a lucid dream, now that he has turned I can see his face, close, just as he saw it this morning after wiping the steam from the mirror at which he was going to shave in the hotel room where he spent four nights and to which he knows he'll never return. Now the doors close forever behind him, and his presence disappears without a trace. He walks along the hotel corridor, turns a corner, and it's as if he'd never been there. I saw him shave this morning at the mirror over the sink in the room he knew he was finally about to leave, thanks to the telegram he'd received a few hours earlier, the one lying open on the night table, next to his wallet and his reading glasses and the letter handed to him yesterday afternoon, the one he almost tore up after he read it. *Dear Ignacio, I hope this letter finds you well your children and I are fine and safe thank God, no small thing these days though it seems you haven't worried too much about finding out how we are.* The telegram contains a brief apology for the days of waiting, as well as information regarding the train and its departure time and the name of the station where he'll be picked up. The letter was written and mailed almost three months ago and reached him at this hotel in New York owing to a series of accidents he cannot quite explain, as if the very density of the rancor its words exhale (rancor or something else that for the moment he prefers not to name, or doesn't know how to) guided it in its dogged search for him. Nothing is how it once was, and there's no reason to think that after the upheaval things will go back to the way they were. A letter sent to Madrid from a village in the Sierra is lost en route and it takes not two days but three months to arrive after passing through Red Cross headquarters in Paris and an office of the Spanish postal service where someone stamped the envelope several times: *Unknown at this address.*

Ignacio Abel has been away from his home in Madrid for so short a time and already he's a stranger. I see the envelope in the light of the lamp on the night table in the gloomy room where the noise of an elevated train sounded regularly. Once again Ignacio Abel packed the suitcase lying open on the bed, and shaved more carefully than in recent days now that he knew people were expecting him, that at six this evening someone would be on a platform trying to make out his face among the passengers getting off at the station with the strange Germanic name printed now on his ticket: Rhineberg. He'll get off the train and someone will be waiting for him. He'll hear his name and a part of his suspended existence will be reimposed on him. It matters a great deal to him not to cave in, not to let himself go, to fight with small acts of resistance the entropy of solitary travel, to tend to every detail as one does when constructing a building but forgoes in the sketch of its model. He must shave every morning, though the shaving soap is running out and the razor is losing its edge and the badger brush its hairs, one by one. He must do what he can to keep his shirt collar from looking soiled. But he has only three shirts and they're wearing out from so much washing. The cuffs and collars are fraying, the creases in his trousers are becoming threadbare, his shoelaces are unraveling. He was fastening his shirt this morning and discovered that one of the buttons had fallen off, and even if he could find it, he wouldn't know how to sew it back on. I see Ignacio Abel as if I were seeing myself, with his maniacal attention to detail, his incessant desire to understand everything, his fear of missing something of consequence, his anguish over the passage of time, its crushing slowness when it becomes waiting. He feels his face after shaving, rubbing it with a little lotion from the almost empty bottle he brought from Madrid, and I feel the touch of my fingers on my face. On a journey things wear out or are lost and there's no time to replace them, or you don't know how or how many days are left before you reach your destination, how much longer you'll have to make your increasingly meager funds last, the bills in your wallet, the coins in your pockets, the trifles kept for no reason and eventually lost: subway tokens or telephone slugs, a train ticket, an unused stamp, the ticket stub from a movie house where he waited out of the rain and watched a film not understanding a word of what was said. I want to enumerate these things just as he does on many nights when he returns to his room and methodically empties his pockets onto the night table as he used to empty them on the desk in his study in Madrid, his office at University City; I want to search Ignacio Abel's pockets, the lining of his jacket, the inner band of his hat, with the touch of his fingers; listen to the clink in his raincoat pocket of the keys to his house in Madrid; know each object and each paper left on the night table and dresser in the hotel room, the ones he has kept as he hurried out to Pennsylvania Station and the ones left behind that will be tossed into the trash by the cleaning woman who makes the bed and opens the window to let in the October air that smells of soot and the river, laundry steam and cooking grease: transient things that contain a fact, an indelible moment, the name of a movie house, the receipt for a fast meal in a cafeteria, a calendar page that has a precise date on the front and on the back a hurriedly scrawled telephone number. In his study, in a drawer he always locked, he kept Judith Biely's letters and photographs along with any small object that had something to do with her or had belonged to her — a box of matches, a lipstick, a coaster from the Palace Hotel nightclub with the circle made by Judith's glass. People's souls are not in photographs but in the small things they touched, in the ones that bore the warmth of their hands. With the help of his reading glasses he searched for her through the columns of tiny names in the Manhattan phone book and was moved when he recognized it among the names of so many strangers, as if he had seen a familiar face in the middle of a crowd or heard her voice. Close variants complicated the search: Bily, Bialy, Bieley. In one of the wooden phone booths that lined the back of the hotel lobby he asked for the number listed next to the name Biely and listened to the ring, his heart racing, afraid he would hang up the moment someone answered. But the operator told him there was no answer and he remained sitting in the booth, receiver in hand, until someone's banging on the glass pulled him out of his self-absorption.

Extreme precision matters. Nothing real is vague. In his suitcase Ignacio Abel carries his architect's diploma, signed by Professors Walter Gropius and Karl Ludwig Rossman in Weimar in May 1924. He knows the value of exact measurements, the calculations of the resistance of materials, the balance between contrary forces that keeps a building standing. What could have happened to the engineer Torroja, with whom he liked to talk about the physical foundations of construction, learning disturbing facts about the ultimate insubstantiality of matter, the demented agitation of particles in the void. The sketches in the notebook he carries in one of his pockets will be worthless if they're not subjected to the illuminating disciplines of physics and geometry. What were the words of Juan Ramón Jiménez that seemed like the summary of a treatise on architecture? *The pure, the precise, the synthesizing, the unambiguous.* Ignacio Abel made note of them on a slip of paper and read them aloud at the Student Residence during the lecture he gave the previous year, October 7, 1935. Nothing occurs in an abstract time or a blank space. An arch is a line drawn on a sheet of paper and the solution to a mathematical problem, weight transformed into lightness through the interplay of contrary forces, visual thought converted into habitable space. A stairway is an abstract form as necessary and pure as the spiral of a shell, as organic as the arborescent veins of a leaf. At the top of a wooded hill, in a place Ignacio Abel has yet to visit, the white structure of a library already exists in his imagination and in the sketches in his notebooks. Beneath the iron arches and glass vaults of Pennsylvania Station, in the air flecked with dust and smoke, shaken by the din of concave spaces, the clocks mark a precise time: in a rapid spasm the eye barely perceives, the minute hand has just advanced to five minutes to four. The ticket Ignacio Abel holds in his lightly sweating left hand is for a train that leaves at four from a platform whose location he still doesn't know. In the inside pocket of his raincoat he has the passport that was on the night table next to his wallet this morning, and a written, stamped postcard he forgot to mail in the hotel lobby is

9

now in a jacket pocket next to the letter he didn't tear into pieces. *Two children growing up without a father at their most difficult age and in these times and my having to rear them all alone.* The postcard is a color photograph of the Empire State Building seen at night, with rows of lit windows and a zeppelin moored to its splendid steel spike. Every time he traveled he sent daily postcards to his children. He's continued to do so this time but doesn't know whether they'll reach their destination; he writes the names and address as if repeating an incantation, as if his obstinacy in sending the cards would be enough to prevent their being lost, like the impetus and aim with which one fires an arrow, or the meticulous resentment with which his wife enumerated each of her complaints in writing. *Dear Lita, Dear Miguel, this is the tallest building in the world. I'd have liked to see New York from the sky, up in a zeppelin with you.* In the ink-blue sky of the postcard a full yellow moon and conical reflectors illuminate the futuristic silhouette of the dirigible. Postcards and letters go astray now in the convulsive geography of the war. Adela's letter and the telegram temporarily rescued Ignacio Abel from his gradual nonexistence in the hotel room, where for four days the telephone didn't ring and no one said his name or even had the most incidental conversation with him. He also carries in a pocket the belated welcoming telegram from Professor Stevens, chairman of the Department of Architecture and Fine Arts at Burton College, the letter in which, through a hallucination of desire, he recognized Judith Biely's hand, if only for a few seconds, as clearly as he heard her voice in Pennsylvania Station. Except he didn't, and the writing doesn't resemble hers at all. Last night, before turning off the light, Ignacio Abel read all of Adela's letter and put it back in its envelope, leaving it on the night table next to his passport and wallet and reading glasses, resisting without difficulty the temptation to tear it up. In the room's imperfect darkness, submerged in the hoarse vibration of the city that enveloped him like the incessant tremor of the ship's machinery during his six-day voyage across the Atlantic, Ignacio Abel watched his wife's old-fashioned delicate writing glide before his eyes, and in his wakefulness the words in the letter took on her monotonous voice with its simultaneous catalogue of reproaches and a sort of indestructible tenderness against which he had no defenses.

After several days of waiting, time again accelerated in a disquieting way. It was almost three-thirty when he looked at his watch, and the train for Rhineberg left at four. It had become so late that he slammed shut the suitcase on the bed and realized only as he was opening the door that he had left his passport on the night table. He shuddered at the thought of leaving without it. An entire catastrophe can be contained in a moment's carelessness. They were less than a minute away from killing him on that night in late July he often dreams about, when a voice saying his name in the darkness saved him: Don Ignacio, calm down, nothing's going to happen. The blue passport with the seal of the Spanish Republic was issued in the middle of June; the year's visa for the United States is dated early October (but everything takes so long, it doesn't seem it'll ever arrive). The photograph is of a huskier man, not exactly younger but less mistrustful, with a less insecure expression and eyes that will always have something furtive about them but rest on the camera lens with serenity, even with a touch of arrogance, accentuated by the excellent cut of his jacket, a crisply folded handkerchief and fountain pen in the breast pocket, the silky gleam of his tie, the obvious quality of his shirt. At each sentry post along the borders Ignacio Abel has crossed in recent weeks, the guards compared more and more slowly the face in the passport to that of the man who presented it to them with a docile expression that gradually grew more nervous. In this accelerated time, photographs don't take long to become unfaithful. Ignacio Abel looks at his passport photograph and sees the face of someone who has become a stranger and ultimately generates no sympathy in him, not even nostalgia. Nostalgia, or rather a longing as physical as a disease, is what he feels for Judith Biely and his children, not for the man he was a few months earlier, and even less so before the war. Ignacio Abel's eyes have seen things the man in the photograph, whose assurance is petulance, or worse, blindness, doesn't suspect. A step away from the future explosion that will turn everything upside down, he doesn't sense its proximity and can't imagine its horror.

Exact details: his passport has suffered the same deterioration as his clothes and suitcase; it has passed through too many hands, received the forceful impact of a good number of rubber stamps. The exit stamp from Spain has the badly printed red-and-black initials of the FAI, the Iberian Anarchist Federation, and the trace of dirty fingerprints. The hands of the French gendarme who inspected it only a few meters away were pale and bony and had shiny nails. His fingers handled the passport with the misgivings of someone who fears an infection. On the Spanish side, the Anarchist militiaman had stared at Ignacio Abel with a glint of threat and sarcasm, with contempt, letting him know he considered him a malingerer and a deserter, and though the militiaman let him pass, he didn't renounce until the last moment the authority to seize the passport that meant nothing to him; the French gendarme, his head rigid above the hard collar of his uniform, had studied Ignacio Abel at length without ever looking him in the eye, without granting him that privilege (it requires training to examine someone's face without meeting his eye). The French stamp, with a polished wooden handle, came down on the open passport with the crack of a metal spring. At every border someone will take his time studying the passport and any other document he feels like demanding, peer over his glasses with distrust, turn to a colleague or disappear behind a closed door, taking the suddenly suspicious document with him — someone who thinks of himself as a guardian, a master of the future of those who wait, admitting some, inscrutably rejecting others, taking his time to light a cigarette or exchange gossip with the clerk at the next table before turning back to the window and examining once again the person waiting, the one who knows he's on the verge of salvation or damnation, of yes or no.

Perhaps today the enemy is in Madrid and the passport is no longer valid. On the floor of the hotel room, beside the bed, Ignacio Abel left a rumpled newspaper that the cleaning woman will throw into the trash without looking at it. INSURGENTS ADVANCE ON MADRID. The news item is three days old. INCENDIARY BOMBS FALL ON BATTERED CITY. In the middle of a sleepless night he listened to a news bulletin on the radio, read without pause in a nasal, high-pitched voice; the only word he could catch was "Madrid." Between the advertising jingles and the whistles of static, the name sounded like a remote, exotic city lit by the brilliance of bombs. Perhaps by now his house is a pile of rubble and the country to which his passport belongs and on which his legal identity depends has ceased to exist. But at least the words "Spain" and "war" and "Madrid" were not on the front pages of newspapers at one of the station newsstands he glimpsed out of the corner of his eye. He looks at arrows, displays; he listens in passing to bursts of trivial conversations that become transparent and seem to refer to him or contain prophecies; one by one he examines the faces of all the women, not because he expects suddenly to see Judith Biely but because he doesn't know how not to look for her. The mellow afternoon twilight descends diagonally through the glass of the vaulted ceiling and traces its broad parallel streaks stippled with dust on people's heads. He tries to ask a porter in a dark blue uniform and red cap a question, but in the confusion his effort isn't noticed. A column of people hurries toward a corridor under a large sign and an arrow: DEPARTING TRAINS.

How long had it been since he'd heard someone say his name out loud? If no one recognizes you and no one names you, little by little you cease to exist. He turned, knowing it couldn't be true that someone was calling to him, but for a few seconds a reflexive impulse continued to affirm what his rational mind denied. The voices of the past, the ones that still reach him in his flight, join in a sound as powerful as the one that echoes beneath the iron-and-glass vaults of Pennsylvania Station. Distance in time and space is their acoustic chamber. He's fallen asleep after lunch one Sunday in July in the house in the Sierra, and his children's voices call to him from the garden where the sound of the rusted swing filtered into his sleep. They tell him it's getting late, that the train to Madrid will come by very soon. He answers the telephone in the middle of the long hall in his apartment and the foreign voice saying his name is Judith Biely's. He walks into the shade of the awning over the café next to the Europa movie house on Calle Bravo Murillo and pretends not to hear the voice behind him calling his name, the voice of his old teacher at the Weimar Bauhaus, Professor Rossman. He has no reason to avoid him but prefers not to see him; he doesn't know that this September morning is the last time Professor Rossman will call him by name on a street in Madrid. His voice is lost in a choral explosion of martial anthems, accompanied by drums and cornets, which emerges from the open doors of the movie theater along with a breath of shade and the smell of disinfectant. But the voice repeats his name, as Professor Rossman pats him on the shoulder, my dear Professor Abel, what a surprise, I thought you'd be in America by now.

Auditory hallucinations (but the voice that spoke his name outside the locked door was not a dream: *Ignacio, for the sake of all you love best, open the door, don't let them kill me*). Ignacio Abel tells himself that perhaps the human brain instinctively hears familiar voices in such situations so that the mind doesn't lose its grip on reality. He heard them this summer in Madrid, at night in his darkened apartment, larger for not being inhabited since the beginning of July, most of the furniture and lamps draped in white cloths to protect them from dust; he didn't bother to remove them. He thought he heard the radio at the back of the house, in the ironing room, and it took him several seconds to realize it wasn't possible, or that his memory had manipulated the sound of another radio in the vicinity and transformed the echo of a recollection into a present sensation. He imagined he heard Miguel and Lita having an argument in their room, or that Adela had just come in and the door slammed behind her. The brevity of the deception made it more intense, as did its unexpected occurrence. At any time, particularly when he abandons himself to restless sleep, the voice of Judith Biely would whisper his name so close to his ear he could feel the brush of her breath. In Paris, on his first morning away from Spain, the unexpected voices combined with the fleeting hallucinations. He would see a figure in the distance, the silhouette of someone on the other side of a café window, and for a second he was sure it was someone he knew in Madrid. His children, about whom he'd heard nothing, played soccer on a sandy path in the Luxembourg Gardens; the day before starting out on his journey, he went to say goodbye to José Moreno Villa, alone and looking older in a tiny office in the National Palace, bending over an old file—and yet now he saw him walking a few paces ahead on the Boulevard Saint-Germain, erect, younger, wearing one of his favorite English wool suits and a felt hat tilted slightly to the side. A second later the illusion disappeared as he came closer to the person who'd inspired it, and Ignacio Abel found it difficult to understand how the deception had been possible: the children playing in the Luxembourg were older than his and in no way resembled them; the man identical to Moreno Villa had a dull face, eyes lacking intelligence, and a suit of mediocre cut. Through the small round window of a restaurant kitchen he saw, and for an instant was paralyzed by, the face of one of the three men who'd come to search his house on one of the last nights in July.

But the experience of the deception didn't make him more cautious. Not long afterward, he again saw in the distance, at a café table or on a station platform, an acquaintance from Madrid, someone he knew was dead. At first the faces of the dead are imprinted deep in one's memory and return in dreams and daytime hallucinations shortly before they fade into nothingness. The bald oval head of Professor Karl Ludwig Rossman, whom he had seen and recognized with difficulty one night early in September at the morgue in Madrid under the funereal light of a bulb hanging from a cord where flies clustered, fleetingly appeared to him one day among the passengers sitting in the weak October sun on the deck of the ship he'd taken to New York: an older bald man, probably a Jew, lying on a canvas hammock, his mouth open, his head twisted to one side, sleeping. The dead look as if they've fallen asleep in a strange position, or were laughing in their dreams, or death came without waking them, or they opened their eyes and were already dead, one eye wide, the other half closed, one eye blackened or turned to pulp by a bullet. Sudden memories are projected in the present before him like photograms inserted by mistake in the montage of a film, and though he knows they're false, he has no way to dispel them and avoid their promise and their poison. Walking along the boulevard that led to the port of Saint-Nazaire—at the end of a perspective of horse chestnut trees rose the curved steel wall of an ocean liner, where a name recently painted in white letters, SS MANHATTAN, gleamed in the sun—he saw a man with a broad face and black hair, dressed in a light-colored suit, sitting in the sun at a café table: through a trick of memory, he saw García Lorca again on a June morning on the Paseo de Recoletos in Madrid, from the taxi in which he was rushing to one of his secret meetings with Judith Biely. One of the last. Distance enlivened the details of memory with the immediacy of physical sensations—the June heat inside the taxi, the worn-leather smell of the seat. Lorca, his legs crossed, smoking a cigarette at a marble-topped table, and for a moment Ignacio Abel thought he'd seen and recognized him. Then the taxi circled Cibeles and drove very slowly up Calle de Alcalá, where traffic had stopped, perhaps for a funeral procession, as there were armed guards at the corners. He looked at his wristwatch and the clock on the Post Office Building; he calculated each minute of his time with Judith that was stolen from him by the slow-moving taxi, the crowd gathered for the funeral with flags, placards, and the convulsive gestures of political mourning. Now he thinks of García Lorca dead and imagines him in the same light-colored summer suit he wore that morning, the same tie and two-toned shoes, dead and curled up like a street urchin in that posture of preparing for sleep displayed by the bodies of some who have been shot, lying on their side with their legs pulled up, face resting on a partially extended arm, sleepers tossed into a ditch or near an adobe wall riddled with bullet holes, spattered with blood.

The same haste he felt then propels him forward now toward the unknown, Rhineberg, a place that is only a name, a hill overlooking a river of maritime width, a nonexistent library that at this stage of the journey is nothing more than a series of pencil sketches and an excuse for his flight. The haste that carried him to his obligations, driving his small car at top speed through Madrid, that made him wake at night, impatient for dawn, distressed at time's passage, the irreparable waste of time imposed by Spanish ineptitude, indifference, and that age-old sullen resistance to any kind of change. Now the haste endures, stripped of its purpose, like the phantom pain that continues to afflict someone who's had an amputation, like the reflexive impulse that carries him to an immediate destiny where he won't find Judith Biely and beyond which he can see nothing: the voices dreamed and real, the minute hand that abruptly advances on all the clocks in Pennsylvania Station, a staircase with metal steps descending into the echoing underground vault where the trains depart, his suitcase in his hand, his knuckles aching, his passport in the inside pocket, touched for a second by the hand that holds his ticket, a conductor who nods as he shouts the name of his destination, a voice drowned by the vibration of the electric locomotive as beautiful as the nose of an airplane, ready to leave with merciless punctuality, roaring like the machinery and sirens of the SS *Manhattan* as it moved slowly away from the pier. Occasionally his haste lessens, but its urgent pang is not erased. The only letup is the moment of departure, the absolution of a few hours or days when you can abandon yourself without remorse to the passivity of the journey, or lie down and close your eyes in a hotel room without taking your shoes off, lie down on your side, your legs drawn up, wanting not to think about anything, not to have to open your eyes again. Soon that period of time will be over, the uneasiness will return: the suitcase has to be packed again or taken down from the luggage net, documents have to be prepared to make sure nothing is left behind. But for now, having just entered the train and taking his seat, Ignacio Abel leans with infinite relief against the window, at least for the next two hours protected and safe. He has placed the suitcase on the seat beside him, and without removing his raincoat touches all his pockets one by one, his fingertips identifying surfaces, textures, the cover and flexibility of his passport, the bulk of his wallet with the photos of Judith Biely and his children and the few dollars he has left, the telegram he will take out soon to reconfirm his travel instructions, the envelope with Adela's letter, packed with sheets of paper he perhaps should have torn up before leaving the hotel room or simply left behind, forgotten, on the night table. There is something he doesn't recognize right away, a fine cardboard edge in his right jacket pocket: it's the postcard of the Empire State Building with a zeppelin moored to the top, which he forgot to slip into one of the letterboxes at the station, each bearing the name of a country in gold letters. He notices now, as he crosses his legs, how dirty and cracked his shoes are, the soles still carrying dust from the streets of Madrid, the hand-sewn soles that are wearing out, just like the crease in his trousers, and his shirt cuffs. The most interesting part of a construction begins when it is finished, said the smiling engineer Torroja, the man responsible for reviewing the structural calculations for the buildings at University City and who had designed a bridge with tall narrow arches like those in a canvas by Giorgio de Chirico. The action of time, the pull of gravity, the forces that continue to interact among themselves in the precarious equilibrium generally called stability or firmness, which in reality has no more substance than a house of cards and sooner or later will succumb to its own internal laws—Torroja would say, aiding the enumeration with his fingers, or a natural catastrophe, a flood or an earthquake, or the human enthusiasm for destruction. The door at the rear of the car opens and a young blond woman appears, slim, hatless, looking for someone, an expression of urgency on her face, as if she had to get off the train before it started moving in less than a minute. For a moment, barely the lapse between two heartbeats, Abel recognizes Judith Biely, re-creates with the precision of a drawing what he didn't know had remained intact in his memory, what exists and is erased without a trace in the presence of an unknown woman who doesn't resemble her at all: the oval of her face, her eyebrows, her lips, her curly hair, a light chestnut color, the red nail polish, her broad shoulders, like those of a swimmer or a mannequin in a display window.

2

THE MIRACLE OF such a sight ends suddenly. That Judith Biely is in the world right now seems as improbable as her appearing in the car of a train about to depart, forcing him to invent the melodrama of her last-minute arrival at the station. He doesn't remember exactly how long ago she left Madrid, but he has a precise count of the days that have passed since he last saw her. He has walked through the city for four days, traveled on streetcars, subways, and elevated trains, and has never stopped looking for her in each young woman who crossed paths with him or whom he saw from a distance, and the repeated disappointment hasn't inoculated him against the hallucination of recognizing her. In Union Square he saw a poster announcing an act of solidarity with the Spanish Republic and the glorious struggle of the Spanish people against fascism, and he made his way through the crowd waving placards and banners and singing anthems only in the hope of running into her. From the deck of the ship he saw the towers of the city emerge from the fog like brightly lit cliffs, and aside from fear and vertigo, his only thought was that Judith Biely might be somewhere in that labyrinth. In the innumerable columns of names in the New York telephone directory, he found hers listed three times; he called two of them, annoyed voices he could barely understand telling him he had the wrong number, and the third rang a long time but no one answered. The mind, however, secretes images and fictions just as the glands in the mouth secrete saliva. Judith running past people in the great lobby of Pennsylvania Station, looking for him, thinking she saw him in any middle-aged man in a dark suit, descending the echoing iron steps with gymnastic agility in spite of her high heels and narrow skirt, and arriving on time. And so he looked for her among the passengers on the express trains about to leave Madrid on the night of July 19, a seemingly ordinary night and not a definitive threshold in time, despite the radios blasting at top volume on the lighted, wide-open balconies, and the crowds shouting down the main streets, and the bursts of gunshots one could still mistake for backfires or fireworks. He'd find her a few moments before her train pulled out, her blond hair billowing from a sleeping-car window in a cloud of steam made iridescent by powerful electric lights, and when she saw him, she'd back down from her decision to break up with him and leave Spain, and throw herself into his arms. Puerile fictions, the subliminal effect of novels and films in which destiny allows the reunion of lovers seconds before the end. Musicals he'd seen with her in the movie houses of Madrid, enormous and dark, smelling of new materials and disinfectant, their surfaces golden under the silver light of the big screen.

They used to meet in one of the theaters on Calle Bravo Murillo, and though it was unlikely anyone would recognize them in a working-class district far from downtown, they entered separately for the first afternoon showing, when the audience was smaller. The bustling, dusty street was hot in early summer and the sun was blinding; all you had to do was walk through the doors lined with garnet fabric and into the artificial delight of darkness and cooled air. It took time for them to become accustomed to the dark, and they looked for each other by taking advantage of the best-lit scenes, the sudden brightness of midday on the first-class deck of a fake ocean liner, the sea projected on a transparency screen, an ocean breeze from electric fans agitating the heroine's blond curls. In the newsreel, two million men carrying olive branches and tools on their shoulders marched along the avenues of Berlin on May Day to the rhythm of military bands. An equally oceanic and disciplined crowd waved weapons, flowering branches, flags, and portraits on Red Square in Moscow. Cyclists with the hard faces of farm laborers pedaled up rocky paths in the Tour of Spain. He searched avidly for her hands in the dark, the bare skin of her thighs; he abandoned himself to the secretive, indecent caress of her hand, her smiling face illuminated by powder flashes from the screen. Insolent Italian legionnaires with black pirate goatees and colonial helmets crowned with feathers marched before the recently conquered palace of the negus in Addis Ababa. Don Manuel Azaña left the Congress of Deputies after his swearing-in as president of the Spanish Republic, dressed in tails with a sash across his distended torso, pale, wearing an absurd top hat and an astonished expression as if attending his own funeral. (Judith had seen the procession pass in the street and recalled the contrast between Azaña's colorless skin in the open car and the red crests of the cavalry soldiers who escorted him.) Ginger Rogers and Fred Astaire glided weightlessly on a lacquered platform, holding each other as they danced in a pose identical to the one on the full-color canvas announcement that covered the façade of the Europa. The evident fakery of the film offered Judith a true emotion to which she gave herself up with no resistance: the mouths that moved without singing, the unlikelihood of a man and woman dressed in street clothes talking as they walked and a moment later singing and dancing and having to protect themselves from a sudden, obviously artificial rain. She knew all the songs by heart, including the ones on Spanish radio commercials, which she studied as meticulously as the traditional ballads or the poems of Rubén Darío she was learning in Don Pedro Salinas's classes. She'd recite the lyrics of the songs in English and asked Ignacio to explain the ones sung by Imperio Argentina in *Morena Clara,* which for reasons he didn't understand she liked as much as *Top Hat.* On the phonograph in her room, she played songs she'd brought from America as often as those of García Lorca accompanying La Argentinita on the piano. That Judith liked those muddled movies about flamenco dancers and smugglers, and the strident voices that sang in them, irritated Ignacio Abel less than the fact that his son, Miguel, at the age of twelve, adored them too. The first time he saw her, her presence had been announced by the music that radiated from her as naturally as her voice or the shine of her hair or the fragrance, between sportive and rustic, of the cologne she wore. One afternoon at the end of September, Ignacio Abel entered the auditorium of the Student Residence looking for Moreno Villa, and a woman with her back to him was playing the piano and singing quietly to herself in the empty hall, flooded by the reddish-gold light of sunset that would remain intact in his memory like a drop of amber, the precise light of that late afternoon on September 29.

It feels like yesterday, but so much time has gone by. He knows now that personal identity is too fragile a tower to stand on its own without witnesses to certify it or glances to acknowledge it. The memories of what matters to him most are as distant as if they belonged to another man. The face in the passport is almost a stranger's; the one he is used to seeing now in the mirror, Judith Biely or his children would barely recognize. In Madrid he saw the faces of people he thought he knew well transformed overnight into the faces of executioners or prophets or fugitives or cattle brought to the slaughter; faces entirely occupied by mouths shouting in euphoria or panic; faces of the dead barely recognizable, half converted into red pulp by a rifle bullet; waxen faces deciding on life and death behind a table lit by a lamp while rapid fingers type lists of names. Like the face of someone in the glare of headlights moments before being murdered, or falling gravely wounded, twisting in the throes of death until a pistol placed at the back of his neck ends the misery. Death in Madrid is sometimes a sudden explosion of gunfire and at other times a slow procedure requiring documents written in administrative prose and typed with several carbon copies and legalized with rubber stamps. As he reminisces about the day a little over a year ago when he first saw Judith there's almost no feeling of loss, because what's lost has ceased to exist as completely as the man who might have longed for it. There is instead a scrupulous striving for exactitude, the desire to leave a mark through the effort to imagine a world that's been erased, leaving behind few material traces, so fragile they too are destined for a swift disappearance. But he isn't satisfied with his attempts to restore that moment to its authenticity, stripping away the additions and superimpositions of memory, like the restorer who cleans a fresco with delicate patience to bring back the splendor of its original colors. He wants to relive the steps that led him to an encounter that might not have happened, to reconstruct step by step that entire afternoon, the prelude, the hours that brought him to this point in his life.

He sees himself as if in a snapshot, frozen in time, as I saw him appearing in the crowd in Pennsylvania Station, or as I see him now, easier to grasp because he's motionless, leaning back in his seat as the train begins to move, exhausted, relieved, still wearing his raincoat, his hat on his lap, his suitcase on the seat beside him, the signs of deterioration visible to an attentive eye, the knot in his tie crooked, his shirt collar worn and a little dark because he perspired on the way to the station, more out of fear of missing the train than from the heat on a sunny October day, its clean golden light looking remarkably like the light in Madrid. When he reaches Rhineberg Station, Professor Stevens, who'll be waiting for him on the platform and who met him the year before in his office in University City, will be amazed at the change he sees in him and will attribute it, out of compassion, to war, while also feeling a certain displeasure, an impulse of rejection that is above all the discomfort produced by the proximity of misfortune. Ignacio Abel felt much the same and tried not to let it show on his face when he saw Professor Rossman, who appeared suddenly in Madrid, having arrived from Moscow after a tortuous journey across half of Europe, looking so different that the only traces of his former self were his round tortoise-shell glasses and the large black briefcase he carried under his arm. But on this late September afternoon in 1935, Ignacio Abel knows nothing yet: it's the extent of his own ignorance he finds most difficult to imagine now, like looking at someone's expression in a photo taken back then, like examining the smiling expressions of those who walk

23

along the street or chat in a café, and though they look directly into the lens and seem to see us, they don't know how to go beyond the boundary of time, don't see what's going to happen to them, what's happening close by, perhaps, without their realizing it or knowing that this ordinary date on which they're alive will acquire a sinister importance in history books. Ignacio Abel stands in his shirtsleeves, so absorbed in the drawing board he doesn't realize he's alone in the office in front of a large window overlooking the construction at University City, and beyond that a horizon of oak groves dissolved by distance on the slopes of the Sierra. Raising his eyes, which are suddenly fatigued, he looked at the rows of empty drawing boards, tilted like school desks, with pale blue plans spread over them, jars of pencils, inkwells, rulers, and the desks where until a few minutes ago phones rang and secretaries typed. An abandoned cigarette still smoldered in an ashtray. The sound of voices and work still floated in the air. In the middle of the room, on a stand sixteen inches high, stood the scale models of what didn't yet exist completely beyond the window: tree-lined avenues, athletic fields, classroom buildings, the university hospital, the hills and valleys of the landscape. Ignacio Abel would have recognized them in the dark just by feeling them, as a blind man perceives volumes and spaces with his hands. He'd drawn and folded some of those scale models himself, studying the elevations on the plans, focusing on the skill of the master model maker, whom he would visit in his workshop every time he had a new assignment for him, simply for the pleasure of watching his hands move and breathing in the smell of Bristol board, fresh wood, and hot glue. Childishly, he had drawn, colored, and cut out many of the trees, some of the tiny human figures walking along the still nonexistent avenues; he'd added small toy automobiles and streetcars like the ones he gave his son as presents (alarmed, he realized he'd almost forgotten that today was the boy's saint's day, San Miguel). For the past six years he'd lived many hours each day between one space and another, as if moving between two parallel worlds governed by different laws and scales, the University City coming to life so slowly because of the labor of hundreds of men, and its approximate, illusory model taking form on a stand with a perfection and a consistency both tangible and fantastic, like the stations and Alpine villages and the electric trains circling past them in the windows of expensive toy stores in Madrid. The model had grown incrementally, as did the real buildings, though at a different pace. At times the scale model occupied its exact site on the surface that reproduced the uneven terrain long before the building it anticipated came to be; at other times it remained for years on the same spot in that large imaginary space, even after the building it anticipated had been rejected: a future no longer possible but somehow still existing, the ghost not of what was demolished but of what had never been erected. Unlike real buildings, the scale models had an abstract quality his hands appreciated as much as his eyes, pure forms, polished surfaces, window cuts or right angles of corners and eaves in which his fingertips took pleasure. On a shelf in his office he kept the model of the national school he'd designed almost four years earlier for his neighborhood in Madrid, the one where he'd been born, La Latina, not Salamanca where he lived now, on the other side of the city.

The workday had also ended beyond the windows of the drafting room, where Ignacio Abel was getting ready to leave, fixing his tie, putting papers in his briefcase. The workers were leaving their jobs in groups, following paths between the clearings on their way to distant metro and streetcar stops. Lowered heads, dun-colored clothing, lunch bags over their shoulders. Ignacio Abel recognized with a rush of old affection the figure of Eutimio Gómez, the construction foreman at the Medical School, who turned, looked up, and waved. Eutimio was tall, strong, graceful in spite of his years, with the slow, flexible verticality of a poplar. When he was young, he'd worked as an apprentice stucco laborer in the crew of Ignacio Abel's father. Among the cement pillars of a building where the partitions had not yet been put up, the rifle of a uniformed watchman could be seen gleaming in the oblique afternoon sun. A truck carrying Assault Guards advanced slowly along the main avenue, which would be called Avenue of the Republic when it was completed. As night fell they'd begin to search the construction site for gangs that stole materials and for saboteurs prepared to overturn or burn the machinery they blamed for their low wages, men inspired by a primitive millenarianism, like the weavers who in another century burned steam looms. Steam shovels, steamrollers, machines for laying asphalt, cement mixers, now motionless, took on a presence as solid as the buildings that already had roofs, where beautiful tricolor flags waved in the luminous late September afternoon.

Before he left, Ignacio Abel used a red pencil to cross out the date on the calendar behind his desk, next to the one for the following year, on which only one date was highlighted, the day in October marked for the inauguration of University City, when the model and the real landscape would mirror each other. Black and red numbers measured the white calendar space that was his daily life, imposing a grid of working days and a line as straight as an arrow's trajectory, at once distressing and calming. Time so swift, work so slow and difficult, the process by which the neat lines of a plan or the weightless volumes of a model were transformed into foundations, walls, tiled roofs. The time that vanished day after day for the past six years: numbers lodged in the identical squares of each calendar day, on the curvature of a clock's sphere, the watch he wore on his wrist and the clock on the office wall, which now showed six o'clock. "The president of the Republic wants to be certain an inauguration will take place before the end of his term," Dr. Negrín, the secretary of public works, had yelled on the telephone. Then bring in more machines, hire more workers, speed up the deliveries, don't let everything come to a standstill with each change of government, Ignacio Abel thought but didn't say. "We'll do what we can, Don Juan," he said, and Negrín's voice sounded ever more peremptory on the phone, his Canarian vowels as powerful as his physical presence. "Not what you *can,* Abel. You'll do what has to be done." Ignacio Abel imagined him slamming down the phone, his large hand covering the entire receiver, an emphatic vigor in his gestures, as if he were walking against the wind on the deck of a ship.

He liked that moment of stillness at the end of the day: the deep stillness of places where people have worked hard, the silence that follows the rumble and vibration of machinery, the ringing of telephones, the shouts of men; the solitude of a place where a crowd rushed through seconds before, people busy with their tasks, fulfilling their duties, doing their part in the great general undertaking. The son of a construction foreman, accustomed since childhood to dealing with masons and working with his hands, Ignacio Abel maintained a practical, sentimental affection for the specific trade skills that were transformed into the character traits of the men who cultivated them. The draftsman who inked a right angle on a plan, the bricklayer who spread a base of fresh mortar and smoothed it with the trowel before placing the brick on top of it, the woodworker who sanded the curve of a banister, the glazier who cut the exact dimensions of the pane of glass for a window, the master craftsman who verified with a plumb line the verticality of a wall, the stonecutter who cut a paving stone or the stone block for a curb or the plinth of a column. Now his hands were too delicate and couldn't have endured the roughness of the materials, and they never had acquired the wisdom of touch he'd observed as a boy in his father and the men who worked with him. His fingers brushed soft Bristol board and paper, handled rulers, compasses, drawing pencils, watercolor brushes, moved quickly on a typewriter, skillfully dialed phone numbers, closed around the curved black lacquer of his fountain pen as he inked signatures on paperwork. But somewhere he'd kept a tactile memory that longed for the feel of tools and objects in his hands. He had an extraordinary ability to assemble and disassemble his children's Meccano sets and toys; on his worktable there were always paper houses, boats, birds; he took photos with a small Leica to document each phase in the construction of a building and developed them himself in a tiny darkroom he'd installed at home, to the excitement and admiration of his children, especially Miguel, who, unlike his sister, possessed a whimsical imagination, and when he saw his father's camera decided that when he grew up he was going to be one of those photographers who traveled to the far corners of the world to capture images that appeared as full-page spreads in magazines.

With a pleasant feeling of fatigue and relief, of work accomplished, he crossed the empty space of the office and went outside, feeling on his face a cool breeze from the Sierra with its hint of autumn. The scents of pine and oak, of rockrose, thyme, and damp earth. To prolong the enjoyment, he left the window of his small Fiat open when he started the engine. A short distance from Madrid, University City would have both the geometrical harmony of an urban design and a breadth of horizons outlined by tree-covered slopes. In a few more years the luxuriant growth of trees would provide a counterpoint to the straight lines of the architecture. The mechanical rhythm of construction work, the impatience to impress upon reality the forms of models and plans, corresponded to the unhurried pace of organic growth. What had recently been completed achieved true nobility only with use and a constant resistance to the elements, the wear caused by wind and rain, the passage of humans, the voices that at first resound with too-raw echoes in spaces still permeated by the smell of plaster and paint, wood, fresh varnish. Partial to technical novelties, Ignacio Abel had a radio in the car. But now he preferred not to turn it on, so nothing would distract him from the pleasure of driving slowly along the straight, empty avenues of the future city, looking over construction work and machines, the progress of recent days, allowing himself to be carried along by a mixture of attentive contemplation and daydreaming, because he saw with an expert eye what was in front of him as well as what did not yet exist, what was complete in the plans and in the large model installed in the center of the drafting room. The School of Philosophy stood out all the more in the chaos of the construction site. Opened barely two years earlier, the building still had the radiance of the new, the light stone and red brick shining in the sun as brightly as the banner on the façade and the clothes of the students who went in and out of the lobby, the girls especially, with their short hair and tight skirts, their summery blouses against which they pressed books and notebooks. In a few years his daughter Lita would probably be one of them.

He watched their brightly colored figures become smaller in the rearview mirror as he drove toward Madrid, though he was in no hurry and didn't choose the fastest route. He liked to go around the edge of the city to the west, then to the north, driving the length of the Monte del Pardo along the suddenly limitless plain and the beginning of the highway to Burgos, over which the Sierra extended like a formidable, weightless mass, dark blue and violet, crowned by motionless waterfalls of clouds. Madrid, so close, disappeared into the plain and emerged again as a rustic horizon of low, whitewashed houses, empty stretches, church spires. He passed only a few cars on the highway, a straight line brighter than the dull terrain on which it had been laid out with saplings along its edges. Rows of hovels beside the highway, long whitewashed earthen walls, doors as dark as the mouths of caves beside which were gathered disheveled women and children with shaved heads who watched the car go by with mouths hanging open. Columns of smoke rising from kilns in the brickyards and emanating from the garbage fermenting in the mountains. To isolate himself from the stink, he closed the window. In the radiant expanse of the sky, the first flocks of migratory birds flew south. The late September sun made dry stalks in fallow fields glow. The first signs of autumn produced a state of hopeful expectation in Ignacio Abel that had no specific cause and perhaps was nothing more than the reverberation in time of a distant schoolboy's joy in new notebooks and pencils, the innocent pull of an unblemished future that emerged in childhood, maintained until the first failures of adult life.

Now the highway took on a more precise meaning, defined by rows of electric and telephone wires. In the flat, unpopulated outskirts of

Madrid, the avenues of its future expansion stretched with the abstract rigor of a drawn plan. Settlements of small hotels emerged like islands among the desert-like lots and cultivated fields along the sinuous lines of streetcar cables, fragile urban outposts in the middle of nothing. He could imagine districts of white apartment buildings for workers among wooded areas and sports fields, the kind of housing he'd seen in Berlin ten years earlier, in a less rugged climate and with gray, low skies — tall towers among fields of grass, as in the cities of Le Corbusier. Architecture was an effort of the imagination to see what doesn't exist more clearly than what you have before your eyes, the rundown buildings that have endured for no reason other than the obstinacy of their materials, just as religion or malaria endures, or the pride of the strong, or the misery of the deprived. *Arise, you prisoners of starvation! Arise, you wretched of the earth!* As he drove he saw, along with the high mirages of clouds over the peaks of the Sierra, the public housing that already existed in his sketchbooks, with large windows, terraces, athletic fields, playgrounds, plazas with community centers and libraries. He saw luminous patches of green — an orchard, a line of poplars along a stream — in the midst of treeless barrens and slopes cracked by erosion, scarred by dry avalanches. More irrigation and fewer words, more trees with roots that can hold down the fertile soil, more pipelines of clean, fresh water, more rail lines brilliant in the sun, along which trolleys painted in bright colors will glide. He saw shacks, garbage dumps where the indigent swarmed, farmhouses with caved-in roofs, wastelands devoured by brambles, a dog tied to a tree with too short a rope cutting into his neck, a shepherd dressed in rags or animal hides guarding a flock of goats as if in a biblical desert — all within two kilometers of the center of Madrid.

He saw the future in its isolated signs: in the energy of what was being built, solidly in the earth, on the still barren plain, broken by the right angles of future avenues, the framework of sidewalks, the lines of streetlights and trolley cables, and pierced by tunnels and underground transport. On the bare horizon the huge outline of a wall rising beneath its scaffolding. In the not too distant future, it would be referred to as the new government offices. Another, more transparent city that wouldn't resemble Madrid, though it would continue to bear its name, would soon extend through those cleared fields in the north. Pockets of the future: to his left, on the other side of the sweeping extension of wasteland, above the row of saplings that delineated like broad ink strokes the extension to the north of La Castellana Boulevard, the Student Residence crowned an undeveloped hill shaded by poplars, at the foot of which stood the School of Engineering and the exaggerated dome of the Museum of Natural Sciences. Diminutive white figures were prominent on the gray-brown expanse of athletic fields. The sun of late September burned with golden brilliance on the windows facing west. Suddenly he remembered that he had to give an answer to José Moreno Villa, who had asked him weeks earlier to give a talk on Spanish architecture. A kind, solitary man, very formal in his dress and manner, older than most of his acquaintances. Moreno Villa would appreciate a letter or personal visit much more than a phone call. He lived in his room at the Residence as if it were a cell in a comfortable lay monastery, surrounded by paintings and books, enjoying with the melancholy of an old bachelor the proximity of foreign students, girls who flooded the halls with the clicking of high heels, sonorous laughter, and conversations in English.

Without giving it another thought, Ignacio Abel turned left and drove up the hill to the Residence. At a snack bar among the poplars — still open, though it was late in the season — the radio played dance music at top volume, but there was almost no one at the iron tables. At the reception desk he was told that Señor Moreno Villa was probably in the auditorium. As he walked toward it, he heard muffled piano music and singing on the other side of the closed door. Perhaps he shouldn't have opened it, at the risk of interrupting what might be a rehearsal. He could have turned away but didn't. He opened the door softly, barely putting his head inside. A woman turned when she heard the door open. She was young and undoubtedly foreign. The sun shone on her light chestnut hair, which she brushed aside. She stopped singing but finished the phrase on the piano. Ignacio Abel murmured an apology and closed the door. As he walked away, he continued to hear a melody at once sentimental and rhythmic.

3

DULL FOOTSTEPS echoing down the hall, getting closer, urgent knocking on the door, like the footsteps of someone looking for something in a hurry, the leather shoes creaking as they walked on the tiles: someone under the pressure of an assignment, unlike him, José Moreno Villa, who felt no urgency about anything and often would find himself forgetting what he was looking for, or searching for something different from what he originally had in mind. Almost nothing touched his heart; he held no conviction about anything. At times he was ashamed of his apathy, and at other times relieved — if it often took away his drive, it also saved him from suffering and mistakes he would later regret. He'd had a passionate love affair late in life and lost her, largely because of his own apathy; when he realized he wasn't going to win her back, the sorrow he felt was tinged with relief. He felt a certain joy at finding himself alone again, as he settled into his cabin on the ship that would sail from New York and carry him back to Spain, leaving behind the woman he'd been about to marry; what a relief, after all the emotional turmoil, to settle down again among his possessions in his simple room at the Residence. So much fury in Spain, so much harshness, passionate crimes and savage Anarchist uprisings drowned in blood, crude barracks proclamations; so many saints, martyrs, fanatics, like the paintings in the Prado in which the skin of ascetics seems as torn as the sackcloth they wear, their eyes rendered unforgiving by a vision of purity incompatible with the real world; and the throats raw from shouting so many "long live"s and "death to"s, the aggressive vulgarity that has been taking over his beloved Madrid, where he ventures less and less frequently, with the displeasure of a man no longer young who experiences change like a personal insult. The coarse ways of politics, the desecration of ideas that, after all, no one had asked him to believe in, though for a time they warmed his heart, as full of rational promises and esthetic dreams as the tricolor flags waving at the tops of buildings against a blue as clean and new as the flags themselves. How typical of him that his political convictions, so easily attenuated by his skepticism—about the selfishness of the human soul, the triviality and profound misery of Spanish life—were so closely associated with esthetic whim, with his preference for the tricolor rather than for the vulgar red-and-yellow flag of the scoundrel king for whom no one yearned, or the red-and-black that for some incomprehensible reason was shared by the Fascists and the Anarchists, or the entirely red flag with a hammer and sickle so favored by some of his friends, sudden enthusiasts for the Soviet Union, for photographic collages of workers, soldiers in greatcoats holding bayonets, tractors and hydroelectric plants, sky-blue shirts, leather straps, clenched fists. Perhaps he didn't understand or, worse, didn't believe in the sincerity or substance of their attitudes because they were younger than him, or because they were more successful; he saw them stand up to sing anthems at the end of literary banquets, and what he felt wasn't ideological disagreement but embarrassment for them. He'd never known how to participate in public enthusiasm without observing himself from the outside. He was a bourgeois, of course, and not only that, he had independent means and was a bureaucrat. But some of them, his old friends, were more bourgeois, idle rich men who'd never really worked but spoke with extraordinary gravity about the dictatorship of the proletariat as they crossed their legs, a whiskey in hand, on the terrace of the Palace Hotel after having a haircut in the barbershop. They predicted the imminent fall of the Republic, crushed by the social revolution, and at the same time they prospered by going abroad on official lecture tours or receiving salaries justified by vague cultural assignments.

But Moreno Villa didn't like his own sarcasm, his inclination toward bitterness; he distrusted lucidity that was born of resentment. As for his own integrity, what merit did it have if it had never been tested by temptation? No diva of the theater had asked him to write a play to the measure of her own success, as Lola Membrives or Margarita Xirgú had done with Lorca; not one of them had ever been interested in reciting his poems, like that irritating Berta Singermann, who filled theaters by grimacing and shouting in a Buenos Aires accent the verses of Antonio Machado, or Lorca, or Juan Ramón Jiménez. And he never would be in a position to turn down a government job offer and dedicate himself body and soul to his writing. No one was going to consider him for the post of general secretary of the Summer University in Santander, as they had with Pedro Salinas, who complained so much about the lack of quiet and time but looked so pleased with himself in photographs of official engagements. It isn't at all difficult for me to imagine him, José Moreno Villa, used to the benevolent hospitality of the Student Residence, a man close to fifty, often no more than a secondary guest in photographs of other, more important people, always discreet, elusive, formal, at times not even identified by name, unrecognized, without the open smile or arrogant pose the others display as if their place in posterity could be taken for granted. He isn't young and doesn't dress as if he were, doesn't have the air of a literary figure or professor but rather of what he actually does for a living: a functionary in a certain position, not a clerk but not a high-ranking employee either, perhaps an attorney or a person of some means in a provincial capital who doesn't attend Mass or hide his Republican sympathies but would never go out without a tie and hat; a man who looked older than he was long before his hair turned gray, who at the age of forty-eight supposes with a mixture of melancholy and relief that no great changes in his life await him.

• • •

The footsteps had taken him out of his self-absorption—profound and at the same time bare of reflection and almost of memory, filled above all with indolence and something else not very different from it, the attentive contemplation of a small canvas where he'd sketched a few tenuous lines in charcoal, and a bowl of seasonal fruit brought up at midday from the Residence dining room: a quince, a pomegranate, an apple, a bunch of grapes. He'd cleared away some papers and books from the table so the clean forms would stand out. He'd been observing the slow descent of light from the window as it made the volumes look denser, their shadows accentuated, every color slightly muted. The red of the pomegranate turned the color of polished leather; the dusty gold of the quince shone with greater intensity as the twilight enveloped the space, no longer reflecting light but radiating it; light slid over the apple as if it were a ball of oiled wood, yet it acquired a degree of moist density when it touched the skin of the grapes. Perhaps the grapes were too sensual, too tactile for the purpose he'd just begun to anticipate, half closing his eyes. They'd have to be ascetic grapes like those of Juan Gris or Sánchez Cotán, carved in a single visual volume, without that slightly sticky suggestion accentuated by the ripe afternoon sun, a Sorolla sun, sifted with the same soft dust that the rough surface of the quince left on his fingers, in his nostrils.

Under the fruit bowl was a page from the magazine *Estampa:* AN ENCHANTER FROM CAIRO WHO BEWITCHES WOMEN AND PREDICTS THE FUTURE COMES TO MADRID. The words "Madrid" and "future" were as spellbinding as the forms of the fruits. Each time he prepared to paint something, there was a moment of revelation and another of discouragement, just as when the first line of a poem appeared unexpectedly in his mind. How can one take the next step in the empty space that is a blank sheet of paper or canvas? Perhaps the very texture, the resistance or softness of the paper, could indicate a way. He could go on and realize he'd ruined the attempt: the second verse was forced, not worthy of the sudden illumination of the first, a useless blot on that grand expanse of paper. The revelation seemed to be lost without his knowing how to recapture it; the feeling of failure stayed with him, and to begin work it was necessary, if not to conquer it, at least to resist it, to take the first steps as if he didn't feel its leaden weight. But in everything he'd undertaken, the same thing occurred: an easy enthusiasm, then the start of fatigue, and finally a reluctance he couldn't always overcome. In the long run, he was a Sunday painter. And if painting demanded such great mental effort and skill, why, instead of putting all his heart and talent into it, did he dissipate his already limited energies writing poetry, where he was not even granted the absolution of manual labor, the certainty of an acceptable degree of technical command? In the heat of the work his unwillingness dissipated, but the next day he had to begin again, and nothing guaranteed that the enthusiasm of the day before would still be there. Work he'd already completed was useless: each beginning was a new point of departure, and the canvas or sheet of paper before which he was transfixed and disheartened remained emptier than ever. A first line, promising but very uncertain, a horizontal that could be a table on which the fruit bowl rested or an imagined distant ocean beyond his Madrid window. An imminent insight disappeared without a trace into pure dejection.

He saw himself as a man without ambition who'd desired too many disparate things. Ambition is needed to fulfill desires; one can't allow incredulity and reluctance to gnaw inside. Others knew how to concentrate their energies. He dissipated his, going from one task to another like a traveler who spends no more than a few days in any city and eventually grows tired of wandering. Others younger than he had approached him, wanting to learn from his experience, and not long afterward left him behind with no thanks for what they owed him: the example of his painting, his knowledge of modern art, and his poetry, innovative before anyone else's, whose unacknowledged imprint was so evident in those who now shone much brighter than he. He'd have preferred none of that to matter to him: his own resentment irritated him more than the success of others, slightly bitter to him even when he considered it deserved. It saddened him not to be on a level with the best in himself, not to be content with the noble stoicism of the personage he imagined, another Moreno Villa, just as disillusioned but with a much more serene heart, an obscure poet, a painter as removed from fame as Sánchez Cotán, whom he admired so much and who had spent his life completing recondite masterpieces in his Carthusian cell, or like Juan Gris, persisting in his rigorous art in spite of poverty, in spite of the clamor of Picasso's obscene triumph.

Without intending to, he'd remained alone. Continuing to live in the Residence, in spite of his age and long after his old friends had moved on, accentuated his sense of anachronism, of dislocation. On the other hand, it was all he desired, and he couldn't imagine himself living anywhere else. In one room he had his studio, in another his bedroom, with the few pieces of furniture, family heirlooms, he'd brought from Málaga. He'd given his share of the family inheritance to his unmarried sisters, who needed it more than he did. He thought it immoral to accumulate more than was necessary, which for him was like talking or gesticulating too much, or showing signs of excessive enthusiasm or suffering, or dressing in a way that would attract attention. A line of Antonio Machado's came to mind: *He who lets go keeps the most, and he who has lived, lives.* Nothing belonged to him more than the things he detached himself from; living was a suspended state in which distant things and lost presences counted most (the loud laughter of the young American woman he called Jacinta in the poems he dedicated to her, poems in which her name is repeated like a spell; her tumultuous red hair). He liked the position of archivist that earned him a living: the work schedule was in no way oppressive, and it gave a solid form to his days, saving him from the certain dangers of boredom and insecurity. He frequented the common areas of the Residence very little, and the duties assigned him were limited. Organizing some conferences, escorting illustrious visitors. He could spend entire afternoons in his room, with all the luxury of solitude and time stretching before him, and the absolution of having worked with dedication and profit, reading, ensconced in the leather armchair already worn by the friction of the nape of his father's neck, his father's arms, or imagining or sketching a still life, or simply looking out the window at the courtyard

with its brick walls and the oleander Juan Ramón Jiménez had planted
— the green of the leaves as ascetic as the faded red of the bricks — or
listening with an attentive ear and half-closed eyes to the sounds of
the city, muffled, like sfumato in a drawing, by their distance from the
hill where the Residence was located, and lacking the wounding indifference of the streets. Car horns, streetcar bells, the shouts of street
vendors, the monotonous chants of blind beggars, paso dobles at bullfights, drums and trumpets at military parades, the rabble's music at
festivals and circuses, church bells, the uproar of workers' demonstrations, gunshots at riots, train whistles, all ascended to his open window,
confused as in the polychromatic haze of a Ravel orchestration, against
which the close, sharp sound of the soccer players' shouts and the referees' whistles on the athletic fields and the bleating of a flock of sheep
grazing in a nearby meadow stood out clearly. If he paid a great deal of
attention he could hear the wind in the poplars and almost make out
the flow of water in the irrigation ditch that ran beside the Residence
and on to the orchards on the other side of the Castellana. He was in
Madrid and in the countryside, on the boundary where the city ended.
He couldn't imagine living anywhere else (little did he know that in less
than a year he'd leave Madrid and Spain, never to return). His immobility accentuated the diaspora of the others, those who'd known how
to concentrate on a single purpose, desire it with an intensity that perhaps was enough to make its achievement inevitable. Now Lorca was a
successful author who had multiple premieres in Barcelona and Buenos Aires and with no misgivings told everyone he was earning a great
deal of money, pleased with a rather puerile shamelessness at the magnitude of his triumph, as if he were still a boy, as if he weren't close to
forty, wearing those loud shirts that made so strong a contrast with his
flat, no-necked peasant's head, as if he didn't notice how other people
looked at him, the physical displeasure with which they moved away
from him. Buñuel had turned into a film producer; he had an ostentatious automobile and received visitors smoking a cigar, his feet crossed
on the enormous desk in his office on the highest floor of a new building on the Gran Vía. Success favored or forgave poor memory: seeing

posters on the façades of movie houses for the films made by Buñuel about Andalusian flamenco dancers or Aragonese rustics with tight sashes and painted eyes, Moreno Villa recalled the malevolence with which, not long ago, he'd heard Buñuel ridicule Lorca for his Gypsy ballads. Salinas accumulated professorships, positions, conferences, official posts, even mistresses, according to the talk in Madrid; Alberti and María Teresa León took a trip to Russia, paid for with money from the Republic, and on their return had their pictures taken on the deck of their ship like two film stars on a world tour, each raising a clenched fist, she wrapped in furs, blond, wearing a good deal of lipstick, like a Soviet Jean Harlow with the face of a big Spanish doll. Bergamín, once so ascetic, had obtained his own official car immediately, before anyone else. One morning during the first month of the Republic — which, after a little more than four years now, seemed so distant — Moreno Villa was walking absent-mindedly under the trees on the Paseo de Recoletos when an enormous black car stopped beside him, the horn sounding hoarsely. The back door opened and inside sat Bergamín, sporting a tailcoat, puffing a cigarette, inviting him in with a big smile. Dalí would soon be as rich and despotic as Picasso: never again would he send him, Moreno Villa, a postcard filled with declarations of admiration and gratitude and spelling mistakes, and Dalí would never say his name when he mentioned the teachers from whom he'd learned, or tell who'd been the first to show him photographs of the new German portraits that with astonishing technique and in a fully modern manner recaptured the realism of Holbein. Lorca would never recognize his debt to him either, but he'd been the first to juxtapose avant-garde poetic expression and the meter of popular ballads, he who had long ago traveled to New York and conceived of a poetry and prose that corresponded to the city's agitation, the noise of elevated trains and the discordant sounds of jazz bands. In fact, Lorca had the nerve to give a reading in the Residence of poems and prose impressions of New York, illustrating it with musical recordings and slides, and not to mention Moreno Villa, sitting in the first row, once as an early pioneer.

• • •

The celebrity of others made him invisible; better to erase his existence so his shadow would not be projected in a revealing way onto the triumphal faces of those who owed him so much. If not greatness, then retirement. Writing verses with a passion that was sabotaged by his own apathy to things, knowing that for some reason they would repel success. Investigating things in archives no one had visited for centuries, the lives of dwarves and buffoons in the gloomy courts of Felipe IV and Carlos II. Not thinking about all the work completed, or the dubious future of his painting, or its probable distance from a style he didn't care about but that pained him like an insult to all the years he'd devoted to painting with no recognition. Not imagining oneself a painter: limiting one's expectations, the field of vision. Concentrating on the relatively simple but still inexhaustible problem of representing on a small canvas that bowl with a few pieces of fruit. But what if he really deserved the mediocre place where he'd been relegated? Perhaps, after all, it wasn't that Lorca had silenced the debt he owed him but simply hadn't read his poems about New York and the book of prose pieces about the city written on his return trip and then published serially in *El Sol,* to unanimous indifference. (In Madrid there didn't seem to be much interest in the outside world: he went to the café the day following his return from New York, excited by all the stories he had to tell, and his friends received him as if he hadn't been away and didn't ask a single question.) What if he'd become old and was being poisoned by what he'd always disliked most, resentment? Juan Ramón Jiménez, who was actually more accomplished, was infected by an ignoble bitterness, an obsessive mean-spiritedness fed by any small slight, imagined or real, by each scintilla of recognition not dedicated to him, muddied water that debased his luminous talent. How sordid it would be if one lacked not only talent but nobility as well and allowed oneself to be hopelessly intoxicated by an aging man's rancor toward those who are younger, by the affront of feeling offended by the jealously observed good fortune of others who didn't even notice him, who insulted him by achieving with no apparent effort what had been denied to him, when he was the more deserving. But did he really want to be like

Lorca, his success hovering between folklore and bullfights, his fondness for the parties of diplomats and duchesses? Hadn't he told himself at some point that his secret models were Antonio Machado and Juan Gris? He didn't imagine Juan Gris as resentful over Picasso's triumph, aggrieved by his obscene energy, his simian histrionics, filling canvases as quickly as he seduced and abandoned women. But Juan Gris, alone in Paris, not merely overshadowed but erased by the other and ill with tuberculosis, probably had possessed a certainty in the depths of his soul that he, Moreno Villa, was lacking, had obeyed a single passion, had known how, like an ascetic or a mystic, to strip away all the worldly comforts he'd never be able to renounce no matter how modest: his functionary's secure salary, his two adjoining rooms in the Residence, his well-cut suits, his English cigarettes. It wasn't true — he hadn't withdrawn from the world. The insight he'd been so close to having while looking at the bowl of autumn fruit and the seductive, vulgar typography of the illustrated magazine would never come simply because he couldn't sustain the required intensity of observation, the state of alertness that would have sharpened his eye and guided his hand on the blank sheet of paper. Someone was coming down the hall, walking with an almost violent determination, then knocking on his door. No matter how short the anticipated visit, he knew he wouldn't be able to recapture that moment of being on the verge of enlightenment.

"Come in," he said, giving in to the interruption, relieved deep down, resigned, the thick charcoal with its creamy tip still in his hand, held close to the surface of the paper.

Ignacio Abel burst into the stillness of his room, bringing with him the rush of the street, the busy life, as if he'd let in a cold current through the door. With a glance that Moreno Villa noticed, he quickly formed an impression of the messy room, a combination of painter's studio, scholar's library, and old-bachelor's den, canvases stacked against the walls and sketches upon sketches in disordered piles on the floor, paint-smudged rags, postcards pinned haphazardly on the walls. Ignacio Abel's suit with its wide trousers and double-breasted jacket, his silk tie, shined shoes, and good wristwatch, made him conscious of the penury of his own appearance in the stained smock and flannel slippers he put on to paint. It comforted Moreno Villa, however, who'd spent perhaps too much of his life with younger people, that Ignacio Abel was almost his age, and even more that he didn't attempt to feign youth. But he knew him only superficially: the architect also belonged to that other world, the world of people with careers and projects, those capable of acting with a pragmatism he'd never possessed.

"You were working and I've interrupted you."

"Don't worry, Abel my friend, I've been alone all afternoon. I was actually in the mood to talk to someone."

"I'll bother you only for a few minutes."

He looked at his watch as if measuring the exact amount of time he had left. He spread papers on the table, from which Moreno Villa removed the fruit bowl that Abel had glanced at, intrigued, followed by another glance at the almost blank canvas, where the only result of several lazy hours of contemplation were a few lines in charcoal. An active man who consulted an appointment book and made phone calls, drove a car, worked ten hours a day on the construction of University City, and recently had completed a municipal food market and a public school. He asked for details: how long his lecture was to be, what kind of slide projector would be available, how many posters had been printed, how many invitations sent out. Moreno Villa observed him as if from his shore of slower time, improvising answers to things he didn't know or hadn't thought about. To come as far as he had from such an unpromising background, Ignacio Abel needed exceptional determination, a moral and physical energy that was evident in his gestures and perhaps in his somewhat excessive cordiality, as if at each moment, and with each person, he were calibrating the practical importance of being agreeable. Perhaps he, Moreno Villa, never had to make too much of an effort, thus his overall apathy toward things, his inability to set his mind to one thing, his tendency to give up so easily. He had the reluctance of an heir to a limited position but one that allows him to live with no effort other than not aspiring to too much, accommodating to the soporific inertia and lethargy of the Spanish provincial middle class. He looked at Ignacio Abel's gold watch, his shirt cuffs, the cap of his fountain pen visible in the breast pocket next to the tip of a white handkerchief with embroidered initials. He'd married well, he recalled someone saying in those Madrid circles where everything was known; he'd married an older woman, the daughter of someone influential. Here in the stillness of Moreno Villa's room, he seemed out of place, his energy intact after so many hours at the office, a day full of phone calls and paperwork, decision after decision, executed by his construction crew at the other end of the city.

I can easily imagine the two men talking, and listen to their calm voices as the afternoon sun slowly leaves the room and disappears behind the roofs of the city. They are not exactly friends, because neither one is particularly sociable, yet they are united by a vague familiarity, by a common air of decorum, though Ignacio Abel is younger, of course. They use the formal *usted* with each other, which is a relief to Moreno Villa now that almost everyone calls him Pepe or even Pepito, reinforcing the suspicion that he's lost his youth without gaining respect. He keeps comparing—he can't help it—his rumpled, stained clothing to Abel's suit; the tense, erect posture the other maintains in the upright chair as he spreads drawings and photos on the table to his own, old man's carelessness in the easy chair that belonged to his father; his two more or less borrowed rooms to Ignacio Abel's apartment in a new building in the Salamanca district, this father of two children whose work gives him a solid, undeniable place in the world.

"And what will you do when University City is finished?"

Ignacio Abel, disconcerted by the question, took a moment to answer.

"The truth is, I don't think about it. I know there's a deadline, and I want that date to come, but at the same time I don't really believe it."

"The political situation doesn't seem very reassuring."

"I prefer not to think about that either. Of course there'll be delays, I have no illusions about it, no matter how many guarantees Dr. Negrín gives me. All construction sites have delays. Nothing turns out the way it was planned. You know what you're going to paint in that picture, but uncertainty is much greater in my work. Each time there's a change of minister or a construction strike, everything stops, and then it's even more difficult to get started again."

"You have plans and models of your buildings. I don't know how this picture will turn out, or whether I'll paint it at all."

"The model doesn't serve as your guide? It's calming to look at the fruit you have before you, the glass bowl."

"But if you pay attention, they're always changing. It doesn't look the same as it did when you came in a little while ago. The old still-life painters liked to put some blemish on the fruit, or a hole with a worm looking out. They wanted people to see that youth and beauty were false or transitory and that putrefaction was at work."

"Don't tell me that, Moreno." Ignacio Abel smiled in his quick, formal way. "I don't want to go to the construction site tomorrow and think I've spent six years building future ruins."

"You're lucky, Abel my friend. I like your things very much, the ones I've seen in architecture magazines, and the new market on Calle Toledo. Once I was passing by and decided to go in just to appreciate the interior. So new, and already so full of people, with the aromas of fruit, vegetables, meat, fish, spices. The things you make are as beautiful as a sculpture and yet also practical and of use to people in their lives. Those vendors endlessly shouting and the women buying enjoy your work without thinking about it. I thought about writing to you that day, but you know sometimes the road to hell is paved with good intentions. In my case, you must be thinking, it certainly wasn't for lack of time."

"I think you judge yourself too harshly, Moreno."

"I see things as they are. My eyes are well trained."

"Physicists say that the things we think we see don't resemble in any way the structure of matter. According to Dr. Negrín, Max Planck's conclusions aren't far from Plato's or those of the mystics of our Golden Age. The reality you and I see is a deception of the senses."

"Do you see Negrín often? He never goes to his old laboratory anymore."

"Do I see him? Even in my dreams. In fact, my nightmares—the only Spaniard who performs his job to the letter. He's informed about everything—the last brick we laid, the last tree planted. He calls me at any hour of the day or night, at the office or at home. My children make fun of me. They've made up a song about him: *Ring, ring, / Is he in? / Tell him it's Dr. Negrín.* If he's traveling and isn't near a phone, he sends a telegram. Now that he's discovered the airplane, he has no limits. He lectures me by underwater cable from the Canary Islands at eight in the morning, and at five he comes to my office straight from the airport. He's always in motion, like one of those particles he talks about so much, because aside from everything else, he's always reading German scientific journals, just as he did when he was dedicated only to the laboratory. You can know at any given moment where Dr. Negrín is, or his trajectory, but not both things at the same time."

It was growing late. In the deepening shadow the two voices became increasingly inaudible and at the same time closer, now two silhouettes leaning each toward the other, separated by the table and the fruit bowl. The residual brightness, still beyond the reach of the dim light coming through the window, reflected off the white canvas on the easel, highlighting the few lines sketched in charcoal. Moreno Villa turns on the lamp next to his easy chair—the lamp and end table are relics of his parents' old house in Málaga—and when the electric light illuminates their faces, it cancels the confidential, slightly ironic tone the voices had been slipping into. Now Ignacio Abel looks at his watch, which he had already furtively consulted once or twice. He has to go; he remembered again that today is San Miguel, and if he hurries he'll have time to buy something for his son, one of those painted tin airplanes or ocean liners he still likes though he's not a little boy anymore, perhaps a new electric train, not the kind that imitates the old coal trains but express trains with locomotives as stylized as the prow of a ship or the nose of a plane, or a complete American cowboy outfit, which would require him to buy his daughter an Indian girl's dress, just to please the boy. She, unlike her brother, is in a hurry not to look like a little girl, but Miguel would like to hold her down hard and keep her from growing, keep her as long as possible in the space of their shared childhood. Ignacio Abel puts his papers and the photographs of traditional Spanish architecture back in his briefcase and shakes Moreno Villa's hand, moving his head away slightly, as if before leaving he'd already stopped being there. An indolent Moreno Villa doesn't walk him to the door but sinks deeper into the easy chair, as if trying to hide his loose, stained painting trousers and flannel slippers.

"You still haven't told me what you'll do when University City is finished," he says.

"I'll let you know when I have time to think about it," says Ignacio Abel, compensating with a smile for the recovered stiffness of a very busy man.

The door closes, and the footsteps storm down the hall, and in the silence of the room the distant noises of the city filter in, along with the sounds of the Residence and the athletic fields where isolated exclamations from players and the whistles of referees can be heard. Closer, though he can't identify where it's coming from, Moreno Villa listens to a burst of piano music that becomes lost in the other sounds and returns again, a song that brings to his mind, stripped now of grief but not of melancholy, a red-haired girl he said goodbye to in New York more than six years earlier.

4

A S SOON AS HE leans back in the seat, Ignacio Abel is overcome
by uncertainty. Suppose he's on the wrong train? The train begins to move and that brief moment of calm turns to alarm. I observe the automatic gesture of his right hand, which had rested, open,
on his thigh and now contracts to search for his ticket; the hand that
so often rummages, investigates, recognizes, driven by fear of losing
something, the one that rubs his face, rough with the unwanted beginning of his beard, touches the worn collar of his shirt, finally closes
with a slight tremor, holding the discovered document; the hand that
has not touched anyone for so long. On the other side of the tracks sits
an identical train that remains motionless, and perhaps that is the one
he should have taken. In less than a second he is a bundle of nerves
again. At the slightest suspicion of a threat, every fiber in his body
tightens to the limit of its resistance. Now he can't find the ticket. He
pats his pockets and doesn't remember that a while ago he put it in his
briefcase to be sure it wouldn't become entangled in his fingers and
fall out accidentally when he looked for something else in his trouser
pockets, jacket pockets, raincoat pockets — the haunts of tiny, useless
objects, breadcrumbs, coins of little value from several countries. He
touches the edge of the postcard he didn't mail. At the bottom of some
pocket, the keys to his apartment in Madrid jingle. He feels the telegram, a corner of the envelope that contains the letter from his wife. *I*

know you'd rather not hear what I have to say to you. He finally opens the briefcase and sees the edge of the ticket, his deep sigh of relief coinciding with the discovery that he's again been the victim of an optical illusion: the train that's started to move is the one at the next platform, an identical train from which, for a few seconds, a stranger has been looking at him. So he still has time to double-check. A porter has come into the car, dragging a trunk. Ignacio Abel goes up to him and shows him his ticket, attempting to pronounce a sentence that's been clear in his mind but breaks down into nonsense as he struggles to articulate it. The porter wipes his forehead with a handkerchief as red as his cap and says something that must be simple but Ignacio doesn't understand it at first. The man's gesture is as unmistakable as his weary, friendly smile, and after a few seconds, like a clap of thunder after lightning, every word acquires delayed meaning in Ignacio's mind: *You can be damn sure you're on your way up to old Rhineberg, sir.*

The ticket is for this train and no other. He knew it, but anxiety got the best of him: like an intruder, it usurped the movement of his hands, accelerated the beating of his heart, and pressed against his chest, lodging like a parasite inside the empty shell of his previous existence. In his heart, he no longer believes he can ever go back. Who'll undo what has been done, raise what's fallen, restore what's turned to ashes and smoke? Would the human flesh rotting beneath the ground rise up if the trumpets of the resurrection were to sound? Who'll erase the words, spoken and written, that sought to legitimize the crime and make it seem not only respectable and heroic but necessary? Who'll open the door no one is knocking on now, pleading for refuge? Sounds travel at a perceptible though infinitesimally slow rate between his ear and the circuits in his brain where words are deciphered. He sits down again, breathing deeply, his face against the window, looking at the subterranean platform, a stab of pain near his heart, trying to calm down, waiting. In his mind two clocks show two different times, like two discordant pulsations he might detect by pressing two different points on his body. It's four in the afternoon and it's ten at night. In Madrid it's been dark for several hours, and only the dim light of a few street lamps, the globes painted blue, can be seen in the deserted streets. Sometimes the headlights of a car driving at top speed emerge from around a corner, the tires screeching against the paving stones, mattresses tied haphazardly to the roof as an absurd protection, acronyms scrawled with a paintbrush on the side panels, a rifle protruding from the window, perhaps the ghostly face of someone whose hands are tied, who knows he is on the way to his death. (They didn't bother to tie his legs; he was so docile they probably didn't think it was necessary.) In the house in the Sierra where his children may still be living, they can hear in the darkness the dry thump of the pendulum and the mechanism of a clock that always runs slow. In the Sierra de Guadarrama the nights are cold now and the smell of damp rotting leaves and pine needles rises from the earth. Over the dark city, on the first clear nights of autumn just a few weeks earlier, the sky recovered its forgotten splendor, the powerful radiance of the Milky Way, which revived old fears from his childhood nested in the memories of a Madrid that predated electricity and the endless streams of headlights running down the streets. With the war, darkness returned to the city along with the night terrors of children's folktales. As a boy, he'd wake up in his tiny room in the porter's lodging and stare at faint yellow gaslights from the small barred window at the height of the sidewalk. He would listen to the footsteps and the pounding of the metal tip of the night watchman's pike on the paving stones, his slow, frightening steps like the steps of the bogeyman himself. Many years later, in a darkened Madrid, footsteps and pounding were once again emissaries of panic: the elevator noises in the middle of the night, the heels of boots in the hallway, rifle butts banging on the door, resounding inside one's chest to the accelerated rhythm of one's heart, as if two hearts were beating simultaneously. *Ignacio, for the sake of all you love best, open the door, they're going to kill me.* Now the train is really moving, but slowly, with powerful majesty and the vigor of its electric locomotive, granting intact the happiness of every journey's start: perfect absolution for the next two hours when nothing unforeseen can happen. A brief future with no potential surprises on the horizon is a gift he's learned to appreciate in recent months. He felt the same way, only more so, in the port of Saint-Nazaire when the SS *Manhattan* pulled away from the pier, the deep howling of the siren in the air, the engine's vibration rattling the metal beneath his feet and the railing where he rested his hands as if on the metal of a balcony on a high floor. When he looked down at the shrinking figures waving handkerchiefs on the dock, he felt not the simple joy of having escaped, of actually leaving for America after so many delays, so many days in that state of fear and anxiety, but the suspension of the immediate past and the near future because he had before him six or seven days to live in the present without having to confront anything, fear anything, decide anything. That was all he wanted, to stretch out on a hammock on deck, his eyes closed and his mind clear of all thought, as smooth and empty as the ocean's horizon.

He was a passenger like any other in second class, still relatively well dressed, though carrying only one small suitcase made him somewhat unusual. Was a person traveling so far with so little luggage completely respectable? *You may encounter problems at the border no matter how many documents you show,* Negrín had warned him on the eve of his departure, with sad sarcasm, his face swollen from exhaustion and lack of sleep, *so you're better off not carrying much luggage in case you have to cross to France over the mountains. You know very well that in our country nothing's certain anymore.* As the ship left the pier, the war's stigmas were left behind, the pestilence of Europe, at least for the time being, faded from his memory as water dissolves writing and leaves only blurred stains on blank paper. In a way, the war had reached the French border, the cafés and cheap hotels where Spaniards met, like sick people brought together by the shame of a vile infection that when shared perhaps seemed less monstrous. Spaniards fleeing from one side or the other, in transit to who knows where, or appointed more or less officially to dubious missions in Paris, which in some cases allowed them to handle unusual sums of money—to buy weapons, to arrange for newspapers to publish reports favorable to the Republican cause — grouped around a radio trying to decipher news bulletins that mentioned the names of public figures or places in Spain, waiting for the afternoon papers in which the word "Madrid" would appear in a headline, but almost never on the front page. They had stormy arguments, slamming their fists on marble-topped tables and waving their hands through the clouds of cigarette smoke, rejecting the city where they found themselves, as if they were in a café on Calle de Alcalá or the Puerta del Sol and what lay before their eyes didn't interest them in the least, the prosperous, radiant city without fear where their obsessive war didn't exist, where they themselves were nothing, foreigners similar to others who talked louder and had darker hair, darker faces, gruffer voices, and the harsh gutturals of a Balkan dialect. On the two nights he had to spend in a Paris hotel, waiting to have his transit visa and ticket to America confirmed, Ignacio Abel did his best not to run into anyone he knew. It was rumored that Bergamín was in Paris on an obscure cultural venture that perhaps disguised a mission to buy weapons or recruit foreign volunteers. But Bergamín was probably in a better hotel. The one where Ignacio Abel stayed, with a profound feeling of distaste, was largely populated by prostitutes and foreigners, the various castoffs of Europe, among whom the Spaniards preserved their noisy national distinction, intensely singular and at the same time resembling the others, those who'd left their countries long before and those who had no country to go back to, the stateless, carrying Nansen passports from the League of Nations, not allowed to stay in France but also not admitted to any other country: German Jews, Romanians, Hungarians, Italian anti-Fascists, Russians languidly resigned to exile or furiously arguing about their increasingly phantasmagorical country, each with his own language and his own particular manner of speaking bad French, all united by the identical air of their foreignness, documents that didn't guarantee much and bureaucratic decisions always delayed, the hostility of hotel employees and the violent searches by the police. With his passport in order and his American visa, with his ticket for the SS *Manhattan*, Ignacio Abel had eluded the fate of those wandering souls, whom he would pass in the narrow hallway to the toilet or hear groaning or murmuring in their equally foreign languages on the other side of his room's thin wall. Professor Rossman could have been one of them if, on his return from Moscow in the spring of 1935, he'd remained with his daughter in Paris instead of trying his luck at the Spanish embassy, where the clerks in charge of residency permits had seemed more benevolent or indifferent or venal than the French. At times during those days in Paris, Ignacio Abel thought he saw Professor Rossman in the distance, his arms around a large black briefcase, or holding the arm of his daughter, who was taller than he, as if he'd continued to have a parallel existence not canceled by the other, the one that took him to Madrid and nomadic penury, gradual loss of dignity, then the morgue. If Professor Rossman had remained in Paris, he'd be living now in one of these hotels, visiting embassies and consular offices, persistent and meek, always smiling and removing his hat when he approached a clerk's window, waiting for a visa to the United States or Cuba or any country in South America, pretending not to understand when a bureaucrat or shopkeeper called him *sale boche, sale métèque* behind his back.

Professor Rossman no longer had to wait for anything. He'd been buried with several dozen other corpses and hurriedly covered by lime in a common grave in Madrid, infected without reason or fault by the great medieval plague of Spanish death, spread indiscriminately by the most modern and most primitive means alike, everything from Mauser rifles, machine guns, and incendiary bombs to crude ancestral weapons: pocketknives, harquebuses, hunting shotguns, cattle prods, even animal jawbones if necessary, death that descended with the roar of airplane engines and the neighing of mules, with scapulars and crosses and red flags, with rosary prayers and the shouting of anthems on the radio. In the tucked-away cafés and rundown hotels of Paris, Spanish emissaries from both sides closed deals on weapon purchases that would allow them to finish off their compatriots with greater speed and efficiency. In the midst of this carnival of Spanish death, the pale face of Professor Rossman appeared to Ignacio Abel in dreams and in the light of day, producing in him a shudder of shame, a wave of nausea, like the one he felt the first time he saw a dead body in the middle of the street under the relentless sun of a summer morning. If he overheard a conversation in Spanish at the cheap restaurant where he ate in Paris, he maintained a neutral expression and tried not to look, as if that would save him from contagion. In the Spanish newspapers, the war had been a daily typographic battle: enormous, triumphant, and colossally untrue headlines printed haphazardly on bad paper, on scant sheets, spreading false reports about victorious battles while the enemy continued to approach Madrid. In the Parisian papers, solemn and monotonous as bourgeois buildings, and secured in their burnished wooden holders under the soothing half-light of cafés, the war in Spain was an exotic, frequently minor matter, news of sheer savagery in a distant, primitive region of the world. He recalled the melancholy of his first trips out of the country, the feeling of leaping in time as soon as he crossed the Spanish border. He relived the shame he'd felt as a young man when he saw pictures of bullfights in a French or German newspaper: miserable horses, their bellies gored open, kicking in agony in a quagmire of guts, sand, and blood; bulls vomiting blood, their tongues hanging out and a sword running through the nape of their necks, turned into red pulp by the failed efforts to kill them with a single thrust. Now it was not dead bulls or horses he saw in Parisian newspapers or in newsreels at a movie theater where he longed for Judith Biely; this time it was men, men killing one another, corpses tossed like bundles of rags into ditches, laborers wearing berets and white shirts, their hands raised, herded like cattle by soldiers on horseback, filthy soldiers wearing grotesque uniforms, cruel, arrogant, driven by a senseless enthusiasm, as exotically sinister as bandits in daguerreotypes and lithographs from the last century, so alien to the worthy European public who had witnessed from a distance the massacre of Abyssinians holding shields and spears and who for months and with perfect impunity had been gunned down and bombed from the air by Mussolini's Italian expeditionary forces. For a time the Abyssinians appeared in newspapers, in illustrated magazines, in newsreels, but once they'd played their transitory part as cannon fodder, as extras in the great masquerade of international scandal, they became invisible again. Now it's our turn, he thought as he leafed through the newspaper in the restaurant, lowering his head behind the large sheets for fear a Spaniard at one of the nearby tables might recognize him. ESPAGNE ENSANGLANTÉE — ON FUSILLE ICI COMME ON DÉBOISE. Among the French words, rebounding like pebbles in the dense typography of the paper, were the names of Spanish towns, the geography of the enemy's inexorable advance toward Madrid, where the flamenco music that played on the radio, broadcast by loudspeakers in the cafés, would be interrupted from time to time by a cornet fanfare and a resonant voice that announced increasingly glorious and unlikely new victories that were received by the public with applause and bullfight *olés*. DES FEMMES, DES ENFANTS, FUIENT SOUS LE FEU DES INSURGÉS. In a blurred, dark photograph he recognized a straight, white highway, figures advancing, laden animals, a peasant woman holding a nursing child whom she tried to protect from something that came down from the sky. He calculated the enemy's distance from Madrid, probably reduced now by the rapid advance of recent days. He imagined the repetition of what he'd seen with his own eyes: wagons, donkeys, cars overturned in ditches, militiamen tossing aside rifles and cartridge belts to run faster through the countryside, officers shouting orders no one understood or obeyed. The highway was an overflowing river of human beings, animals, and machines pushed forward by the seismic upheaval of an enemy that was close but still invisible. Beside him, in the back seat of the official automobile caught in a traffic jam of trucks and peasant wagons, among which, absurdly, a flock of goats wandered, Negrín contemplated the disaster with an expression of dejected fatalism, his profile morose against the window, his chin thrust into his fist, while the uniformed driver uselessly blew the horn in an attempt to inch forward. A little beyond the highway stood a white house with a grape arbor, a gentle slope of dark earth recently tilled for autumn planting. In the background, against the clear afternoon sky, rose a great column of thick, black smoke that gave off a smell of gasoline and burned tires. "They're much closer than we thought," said Negrín. Hostile or terrified faces pressed against the car windows trying to peer inside. Furious fists and rifle butts struck the roof and sides. "I don't think they'll let us get through, Don Juan," said the militiaman who was their bodyguard and sat beside the driver.

Perhaps Professor Rossman decided to try his luck in Spain because he trusted in the help of his former student Ignacio Abel, who could have saved his life yet did nothing, or almost nothing, for him. Who could have warned him at least, advised him not to talk so loud, or make himself so visible, or tell anyone what had happened in Germany, what he'd seen in Moscow. Abel could have supported him with more conviction and not merely arrange job interviews that led nowhere or hire his daughter to give Lita and Miguel German lessons. But the favors granted least frequently are those that would cost almost nothing: need that is too apparent provokes rejection; the vehemence of a request guarantees it will receive no response. Professor Rossman's eyes were more faded than he remembered, and his skin was whiter, a little viscous, the skin of someone who's grown accustomed to living in damp shadows, without the military luster his bald head once displayed, shining under the electric light of a lecture hall on the early nights of winter. Ignacio Abel raised tired eyes from the worktable covered by blueprints and documents in his University City office, and the pale man dressed with funereal severity who called him by name and held out his hand wore the uncertain smile of someone hoping to be recognized. But Dr. Rossman was not an older version of the man Ignacio Abel had met in Weimar in 1923 or to whom he'd said goodbye one day in September 1929 in Barcelona, at the France Station, after visiting the German pavilion at the International Exposition with him and spending hours talking passionately in a café; less than six years later, in April or May of 1935, he was another man, not changed or aged but transfigured, his skin pale as if his blood had been diluted or extracted, his eyes like slightly cloudy water, his gestures as frail and his voice as faint as a convalescent's, his suit as worn as if he hadn't taken it off, even to go to sleep, since leaving Barcelona in 1929. When one no longer has a bathroom, a clean bed, and running water, deterioration comes quickly. Very quickly, and at the same time very gradually. Your shirt collar turns darker even though you scrub it in a sink; your shoes stretch, crossed by cracks resembling the wrinkles in a face; the elbows of your jacket, the knees of your trousers, take on the shine of an old cassock or a fly's wing. Ever since he was a child, Ignacio Abel had instinctively spotted misfortune that afflicted impoverished decent people, respectable tenants late in paying rent in the building where his mother worked as porter: gentlemen with slicked-back hair and misshapen boots who would bend down rapidly to retrieve a cigarette butt from the ground or look furtively inside a garbage can; aging widows who went to Mass, leaving on the staircase a trail of unfathomable stench, their greasy chignons held by combs under mended veils; clerks wearing ties and celluloid collars, their nails dirty, their breath smelling of sour café con leche and ulcers. Seeing Professor Rossman appear without warning in his University City office as if he'd just returned from the land of the dead, Ignacio Abel felt the same mixture of pity and revulsion those people had inspired in him when he was a boy. Professor Rossman's smile seemed strange now that almost all his teeth were missing. The only thing that remained of his former presence, aside from his formality — the bow tie, hard collar, high shoes, the suit tailored before 1914 — was the large briefcase he held with both hands against his chest, the same one he'd drop on his desk in a lecture hall at the Bauhaus, producing a metallic noise of random objects and junk, but more worn now, with the consistency of cracked parchment, as soft as his toothless mouth but still maintaining all the Germanic severity of a professor's briefcase with its metal buckles and clasps and reinforced corners, the briefcase from which the most unexpected objects would emerge during his classes, like the doves or rabbits or scarves that come out of a magician's top hat.

One by one, with the comic astonishment of a silent film, Professor Rossman would remove from his apparently bottomless briefcase perfectly ordinary objects that in his hands took on the miraculous quality of the newly invented. In his Weimar class in an unheated lecture hall, where the cold wind blew through broken windowpanes, Professor Karl Ludwig Rossman, without removing his overcoat or scarf, examined as if they were pristine inventions or recently discovered treasures the most mundane tools, the kind that everyone uses every day and no one notices because their invisibility, he'd say, was the measure of their efficiency, the test of a form corresponding to a task—a form often shaped over centuries, even millennia, like the spiral of a shell or the almost flat curvature of a pebble polished by the friction of sand and water at the ocean's edge. No books, sketches, or architectural magazines came out of Professor Rossman's briefcase but the tools of carpenters, stonecutters, and masons, plumb lines, spinning tops, clay bowls, a spoon, a pencil, the handle of a coffee grinder, a black rubber ball that rebounded off the ceiling after popping up like a spring before the infantilized eyes of the students, an artist's brush, a paintbrush, an Italian vase of heavy green glass, a crank of corrugated brass, a packet of cigarette papers, a lightbulb, a baby's bottle, a pair of scissors. Reality was a labyrinth and a laboratory of objects that were prodigious but so common you easily forgot they didn't exist in nature but were products of the human imagination. A horizontal plane, he'd say, a staircase. In nature the only horizontal plane was motionless water, the distant horizon at sea. A natural cave or a treetop can suggest the idea of a roof, a column. But what mental process first produced the concept of a staircase? In the icy lecture hall, his hat pulled down to his eyebrows, not removing his overcoat or wool gloves, Professor Rossman, who was susceptible to the cold, could spend an entire class voluptuously concentrating on the form and function of a pair of scissors, the manner in which the two sharpened arms opened like a bird's beak or an alligator's jaws and cut a sheet of paper perfectly, cleanly, following a straight or curved line, the sinuous profiled lines of a caricature. His coat pockets were always stuffed with everyday objects, things he would pick up from the ground, and when he probed them with his glove-covered fingers, looking for something specific, he'd usually come across another unexpected object that demanded his attention and fired his enthusiasm. The six sides of a die, dots bored into each one of them, contained the infinite possibilities of chance. Nothing was more beautiful than a well-polished ball rolling on a smooth surface. A tiny match contained the marvelous solution to the millenarian problem of producing and transporting fire. He extracted the match from its box with care, as if he were removing a dried butterfly whose wings could be destroyed if handled too casually, held it between his thumb and index finger, showed it to the students, raising it in a somehow liturgical gesture. He pondered its qualities, the delicate, diminutive pear shape of the head, the body of wood or waxed paper. The box itself, with its complication of angles and the master stroke of intuition it had been to invent two parts that adjusted to each other so effortlessly and at the same time were easy to open. When he struck the match, the tiny sound of the match head running along the thin strip of sandpaper was heard with perfect clarity in the silence of the lecture hall, and the small burst of flame seemed like a miracle. Radiant, like someone who's successfully completed an experiment, Professor Rossman displayed the burning match. Then he took out a cigarette and lit it as naturally as if he were in a café, and only then, once he had put out the match, did those listening to his exposition emerge from the hypnotic trance they'd been led into without realizing it.

Professor Rossman was like a peddler of the most vulgar, most improbable things. He lectured as easily on the practical virtues of a spoon's curvature as on the exquisite visual rhythms of the radii of a bicycle wheel in motion. Other professors at the School proselytized for the new, while Professor Rossman revealed the innovation and sophistication that remain hidden and yet produce results in what has always existed. He would clear the middle of the table, place on it a top he'd bought on his way to the School from some children playing in the street, start it twirling with an abrupt, skilled gesture, and watch it spin, as dazzled as if he were witnessing the rotation of a heavenly body. "Invent something like this," he challenged the students with a smile. "Invent the top, or the spoon, or the pencil. Invent the book that can be carried in a pocket and contains the *Iliad* or Goethe's *Faust*. Invent the match, the jug handle, the scale, the carpenter's folding ruler, the sewing needle, the scissors. Perfect the wheel or the fountain pen. Think of the time when some of these things didn't exist." Then he looked at his wristwatch—he was enthusiastic about this new gadget, which had appeared, according to him, among British officers during the war— picked up his things, placed his lunatic inventor's or junkman's objects back in his briefcase, filled his pockets with them, and dismissed the class with a nod and a mock-military click of his heels.

"My dear friend, don't you remember me?"

But it hadn't been that long. In Barcelona, less than six years earlier, Professor Rossman, stouter and balder than in Weimar, in one of the suits probably cut by the same tailor who had made them for him before 1914, inspected the final details of the German pavilion at the International Exposition with bird-like gestures and an owl's pale eyes behind his glasses. He had to be sure everything would be just right when Mies van der Rohe made his grand appearance there, wearing the monocle of a Prussian officer, chewing the long ebony holder into which he inserted cigarettes with a surgical flourish. Professor Rossman took Ignacio Abel's arm, asked about his work in Spain, lamented that he hadn't returned to the School now that things had improved so much and there was a new, magnificent campus in Dessau. He passed his hand over a polished surface of dark green marble to check its cleanliness, studied the alignment of a piece of furniture or a sculpture, brought his eyes close to a sign as if to make certain the typography was exact. In the austere, limpid space no one had visited yet, Dr. Rossman seemed even more anachronistic with his stiff collar, high shoes in that 1900 style, and the aloof courtesy of an imperial functionary. But his hands touched objects with the same old avidity, confirming textures, angles, curvatures, and in his eyes was the same permanent mixture of interrogation and amazement, a brazen urgency to see everything, a childish joy at incessant discoveries. Now his jovial disposition had been strengthened along with his physical presence, and he recalled with relief the not so distant past of uncertainty, inflation, hunger, days when he carried a boiled potato, his only food for the day, in his bottomless briefcase or in a coat pocket, when in the unheated lecture halls of the School it was so cold he couldn't hold the chalk between his frostbitten fingers. "But you remember as well, my friend, you spent the winter of 1923 with us." Now Professor Rossman looked at the future with a serenity tempered by the basic mistrust of someone who's already seen the world drown once. "You have to come back to Germany. You won't recognize Berlin. You can't imagine the number of new, beautiful buildings being built. You can see them in the magazines, of course, but you know it's not the same thing. Berlin resembles New York. You have to see the new neighborhoods with workers' housing, the big department stores, the lights at night. Things we dreamed about at the School in the middle of the disaster seem to have become reality. A few, not many. But you know how something well made, even if small, can make a difference."

The value of objects, instruments, tools. The beauty of the pavilion that took one's breath away, staggered the soul, something tangible and of this world though it seemed not to belong to it entirely, too pure perhaps, too perfect in the purity of its right angles and smooth surfaces, alien not only to most of the other buildings in the Exposition but to reality itself, to the raw light and harshness of life in Spain. There may be a depraved, baroque quality in poverty, just as there is in ostentation. One September morning in 1929, Ignacio Abel strolled with Professor Rossman through the German pavilion, where hammers still sounded and laborers were hard at work, where footsteps and voices echoed in the uninhabited spaces, and he noticed a sting of skepticism in his own enthusiasm. Or perhaps it was simply resentment at not being able to imagine anything similar, a building that would justify his life even though it was destined to be demolished after a few months. Like a brilliant composition that won't be played again after its premiere, the score would remain, perhaps a recording, the inexact recollections of those who heard it. Active, loquacious, attentive to everything, Professor Rossman supervised the construction so that everything would be ready when his colleague Mies van der Rohe arrived from Germany, and afterward Rossman toured Barcelona with his wife and daughter, whom he photographed in front of Gaudí's buildings, which seemed to him nonsensical, yet were endowed with a beauty that struck him all the more because it contradicted all his own principles. His wife was fat, short, and phlegmatic, his daughter tall, thin, and ungainly, with an intense look behind her gold-framed eyeglasses. And Professor Rossman between the two, cheerful to no end, asking a passerby to take a picture of the three of them, extolling buildings and views that neither mother nor daughter looked at, praising the local delicacies they both wolfed down mindlessly, waiting for an opportunity to drop them off at the hotel and allow himself to be carried downriver to the port by the human current on the Ramblas.

"How are your wife and children? A boy and a girl, isn't that so? I remember your showing me pictures of them when we were in Weimar and they were very small. Still too young to argue politics with you. My wife misses the kaiser and feels sympathy for Hitler. The only defect she finds in him is that he's so anti-Semitic. And my daughter belongs to the Communist Party. She lives in a house with central heating and hot water but longs for a communal apartment in Moscow. She hates Hitler, but much less than she hates the Social Democrats, including me: she must think I'm the worst of the bunch. What a magnificent Freudian drama to be the daughter of a Social Fascist, a Social Imperialist. Perhaps deep down my daughter admires Hitler just as much as her mother does, and the only defect she finds in him is that he's so anti-Communist." Professor Rossman laughed with some benevolence, as if at heart he attributed the muddled politics of his wife and daughter to a certain congenital intellectual weakness of the female mind, or as if over the years he'd developed a tolerance somewhere between being resigned to and sardonic about the extremes of human foolishness. "But tell me what you're working on now, my friend, what projects you have. I'm happy to know you're completely innocent of the esthetic crime that is the Spanish pavilion at the Exposition." Professor Rossman's oval head stopped moving, and his eyes, enlarged by his glasses, focused on him with an affectionate attention that made Ignacio Abel feel bewildered as someone much younger, a student not certain he can endure the scrutiny of the professor who knows him well. What had he done in those years that could measure up to what he'd learned in Germany, to the expectations he'd had for himself and his work? The nocturnal lights and strong colors of Berlin, the calm of Weimar, the libraries, the joy of finally penetrating a language he'd handled until then only laboriously and to which his ears suddenly opened up as naturally as if he'd removed plugs of wax, the lecture halls at Weimar, those rainy nightfalls of self-reflection, lamps lit behind curtains, bicycle bells echoing in the silence. The cold, too, and the scarcity of everything, but he didn't care or notice very much. The hooves of policemen's horses raising sparks on the paving stones, the solemn, angry demonstrations by unemployed workers in berets and leather jackets and red armbands, the placards and red flags lit by torches, the veterans with amputated limbs begging on the sidewalks, displaying stumps under the rags of their uniforms or faces doubly disfigured by war wounds and surgeries. The young women in short skirts, eyes and lips painted, chin-length hair, sitting on the terraces of Berlin cafés with their legs crossed, smoking cigarettes on which they left red lipstick marks, walking with determination along the sidewalks without male companions, jumping onto streetcars after the offices closed, heels clicking as they hurried down the metro steps.

He didn't think about Spain during those months of great intensity. He was thirty-four years old and felt a physical agility and intellectual excitement he hadn't known when he was twenty. He imagined for himself another life, limitless and also impossible, in which the weight, the extortion of the past didn't count, the sadness of his marriage, the perpetual demands of his children. After a few months his time in

Germany was gone like a sum that would have seemed inexhaustible to a man accustomed to handling only small amounts of money. He returned to Madrid in the early summer heat of 1924, and nothing had changed. His son had begun to walk. The girl didn't recognize him and took frightened refuge in her mother's arms. No one asked him anything about his time in Germany. He went to the office of the Council for Advanced Studies to submit the required report on his travels, and the bureaucrat who received it filed it away promptly and handed him a stamped receipt. Now, in Barcelona, Professor Rossman asked what he'd done in those five years, and his life, full of tasks and compromises, seemed to dissolve into nothingness, like the feverish expectations of his months in Weimar, like those dreams in which one feels exalted by a splendid idea that on waking turns out to be insignificant. Efforts that at some point end in frustration, assignments without result, projects in ruins — or, to quote from an article by Ortega y Gasset, Spain was a nation of projects in ruins. But at least there was a promising expectation, he told Professor Rossman, superstitiously fearing it would come to nothing because he'd mentioned it: a market in a working-class district of Madrid, close to the street where he'd been born, and something even more improbable, but also more tempting, which almost made him dizzy: a position in the Department of Design and Construction at Madrid's University City. Professor Rossman, with his versatile, polyglot curiosity, with his interest in everything, had already heard about the project, which had an unusual breadth for Europe — he'd read something in an international magazine. "Write to me," he told Ignacio Abel when they were saying goodbye. "Let me know how everything goes. I wish you could come sometime to teach a course at the School. Let me know how your ideal city of knowledge progresses."

But neither wrote to the other. The promises, the good things they wished each other as they were leaving, were as abundant and unreal as the stacks of German bills that filled one's pockets and weren't enough to buy a cup of coffee. Suddenly time accelerates, and the children have grown without your being aware of it. On land where nothing existed—where pine groves had been uprooted by steam shovels, the ground leveled, the plain subdivided by imaginary lines—there are now streets with sidewalks, but no houses, young trees, buildings emerging from the mud, some completed but still empty, some inaugurated and put to use, the School of Philosophy and Letters Building is occupied, though masons, carpenters, and painters continue to work there, though students have to cut across open country and walk around ditches and piles of building materials to reach it. Through the windows of his office he could see the red blocks of the Schools of Medicine and of Pharmacy, almost finished on the outside, the structure of the University Hospital, surrounded by swarms of laborers, donkeys, trucks carrying materials, armed guards patrolling the site. Farther on past the somber green of oaks and pines, and above that, on a more distant plane, the outline of the Sierra, its highest peaks still snow-covered. It's almost six on the large office clock, too late to receive a visitor who doesn't have an appointment. The calendar shows a date in May 1935, which Ignacio Abel will cross out just before he leaves. He looked up from the board on which a student had spread a plan, and the pale old man from the other world smiled at him awkwardly, his eyes watery, stretching wide a mouth filled with ruined teeth, extending his hand, the other pressing against his chest the black briefcase, as immediately recognizable as his accent and stiff comportment from another century, the briefcase in which he no longer kept dazzling objects with which he'd transmit to his students the mystery of the practical forms that make life better: now he kept documents, certificates in Gothic print and gilt seals no longer worth anything, printed requests for visas in a variety of languages, copies of letters to embassies, official letters that denied him something in neutral language or demanded yet another certificate, some insignificant but inaccessible paper, some consular stamp without which the months of waiting and delays would have been in vain.

"Professor Rossman, what a pleasant surprise. When did you get here?"

"My friend, my dear Professor Abel, you wouldn't believe what has happened. But don't worry about me, I see you're busy, I don't mind waiting."

5

A BLACK SILHOUETTE crossed the illuminated rectangle of the screen where the slides were being projected, next to the podium from which Ignacio Abel gave his lecture. His nerves settled down when he began to speak. He was calmed by the clear sound of his own voice, the sturdy podium on which he rested his hands. Before walking onstage he'd been comforted by the warm sound of the audience filling the hall, after having been afraid that no one would attend the lecture, his fear growing as the day approached; how embarrassed he felt that morning trying to hide his anxiety from Adela and the children during breakfast and then excusing himself from the table, explaining he would rather walk to the Student Residence by himself. He'd been speaking only a few minutes when he'd asked that the lights in the auditorium be turned off, and the murmur of the audience dissolved into silence. On the podium, a lamp with a green shade reflected the white of the written pages onto his face, hardening his features with areas of shadow. He looked older than he was, as seen from the first row where Adela and their daughter were sitting, both nervous, Adela with a shy, protective tenderness, uneasy about his male vanity, the girl proud of the high, solitary appearance of her father onstage, distinguished in his bow tie and reading glasses, which he put on and took off depending on whether he consulted his notes or spoke without looking at them. The girl, Lita, who at the age of fourteen has a precocious love of painting, encouraged by her teachers at the Institute School, appreciates the composition of the scene whose fleeting center is the profile of a female shadow, moving in front of a slide projected on the screen behind her father's back. She's flattered that they've allowed her to attend the talk; that her father is aware of her and has signaled to her from the podium; that these cultured, amiable ladies whom her mother invites to tea from time to time have come this evening—Doña María de Maeztu, Señora Bonmati de Salinas, Juan Ramón Jiménez's wife, who has such a pretty name, Zenobia, Zenobia Camprubí—and accepted her without condescension, remarking on how grown-up she looked. (Adela phoned the ladies to make certain they'd attend; she'd been infected by the fear she guessed at in him, the fear there would be no audience; she made the calls without his knowledge in order not to wound his pride.) Lita hoped the interruption hadn't distracted her father, who complained so often at home about how loudly the maids played the radio, about the arguments between Lita and her brother. He remained silent, his glasses in one hand and in the other the pointer he used to indicate details in the slides, like a teacher in front of a map, wearing an irritated expression that Adela and the girl recognized, though it was subtle, when the door of the hall opened and a woman in high-heeled shoes walked in, her steps resounding on the wooden floor in spite of the caution of her movements. Caution and a certain insolence, or simply the awkwardness of someone who arrives late and has to move about in semidarkness. She passed in front of the beam of light from the projector, the entire length of the first row, toward an empty seat in the corner. I see the silhouette, moving and at the same time frozen, the profile against the screen as in a shadow play, the skirt made of light fabric like an inverted corolla. Ignacio Abel made it a point to stay silent, following the newcomer with his eyes and not hiding his annoyance. That evening in the Residence, in the darkened hall where he could barely make out the familiar faces in the audience—Adela, his daughter, Señora de Salinas, Zenobia, Moreno Villa, Negrín, the engineer Torroja, the architect López Otero, Professor Rossman, far in the back, his bald oval head among women's hats—he was pleased by the strong, clear sound of his own voice and the attention he was getting, which had a lightly euphoric effect after the first few minutes of settling in, after the noise in the hall and the scraping of chairs, and after the several days of insecurity he wouldn't have admitted to anyone came to an end. The silhouette of the newcomer was outlined on the slide of a peasant façade, a house built in the middle of the eighteenth century, he explained, looking at his notes, in a southern city, conceived not by an architect but a master builder who knew his trade and, literally, the ground he walked on: the earth that produced the sandy, golden stone of the lintel over the door and windows, the clay for the bricks and tiles, the lime that had whitened the façade, leaving exposed, with admirable esthetic intuition, only the stone of the lintels, delicately carved by a master stonecutter who'd also sculpted, in the center of the lintel, a calyx situated exactly at the axis of the building. He signaled for the next slide, a detail of the angle of the lintel. With the pointer he indicated the diagonal of the joint of two ashlars that formed the corner, where two contrary forces balanced with a mathematical precision that was even more astonishing given that the men who conceived and built the structure probably didn't know how to read or write. Stone and lime, he said, thick walls that insulated against both heat and cold, small windows avoiding obvious symmetry and distributed according to an irregular order related to the slant of the sun's rays, and white lime that best reflected the sunlight and eased the interior temperature during the summer months. With mortar and reeds that grew along nearby streams, they created natural insulation for the roofs of the highest rooms—the technique essentially the same one used in ancient Egypt and Mesopotamia. Architects of the German school—"myself among them," he noted with a smile, knowing that isolated laughter would be heard in the hall—always speak of organic construction. What could be more organic than the people's instinct to use what was closest at hand and flexibly adapt a timeless vocabulary to immediate conditions, the climate and ways of earning a living and the demands of the work, reinventing elemental forms that were always new yet never yielded to whim, that stood out in the landscape and at the same time fused with it, without ostentation or mechanical repetition, transmitted throughout the country and from one generation to the next like old ballads that don't need to be transcribed because they survive in the current of the people's memory, in the discipline without vanity of the best artisans. At the rear of the hall, in spite of the darkness, he guessed at or almost discerned the approving smile of Professor Rossman, leaning forward so as not to miss any of the Spanish words: the intuition of forms, the integrity of materials and procedures, courtyards paved with river pebbles tracing a rotating visual rhythm, tiles fitted together with the organic precision of fish scales. (He'd said that word again; from now on he had to avoid it.) As he spoke, he became less self-conscious and his gestures lost their initial rigidity, which perhaps only Adela had noticed, just as she noticed how his voice became more natural. He showed a paved courtyard with columns and a fountain in the center, which could have been in Crete or Rome but belonged to an apartment house in Córdoba, its form so well adapted to its function that it had endured with only minor variations for several millennia. Light and shade shaped just like the material—light, shade, sound, the flow of water in a fountain refreshing a courtyard, the opacity of the outside walls, the daylight that enters from above and spreads through rooms and hallways. Who'd be presumptuous enough to affirm that functional architecture—he almost said "organic"—was a twentieth-century invention? But it was fraudulent to imitate external forms by parodying them; one had to learn from processes, not results, the syntax of a language and not isolated words. Iron, steel, wide sheets of glass, and reinforced concrete would have to be employed with the same awareness of their material qualities that the plebeian architect possessed when he used reeds or clay or stones with sharp edges to erect a dividing wall, instinctively taking advantage of the form of each stone to fit it to the others, not feeling obliged to force it into an external mold. He showed a slide of a shepherd's hut made of interwoven straw and rushes, another of the interior of a mountain shelter where with stones but no mortar a vault had been built that had the rugged solidity of a Romanesque apse. The chance form of each slab was transformed into necessity when it was fitted as if by magnetic attraction to the form of another. And at the heart of everything was the people's instinct for making full use of scarcity, their talent in turning limitations into advantages. Until now the slides had shown only buildings. The click of the projector sounded and the screen was filled by a peasant family posing in front of one of the huts with eaves of admirably woven straw and rushes. Dark faces stared into the hall, the large eyes of barefoot, big-bellied children dressed in rags, a gaunt pregnant woman holding a child, a lean, dry man beside her in a white shirt, trousers tied at the waist with rope, and sandals made of esparto grass. In the Residence Hall the picture was something like documentation of a trip to a remote country sunk in primitivism. Just as he used the pointer earlier to indicate architectural details, Ignacio Abel now pointed out the faces he'd photographed only a few months earlier in a village of phantasmagorical poverty in the Sierra de Málaga. Architecture, he said, didn't consist of inventing abstract forms, and the Spanish plebeian tradition wasn't a catalogue of the picturesque to be shown to foreigners or used decoratively in the pavilion of a fair. The architecture of a new time had to be a tool in the great task of improving people's lives, alleviating suffering, bringing justice, or better yet, or said more precisely, making accessible what the family in the slide had never seen and didn't know existed: running water, airy spaces, a school, food that was sufficient and, if possible, tasty; not a gift but restitution, not charity but an act of reparation for unremunerated labor, for the skill of hands and the fineness of minds that had known how to choose the best rushes and braid them to hold up a straw roof or make a basket, the proper clay to whitewash the walls of a hut. From what those people have created over the centuries come almost the only solid, noble things in Spain, he said, original and incomparable, music and ballads and buildings. He was moved, Adela noted from the first row and privately shared his emotion. Ignacio Abel forced himself to contain an effusiveness that took him by surprise. He wasn't quite sure where it came from, rising from his stomach, as if he were suddenly possessed not by memories of his father and the masons

71

and stonecutters who worked with him, the ones who erected buildings and paved streets and dug foundations and tunnels and then disappeared from the earth without a trace, but by the awareness of those who'd lived before, several generations of peasants from whom he descended, those who'd lived and died in mud huts identical to the one in the slide, as poor, as obstinate, as lacking in a future as those people whose faces were fading, now that the lights in the hall had been turned on but the slide projector had not yet been turned off.

In a drawer in his study locked with a small key, useless now, which Ignacio Abel continues to carry in his pocket, is the folded sheet announcing the lecture. The smallest things can last a long time, immune to abandonment and even the physical disappearance of the person who held them in his hands. A yellow sheet, somewhat faded, the line of the fold so worn that after a few years it will fall apart if someone attempts to open it, if it hasn't been burned or tossed in the trash, if it doesn't disappear beneath the rubble of the house after one of the enemy bombing raids the following winter. He found the handbill in a pocket of the jacket he hadn't worn since then, but by now it was a secret clue, the material proof of the start of another life that began that evening, without anything announcing it, not even the silhouette crossing in front of the slide projector. The day and the year, the place and the hour, like an unearthed inscription that permits the dating of an archeological find: Tuesday, October 7, 1935, 7:00 in the evening, the Auditorium of the Student Residence, Pinar 21, Madrid. Ignacio Abel folded the sheet carefully, with a certain clandestine feeling, and locked it in the same drawer that held his first letters from Judith Biely.

If not for that paper printed in the Residence's noble, austere typography, perhaps he wouldn't have proof of the date he heard her name for the first time. But a few minutes before someone introduced them, he'd already recognized her in a kind of flash when, as he concluded his talk, the lights in the auditorium went on and he bowed with some discomfort when he heard well-mannered applause and woke from a fervor he now privately regretted or was embarrassed by, looking sideways toward the end of the first row where Adela and the girl, Señora de Salinas, Zenobia Camprubí, and María de Maeztu in her twisted hat were all sitting, and next to them, incongruous and young, exotic with her fair hair, pale skin, and energetic applause, the stranger who'd irritated him when she came in late. He remembered the woman at the piano, her back to him, who'd turned around, just as he recalled the ripe autumnal quality of the sunlight shining on her hair.

He embraced his daughter, who ran toward him as soon as he came down from the stage. "Why isn't your brother here with all of you?" "He had a German lesson with Señorita Rossman. Have you seen her father? Mamá couldn't get away from him." Professor Rossman made his way through the crowd, enveloped him in his oppressive Germanic cordiality, his sour smell of unwashed clothing, a squalid pensión, and prostate disease. ("Professor Rossman smells like old cat piss," his son once protested with the savage sincerity of a child.) "An excellent speech, my dear friend, excellent. You don't know how grateful I am for your invitation, yet another courtesy I can't reciprocate." Behind the thick lenses of his round glasses, Professor Rossman's colorless eyes were wet with emotion, an excessive gratitude Ignacio Abel would have preferred not to receive. He did, in fact, smell of uric acid and had on a suit he had worn too much, and his bald oval head shone with sweat. He now scraped a living by selling fountain pens in cafés and with the small amount of money Ignacio Abel paid his daughter to give German lessons to Miguel and Lita. "But I don't want to keep you, my friend —you have many people to greet." Ignacio Abel moved away, and Dr. Rossman remained alone, isolated by his obvious state of impoverished foreignness and misfortune.

While he looked after the ladies and accepted congratulations, agreed with comments, thought before responding to questions, Ignacio Abel looked through the crowd for the blond woman, fearing she'd left. It comforted his vanity that so many people had attended. The booming voice and corpulence of Don Juan Negrín stood out from the civilized murmur of the others. "I was the one who proposed to López

73

Otero that he hire our friend Abel when we began construction of University City, and as you see, I wasn't wrong," he heard Negrín say, in the center of a vaguely official group, with his mouth full. Waiters in short jackets held trays of small sandwiches and served glasses of wine, grenadine, and lemon soft drinks. Professor Rossman bowed stiffly to people who didn't know him or didn't remember that they'd been introduced, and took canapés as the trays passed, eating some and putting others in his jacket pocket. When he returned to the pensión that night, he'd share them with his daughter. Ignacio Abel looked at him out of the corner of his eye, conscious of too many things at the same time, constantly torn by feelings that were too disparate.

"Juan Ramón would have liked so much to hear the lovely things you said this evening," Zenobia Camprubí commented. "'The cubist rigor of white Andalusian villages'—how beautiful. And how grateful I am that you quoted him. But you know how delicate his health is, how difficult it is for him to set foot outside."

"Ignacio always says your husband has an instinctive sense of architecture," Adela said. "He never tires of admiring the composition of his books, the covers, the typography."

"Not only that." Ignacio Abel smiled, looked furtively beyond the circle of ladies who surrounded him, and didn't notice his wife's annoyance. "The poems, above all. The precision of each word."

Moreno Villa spoke with the blond foreigner, gesticulating a great deal, leaning against the piano, and she, taller than he, nodded and occasionally let her glance wander over the crowd.

"I thought it went without saying that we don't admire Juan Ramón because of the external beauty of his books," said Adela, suddenly very shy, deeply humiliated, like a much younger woman. Zenobia pressed her gloved hand.

"Of course, Adela darling. We all understood what you meant."

A photographer circulating through the crowd asked Ignacio Abel to allow him to take a picture. "It's for *Ahora*." Abel moved away from the ladies and observed that his daughter looked at him with pride, and the blond woman turned when she noticed the flash. The following day he was irritated to see himself in the newspaper photo with an overly complacent smile he hadn't been aware of and perhaps gave other people an idea of him that he disliked. The esteemed architect Señor Abel, associate director of construction at University City, spoke brilliantly last night on the rich history of traditional Spanish popular architecture to a select audience who gathered to hear him in the auditorium of the Student Residence. Cigarette smoke, the clink of glasses, the gloved, mobile hands of the women, the delicate veils of their hats, the civilized sound of conversations. Judith Biely's laugh burst like a glass breaking on the polished wood floor. He would have liked to detach himself heedlessly from the admiring circle of ladies and walk straight across the hall to her.

"I liked the comparison of architecture and music," said Señora de Salinas in an almost inaudible voice; she always had an air somewhere between fatigue and absence. "Do you really believe there's no middle ground between the popular tradition and the modern objects of the twentieth century?"

"The nineteenth century is all bourgeois adornment and bad copies," the engineer Torroja interrupted. "Pastry decorations made of stucco instead of cream."

"I agree," said Moreno Villa. "The trouble is, the fine arts in Spain haven't come into the twentieth century yet. The public is bullheaded and patrons are backward."

"You only have to look at the villa with fake Mudéjar tiles where his excellency the president of the Republic has his private residence."

"Architecture for the bandstand."

"Worse, the bullring."

Moreno Villa and the blond woman had gradually approached. She wasn't as young as she'd seemed at a distance because of her haircut and self-assurance. Her features looked as if they'd been drawn with a precise, fine pencil. An old acquaintance of the ladies and their eminent husbands, Moreno Villa carried out with old-fashioned ease the protocol of introductions. *I looked at you up close for the first time and it seemed I'd always known you and that no one but you was in that hall.*

With secret male disloyalty, Ignacio Abel saw his wife comparing herself to the young foreigner whose strange name he heard for the first time without catching the surname. A Spanish woman, mature, widened by motherhood and the neglect of age, her hair waved in a style that had become out-of-date, so similar to the other women, her friends and acquaintances, fond of midafternoon teas, artistic and literary talks for ladies at the Lyceum Club, the wives of professors, midlevel government dignitaries, inhabitants of an enlightened and rather fictitious Madrid that took on something of reality only in places like the Residence, or in the shop of popular Spanish crafts run by Zenobia Camprubí.

"Will you forgive me for coming late to your lecture? I'm always in a rush and I lost my way in the halls," Judith said.

"If you'll forgive me for interrupting your rehearsal the other day."

But she hadn't noticed, or didn't remember.

"My dear Abel, give me a hug. You've won two ears and a tail in a very demanding bullring—excuse the metaphor, since I know you hate the national pastime." Negrín broke in with his excessive presence, the physical pride of a large man in a country of short men. Moreno Villa made the introductions, and this time Ignacio Abel listened closely to the foreigner's name.

"Biely," said Negrín. "Isn't that Russian?"

"My parents were Russian. They immigrated to America at the beginning of the century." Judith spoke a clear, careful Spanish. "Don't you like bullfights?"

When she asked the question she looked at Ignacio Abel in a way that canceled out the presence of Negrín and Moreno Villa. His daughter came toward him, took his hand, told him in a quiet voice that her mother was a little tired. The time he spent with Judith would always be measured, threatened, always subject to someone's questioning, to an anguished usury of hours and minutes, of wristwatches you don't want to look at yet glance at sideways, public clocks that slowly approach the hour of an appointment or mark with indifference the inexorable moment of saying goodbye that can't be put off any longer.

"Our friend Abel feels the same as the eminent husband of Señora Camprubí, who's here now," said Negrín. Adela and Zenobia had approached the group. Adela looked at the foreigner to whom she hadn't been introduced with the distrustful curiosity she frequently displayed with strangers, men or women. "His secular, anti-military, and anti-bullfight principles are so solid that his worst nightmare would be a battlefield Mass in a bullring."

Negrín celebrated his own joke with a laugh. He could no more control the volume of his voice than the pressure of his hand, and didn't realize that Judith Biely hadn't completely understood what he said, spoken rapidly and enveloped in the noise of nearby conversations.

"Great Spanish intellectuals have written beautiful things about bullfighting." Judith had thought out the entire sentence in Spanish before daring to say it.

"It would be better for everyone if they wrote about things that were more serious and less barbaric," said Ignacio Abel, regretting it immediately because he noticed that she blushed, the foreign pink of her skin more intense on her cheeks and neck, like a rash.

Adela reproached him afterward in the taxi, as they were crossing the deserted edges of Madrid at night, with stretches of unlit building lots and streetcar tracks that would be lost in rural darkness beyond the last illuminated corners. "How cold you are sometimes, my dear. You don't moderate your words or realize the overly serious face you put on. First you make me look ridiculous in front of Zenobia and then you say something rude about the bullfights to that poor foreign girl who was only trying to make polite conversation. She must have felt awful. You never gauge your strength. You don't seem to realize how much you can wound. Or maybe you do, and that's why you do it." But what she was rebuking him for, not with her words but with the tone in which she pronounced them, was that he'd looked to her to alleviate his insecurity but afterward hadn't shared his relief and satisfaction at his success, hadn't bothered to thank her or even to notice the deep conjugal emotion that she, docile and at the same time protective, felt, the too-comforting admiration he no longer seemed to need. Leaning back in the cab, exhausted, lightheaded, Ignacio Abel looked with some private hostility at Adela's profile, so close, so overly familiar, the face of a woman he suddenly realized he didn't love, with whom he hadn't associated the idea of love for many years, if he ever had. He couldn't recall. He could perhaps recover a trace of old tenderness by identifying in the faces of his children the features of a much younger Adela. But he was reluctant to think about the past, the years of their engagement, and perhaps he was ashamed of having loved her more than he was now willing to remember, with an antiquated, verbose love, almost the kind found on a hand-colored romantic postcard, the love of the young, ignorant man it had been difficult for him to stop being, the man Adela recalled with a memory that was both compassionate and ironic. What she saw in him couldn't be detected now by anyone who knew only the accomplished, solid man of today, none of the ladies who'd watched and listened to him this evening at the Residence, tall on the platform, well dressed in his pinstriped suit and handmade shoes, his flexible high-quality collar and English bow tie. She'd tied the bow before he left the apartment. They saw the finished man, not the precarious rough drafts that had preceded him, the architect who projected images of old Andalusian houses and German buildings with right angles, broad windows, and nautical railings on the terraces, who knew how to pronounce names in German and English and appropriately interrupt a serious exposition with an ironic aside that flattered the audience by presupposing their ability to catch it. But she, Adela, sitting next to their daughter and her friends in the first row, pleased by her husband's brilliance, knew things about him the others did not, and could measure the distance between the man of this evening and the unpolished, half-grown boy he was when they first met, calibrate the degree of artifice in his manner and worldliness, for at those moments everything in him was too irreproachable to be completely true. *Although it may not matter to you, there's no one in this world who can love you more than I because there's no one who has known you so in-*

timately your whole life and not just a few months or a few years. The scorned lover is a legitimist who vainly defends ancestral rights no one believes in. She doesn't see the signs, doesn't suspect what's incubating inside him, in the still unmodified presence of the other, doesn't perceive the slightly greater degree of ill will in his silence, the secret, not fully conscious disloyalty of the man who rides beside her in the taxi, tired and content, relieved to be returning home, mentally listing the people he knew who attended his lecture, the ones *Heraldo, Ahora,* and *El Sol* will mention tomorrow in articles he'll look for with disguised impatience, for his vanity lies in not showing his vanity, and it disconcerts him not to be immune to the weakness that he finds so unpleasant in others. Now the taxi was driving down Calle Príncipe de Vergara, advancing more slowly along the row of young trees on the central promenade, some displaying the dimmed bulbs and paper pennants of a recent festival. "We're close to home now," said the girl, who sat next to the driver, erect and attentive, as if responsibility for their ride home had been entrusted to her. Coming toward them on the sidewalk were an older man and a tall, thin woman holding his arm, walking close to the wall on their way to the metro station. "Look, Papá, we're lucky, Professor Rossman got here ahead of us and has already picked up his daughter."

6

THE SAME MUSIC had brought him to Judith for a second time. In the echoing corridor of an office building in Madrid, a distant song had invoked a feeling of familiarity at first, clarinet and piano becoming more distinct, then fading as if the wind had changed. He looked at the numbered doors of offices where he heard the ringing of telephones and the clatter of typewriters, and it took him a while to identify where the sudden vibration of recognition came from; he'd heard the same song just before he opened the door to the auditorium in the Residence, expecting to find Moreno Villa, on that afternoon whose date he was certain of because it was the day of San Miguel. But he didn't know the song had stayed with him. He knew it now, as the isolated thread of the melody joined the two images he had of Judith and wakened a vague expectation of seeing her again. Even after seeing her again at the Residence and desiring her, he could have forgotten her in the end. During that period of obsessive immersion in his work, his states of mind were as transient as the shapes of clouds. Beyond his drawing board and the large model of University City, the external world was a confused hum, like a landscape in the window that becomes more blurred as the speed of the train increases. Political passion, which had never put down deep roots in him, had been dampened over the years, tempered by skepticism and a distrust of exaggerated emotions, guttural manifestoes, and Spanish torrents of words. As distractedly as he looked over newspaper headlines or listened to the eight o'clock news on the radio, he withstood erratic squalls of dejection or impatience, familial annoyance, remorse with no visible motive, longing with no object. Urgency carried him from one place to another, as isolated in his tasks as he was inside the small Fiat he drove fast across Madrid. With no effort the attraction he'd felt for the foreign woman he saw in profile, crossing the projector's beam of light, had weakened — the attraction of an exotic presence that was intensely carnal and at the same time as intangible as a promise was contained not in her attitude or words but in her very presence, the shape of her face, the color of her hair and eyes, the timbre of her voice, and something else not in her, the promise of so many unfulfilled and often unformed desires in him, roused by Judith's proximity as if by a clap of hands or a voice revealing the dimensions of a great area of darkness. In the promise was a portion of nostalgia for what had never happened, and regret for what probably wouldn't happen now. Life could not be only what he already knew; something or someone had to be waiting for him down the road, just around the corner, in the narrow swaying streetcar he watched coming up an avenue, tracks shining in the sun on the paving stones, or behind the revolving door of a café, something or someone in the mists of the future, as soon as tomorrow or the next minute. No longer believing, he continued to wait; the loss or decline of faith didn't eliminate expectation of the miracle. Something would come leaping over everything: the project for a building that would resemble no other; the richer, denser life of excitements and textures he'd glimpsed, almost touched, in Germany for barely a year, the time that had seemed the start of his true existence and turned out to be simply a parenthesis that disappeared with the passage of the years, the delayed conclusion to his youth. Slim, independent, foreign, talking to a group of men with a naturalness that would have been unusual in a Spanish woman, Judith Biely had attracted him perhaps because she reminded him of the young women in Berlin and Weimar, coming out in groups in the late afternoon from department stores and office buildings, typists, secretaries, salesclerks, leaving behind them a scent of lipstick and the sweet smoke of American cigarettes, the brims of their hats tilted down to their eyes, their light clothing and athletic strides, dashing fearlessly across streets and past automobiles and streetcars. What excited him most was that easy confidence he'd never seen in Spain, which stimulated and intimidated him at the same time. When he was in his thirties, an architect and a family man, with a grant from the government to study abroad, dressed somberly in the Spanish manner, the women who walked along the streets or chatted in cafés with their cigarettes and drinks, their short skirts, crossed legs, and red lips, tossing their straight hair as they gestured, awakened in him an excitement and fear very similar to those of adolescence. Sexual desire was indistinguishable from enthusiasm for what he was learning and the tremors of discovery: night lights, the sound of the trains, the joy of truly submerging himself in a language and beginning to master it, his ears opening as well as his eyes, his mind overflowing with so many stimuli he didn't know how to avoid, and when he spoke German with a little fluency, without realizing it he acquired an identity that was not completely the one so tediously his, but lighter, like his body when he went out each morning, ready to take in everything, giving himself over to the clamor of Berlin or the tranquility of the heavily tree-lined streets of Weimar where he would pedal his bicycle on the way to the School, delighting in the sound of tires on the paving stones and the soft wind on his face. In the unheated lecture halls of the Bauhaus almost half the students were women, all of them much younger than he. At a party, a woman named Mitzi had kissed him, putting her tongue in his mouth and leaving in his saliva an aftertaste of alcohol and tobacco. Later she sneaked back with him to his room at the pensión, and when he turned around after looking for the book he'd promised to lend her, she was naked on the bed, slim, white, shivering with cold. Never before had a woman undressed in front of him like that. He'd never been with so young a woman, who took the initiative with a spontaneity at once delicate and obscene. Under the blankets she seemed about to come apart in his arms, as open and succulent as her mouth had been a few hours earlier at the party. She said she came from a large family in Hungary that had been ruined. She communicated by moving at will from German to French, and he heard her murmuring incomprehensible words in Hungarian, like phonetic splatters in his ear. She'd begun studying architecture, but at the School discovered that photography mattered more to her. She searched in nature and in ordinary places for the abstract visual forms her compatriot Moholy-Nagy, who also was or had been her lover, taught her to see. She gave herself in love with her eyes open and as if offering herself for a human sacrifice in which she was both priest and victim. When she took the initiative, she'd come with a shudder as if in a methodical trance that was somewhat distracted, even indifferent. Afterward she'd light a cigarette and smoke stretched out on the bed, her legs open, a knee raised, and just by looking at her he'd be consumed again with desire. The presumed Hungarian ex-countess or ex-marquise lived in a basement that had only a straw mattress and an open suitcase with her clothing, and above that a sink and mirror. In a corner, on an imposing porcelain stove that rarely gave off adequate heat, a pot of potatoes simmered. No salt, no butter, nothing, only boiled potatoes that she ate in an anarchic way throughout the day or night, piercing them with a fork and blowing to cool them before she began chewing. He remembered her sitting on the mattress with his overcoat around her thin shoulders, hair disheveled, leaning over the pot and stabbing a potato with the fork, a lit cigarette in her other hand, chewing with a purr of contentment. What most disconcerted Ignacio Abel was her lack of any trace of modesty. She burst into laughter the first night when he tried to turn off the light. For years he became inconsolably excited on sleepless nights as he lay next to Adela's wide, sleeping body, remembering the intoxicated smile that sometimes was in her eyes when she raised her head between his thighs to catch her breath or see in his face the effect of what she was doing to him with her tongue and thin lips, where the line of color had been erased; what no woman had done to him before and, he imagined, what wouldn't happen to him again; what she did with the same surrender and indifference, he soon discovered with an attack of rustic Spanish jealousy, to other students at the School in addition to her professor of photography. At some point Mitzi disappeared, and he, humiliated and ridiculous, went looking for her. He was wounded in particular by the astonishment and slight mockery with which she listened to his old-fashioned, offended lover's complaints expressed in awkward German. No one had an exclusive right to her. Had she put any conditions on him, ever asked him to turn the photo of his wife and two children on the night table to the wall? How was he so sure he was enough to satisfy her? When he tried to hold her she got away, slipping her sweaty, agile body out of his coarse male embrace like a swimmer kicking free of an undulating underwater plant that was entangling her feet. Perhaps Mitzi went to bed with other men to sleep occasionally in less inhospitable rooms than his, or eat something other than potatoes, or smoke cigarettes less toxic than the ones she bought on the street from war veterans missing an arm or leg or half a face who rolled them with tobacco from the butts they picked up from the ground. Perhaps that was why she'd gone to bed with him, who found his hands full of enormous bills worth millions of marks each time he changed a few francs of his paltry Spanish scholarship. Hunger exaggerated the collective hallucination and heightened the brilliance of bright nocturnal lights and the cascades of pearl necklaces on women who descended from black cars as long as gondolas at the doors of luxury restaurants. There was a sexual palpitation in the air that corresponded to a kind of perpetual rutting that drove him, when he was alone, to wander the streets where there were cabarets and brothels from which came bursts of syncopated music and splashes of light in strong colors, reds, greens, blues sometimes blurred by fog. Women with platinum hair and long legs, bare in spite of the cold, turned out to be men with shadowy chins and deep voices when he passed close to them, looking away and ignoring their invitations. At two or three in the morning he'd rap his knuckles on the little window of the basement where she lived, caress and open her in the darkness, and never know whether she was completely awake or moaned and murmured and laughed in her dreams as she held his waist with thin, supple thighs. Then he'd lie next to her, oppressed by stupefaction at himself and his own fury, now placated, with its share of Catholic remorse. But other times he looked for her and couldn't find her, or, even worse, saw light in the dirty window and knocked but obtained no reply, and what became physically intolerable was the certainty that she was in bed at that moment with another man, the two of them lying there in silence, looking at the shadow on the glass, she placing her index finger on her painted lips, mockery on her face. In ten years Ignacio Abel hadn't felt anything resembling that physical upheaval and hadn't forgotten any of its details. He told no one of his adventure; he always stayed silent in men's conversations about sex. But several years after his return from Germany, he saw his own derangement in a film of Buñuel's shown privately in a small room at the Lyceum Club, not without great embarrassment on the part of the ladies. In the film a young woman, whom he found easy to confuse with his transient Hungarian lover, voluptuously sucked the foot of a marble statue; the two Buñuel lovers looked for each other, and when they found each other were separated again and harassed again and desired each other so much they dropped to the ground, embracing, not noticing the scandal they caused around them. He returned to Madrid early in the summer of 1924, and things and people seemed at a standstill, exactly where he had left them a year earlier. Even his former spirit was waiting for him, like a suit from several seasons ago hanging in a closet. He realized, like someone coming out of a drunken binge, that in Germany he'd sunk feverishly into a collective state of delusion and vigilance. As soon as he crossed the Spanish border, presenting his passport to Civil Guards with the surly faces of the poor under their three-cornered hats, and climbed into a train, excessive stimulation turned into dejection. He found strength only in the suitcase filled with books and magazines he'd dragged like a stone through the stations of Europe; they'd be nourishment for his mind in the years of intellectual penury that were approaching. In Madrid it was as hot as a desert and the streets in the city's center were filled with the slow, baroque Corpus Christi procession: canons in heavy capes raising crosses and swinging ornate silver censers; women in black mantillas, with African down on their fleshy lips (among them his own mother-in-law, Doña Cecilia, and the unmarried sisters of his father-in-law, Don Francisco de Asís); soldiers in full-dress uniforms presenting arms to the Holy Sacrament. He went into his house and the air had the dense smell of the muscle ointment Adela's father used and the garlic soup he enjoyed when he came over during her husband's absence. Miguel, his face red, cried constantly, and Adela listed the symptoms of a possible intestinal infection, as if Ignacio Abel or his absence were responsible for it. The girl, four years old now, was frightened and threw herself into her mother's arms when she saw the tall stranger who left two enormous suitcases in the entrance and came down the hall reaching for her, his big arms spread wide.

After so much time he was still searching as he had then, hoping for something he couldn't name but that corroded or undermined his stability of thought, not allowing him real rest, injecting doubt and suspicion into the evident satisfaction of everything he'd achieved. In some German or French magazines he'd sometimes see photographs by his lover of so many years ago, signed with a short, clear pseudonym. Very calmly he pondered the asymmetry of memory: what had mattered so much to him was probably nothing to her. Time had erased his resentment and male suspicion of ridicule, leaving him with secret gratitude. He continued searching because of a youthful habit of his spirit transformed now into a character trait, separate from the expectations of his real life, which had flattened as it became more solid, stripped of risk and also of surprise, like a project that acquires a firm, useful presence when it materializes and at the same time loses the originality and beauty that were such powerful possibilities at the start, when it was no more than a sketch, a play of lines in a notebook, or not even that: the lightning flash of an intuition, the vacant space where foundations will not be dug for a long time to come. Somehow what was accomplished was frustrated, the work finished but omitting the best of what might have been. Perhaps the cutting edge of his intelligence had dulled, just as his sight was weaker and his movements clumsier, his body heavier and blunter, not pierced for so long by the stab of true desire. The tension of expectation remained unchanged, but it was likely that what awaited him in the future would not be much more than what had happened to him in the past. He wouldn't feel again the suspense of the unknown, the feeling of unlimited possibility he'd had during the time he spent in Germany, so luminous and brief in memory. He had put his talent and ambition into his work and tended to his personal life distractedly, like someone who delegates to others the subordinate details of a complex assignment. Moving up with almost no one's help — with only his enterprising illiterate mother, his prematurely dead father, and the decision his father never expressed but arranged for efficiently and in secret: his son would have a future less harsh than his — studying first for the bachelor's degree and then the diploma in architecture, living with a kind of fanatical asceticism, had required so great a degree of concentration and energy that by comparison the rest of his life seemed a long period of idleness. Once he'd achieved the diploma and obtained his first position, constantly doing what was required or expected of him had demanded no more effort than allowing himself to be carried along with a certain strategic cleverness in the general direction of respectability. Perhaps, when the two of them were young, he'd been fonder of Adela than he remembered now. Their engagement, marriage, children, a girl and then a boy, had followed one another at decent intervals. With a combination of calculation and private irritation he'd complied with the norms of Adela's family — attended his children's baptisms, confirmations, and laying on of scapulars, languished through countless family celebrations, weddings and saints' days and Christmas and New Year's dinners, adopting a well-bred and increasingly absent air that everyone accepted as proof of his oddity, perhaps his talent, and maybe as a remnant of the indelicacy typical of his plebeian origins, to which no one alluded but no one forgot. In spite of his being the son of a woman who worked as a porter on Calle Toledo and a mason who'd done well, they were magnanimous enough to accept him as one of their own; they'd presented him with the most distinguished (though somewhat frayed) daughter of their irreproachable family and facilitated his access to the first rungs of a profession to which he otherwise could not have aspired no matter how many academic honors and diplomas in architecture he might have. They expected him to fulfill his responsibilities, to pay in regular installments and for the rest of his life the formidable interest on his debt: dignified behavior, observable conjugal ardor, rapid fatherhood, a profitable and brilliant display of his abilities, in principle only theoretical, by virtue of which he'd been accepted without too many reservations into a class that wasn't his.

For years he performed the role so literally and with no detectable effort that he almost forgot another life might have been possible. Deception and conformity quickly became stable traits of his spirit, along with a profound indifference toward everything that wasn't the solitary intellectual exaltation his work afforded him. Tedium without histrionics, sex without desire, and a shared and excessive concern for the children sustained his conjugal life. Unthinkingly, he imagined that his self-involvement and impassivity, gradually transformed into indifference, didn't trouble Adela, that she even accepted them with relief, for she was a woman who always seemed insecure about and rather ashamed of her body, convinced it was typical of men to leave home early and return late and occupy the intervening time with incomprehensible tasks whose only result worthy of interest was the family's welfare. The idea of patronizing prostitutes would have offended him even if he'd been able to ignore the undeniable hygienic arguments against it, which to his surprise didn't faze other men. What he'd experienced in a room in Weimar with a young, determined, naked woman who shivered and embraced him and looked smilingly into his eyes as he moved rhythmically on top of her, adapting his thrusts to the knowing undulation of her hips — that wasn't going to happen to him again, in the same irrevocable way he wouldn't relive his youth. He looked attentively at all women but rarely felt deeply attracted by one or turned to continue looking at her after she passed. He supposed age was dampening his physical desire as much as his ambitions and the wildness of his imagination. He'd liked an American stranger a great deal for a few minutes and they exchanged a few words, and he'd been satisfied to think about her in the darkness of a taxi while Adela sat beside him and spoke with a hostile tone in her voice, as if she'd guessed, as if she'd been capable of catching in her husband's eyes an instantaneous flash that hadn't animated them in many years, just as Lita had noticed the foreigner's narrow skirt and haircut and accent when she spoke Spanish, so different from Señorita Rossman's severe Germanic consonants. He thought about her again as he lay in silence next to his wife that night, forcing himself to fix in his memory the details of her face — the freckles around her nose, the gleam of her eyes behind a lock of curly hair, which he'd been madly tempted to brush aside with his fingers — at the same time noting an indubitable beginning of physical excitement that soon languished, a flame fed by the very weak materials of his adult imagination. The following day, in his office at University City — on his desk was a newspaper with a review of his talk and a dark photo in which his face could hardly be seen — he asked to be connected to Moreno Villa's telephone while he thought of the pretext for a conversation that would veer easily toward Judith Biely. But he hung up immediately, indecisive, cutting off the operator, unaccustomed to those kinds of tricks, and he didn't have the opportunity to repeat the call or carry out a vague intention to invent an excuse for returning to the Residence in the childish hope he'd run into her.

The days go by and the possibility of something that was about to occur dissolves like a drawing traced in one's breath on glass. Ignacio Abel might never have seen Judith Biely a second time and neither would have thought of the other again as they moved into the labyrinths of their own lives. Now he was walking along a corridor on the tenth floor of a new building on the Gran Vía — dark suit, double-breasted jacket, hat in hand, gray hair flat against his temples, the distracted, energetic appearance of someone who at heart doesn't fear very much or expect too much, except for what's appropriate. Surrounded by the predictable sounds of footsteps, secretaries' clicking heels, bursts of announcements on radios, ringing telephones, the clatter of typewriters behind frosted-glass doors, he could distinguish more clearly the music he'd begun to hear when he left the elevator. The song reminded him of Judith Biely even before he knew it was guiding him to her. He remembered her first name but not her second — the sunlight coming in through the large window facing west as she turned her head without interrupting the melody she was playing on the piano, Negrín saying that her last name was or sounded Russian. The silent elevator had opened on a wide expanse of polished floor and a wall of glass bricks that diffused the light from a large interior courtyard. The elevator operator touched his cap and stepped aside to let him pass. It smelled promisingly new, just completed, with odors of recent varnish, fresh paint, and wood. Even footsteps had the resonance of a space not yet completely occupied, its bare walls returning echoes and accentuating sharp sounds.

The music came from the other side of one of the numbered doors along the corridor where Ignacio Abel was looking for the name-plate of the person who'd made an appointment with him, the effusive voice with a strong Mexican accent that called him on the phone two or three days after his lecture. "You don't know who I am, but I know a great deal about you," the voice said. "I know and admire your work. We have mutual friends. Dr. Negrín was kind enough to give me your number." Ignacio Abel accepted out of curiosity, yielding to flattery, and because that Friday afternoon he was going to be alone in Madrid. Adela and the children had left for the house in the Sierra in preparation for one of the great yearly family celebrations, the saint's day of her father, Don Francisco de Asís. He imagined the appointment would be in an office. There were many in the building, the headquarters of foreign businesses, film producers and distributors, travel agencies, and steamship companies. The typewriters and telephones sounded in gusts, as when a door is opened and closed and the sound of the rain comes in. Young secretaries passed him, wearing makeup and moving fast like the ones he'd seen ten years earlier in Germany: uniformed pages, telegram deliverymen, clerks with briefcases under their arms, workers putting the finishing touches on installations. The activity pleased him, the suggestion of urgent tasks, so different from the lethargic calm of the ministerial offices where he sometimes had to go to take care of matters related to the construction at University City: records of payments that were never resolved, transactions that ground to a halt because a signature was missing, or a certificate, or the purple oval of a stamp, or medieval red sealing wax at the bottom of a document. On the outside this building, like so many recent ones in Madrid, had a noble mass but was complicated and affected, with columns and cornices that held up nothing and stone balconies where no one would ever stand, plaster filigrees whose only purpose would be to immediately collect pigeon droppings and soot from chimneys and cars. The interiors, however, were diaphanous, right angles and clean curves, arithmetical sequences that unfolded before him as he walked along the corridor and approached the door from which the music came; it wasn't frosted glass and didn't have a commercial sign but a discreet plaque with a name written in cursive script: *P. W. Van Doren.*

He recognized the song at the same time he recalled her musical and forgotten last name: Biely. And a moment later, when the door opened, he saw her, with no prior warning, as if her presence had been an emanation of the music and her suddenly remembered name. Instead of an office he found himself in the middle of what seemed to be a party, somewhat incongruous at that early hour, still part of the working day. He had the feeling that when he crossed the threshold he was entering a space not continuous with the corridor that brought him there; it didn't seem Spanish, didn't seem completely real: a large living room with white walls and abstract masses, like an interior in a modern film. The people, the guests, looked like extras, arranged in small groups and conversing in several languages and on different planes, as if to occupy the set in a convincing way. Unexpected, recognized, carnal among those figures who didn't notice the presence of the new arrival—not because they intended to act as if they didn't see him, but because they moved on another plane of reality—Judith saw him as soon as he came in and from a distance made a gesture of welcome. She held a gleaming record in her hands and stood next to the gramophone, lost as well among strangers though he didn't realize it at the time, in front of a large window overlooking a provincial Madrid of tile roofs and bell towers and church domes, keeping the rhythm of the song with nods of her head. The clarinet, the piano, Benny Goodman accompanying Teddy Wilson on a disk recorded in New York only a few months earlier, discovered by her with a rush of nostalgia in the listening booth of a music store in Paris at the beginning of the summer, when she didn't yet know she would travel to Madrid in September, when Spain for her was still the place dreamed about in books, a country as illusory and anchored in her youthful imagination as Treasure Island or Sancho Panza's Ínsula Barataria. The maid in the black uniform and white cap who opened the door moved away discreetly, carrying Ignacio Abel's hat and umbrella. His quick, expert glance simultaneously assessed the dimensions of the space and the quality and disposition of the objects, identifying the creators of the paintings and furniture, almost all German or French of the past ten years except for a distinguished Viennese or two from the beginning of the century. Everything had the attractiveness of excessive premeditation, of calculated disorder, with a shine like that of photographic paper or an international design magazine. A young waiter, his hair lacquered with pomade, offered him a glass of transparent liquid that smelled of iced gin, a small tray with canapés of fresh butter and caviar. Judith seemed to take a long time to reach him through groups of people who separated without seeing her to let her pass or whom she skirted, guided only by the melody she'd played tentatively on the piano in the Residence. The closer she came, the more real and exciting she was, dressed in a plain white blouse and wide trousers. Then she shook his hand with masculine assurance. Her warm hand, with slim fingers and fragile bones when he pressed it slightly, caught in his for a moment that was prolonged without either one doing anything about it, not knowing anything about the other and alone again in the sound made by invisible people, just as they'd been a few nights earlier at the Residence. When she looked at him, Ignacio Abel became uncomfortably aware of his own appearance, too severe and too Spanish in that environment, among people younger than he and, like Judith, dressed in sports clothes — close-fitting sweaters, bright ties, checked trousers, two-toned shoes. Occasionally a laugh or an American exclamation rose above the conversations and the clink of glasses.

"The man who doesn't like bullfights," said Judith. "I'm so happy to see you again, among so many strangers."

"I thought they were all compatriots of yours."

"But in my country I wouldn't have known any of them."

"One isn't the same away from one's country."

"What are you like when you're away from Spain?" Judith looked at him over the glass she held to her lips.

"I almost don't remember. I haven't traveled for a long time."

"You say that sadly. Your face lit up when you showed photographs of modern German buildings in your talk."

"I hope you weren't too bored." Alcohol, which he wasn't accustomed to drinking, caused a warm surge in his chest each time he took a sip. The smell of gin mixed with the scent of Judith's cologne or soap. The physical desire her closeness provoked was as new and as immediate for him as the alcohol in his blood, and it produced a comparable bewilderment. He was waking after more than ten years, astonished at having been asleep for so long.

"*Now you're fishing for compliments.*" Judith had moved instinctively to English and began to laugh at her own linguistic confusion: she wiped her lips with a small napkin, sorry now for her laughter and perhaps her remark. "You know very well no one was bored."

He liked her even more than he remembered. He hadn't known how to keep in his memory the exact color of her eyes, the brightness of her ironic and alert intelligence, the way her thick, curly hair was cut at a right angle at her cheeks, the luminous timbre of her voice in Spanish. Enthusiasm made her beautiful. She'd been in Madrid for a month and felt all the ardor of an unexpected love affair with the city. She was one of those people able to take pleasure in everything, to be grateful for the new with no shadow of mistrust toward the unknown. Talking to her that afternoon, Ignacio Abel thought she resembled Lita in her balance between a rigorous vocation for learning and a good-natured aptitude for receiving the gifts of the unforeseen, for serenely enjoying life. She'd spent two years traveling in Europe and planned to leave a six-month stay in Spain for the end. But a former classmate from Columbia University, where Judith had abandoned her doctoral studies a few years earlier, called at the beginning of the summer: she was ill and couldn't take charge of the group of students whom she had to accompany during a semester of exchange studies in Madrid. So many pieces of chance required to weave a decisive moment in life. Since the beginning of September, and contrary to all her recent expectations, Judith Biely was a teacher living in a pensión in Madrid, in an austere, bright room overlooking the Plaza de Santa Ana, while she waited for a room to become available at the Residence for Young Ladies. She was perfecting her Spanish, which she had begun to study on her own as a child after reading a student edition of *Tales of the Alhambra;* she attended classes in literature at the Faculty of Philosophy and Letters and in Spanish history at the Center for Historical Studies on Calle Almagro, and went to lectures and concerts and film screenings at the Student Residence; she ate delicious, indigestible stews in the taverns along Cava Baja; she strolled at dusk along Vistillas and the Viaducto and the Plaza de Oriente to watch the sunsets that in this inland city took on the delicate breadth of ocean horizons sieved with mist. The purples and grays of the Sierra seen through her window on the first rainy days of October she recognized a short time later in the backgrounds of Velázquez's hunting scenes. The joy of leaving her pensión and spending a morning in the museum was not very different from the pleasure afterward of having a sandwich of fried squid and a glass of beer at a stand on the Paseo del Prado, watching the talkative, active people of Madrid walk by, attempting to decipher their turns of phrase, reviewing in a small notebook the new words and expressions she was learning. When she was ten or twelve years old and her family lived in Brooklyn she read Washington Irving, bent for hours over a table in a public library, looking at illustrations in which the Alhambra was an Oriental palace, sitting by a window through which she could see courtyards covered with clotheslines of sheets in a neighborhood of Italian and Jewish immigrants; now she was impatient to take an express train one night and wake up in Granada. A little before enrolling at City College she discovered a book of travels through Spain by John Dos Passos, *Rosinante to the Road Again,* and now she carried it with her and at times reread it in the very places described in its pages. Thanks to Dos Passos she'd learned about Cervantes and El Greco, but in the Prado was moved much more by Velázquez and Goya. Had she seen Goya's frescoes in the dome of San Antonio de la Florida, his less famous but equally powerful canvases in the Academia de San Fernando, his several series of etchings? Ignacio Abel surprised himself by offering to act as guide. They were very near San Fernando, and they could reach the hermitage of San Antonio in just a few minutes by car: you crossed the river, and the landscape of the Pradera, with the city in the background and the great white smudge of the Palacio de Oriente, was the same one Goya painted. His own boldness disconcerted him: it would in no way be difficult to put out his hand and touch her face, so close, to move away the lock of hair that brushed the corner of her smiling mouth. Judith nodded, very attentive in order to understand each word, her thin lips moistened by her drink, her eyes shining, or was it simply the euphoric effect of alcohol and conversation in a foreign language, the same boldness that was urging him on, irresponsible, a little dizzy, insisting that his car was nearby, and besides, because of his work, he knew the chaplain at the hermitage, who would allow them to climb up to the dome to see the frescoes more closely. He was not in love yet and already he was jealous of others who might touch her, other men joined to her by the complicity of language. A husky man with a shaved head embraced her from behind.

"*Judith, my dear, would you please introduce me to my own guest?*"

How did he know her, for how long? Why did he rest his square chin on her shoulder and brush her hair with his lips with no awkwardness and put his arms around her waist, his two large, thick hands with black hairs (but pink, glossy manicured nails) closing just above her trousers? She made a gesture of detaching herself but without much conviction, perhaps somewhat uncomfortable though not enough to move her face away, to separate the hands that pressed her against the male body adhering to her back. How would it feel to be in his place, pressing that slim body, feeling the rhythm of her breathing beneath the fabric of her blouse? He was surprised by this confusion of sudden emotions, as impervious to the control of his will as the beating of his heart or the rapid surges of pressure at his temples.

"Phil Van Doren," said Judith, looking at Ignacio Abel as if begging his pardon. "Philip Van Doren the Third, to give his complete name."

"I couldn't attend your lecture the other day, but I read about it in several newspapers, and Judith gave me all the details."

I would have liked to separate those two hands that touched you so confidently, with their black hairs and rings and polished nails, make him move away from you and not put his mouth so close to yours, and not keep brushing against you with that proprietary air he had toward everything, his house, his guests, even me, who didn't even know why he'd called me and didn't care, it was enough to have found you again.

"As I told you on the phone, I've made some inquiries about you. I've seen some of your work in Madrid." Van Doren spoke excellent Spanish, with a Mexican accent. "The public school in that southern neighborhood, the Marketplace. Magnificent works, if you'll permit the opinion of an *amateur*."

He pronounced *amateur* in perfect French. He had light eyes and a penetrating gaze that could easily turn suspicious or sarcastic, and he depilated his eyebrows as carefully as he shaved his skull. No matter how sharp his razor, it would never mitigate the black shadow of his beard. From a turtleneck sweater that emphasized his pectoral muscles emerged the tanned, powerful head of an athlete. Ignacio Abel immediately felt relief tinged with discomfort: in those solidly masculine hands embracing Judith there was probably no desire, but his gaze had the excessive fixity of someone prepared to make quick, irrevocable judgments regarding whoever was in front of him, subjecting that person to tests for which he was the only judge; a brazen, covetous, indiscriminate, incautious curiosity, an instinct for discovering what was most hidden and learning what no one else knew.

"Things never turn out as one would like," said Abel, flattered, especially because Judith was there, and unaccustomed to praise. "There's always a lack of money, and delays, and you have to fight with everybody. Not to mention the strikes, the ones that are justified and the ones that are not . . ."

But once he was no longer the person speaking, Van Doren became instantly distracted. He looked at the guests, the waiters, attentive to every detail, making abrupt movements with his head as if constantly adjusting the angle and distance of vision. He nodded a great deal, he greeted someone briefly, he looked toward the large windows as if the brightness of the day or the condition of the atmosphere also depended on him. He asked Ignacio Abel to accompany him to his study. When he'd taken him by the arm to lead him there, he seemed to remember Judith, signaled her to join them, and put his arm around her waist, affectionate again, noticing her glass was almost empty, ordering a waiter with an authoritative gesture to give her another, his face animated by a wide smile one moment and very serious the next, frowning in anger. Ignacio Abel allowed himself to be carried along. The hand leading him was as strong as his sexual desire, and the gin he drank unexpectedly weakened his self-control. He was confused by the strangeness of the place, the bubble of space he'd entered when the maid opened the door and he saw Judith in the back of the room, gesturing as if she had been expecting him all along; she knew he'd come; somehow it was part of a purpose that involved him without his knowledge; she was going to change the record on the gramophone and turned when she heard the doorbell over the music and the guests' voices.

Van Doren closed his door more energetically than necessary, and when he sat across from them in a tubular easy chair covered in calfskin and placed his hands on his knees, he had the serenity of a dancer who has completed a leap without visible effort. Resting on the sporty fabric of his trousers, his hands stood out with obscene crudeness. The sound of the party was faint, intensifying in Ignacio Abel the sensation of distance, of losing his footing, of advancing in the darkness along a passage, extending his hands and not finding a solid point of reference to define the space. The close-fitting sleeves of Van Doren's sweater revealed a portion of his muscular, hairy forearms. The watch on his left wrist and the bracelet on his right were gold, and both shook when he moved his hands. The pale light of the October afternoon shone on her hair and the taut skin of her cheeks and chin. Van Doren had rung a bell when he observed Judith lighting a cigarette and followed with his eyes the hand that left the burned match on the glass tabletop. The waiter came in, and Van Doren signaled to him to bring an ashtray, always in a hurry and with a touch of rage that his smile couldn't conceal, not because he didn't know how but because he didn't try. Perhaps what he didn't know was how to live without the sensation of frightening whoever was near him. The waiter changed Ignacio Abel's unfinished, by now warm glass for another in which the cold left a cloud of condensation on its delicate, inverted-cone shape. Judith tasted hers in short sips, like her puffs on the cigarette, which she kept far from her face.

"Modern architecture is my passion," said Van Doren. "Painting, too, as you may have noticed, but in another way. Do you like Paul Klee?"

That vigilant stare had followed his, incredulous, overwhelmed by five small canvases by Paul Klee, watercolors and oils, and not far from them a drawing of a still life, probably by Juan Gris.

"Klee was my drawing professor in Germany."

"You studied at the Bauhaus?" Now Van Doren granted him the consideration that until then, for one reason or another, out of mistrust or simple arrogance, he'd only feigned.

"One year, during the early period, in Weimar. I learned more in a few months than I had in my entire life."

But Van Doren had already lost interest. Still smiling, he was elsewhere, like someone who closes his eyes for a second, is asleep, and wakes with a start. He contracted his facial muscles and in an instant picked up the interrupted thread of his monologue.

"But painting is a private pleasure, even when it's enjoyed in a museum. You're alone before the canvas, and the world around you no longer exists. Painting demands a degree of contemplation that at times is a problem for active people. When you're still for a few minutes, don't you regret it, feel you're losing something? Of course a building can be enjoyed as privately as a painting. As you know, the esthetic emotion tends to be reinforced by the privilege of possession. But architecture always has a public part, accessible to anyone, on the street, outdoors. It's an affirmation. Like a fist coming down on a table . . ."

Van Doren made a fist with his right hand and held it up, pushing up the sleeves of his sweater almost to the elbow.

"Look at that magnificent Telephone Company tower. Perhaps Judith has told you we own shares in it. My family, I mean, through American Telephone and Telegraph. The tower is a statement—the power of money, our dear Judith, who has radical sympathies as you know, would say. And she's correct, of course she is, but there's also something else. The marvel of telephone communications, and better still, radio waves that don't require the laying of cables to transmit words through the atmosphere, making them resonate like echoes in the stratosphere, then retrieving them. A miracle for people our parents' age, an act of witchcraft. But that tower is saying something else as well, and you as an architect are aware of what it means: the drive of your country, as powerful now as when the cathedrals were built. You approach Madrid and the Telephone Company Building is its cathedral. A tower of offices and a warehouse filled with machinery and cables, a symbol too, just like a church or a Greek temple or a pyramid."

He took a final sip of his drink, clicking his tongue, and looked sideways at his watch. Ignacio Abel studied the somewhat absent face of Judith, whose eyes were fixed on her cigarette smoke. Perhaps their mutual excitement had dissipated. Perhaps when the effect of alcohol and physical proximity had passed, neither would feel anything for the other.

"But I see you're impatient. I don't want to waste your time or mine. I haven't forgotten that you're not a contemplative soul either. I suppose you haven't heard of Burton College. It's a small school, very select, about two hours by train north of New York, on the Hudson River. Beautiful country. The campus is in the middle of a natural landscape, the houses and farms of the early colonists surround it—"

"And before that, those of the Indians expelled by the early colonists," said Judith.

Van Doren looked at her with absolute serenity, examining her slowly, then looking at Ignacio Abel as if to make certain he'd witnessed his magnanimity. It pleased him to give the impression that some kind of familiarity existed between Judith and him.

"It was inevitable when we reached this point that our dear Judith would bring up the Indians. Sadly disappeared. You Spaniards know something about that. But if Judith permits, I'd prefer to go on with my story about Burton College. Right now the woods are turning red and yellow. I'm not sentimental, and I like Madrid a great deal, but I miss the autumn colors in that part of America. Judith knows what I'm referring to. Haven't you ever been to the United States, Professor Abel? Perhaps the right moment is now. My family has been connected to Burton College for several generations. At one point, in fact, it was almost called Van Doren College. The land for the campus was a gift from a great-grandfather of mine. As you know, we settled there before the English arrived. We Dutch, I mean. Their New York was our New Amsterdam first, just as today's Mexico was your New Spain—"

"That's why that part of the state is filled with Dutch names," Judith interrupted, perhaps with some annoyance at his display of ancestors, she whose only forebears in America were her parents, immigrants who spoke English with a terrible accent and argued in Russian and Yiddish.

"The Roosevelts, to name some prominent neighbors," and Van Doren laughed. "Or the Vanderbilts. Or the Van Burens. Except in our family we've been more discreet. No politics, no speculative transactions. The last crisis barely affected us."

"It affected *us*," said Judith, but Van Doren decided to ignore her.

"Burton College has been the preferred area for our philanthropy. There's a Van Doren Hall where symphonic concerts are given regularly, a Van Doren Wing in the hospital, specializing in pioneering treatments for cancer. And for years, since my father's time, a project has existed that I love dearly because my father wanted to build it and died too soon: a new library, the Van Doren Library, the Philip Van Doren the Second Library, to be exact. Several architects have already done work for us, but I don't like any of the proposals. Of course I'm not the one who decides, but what I say carries a good deal of weight with the board of trustees, and in the end, I'm the one who holds the purse strings."

"The one who has the frying pan by the handle," said Judith, happy to correct Van Doren for his literal translation from English with a straightforward Spanish expression she'd learned not long before and liked very much.

"So far everything they've presented to us has been a *pastiche,* as you can imagine." Van Doren again pronounced a French word with mannered correctness. "Gothic *pastiches,* imitations of imitations, Greek temples, Roman baths, railroad stations, or exposition halls imitating Greek temples and Roman monuments, pastries in the *Beaux-Arts* style. But I don't want that land profaned by a monstrosity that resembles a post office. I'd like you to see it. I'll have photographs and plans sent to you. It's a clearing in a forest of maples and oaks, high ground beyond the western edge of the campus, with a view of the Hudson. The building will be seen from the trains that run along the riverbank, from the ships that sail up and down the river. Even from the New Jersey side. It'll be the most visible building of the college. I picture it above the treetops, more hidden when they're full of leaves, at the end of a walk that will lead away from the central quadrangle, a secluded, elevated path to books, its lights on until midnight. There will be books but also records of any kind of music, from anywhere in the world. Judith, with her excellent ear, will undoubtedly help me find recordings of Spanish music. My family has shares in some gramophone companies. I imagine soundproof booths for listening to the records, projection rooms where anyone can watch films. I'm interested in the project you have now in Spain to record the voices of your most eminent personalities. There'll be reading rooms with large windows offering views of the woods and the river, the other buildings on campus. Not one of those lugubrious libraries like the ones in England that are mindlessly imitated in America, with smells of mildew and crumbling leather, stacks and card catalogues of dark wood, like coffins or funerary monuments, low lamps with green shades that give faces the color of death. I see a bright library, like those buildings and shops your teachers built in Germany, like the school you built in Madrid. A library that's practical, like a good gymnasium, a gymnasium for the mind. A watchtower and a refuge as well."

"I want to work in that library," said Judith, but Van Doren had no time to listen. He moved his large hands with their pink manicured nails and pushed up the sleeves of his sweater as if impatient to begin work on his imaginary library, to dig the foundation, level the uneven terrain, lay rows of red bricks or blocks carved from the gray stones found in the forest.

"I didn't invite you here today for you to say yes, to make a commitment to me," Van Doren said. "You have many things to do, and so do I. Dr. Negrín has told me that this year will be particularly difficult for all of you, because he promised to inaugurate University City next October. Difficult, if you'll permit me. Almost impossible."

"Have you visited the construction site?"

Before answering, Van Doren smiled to himself, like someone who hasn't decided to reveal completely what he knows, or who wants to give the impression that he knows more than he does.

"That's one of the reasons I came to Madrid in the first place. I've visited the site and consulted plans and models. A magnificent project, on a scale that has no equal in Europe, though its execution is slow and perhaps chaotic. I liked your building very much, of course, the one designed exclusively by you. The steam power plant, if I'm not mistaken."

"It's almost not a building. It's a box for holding machinery and controls. It's not operating yet. Who showed it to you?"

"Phil isn't going to answer that question," said Judith. Van Doren gave her a quick smile, a gesture, approving, not without flattery, what she'd said. He was a man who liked above all to know what others didn't know and to have privileged access to what was unavailable to the rest. Ignacio Abel didn't like Judith calling him "Phil" again.

"It's a cubic block and yet looks as if it emerged from the earth, was part of the earth," Van Doren said. "It's a fortress but doesn't seem to weigh too much, this vigorous heart that pumps hot water and heat to the city of knowledge. One wants to knock on that gate in the wall and enter the castle. One sees immediately that you've worked with competent engineers. And that aside from your German teachers, you must admire some Scandinavian architects, I would assume. Was it difficult to have your project accepted?"

"Not too bad. It's a practical construction, so no one pays much attention to it. There was no need to add volutes or Plateresque eaves or to imitate El Escorial."

"A terrible building, don't you agree? Compatriots of yours who are very proud of it took me to see it last week. It was like entering a sinister set for *Don Carlo*. One feels the weight of the granite as if it were the hand of Philip the Second in an iron glove. Or perhaps the hand of the statue of the Commendatore in *Don Giovanni*."

Van Doren burst into laughter, looking for Judith's complicity, then turned to Abel, completely changing his tone.

"Are you a Communist?"

"Why do you ask?"

"*Checking up on me*," Judith said quietly in English, visibly irritated. She stood and went to the window, uncomfortable because of what seemed to be the beginning of an interrogation for which she perhaps felt partially responsible.

"Some of your classmates and professors at the Bauhaus were. And I think you're a man who likes to get things done. Who has practical sense and at the same time a utopian imagination."

"Do you have to be a Communist for that?"

"Communist or Fascist, I'm afraid. You have to love big projects and immediate, effective action, and have no patience for empty talk, for delays. In Moscow or Berlin your University City would be finished by now. Even in Rome."

"But probably it would make no sense." Ignacio Abel was aware of Judith's gaze and attention. "Unless it was like a barracks or a reeducation camp."

"Don't repeat propagandistic vulgarities that are unworthy of you. German science is the best in the world."

"It won't be for very long."

"Now you're talking like a Communist."

"Are you saying you have to be a Communist to be against Hitler?" Judith Biely said. She was standing by the window, angry, serious, agitated. Van Doren looked at her, not responding. The one he stared at intently was Ignacio Abel, who spoke without raising his voice, with the instinctive diffidence he felt when he expressed political opinions.

"I'm a Socialist."

"Is there any difference?"

"When the Communists came to power in Russia, they sent the Socialists to prison."

"The Socialists shot Rosa Luxemburg in Germany in 1919," Judith said. The discussion produced a somewhat histrionic comic effect in Van Doren.

"And when the Fascists or the Nazis win, Communists and Socialists will end up together in the same prisons, after having fought so much with one another. You cannot deny there's a certain humor in that."

"I hope that doesn't happen in my country, and we'll inaugurate University City on time with no need for a Fascist or Communist coup." Ignacio Abel would have liked to end the conversation and leave, but if he left now, when would he see Judith again?

"I like your enthusiasm, Ignacio, if you'll permit me to use your first name. I've heard you ended your lecture eloquently, with a revolutionary declaration. Judith didn't tell me this, don't blame her. I'd be delighted if you called me Phil and if we used informal address with each other, though I know we just met and Spain is a more formal place than America. I like it that you don't seem to care about staying on the margins of the great modern currents, politically speaking."

"They seem horribly primitive to me."

"I visited the Soviet Union two years ago, and I've traveled extensively through Germany and Italy. I believe I'm a person without prejudices. An American open to the new things the world can offer. An innocent abroad, as Mark Twain, one of the great travelers of my country, put it. We're a new nation compared to you Europeans. We feel sympathy for everything that's a valiant break with the past. That's how we were born, breaking with old Europe, putting an end to kings and archbishops."

"We did that in Spain just four years ago."

"And with what results? What have you brought to completion in this time? I drive through the country and once I leave Madrid I see only miserable villages. Skinny peasants on burros, goatherds, barefoot children, women sitting in the sun picking lice out of each other's hair."

"You're exaggerating, Phil," Judith said. "Señor Abel's feelings may be hurt. You're talking about his country."

"About a part of it," Ignacio Abel said quietly, furious with himself for not leaving, for continuing to listen.

"You waste your energy on parliamentary battles, on speeches, on changes of government. You say you're a Socialist, but inside your own party you're fighting! Are you a Socialist in favor of the parliamentary system or a participant in the uprising last year to bring the Soviet revolution to Spain? I had the pleasure of meeting your coreligionist Don Julián Besteiro last year at a diplomatic dinner, and he seemed a perfect *gentleman*, but I also thought he was living in the clouds. Forgive me for speaking frankly: part of my work entails looking for information. We have a good deal of money invested in your country and wouldn't like to lose it. We want to know whether it's advisable for us to continue working and investing money here, or would it be more prudent to leave. Is it true that new elections will be held soon? I arrived in Madrid last month and the papers were full of photographs of the new government. Now I've read that a crisis has been announced and the government will change. Look at what Germany has accomplished in the same time. Look at the highways, the expansion of industry, the millions of new jobs. And it isn't a question of racial differences, of efficient Aryans and lazy Latins, as some people believe. Look at what Italy has become in ten years. Have you seen the highways, the new railroad stations, the strength of the army? I also don't have ideological prejudices, my dear Judith — it's simply a practical question. In the same way I admire the formidable advances of the Soviet five-year plans. I've seen the factories with my own eyes, the blast furnaces, the collective farms plowed with tractors. Ten, fifteen years ago, the countryside was more miserable and backward in Russia than in Spain. Just two years ago Germany was a humiliated nation. Now once again it's the leading power in Europe. In spite of the terrible, unjust sanctions the Allies imposed on it, especially the French, who wouldn't be so resented if they were not also incompetent and corrupt —"

"And the price doesn't matter?"

"Don't the democracies pay a horrifying price as well? Millions of men without work in my country, in England, in France. The breakdown of the Third Republic. Children with swollen bellies and eyes covered with flies right here on the outskirts of Madrid. Even our president has had to imitate the gigantic public works projects of Germany and Italy, the planning of the Soviet government."

"I hope he doesn't also imitate the prison camps."

"Or the racial laws."

"Dear Judith, in that regard I'm afraid you have an insurmountable prejudice."

It took Ignacio Abel a moment to understand what they were saying. He observed that Judith Biely had turned red, and that Van Doren was enjoying his own cold vehemence, the sense that he was controlling the conversation. He wasn't accustomed to the North American ease in combining courtesy with crudeness.

"Do you mean I despise Hitler because I'm a Jew?"

"I mean that things have to be considered in their exact proportions. I don't have prejudices, as you well know. If you wanted to leave the position you have now in a university that in my opinion is mediocre, I would recommend immediately that you be offered a contract at Burton College. How many Jews were there in Germany two years ago? Five hundred thousand? How many of them will have to leave? And if there's no place for all of them in Germany, why don't their coreligionists and friends in France, England, or the United States rush to take them in? How many Russian aristocrats and parasites had to leave the country, voluntarily or by force, when the Soviet Union began to be created in earnest? And the Spaniards, didn't they burn churches and expel the Jesuits when they started out? How many Germans found themselves forced to leave the land where they were born so that Beneš and Masaryk could have their beloved Czech homeland complete? In America, we also expelled thousands of Britons, a great many colonists who were as American as Washington or Jefferson but preferred to continue as subjects of the English crown. It's a question of proportion, my dear, not individual cases. As we say in our country, *there's no free lunch*. Everything has a price."

Van Doren had been glancing sideways at his watch as he spoke. He inspected in dry flashes of attention everything that happened around him, what he could deduce from the gaze, the gestures, the silence of his interlocutor. There was a suggestion of imposture in his conviction, as if he were capable of defending with the same intensity the opposite of what he was saying, laying a trap to find out their hidden thoughts. The servant in the short jacket and carrying a tray came in silently and leaned over to whisper in his ear. Ignacio Abel suspected he came in at a prearranged hour to interrupt a meeting that shouldn't be prolonged. In Judith's eyes he saw a complicity that hadn't existed when they entered the room: something that had been said there placed them on the same side. Her sharing with him something that excluded Van Doren not only flattered him, it produced an intense sexual desire, as if they'd dared an unexpected physical closeness that no one else saw. Van Doren looked at his watch again and spoke to the servant, detached from what was happening between them. Or perhaps not—nothing escaped his cynicism or his astuteness, his habit of controlling, subtly or rudely, the lives of others.

"You don't know how sorry I am, but I have to leave. An unexpected appointment at the Ministry of Information. The question is whether the minister will still be minister when I get there ... Seriously, *my dear* Ignacio, I'm sorry we talked about politics. It's always a waste of time, especially when there are more serious things to be discussed. Judith, how do you say *to make a long story short* in Spanish?"

"*Ir al grano.* To get right to the point."

"An admirable woman. To get right to the point, Ignacio, I'm authorized to offer you a position as visiting professor in the Department of Fine Arts and Architecture at Burton College next year, the fall semester if that's convenient, and if University City is inaugurated on time, which I hope with all my heart. And during that time I'd like you to study the possibility of designing the new library, the Van Doren Library. The project will have to be approved by the board, of course, but I can guarantee you'll be able to work with absolute freedom. You're a man of the future, and if the future, by your calculation, doesn't belong to Germany or Russia, perhaps the best thing for you is the future in America. Now I have to go, if you'll both forgive me. Make yourselves at home. This is your house. I'll be waiting for your reply, my dear Ignacio. *À bientôt,* my dear Judith."

Van Doren stood, extended his arms, and with no effort put on the sports jacket the servant held for him. In the sharp, acute look of his eyes, in the movement of his depilated eyebrows, was a quick suggestion of obscenity, as if offering to Judith Biely and Ignacio Abel the room he was about to leave, as if he'd already guessed and taken as certain what they themselves still didn't dare to think.

7

J UDITH BIELY SITS at a piano, her face and hair lit by the late afternoon sun. It is September 29, 1935; she's a silhouette crossing the bluish light that emanates from a slide projector, the hurried handwriting on the envelope Ignacio Abel keeps in one of his pockets, in the luggage of one who possesses only what he carries with him, a fugitive or deserter, one who doesn't know how long his journey will take or even if he'll return to the country in ruins that he left only two weeks before. Judith Biely's is the explosive writing on the pages of that letter, which Ignacio Abel would have preferred not to receive, dated in Madrid, less than three months earlier, and not entrusted to the mail but left with somebody who handed it to him with the combined slyness and delight of one who knows she's offering the pain of a knife blade. He saw the hands offering it to him in the vestibule of the house of assignation where they'd agreed to meet one last time, the red nails and arthritic fingers like stains on the envelope where Judith's hand had written his name with a formality that did not bode well, *Sr. D. Ignacio Abel*. A letter can be a delayed curse; someone for whom it wasn't intended opens a drawer and sees it by mistake, and if that person dares to read it, it's as if her hand had been thrust into a scorpion's hole; the drawer can't be closed again; the letter can't not be removed from the envelope, it can't not be read, deciphering that writing, those words that will burn in her memory for a long time. Someone finds it many years later, in a suitcase covered with dust or in a university's archive, and the letter continues to preserve its ardor or its hurtfulness even though the one who wrote it and the one who received it are dead by then. *Sr. D. Ignacio Abel:* as if suddenly they no longer knew each other, as if the past nine months hadn't existed. Right now Judith Biely is a woman seen from behind who turned around, an irreparable absence haunting the man who leans his face against the train window looking at the breadth of the Hudson River, his eyes half closed, his mind dissolving in fatigue and contemplation. I see his black shoes wrinkled in the shape of his foot and by the way he walks. Traces of the dust of Madrid and mud from the construction at University City. In his hotel room in New York he found a needle and thread in a small box and attempted to darn a hole in his sock, discovering he didn't know how, that his hands were useless. He didn't know how to sew a button back on a shirt and had spotted with alarm that the right pocket of his jacket was beginning to shred. Materials deteriorate in a subtle way; the pockets of a man with no fixed address become misshapen because he keeps too many things in them; a few loose threads, like an almost invisible crack in a wall, are the first sign of the next phase of ruin. He remembers when clothing would appear miraculously clean and ironed in his closet, in the drawers of the dresser with an oval mirror in which the somber double bed was reflected, its headboard of wood carved in imitation Spanish Renaissance fashion, the time-honored style of the Ponce-Cañizares Salcedo family. You don't know how to do anything; you'd die of hunger if you had to earn a living with your hands or cook a meal. When he was a boy, his father would make fun of him when he saw his vertigo climbing even the lowest scaffold, his clumsiness in carrying out the simplest manual tasks. "Eutimio, either this son of mine becomes a rich kid or he'll die of hunger," he'd say to the apprentice who looked after Ignacio like an older brother each time his father took the boy to a site. Professor Rossman at least was dexterous and managed to eke out a poor living during his worst times in Madrid by repairing pens, selling them on commission in the cafés, coming across them in his pockets or his bottomless briefcase as if by surprise, like a magician who keeps repeating old tricks. He hadn't carried the briefcase with him when they took him out of the pensión in a gruff but not violent or brutal way and put him in the back seat of a confiscated car, a Hispano-Suiza, his daughter recalled. With no political slogans painted on the doors or hood, no mattresses on the roof as a slapdash precaution against snipers or shrapnel from enemy planes. The doors still bore the noble coat of arms of the aristocrat from whom it had been confiscated and who probably had fled the country or was dead. Serious men who didn't waste time or make a fuss or imitate film gangsters, who had a signed search warrant with an official-looking purple stamp that Señorita Rossman couldn't make out. Professor Rossman's pockets were filled with things (as were Ignacio Abel's now on the train, bulging, fraying). The men had given Professor Rossman time to put on his jacket but not his vest or hard collar, which in any case he wouldn't need in the Madrid heat. Either they didn't allow him to put on his German boots with the worn-down heels, or he was so frightened he forgot to put them on, and left wearing his socks and old felt slippers. In the morgue on Calle Santa Isabel, one of Professor Rossman's feet still had a slipper on, and the big toe of his other foot, yellow, rigid, the nail like a contorted claw, jutted out of the sock. The morgue smelled of death and disinfectant, and all the bodies had numbered cards hung around their necks. The corpses' shoes were missing. Looters were up by daybreak to steal shoes and watches from the dead, tie pins, even gold teeth. Some were more difficult to identify because their faces had been blown away or their wallets stolen. "It's the people's justice," said Bergamín, looking at Ignacio Abel with ecclesiastical misgiving from the other side of the desk in his office, a hall with a Gothic ceiling in the Alliance of Anti-Fascist Intellectuals, his hands together at the height of his mouth as he surreptitiously sniffed his nails. "A flood that levels everything, that washes away everything. But it was the others in their uprising who opened the sluice gates of the flood where they now perish. Even Señor Ossorio y Gallardo, who's as

Catholic as I and much more conservative, has understood this and put it in writing: it's the logic of history." Individual lives didn't count now, he said, and neither do ours. Perhaps he was protecting his own in an office instead of risking it closer to the front, Ignacio Abel wanted to say, though he had been close to dying too, interrogated a few times during the summer, the barrels of old rifles pointing at him, pushing into his chest. The rifles could have easily gone off, as the men who held them barely knew how to use them, and one night he'd been shoved in front of some headlights a few seconds before the voice that saved him pronounced his name. He still looked like a bourgeois, even if as a precaution he always went out not wearing a tie or hat, feeling as unprotected at first as when one dreams of going out on the street naked. When one has been on the verge of dying, the world acquires an impersonal quality: whatever one looks at would still exist even if a few minutes earlier a bullet had blown one's head or chest open. He thinks with detachment, with the objectivity of a camera with no eye behind it: I could be dead and not sitting on this train, next to the window where a view flashes by, a sight that overwhelms these Spanish eyes, accustomed to dry lands and shallow streams. "The uncontrollable flood of the people's just anger, Bergamín wrote," he said aloud in a faint, muffled voice. Ignacio Abel knows beyond any doubt that he could have died at least four or five times that summer, and Judith and his children wouldn't have known. They might have thought or assumed he was dead; maybe he is dead in a way and doesn't know it. Erased into oblivion by others' forgetfulness while he imagines his identity remains intact. *The terror, to think that at this very instant, in some unknown place, memory is working against me, slowly fading away,* he has written to Judith, but he doesn't know if she will ever see those words. If I'd died in Madrid, this river, this horizon would speed past this window at this exact moment without anyone looking at it. I'd have been taken to a morgue inundated with nameless corpses piled in hallways and even in broom closets, beneath a buzzing cloud of flies, around my neck a crumpled card with a registration number. Whatever had not been stolen from my corpse by daybreak would have been placed in a filing cabinet by someone after he'd typed a list with several carbon copies.

I catalogue Ignacio Abel's pockets—everything a man carries, what he hasn't thrown out, what he cares about, and what for no reason stays there, making his pockets bulge, creating excess weight that begins to loosen a few threads, and once loose the slackening can turn into a tear, what would help him establish his identity and reconstruct his steps and is as ephemeral as any piece of paper the October wind blows down the street, like the contents of the wastebasket the cleaning women in the New Yorker Hotel empty into a trash can. Suppose you died and only those things spoke of you. But in Madrid the suicides on the Viaducto tended to empty their pockets and leave their documents and valuable personal possessions in good order before jumping into the void. Some took off their shoes, but not their socks, and left them lined up together, as if at the foot of a bed. (Adela didn't take hers off; she jumped into the water, or rather took a step and let herself fall, wearing her high-heeled shoes, her handbag clutched between her hands in light summer gloves, the small hat that would remain floating and from a distance look like a paper boat.) He recalls Adela's letter, which he should have torn to pieces but still carries in his pocket with the tenacity of memory or remorse. *Why should I hide the fact that I'm no better than you, what frightens and angers me the most is not the thought that those savages you believed to be your people have killed you and that your children will grow up without a father but that right now you're alive and happy in the arms of that woman.* He remembers Judith's letters, stupidly kept in his study, in a drawer locked with a small key that at some point he would forget and leave in the lock. *I knew very well I couldn't give you many things you desired, but then neither will any other woman because what you want doesn't exist and you don't know how to want what's closest to you.*

Archeology of the passenger on a train that left Pennsylvania Station at four o'clock on a specific day in October 1936, not what's in his suitcase

113

but the contents of his pockets: the train ticket; a card with emergency instructions in the event of shipwreck, distributed to each passenger on the SS *Manhattan* upon embarkation; a stamped postcard he's promised himself to mail as soon as he reaches his destination, guilty for not having written to his children in so long, though he doesn't know whether any of the postcards he's been sending since the morning after his departure from Madrid have reached them; a few French centimes; a small copper penny hidden in the hindmost gap, where the hardest crumbs of bread lodge, in an opening where one's nails cannot reach; a postage stamp; a fountain pen Adela gave him for his last birthday, a gift suggested — and sold, with a small commission — by Professor Karl Ludwig Rossman, taking advantage of one of the occasions when he went to Ignacio Abel's house to pick up his daughter after the German lesson she gave the children; a token for the elevated train; two letters from two women, as different from each other as their handwriting (both announce the end of something on each of the two sides of his life, which for a time he thought would never collide or meet, contiguous rooms in the same hotel with a soundproof wall between parallel worlds). Photos in his wallet, worn and stuffed with useless documents and credentials: identity card; membership cards in the UGT, the Socialist Party, and the Association of Architects; a safe-conduct pass, dated September 4, 1936, to travel to Illescas, province of Toledo, *for the purpose of saving valuable works of art belonging to the national patrimony and threatened by the brutal Fascist aggression.* The safe-conduct mentions aggression, not advance. Words were modified in the hope that the facts words can no longer recount would cease to exist. That the enemy came and there was no effective force to stop them, or at least hamper their advance, except for unruly groups of militiamen who passed from boasting to panic to scattering after the first shots; who died with a generous, useless heroism, not knowing where the enemy was or even that the confusion suddenly surrounding them was a battle; who fell backward when their rifles recoiled against their shoulders or had rifles with no bullets or only wooden rifles or enormous pistols stolen in the looting of the Montana Barracks, foolishly aimed at an airplane flying low over the straight highway and firing shrapnel, or at some poplars shaken by the wind that appeared to be teeming with the enemy. *The squares the rebels consider decisive bulwarks of their position look more and more desperate each day. If they have not yet surrendered, it is simply because our victorious forces do not wish to destroy those cities but conquer them for Civilization and the Republic.* Perhaps they've already reached Madrid and this is the first night of the occupation, the night six hours later will fill the silent streets with the darkness of an inkpot or a well. Perhaps when the train reaches the Burton College station the newsstand will display headlines in fresh ink announcing the fall of Madrid.

Judith Biely is a photo in his wallet, taken in Paris when the possibility of their meeting didn't exist, days or weeks before she received the unexpected invitation to travel to Madrid, overnight, when she imagined she would spend the autumn in Italy, writing articles for an American magazine that would pay her very little but offered at least the double recompense of not spending the money she had left and seeing something she'd written in print; she'd see it and so would her mother, who kept in an album the photographs and letters Judith had been sending her for the past two years and the few published articles with her byline — compensation, at the moment so doubtful, for the sacrifice she had made so that her daughter could travel and give herself the education in the world she deserved and needed. The most fragile things have an extraordinary capacity to endure, at least by comparison to the people who use and make them. In some New York archive no one visits, clerks are probably binding the small radical magazines that between 1934 and 1936 published accounts of journeys or brief descriptions of European cities written by Judith Biely, never overtly political though endowed with sharp observations of life in a witty, breathless style, typed on a portable, the Smith-Corona that had also been a gift from her mother, as was the entire trip and the impulse to undertake it. She gave her daughter the typewriter when they were on the pier waiting for the gangplank to open, when the huge siren had sounded and a great column of smoke rose from one of the ship's funnels. She imposed no conditions and demanded no results; she simply offered her this gift with an unrestrained devotion similar to what she felt twenty-nine years earlier when she had given her life. Judith turned twenty-nine in the middle of the ocean, enclosed in her cabin before the typewriter in which she'd placed a sheet of paper and then written nothing, dizzy with the movement and heat of the ship, overwhelmed by the magnitude of the gift and the responsibility of deserving it. Leaning his elbows on a railing on the first-class deck, Philip Van Doren had been observing her during the voyage. It was Judith's life that would acquire a decisive form as a consequence of the gift, but it was also, by proxy, the life her mother hadn't been able to have; crossing to a Europe where she'd never been was the return journey her mother wouldn't make now. Judith, the youngest, unexpected daughter who had come when she was in her thirties, would now fulfill the expectations and possibilities she'd renounced under the weight of rearing her children, caring for the house, and feeling pressure from a husband who couldn't explain to himself why other, more recent arrivals triumphed in America and he didn't, or not on the scale he would have wished; who in Russia had been a shrewd and respected merchant, capable of closing critical deals as easily in French and German as in Polish or Yiddish, but who in the new country found himself to be as dimwitted in doing business as he was in handling the English language. The bitterness of a proud man enveloped his presence, filled his house like a suffocating shadow. Being a girl and the last born, Judith was safe from the violent pressure her father put on his sons: he demanded they be what he hadn't been and at the same time was very sensitive to the humiliation they inflicted on him by soon going beyond his discredited teaching; speaking English with no accent, becoming ashamed of him, moving ahead with an inexhaustible capacity for giving themselves over to work, for trading in goods that in Russia he would have scorned — scrap, old clothes, building materials, any merchandise that could be easily bought and sold in large quantities. At the family table he spoke loudly and listened to no one, indoctrinating his sons with useless advice that always began and ended on the same note, the relationships he'd known how to cultivate throughout Europe, conducting his own correspondence in French and German; he told them how to write their letters, as if unaware he was in Brooklyn and not St. Petersburg, as he still called his native city. The farther outside the world he found himself, the more aggressive he became; the more terror he felt at venturing into a city that would never be his, the more defiantly he refused to follow his sons' instructions in the limited tasks they gave him. His egomania swelled with the constantly repeated and increasingly exaggerated recollections in which he was always the center. His sons exchanged glances or simply looked away, became distracted playing with crumbs of bread or smoking cigarettes; they left quickly, they always had things to do, and got up so early in the morning they were snoring into their plates as soon as supper was over. The mother remained at the table, nodding, not daring to leave him without an audience for his ravings; sometimes she became absorbed in playing piano scales on the oilcloth. In time little Judith was the only one who listened to him, unable to escape the eyes that had wandered from one face to another searching for an attentive gaze where he could anchor his monologue. She understood him only in part, because he spoke fast in Russian, or rambled in French or German to demonstrate his command of those two languages which for him represented civilization, or to cite the praise for him in letters sent from business associates in Paris or Berlin many years earlier. Being a girl and having come last gave her a somewhat feline freedom denied to the others, from which she observed them all, absolved of the brutal obligations to which her brothers and father devoted themselves — the early risings, the trips to junkyards and dumping grounds, the fury of male celebrations, always harsh and threatening, the vodka, beer, tobacco, the athletic competitions. But she was also saved for the most part from the work of her mother, who lived in silence as her husband lived in words, but in ever greater isolation, which Judith began to understand when she grew older and could explain to herself what she had only sensed as currents of sadness when she was a little girl, sensitive to them but unaware of their origin. After spending the whole day working in the house, when the others were asleep her mother would remain in the spotless kitchen, and her face would change once she put on her eyeglasses and sat up straight to read a book in Russian, usually some thick tome with black covers, like a Bible. What she felt toward her husband was not fear of his unfocused and violent energy but a profound contempt that made her boredom more tolerable, allowing her to confirm that his command of languages was not as good as he asserted, his boasting nothing more than secret, pathetic fear. She took her revenge by seeing him as ridiculous, noting each indication of his vulgarity, predicting in advance and word for word the lies he would tell night after night. She would look at him and make a face, and knew her children had seen it and taken it as a signal to share with her the discredit of their father, against whom she held grudges immune to the passage of time and dating to long before he'd forced her to leave her beloved native city. It was he who had foolishly insisted on taking her to America. It was his fault she stopped being a lady with a love of music and literature, and with domestic servants who efficiently and silently attended to household tasks, to become little more than a scrubwoman. From occupying the main floor of a building in St. Petersburg she had come to live in a foul-smelling, noisy tenement of immigrants, in an apartment with low ceilings and walls like cardboard where almost all the windows faced an interior courtyard that was a black hole of garbage and screams. She who had been a lady had to fight not to lose her turn at the washbasin or the toilet with unkempt, loud women who despised her because they sensed her superiority and reserve, because they saw her returning from the public library carrying books under her arm, because she occasionally received in the mail a Russian magazine or a sales catalogue from a piano company. She spent years saving, penny by penny, to buy the piano. She'd brought musical scores from Russia, and some nights, instead of reading, she opened one on the kitchen table, leaning it vertically against a jar or box of biscuits and rapidly moving her fingers over a nonexistent keyboard, murmuring the music in a voice so low Judith barely heard it. When she was little she was hypnotized by the invisible piano that disappeared as if by magic but remained present in the strange markings on the score and in the delicacy with which her mother's hands moved over the cheap oilcloth or scoured wood. Sometimes her mother did piecework in a sweatshop where the sewing machines never stopped, night or day. It was important not to injure her fingers, not to let them become dull and slow, and to keep the music in her head, though no instrument would make it sound. Judith watched her reading or playing the nonexistent piano and understood that her mother, though so concerned about her—she wasn't to miss school or leave the house without completing her homework, she was to be neatly combed and clean and dressed like a young lady—in reality lived in another world from which she, her daughter, just like her husband and the boys, was excluded, a bubble of silence inside which floated the Russian novels she read in a low voice, the notes on the piano that perhaps no longer sounded in her head as clearly as she might have wished. Long after the Petersburg of her youth had become Petrograd and then—barbarously, in her opinion, a profanation she took as a personal insult—the Leningrad of the Soviets; when letters from relatives and friends stopped arriving and she learned in retrospect the fate of many of them—deported, imprisoned, dead of cold and hunger in the streets, disappeared—even then she continued to nourish the same circular denunciations of her husband for having uprooted her from her city and her life: a city that no longer existed, a life that eventually would have been much worse than the one she had in America. Her husband boasted at the table of having foreseen what was happening twenty years before the fact. It seemed incomprehensible to him that the czar hadn't asked for his advice, that Kerensky in 1917 had allowed himself to be guided by an ingenuousness with such disastrous consequences when he might have heeded Biely's warnings, though he'd been out of the country for many years, because he had knowledge of the world and an eye for business, an ability to penetrate the most secret intentions of men and read between the lines of the newspaper reports. When Fanny Kaplan attempted to kill Lenin in 1918, he maintained that in reality she'd assassinated him and the Soviets, masters of propaganda, gained time by deceiving the entire world except him. When it was learned several years later that Lenin had died, he predicted the immediate collapse of a system of Asiatic tyranny dependent on just one man: this was how the empire of Genghis Khan fell apart after his death, and this was how Attila's hordes dissolved into nothingness. Unlike others, he didn't base his opinions on the banalities published in the papers; one needed to have a broad perspective, to read history books in several languages. By this time Judith was already a brilliant student at City College, not because her mother's insistence that she have an education would have prevailed over her father and brothers, but because none of them paid much attention to her when she was growing up, quiet and reserved, subdued and pliant; she was the only one of them born in America. They accepted as part of her singularity that she won all the prizes in high school and with no difficulty would excel on the entrance examination for City College. In fact, they thought it a minor achievement, a thing for girls or unmanly men. At first her father bragged about her, much more than her mother did. He explained that his daughter's achievements in one way or another were due to him, and he altered his memories to fit the new version of events; in front of her, her mother, and her brothers, he recounted what everyone knew wasn't true, and the more he sensed their disbelief, the more he adorned and exaggerated his account, as if defying them to contradict him, to not agree to remember as well — she, Judith, above all — what never happened: how her father had walked her to school every winter morning when she was little, how he'd helped her with her homework, how he'd actually been more responsible for her excellent grades than she was. As his daughter progressed toward her degree, he began to display an offended mistrust that manifested itself in disdain for what he called "book knowledge," the lack of true education in professors who in many cases achieved their positions thanks not to personal merit but to family connections or the corrupting influence of money. Had he needed to go to the university to direct an expanding business in St. Petersburg with branches in the great cities of Europe and the capitals of the Levant from which he imported, at an excellent profit, olive oil, almonds, olives, and oranges? What degree had he needed to make his way in America, having foreseen before anyone, and contrary to the opinions of pompous university professors, that the days of czarism were numbered and that when the monarchy fell it would be replaced not by a European-style parliamentary system, as so many deluded men with doctorates had maintained, but by Asiatic despotism. At the family table, beneath the circle of light from the lamp, one of the brothers, exhausted by fourteen hours of work without respite, snored with his chin resting on his chest. The other smoked a cigarette, paying close attention to the ash. The mother looked sideways and practiced fingering exercises with her right hand on the edge of the table. Only she, Judith, held her father's gaze, acted as an audience, nodded without much effort at his questions that always implied the answer. But she felt no real rancor toward him and didn't lose her patience, and this tolerance of hers hurt her mother, who would have wanted her to be more indignant with him, more wounded by his miserliness, his vanity, his indifference toward everything that was not himself. She, who had actually done so much for her daughter, wasn't she entitled to have Judith place herself openly on her side, become her accomplice in resentment and in the care of the archive of all the affronts catalogued since a few years before the end of the previous century, in a world of corsets and horse-drawn carriages and byzantine solemnities in honor of the czar? But if she spoke against her father, Judith didn't second her, and if she enumerated his displays of vulgarity, Judith agreed and then smiled, making a comment that in some way exculpated him, presented him as picturesque or eccentric rather than arbitrary and cruel. He'd never given her a cent to buy a notebook, a pencil, a book. And still she wasn't resentful, and if despite everything she felt a private impulse to complain, she smothered it in remorse. The day before Judith left for Europe, he caressed her hair in his usual awkward way and said in Russian, "My girl," before turning away to hide the wet gleam in his eyes.

But it was her mother who made the trip possible, encouraged her, assisted her when she felt most lost; who observed her with worried expectation during the years when she saw her adrift, in danger of eventually being buried forever, as she had been, wanting to warn her and not knowing how. What good was her insight into the character and weaknesses of her daughter if she, her mother, was powerless to prevent the disaster? How easily she tied herself down, someone very young who'd never had any obligations, who didn't know the magnitude of the treasure she was squandering for no reason other than her stubbornness, and not even because passion blinded her. In 1930, instead of completing her doctorate, Judith Biely married a classmate who worked ten hours a day in an office that published cheap detective novels. In 1934 she called her mother and told her she'd been divorced, that perhaps she'd accept a job taking care of children or giving English lessons in Paris, and from there she would travel to Spain, where she'd wanted to go ever since she was a little girl reading Washington Irving. She wanted to revive her Spanish, which she'd studied in high school and then in college, perhaps take up again a doctoral dissertation in Spanish literature. They'd seen little of each other in recent years: her father, mother, and brothers, who tended to argue furiously about everything, had agreed, though for different reasons, that her marriage was a mistake and her husband undesirable, and Judith had broken angrily with all of them. She and her mother agreed to meet at a large, noisy cafeteria on Second Avenue in Manhattan, decorated with posters and photographs of actors in the Yiddish theater. Her mother came in with a black leather handbag held tightly inside her coat, an elegant, worn handbag brought from Russia. She'd been working as a seamstress in recent years, had saved her money and chosen a piano. But when she looked at it in the store and extended her hands over the keys, she realized it was too late: her fingers, which had been strong and flexible, were now clumsier than she'd imagined, their joints swollen by arthritis. Her scores had accustomed her to music that was now only in her head, just as she listened to the sweet Russian phonetics of the novels she read in silence, sitting in the kitchen wearing the eyeglasses she now had to use all the time. She moved the coffee cups and cake plates to one side of the table and on it she placed her handbag with the bulky bills in perfect order, which constituted her personal savings of the past thirty years. "For your trip," she said, pushing the bag toward Judith, "so you don't come back until you've spent it all." *Down to the very last cent,* she said, Judith repeating this to Ignacio Abel, feeling only then, long afterward, the relief of restitution, the certainty of having learned to return her mother's tenderness with no disloyalty to her father, who would never have done anything like that for her.

I see her more clearly now, not as a silhouette outlined in black. I see her face, luminous with expectation in the photograph taken in an automatic booth on a street in Paris, the face and look of someone who hopes for something intensely, not because she can't see the shadows but because she had the courage to overcome misfortune and a spiritual health resistant to both deceit and desolation. But perhaps that face belongs to the past now, or continues to exist only in the chemical illusion of the photograph: it's the face of a stranger Ignacio Abel hasn't seen yet and might very well never see, someone who perhaps no longer resembles her and has entered another life, who at this moment speaks and looks and breathes in a hostile place where he'll never find her, where she dedicates herself to erasing him from her life, effortlessly, as you erase things written on a blackboard when you enter a room to teach a class, white chalk dust falling to the floor and speckling one's fingers, a physical trace much more tangible than the faded presence of the lover she left in the middle of July, in another city, another country, another continent—if in fact she's returned to America—in another time.

8

HE DOES NOTHING, he only waits, letting the train carry him. He waits and is afraid, but most of all he abandons himself to the momentum of the train, the inertia of being carried and not deciding, leaning back against the worn upholstery, his face turned to the window, his hat on his lap, his hands on his knees, his entire body registering the rhythmic bump of the wheels on the rails, the abruptness of a curve. This was how he spent six days on the ship that crossed the Atlantic, absolved of all obligation and all uncertainty for the first time in who knows how long, from the moment he saw with relief how the coast of France was disappearing and before the uneasiness about his arrival in America began, six days of not showing documents or responding to lists of questions, without the torment of having to decide anything, the past and the future as clear and empty as the ocean's horizon, lying on a hammock on deck feeling all the weariness stored up in his body, a weariness much deeper than he'd imagined, in the weight of his eyelids, his arms and hands, his feet swollen after whole nights on trains when he couldn't remove his shoes, his body exhausted inert matter demanding its own immobility after hurrying so much from one place to another.

He thinks of a convalescent opening her eyes as she emerges from unconsciousness or anesthesia, and turning her head that rested on a pil-

124

low toward the window of the hospital room; the image becomes more precise and it's Adela. Beyond the window is a landscape of dark groves of pine and oak, flecked by the large white flowers of rockrose. The window is partially open, and a soft breeze scented with rockrose and resin enters and gently brushes a gray lock of hair off her pale face. He doesn't know if the gray strands have just come out or if she's been careless about dyeing her hair; maybe the color has faded because of her immersion in water where she almost drowned. He looks at her and knows nothing about her. She's his wife, he's lived with her almost every day for the past sixteen years, and she's as unfamiliar and anonymous as the sanatorium room or the bed with white bars she's lying in. Farther away, toward a Madrid barely silhouetted in the distance, the air has a chalky light that vibrates in a fog of suffocating heat. When he came in, Ignacio Abel closed the door, took a few steps toward the bed, but remained standing, his hat in one hand, in the other the small bouquet of flowers he hasn't yet resolved to give her, perhaps because he doesn't know how. How do you give flowers to a woman who didn't move at all when she saw him come in but simply looked at him for a moment and then turned her eyes back to the window, both arms next to her body, on top of the cover, her hands doing nothing to take the flowers. *You stood next to the door as if you were making an obligatory call. You didn't even come to put your arms around me and say you were glad I was all right. Who knows if maybe you would have preferred that they hadn't saved me. You would be rid of the obstacle.* Leaning against the window, noting the vibration of the glass against his forehead, he doesn't know whether what he remembers is Adela's voice that day in June or lines from the letter he carries in his pocket and should have torn up. Maybe he's projecting onto her silent image the written words he imagined in her voice, the ones Adela wanted to say to him that day but didn't, or the ones she murmured in the half-sleep of her fever and then, without relief or consolation, wrote down much later, when the outbreak of the war had already separated them like a great geological fault, he in Madrid and she in the Sierra house with the children and her parents, back inside that familial cocoon where she felt so protected and perhaps should never have left, except that then she wouldn't have had those two children who'd welcomed her with such sweetness when she came home after a week in the hospital, not asking questions about what everyone in the family was calling "the accident," filling her with remorse for what she'd attempted. *If there is anything I regret, it's not having thought about them when I was blinded by my desire to hurt you. They are the ones who would have really suffered. Not you. You would have been spared my presence. Your path would have been cleared. And yet, deep down I didn't want to hurt you, fool that I am. I was simply mad with love and couldn't bear the thought of you leaving me.* It's not really her voice, they're words written in a kind of long, unrelenting paroxysm, perhaps on a sleepless night, by the light of an oil lamp, possibly hearing like the muffled noise of a storm the shelling at the front that couldn't have been very far away. The children sleeping, Don Francisco de Asís and Doña Cecilia snoring in their room, the village with all its lights out, perhaps a small lantern in the narrow window of a barn, the railroad station dark, no trains going back and forth to Madrid for over a month, not since the day in July when Ignacio Abel left as he would have done on any other Sunday afternoon that summer, like so many men who leave their families in the Sierra and return to the city to work, in his light suit, holding his briefcase, waving goodbye with his hat on the other side of the gate. *You must have thought I didn't notice your impatience when you wanted to leave. You didn't dare say so because you promised the children you'd stay until early Monday morning but I knew you wouldn't be able to stand it. What called you was so strong you didn't care about the news from Morocco and Sevilla and the danger in Madrid with so much gunfire and horrible crimes. All you cared about was that the train not leave without you so you could meet that woman waiting for you.* She wrote so quickly her handwriting lost its regularity and straight lines and took up all the space on the paper. She crossed out words carelessly, leaving ink stains and scrapes at the places where the almost dry pen point became clogged, like a mouth without saliva, possessed by the impulse to say what she'd never said, to break immodestly with her timidity and sense of propriety, *she must do things to you it would disgust me to do. It seems that's what all you men want. That's why you go to those indecent houses.* That's what she must have been thinking when he entered the room at the sanatorium and saw her turned toward the window, indifferent to his presence, letting herself be carried away by exhaustion, complete surrender, pure physical inertia, obedience to the weight of her body, its immobility after asphyxia, the turbid water that entered her nose and mouth and flooded her lungs: still water where her body was reflected, outlined against the sky before she took that step into the void, letting herself fall like a sack of clay, relieved at last of the awkward, sweaty burden of herself.

The train moves forward along the river that pulls in the opposite direction, toward the sea, great barges loaded with minerals or mountains of scrap metal or garbage, and light sailboats suspended over the water, tossing like paper boats, white sails agitated by the wind in undulations similar to those on the surface where, half submerged like the back of an alligator, an enormous tree trunk is floating, perhaps torn away from the bank, gulls flapping over its thatch of roots. If someone were to jump into the water here, rescue would be impossible. He would prefer simply to observe: not to have memories or desires or regrets (desires for what will not be granted him now, regrets for what he can no longer remedy), not to calculate the time remaining in the trip, not to feel nervous about missing the station or not being ready to get off when the train arrives because the conductor told him the stop is brief and he ought to walk to the exit door ahead of time. But he hasn't been traveling very long. He looks at his watch as often as anxious men puff on or light cigarettes; he looks at it and so little time has passed since he last looked, he thinks time has stopped and brings the watch up to his ear in a gesture of alarm. A pronounced curve of the train tracks now allows him to see the entire breadth of the river and the two banks at the same time, and above them, as light as a drawing or a mirage, the most beautiful bridge he's ever seen, its columns and arches and the metal framework of its two towers shining in the sun like a weightless structure of steel plates, the cables prominent against the blue or almost disappearing in the blinding light like the silk threads of a spider's web vibrating in the wind. He recognizes the George Washington Bridge, more perfect in reality than in photographs and plans, with the radiance of a recently completed Gothic cathedral, still white, as in Le Corbusier's evocations, but more beautiful than any cathedral, delicate in its formidable scale, in its form, as pure as a mathematical axiom, as necessary as those marvelous everyday objects placed on the table in the lecture hall by Professor Rossman, who will never know the emotion of seeing the bridge in the distance. He presses his face to the window for a better view. For his saint's day two years earlier he bought his son Miguel a Meccano kit of the George Washington Bridge, and the boy was so excited, so overwhelmed by the gift that he couldn't assemble it: all the pieces fell when it finally seemed he'd begun to succeed, and he burst into tears. The inverted bow of the cables cross from one bank to the other with the exactness of a compass curve drawn in blue ink on white Bristol board. There's no stone facing to hide or ennoble the structure: light passes through the towers like the geometrical filigrees of a latticed shutter. The naked towers, pure prisms of steel, their verticality as firm as the lightly bent horizontal that extends with only their support between the two banks, the cables like bows and the double strings of a harp, vibrating in the wind. Mathematical purity: two vertical lines crossed by a horizontal, a bow inverted at approximately thirty degrees, its far ends at the points of intersection of the horizontal and the verticals. Gradually, as the train approaches, lightness is transformed into weight, into the tremendous gravitation of steel girders on the gigantic columns that support them, sunk into the living rock beneath the riverbed and the mud, their granite blocks pounded by waves created by a freighter as it passes under the bridge, but the train immediately pulls ahead of it. Perhaps he chose the wrong occupation. An architect's work has room for frivolities and whims that the ascetic art of engineering doesn't allow ("You architects, aren't you really decorators?" the engineer Torroja had said to him, and it wasn't entirely a joke): no building can be more beautiful than a bridge, a form purer and at the same time more artificial, superimposed on nature's lack of moderation like a sheet of transparent paper where a sketch has been traced. For a few seconds he can appreciate up close, through the window, the carved surface of the large ashlars as magnificent as those in a Florentine or Roman palace, or the blocks of primitive rock the size of the tightened bolts along the length of the girders; he has the sensation of touching the rough spots and cracks on the coat of paint worn away by the weather, its texture as rich as the bark of a great tree; he tilts his head in an attempt to take in the height of the columns and feels the dizziness of their gravitation. The scale of the bridge is measured against that of the river, as wide and powerful as a sea, the palisades, the woods the train enters, faster now that the city has been left behind. He'll send his children a postcard in color, like the ones he's already sent of the Brooklyn Bridge and the ocean liners along the docks against a backdrop of skyscrapers, and of the Chrysler Building, a postcard like the one of the Empire State Building he forgot to mail though he'd already put a stamp on it. He'll mark a dot at the bottom of one of the towers of the George Washington Bridge to give them an idea of the size of a human figure, as small as an insect, lost in a colossal world and at the same time exalted in intelligence and imagination because nothing of what overwhelmed him belonged to the realm of nature. Equally diminutive men had conceived of the bridge, imagined it, drawing indecisive lines in a sketchbook; they had calculated stress and resistance with great precision, then drilled into the earth with machines, gone underwater in diving suits and lead shoes, climbed oscillating metal structures to solder girders, tighten cables, pound rivets with powerful hammers. Human work was sacred: the courage to confront icy winds, fatigue, and vertigo, not in the name of any ideal or passion but to complete a job and earn one's daily bread; the unanimous commitment to erecting something where nothing existed before — a bridge, the rails and ties of train tracks nailed one by one into the earth, a house, a library at the top of a hill. Building something and knowing that from the moment the work is completed, time and the elements are already beginning to undermine it, wear it out with the expansion of heat or the aggression of wind and rain, with insidious damp, the oxidation of iron, the decay of wood, the slow pulverization of brick, the corrosion of stone, the sudden disaster of fire. Teams of men up on the cables, black dots like notes on a score or birds on telegraph wires, repairing something, perhaps repainting, because the most solid paint would degrade quickly in this climate attacked by the ocean's saltpeter, cracked by extreme cold and ice, softened by the unforgiving summer heat. But it was time that completed the work; the passage of time, heat and cold, constant use; time that revealed and consumed the beauty of a brick wall eroded by weather, or flights of stairs worn by footsteps, or a wooden railing burnished by the constant slide of hands. So many years driven by an obsession to finish things immediately, to leap from one minute to the next as if leaping between cars on a moving train. Only now does he begin to realize that perhaps what he'd lacked wasn't speed but deliberation, patience and not perplexed agitation.

Yet building something is so arduous. There's a silent resentment against the effort, a destructive underground current, the impulse of the child who tramples his recently completed sandcastle at the beach, the joy of flattening towers with the sole of the foot, destroying walls with a kick; Miguel crying in his room, red-faced, surrounded by the ruins of the Meccano, too much crying for his age, his sister looking at him with annoyance from her desk; teams of dynamiters in the late July heat and the first hallucinatory days of the war attempting to blow up the monument to the Sacred Heart of Jesus on Los Angeles Hill, bringing large augers and hammer drills on trucks from Madrid, squads of militiamen firing their rifles in successive volleys at the enormous statue, its arms spread wide; the crowd illuminated by the brilliance of the flames, eyes shining, the unanimous uproar that burst from open mouths on the night of July 19 when they saw the dome of a church collapse amid brilliant embers and a lava of melted lead. In the heat of the summer night the fire, like blasts from a furnace, made the air tremble. How much time, how much labor, how much ingenuity had gone into building that dome a little more than two centuries ago, how many men breaking stone, how many mules and oxen dragging huge blocks from the quarry, how many trees and how many axes needed to prepare the rafters, how many callused hands skinned, tugging on pulley ropes, in which furnaces was lead molded for the roofs or the red clay and glazed tiles baked? But everything burned so quickly; the fire sucked in hot air to keep feeding its own voracity; around Ignacio Abel men and women danced as if celebrating the apotheosis of a primitive deity, some shooting rifles or pistols into the air, as intoxicated by fire as by words or anthems, celebrating not the literal collapse of a church dome in Madrid but the imaginary downfall of an old world that deserved to perish. He recalls the sensation of the fire stinging the skin on his face, the smell of gasoline, the suffocating smoke after a gust of wind, the taste of ash in his mouth, and afterward the stink of smoke on his clothes. The other side destroys with more modern methods, not with the fire of medieval apocalypses but with Italian and German planes that machine-gun refugees on the roads and drop bombs from a comfortable height over a Madrid that lacks not only antiaircraft defenses but also effective searchlights and sirens. Our side executes crudely, with fury, the other side with the methodical deliberation of butchers, shooting from a distance and with infallible marksmanship at terrified militiamen who run away, then using sharpened bayonets up close. Neither side rests at night. At night the designated victim offers even less resistance. He waits motionless, apathetic, like an animal transfixed by the headlights of the car that will knock it down. On both sides, headlights are the last thing those who are going to be executed see. As for Professor Rossman, whose glasses had been stomped on, the light must have hurt his poor colorless eyes. In the darkness Ignacio Abel heard a voice saying his name, and it took him a moment to realize that if he didn't see anything, it was because he was covering his eyes with both hands.

He looks at his watch again, though he looked at it only a minute ago, like the smoker who doesn't remember that he has a cigarette and anxiously lights another. If they haven't attacked the city yet, it's likely that the engines of the planes can already be heard in the frightened silence of a night without lights. Moreno Villa must hear them behind the closed window in his room at the Residence, where on other nights he's heard the orders and guns of nearby firing squads, the purr of cars that light the scene and wait with their motors running for the job to be over. Perhaps the planes fly in from the north and Miguel and Lita hear them passing over the peaks of the Sierra, knowing they're going to bomb Madrid, imagining their father is still in the city, or has died, that they won't see him again, their last image of him a badly made photo that disappears in the developing fluid, the light suit, the black briefcase, the summer hat waving on the other side of the gate as the train whistle sounds again.

With a whistle like a ship's siren the train moves away from the riverbank and plunges at higher speed into the tunnel of yellow, ocher, orange, blue, and red leaves of a forest so dense the afternoon light can barely penetrate. The wind caused by the power of the train raises eddies of leaves that flutter like clouds of agitated butterflies, collide with the window, and are rapidly left behind. Leaves of oak, maple, elm, trees he's never seen, still plentiful at the treetops and floating through the air or covering the ground like a great snowstorm of reds, yellows, ochers, among tree trunks as extravagant as primitive columns and impenetrable thickets where it seems primordial nature has been preserved only a few steps from the train, like the river's oceanic current that breaks in diminished waves against the bank adjacent to the rails. His eyes are lost in the density of the woods, as if suddenly there were no traces of the city only a few minutes behind them, or the bridge that testifies to a proximate human presence, as if the continent had closed in on itself in a flood of rivers and forests, erasing the scars of the invaders' presence. The ruins of an abolished civilization might be concealed under vegetation this dense. Coming in through the window now isn't the smell of algae and the ocean but the odor of leaves, damp earth, and fertile soil where vegetable matter rots in the shade of impenetrable undergrowth. Entire forests of pine groves in the Sierra

Morena and the Sierra de Cazorla were cut down to build the ships of Philip II's armada, which a storm sank in just a few hours near the English coast. Dead animals, birds without shelter, rain washing away soil on slopes the tree roots had held in place, finally thankless bare rock, the harsh homeland of goatherds, rachitic peasants, the ecstatic, determined to cut and burn more and leave no refuge even for scorpions.

He took Judith Biely for a walk in the Royal Botanical Garden the second time they met. She recognized American trees, the identical fall colors, though it surprised her that the forest ended abruptly and they immediately came upon the straight paths, fences, and pergolas of a French garden. She walked by his side and both were silent, listening to the rustle of dry leaves under their feet. They'd done no more than caress and kiss with apprehensive awkwardness in the greenish half-light of the bar at the Hotel Florida, and then in the car when Ignacio Abel drove her for the first time to her boarding house, the two of them surprised and silent following their boldness. They hadn't seen each other naked. Conversation had distracted them from the fact of being together and permitted them to suspend the connection affecting them behind their words. They'd agreed to meet at the entrance to the Botanical Garden, and the impulse for one to go to the other had been halted in the prelude to physical intimacy. Indecisive or diffident, they didn't kiss or take each other by the hand. A renewed timidity wiped away the closeness of their first meeting; it seemed impossible that they'd embraced and kissed at length. They had to begin again, probe the re-established limits one more time, the invisible restraints of good manners. How strange that all of it had occurred, that only a year had gone by since then, that the October afternoon light was almost identical, like the smell and colors of the leaves. "And the strangest thing of all is that I feel so at home in Madrid," Judith had said just before she fell silent, her hands in the pockets of her light coat, her head bare, looking around as calmly as on the first day they were together on the street, on the sidewalk of the Gran Vía when they'd left Van Doren's apartment, in front of the movie posters covering the façade of the Palacio de la

Prensa. In the Garden, on a cool, damp October morning with the subtle scent of smoke and fallen leaves in the air, they read the labels with the names of the trees in Latin and Spanish. Judith pronounced them aloud, uncertain, allowing herself to be corrected, taking pleasure in names that alluded to distant origins: the elm of the Caucasus, the weeping pine of the Himalayas, the giant sequoia of California. She told him she felt more at home in Madrid than in any European city she'd visited in the past year and a half, and it had been true from the moment she got off the train in the North Station and went out to a sunny, damp street in the first light of a September morning and took a taxi to the Plaza de Santa Ana, filled with produce and flower stands covered by awnings, the shouts of vendors and the warbling of birds for sale in their wire cages, the cries and flutes of knife grinders and the sound of conversations coming through the wide-open doors of the cafés. Her New York neighborhood had been like that when she was a girl, she said, but perhaps with a more anguished vitality, a more visible fury in the daily search for sustenance or profit, in the harshness of social relationships, men and women from remote places in the world having to earn a living from the first day and without anyone's help in a city that for them was strange and overwhelming beyond the familiar streets where immigrants crowded together, dressed as they had dressed in the villages and ghettos of the far eastern reaches of Europe, surrounded by signs, shouts, and cooking odors that reproduced those of the old country. In Madrid the street peddler standing on a corner or the patron leaning on the bar in a tavern gave Judith the impression of always having been there, inhabiting an uneventful indolence, like that of the men in dark suits who looked out at the street through the large windows of cafés or the drowsing guards in the rooms of the Prado. He asked her whether, in the matter of Oriental indolence, she'd tried the clerks in public offices yet, gone at nine to take care of some transaction and waited until after ten, and found herself looking, beyond the arc of a small window, at a face both embittered and impassive, a nicotine-stained index finger moving back and forth, negating something, or pointing accusingly at a missing stamp on a document, a seal, the signature of someone you'd have to look for in another, more obscure office where the window for serving the public wasn't open yet.

"Don't mistake backwardness for exoticism," Ignacio Abel said, uncertain at having used the familiar form of address, as if it were an inappropriate move, not daring merely to touch her but to desire her fully. "We Spaniards have the misfortune of being picturesque."

"You seem and don't seem Spanish," said Judith, and she stopped, looking at him with a smile of recognition, more adventurous than he, impatient, wanting to let him know she did remember that what happened the last time wasn't forgotten.

"Do I seem American to you?"

"More American than anybody."

"Phil Van Doren would have his doubts. His family came to America three centuries ago, and mine thirty years ago."

He didn't like her saying that name, Van Doren, and even less the casual name Phil. He thought of the fixed, sarcastic eyes under depilated brows, the blunt, hairy hands with rings pressing Judith's waist, the moment when, just having walked out of his study and leaving them alone, he looked in again, pushing the door abruptly as though he'd forgotten something.

"For him we Spaniards must be something like Abyssinians. He talks about his trips through the interior of the country as if he had to take along native carriers."

He realized his hostility was a deep personal ill will caused by his jealousy of a link between Van Doren and Judith from which he was excluded and about which he didn't dare question her—what right did he have? If Van Doren didn't like women, why did he touch her so much? How could Ignacio Abel feel confident next to her when they were alone, if he didn't dare touch her or look her in the eyes? He heard train whistles in the nearby station, and car engines and horns on the Paseo del Prado, muffled by the dense trees, like the rustle of the dry leaves beneath their feet that sank slightly into the damp earth, only a year ago, a year and a few days, in another city, another continent, another time. And if she had regrets or simply considered it unimportant, or thought there was something embarrassing or ridiculous in the eagerness of a well-known married man with children, a man in his late forties who couldn't risk being seen in public with a woman who wasn't his wife, a foreign younger woman observed by the vigilant faces of Madrid in taverns and cafés. What was he doing, he must have asked himself when they both fell silent and conversation no longer stretched the ruse of a pretext beneath them like a net, leaving the office much earlier than he should have, making a date with Judith with an excuse of almost pathetic puerility, showing her the Botanical Garden, his favorite place in Madrid, he told her, the best of Spain, better than the Prado, better than University City, his motherland full of statues of naturalists and botanists, not bloody generals or cretinous kings, his island of civilization dedicated to the knowledge and patience to classify nature according to the scale of human intelligence. Then Judith stopped, facing him on the other side of one of those basin fountains where red fish swam and a weak jet of water rose, and before she said anything, he knew she'd refer to what hadn't been mentioned so far, the other night in the bar at the Florida.

"I wasn't sure you'd call me."

"How could I not call you?" Ignacio Abel felt himself blushing slightly. He spoke so softly it was difficult for her to understand what he was saying. "What made you think that? I haven't stopped thinking about you."

"You were so serious while you were driving, not saying anything, not looking at me. I thought you must have regretted it."

"I couldn't believe I dared kiss you."

"Will you dare now?"

"How do you say *me muero de ganas* in English?"

"'I'm dying to.'"

But in the boldness he'd felt on the afternoon of their first meeting, there was not only desire but also alcohol, the clear liquid in the cone-shaped glasses served in Van Doren's apartment by the waiter following his employer's instructions, his subtle, imperious gestures. The intoxication of drink, the novelty of words, the same song playing again on the phonograph, his own voice slightly changed, the October sky over the roofs of Madrid, the faces of the guests, most of them American, the works by Klee and Juan Gris, the blank, diaphanous space that took him back to his time in Germany, just as his desire for Judith wakened the part of him that had been sleeping since his affair with his Hungarian lover. He said, looking at his watch when Van Doren had left them alone in his office, "Now I really do have to go," and was grateful as if for a disproportionate gift when Judith replied that she did, too, and would leave with him, and in the elevator she sighed with relief, arranging her hair in the mirror. Out on the street they'd walked together for the first time, in the light of day and among people, with no need for caution, even when it was time to say goodbye and nothing happened, time for each of them to walk away into the crowd on the Gran Vía at five o'clock on a Friday afternoon, store windows and large, hand-painted canvas banners on the façades of movie theaters, honking, the sun shining on the silvery metal of automobiles, a present without a future, the inevitable future unleashed by a word that might not be said. He could say what was true, that it was urgent for him to go back to the office, to documents and blueprints and urgent calls he had to answer. He felt lightheaded: if he drove with the window down, the air would clear his mind. At each moment possible futures unfolded that burn like flares in the darkness and a second later are extinguished. He wanted to go on listening to her voice, the peculiar way her Spanish vowels and consonants sounded, to prolong the state of gentle physical intoxication, her proximity the powerful imminence of something, the exciting, mysterious ambit of the feminine. Judith stood looking with a smile of recognition at the sunlight on the terraces of the tallest buildings, the limpid blue of the sky against which the tower of the Capitol Theater was outlined.

"I look up and it's as if I were in New York."

"But the buildings must be much taller there."

"It's not the buildings, it's the light. This is the same light as in New York right now. I mean, that will be there in six hours."

He could suggest they have a drink and Judith would smile and thank him and say she was late for an appointment with her students or a talk at the Residence or at the Center for Historical Studies. He thought about his dark, empty apartment when he'd go home that night, when he'd open the door and not hear the voices of his children; perhaps they were exploring the garden of the house in the Sierra, or planning an expedition, like the ones in Jules Verne's novels, for his arrival the following day. In a lighthearted tone that surprised him and hid his fear, he told Judith he was inviting her to have a drink at the Hotel Florida across the street. After a moment of hesitation she agreed, shrugging with a smile, and took his arm to cross the Gran Vía in the middle of traffic.

Words are nothing, the delirium of desires and phantasmagoria whirling in vain inside the hard, impenetrable concavity of the skull; only physical contact counts, the touch of another hand, the warmth of a body, the mysterious beat of a pulse. How long has it been since someone touched him, a figure folding in on himself on the train seat, as hard and mineral-like as a thick, closed seashell. He's dreamed of Judith Biely's voice (which he hardly remembers after only three months), but its sound was less true than the sensation of being brushed, touched by her hand, pressed against her smooth skin, kissed by her lips, caressed by her curly hair almost as immaterially as by her breath, like a faint breeze that has silently come through an open window. He was walking beside her along an avenue in the Botanical Garden and suddenly they were silent and all that could be heard were the leaves beneath their feet: the leaves of trees brought as seeds or frail shoots from America in the eighteenth century, housed in the dark holds of ships, waiting to germinate in this distant land where Judith Biely, after almost two years of traveling, feels at home, in a homeland she never knew she had until now, recognizing the trunks and the shapes and colors of the leaves, learning their names in Spanish, saying them in English so he could pronounce after her. He seemed awkward now and much younger than the first few times she saw him, younger and softer at each meeting, as if his life were being projected backward: the tall, professorial figure behind a podium at the Residence, with his dark suit and gray hair and judgmental appearance. The man who afterward looked at her across the crowd from the other end of the room, who left without saying goodbye, beside his wife, who was visibly older than he; who appeared in the doorway of Van Doren's apartment; who leaned stiffly toward her in a private booth in the bar of the Hotel Florida and almost didn't dare kiss her; who now, only a few days later, disconcerted, erudite, pronounces the names of trees in Latin, not realizing the mud on the ground was dirtying his shoes and the cuffs of his trousers, stopping because she'd stopped and not daring to meet her eyes, perhaps regretful, overwhelmed by the responsibility of having gone so far, of having called her again, unable to continue talking, to go on pretending he was some kind of teacher or mentor of botany or Spanish customs and she a foreign pupil, paralyzed by the recognition of a desire that couldn't be contained and that he couldn't manage, a desire he barely remembered existed.

"*I'm dying to.*"

9

NOT USED TO LYING, the ease of concealing something for the first time in a long while surprised him. The novelty of pretense was as stimulating as his resurgent desire and the signs of falling in love. There was a kind of innocence in such perfect impunity. What no one could know had occurred only a few hours earlier, and was clear and fresh in his memory, and still had left no trace in his external appearance. The mind's secrecy was a prodigious gift. Lying on the grass in the mild sun of a Saturday afternoon, he talked distractedly with Adela about the children's new school term, and though she was looking into his eyes she couldn't know what he was thinking, what he was reliving, delighting in the precision of each detail, each minute. His memory was a camera obscura where only he could see Judith Biely, a gallery of murmurs where only he heard her voice, as close as if she were talking into his ear. Adela was probably grateful for his talkative, friendly mood when he arrived that morning at the house in the Sierra, his rested, almost smiling air, his amiable disposition toward her and her relatives, which came as a surprise since he often seemed uncomfortable around them. She was in the kitchen helping the maids peel quinces — she liked the brown and gold down that remained on her fingertips and had so delicate a scent when she brought her fingers to her nose — when she was startled by the sound of a car's engine. Pleasantly surprised that her husband had arrived earlier than expected, fearful he would be unsociable, in a bad mood, sleep-deprived. She would have liked not to have so acute a perception of the variations in his state of mind, not to respond so immediately to any indication of a change of mood, of anger or dejection, as if over the years she'd sharpened an instrument of detection so sensitive it approached prophecy, because it warned of certain symptoms before they occurred. Her children's footsteps resounded as they galloped down the stairs. "Ah, my faithful vassals at the battlements, a knight-errant approaches the castle, if not an inn or station snack bar," Don Francisco de Asís declaimed with theatrical exaggeration under the squat granite columns of the porch when his grandchildren crossed the garden on their way to the gate. Ignacio Abel stopped the car in front of it, looking at himself for a moment in the rearview mirror, prepared without remorse for the novelty of lying. In the seat next to him was no trace of the woman who only the night before had sat there, half closing her eyes to feel the cool air coming through the lowered window and blowing her hair away from her face while he drove up the Castellana. She'd looked into the same mirror to fix her lipstick and comb her hair with her fingers before getting out. The eyes that a few hours earlier had looked at her with so much attention and desire now revealed nothing, the same eyes that had seen her come near, opening her lips and tilting back her head. How strange that this memory wasn't visible to others, that it was so easy to keep the secret, like a thief who shakes your hand and steals something valuable with no effort and in view of everyone and then walks away in the full light of day. He got out of the car and his daughter ran toward him and hung around his neck to kiss him. The boy remained standing by the gate, expectant and serious, more timid than his sister, weaker, perhaps suspecting something, alert to any sign that his father's presence was not completely certain, for he tended to arrive later than he'd announced, and probably this time, too, his stay would be shorter than he'd promised. Embracing his father, he then clung to him as if to make sure he really had arrived, as if deep down he'd feared he wouldn't appear. In the clear space of the garden in front of the house, Don Francisco de Asís received Ignacio Abel with open arms in a melodramatic gesture of welcome, like a parody of the classic Spanish theater he liked so much. "What a surprise, my illustrious son-in-law! Your presence honors this humble rustic dwelling, ancestral home of my elders!" He gave his son-in-law two loud, wet kisses, too absorbed in himself or too innocent or childish to notice Abel's physical displeasure, his attitude of rejection. But Adela noticed it, waiting in the doorway, drying her hands, which smelled of quince, on her apron. She heard her father's hackneyed declamation through her husband's ears, and what otherwise would have been no more than one of an old man's tiresome habits that awaken only patience and some tenderness sounded to her like embarrassing nonsense. She noticed her husband's expression as he pulled back slightly; she knew what he must be thinking and was ashamed of her father's eccentricities, guilty about the embarrassment and disloyalty to him that muddied the otherwise loving resignation with which she would have accepted those eccentricities if not for Ignacio Abel. Too sensitive to the states of mind of someone who paid little attention to hers, as inclined as her son to depend too much on an undependable affection. The girl didn't suffer from these kinds of insecurities: she walked with her father along the gravel path, carrying his briefcase like a page in his service, certain of the preference bestowed on her. She became pleasingly childish in his presence, to the same degree that with her mother she defended somewhat defiantly her right not to be treated like a little girl.

How strange that in this part of his life nothing had been altered by what only he and Judith Biely knew, that he didn't have to pretend in order to conceal — as if he'd crossed the invisible border between two contiguous worlds, the inhabitants of one not suspecting the existence of the other. And though he missed Judith and would have liked to wake beside her, he delighted in the presence of his children and the scent of rockrose and resinous wood smoke in the Sierra air, the first autumn colors in the garden. The Japanese creeper climbed like a flame curling around a column at the entrance and along the balcony railing, the vibrant red of its leaves standing out against the granite and whitewash on the façade of the house that had a certain rustic nobility in its proportions. On Saturday morning, time in this other world seemed suspended. A cowbell's slow clang, the lowing of cattle from nearby pastures, and occasional shooting by hunters didn't disturb the autumnal stillness. Ignacio Abel was self-absorbed, doing nothing, the newspaper on his lap, sitting on the porch that faced south, and the sun had a slow density of honey that warmed the air, turned things golden, revived dozing insects. The last figs were opening on the fig tree, revealing the red pulp that sparrows and blackbirds pecked at and wasps sucked. Inside the house the family chattered noisily, Doña Cecilia's shrill tones rising above the others, supported by Don Francisco de Asís's booming organ voice, like a basso continuo. There would be elections, he declaimed, in a long-sleeved undershirt and slippers, his suspenders hanging down on each side, the paper in his hands like a banner ruined by the misfortunes of Spanish politics. There would be elections, and if the right won again, the left would rise up in another attempt at a Bolshevik revolution, and if the left won, the Bolshevik revolution would also be inevitable, a collapse of civilization as terrifying as in Russia. Don Francisco de Asís liked the word "terrifying," the word "civilization." Doña Cecilia asked him please not to talk about those things: in her husband's booming voice, apocalyptic prophecies gave her, she said, an upset stomach. Don Francisco de Asís voted sensibly for the Catholic and somewhat cajoling right of Gil Robles, but what truly moved him was the oratory of Don José Calvo Sotelo: what emotion when that man said "ship of state" or "the backbone of the nation," with what good judgment had he reformed and strengthened public administration throughout his mandate as minister during the dictatorship of Don Miguel Primo de Rivera. The boy played ball in the garden, imagining he was eluding famous soccer players, happy to be at the house in the Sierra, happy his father had come. The girl sat on the swing, balancing slowly as she read a book, the tips of her sandals brushing against the ground. Bluish oak groves in the distance; from the pastures the echoes of isolated shooting; on the ground quinces and burst pomegranates, their skins red and dry; on the grapevine

143

that shaded the entrance to the house the last grapes had the same rich honey color as the October sun (he recalled the fruit bowl of grapes and quinces in Moreno Villa's room). His briefcase filled with documents and drawings lay on the table outdoors where the family had supper on summer nights, but Ignacio Abel felt too lazy to open it. Time had paused in a sweet somnolence that weighed on his eyelids. In Madrid Judith Biely would be thinking about the same things, wondering where he'd gone. They hadn't spoken about seeing each other again when they said goodbye. As if satisfied with what had already happened, first in the half-light of the private booth, when they suddenly faced each other in silence after a lively conversation, then in the uncomfortable interior of the car. Looking for a continuation, making plans, would have profaned the unexpected paradise where they suddenly found themselves, not as if they'd traveled there but had awakened and were not completely certain where they were. Concealment was so easy: to think about Judith Biely's bare thighs above her stockings and at the same time to smile at Adela, who came out of the house bringing him a glass of wine and an appetizer, a foretaste of the meal being prepared, Doña Cecilia's renowned arroz con pollo. And it hadn't been difficult, when he arrived, to kiss Adela on the lips while he passed his hand along her waist in an unusual gesture that the boy's vigilant eyes noted with approval. He was so unaccustomed to lying, he hadn't even devised a response for when Adela or his father-in-law or the children asked him what he'd done yesterday afternoon. But it wasn't at all difficult to invent something on the spot, and he was astonished it was all so easy, that something unforgettable could have occurred with no consequences and flowed with as little premeditation as the words they'd said in a dim corner of the bar at the Hotel Florida, which they chose with tacit complicity. That was how they'd talked as they rode down in the elevator of the Palacio de la Prensa, how Judith Biely had held his arm when they crossed the Gran Vía, dodging traffic.

He'd forgotten the sensation of novelty, the thrill of desiring a woman so intensely it was the pure magnetism of her female presence that made him tremble, more than her physical beauty or the slightly exotic elegance of her dress or the spontaneity with which she had leaned on his arm, holding it tighter when a speeding car passed close to them. It was her singularity as a woman, possessed of a life that seemed richer and more mysterious because he knew nothing about it, with a language and accent in Spanish that didn't belong to anyone with her same background but only to her, as intrinsic to the attraction she exercised as the shape of her eyelids or her large mouth. With impunity he felt he inhabited two worlds. The emotional intoxication of yesterday afternoon in Madrid was transmitted without guilt to his perceptions this morning in the house in the Sierra, just as it had accompanied him on his drive along the highway to La Coruña, the car's speed as assuring and joyful as his self-awareness. The freshness of the air on that October morning, the oak groves and houses as clear in the distance as if etched in diamond, a motionless swelling of clouds overflowing the mountains of El Escorial with the magnificence of an ice cliff.

Judith had liked listening to music on the radio as they drove across Madrid. With concealed vanity Ignacio Abel pressed the accelerator and handled the controls of the recently installed radio. The speed and the music seemed to feed on each other. In the headlights the straight rows of trees along the Castellana and the palaces behind the gates and gardens became visible; streetcar tracks gleamed on paving stones. He was lucky to have become an adult in an age of extraordinary machines, more beautiful than the statues of antiquity, more incredible than the marvels in stories. Very soon they'd all conspire to facilitate his love for Judith Biely. Streetcars and automobiles would rapidly carry him to her, prolonging the meager time of their meetings; telephones would secretly bring him her voice when he couldn't have her with him and he'd call her from his house, covering his mouth with his hand, feigning a conversation about work if anyone came near; movie theaters would welcome them in their simulacrum of hospitable darkness when they wanted to hide from the light of day; telegraph offices would remain open late so he could send her a telegram on the spur of the moment. Mechanized belts transported the letters they soon began to write to each other and canceled the stamps automatically, allowing their messages to traverse distances with more accurate speed. Thanks to a splendid Fiat motor, he'd driven from one world to another in less than two hours. Adela noticed he was talking more than usual that morning. He greeted his mother-in-law, the maiden aunts, distant relatives whose names he never remembered. The family began to prepare early for the celebration — moved back to Saturday to make it more resplendent — of Don Francisco de Asís's saint's day. From the kitchen came the bubbling aroma of the stew, along with Doña Cecilia's melodramatic voice deliberating with Adela, the maids, and Don Francisco de Asís regarding the advantages and disadvantages of starting the rice, for fear that if her son Víctor arrived late, as he so often did, he'd find it overcooked when after all he liked it so much and it was so easy for rice to be overdone and then it lost all its savor. In this family there was nothing that wasn't a tradition, a commemoration. Every time Doña Cecilia prepared her stew — "legendary" in the opinion of Don Francisco de Asís — the conflict regarding the proper moment to put in the rice was repeated almost word for word, what Don Francisco de Asís called "the burning question": whether to add the rice to the bubbling liquid now or wait a little longer; whether to send the maid to the gate to see if Señorito Víctor was arriving from Madrid; whether to hold off at least until they heard the next train at the station. Ignacio Abel thought about Judith Biely — but he didn't have to invoke her, she was a constant, secret presence in his memory — and he greeted and chatted like an actor who doesn't need to make much of an effort to perform his assigned role. He listened, agreed without understanding anything, refined his capacity for resignation and self-absorption. When Víctor finally arrived — on an almost telepathic hunch Doña Cecilia had put in the rice only a few minutes earlier — it was in no way difficult for him to accept the excessive grip of his handshake and not show displeasure. He didn't even lie; he told the partial truth, explaining to Adela and the children that he'd spent all of Friday afternoon at the home of an American millionaire who lived in Madrid and had invited him to travel to America to teach some classes and design a building.

"A skyscraper?" said the boy. "Like the Telephone Company?"

"Bigger, dummy. In America skyscrapers are much taller."

"Don't talk like that to your brother."

"A library. In the middle of a forest. On the banks of a very wide river."

"The Mississippi?"

"You think that's the only river in America?"

"It's the one in *The Adventures of Tom Sawyer.*"

"The Hudson River."

"That has its mouth right at New York."

"She thinks she knows all about geography."

"Will you take us with you?"

"If your mother agrees, this afternoon I'll take you to the irrigation pond—that's much closer than America."

He didn't pretend. It was easy for him to talk to Adela and his children and not feel the sting of imposture or betrayal. What happened in his secret life didn't interfere with this one but transferred to it some of its sunlit plenitude. And he didn't care too much about the ominous prospect of immersion in the celebrations of his in-laws, usually as suffocating for him as the air in the places where they lived, heavy with dust from draperies, rugs, faux heraldic tapestries, smells of fried food and garlic, ecclesiastical colognes, liniments for the pains of rheumatism, sweaty scapulars. A sharp awareness of the other, invisible world to which he could return soon made more tolerable the painstaking ugliness of the one where he now found himself and where, in spite of the passage of years, he'd never stopped being a stranger, an intruder. The maiden aunts swarmed in the sewing room, which had an oriel window facing south. They covered their mouths when they laughed, leaned toward one another to say things in a subdued voice, embroidered sheets and pillowcases with romantic motifs of a century ago, marked patterns with slivers of soap polished to the same shine as their faces of girls grown old. Ignacio Abel kissed them one by one and still wasn't sure of their number. The uncle who was a priest would arrive when it was time to eat, with a good appetite but a somber face, recounting tales of ungodliness or assaults against the Church, predicting the return to government — if it was true that elections would be called — of the same men who in 1931 secretly encouraged the burning of convents. Abel's recently arrived brother-in-law, Víctor, dressed for a Sierra weekend in a kind of hunting or riding outfit, extended his hand with the palm on the diagonal, turned partially downward, in a gesture he must have thought athletic or energetic. "Ignacio, how good to see you." His thin hair, lying close to his scalp, formed a widow's peak. He was younger than he looked; what aged him was a rather perpetual scowl and the shadow of a beard on his bony, prominent chin, the hardness of his features, a product of his determination to display manliness without weaknesses or cracks. His Hispanic, virile brother-in-law's cordiality contrasted with a deep distrust of Ignacio Abel that was only in part ideological: Víctor gave the impression of lying in wait, looking for some threat to the honor or well-being of his sister, toward whom he felt protective although ten years her junior. Adela treated him with the limitless indulgence and docility of a pliant mother, which irritated Ignacio Abel. Víctor carried a pistol and a blackjack. Sometimes he came to eat at his parents' house in the shirt and leather straps of a Falangist centurion. Adela was both submissive and protective: "He always liked uniforms, and the pistol doesn't even have bullets." He raised his chin as he shook Ignacio Abel's hand and looked into his eyes, searching for signs of danger, not suspecting anything. He showed them the gift he'd brought for his father: a pseudo-antique *Quijote* bound in leather, with gilt letters and edges and reproductions of Doré. The family possessed an insatiable appetite for atrocious objects, fake antiquities, Gothic calligraphy on parchment, luxury bindings, and illusory genealogies. On the façade of the house, behind the two granite columns that held up the terrace, were embedded the heraldic coats of arms of the two family names, those of Don Francisco de Asís and of Doña Cecilia: Ponce-Cañizares and Salcedo. In the family the distinctive traits of each of the two branches were passionately debated: My son Víctor has the unmistakable Ponce-Cañizares nose; you can tell the girl came into this world with a pure Salcedo character. From the time they were born, the children of Ignacio Abel and Adela were picked up by their grandfather, the maiden aunts, Abel's brother-in-law Víctor, and the uncle who was a priest, and scrutinized as they discussed to which of the two lines a nose or a type of hair or dimples belonged, from which Ponce or Cañizares or Salcedo the baby had inherited the tendency to cry so loudly—those strong Cañizares lungs! No sooner had the child taken a few hesitant steps than the exact resemblance to some especially graceful ancestor was recognized, or its Ponce or Ponce-Cañizares or Salcedo origin vehemently argued over with the attention to detail of philologists debating an obscure etymology. In the heat of these gratifying diatribes they tended to forget the inevitable genetic contribution of the children's father, unless they could relate it to the hint of a defect: The boy seems to have inherited his father's eccentricity, one of them would say. At family meals Adela would look at her husband out of the corner of her eye and become irritated with herself for not knowing how to overcome the stress of imagining what he must be thinking, what he must be seeing. *You despise my parents, who love you like a son, who love you even more because your parents aren't alive. You see them as foolish and ridiculous and don't realize they're not young anymore and are developing the manias of old people like the ones you or I will have when we're their age. You think my brother is a Fascist and a parasite, and when he says something to you your answer is so dismissive even I feel embarrassed. You can't see any goodness or generosity in them, or how much they love your children and how much your children love them. You can't imagine how they suffer when they hear about the horrible things your people or the people you think are your people are doing in Madrid, and they're in distress just like me and your children at not knowing where you are or if those savages have done something to you. I think they make you angry and jealous. You don't know how happy each of your professional accomplishments makes them. They respect you and don't care if you're a Republican and a Socialist and don't go to Mass on Sunday or want our children to have a religious upbringing, as if my opinion didn't matter. You despise them just because they're Catholic and vote for the right and go to Mass and recite the rosary every day, even though they don't hurt anybody. But you didn't turn down the money my father gave us when we didn't have anything, or the commissions you received thanks to him, and when you got it into your head to go to Germany even though the children were so young, you didn't think twice about asking my father to let us live in his house while you were away because that would allow you to leave with no sense of guilt, besides saving you money as you wouldn't have been able to live for a whole year in Germany on the grant the Council for Advanced Studies gave you. You aren't grateful to them for accepting you with open arms even though other people in my family and from our class told them you didn't have a cent when you courted me and were the son of a Socialist construction foreman and a caretaker on Calle Toledo. They're reactionaries as all of you call them but they've always been much more generous with you than you've been with them. Had it not been for them and our children I would have rotted with loneliness all these years. What would I do without them now that you have gone back to Madrid even though you knew as well as we did that something very bad was going on there, you cared more about seeing your mistress than staying with your own children.*

But he wouldn't have been able to explain to his wife that the antagonism he felt toward her family was due not to ideological but to esthetic differences, the same silent antagonism he felt toward the inexhaustible Spanish ugliness of so many commonplace things, a kind of national depravity that offended his sense of beauty more deeply than his convictions regarding justice: the stuffed heads of bulls over the bars in taverns; the paprika red and saffron-substitute yellow of bullfight posters; folding chairs and carved desks that imitated the Spanish Renaissance; dolls in flamenco dresses, a curl on their forehead, which closed their eyes when leaned back and opened them as if resuscitated when they were upright again; rings with cubic stones; gold teeth in the brutal mouths of tycoons; the newspaper obituaries of dead children — *he rose to heaven, he joined the angels* — and their tragic white coffins; baroque moldings; excrescences carved in granite on the vulgar façades of banks; coat and hat racks made with the horns and hooves of deer or mountain goats; coats of arms for common last names made of glazed ceramic from Talavera; funeral announcements in the *ABC* or *El Debate;* photographs of King Alfonso XIII hunting, just a few days before he left the country, indifferent or blind to what was happening around him, leaning on his rifle beside the head of a dead deer, or erect and jovial next to a sacrifice of partridges or pheasants or hares, surrounded by gentlemen in hunting outfits and gaiters and servants in poor men's berets and espadrilles and smiles diminished by toothless mouths. He sometimes thought his excessive anger had more to do with esthetics than ethics, with ugliness than injustice. In the rotunda of the Palace Hotel monarchist gentlemen raised their teacups and extended their little fingers adorned with a small ring and a very long polished nail. In the most successful movies characters profaned the marvelous technology of sound by breaking into folksongs, dressed in awful regional outfits, mounted on donkeys, leaning against window grilles hung with flowerpots, wearing broad-brimmed hats or berets or rustic bandannas. The *Heraldo* reported with patriotic fervor that at the beginning of the great bullfight for the festival of Our Lady of the Pillar in Zaragoza the matador's team had performed the promenade to the vibrant rhythms of the "Himno de Riego," the national anthem. In the house of the Ponce-Cañizares Salcedo family, at the end of a gloomy hallway, tiny electric candles burned in the small lamps framing a full-color print of Jesus of Medinaceli that had an artistic roof of Mudéjar inspiration and a small railing simulating an Andalusian balcony. In the Renaissance armchair in the dining room filled with dark wood furniture that imitated a style between Gothic and Moorish and had inlaid medallions of the Catholic sovereigns, Don Francisco de Asís Ponce-Cañizares, retired member of the Honorable Provincial Delegation of Madrid, read aloud in a grave voice the lead articles and parliamentary accounts in the *ABC*, and Doña Cecilia listened to him, half bewildered and half impatient, and said "Good" or "Of course" or "How shameful" each time Don Francisco de Asís concluded a paragraph in the cavernous tone of a sacred orator and at the same time noted the pangs of emotion and those of stomach upset, about which he'd inform the family in detail. Don Francisco de Asís was intoxicated by the apocalyptic prose of Calvo Sotelo's speeches in Parliament and of reporters who spoke of Asiatic hordes or mobs filled with Bolshevik resentment or the virile martial joy of German youth cheering the Führer, waving olive branches, raising their right arms in unison in the stadiums. He liked words like "horde," "mob," "vortex," "collapse," and "collusion," and as he read and became more emotional, his voice deepened and he accompanied his reading with oratorical gestures, angry blows on the table, an accusatory index finger. He loved sonorous verbal turns and expressions in Latin: *alea iacta est; sic semper tyrannis;* he who laughs last laughs best; better to die with honor than to live in shame; better honor without ships than ships without honor; the clarions of destiny; the moment of truth; the straw that broke the camel's back. The fervent articles by correspondents in Germany and Italy and the Falangist publications his son Víctor brought home provided him with a poetic prose somewhat less old-fashioned but just as intoxicating and allowed him the gratification of feeling in tune with the youthful dynamism of the new day. But it was true that toward Ignacio Abel he'd always demonstrated a resounding affection of bear hugs and kisses that included a curious mixture of admiration and indulgence: admiration of his son-in-law's brilliance and the tenacity with which he overcame the difficulties of his origins and the early deaths of his parents; indulgence of his political convictions, which he attributed, if he thought about them at all, more to a sentimental loyalty to the memory of his Republican and Socialist father than to real personal radicalism. How could he be an extremist and still be so fond of well-cut suits and good manners? If Ignacio Abel was a Socialist, he had to be one in the civilized, semi-British mode of Don Julián Besteiro or Don Fernando de los Ríos. But according to the uncle who was a priest, he shouldn't let himself be deceived, because those Socialists were the worst ones, the most insidious! Who but Fernando de los Ríos, with all his unctuous manners, had devised the blasphemous divorce law when he was minister of justice? Deep down, Don Francisco de Asís must have compared the perseverance and integrity of his son-in-law, who came from nothing and created himself, with the uselessness of his own son, who always had everything but couldn't complete his law degree and spent years bouncing from one job to another, not understanding anything, his head filled with stupidities, becoming involved in futile projects and dubious business schemes, dazzled now by a Falangist enthusiasm that in Don Francisco de Asís's heart provoked not sympathy but alarm and distrust. He was afraid something awful would happen to his son, that he'd take part in a conspiracy and be sent to prison, or that one day he'd end up dead in the street after one of those gunfights between Falangists and Communists, he was always so inept, as a boy so easily intimidated in spite of his bravado.

How different from his son-in-law, almost his other son, so serious and aloof, walking into the garden that morning with his firm bearing, his solid way of being in the world, his dark double-breasted suit, his shoes—made to measure in the best English shoe store in Madrid—stepping on the gravel, holding the briefcase that the girl took from him so she could carry it, heavy with documents and blueprints that required his attention even on a day off, for he had a position with a great deal of responsibility in the construction of University City, as Don Francisco de Asís took pleasure in telling his friends. In fact, *El Sol* had published Ignacio Abel's photograph a few days earlier, and Don Francisco de Asís—breaking with custom because he defined himself as an unyielding reader of the *ABC*—had bought that paper and read aloud to Doña Cecilia the article on their son-in-law's talk at the Student Residence, and then cut out the page and kept it in a folder in the imitation Renaissance desk in his study. Not very shrewd, in no way inclined to think ill of anyone, because of elderly innocence or lack of imagination or excessive reverence for the formalities, Don Francisco de Asís, as he himself said, would have put his hand in fire for his son-in-law, who didn't smoke, barely drank more than a glass of wine at meals, never raised his voice, not even when discussing politics, which rarely happened, not even at meals when his brother-in-law Víctor or the uncle the priest would hotly argue the calamity of the Republic, the constant anarchy, the insolence of the workers, the need in Spain for a providential figure like the Duce or the Führer, or at least the sadly missed General Primo de Rivera, a strong man. On such occasions his son-in-law didn't respond, never used an uncouth word; he was a Socialist but thanks to his work had been able to buy a car and a spacious apartment with an elevator in the most elegant section of Calle Príncipe de Vergara, between Goya and Lista no less; he sent the children to the Institute School so they'd have a secular education, and didn't permit scapulars to be hung around their necks, but he hadn't opposed their taking Communion or their mother teaching them prayers; he didn't waste his evenings sitting idly in cafés; the time he didn't devote to his work he spent with his wife and two children, Don Francisco de Asís's only two grandchildren, who sadly wouldn't carry to the next generation the family name of Ponce-Cañizares. Last night he probably worked late at University City and early this morning drove to the house in the Sierra. Immune to his habitual coldness, Don Francisco de Asís offered a festive celebration when he saw his son-in-law, and gave him a wet kiss of welcome on each cheek. The two children struggled to be closer to him, to carry his briefcase and recount the adventures and explorations of the past few days, and they competed to mention the books they had read. They reminded him to take them and their mother that afternoon to the irrigation pond; they asked him if what he'd promised before his arrival was true, that he wouldn't leave tomorrow, Sunday afternoon, but would drive them back to Madrid on Monday morning. When he saw his wife, he looked her in the eye and kissed her on the lips, and his son saw from behind how he put his hand on her waist and pressed her lightly to him.

• • •

The benevolent attitude that Adela's extreme sensitivity to him detected with relief and almost with gratitude was in fact the consequence of his deception. Perhaps her husband wouldn't have placed his hand on her waist when he kissed her if he hadn't embraced another woman the previous afternoon; his gestures of tenderness compensated for the offense she didn't know she'd received; they were the remnants of an effusiveness another woman had awakened; the result of the liar's relief at not being caught; the joy of the man who has seen in himself the surge of a desire he no longer imagined possible in his life and has reached a satisfaction he didn't recall ever experiencing. As they'd often done when the children were small, that afternoon they walked with them on the path that led through pine groves and thickets of rockrose to the irrigation pond — the reservoir that had fed the old electrical power plant, a half-abandoned building at the edge. From time to time they caught sight of an unsociable custodian who once frightened the children and served as a character in their stories about enchanted houses beside a lake. That Ignacio Abel had so readily agreed to the excursion was another indication of his good mood and not merely his impatience to leave the close familial ambience, which after the snores of siesta culminated in praying the rosary, followed by a comforting snack of thick hot chocolate and anise biscuits, the work of Doña Cecilia's legendary confectionery talent. The four of them, away from the others, seemed to commemorate an earlier time it wasn't difficult to imagine as happier, the summers when the children were small, when their hands had to be held on the path and they tired so quickly that their father carried them on his shoulders, so small they had to be watched constantly so they wouldn't go in the deep parts of the pond. They played Hansel and Gretel and left breadcrumbs along the path, and on the way back they would see whether birds had eaten them. But if they went too far into the game, the boy would burst into tears because he really was afraid his parents would abandon them, and he'd put his arms around Adela's legs, his little face red and wet with tears while his sister laughed. The water in the pond had a green transparency and reflected on its surface the tops of the pines and the dark mass of the brick building that once housed turbines. The October sun was still high, gilding the bluish distances, the soft afternoon colors. The children looked for flat stones along the edge, then threw them at well-aimed angles over the smooth surface of the water, shouting their disagreement, returning to the old complicity of games now that both had left early childhood but were closer to it than either imagined. His father's camera hung around Miguel's neck, and as they walked in the woods he imagined he was making his way through the Amazon jungle or the heart of Africa, a solitary reporter because his sister didn't want to join him in the game. Sitting on the grass in the warm afternoon air, Ignacio Abel and Adela also seemed to have returned to an earlier time, the young father and mother the children see at a protective distance, engaged in their mysterious conversations but also vigilant, perhaps anxious, afraid an accident or a mishap might occur if they looked away even for a moment from the children. How strange to have Adela so close when she didn't know anything, to hold her open, melancholy gaze and not awaken any suspicion in her, to speak to her so naturally with no need to pretend or lie. He observed Adela while he listened to her. As had happened a few nights earlier in the Residence, he saw her as he hadn't seen her for some time, precisely the time when she lost the last embers of her youth. A click sounded and Miguel had taken their picture from the edge of the pond.

"Are you really planning to go to America next year? And can you take us with you?"

She knew him too well not to be aware that his mood could be temporary. She was grateful for the gestures of tenderness, the quick kiss on the lips, the hand at her waist, but she protected herself instinctively against disappointment and at the same time protected her children, especially the boy, who was more fragile and also closer to her, with a more excitable imagination: now, at the pond's edge, he talked to his sister about traveling to America on ocean liners or airplanes, made exaggerated gestures with his arms to suggest the size of things, the Empire State Building, the Statue of Liberty.

"I have to consult with Negrín first. And I have to see what they offer and how long I'll have to stay. However it turns out, you'll all come with me."

But Adela detected a touch of insincerity in his voice, though he himself didn't know he wasn't telling the whole truth. Now he was in the two worlds, two simultaneous times, yesterday afternoon with Judith and today with Adela and the children, in the dim light of the bar at the Florida and in the comfortable sun at the edge of the pond, smelling rockrose and thyme and resin, not divided but duplicated, ablaze with love and at the same time settled into the solid routine he'd constructed over the years, which that afternoon reached a kind of visual plenitude, like a completed painting, like the maturation of the last fruits of October, pomegranates and quince, yellow squash, persimmons, bursting golden grapes in the garden. He had so little experience, or so little capacity for real introspection, he didn't imagine the guilt and anguish lying in wait; he didn't even ask himself what Judith Biely might be feeling. She didn't exist for him in an autonomous, complete way but only as a projection of his own desire.

"What are you thinking about?"

"Nothing, work."

"You seemed to be in another world."

"Perhaps I ought to go back to Madrid tomorrow afternoon."

"You promised the children we'd drive back together early on Monday."

"If I go back, it's not on a whim."

"Don't tell them you'll take them to America if you're not going to do it. Don't make promises you know you won't keep."

"And you, would you like to make the trip?"

"What I'd like is never to be separated from you. Where we are doesn't matter."

She blushed when she said this and looked younger. She resembled the overly shy woman who no longer counted on finding a man, which she'd been when they met, the one for whom her parents predicted the same familial destiny as the maiden aunts, with whom she sometimes spent Sunday afternoons praying the rosary. With her wide hips settled on the warm grass beside the pond, her ankles tended to swell. Her black hair styled with an out-of-date wave made her seem older. But her eyes suddenly looked as they had fifteen years earlier and had a passionate, vulnerable expression, as if she'd passed from not expecting anything to wanting it all, from conformity to audacity, and from there to anticipated disillusionment, to skepticism regarding what life could offer her. Now she might have wished that her children weren't so near, that they didn't shout so much while they looked for smooth stones along the edge and then threw them at the water. For her it was a contretemps when they approached, tired and hungry, their cheeks reddened by exercise and the Sierra breeze, demanding the snack they'd brought in a wicker basket. For Ignacio Abel it was a relief. The sun began to go down behind the pines, the air acquired a touch of dampness that intensified the mountain odors, the smell of thyme and rockrose and dry pine needles. The bells and the lowing of cows, the smaller bells of sheep, emphasized acoustically the sensation of amplitude and distance. If the air had been clearer, the white smudge of Madrid would have been visible on the horizon. It would be cold as soon as the setting sun no longer reached the pond, raising a faint golden mist over it. Secretly disloyal, unpunished in his dissimulation, Ignacio Abel decided he'd invent an excuse to return to Madrid on Sunday afternoon. He wouldn't wait until then to hear Judith Biely's voice; he'd go to the village to buy something and try to call her from the only phone, located in the station café. He looked up, coming out of his absorption, his secret trip to that other, invisible, contiguous world. Sitting on a rock, his daughter ate a sandwich and read a novel by Jules Verne. Adela took a few awkward steps along the bank, ridding her legs of numbness, brushing pine needles and grass stems from her skirt. His son was looking at him with wide-open eyes, as if he'd read his mind and was aware of his deceit, as if he already knew that the next afternoon his father would go back to Madrid alone, and if he went to America, he would also go alone.

10

WHERE HAD JUDITH come from, bringing with her a different world, bursting into his life like someone who abruptly enters a room, someone unexpected who opens the door and is followed by cold outside air that in a few seconds has altered the closed atmosphere. Her very presence was an upheaval, the new arrival who rings the bell brusquely and makes all eyes look. Judith Biely always moved quickly among much slower people, like an emissary of herself, detached from her will and character, the luminous advance of something that might be a promise of another life in another, less harsh country whose colors were less gritty or mournful, a tangible woman and at the same time the illusion and synthesis of what Ignacio Abel found was most desirable in women, in the very substance of the feminine: changing, unpredictable, entering unexpectedly, leaving so quickly that trapping an image of her on his retina, one that would remain fixed in memory, was as impossible as stopping time, or suspending it so a secret meeting might last longer. Judith Biely was like that in the only photograph of her Ignacio Abel keeps in his wallet, slightly out of focus because she was turning to one side at the moment the automatic camera shot the picture, a faint mist around her eyes, her smiling mouth, responding with a lighthearted expression to something that attracted her attention and forgetting for an instant that she was posing for a photograph, the precise instant captured in it. She must have been waiting uncomfortably for the flash to go off inside the booth on the street when something or someone made her turn her face slightly and smile, and the light exploded on her chin and cheeks, the curls in her hair, her slightly smudged eyes where a gleam of light stands out, as does one on her lips. It's the imperfection of the photo that appeals to Ignacio Abel: the impersonal quality of chance causes Judith to be more present without the interference of a photographer's eye and intention, as if she were really there, in that rescued moment. And to make the photo even truer, it's not of the Judith he remembers but the one who hadn't yet traveled to Madrid, the one not yet distorted by familiarity or the obsession of desire, intact in her distance and as much herself as when she burst into his life a few months later, in a future about which she still knows nothing when she smiles in the photograph, because she doesn't know she's about to receive the offer that will make her change her plans by moving forward the trip to Spain.

Where had she come from? Recounting her life in a new language limited the amount of detail she could provide and forced her to simplify her story. Listening to herself from the perspective of this man granted her an objectivity that was liberating. Her life experiences, when told, took on something of a novel's rigor and sense of purpose. The uncertainty of so many years acquired the curve of an arc that emerged from the murky past to rise above time and bring its far end to rest in the present moment, on the other side of the world, in Madrid during the days of October 1935, in a shadowy private booth in the Hotel Florida, in the gentle dizziness of driving along a straight, tree-lined avenue that opened like a tunnel in the headlights, her eyes half closed, seeing things through a light mist he'll recognize afterward and want to treasure in an ordinary photo from an automatic picture booth. Images and words flow, appear, are lost, just like the treetops and façades and lights shining in the windows of the mansions along the Castellana; Judith Biely is in a car moving through Madrid but she could also be on an avenue in Paris, or in any of the European capitals she's visited in the past two years that are becoming confused in her fatigued memory; the headlights illuminate black paving stones as brilliant as patent leather, the rails and cables of streetcars; she's silent beside the man at the wheel, who seems much younger now than just a few hours ago, when he appeared alienated, almost frightened in the foyer of Philip Van Doren's apartment (where Van Doren must be now; how shrewdly he'd suspected and understood, almost prophesied). She's fallen silent, but turning over in her head is the sense of having talked a great deal; her life, as recounted, extends before her like the avenue along which the car is driving, opens up with a feeling of symmetry and purpose that she knows is false but for now doesn't mind enjoying, like the speed of the car or the music from the radio. Ignacio Abel finds Judith's hand and holds it gently, though she doesn't respond, doesn't quite acknowledge what's happening. How strange, the play of hands at this age.

Suddenly she sees all the distance she's traversed. In a language she's becoming truly familiar with only now, she recounts her life to the man who listens and looks at her attentively. In her narrative, events acquire an order she knows is false, a suggestion of inevitability that conceals but doesn't extenuate her awareness of its improbability. She comes from a room with a low ceiling where, as a little girl, she would read by the light of a candle in the small hours; from trains to Manhattan that would disappear into tunnels and emerge into the limitless vertigo of the graceful pillars of a bridge suspended over the East River, and the sight of the oceanic bay and the steep cliffs of buildings through the windows, and beneath and beyond the vibrating framework of the Williamsburg Bridge the row of ocean liners along the piers emitting bellowing sirens and columns of smoke above funnels painted black and red, white and red. She comes from the lecture halls and grassy campus under colossal trees of a university for the children of immigrants, torn between the only world they know and the one that cast a shadow of insecurity and persecution over their lives, the remote world their

parents brought with them. But she comes above all from the awareness of a mistake she can't blame on anyone but herself, one she easily
could have avoided and in which she persisted, not out of blindness or
passion but out of pure, senseless pride, simply to resist pressure she'd
trained herself to rebel against. How easily she squandered the treasure
of her own will, not for love but to be contrary, to do what her elders
asked her not to do and what consequently became the very incarna-
tion of her freedom. She married a former college classmate somewhat
older than her, and knew she was making a mistake, she told Ignacio
Abel, and as she said it she recalled the image of the woman with wide
hips and melancholy eyes and the girl in old-fashioned clothes and a
ribbon in her hair who came up to him after his talk at the Residence;
the empty seat next to the woman was the one she, Judith, had occupied; the woman looked at her for a moment, her eyes moving up and
down with instinctive mistrust when Judith asked Moreno Villa to introduce her to Ignacio Abel. Who can know the reason for her actions?
Before she left the desolate court building where with full knowledge
she accepted the bonds of marriage, Judith Biely knew she'd made a
mistake and that renouncing her last name was an unacceptable humiliation. She preferred not to see, of course. No one puts a blindfold
on you by force and then knots it at the back of your neck so tightly
you couldn't take it off even if your hands weren't tied. You're the one
who weaves the blindfold and the rope, who extends her hands voluntarily and waits until the knot is tight. No one erects the walls of the
cell and locks it from the outside and makes certain the bolt is in place.
You take the necessary steps, one after the other, and if anyone signals
to warn you of danger, all that's accomplished is the reinforcement of
your determination to keep approaching disaster. At times you're relieved to know you haven't arrived yet, at others, that there's no turning back. Doubt is transformed into disloyalty you don't acknowledge
even to yourself. She'd graduated with honors from City College; she
could easily have completed her doctorate in Spanish literature under
Professor Onís at Columbia and at the same time teach the language to
beginning students. Henry James's heroines who'd awakened her imag-

ination and whom she wanted to resemble when she was fifteen or sixteen years old inherited fortunes that allowed them to travel alone in Europe. Now her model in life was Virginia Woolf's room of her own, the emancipated solitude of a woman who earns enough money not to depend on anyone and fearlessly cultivates her enthusiasms or her talent. Her mother hadn't had a piano, let alone her own room. The narrow cubicles held the children's beds and she had to wait until everyone fell asleep to read her beloved Russian novels or review in silence the unbound scores that had come from St. Petersburg in a trunk more than thirty years earlier.

But overnight what had mattered to her most was no longer of interest. She said she didn't want to devote several years to a doctoral dissertation and then find herself buried in some girls' college, that academic study surrounded by dusty books was less valuable in shaping her vocation than real-life experience and work. (She didn't forgive her mother for saying that those words didn't seem to be hers, that she, Judith, was moving her lips but someone else was speaking through her mouth.) Her own room couldn't be in the middle of the woods or a sleepy expanse of cornfields. It had to be an austere room well insulated against interruptions, favorable to a solitary pursuit whose exact nature she couldn't define yet; in her room she ought to hear the noises and voices of the street, the clamor of the trains, the sirens of ships at the docks and police cars and red fire trucks. She wanted to travel to Europe to learn about life and create her destiny, like Isabel Archer in the Henry James novel she'd read several times, or like the women reporters who sent articles from Paris to *Vanity Fair* or *The New Yorker*. But she also loved more than ever the moving crowds, the excitement of her native city, she omitted nothing, enjoying it all, the neon lights going on at dusk, the fog into which the tallest buildings disappeared in whirlwinds of snow, the human waves erupting from the ferry buildings, the luxury-store windows on Fifth Avenue, the crowds waving red flags and union placards in Italian and Yiddish under shade trees in Union Square, the harshness, the helplessness, the cordiality of strangers, the pleasure of not choosing and letting herself be carried along with no purpose, no urgency, with the same sense of fervor she felt whenever she read a poem by Walt Whitman aloud. At one point in her tale a man's name came up that perhaps she'd already mentioned, or that Ignacio Abel hadn't heard, one of those times when he was lost or absorbed in a thought that carried him far away or he disliked the idea that she'd been married and loved another man passionately enough to break with her family, abandon her teaching job and doctoral dissertation, and go live in a rented room at the top of five flights of stairs, with a communal toilet at the end of the hall, a single cold-water faucet in the sink, and a tub in the kitchen covered with a board that served as desk and dining room table. Wanting to run away to search for a room of her own, Judith Biely found herself in a kitchen more uncongenial than her mother's, at times as alone as her mother had been, at other times as invaded: instead of her brothers' anxiety about work and money and her father's delusions, the equally masculine invasion to which she now was subjected dragged with it ill-tempered literary and political babble. The acrid cigarette smoke was the same, as was the aggression of the gestures. In the family kitchen she'd spent so many years wanting to run away from, her father and brothers celebrated the glory of capitalism like believers in a despotic god who could as easily demolish as exalt them; in her own room the guests sat on the floor and put out their cigarettes on the linoleum while they argued about revolutionary art of the future and the imminent collapse of the Great Golden Calf of America, staggering through the disaster of the Depression. The equality of men and women was one of the banners they wielded, but the women, though they smoked just as much and sat on the floor too, either didn't speak or weren't listened to, and when they all left, she was the one who swept the floor and picked up the glasses and the empty bottles of cheap wine and opened the windows to air out the room. Judith left the university and abandoned her dissertation and obtained a badly paid job correcting and typing stories about gangsters and crimes from morning to night for a publisher of cheap novels. The husband whose name Ignacio Abel took so long to identify was spending years completing a dense, rambling novel about New York, fragments of which he'd published in some magazines. It wasn't unlikely that John Dos Passos had read them, but in spite of his apparently advanced ideas, Dos Passos had settled into commercial success and would never acknowledge the influence of an almost unknown author on the rhythm and general outline of *Manhattan Transfer*. If their paths happened to cross at a literary party in the Village, Dos Passos looked away and acted as if he hadn't seen him. That others doubted her husband's talent infuriated Judith so much that she ignored her own still indistinct doubts and belligerently defended him. Gradually she realized she'd married him not in spite of her parents' and brothers' opposition but because of it. It didn't surprise her that her father and brothers looked on him as a despicable individual from the instant he'd walked into the apartment with her and hurried to make his political convictions known. If America was a plutocracy without hope or opportunity for the workers, they said, why didn't he go back to the Russia his parents had come from? It hurt Judith more that her mother didn't trust him either although he could quote in Russian from her favorite novels and had an awkward, almost sickly air that should have awakened her protective maternal instinct. What would they live on if he thought any ordinary job was a betrayal of his political principles and writer's calling? And why did she, Judith, abandon so easily what had cost her so much, the promising position at the university, the beautiful campus at Columbia, her doctoral research? It was clear that no matter how much it hurt her, she had to break with all of them; wanting to get away was one thing, considering the way back closed was quite another. Stubborn pride sustained her. The sudden deterioration of sexual passion at first produced more perplexity than bitterness in her, and perhaps also the suspicion of not being equal to the erotic ideal debated at their gatherings as freely as the dictatorship of the proletariat, social realism, and the stream of consciousness. In the man beside her she began to find not strength but weakness, the indifference of cold skin, resentful vanity beneath his professed rebellion, and the incorruptible renunciation of temptations that in reality didn't exist. Anger too, sometimes directed at her; again she felt panic in the face of male aggression, the rage of alcohol, fists pounding the table, hoarse voices, the loss of a sense of reality induced by narcissism and resentment. Words that, once said, couldn't be remedied, facial expressions that forgetting couldn't erase. The secret difference she fed between herself and the people she now moved with — her husband's friends and comrades, artists with radically inventive projects who devoted more time to explaining them than to executing them — wasn't it identical to what she'd felt in childhood, when she was aware of things that mattered only to her, when she liked to imagine she was not her parents' daughter or her brothers' sister? Just as when she was a little girl, many things moved her now that others couldn't see. A bouquet of fresh flowers in a glass pitcher; a dress that fit close to the body and at the same time seemed to float around it; the lit sign of an Automat in daylight, the pink neon in the tube barely visible, diluted in the light like ink in water; the mystery of continual renewal and the evanescence of style crossed with similar things and things very different from one another, transforming everything in a continual yet invisible rhythm, transforming the immediate past into an anachronism. She liked some paintings she saw in avant-garde magazines but also a set of porcelain cups in a shop window, or summer sandals she tried on in a shoe store for the simple joy of feeling her feet slip into them, knowing she couldn't afford them. She enjoyed movies based on Broadway musicals more than Soviet or German films, and abandoned herself to the prose of Henry James or a new tune by Irving Berlin. She secretly enjoyed these things but also felt guilty for a frivolity that might be a basic intellectual weakness or political indifference. And could she help pausing, when she was alone, at the windows of fashionable dress shops on Fifth Avenue or near the revolving doors of hotels from which well-dressed and perfumed women emerged along with bursts of dance-band music. Why did the cause of justice imply the choice of ugliness and a somber mood? She would spend hours walking, looking at the bronze color of a cornice outlined against the clean sky on a winter afternoon, watching a shoeshine man leaning over a pair of men's patent leather shoes and whistling a Broadway tune. She didn't believe those hidden enthusiasms made her exceptional, but she also didn't want to be judged harshly because of them. Concealing them, as she had when she was a young girl, gave her the comforting sensation of living in a place only she knew about.

For some time the secret cultivation of her individuality allowed her to postpone acknowledgment of an error that became more serious when it proved to be inexplicable. Her commitment to personal independence, her renunciation of her studies, the drive and complicity of her mother had brought her to a circumstance for which no effort had been required: the ache in her back after sitting for many hours at a typewriter in the office, the five flights of stairs, her irritable, hermetic husband, offended by injustice, his pride wounded by the world's indifference and countless rejections from publishers. She looked around and couldn't understand how she'd reached this point, by what sum of errors, as if after a long, difficult journey she found herself in the wrong station, her suitcases on the ground, the train she'd been on disappearing in the distance and no other in sight, and nobody in the station, not even an open clerk's window where she could consult timetables or buy another ticket. No one else had put the blindfold around her eyes. She didn't even need the effort of will, the dexterity, to grope at the knot at the back of her head to untie it. The blindfold, loosening, fell off of its own accord. And one day Judith Biely found herself in a room where nothing invited her to stay or seemed to be hers, with an unattractive man who talked endlessly, gesticulating, shaking his head, holding a cigarette between nicotine-stained fingers, scattering ashes, tossing the butts on the floor. The things he said weren't particularly brilliant; they weren't even his. They floated in the air, passing from one mouth to another, from one pamphlet to another, enlarged sometimes on posters, shouted in the cold passion of a political discussion in which it was urgent to annihilate the adversary, leaving him with no arguments, condemning him to an inclement darkness. Her eyes saw the man who spoke without looking at her, his hair curling over his forehead, his hands waving away the cigarette smoke in front of his face. She heard his words as a steady buzz, not distinguishing many of them. At that moment she thought she might be pregnant. She'd done the calculations on her fingers, looked at the record of previous months on the calendar. Three, four days late. While the man who was almost a stranger talked, the germ sowed by him probably was growing in her womb, a tiny clot of cells, a seed awakened in the dense blackness of the soil that it will make its way through. The enormous consequence of what? Of something she hadn't paid much attention to and that didn't give her much pleasure, only relief at its being over. Calmly she decided to conceal what she had been about to say. She would get an abortion. Soon, right away, in secret, to shorten the sadness, the crushing sorrow. The child she wanted, the robust, noble human being she sometimes glimpsed growing beside her in a vague future, shouldn't be born from so much wretchedness. She slept badly, and the next day, on her lunch hour, she had a sandwich on the steps of the Forty-second Street library. It was sunny and the air was unusually mild for the middle of March. She looked at the people around her, thinking no one could fathom her secret or share her dejection: typists, salesclerks, girls younger than she, dressed with an assurance she'd lost in the past few years, exchanging looks and laughter with the office workers on nearby benches, the marble steps and iron chairs. She finished her sandwich, closed the thermos of coffee, stood, and brushed crumbs from her skirt. A little while before, when she crossed the avenue, she'd felt dizzy, the beginning of nausea. Now, as she walked down the stairway, she noticed something in her belly, like a mild cramp, the pleasurable discharging of something. With disbelief, with sweetness, with a relief that almost raised her off the ground, she felt that her flow had begun and the yoke of regret and resignation she'd felt condemned to was dissolving, leaving before her a diaphanous future she wouldn't waste this time. She saw it clearly, effortlessly, just as she could see the traffic on Fifth Avenue, the sun on the windows and steel inlays of a recently completed skyscraper, the errors of a life she was ready to leave behind and the new future before her, all the shadows that had surrounded her with the consistency of walls or tunnels excavated from living rock suddenly dissipated like a cloud blown away by a light breeze.

On that morning she came toward him in the same straight line she'd taken across Fifth Avenue from the stairway of the library: her back erect, her pace the bold, determined walk of people in her city, her mouth partially open, wearing the same expectant expression Ignacio Abel saw from the table at the back of the café where he was waiting for her, or when he remained standing, not taking off his jacket and often not even his overcoat, in the room rented for the secret meetings where he saw her naked for the first time, in the semidarkness of heavy curtains and half-closed shutters through which the afternoon light filtered as faintly as the noises of the city and the sounds in the house. Each of the steps she'd taken preceded her silent walk on bare feet across the worn rug toward the man who hadn't moved or begun to undress. Only weeks earlier, a little more than a month, she'd arrived at a pensión on the Plaza de Santa Ana, not knowing anyone in Madrid and exhausted after an entire night on the train that brought her from Hendaye. How different from Paris this city smelled, how different the odor in the air since she'd crossed the border. Early on that September morning, Madrid had the damp smell of an earthenware jug set to cool in a kitchen window. It smelled of paving tiles recently watered by a municipal tank pulled by two old horses; it smelled of horse manure, oil, dry dust, of the stubble on which there was still dew as the train pulled into Madrid; of rockrose and pines in the Sierra; of the damp half-light and wooden steps of the building where the pensión was located, steps scrubbed and scoured with bleach, half-light invaded by the smell of sausage and spices from a grocery store downstairs whose shutters were just being raised when she arrived, suitcase in hand, receiving as a welcome, almost an embrace, the dense aroma of the coffee the shopkeeper was grinding in the doorway. The room she was given faced a narrow street that led to the plaza. A noise rose from it that at first she couldn't identify, still disoriented by strangeness and fatigue:

people chatting in groups looking for shade, peddlers, street vendors announcing repairs of umbrellas and tin pots, radio speakers in stalls selling drinks, the songs of maids cleaning, hanging clothes on the flat roofs, beating carpets or shaking out sheets on nearby balconies. Happiness settled in her: it was the sense of ample, austere space in the room, more welcoming than the increasingly smaller ones she'd been able to afford in Paris. As in the landscapes she saw at daybreak from the train window, in the room things seemed arranged in an order that defined space. In other countries in Europe, the countryside, like the cities, appeared too complete, too full, too cultivated and inhabited. In Spain empty spaces had the amplitude of America. Above the iron bed in the room was a crucifix, and a painted plaster Virgin Mary stood on a bureau in which she put her clothes, its deep drawers lined with sheets of newspaper. The walls were white, painted with lime, and had black paneling that reached as high as the window; the floor was of red clay tiles interspersed with smaller ones of polychrome ceramic. The straight bars of the bed ended in gilded tin balls that jingled when footsteps made the floor vibrate. On the bureau, next to the Virgin with a smooth bosom and blue mantle who crushed the head of a serpent with her small, unshod foot, was a kind of bronze or tin candelabrum holding candles. The electric cable crossed the wall in a straight line to a black bakelite switch above the bed and the bulb with a blue glass shade hanging from the ceiling. The top of the bed sheet was folded over a light quilt, under the pillow, with a solemn suggestion of whiteness and volume that Judith would recognize that same morning, on her first visit to the Prado, in the habits of Carthusian friars painted by Zurbarán. Opposite the bed was a bare pine table, solid, its legs resting on the tiles, with a drawer that emitted a smell of resin when it was opened. In front of the table was a chair with a straight back and a rush seat that invited you to sit down. Before she finished unpacking the suitcase, she placed her typewriter on the table, along with a folder of blank sheets, an ink bottle, her fountain pen, a blotter, a pencil case, her notebook, the small round mirror she always had at hand when she sat down to work. Each object seemed to fit with an effortless precision that anticipated writing and made it inevitable: all the things on the wooden table in the golden, slightly damp light of a Madrid morning related to one another like the random objects in the flat space of a cubist painting. The armoire, tall and gloomy, had a full-length mirror, and Judith looked at herself, benevolently studying the signs of weariness, the contrast between her foreign presence and the background of the room. The washbasin and pitcher of water on the washstand were of white porcelain with a delicate blue edge. She felt a sensation she hadn't yet experienced on her journey: an immediate affinity with the place where she found herself, a harmony that alleviated the solitude and at the same time confirmed for her the privilege of not needing anyone. On the roof opposite the window a cat lay dozing in the sun. Farther away, at a dormer window, a woman was wrapping her black hair in a towel, her eyes and face turned to the sun. A few days later, Judith had learned to identify the buildings outlined against the roofed horizon: the large tower with columns and the bronze Athena of the Fine Arts Circle, the battlements on the Palace of Communications, and above them a flag waving that had awakened in her an unwarranted affection from the moment she first saw it when she crossed the border at Hendaye — red, yellow, purple, shining in the sun with something of the proletarian boldness of the geraniums on the balconies.

She wanted to do everything at once, that very morning, she later told Ignacio Abel. Go out to the street, lie down on the white, fragrant sheet, write a letter to her mother, write an article about her trip: the sensation of having come to another world simply by crossing a border; of finding people with darker faces and eyes with an intensity that at first disconcerted her; of glimpsing through the train window, in the darkness, the shadows of bare rocks and precipices; of being awakened by the violent shaking of a train much slower and less comfortable than French trains and seeing at first light a level, abstract landscape in earth tones, flat and dry like a juxtaposition of autumn leaves. She wanted to read the book by Dos Passos she'd brought with her but also wanted to sit at the table with a dictionary at hand to read a novel by Pérez Galdós that her professor at Columbia had introduced her to, or go outside holding the novel and find the streets his characters had walked along. Sitting in front of the typewriter and the open window, she felt for the first time, in her consciousness and at the tips of her fingers, barely brushing the keys, the imminence of a book that would include each of the things she was feeling at that moment. It wasn't a chronicle or a travel story or a confession or a novel; the uncertainty both wounded and stimulated her; she sensed that if she stayed alert but also allowed herself to drift, she'd find a beginning as tenuous as the tip of a thread; she'd have to squeeze it between her fingers not to lose it, but if she squeezed it with a little more strength than necessary, the thread would break and she wouldn't be able to find it again. Through the window came the voices of street vendors, the cooing of pigeons, the noises of traffic, the ringing of bells. The sounds of the bells changed every few minutes or became confused with one another: the horizon over the roofs was filled with bell towers. Someone knocked at the door, startling her. A maid came in with a tray and Judith tried to explain in her awkward Spanish that there must be some mistake, she hadn't ordered anything. "It's from the landlady," the maid said, "in case the señorita arrived with an empty stomach after traveling so much in foreign countries." She put the tray on the table, using her elbow to move the typewriter, which didn't fail to attract her attention because she didn't associate it with a woman. "I hope you enjoy it": a large cup of coffee, a small pitcher of milk, a toasted white-flour roll, cut in half, dripping a gold-green oil, the grains of salt on top gleaming in the light. Suddenly she discovered how hungry she was. The bread covered in oil crackled as it dissolved in her mouth, the grains of salt bursting on her palate like seeds of delight. With a checked napkin she wiped the oil from the corners of her mouth, the muzzle of cream the milk left on her lips. Everything conspired for her happiness, including her exhaustion, the sweet somnolence, the din of the church bells that provoked flights of pigeons over the roofs. She took off her shoes and sat on the bed, to massage her feet, swollen and painful after so many hours of traveling. She lay down, holding the novel by Pérez Galdós, searching its pages for place names in Madrid that wouldn't be too far away, and in less than a minute she was sleeping as soundly as she had when she was a little girl on those winter mornings when she didn't feel well and her mother brought her breakfast in bed, after the men had gone and a peaceful silence had descended on the apartment.

11

WHEN HIS CHILDREN were small, Ignacio Abel liked to make for them drawings and models, cutouts of houses, automobiles, animals, trees, ships. He'd begin by drawing a tiny dog in his sketchbook, and next to the dog a street lamp would emerge like a tall flower, and near it a window, and from there the entire house would take shape, and above the roof and chimney, beside which a cat was outlined, the moon appeared like a slice of melon. Lita and Miguel would look at those prodigious creations, their elbows on the table, leaning so close to the sketchbook they barely left him room to continue drawing, competing for a proximity they rarely enjoyed. They lived in their shared bedroom that was also their homework room and playroom, and in the back rooms where the maids reigned, not observing the severe norms of silence or things said in quiet voices that the children had to submit to when entering adult territory: in the kitchen, in the laundry room, where Miguel spent all his spare time, the maids talked loudly and the radio played all day long, and through the window overlooking an interior courtyard came the voices of the servants in other residences as they called to one another, slurring their speech in an accent Miguel imitated perfectly. In the rest of the house the children had to close and open doors gently, walk without making noise, especially near their father's study or the bedroom with closed curtains where their mother often had to withdraw because of endless headaches or ailments that rarely had a precise name or were serious enough to require the doctor's presence. In the kitchen the maids' voices and those on the radio fused with the splatters and smoke emanating from the stoves, and colorful characters would appear at the service door, delivery men from the stores, peddlers loaded down with cheeses, pots of honey, sometimes chickens or rabbits, heads down and feet tied. But the door separating the service area from the rest of the apartment had to be kept closed, and the children, above all Miguel, who had a more confused idea of his place in the world, were fascinated by this rigorous frontier that only they moved across freely. Not only faces and sounds changed but accents and odors, the odors of things and of people: on one side it smelled of oil, food, fish, the blood of a recently slaughtered chicken or rabbit, the maids' sweat; on the other side it smelled of the lavender soap their mother used to wash her hands, their father's cologne, furniture polish, the cigarettes visitors sometimes smoked.

As she grew older, the girl ventured across the frontier less and less frequently, for the most part in order to remain true to the character of a distinguished intellectual señorita she'd invented for herself, and instead of flamenco verses about jealousy and crimes and great black eyes playing on the kitchen radio, Lita listened with her mother to symphonic broadcasts on Unión Radio. While Miguel, enthralled, read about film stars and advertisements for exorcisms and astrological remedies in the cheap magazines the maids bought (LOVE and LUCK are yours FREE OF CHARGE if you possess the mysterious RADIATING FLOWER prepared in accordance with the millenarian rites of PAMIR and the immutable astrological principles of the MAGI OF THE ORIENT), Lita read novels by Jules Verne, knowing she'd earn her father's approval, and interpreted for the family the popular ballads she learned to sing at school. But both had felt attracted to their father's study, whose mysterious spaces their childish imaginations had enlarged. He was fast and sure with the pencil, as absorbed as his children in what he was doing. He would shade the outlines of the drawing and add the form of a foldable base, then cut everything out, house, tree, balloon, animal, automobile with its convertible top and headlights, the radii of the wheels perfectly detailed, even the profile of a chauffeur in a visored cap at the wheel, a Western outlaw on horseback, a motorcycle with the driver leaning forward, wearing a leather jacket and aviator goggles. Once he drew an airplane, and when he finished cutting it from the sketchbook, flew it between his fingers above the heads of the children, each desperate to hold it first. In stationery stores he looked for cutouts of famous buildings, bridges, trains, ocean liners; he taught them to handle scissors, in which their pudgy child's fingers became entangled, to follow with cautious precision the edges of a drawing, to distinguish between cutting and folding lines, to gently squeeze the bottle of glue so that only the small drop that was needed came out. And when they became impatient or gave up, he'd take the scissors and show them again how to cut out a drawing, recalling Professor Rossman, his teacher in Weimar, who would go into a comic ecstasy when he heard the sound and observed the resistance of the sheet of paper he was cutting.

He brought them old models from the office, drew cutouts of buildings he'd studied in international magazines. When they were older, perhaps they'd remember that as children they played with models of the Bauhaus in Dessau and Erich Mendelsohn's Einstein Tower, which they liked more because it resembled a lighthouse and a castle tower. But it wasn't that Ignacio Abel condescended to entertain his children or showed them praiseworthy patience. His own love of architecture had a portion of self-absorbed childish play. He liked to cut and fold. The flexible angles of an empty pillbox gave him immediate tactile pleasure, pure forms as perceptible with one's fingertips as with one's eyes: angles, stairways, corners. How strange the invention of the staircase, a concept of something so remote from any inspiration in nature, space folding over itself at right angles, a single broken line on blank paper, as limitless in principle as a spiral, or those parallel lines whose definition had overwhelmed him at school: "No matter how far they extend, they will never meet." So close one to the other, yet condemned never to meet by an unexplained curse. From his able hands, from the shadows of words and childish fears, an emotion receded to the bottom of time: as if advancing along a very long passage toward a faint light, he saw the boy he had been, sitting in a room with a low ceiling, bent over a notebook, wielding a cheap pen, dipping it into an inkwell, objects near him erased beyond the small circle of the oil lamp. The sun didn't come in the basement window, but the sound of people's footsteps did, and animals' hooves, and wagon wheels, the permanent yelling of street vendors, the monotonous chant of blind men singing. One night hooves and wheels stopped at the window. Someone knocked at the door and he remembered that his mother had gone out and he had to go up and open the street door. In the wagon was a shape covered with sacks.

He made a small building and told his children it was a house for fleas; next to it a tree, an automobile, a bridge a little farther away, its raised arch identical to the one in the Viaducto, or the one the engineer Torroja had designed to save the gully of a stream in University City; the marquee of a train station, its clock hanging from the beams, the tiny Roman numerals drawn inside the sphere with a pencil he'd sharpened to an extremely fine point. With the same joy he studied the scale model of University City that had been growing in one of the drafting rooms at his office, a replica of the space visible through the windows, at first not a blank page but a wasteland of bare earth covered with the stumps of thousands of pines. Like Gulliver in Lilliput he supervised a diminutive city where his footsteps would have reverberated like seismic shocks, the city that had begun as cardboard and ink, glue, blocks of wood, the faithful model of a fragment of the world that was three-dimensional but didn't exist yet or was being created slowly, too slowly. On the other side of the windows, steam shovels opened great trenches in the barren earth, lifting roots like manes of hair, like naked branches of trees that would have grown in the subsoil (to build, one first had to clear away and cut down, clean out and flatten, make the earth as smooth and abstract as a sheet of paper spread on a drawing table). Laborers swarmed along the esplanades, on the embankments; with agility they climbed the scaffolding of buildings under construction, thronged in corridors and future lecture halls, applying cement, installing tiles, completing a row of bricks, beginning another; monarchs of their trades, experts in giving real form to what began as capricious fantasy in a sketchbook, copper-colored men in berets with cigarettes glued to their lips; powerful dump trucks and droves of donkeys that transported loads of plaster or jugs of water in their panniers; armed guards who patrolled the construction sites to chase away the crowds of laid-off workers who demanded jobs or tried to overturn or burn the machines that had replaced them and condemned them to starvation. Primitives and millenarians, like them, deluded now not by the expectation of the End of Days but by Libertarian Communism. With a slight effort of his rational imagination, Ignacio Abel could see the completed buildings when bricklayers were still hard at work on their scaffolding and cranes with electric motors swayed over them: beautiful blocks of red brick shining in the sun, along with the exact visual rhythm of the windows, against the dark green background of the Sierra's spurs. He saw avenues with large trees that now were little more than weak shoots or not even that, cardboard trees he'd cut out himself and glued to the sidewalk of a model. The School of Philosophy students crossed felled trees to reach their building, inaugurated in a rush (in the lecture halls one could still hear the workers' shouts and pounding hammers). He imagined the students arriving in high-speed streetcars along the straight, wide avenues, strolling in the shade of the trees, lindens or oaks, dispersed on the grass that would grow someday on that bare ground: young, well-fed men and women with strong bones, children of privilege but also workers' children, educated in solid public schools where knowledge wouldn't be corrupted by religion and merit would prevail over family background and money. He preferred the vigor of sap to boiling Spanish blood, botany to politics, irrigation projects to five-year plans. Running water, electric streetcars, trees with broad, dense foliage, ventilated spaces. "Abel, for you the social revolution is a question of public works and gardening," Negrín once said to him, and he replied, "And it's not for you, Don Juan?" He could almost see his daughter, in a few years' time, destined for the School of Philosophy and Letters, good-natured and mature, jumping off the streetcar, books under her arm, her hair under a beret slanted to one side, her raincoat open, still an uncommon sight among groups of male students. The future wasn't a fog of the unknown or a projection of senseless desires, not the predictions of cards or lines on one's hand, not preachers' sinister prophecies of the end of the world or paradise on earth. The future was foreseen in the blue lines on plans and in the models he'd helped to build, seeing something in a single glance, understanding with one's eyes, guessing at a form with the touch of one's fingers. Ignacio Abel loved the blocks of wood in his children's building sets, the typography in the books of Juan Ramón Jiménez, the poetry of right angles in Le Corbusier. The flat outskirts of Madrid were a clear drawing table on which the future city could be laid out beyond the plans for the university. Straight perspectives that would dissolve in the horizon of the Sierra, vanishing lines of streetcar tracks and electric cables, the workers' district and its white houses with large windows surrounded by plazas and gardens. To the same extent that he distrusted the vagueness of words, he loved concrete acts and tangible, well-made constructions. A school with bright, comfortable classrooms, a spacious playground, a well-equipped gymnasium; a bridge built with solidity and beauty; a rationally conceived house with running water and a bathroom—he could not imagine more practical ways of improving the world.

He had accomplished things that could be measured and judged, that had an undeniable lasting presence in reality. How unsettling the thought that time would run out, that he wouldn't have the intellectual clarity or presence of mind or courage to carry out what he dreamed of: a house where he and Judith Biely would live both in the world and separate and safe from it, a library in a clearing in the woods beside a great river. The tiny human figures he'd placed on the model to give an idea of scale—he saw them as animated and enlarged to the size of adults, young men and women carrying books, his own children. He was impatient for that future to arrive sooner. He'd heard Juan Ramón

Jiménez speak of *an unhurried hurry*, of *joyful work*. He wanted to see them concluded: the University Hospital, the School of Medicine, the School of Sciences, the School of Architecture (so close to completion); he wanted that open ground with trenches like scars and harsh brambles to be an athletic field; he wanted the sticks of trees to grow and give more shade to the barren land of Madrid (other trees had been cut down earlier, other walls demolished by pickaxes and steam shovels, but in a short time the wounds in the landscape would heal, and what existed before would be forgotten). How painful the slowness of the work, what impatience with administrative procedures, with the dilatoriness of the human effort required for any task, even more so with such primitive methods of construction. Picks, hoes, shovels scratching at the hard earth of Castilla, malnourished laborers in filthy berets, with ruined mouths from which hand-rolled cigarettes hung. Early on Monday the work would start up with a show of energy, and a week later all was left hanging because of a government crisis or because another construction strike had been called.

Sometimes he thought: you could have been one of them, your son could have been born to earn a scant wage as a bricklayer in University City or to throw rocks at the mounted guards and not study for a career. (What would Miguel study? What would he be suited for?) As a boy he'd worked with his hands during school vacations with the crews under his father, the foreman respected by his bricklayers because even if he'd prospered enough to wear a vest and jacket, he still had a face burned by weather and blunt, hard hands, and was more skilled than anyone in tracing the line of a wall with squinting eyes and no more help than a cord and a lead weight. Accompanying his father as a boy, he'd learned the physical effort demanded by each shovelful of cement and moved earth, each paving stone in its precise place, each brick in its identical row. Everything was easy, dazzling on the plan: the lines of ink and patches of watercolor culminated in a building in a couple of afternoons of joyful work, an entire city invented in a few days. Avenues crossing at right angles, receding to the vanishing point; trees in the tender greens of watercolor; small human figures to indicate scale. But in reality the figure seen through the windows of the drafting room is a man who tires easily and isn't well fed; who left his wretched living quarters in an outlying suburb before dawn to walk to work and save the few céntimos a streetcar or the metro would have cost; who at mid-day eats a poor stew of garbanzos boiled in a broth made from an old bone; who could fall from a scaffolding or be crushed by an avalanche of bricks or stones and become an invalid and spend the rest of his life lying on a straw mattress in a room at the end of a foul-smelling hall while his wife and children go hungry and find themselves condemned to the humiliation of public charity. When he inspected a construction site, passively observing the physical effort of other men, Ignacio Abel became uncomfortably aware of his well-cut suit, his body fresh from his morning shower and absolved from the brutality of labor, his shoes dirtied by dust, the shoes the bricklayer bent over in a trench would see at eye level when he passed: gentlemen's shoes, so insulting to the man who wears espadrilles. "You don't understand the class struggle, Don Ignacio," Eutimio had told him, the foreman who forty years earlier had been an apprentice on his father's crew. "Class struggle is when a few drops of rain fall and your feet get wet." He felt shame and relief, wished for social justice, and feared the rage of those hoping to make it happen through the violence of a bloody revolution. How many men had died in the Asturias uprising, how many suffered torture and prison? For what? In the name of what apocalyptic prophecies translated into the language of tabloids, at the hands of such brutal uniformed avengers, drunk on other degraded words, or not even that, mercenaries paid as miserably as the rebels they hunted down. He feared that cruelty or misfortune would crush his children, dragging them into the penury from which he'd escaped but that was still so close, like a certain, vis-ible threat: in the scabby, barefoot children who circled the site looking for something to steal or approached the workers to beg for something to eat, who walked with their heads down, holding the hand of a fa-ther who'd been laid off. He wanted his children to become strong, to learn something about the harshness of real life, particularly the boy, so weak and vulnerable, but he also wanted to protect them beyond any uncertainty, save them forever from evil and sorrow. Sometimes he took the children to the office, especially after he'd bought the car. He took them for rides along the future avenues, pointed out the places where perhaps they would study. He'd accelerate so the wind would hit them in the face, drive to the dusty green of the Monte del Pardo, then return to University City. Their mother had dressed them as if they were going to a baptism: the boy with straight bangs across his forehead, his small man's jacket, his loose-fitting trousers; the girl's hair arranged with a part and a ribbon, wearing patent leather shoes and socks. He'd continue working after the other employees had left and the children played like giants in the model of the city. At home, the maids were surprised to see the señor take care of the children while the señora attended her social gatherings, the lectures and expositions at the Lyceum Club, or spent the entire day in the darkened bedroom; surprised that he would go down on all fours with the children in the hallway, or move aside the papers on his worktable to make room for their constructions of paper and cardboard and their toy car races.

It hadn't always been this way. For a long time he wished they hadn't been born, during anguished nights of crying and fever when he felt suffocated under the weight of his responsibility. He went far away, but with distance guilt became sharper. In Weimar, each time he saw his wife's handwriting on a letter he was afraid he would find out that one of them was sick (surely the boy, not only younger but more fragile). At times he'd walk along the street enjoying the silence after a day of hard work and study and suddenly have the presentiment that when he reached the pensión the landlady would hand him an urgent telegram. He feared misfortune, and punishment even more. For having gone away, for not feeling homesick. For surrendering to the embrace of his Hungarian lover, who, when they had finished, pushed him away, lit a cigarette, and seemed to forget his existence. For having applied for the study grant without consulting Adela and putting off the moment of telling her in the cowardly hope he'd be turned down, avoiding both the need for courage and the certain melodrama. He was afraid of telegrams, unexpected phone calls, knocks on the door, the signs that he'd soon learn something that would ruin everything.

The wagon with wooden wheels and iron reinforcements had stopped at the low window of the porter's lodging, and the hooves of a horse had struck the paving stones, but he didn't look up from the notebook where he was copying an exercise in geometrical drawing, going over in ink the lines he'd previously drawn in pencil (two parallel lines, regardless of how far they extend, never meet), wetting just the tip of the nib in the inkwell to avoid the error of a blot on the white paper. It was another time, almost another century, and he was thirteen years old in the winter of 1903. (The king had been crowned a few months earlier. Ignacio Abel had seen him go by in a carriage surrounded by golden shakos with crests of feathers and noticed that he wasn't much older than himself: the king had the long, pale face of a boy beneath the visor of his high military shako.) There was knocking at the entrance door and he didn't look up because his mother was the one who took care of the porter's lodging. There was more knocking, louder this time, and then he remembered that his mother had gone out, telling him to look after things. A stranger wearing a beret and a bricklayer's smock asked for her and looked at him when he said she wasn't in, and he was her son. He was still holding the pen with the wooden shaft when he approached the wagon where the shape covered in empty plaster sacks lay. Wagon wheels will leave two parallel lines that will never meet as they carry on bare boards that bounce over potholes a dead body covered with a sack. His father, always so agile, so impatient with his son who had vertigo when he climbed a foot or two, had broken his neck falling from a scaffold. After many years Ignacio Abel still sometimes dreamed he had to move aside the cloth of the dusty sack with the large, dark stain to see the face underneath. In the soft palm of his child's hand the shaft of the pen broke in two, a sharp splinter piercing his sweaty skin. His guilt as a father mixed with his fear of misfortune. Vertigo in the face of those fragile lives to whom he was tied by an overwhelming responsibility was revived by his retrospective compassion for the boy who had bent his head over a notebook in that poorly lit room moments before the knocking at the door, ignorant of the fact that he was now the only child of a widowed mother, an exemplary student at the neighborhood Piarist school, rescued from a sentence to manual labor thanks not only to his intelligence but to the money his father had saved for so many years, knowing he wasn't well, knowing he'd leave a defenseless child too delicate to earn his living as he'd done. He had been ill. When he fell from the top of the scaffolding, it wasn't because he tripped or because of a loose board but because his heart burst.

Slowly, Ignacio Abel had been coming to terms with the presence of his two children and discovered, as time went on, that they were the most luminous part of his life. Watching them grow taught him to mistrust disappointment and be thankful for the unexpected. What real life imposed on his desire and the project were not only limitations but also possibilities, the gifts of risk and the unforeseen. The anonymous masters of architecture had worked with what they had closest to hand, not with materials they'd selected but with those provided by chance, stone or wood or clay for adobe bricks. His father would touch a dressed stone of granite with his large open palm as if he were stroking an animal's back. There was discipline, a pride in the struggle to execute a project exactly according to plan. In 1929 he'd traveled to Barcelona expressly to see the German pavilion at the International Exposition, and as he studied with Professor Rossman the rooms of marble and steel and glass walls, he'd discovered in himself, beneath the admiration, an element of rejection. The perfection that only a few years earlier would have seemed indisputable disturbed him now for its coldness, over which it seemed the human presence would slide without leaving a trace. He loved the reinforced concrete, the extensive sheets of glass, the firm, flexible steel, but he envied the talent and skill when he saw at the side of a road a melon patch with a watchman's shack made of straw and reeds, woven with an art that had existed four thousand years ago in the salt marshes of Mesopotamia, or a simple wall built with stones of different sizes and shapes that fit solidly together with no need for mortar. There was no plan so perfect that uncertainty could be discarded. Only the test of time and the elements revealed the beauty of a construction, ennobled by weather and worn by the movement of human lives, just as a tool handle was worn by use, or the treads of a staircase. And if the fulfillment of what he'd desired when he was very young resulted in disappointment and wariness over the years, the best he had was the consequence of the unexpected: the Hungarian woman who pressed her flat belly and meager hips against him in an unheated room in Weimar; Judith Biely; Lita and Miguel, who perhaps are forgetting his face and the sound of his voice or think he's dead and are beginning to erase him from their lives, strengthened by a will to survive despite his absence.

No sign warned him of the appearance of Judith Biely. He'd never dreamed of or wished for children, who arrived by chance in the inertia of his marriage. No project, no fulfilled desire, not even those that without much hope inspired him at the age of thirteen or fourteen in the porter's lodging (his schoolbooks and notebooks on the oilcloth-covered table with the built-in foot warmer, the inkwell and pencils, the oil lamp always lit in the damp basement apartment, the photograph of his dead father on the fireplace mantel, a black ribbon at a corner of the frame), had offered him as much happiness as watching his daughter grow, an unexpected masterpiece in which he could take pleasure with no hint of vanity or fear of disappointment. She lived in a self-determined, autonomous way, born of parents but independent of them, with a vague family resemblance — her hair identical to that of the Ponce-Cañizares clan, her rounded nose as unquestionably Salcedo as the hazel color of her eyes. From whom had she inherited her serenity, her consideration of people over and above the familial or the social, her equable instinct, her balance between a sense of duty and a disposition for joy? She'd inherited none of that from him, of course, or from Adela or her family, whom she nonetheless adored, especially her grandfather Don Francisco de Asís. As a little girl she'd been protective of her brother, tender with him, perhaps because the boy was younger and rather frail. Adela was frequently ill after Miguel's birth. The wet nurse fed him and kept him clean, the maids hovered over him, but it was his sister who from the start concerned herself with caring for him, teaching him to play, urging him to walk, guessing his desires, understanding his language. She cared for her brother with the same satisfaction she took in jumping rope or cutting out a childish figure or arranging the furniture in her dollhouse. When he was a baby she'd take him in her arms, pressing him firmly against her and placing her hand at the back of his neck to protect his tender head. She cradled him, pressing her chubby cheeks against the boy's pale little face, kissing him with a spontaneity her parents lacked. From early on, the boy admired her, and was as unconditional in his love as a dog to his owner, from whom he expects all good things and to whom he attributes all powers. It was she who helped him take his first steps and wiped away his tears and snot every time he fell. She played school and sat her brother in a low chair, in the same row as the dolls to whom she gave sums to do, or dictations, writing with chalk in her neat round hand on a blackboard the Three Kings had brought for her. The boy grew up adoring her, imitating her, so close to her in age and at the same time small and docile enough to obey her and learn from her. But he didn't learn her social skills, her capacity for making friends and establishing intense relationships, as rich in embraces and promises of eternal friendship as in dramatic fights and reconciliations.

When they were small, Ignacio Abel had looked at his children with distraction and alarm, too impatient to pay much attention to them. He became more interested when they began to speak. The most lasting memories he had of their early years arose from the terror their illnesses caused in him. Attacks of fever in the middle of the night, endless fierce crying, blood spurting from a nose with no way to stop it, incessant diarrhea, the cough that seemed to calm down after several hours and then started again, so deep it seemed to be tearing apart their small lungs. He vaguely imagined that Adela or the wet nurse or the maids must have had some way of controlling the danger, must have known how to provide remedies or decide when it was time to call the doctor. He felt awkward and annoyed, sick with fear and consumed with irritation. The boy had been weak since birth, following an extremely long labor when it seemed Adela or he or both would die. When the midwife came out of the bedroom she placed the baby in his arms, tiny and red, his hands so small, so wrinkled, his fingers as fine as a mouse's, his legs and feet tiny; his purple flaccid skin, too loose for his newborn's bones, seemed covered with scales. "He's very small, but even if he doesn't look it, he's very healthy," said the midwife as she wrapped a woolen shawl around the form who weighed almost nothing, who seemed not to breathe, who moved in an abrupt spasm. Adela spent weeks in a feverish and delirious state, and when it seemed she was recovering, it was only to succumb to a lassitude not even the boy's helpless presence could drive away. Wet nurse, servant girls, midwives, and doctors were summoned at all hours. Don Francisco de Asís and Doña Cecilia, the maiden aunts, the uncle who was a priest, all invaded the house that was much smaller than the future apartment on Calle Príncipe de Vergara, roused to relentless activity, boiling pots of water, preparing baby bottles, diapers, medicines, damp compresses for Adela's fever, household remedies for the boy's diarrhea, as constant as his inconsolable crying, reciting the rosary and prayers for women who have given birth, the primitive incantations of old women. Ignacio Abel spent the nights lying awake beside his silent, prostrate wife, and early in the morning, relieved, exhausted, left for work. He'd applied to the Council for Advanced Studies for a grant to spend a year in Germany, at the new School of Architecture founded by Walter Gropius in Weimar. He reviewed over and over the documents he'd presented at the Ministry of Education, calculating the possibility of receiving the official letter that would notify him of the grant. The boy would get better; the girl was almost three years old and had always been strong and healthy. In disbelief, he imagined himself taking a train at the North Station, leaning against the cold

187

window as dawn broke over a landscape of green fields and gray mist while the train advanced along a wide river. He practiced German, trying to remember what he'd learned during his university studies. He read German books, looking up difficult words in the dictionary. He prepared in secret for something he wasn't sure would happen; he wasn't even sure he'd find the courage if the time came. Why had he supported Adela's eagerness to become pregnant, then to have another child, frightened because she was no longer young, because she was uncertain of keeping her husband? More than a minute had gone by and the boy wasn't crying; if he closed his eyes, perhaps he could sleep one or two uninterrupted hours tonight. But the crying returned, ever more relentless, with a muscular vigor that didn't seem possible in an infant who had weighed less than two and a half kilos at birth. Very small but very healthy, the midwife had said, perhaps to deceive him. "We'll have to baptize him right away," said Don Francisco de Asís, putting his hands on the shoulders of his afflicted son-in-law, emerging from the dark corner where aunts and relatives recited the rosary in anticipation of the imminent misfortune. One night the uncle who was a priest appeared in full liturgical dress, accompanied by an altar boy, and the odor of incense mixed with the smell of medicine and the baby's diarrhea. "It's difficult to accept, my son, but if this angel leaves us, we must be certain he'll go straight to heaven." They brought holy water, a silver basin, embroidered cloths, candles on which the name of the boy was written. Not consulting him, and probably not Adela either — she was in a daze, her eyes lost on the wall opposite the bed — the maiden aunts helped the wet nurse dress the tiny baby in a long gown with blue ribbons and embroidered skirts in which his body disappeared, his chest swelling the cloth, his legs like matchsticks kicking beneath the skirts, his diminutive purple feet with the dry patches no cream could alleviate. Doña Cecilia, the maiden aunts, the wet nurse, and the weeping maids had put on veils as if for a funeral, and Uncle Víctor stood erect in his position as godfather, though his dislike of the boy's weakness and crying was evident, as was his conviction that the feeble blood of the paternal line had prevailed. The boy, the first grandson, had come into the world sickly and crying, more proof of how untrustworthy the intruder was, the external inseminator, as suspect in his male capabilities as in his ideas. "Courage, brother-in-law, the kid will come out of this. In our family there hasn't been a single case of premature death."

In the midst of that upheaval only the girl seemed to remain calm, going from room to room, her pacifier in her mouth, observing the maid as she cleaned the baby's bottom and washed the diapers under the tap in the kitchen, watching the wet nurse when she brought the small red face to her large, swollen white breast, the translucent skin crossed with blue veins, the enormous dark nipples, the broad hands that caressed the baby's sweaty, flattened hair and delicately put the mouth at her nipple from which surged a rich, white thread of milk. The girl went down the long hallway and stole into the bedroom where her mother lay. She sat next to her on the edge of the bed, caressed her hands or smoothed her hair, damp with sweat, uncombed, dirty after so many days of convalescence. She seemed not to think it strange that her mother didn't respond to her gestures of affection or give any sign she was aware of her presence. They put a white veil on the girl and had her hold a candle at her brother's baptism, and she stood on tiptoe to watch as the priest poured water on the baby's head and then dried it lightly with an embroidered handkerchief on which he also wiped his fingertips. That night, when her brother cried, she went to him and, instead of rocking the cradle, took his hand, and the baby calmed. From then on, the girl slept with the cradle beside her bed. When she heard the beginning of a whimper in the dark, her hand would feel its way between the bars. The boy's tiny hand would close around his sister's thumb, and, feeling safe, he went back to sleep. Meanwhile, awake in his bedroom, Ignacio Abel counted the seconds of silence, fearing that before he reached a minute the crying would start again. He could imagine himself dozing on a long train journey at night, autonomous and alone in a European city, as clearly as if that future were part of a memory, the way he saw himself as a boy, elbows propped on a table, in front of his notebook, the pen drawing two parallel lines on the blank page a moment before the knocking sounded on the door, in the light of the oil lamp that seemed to burn forever at the heart of time.

12

How strange that he remained guilt-free for so long; the unshadowed gift, limitless and full of secret places, became sweeter the more he enjoyed it: dark movie theaters and open-air cafés from which one could see in an expanse as broad as a marine horizon the oak trees of the Casa de Campo and the Monte del Pardo and the hazy distances of the Sierra; the room rented by the hour in a private hotel at the end of Calle O'Donnell (streetcar bells and car horns heard faintly through heavy curtains drawn to achieve a pretense of night during the day's working hours); and the public space of the Velázquez rooms at the Prado, early on winter mornings when the museum had just opened and before tourists had begun to come in. He awoke when it was still dark with an instinctive feeling of happiness waiting for him, and when he looked at the time on the alarm clock, he remembered he would meet her in only three hours. How strange that fear hadn't intruded yet: the presentiment that something unexpected would happen and he wouldn't be able to see her that day, or ever again, that she was separated from him by fate or because another man had taken her from him or because she herself had decided to leave, exercising the same freedom that had brought her from America to Europe and moved her to become his lover. He shaved after his shower, savoring his secret, looking in the mirror at the face of the man at whom Judith Biely would smile in a little more than two hours, and no one else would know. Time and the order of things conspired in his favor: breakfast waiting on the table, his two children healthy and obedient, his wife, who handed him his briefcase and hat in the entrance hall and told him to button up, it was foggy and damp this morning, and was satisfied, or at least seemed satisfied, with a domestic kiss that barely brushed her lips and a wave goodbye in which no smile and hardly a glance intervened. Efficient, involuntary accomplices acted on his behalf: the new elevator with its electric mechanism and gentle hydraulic brakes, the porter's son who had gone to the garage for his car and had it ready for him at the door, the Fiat motor that in spite of the morning cold started with just a turn of the ignition key, the straight streets, still clear of traffic, that allowed him to arrive quickly at his appointment, not wasting a single minute. Even though it was early, someone was at the museum's ticket office, ready to sell him an admission, and a sleepy porter in a blue uniform was there to tear it for him. In the light of the deserted central gallery footsteps echoed before he could see at a distance the figure they announced. One of them would arrive, and the other was waiting, feeling observed in the empty galleries by personages in the paintings, saints and kings whose names Judith Biely didn't know, martyrs of a religion that to her was sumptuous and exotic. One of them walked down the long museum corridor in the gray illumination from the skylights, and the other arrived at the same time, appeared in a doorway and was recognized in the distance with a skipped heartbeat by sharp eyes proficient in searching. Ignacio Abel arrived first so he'd be sure to see her arrive. Judith Biely's broad shoulders, her determined walk, her head tilted slightly to one side, and her hair covering half her face; her eyes large, and as she came closer, widely separated; her cheeks; her thin lips parted at the corners, with a suggestion of expectation, like a word or smile about to be formed; her face serious and angular and yet illuminated by the beginning of a smile, still only hinted at, like the morning light becoming more intense inside a tenuous fog, the one they'd passed through as they walked to the museum along different streets. Alone and self-confident, determined to give herself with all the deliberation of a will that both flattered and frightened him. It frightened him and aroused him just to see her walk toward him, provocative and carefree. In a corner safe from the eyes of the guards they kissed greedily, noticing the winter cold on skin, the smell of cold on breath and hair, on outer clothing damp from the fog.

On another day he watched her approach from a distance along an avenue in the Botanical Garden, listening to the dry sound of fallen leaves blown by the wind and covering the ground under her feet, a cold, sunny morning early in December when the frost made the grass silver in the shaded areas and the air shone with ice crystals. She came muffled against the winter, the brim of her hat over her forehead, coat lapels raised, a scarf concealing her chin and mouth, showing only her bright eyes and her nose red from the cold. He wanted to go to her but remained still, his hands in his overcoat pockets and his breath cold, conscious of each step she took, the distance that separated them lessening by the second, the imminence of her body pressing against his, the two cold hands that held his face so she could keep looking at him until she closed her eyes to kiss him. Halfway through their day they would make room for a quick escape, a phone call, a taxi ride into the always-too-brief parenthesis of a meeting. How strange that it took them so long to begin to measure what was denied to them, to not be grateful for what had been granted them, what they might not have known. If there was no time for anything else and the winter weather was too inhospitable, they took refuge in one of those remote cafés frequented by office clerks, retirees, other pairs of lovers meeting in secret; cafés half empty and gloomy, in ambiguous areas of Madrid that weren't centrally located but didn't quite belong to the outskirts, on streets only recently urbanized that still had rows of young trees and fences around undeveloped lots with posters announcing the circus or boxing matches or political propaganda, and the final stops of streetcar lines, and corners that bordered open countryside. They had to tell each other everything, ask about everything, their entire lives up to the day a few months earlier, the first of their common memory. There was only one boundary neither of them crossed, by a silent agreement that seemed humiliating to Judith, though it took her a long time to breach it, perhaps not until she realized it was she who was telling, who asked questions: there was a boundary, like the empty space of a silhouette cut out of the center of a family photograph, a name neither mentioned. Ignacio Abel spoke occasionally of his children but never about Adela. How strange that it took them so long not to mention her name or her status—"my wife," "your spouse"—but to sense her shadow, to remember she existed, strange that they were able for so long to wipe away with no trace, from the moment they met, the home and life he came from. For him, Judith lived in an invisible world he could reach instantaneously, as if he could cross to the other side of a mirror by virtue of a secret password he alone possessed. The password at times was a material object: he'd close the door to his study to talk to her on the phone; he kept Judith's letters and photographs under lock and key in his desk; he turned the key on the inside of the bathroom door, and as Adela's silhouette passed the frosted glass, he thought of Judith Biely, whom he would see shortly, as he stood under the running water. How close the other side was, the inviolable secret, a distance of a few minutes, a few hundred heartbeats, the topography of desire superimposed like a transparent sheet on the places in his daily life. He went down to the street and the porter's son who brought his car from the garage didn't know he was acting as his accomplice. He gave him a tip, and before he got in the car he looked up and Adela was on the balcony. She watched every morning because she was afraid: gunmen often chose the moment their victims left home to attack. ("But what ideas you have! Who'd ever think of shooting me?") He drove to the corner of Calle de Alcalá and parked the car in front of the Moderna Barber Shop. The face he saw in the mirror while the barber, who welcomed him with a nod and respectfully said his name, leaned over him was the same one Judith Biely would look at very soon. But only he knew that. The secret was a treasure, and the crypt and palace that contained it the inviolable house of time only Judith and he inhabited. Instead of driving down Alcalá, he turned up O'Donnell and left the car a certain distance from the private hotel with a high fence enclosing a garden with palm trees and dense hedges that protected shutters as thick as jalousies and painted an intense green, with workable slats that filtered an aquatic light when partially opened. To reach the hidden other world he had only to drive a few minutes, then pass through successive doors, visible and invisible, each provided with its own password. When he crossed the last threshold, Judith Biely was already waiting for him, seated in a chair near the bed, beside a lit blue-glass lamp on the night table, in the artificial darkness of nine in the morning.

The guilt-free intoxication corresponded to a reckless assurance: when they saw only themselves, they often behaved as rashly as if no one else could see them. At night they'd go to dimly lit bars near the large hotels, frequented for the most part by foreigners and wealthy young night owls who'd scarcely have recognized Ignacio Abel. In the cabaret at the Palace Hotel, sitting close together under the cover of a reddish half-light, they drank exotic mixed drinks that left a sweet aftertaste and conversed in Spanish and English while on the narrow floor couples danced to the rhythm of a small band. At a nearby table, surrounded by a chorus of his friends, the poet García Lorca laughed aloud, his broad face gleaming with sweat. Ignacio Abel had never been in that kind of place, hadn't known they existed. With the apprehension of a jealous man, he saw the ease with which Judith Biely moved among those people. In reality, she resembled them much more than she did him: the Americans and the English especially, young men and women united by a strange egalitarian camaraderie and a similar tolerance for alcohol, travelers in Europe who became involved with and then disentangled from one another as casually as they passed from one country to another, from one language to another, discussing with the same ardor the expectations of the Popular Front in France and a Soviet film, shouting the names of writers not familiar to Ignacio Abel, and about whom Judith Biely held impassioned opinions. With pride and a nebulous fear of losing her, he watched her gallantly defend Roosevelt to a drunken American who'd called him a covert Communist, an imitator of the five-year plans. She was so desirable, entirely his when she gave herself to him, yet fully independent, shining before others who didn't see him, a Spaniard of a certain age in a dark suit, a foreigner in that polyglot country of fluid borders and ambiguous norms they inhabited; for them Madrid wasn't much more than a way station. At times Ignacio Abel saw among them men with tweezed eyebrows and light rouge on their cheeks and women dressed as men, and he felt he was witnessing a corrected version of his time in Germany.

Reasons for returning home later came easily and without remorse — a delayed appointment or some last-minute work — and when he hung up the phone he promptly forgot the hint of reluctant disbelief in Adela's voice. With Judith Biely everything happened to him for the first time, the exaltation of the night beginning at an hour when not long before he'd resigned himself to domestic somnolence, the taste of her mouth or the dense sweetness of entering her or the gratitude and surprise of feeling how her body tensed like a bow when she came with a generous abandon that didn't resemble anything he'd known in his experience of lovemaking. Guided by her, he discovered worlds and lives he'd never imagined in the city that was his and yet became a promising, unknown place on the nights when he explored it beside her. (The lie hadn't stained them yet. Between his old life and the one he led with her there were no dark zones or points of friction. He passed from one to the other as easily as he jumped from a streetcar a short time before it stopped, adjusting his jacket or hat, perhaps blinking to adapt his eyes to the sudden abundance of sun.) But he was also the same man he'd always been, the one he'd be again after a few hours or the next morning (breakfast at the dining room table, the children ready to go to school; the agitation of typewriters and ringing telephones in the drafting room at University City, plans on the drawing tables, crews of men on scaffolds and in trenches, going up in cranes to the terraces of buildings almost completed), and yet he was another man, younger, passionate, dazed, not fully responsible for actions he sometimes observed with alarm, as if looking at himself from the outside while he let himself be carried away by an impulse he didn't want to resist. Holding Judith's hand, he went down narrow steps to basements filled with music and smoke, occupied by pale faces in a semidarkness that was greenish, bluish, reddish, in a submerged Madrid that left no traces in the light of day, that didn't know his secret and to which he gained access by crossing hostile doors, passageways so dimly lit he would have been lost if Judith Biely hadn't led him. He'd been one of those daytime men for whom night falls earlier and earlier in their lives: the return home after work, the key in the lock, the familiar voices and smells coming to receive him from the end of the hall, supper at the table, heads bent over plates in the light of the lamp, the somnolence of conversation punctuated by domestic sounds, the light squeak of a fork's tines on porcelain, a spoon against the side of a glass. From the window of his conjugal bedroom, Madrid was a far-off country whose bright lights were lost in the distance and from which he occasionally could hear, in the silence and in his insomnia, bursts of laughter from people out late, car engines, hands clapping for the *sereno,* the watchman, then the sound of his pike against the paving stones. Now the night expanded before him like those spacious landscapes that dominated dreams, or revealed labyrinths extending beneath or to the other side of the city he'd always known as he knew metro tunnels and the galleries of subterranean pipelines. A simple lie was the password that gave him partial access to the guiltless paradise of a Madrid that was his own and more foreign than ever, where the presence of Judith Biely walking with him and holding his arm granted him an unaccustomed right to citizenship. It took very little drink (or none at all, just breathing the damp, cold night air, looking at the constellations of neon signs and their reflections on the hoods of cars) for him to become giddy, just as he didn't need more than a certain glance or the brush of her hand or her mere proximity to awaken desire. In those places the light was always more subdued, the faces paler, the heads of hair shinier, the voices more foreign. Sexual tension and alcohol blurred everything, and matters flowed with the swift broken rhythm of the music. Judith knocked on an apartment door in a building with a marble staircase on Calle Velázquez, and as soon as they entered they were submerged in a dark space crossed by shadows, where the sound of conversations in

English mixed with smoke that had a resinous aroma, and the lit ends of cigarettes illuminated young faces that seemed to nod in time to the pulsations of music that could be heard from the street. Under the low light of a private room in a flamenco tavern, a woman wearing a great deal of makeup stamped her heels — and seen more closely turned out to be a man. Under the bare brick arches of an American bar installed in a basement behind the Gran Vía (a flickering light shaped like a red owl lit the doorway) he saw with alarm that Judith Biely was embracing a stranger with a shaved head wearing a dinner jacket. It was Philip Van Doren, who said something to him but the music was too loud, the drumbeats as dry and fast as the heels pounding the wooden platform in the flamenco tavern. Ignacio Abel felt Judith's hand squeezing his in a visible, proud affirmation of her love for him. "I hope you've made your decision," Van Doren said close to his ear, and it took Abel a moment to realize he was referring not to Judith but the invitation to travel to Burton College. Van Doren looked sideways at their clenched hands, at Ignacio Abel's bold gesture when he put his arm around Judith's waist. He smiled approvingly, with the air of a conspirator or an expert in human weakness, pleased by the success of his prediction. He asked them to join the other guests at his table and summoned a waiter with the same cold, peremptory gesture he used with his valet. "How nice to see you, Professor, you make me envious. You've become younger since I last saw you. Can it be expectations of an electoral victory by your Socialist comrades?" Suddenly Ignacio Abel thought that Judith and Van Doren had been lovers and were still seeing each other. The drinking and his jealousy filled him with unseemly suspicion: wasn't there something mocking in that approving smile, something condescending? Judith and Van Doren spoke in English and there was too much noise for him to hear what they said. He looked at her lips moving, curving to inhale a cigarette that Van Doren lit with a flat gold lighter. In the oppressive atmosphere under the low ceiling the alcohol made him as dizzy as the music, the voices, the too-near faces of strangers who elbowed their way to the bar. Someone was talking to him in a loud voice, yet he couldn't hear: a redheaded man with glasses in Van Doren's group, a secretary at the American embassy who had just given Abel his card and insisted on holding a formal conversation. "Do you believe, Professor, that the Popular Front has any chance of winning the elections?" He responded vaguely as he looked past the man: still holding her glass, Judith was dancing with Van Doren on the tiny floor; facing each other, they made identical gestures. Her tousled hair covered half her face, the twirl of her skirt revealed her knees burnished by silk stockings. The undaunted secretary was commenting on the Spanish government's diplomatic responses to the Italian occupation of Abyssinia. Ignacio Abel watched Judith dance, consumed with desire and pride, jealous of Van Doren and the other men who looked at her. The League of Nations had once again demonstrated its lamentable irrelevance, the secretary said self-importantly. The trumpet and saxophone hurt Abel's ears. Did he think there was a real threat in Spain of a new revolutionary uprising like the one in Asturias, this time more violent and better organized and perhaps with more likelihood of success? Judith whirled around, led by Van Doren, her skirt lifted and revealed her thighs. And if the left won next February's elections, which seemed possible, wouldn't that cause a military coup? Drum rolls and the metallic crash of cymbals buffeted the inside of his skull. The American government would view with pleasure the formation in Spain of a stable parliamentary majority regardless of its political identification. A final drum roll and applause ended the dance. Her face glowing with perspiration and her hair disheveled, Judith Biely came toward him and looked at him as if no one else were there.

He remembered her most clearly walking toward him, and memory became even more precious when he realized he wouldn't see her again. He imagined her, saw her coming from the bathroom in the room in Madame Mathilde's house, from the vanishing point at the end of the gallery in the Prado, from the revolving door of a café, or in places where they'd never been, Judith Biely in the hallway of his apartment in Madrid, which had been taken over by solitude and disorder in the course of the summer, in the turbulent time when the word "war" was not yet current. Judith outlined against the window of the auditorium in the Student Residence, where he'd seen her for the first time less than a year ago, the room where the piano was now covered and pushed into a corner of the stage on which she'd walked, heels clicking, because the space was now occupied by hospital beds. She came toward him from a distance and he watched her, eager, concentrated in his desire, avidity in his eyes, sitting on the divan in a café where he'd arrived early, not only because he was impatient to be with her but also because he loved to see her arrive, coming in from the street, slim and foreign, disoriented by the semidarkness, and he saying, as he stood to welcome her, with the out-of-date courtesy of a man older than she, "I never tire of looking at you."

The Madrid they saw when they were looking for each other or were together was only partially the city each would have lived in if they hadn't met. Before she arrived, Madrid had been a fantasy for Judith Biely, resplendent with promise and literature, the city of books and a language she loved; for Ignacio Abel, Madrid was the city he'd lived in reluctantly since he was born and for which he felt an uncomfortable mixture of frustration and tenderness. He wanted to leave Madrid — and, if possible, Spain — with the same intensity he wanted to engage in urban design projects that, in spite of gradual skepticism and accommodation to the bourgeois life into which he'd settled, continued to be nourished by his impulse toward social justice and improvement of the world and the lives of ordinary people. The city Judith Biely had imagined by studying maps and photographs, and by reading Galdós at the university with the same passion she had brought to reading Washington Irving when she was in school, became interwoven with the one Ignacio Abel rediscovered because he was showing it to her and looking at it through her wondering eyes. He thought of his own experience when he had arrived in Germany, about the celebratory quality the most trivial acts had for him, buying a newspaper and laboriously reading it in a café, exchanging polite words with the landlady at his pensión; about the permanent joy of learning something new, a word or turn of phrase in German, a secret of the art of drawing or geometry explained by Paul Klee, the rational miracle of an ordinary object suddenly revealed in the hands of Professor Rossman. He understood Judith Biely's love of Spain by recalling the man he'd been, by wanting to recover the part of himself that contained the best of his spirit and had become lethargic since his return. The intensity of his desire for Judith brought back the enthusiasm that sustained him during his time in Germany: the charm of expectation, the sensation of having before him something tangible and at the same time without limits, of once again looking through a wide window in his life that later closed. He understood Judith without her having to explain: as free in Madrid of the weight of the past as he'd been in Berlin and Weimar, the present took on a dazzling sensory quality for her. She'd just turned the age he'd been when he went to Germany: love and the desire to know made her even younger. Infected by her, Ignacio Abel now perceived differently the texture and density of life in familiar places, prepared to love things as she saw them — free of shadows from the past, the regrets of memory, and associated with her love for him. Madrid was the joyful present in which she, too, lightened almost all the weight of her personal identity. She was what Ignacio Abel saw in her, what she herself told him, and more so because when she spoke Spanish she became in part a new person, temporarily divesting herself not only of her usual language but of her former existence. Still immune to suspicion and guilt, though later she didn't know whether it had been a state of innocence or insensitivity — she was grateful it lasted as long as it did but also reproached herself for the pain inflicted, her sordid complicity in deception, she who'd been so honest until then, her conscience so clear — she observed her own life in another country and language as if it were a novel, her immersion in the book she was always about to write: similar to when she'd been an adolescent and stopped reading or came out of a movie theater but continued to reside inside the fiction that had so powerfully bewitched her. What happened to her in that other existence was real, but like events in a film, it had no consequence in the outside world and wasn't governed by its rules. Walking through this city where she knew no one and where nothing had associations in her memory, finding herself in it with a lover she was never sure of seeing again, were acts that belonged to an order of things as distant from her life in America as the episodes of a novel: a novel that continued to unfold without anyone writing it, in which she was the protagonist and only reader; a film shown in a theater where she was the only spectator, a film that absorbed her so much it canceled what it was hard to believe still existed — the wounding light of day, the harsh, hostile weather of the outside world.

But in Madrid novels bore a closer resemblance to truth. Judith Biely attended Professor Salinas's classes on *Fortunata y Jacinta,* and the names of places that in her earlier readings had seemed improbable and fantastic she now found on metro maps and corner street signs. She read on the streetcar, and when she got off at the Puerta del Sol and took just a few steps, she was already in the heart of the novel. The streetcar's route, the walking, the street noise made the book come to life for her. Calle de Postas, Plaza de Santa Cruz, Plaza de Pontejos existed, incredibly, with the same exquisiteness as the Alhambra of Washington Irving and the Manchegan plains John Dos Passos had traveled in search of Don Quijote's fictional trail. On the Plaza de Pontejos, Assault Guard vans and police wearing high boots and blue uniforms with gold buttons moved back and forth. Election posters pasted one over the other covered the walls and reached as high as the first balconies in a chaotic melodrama of typographies and the signs and symbols of political parties. From the novel she recognized the gloomy shops that sold fabrics and images of saints and religious objects, the street peddlers shouting under the arcades on the Plaza Mayor, and at one of its corners she looked for the pharmacy that served as the entrance to the house where Fortunata lived. On Calle Toledo she followed in the footsteps of the garrulous Estupiñá. At the foot of the granite buttress of the Arco de Cuchilleros, she read the description of the arrival of Juanito Santa Cruz to the tenement where he was about to see the girl who would change the course of his life. Young women as beautiful as that fictional character hawked in shrill voices the things they sold at street stalls: swarthy, with eyes as dark and faces as sensual as the paintings of saints by Velázquez and Zurbarán at the Prado, hair disheveled, wearing wide black skirts and shawls over their shoulders, some sitting on a step and casually revealing the swollen white breast on which a child with a red round face and blessed sleep on his eyelids was nursing. Madrid became suburban and rustic: an odor of esparto grass and leather came from mysterious stores of agricultural implements and harnesses for animals. Hammer blows and clouds of smoke from metal submerged in water reached her from the dark mouth of a blacksmith's shop in whose interior glowing coals and white-hot tips of metal gleamed. Peasants' somber faces behind the windows of a bus, wagons pulled by mules beaten mercilessly by drivers in sheepskin coats shouting obscenities, cars honking, the monotonous chant of blind men who sang ballads in the doorways of taverns, flamenco songs and advertisements played at top volume on radios, barefoot boys with shaved heads who had fistfights over a cigarette butt. A car with two loudspeakers on its roof blared "The Internationale," and the air filled with leaflets that fluttered in the wind like an invasion of white butterflies. MADRILEÑOS! VOTE FOR THE CANDIDATES OF THE POPULAR FRONT! The anthem was interrupted to make way for a voice that declared with deficient metallic amplification over the street noises: FOR THE FREEDOM OF THE WRONGFULLY IMPRISONED HEROES OF OCTOBER, FOR THE PUNISHMENT OF THE ASTURIAS EXECUTIONERS, FOR THE TRIUMPH OF THE WORKING CLASS. Attentive to everything, a foreigner, stared at, her head uncovered and a novel under her arm, Judith Biely discovered Madrid, and the streets of New York rose in her memory: on the other side of the ocean, and at an even greater distance in time, she recognized cadences of shouts, the poverty-stricken density of human lives, the stink of manure and rotten fruit and frying grease, the juxtaposition of voices, signs, businesses, trades, the anxieties of survival, perhaps less anguished here, just as the crowds of people were less suffocating, perhaps because the climate was more benign.

She was moving through a real city, the plot and subject matter of a novel, and the oldest part of the memory of the man she loved. On that February afternoon Judith walked, carried along by joy and curiosity, on the same streets where her lover had been a boy at the end of another century, in a city of streetcars pulled by mules and street lamps lit by gas. In the book she had to write, there would also be the resonance of that memory: although it didn't belong to her, it had turned out to be extremely intimate. She would have liked to walk with him here, asking questions: on the far side of the square she saw the entrance to the Plaza Mayor through the Arco de Cuchilleros and recalled his telling her that he had used it as a guide so as not to get lost the first few times he went to school by himself, a boy not very different from the ones she saw now playing in the street, with gray shorts and espadrilles and shaved heads, scarves and berets and faces red with cold, approaching her, attracted by her foreignness, like the men who stood looking at her and muttering in low voices words she didn't understand, as she moved faster past the doors of taverns. She savored the street names, pronouncing them softly to practice her Spanish and underlining them on the pages of the novel. Ignacio Abel thought it strange that Judith found so much beauty in them, surprised at her discovery, uncomfortable when she insisted on asking him things he had long forgotten: the address of the house where his mother had worked as a porter, the location of the window through which a perpetual gray light entered the basement where he studied feverishly in the light of an oil lamp, listening to people's footsteps and horses' hooves on the paving stones, and the wheels of wagons like the one that brought his father home dead. He was awkward or reluctant when remembering; what excited him was what he saw in front of his eyes or what didn't exist yet. He didn't ask Judith about her past so that he wouldn't have to imagine her with other men. Of his own past he recalled with her his first trip through Europe, the year he spent in Germany, and the trunk filled with books and magazines he brought back when he returned and that still nourished him. "Like you now in Madrid, almost as young as you." He wasn't the one who told her about the two buildings erected in recent years that filled him with a pride too private to degrade by talking about them or becoming arrogant. It was Philip Van Doren, whom he distrusted so intensely, feeling himself observed, judged by eyes where an intelligence gleamed, at once piercing and cold, which he found unsettling because he couldn't understand it, the intelligence of someone who knows he has enough money to buy anything and perhaps imagines he can control from a distance the lives of others: his life and Judith's. It was Philip Van Doren who showed Judith photographs of the public school and the marketplace designed by Ignacio Abel for the neighborhood where he'd been born. That afternoon she looked for the two buildings as intently as she had followed the trail of Galdós's characters. Each imposed its presence in a different way, suddenly appearing on a square or around a corner, singular and at the same time blending with the tenements, the modest rows of balconies, the horizon of tiled roofs. The school was all right angles and large picture windows: the children in their blue smocks flooded out when she stopped in front of the building, imagining the care Ignacio Abel must have used in selecting the exact color of the bricks, the forms of the letters carved into the white stone over the entrance: SPANISH REPUBLIC. NATIONAL COEDUCATIONAL SCHOOL "PÉREZ GALDÓS." The concrete roof arched against dark tiles and chimneys like a great animal emerging from the water. She recognized him here, just as she did in the abrupt strokes of his handwriting, the turbulence repressed and concealed beneath his correct manners, beneath his crushing formality, in his impatience when he undressed her the minute they were alone, and kissed and bit her, probed her as feverishly with his eyes as with his fingers and lips. Right angles, wide picture windows, concrete and brick already bruised and ennobled by the weather, massive tensions supported on the buoyancy of a mathematical key, on the pure force of gravity and the solidity of foundations driven into the earth: where others saw a market filled with people and loud voices, filthy

with refuse, occupied by mountains of produce and butchered animals oozing blood on white tile counters under the wounding light of
electric lamps, she found a personal confession, the hidden lines of a
self-portrait.

Night had fallen. The last doors of the market closed with a clang of
metal shutters. On the ground slippery with rotten fruit and fish scraps,
the typography of political leaflets stood out, spiked with symbols and
exclamation points. She'd become disoriented and was walking down a
narrow street where the only light was a dim bulb at the far corner. With
her head erect and eyes looking straight ahead she crossed the stain of
dirty electric light from a tavern that exuded an odor of acidic wine
and the sounds of drunkards' conversations. A shadow brushed against
her at the same time as a fetid breath. A rough, roguish male voice said
something she didn't understand but that instinctively made her walk
faster. At her back, very close, someone called to her, footsteps echoed
hers. A woman alone and young, in high heels, her head uncovered, a
foreigner: she quickened her pace and the shadow following her lagged
behind and the voice fired an insulting interjection, but a moment later
the footsteps approached and with them the breath and the filthy muttered words that frightened and offended her, alone in a strange city
that had suddenly become hostile, doors closed the length of the street,
and behind the windows covered with shutters and curtains, sounds
of conversations, dishes and glasses at suppertime. She wanted to run
but her legs felt heavy as in a dream. If she attempted to escape, she'd be
acknowledging the proximity of danger, she'd provoke her pursuer and
achieve nothing but trouble, the terror of physical harm. A shadow, or
perhaps two shadows, now she wasn't sure, footsteps to her right and
to her left, as if to keep her from running, a touch that provoked revulsion, of rage at the insolence, the sexual pursuit. She could confront
them, shout insults, call for help at the closed doors and the windows
screened by curtains. If only he'd come, if only he'd appear at the end of
the street, his silhouette tall and strong against the light at the corner,
his open arms offering her refuge and enclosing her in caresses, at first

so timid, so incredulous, the caresses of a man grateful for love who can't fully understand that it has been granted him. They were drunk, alcohol made them bold and weakened them too. Beyond the corner, the street widened into a little square, and on the other side she saw the large windows of a café frosted with steam. A rough hand squeezed her arm, the drunken voice came so close to her ear she felt on her neck the damp touch of breath or saliva. She shook off the hand without looking back and ran across the street, dodging a cold blast of wind and the horn of a car she hadn't seen coming. Inside the café she was enveloped in air thick with voices and smoke. Male eyes lingered on her, she felt them on her back and the nape of her neck as she walked to the rear, to the arch covered with a curtain behind which must be the lavatory and a telephone booth. She knew his home number by heart but had never used it. She asked for a token, not hiding her urgency, the intensity of her fear. She imagined him in the interior of his other life, as if she'd walked down a dark street and looked through a wide, tall window where a domestic scene took place in silence. She wasn't going to leave the café until he came for her, wouldn't abandon the protection of the telephone booth. Impatient, drumming her nails on the glass, trying to catch her breath, she listened to the rings. Someone picked up and Judith paused as she was about to say his name. In silence, the earpiece in her hand, holding her breath, she heard a curious voice asking who it was, Adela's voice, which she'd heard only once, long before, at the start of everything, the voice of the woman she'd met briefly at the Student Residence.

13

LULLED TO SLEEP by the rhythm of the train, he saw his children vividly in the lightning flash of a dream. Perhaps he heard their voices too, because now he remembers that they were close, somewhat weakened, like voices in an open space, perhaps the garden of the house in the Sierra or the edge of the irrigation pond; voices heard in the late afternoon, with an echo of withdrawal and anticipated distance; the past and present collapsed, the recovered voices and the sound of the train filtering into his half-sleep, lit by an alloy of light from the Hudson and the Sierra de Madrid. A voice no longer heard fades away in memory, after a few years it's forgotten, as, they say, people who lose their sight gradually forget colors. Ignacio Abel can no longer remember his father's voice and doesn't even know when he forgot it. His mother's he can invoke in association with words or phrases peculiar to her: the way she shouted *I'm coming* when an impatient tenant called for her from the doorway, when someone knocked on the glass of the porter's lodging. He does remember that: the vibration of the frosted glass, the ringing of the bell, and his mother's footsteps, slower and slower as she aged and grew heavier and clumsier because of arthritis, yet she preserved a sharp, young tone and streetwise inflection in her voice. *I'm coming,* she shouted, adding, under her breath, *We're not airplanes.*

• • •

He wonders whether his children will begin to forget his voice as well, his face gradually replaced by the frozen image in a photograph. Distance makes his return that much more difficult. Minutes, hours, days, kilometers, distance multiplied by time. Right now, immobile, leaning back in the train, his face next to the window, he continues to leave, to go away. Distance is not a fixed, stable measurement but an expansive wave that pulls him in its centrifugal current, its icy vacuum of unlimited space. Trains, ocean liners, cabs, subway cars, rambling steps to the end of unknown streets. Hotel room after hotel room always at the end of similar flights of steep stairs and narrow halls with identical smells, a universal geography of desolation. But his children, like Judith Biely, are also moving away at the same velocity in different directions, and each instant and each step added to the distance makes his return more improbable. There's no way to undo the kind of destruction that can sweep away and overturn everything, no way to overcome the accelerated course of time. Doors closing behind him, rooms where he'll never sleep again, corridors, customs barriers, nautical miles, kilometers traveled north by the train carrying him to another unknown place, just a name now, Rhineberg, a hill in a forest beside steep banks and a white building that doesn't yet exist, whose initial sketches are in his briefcase: rough, essentially reluctant drafts of a project that might never be built. Constantly going forward, never going back, adding distances, geographical accidents, plains, mountain ranges, cities, battlefronts, countries, entire continents, oceans, modest hotel rooms.

Memory, like any construction material, has degrees or indices of resistance that in theory one should be able to calculate. How long does it take to forget a voice and not be able to invoke it at will, its unique, mysterious timbre, its tone when it says certain words, whispers in one's ear or calls from a distance, at once intimate and remote in a telephone receiver, saying everything when it pronounces a name, sweet words it had not spoken to anyone until then. Or perhaps it has: perhaps others remember that same voice, unknown men who haunt like shadows the unexplored country of the past, the earlier lives of Judith Biely, the one she must be living now; eyes that also rested on her naked body, hands and lips that caressed her and to which she surrendered with abandon. To whom else had she said those words, even more singular and exciting because they belonged to another language, *honey, my dear, my love.* To whom was she saying them now, to whom had she said them in the three months she'd been away from Spain, back in America or perhaps wandering again through European cities, gradually forgetting him, not contaminated by the Spanish misfortune, free of it just by crossing the border, equally immune to the suffering of love and the mourning of a country that, after all, isn't hers. As spontaneously as she'd decided to become his lover one early October afternoon in Madrid, she decided to break things off a little more than eight months later, toward the middle of July, with a determination that left no room for ambiguity or remorse, and perhaps has also made her immune to pain. So little time, if you stop to think about it. Ignacio Abel continues to see her in his dreams but doesn't hear her voice. Perhaps it was Judith Biely's voice he heard saying his name so clearly in Pennsylvania Station, and yet a moment later he couldn't identify or remember it. Without the photographs, the voice fades before the face. The photo is absence, the voice is presence. The photo is the pain of the past, the fixed point left behind in time: the frozen image, invariable in appearance, yet more and more distant, more unfaithful, the semblance of a shadow vanishing almost as rapidly on photographic paper as in memory. Feeling his pockets, tormented by the thought of losing any of the few things he now possesses, Ignacio Abel finds his wallet and with his fingertips seeks the photo Judith Biely gave him shortly after they met. In it she smiles just as she'll smile at him only a few weeks later, with confidence, not holding anything back, openly showing the plenitude of her expectations. The photo awakened Ignacio Abel's jealousy of Judith's earlier life in which he didn't exist and about which he preferred not knowing, not asking, fearing the inevitable male shadows that were there. Perhaps what made her smile and turn, forgetting about the automatic click of the camera, was a man's presence. What had excited him most about her from the start was what made him most afraid and what had eventually taken her away from him: the strength of her will, which he'd not seen in any other woman, manifested in each of her gestures as clearly as her physical beauty. The flash in the automatic photo booth gleamed on her curly hair, teeth, shining eyes; it rebounded off the line of her cheekbones. That photo was the same one Adela had held in her hands, bewildered, in a kind of fog that threw her features out of focus, and was about to tear up but merely dropped to the floor, along with two or three letters, leaning against the desk in his study whose drawers Ignacio Abel had forgotten to lock.

Unlike Judith's voice, Adela's remains intact in his memory. He's often heard it calling to him, as she sometimes called to him when she had a bad dream and clung to him in bed, her eyes closed, to be certain he was near. He's heard it coming from the end of the hall in the apartment in Madrid, as clear in wakefulness as in dreams, on summer nights when the noises of war were gradually becoming routine, waking him at times with the feeling that Adela had come back, crossed the front line, returned to claim him and demand an explanation. How dirty the house was, how disordered the rooms. (There were no longer maids who came in to clean, no cook to prepare food for the señor, soon there wouldn't even be food.) Too bad he'd let the plants on the balcony die. What a shame he hadn't made more of an effort to get in touch with his wife and children. The complaints written in the letter he should have torn up or at least left behind in the hotel room in New York, those remembered and the ones imagined, intertwine in the monotonous sound of a voice that belongs to Adela and to his own guilty conscience. How strange not to have felt in her voice that she suspected, that she knew. How could she *not* have known? How strange not to be able to see oneself from the outside, in the looks of others, those who are closest and suspect though they would have preferred not to find out, who discover without understanding. The boy so serious in the last few months, so withdrawn, observing, standing at the door of his room when his father lowered his voice to speak on the phone in the hall. Ignacio Abel turned to wave a last goodbye after the gate closed at the house in the Sierra, and Miguel, standing next to his mother and sister at the top of the steps, looked and didn't look at him, as if not wanting to believe that gesture of farewell, as if wanting to let him know he wasn't deceived, that he, his scorned twelve-year-old son, knew with incongruous lucidity about his father's impatience, his desire to leave, the relief he felt getting into the car or quickening his pace on the way to the station so as not to miss the train that would take him back to Madrid. His mother, next to him, remained enveloped in a fog of sorrow that rarely lifted, and Miguel could not grasp her motives no matter how much he scrutinized her; Lita became quite emotional, uncharacteristically so, and perhaps somewhat superficially, just as she did when she saw her father arrive and ran out to embrace him and tell him right away the grades she'd received, the books she'd read.

With clarity Ignacio Abel now relives a scene, the paused image in a documentary film: night in the apartment, the white cloth on the dining room table illuminated by the chandelier, the gold-green light reflecting on place settings and white china plates, the crystal of glasses. The time is February, a few days before the elections. He sees it from the outside, from a distance, a domestic scene glimpsed by the solitary stranger on a street in a city where he doesn't know anyone, where nothing awaits him but a hotel room. He's at the head of the table and Adela faces him, the children at the sides in their assigned seats, holding a quiet, trivial conversation while the maid walks down the hall after serving the soup, the maid who was now putting on a white cap and apron, ordered to do so by the señora, who was becoming more and more strict about such details, who a short while before had reprimanded the cook for going out in a hat instead of the kerchief or beret appropriate to her position. Miguel moved his left leg nervously under the table and attempted with little success not to make noise eating his soup. He observed out of the corner of his eye, in a permanent state of alert, attentive to the smallest detail or hint of danger with a sensibility much more acute than his capacity to reason, and therefore more restless. He imagined himself transformed into an invisible man like the one in the movie he'd seen a few Saturdays before with Lita and the maids, behind the back of his father, who, like a distracted, arbitrary monarch, forbade excursions to the movies whenever he heard about an epidemic of something or other in Madrid. *The Invisible Man*! Miguel was easily overwhelmed when he liked a film a great deal. He couldn't sit still; he leaned forward in his seat as if trying to be closer to the screen, to sink into it, convulsed with laughter or trembling with fear, pinching Lita, punching her, so enthralled by the film that when they left the theater he was lightheaded, agitated, and that night there was no way to keep him quiet when the lights were turned off; he wanted to keep talking to Lita about the scenes and characters, and when she fell asleep he was still too excited to close his eyes, and he relived the film, imagining variations in which he himself played a part. The chilling enigma of a scientific discovery that offers superhuman powers to the person who controls it! How marvelous to spy without anyone seeing you, to watch everything with no danger of being caught. On his way home from school he'd seen on the door of the shabby theater he was allowed to go to with Lita and the maids the ferocious poster for a film with a black silhouette holding a letter and a large magnifying glass. THE SEALED ENVELOPE (*The Secret of the Dardanelles*). COMING SOON. How fantastic that phrase was — coming soon — what excitement it unleashed in him when he simply thought about it, about the days left until the film opened, about the possibility of being sick or coming home from school with a failing grade and as punishment not being allowed to go to the movies. If his father became aware of his jiggling leg, he'd scold him, but Miguel hoped the tablecloth would hide it, and in any case he was incapable of sitting still or ordering his leg to stop. "You're sewing on the Singer," his father would say. "It seems the boy will have a tailor's vocation after all." They all acted in their predictable ways, repeated themselves, the same gestures, but Miguel was the one they all noticed — the scapegoat, he thought, feeling sorry for himself, the black sheep. He thought the Dardanelles in the title of the movie must be members of some secret society of spies or international traffickers, and Lita had laughed at him, calling him ignorant, and told him the Dardanelles was the name of a strait. "And why do you care if your son moves his leg, it's not serious," his mother would say, giving his father a look at once concerned and resigned, different from the one she gave the boy, with whom she had to be both indulgent and severe. Dinner became a series of increasingly difficult tests, a race of exasperating slowness, and as he weakened, tripping over obstacles, jiggling his leg without a moment's rest under the table, unable to sit still in his chair, Lita sat across from him, gliding as if on a magic carpet, smiling and self-confident, eating her soup in silence, handling her knife and fork without leaning her elbows on the table, politely attentive to the adults' conversation and at times asking a question or making an observation that didn't provoke an ironic or condescending reply, the kind he'd become used to hearing from his father. He would have liked to run out, not leaving his napkin folded beside the plate, not asking permission to leave the table, just becoming invisible, floating along the hall toward the partially prohibited territory filled with promise at the back of the house, the kitchen and laundry room and tiny room the cook and the maid shared, where he could hear the sound of the radio, with Angelillo singing a song that brought tears to his eyes, the story of the gravedigger Juan Simón, who one day finds himself obliged to bury his own daughter, dead in the bloom of life:

> *I'm a gravedigger coming back*
> *Oh, I'm a gravedigger coming back*
> *From burying my own heart.*

Miguel wanted to see that film at all costs. He wanted to see it because he liked the song and because the cook and maid had already seen it and told him about it in detail, both of them moved as they remembered it, pausing to recall some dramatic moment. He wanted to see it even more because his father, mother, and sister seemed to have agreed to dislike it without having seen it. His mother wouldn't ridicule him or become angry if she caught him beside the radio, his eyes filled with tears. But she wouldn't have defended him either. She was distressed by his lack of masculinity, by the possibility he would awaken his father's distaste and contempt. But what hurt Miguel most was that Lita had taken the adults' side. She, his accomplice in loving movies on the afternoons they laughed and laughed at the theater watching the Marx Brothers, Laurel and Hardy, and Charlie Chaplin, or shivered with fear as they watched Frankenstein and Dracula and the Wolf Man and the Invisible Man, also disliked movies with flamenco songs and regional dancing, precisely the ones the maids and Miguel liked best. She'd refused to go with him to *Juan Simón's Daughter*. She'd listened with an approving expression when their father said to their mother a few nights earlier during dinner:

"Look at Buñuel, who was so much a surrealist and so modern, and now he's not embarrassed to earn a pile of money producing that piece of folkloric idiocy, *Juan Simón's Daughter*."

Folkloric idiocy. Miguel knew he was going to say or do something wrong, and precisely because he knew it, the transgression was inevitable. How hard would it have been for him to remain silent when his father made that scornful comment about Buñuel? But he couldn't help it, he didn't even think about it; he knew what he was going to say, and he said it, and as he did he became aware of the inevitable reprimand he'd receive and the fact that his mother and sister weren't going to defend him:

"Well, Herminia says it's a picture you cry over and it has pretty songs."

"Herminia." His father repeated the maid's name with burlesque seriousness. "A great cinematic authority."

Now the song was coming from the end of the hall, and they all acted as if they didn't hear it. Or perhaps Miguel was the only one who did, nervously shaking his leg under the table, watching his father's face out of the corner of his eye, noting that his mother, beneath her air of absent placidity, was becoming tense, and Lita, far removed from the possibility of disaster, was recounting a recent excursion with her classmates to the Prado. He admired her as unconditionally as he had when he was little; he admired her even when he resented and despised her because she fawned over their father, when he was tempted to spill ink on her impeccable exercise notebook, or step as if accidentally on one of those school albums in which Lita glued leaves and dried flowers. If she could concentrate on everything she did, and move with so much serenity and in a straight line, it was because she wasn't distracted or alarmed by the sounds of danger, because she lacked the invisible antennae that detected the turmoil he always provoked. His father was going to be ir-ritated because the music on the radio was too loud, because the maid, when she left the dining room, didn't close the door behind her, and because the kitchen door was open. That's why it was so difficult for him to concentrate: because he was mindful of too many things at the same time, because he guessed what the others were thinking or sensed changes in their states of mind, like those barometers in school with fast-moving needles that registered atmospheric disturbances.

Then the telephone rang, just as Miguel was swallowing a mouthful of water, so focused on not making noise that the first ring startled him and made him choke. Sitting across from him, Lita put her hand over her mouth to hide her laughter. The telephone didn't stop ringing, shrill in the silence that had fallen after his coughing had stopped. How was it possible that his father and sister didn't hear it? His father, rigid with anger, concentrated meticulously on chewing. With an abrupt gesture his mother placed her fork and knife on her plate and left the dining room, and a moment later the ringing stopped and her voice was heard in the hall, uneasy because it was unusual for people to call so late: "Who's calling? Who? One moment." She returned to the din-ing room unhurriedly, seemed more serious and more tired than a mo-ment earlier, looking at his father in a strange way when she gave him the message.

"It's for you. From your office, a woman who sounds foreign."

"Well, it's a fine time for people to be calling," said Lita, unaware of what Miguel's eyes saw but his mind couldn't decipher, innocent of all uncertainty, of any suspicion of danger, sure in the world.

Inside his apartment, Ignacio Abel crossed the invisible border to his other life, walking down the dark hallway to the phone on the wall, to the unexpected voice of Judith Biely, leaving behind the family scene in the dining room, interrupted and blurred on the other side of the glass that filtered light and voices. In a few seconds and in so small a space, his heart pounding in his chest, he took on his other identity; he stopped being a father and husband to become a lover; his movements became more secretive, less confident; his voice was changing to become the one Judith would hear—hoarse, anxious, altered by a mixture of bewilderment, happiness, and the sudden fear that it wasn't she who called, breaking an unspoken agreement for a reason that must be serious. His hand trembled when he picked up the earpiece, still swaying against the wall; his voice sounded so low and rasping that Judith, equally anxious in the telephone booth in a café whose location she didn't know, at first didn't recognize it. She too spoke quietly, quickly, in English and a moment afterward in Spanish, short phrases, murmured so close to the mouthpiece that Ignacio Abel heard her breathing and could almost feel on his ear the brush of her lips. "Please come and rescue me. *Casi no sé dónde estoy. Unos hombres venían siguiéndome.* I want to see you right away."

He'll always long for that voice, even when he can no longer recall it at will and has stopped hearing it in the unpredictability of certain dreams or turning when he thinks he's heard her saying his name. During the demented, bloody summer in Madrid, when he went about like a shadow, what he missed most was not the reasonable certainty of not being murdered, or the solid routine of a former life that had disintegrated overnight, but something more secret, more his own, more irretrievably lost: the possibility of dialing a certain number and hearing Judith Biely's voice, the miracle that somewhere in Madrid, at the end of an automobile or streetcar ride, an impatient walk, Judith Biely would be waiting for him, much more desirable than in his imagination, surprising him with the joy of her presence, as if no matter how persistently he tried, he could never remember how much she meant to him.

"It was a secretary, a new girl," he said, back in the dining room, not looking at anyone in particular, putting on his jacket, reckless, a liar, indifferent to the mediocrity of his performance. "There was an emergency at a construction site. A scaffold collapsed."

"Call if you see you'll be back late."

"I don't think it's all that important."

"Papá, are you going in the car? Will you take me with you?"

"What ideas you have, child," Adela said. "You're just what your papá needs now."

"I'll take a taxi and get there faster."

Just a few minutes earlier the night had been closed off for him, the predictable, dull night of family routine: supper, conversation, the distant sounds of the street, the resignation to the details of tedium. The warmth from the heating system, the lethargic, enveloped life, lined in the felt of house slippers and pajamas, the tenaciously won comfort of a house protected against the winter cold. And now the unexpected happened, stillness was transformed into motion, warmth into the knife wound of cold when he stepped out of the building, resignation into temerity, Madrid at night opening like a limitless countryside he'd cross at top speed in a taxi to meet Judith Biely, so the promise would be kept, enunciated not in her words but in the tone of her voice: the desire, the urgency, the certainty of embracing her and kissing her a few minutes later. Through the taxi window he saw the city as if he were dreaming it. Light fog swaddled the lights and made the paving stones and trolley tracks glow with a damp luster. He looked at the solitary displays in store windows, lit in empty streets, the large windows of cafés, the electric light in dining rooms where family suppers were taking place, identical to the one he'd just left and that now seemed like a painful episode in a uniform servitude he'd escaped. Not forever, of course, and not for the whole night, but any measure of time was enough for him now, two hours, even just one hour. There was no currency of minutes his covetousness wouldn't be thankful for, minutes and seconds that decreased with the clicking sound of the numbers as they changed on the meter, with the accelerating beat of his heart. Election posters covered the façades in the Puerta del Sol. In the drizzle, violent searchlights lit the gigantic round face of the candidate Gil Robles, occupying an entire building, crowned with involuntary absurdity by a neon advertisement for Anís del Mono: *Grant Me Your Vote and I'll Return a Great Spain to You.* He recalled Philip Van Doren's fixed stare and sarcastic tone amid the smoke and the noise of a jazz band: "Do you believe, Professor Abel, like your coreligionist Largo Caballero, that if the right wins the elections, the proletariat will start a civil war?" The icy wind shook the cables from which the streetlights were suspended, lengthening convulsive shadows on the sidewalk. The taxi moved slowly toward the Calle Mayor, making its way through a labyrinth of streetcars. His imagination anticipated illusions of what was now imminent: the arches and gardens of the Plaza Mayor, the lanterns at the corners of Calle Toledo, the café where Judith Biely waited for him, her profile standing out in spite of the smoke inside and the steam that covered the glass, the young woman, alone and foreign, whom the men looked at brazenly and approached, almost touching her, to say things in a low voice. In the city where one has always lived, ordinary trips can be equivalent to profound journeys in time: crossing Madrid to meet his lover one inauspicious night in February, Ignacio Abel traveled from his present life to the streets of his distant childhood, to which he almost never returned, along which he'd never walked with her. The impulse of the taxi in the direction of the future returned him to the past, and along the way he got rid of so many years to reach her with the truest part of himself. He erased what at this moment didn't matter to him at all, what he would have given without hesitation for the time with Judith Biely: his career, his dignity, his bourgeois apartment in the Salamanca district, his wife, his children. Before the end of the trip he was searching his pockets for coins to pay the driver, leaning forward to see the exact corner and the café, the silhouette of Judith Biely. He was surprised to find himself moving his left leg as nervously as Miguel, who'd looked at him so seriously when he left the dining room, adjusting his tie, making sure the keys were in his pocket.

He said, "I won't be back late," and in Miguel's neutral gaze was a disbelief all the more wounding because it was completely instinctive and revealed like an unexpected mirror the mediocre quality of his imposture, the gestures of an actor who convinces no one. But that sting of alarm and disgust with himself was quickly suppressed, wiped away by haste, by physical exaltation that carried him down the stairs, the road to the invigorating cold of the street that filled his lungs as he ran to the next corner, looking for a taxi. Standing next to the window of his room while Lita slept, Miguel was looking at the same deserted corner of Calle Príncipe de Vergara, lit by a street lamp, listening in silence to the beat of footsteps on the sidewalk, imagining they were his father's when in fact they belonged to the watchman who checked the building entrances, striking the ground at regular intervals with the iron tip of his pike. He'd awakened in the dark, thinking he heard the elevator's motor when it stopped, recalling something he'd read before he fell asleep, hiding the magazine under the pillow when their mother came in to say good night, an article on people buried alive, from which he learned a word that in itself frightened him — catalepsy — a word whose meaning Lita knew, of course. *How many people have been buried alive? How many have consummated their agony — the most terrible one of all — in the place of their eternal rest?* He was fascinated to discover that for attentive eyes and ears, there was no such thing as total darkness or total silence. As he looked at the room in shadows it became filled with light, just as when slow-moving clouds drift away from the face of the full moon. He'd read in one of the cheap magazines about crimes and wonders that the maids bought that in a secret laboratory in Moscow, scientists were developing x-ray glasses that allowed you to see in absolute darkness and a magnetic-wave pistol that killed silently. THE ENIGMA OF MYSTERIOUS RAYS THAT BRING LONG-DISTANCE

DEATH. What had been at the moment he awoke an oppressive silence was transformed into a jungle of noises: Lita's breathing, wood
creaking, the vibration of the windowpane when a car passed on the
street, the strikes of the *sereno*'s pike, the growl of the heating pipes,
the muffled echo of the opposing forces that, according to his father's
explanation, kept the entire building standing, never at rest, expanding
and contracting like a great animal breathing; and farther away, or at
least in a space difficult for him to locate, another sound that Miguel
couldn't define, that stopped and then started again after a while, like
the sound of his blood when he rested his ear on the pillow. He sat
up in bed very quietly, making certain it wasn't the elevator he heard.
He stood up slowly, the cold of the wood floor on the soles of his feet,
the annoying need to urinate that would force him to go out into the
hall. His father and mother reproached him for not reading, but his
head, when he couldn't sleep, was full of disturbing things he'd read
in the paper. SCOTLAND YARD INVESTIGATES A CASE OF CRIMES
COMMITTED BY SLEEPWALKERS. The sound of labored, intermittent
breathing returned, something that never changed into a voice but did
contain a lament. When he left the room he was the Invisible Man,
invisible and wrapped in silence, walking barefoot, turning cooperative doorknobs. It frightened him to be a sleepwalker and be dreaming
as he walked toward a victim who'd be found dead at dawn, *his face
contorted in terror.* The clock in the living room rumbled and struck
five, one strike after the other, leaving a resonance that took a long time
to disappear. From the end of the hall, as long and black as a tunnel,
came the double snores of the maid and the cook, as methodical as
a bellows machine, with interruptions of quiet in the midst of which
he still heard the other sound, the intermittent breathing, the lament.
Suspended like the Invisible Man at his parents' bedroom door, free
of the force of gravity by virtue of another invention no less decisive
— *an anti-gravitational injection will facilitate space travel* — he leaned
against the door to hear better, to be certain it was his mother's voice he
was hearing, familiar and at the same time unfamiliar, a high-pitched
moan that suddenly became deep, as if it had come from someone

else's throat: a long moan muffled against a pillow, a lament that broke into weeping or isolated words it was impossible to decipher. Perhaps his mother would die if he didn't go in and wake her. Perhaps she was suffering from a horrible disease and hadn't told anyone. He wanted to stay and he wanted to run away. He wanted to save her from the disease or an affront he couldn't imagine, and he wanted not to hear her, not to be awake with icy feet by the door, to enjoy the tranquility of his sister's sleep right now, immune to uneasiness and danger. Suppose his father had come back and his mother was arguing with him? With a rush of panic he saw the landing light go on beneath the entrance door and heard the elevator start up. That would be the last straw: to have his father come back and find him in the hall, standing in the dark, at five in the morning. He'd have to hurry back to his room, but that would bring him to the front door, and his bad luck would turn his retreat into a trap. What he couldn't afford to do was stand there, paralyzed. He rushed forward blindly and closed the door of his room behind him just as the elevator stopped at the landing. His heart pounded in his chest like the beats of a kettledrum in a scary movie. His father turned the key in the lock, walked slowly down the hall in the dark, leaving a long interval between steps as unfamiliar as those of a stranger. Motionless on the bed, his feet cold, his hands crossed over his chest, his eyes closed, Miguel achieved a state of perfect catalepsy.

14

THERE WERE SIGNS but he didn't see them, or rather, chose not to see them. Just a few steps removed from Judith Biely's presence, from the fleeting time he spent with her, reality became as blurred as the background of a photograph. He is amazed at his confusion: so far from Madrid and from her, stripped of the drama of all he'd taken for granted, believed was his, now dissolved like salt in water, Ignacio Abel insists on sizing up the past, an exercise as useless for alleviating remorse as for correcting mistakes. He would have liked to know the moment when the disaster became inevitable, when the monstrous began to seem normal, as invisible as the most ordinary acts in life, when the words that encouraged the crime, which no one took seriously because they were repeated and were nothing but words, turned into crimes, when the crimes became so routine they were now part of normal life. Today the army is the foundation and spine of the nation. When civil war breaks out, we won't accept cowardly defeat by offering our neck to the enemy. There's one moment and not another, a point of no return; a hand holding a pistol is raised and moves to the back of someone's neck, and a few seconds go by before the shot is fired; even when the index finger begins to squeeze the trigger, the possibility of turning back is still there, if only for a second; over months or years, water gradually seeps into the roof of a building that no one repairs and it takes only an instant for it all to come to a head, a beam splits in half and the ceiling falls; in tenths of a second the flame that almost went out revives and sets fire to a curtain or a handful of papers that will feed the blaze that will destroy everything. In the period of transition from a capitalist to a socialist society the form of government will be a dictatorship of the proletariat. Things are always on the verge of not happening, or happening in another way; very slowly or very quickly they are carried out or drift toward paralysis, but there's a moment, just one, when a remedy can be found, when what will be lost forever can still be saved, when the irruption of misfortune, the advent of the apocalypse, can be stopped. When the inflexible justice of the people is carried out, the exploiters and their followers will die with their shoes on. A man will leave his house one morning at the usual hour and his executioners will be waiting inside a car. He will pause in the doorway to adjust his gloves and hat as the men clutch their pistols with sweaty hands. The car window will open just enough to let the cigarette smoke out and then the signal will come. The men will get ready to shoot but a truck might suddenly drive by and disrupt the whole operation. The victim will get a chance to flee, a guard's life will be spared.

During a raw spring of gales and rainstorms that decimated the recently flowering branches of chestnut trees and acacias and peppered the pavements with seeds like white elm petals, almost every day Professor Rossman sent Ignacio Abel newspaper clippings heavily underlined with pencils of different colors and punctuated with exclamation points and question marks: reports of shootings or assaults cut off in the middle by censors, delirious statements amplified by the size of the headlines and by the volume of loudspeakers booming at meetings above the fervor of the crowds in bullrings. When we take to the streets for the second time, let there be no talk of generosity and no blame if revolutionary excesses go to the extreme of not respecting lives. Professor Rossman went around Madrid, his briefcase full of newspapers in several languages and handbills with senseless proclamations picked up on the streets, obsessed by the magnitude of the collective madness, the lies of German or Italian or Soviet propaganda. The USSR is the bright watchtower that lights our way, a free people that suffers neither exploitation nor hunger, a liberated people, marching in the vanguard of the working masses. Professor Rossman realized that the very scale of the lies was overwhelming. In cafés he'd begin a conversation, try to explain international politics that no one understood or cared about. But he'd seen with his own eyes, he knew the lies firsthand, and yet no one believed his status as witness, no one asked him about what he'd seen first in Germany and then in the Soviet Union. They looked at him with disbelief, at the most with impatience or annoyance or suspicion. Ignacio Abel looked at the tray with the mail in the foyer when he came home from work and almost always found an envelope with Professor Rossman's writing, often containing only a clipping of a small square lost among the columns of some Spanish or European newspaper, which no one but he would have noticed: a political assassination in a distant province, a gunfight between Socialist and Anarchist fishermen in the port of Málaga, an administrative measure taken against Jewish professors at a German university, an obscure statement by Stalin at the Komsomol Congress, an article about the Japanese infiltration of Manchuria, an article by Luis Araquistáin in the journal *Claridad* predicting the imminent fall of the bourgeois Republic in Spain and the inevitable advent of the dictatorship of the proletariat, a photo of the tiny king Victor Emmanuel III declaring himself emperor of Abyssinia before a backdrop of Roman splendor from a movie set. Sometimes the envelopes hadn't been stamped: Professor Rossman preferred to deliver them in person to the porter's office in Ignacio Abel's building so his former student could see them without delay. Priests and nuns swarm over the surface of the country like flies in a village that smells of putrefaction. The banner of the Spanish right has as an essential tenet the restoration of Christian spirituality in the face of efforts—dominated by hidden international forces that correspond to the symbols of the hammer and sickle, the Masonic triangle, and the Judaic golden calf—to make society materialistic. Yet Professor Rossman restrained from phoning Ignacio Abel or going to his office or to his apartment when he met his daughter after German lessons. Armed with scissors and pencils, he hunched over the newspapers lying open on a café table, pushing his glasses up onto his bald head, and when he was finished, he stuffed everything into his large black briefcase and went out with pointless urgency to meet someone or visit one of the offices or embassies where he had applications pending, to sound the alarm about the state of the world while it was still possible to do something about it.

But who stops the fire when it has already started and flames climb the walls and heat shatters the windowpanes? Who can quench the fury of someone who has been injured or stop the spiraling casualties? Who will keep count or make the alphabetical list of names growing by the minute like the telephone directory of an immense city, the Spanish city of the dead still expanding—as the train moves north along the banks of the Hudson River and its wheels pound rhythmically on the rails—in the distant night of Madrid, in open country and in the ditches, on both fronts, though it is difficult to imagine and seems impossible, looking at the broad serenity of the river, the expanse of copper and gold in the woods on the other side of the window, that at this very moment darkness and crime are swooping down on an entire country where night fell several hours ago. On sinister summer nights in Madrid, Ignacio Abel waited in vain for sleep to come; from the dark bedroom he could hear bursts of gunfire and the engines of cars racing along the deserted streets, rebelling with belated and useless rage against the inevitable, against the fatalistic necessity of disaster. Humiliated by his own impotence, in his mind he insisted on altering the course of the past: he alone, debating with phantoms, changing his own actions and those of the people he knew and even of public figures, rising up against his own blindness and feeling ashamed of it too late, passionately contradicting someone he hadn't wanted to argue with months earlier, someone he heard saying the same thing everybody said, that in reality nothing was going on and the situation wasn't all that serious and not worth worrying about, or perhaps that something terrible would happen, though nobody knew what, but it was too late now to avoid it, and maybe it was better this way because a torrential rain is preferable to the oppressiveness of an imminent storm that doesn't arrive and makes the air increasingly hard to breathe. You can't stop the implacable March of History, they said — Now or Never; Not One Step Back; Revolution or Death; Crush the Bolshevik Hydra; Workers Will Give Birth with Blood and Pain to a Glorious New Spain; The Army Must Once Again Be the Backbone of the Nation. Posters with large red or black letters recently posted on walls; muscular arms, violent jaws, open hands, clenched fists; swastikas, fasces and arrows, sickles and hammers, eagles with outstretched wings; advertisements for brandy; bullfight posters; effigies of giants painted on huge canvases that covered building façades and proclaimed the coming of the revolution or the opening of a film about Andalusian bandits. The radio played political anthems and military marches ad nauseam, a flamenco-style, shrill voice singing "My Pony" or "Juan Simón's Daughter," and the hoarse proclamations of orators rebounding in a bullfight arena: Let us tear down everything to make room for the flowering of the liberating revolution! Let us destroy those who, by simply thinking about destroying us, have joined the struggle! From the blood of our martyrs who fall under the vicious bullets of Bolshevik assassins the vigorous seed of a new Spain will grow!

He lived like everyone else, bewildered and worried, suffering attacks of disgust and fear as well as tedium, trapped by his obligations and desires, with no time to look around, perhaps seeing some signs but not stopping to reflect on what they foretold. It's the time for liquidations, and these must be total and absolute. What could he know or remedy if he saw nothing, if he hadn't even been able to keep Adela from finding the small key in the lock of his desk drawer, if for several months he hadn't seen her face change day after day, the tone of her voice, the way she looked at him. What might have been avoided couldn't be remedied. Let no traitor hope for clemency, because there will be none, not for any of them. On March 12 at eight-thirty in the morning, the police escort José Gisbert looks at the Socialist professor Luis Jiménez de Asúa, whose life he's just saved by throwing himself against the man to shield him from the bullets; before dying, a gush of blood bursting from his open mouth, Gisbert says with a kind of astonishment, as he clutches the lapels of the professor's overcoat with both hands, "They killed me, Don Luis." The already-dead were a minority compared to all those who would inevitably have to die. Second Lieutenant Reyes, a fifty-year-old Civil Guard about to retire, attends the parade for the Day of the Republic in civilian clothes and stands close to the presidential stand, when suddenly a few men he doesn't know shoot him down and disappear in the crowd. No one can identify the killers. On the hot night of May 7, Captain José Faraudo, a well-known Republican and Socialist, goes out with his wife after supper for a stroll along Calle de Lista; at the corner of Alcántara some young men come up behind him and shoot him point-blank. An avalanche or landslide or earthquake, all obey their own dynamic laws. After a certain catastrophic point, a fire doesn't cease until it has consumed the material that feeds it. Diminutive human figures gesticulate at the edges of its glare, throw water that evaporates before it reaches the flames or even enlivens them, shout as loud as they can, but the roar of the fire obliterates their voices. Captain Faraudo fell face-down on the ground, close to the illuminated window of the travel agency where Lita Abel and her brother looked every afternoon at the model of a Hamburg–New York ocean liner like the one they imagined would carry them to America early in the fall. Ignacio Abel first felt the sensation of physical alarm at words magnified by typography or amplified by microphones soon after his arrival in Germany in 1923; words written on posters and signs at demonstrations, filling entire squares with a deafening sound he'd never experienced before; words like weapons discharging, waking the roar of a crowd or silencing it, bursting above it with the metallic violence of enormous loudspeakers, multiplied and omnipresent on radios. When he left for Germany there were few radios in Spain, and those weren't powerful. In Berlin and then in Weimar, his initial difficulty with the language and his ignorance of the country's circumstances transformed political parades into spectacles of a threatening, primitive crudity: gales of flags, war-like anthems played by bands, millions of steps at a martial pace, crowds of veterans in old uniforms displaying the horrifying variety of their mutilations, and on a balcony, in the rear, almost invisible, a gesticulating doll who could barely be seen but whose shouts were exaggerated by loudspeakers above unmoving heads and then lost in the distance like the echoes of a distant battle. Thirteen years later, Ignacio Abel saw with horror his city and country inundated by that same flood. In the bullfight arena in Zaragoza, in the heat of a May noon, the feverish, hoarse voices of Anarchist orators proclaim the imminent approach of free love, the abolition of the state and of armies, and Libertarian Communism. In the bullfight arena in Madrid, in a vast eddy of red flags, before a huge portrait of Lenin, Don Francisco Largo Caballero, acclaimed by tens of thousands of throats as the Spanish Lenin, foresees, like an old apocalyptic prophet, the advent of the Union of Iberian Soviet Republics, the collectivization of land and factories, the annihilation of the bourgeoisie and man's exploitation of man.

Alone in Madrid, dedicated to assignments that were, for the most part, illusory — during the first months of the war he still went almost every day to his office in University City, examining plans and documents that were worthless now, inspecting abandoned construction sites — he spent the summer withdrawn into a fearful silence. The rational words he would have liked to say in a serene voice, the sweet ordinary words of his previous life, no longer mattered. At times he spoke aloud just to hear a voice in his empty house, his abandoned office; he imagined he was talking to his children, to Adela; he told them about his strange, solitary life in Madrid, the changes on the street and in people's clothing, the new attire that didn't exist a short while ago and yet formed part of a hallucinatory normality. He imagined conversations with Judith Biely as futilely as he wrote her letters he didn't know where to send and often didn't put down on paper. Perhaps there was a word he didn't say that might have prevented Judith's leaving Madrid. Perhaps he came close to finding her on the night of July 19 and leaping with her onto a train or persuading her not to take it. Things are about to happen but don't. The first flame is extinguished and doesn't cause the fire. The man grasping the pistol in his pocket doesn't take it out because of fear or nervousness, or because he thinks he sees someone who looks like the secret police watching him. His intended victim will walk past him and never know he was about to die. On Friday, July 10, Ignacio Abel finally gets in touch with Judith, after two weeks of not hearing from her. As they talk on the phone and she agrees to meet, Lieutenant José Castillo of the Assault Guard — slim, his hair combed straight back, round glasses, impeccable uniform, leather straps and boots gleaming — is sipping his coffee. At the end of the bar he sees some strangers who look suspicious and instinctively reaches for his pistol. He frequently receives anonymous letters and knows that at any moment he could be killed, just like his friend Captain Faraudo two months earlier, yet he still has the gallantry to go out alone and on foot to his quarters, crossing the center of Madrid. The strangers finish their coffee and leave. At the very last moment they were ordered to abort the attempt on Lieutenant Castillo's life.

He found no excuses even for himself. Having lost what mattered to him most, and knowing that he, too, could become one of the murdered, gave him no right to innocence. When did he begin to lie without effort or remorse? When did he become accustomed to hearing shots and calculating their distance and danger without going to the window? When did he see a pistol up close for the first time, not in a film, not in the holster of a police officer, but in the hand of someone he knew, bulging in a pocket, the front of a jacket, a pistol or revolver shown with almost the same ease as a lighter or fountain pen. In May, in the Café Lion, a few days after the murder of Captain Faraudo, Dr. Juan Negrín searched the pockets of his jacket, too tight for his Herculean bulk, after summarily cleaning his fingers, stained by red juice from the prawns he'd been eating, and instead of the pack of cigarettes Ignacio Abel imagined, he took out a pistol and put it on the table, next to the plate of prawns and mugs of beer, an unlikely pistol, so small it looked like a toy. "Look what I have to carry," he said, "and I can't even be on the street by myself anymore," and he pointed to the plainclothes policeman sitting alone at a table near the entrance, engrossed in sucking on a toothpick. In the gangster films he went to see with Judith Biely, pistols were objects with a lacquered shine that had a symbolic, almost immaterial quality, like lamps or flashlights, providing a bewitched immobility with their brightness, an abstract death without traces, not a hole or a tear or a stain in the close-fitting suit of the character who was shot, the silky evening dress of the beautiful but deceitful woman who deserved to die in the end. Gradually pistols were becoming real, without his paying attention, without his knowing how to notice them. He went to the Congress of Deputies to look for Negrín — he left, a secretary told him with a smile, he was dying of hunger and asked me to tell you he's waiting for you at the Café Lion — and on the counter of the checkroom he saw a wooden box filled with pistols under a neatly hand-lettered sign: *The honorable deputies are reminded that it is not permitted to carry firearms inside the parliamentary area.* Leafing through a copy of *Mundo Gráfico* in the anteroom of the dressmaker where Adela and the girl were trying on outfits, he saw the advertisement for Astra pistols among those for skin creams and pills to regulate menstruation and increase the size of one's breasts. *Protect your possessions and the security of your loved ones.*

In the photographs of the funeral of Second Lieutenant Reyes, murdered for unknown reasons during a disturbance in the crowd watching the military parade on the Day of the Republic, one can see that many of those accompanying the coffin, both military and civilian, carry unsheathed pistols. Although it's April 16 and the leaves have come out on the trees along the Paseo de la Castellana, everyone is in dark winter clothing. From the scaffolding at a construction site, pistols and machine pistols are fired over the heads of the funeral procession, and people run in all directions, seeking shelter in gardens and behind trees, and for some minutes the coffin of Second Lieutenant Reyes is abandoned in the puddles on the pavement. When the funeral reaches the East Cemetery several hours later, it has left a trail of more than twenty corpses on the streets. "You shouldn't be so confident, Don Ignacio. If you give me your authorization, I'll arrange for a couple of comrades from the union to escort you when you inspect the sites." Eutimio, the construction foreman at the Medical School, had come into Ignacio Abel's office with his cap in hand and before speaking had closed the door. "A lot of maniacs are running loose, Don Ignacio. None of us is safe." In the wind and rain, the crowd accompanying the funeral of Second Lieutenant Reyes goes up Calle de Alcalá, and when it reaches the Plaza de Manuel Becerra, a formation of Assault Guards armed with rifles bars the way. The shouts of "Long live" and "Death to" become more violent, as do the chanting of the rosary and the hymns. The crowd advances on the barrier of uniforms and the Assault Guards open fire at point-blank range. A slender, pale lieutenant with glasses and a close-fitting uniform pulls his pistol from its holster and fires into the chest of a young man with the look of a Fascist student who was advancing on him, his face red from singing a hymn. But there is a state of emergency and newspapers are censored, so the next day one can't find a clear report of what happened or the number of casualties. Or the announcement of a funeral is published but no one understands it because it was censored a day before news of the killing was published. Besides, you're in a hurry, you have no time and decide not to see what's in front of your eyes. Perhaps you're in a taxi, impatient to reach the appointment with your lover, and you pay no attention to the crowd in your way and aren't curious to know whose funeral it is, only irritated because you'll arrive late, because on account of that disturbance you'll lose some of the precious minutes of your meeting with her. From the shadows of the bedroom in Madame Mathilde's house, on the other side of the thicket, the closed shutters, the curtains, gunfire and panic at the end of the funeral of Second Lieutenant Reyes may have been a distant background noise for Ignacio Abel as he embraces Judith Biely, naked on a red quilt. You leave hurriedly at eight-thirty in the morning to go to work and don't see that across the street a car is parked with its windows down despite the cold and wind, and don't hear that the engine has just started, or when you do and look up, you see the barrels of the pistols ready to shoot. The police escort throws himself on Professor Jiménez de Asúa, wanting to push him out of the way of the bullets, and is shot instead and lies dying on the sidewalk as the killers flee on foot because the driver is clumsy or nervous and floods the engine. How long did it take Adela, not to accumulate small bits of evidence and clues, but to accept what she knew, to dare see what was in front of her? How many times did she go into his study and see that he'd forgotten to lock the drawer and decide not to open it? Only a few meters from where the police officer has died in a pool of blood that stains the hands and shirt cuffs of Jiménez de Asúa, the men at a bar discuss soccer, a fruit seller raises the metal shutters of his store—no one knows what just happened. A month later, the judge who sentenced the Falangist gunmen, easy to arrest because they fled on foot after failing to start the getaway car, leaves his house one morning, barely takes a few steps on the sidewalk, raises his hand to hail a taxi, and is struck by bursts of fire from a machine pistol. At the house of the lawyer Eduardo Ortega y Gasset, a child delivers a basket of eggs with a lid in the shape of a hen, saying it comes from a grateful client. The lawyer lifts the lid and a bomb explodes that destroys half his house and leaves him uninjured.

"Nobody wants to see anything, my friend, and the person who has seen is quiet and does everything possible to forget," Professor Rossman said one afternoon in the Café Aquarium de Madrid, a few minutes after shots were fired in the street and a young man was left dead, blown apart on the sidewalk of the Gran Vía, his skull shattered, blood and brain matter oozing down a shop window, "and if he does say anything they ridicule him or call him crazy or accuse him of provoking the disaster by irritating those at whom he points a finger. It's not so bad, they say, you're exaggerating, and with your exaggerations and warnings you put us all in danger. I didn't want to see or understand either. I saw when it was the only thing I could do. I saw and acted in time and managed to escape, but even then I was blind, I knew I was going to make another, more serious mistake but let myself be carried along, telling myself that perhaps I was wrong, perhaps my daughter was right, my daughter and her comrades. Back then, three years ago, we could have immigrated without much difficulty to America —you know that some distinguished colleagues are already there. Or we could have gone to Prague, or Paris, or come directly here, to this beautiful Madrid. I planned to write to you then. I read that the government of the Spanish Republic offered a chair to Professor Einstein and opened its arms to other exiles from Germany. But I did nothing. I didn't heed the warnings of my instinct, and even worse, of my rational intelligence. I didn't dare contradict my daughter. And not to contradict her, I didn't want to see what she didn't see. We reached the Soviet border and an official delegation boarded the train to welcome us. They embraced us, opened bottles of vodka to toast us, representatives of the anti-Fascist German people, they presented my daughter with a large bouquet of red roses. But I looked and I saw. I saw the beggars in the station, was aware of the fear in the other passengers' eyes at the approach of my daughter's comrades who boarded the train to welcome us, aware of their rancor when they looked at us, their panic if you spoke to them. But I didn't want to know what I was seeing. Forgive me, a foreigner, for saying this to you: you Spaniards don't want to see either, you pretend not to hear."

Perhaps that was also the afternoon when he saw the first dead body. That was why he still remembered the face, or what was left of it, with more detail than almost all the faces of the dead he saw in Madrid during the summer and the first weeks of that golden, sanguinary autumn before his flight, his anxiety-ridden and shame-filled desertion. Ignacio Abel hadn't heard the first shot, hadn't recognized it in the midst of the traffic noise on the other side of the large window in the café where he was talking with Professor Rossman, close to the intersection of Calle de Alcalá and the Gran Vía, at the hour when people were beginning to leave their offices. The ear must be trained: at first it doesn't recognize gunshots. They sound more like small rockets, like a car backfiring. At a sidewalk café on Calle Torrijos, some young men fired at a group of Falangists drinking wine in the shade of an awning, and in the shooting a girl was killed who was sitting alone at a nearby table and whom no one knew. A dry, brief crack that in no way resembles gunshots in films or the pathetic click heard when someone pretends to fire a weapon on the stage. In retaliation for the attack on Calle Torrijos, a car stopped on the sidewalk in front of the General Union of Workers and some milkmen walking out of the building were riddled with bullets, the spilled milk slowly combining with blood. Ignacio Abel realized something was happening when heads looked up at the other tables in the Café Aquarium: the next series of shots was more recognizable because of the confused shouts that accompanied them, and because a moment later the traffic came to a halt — car engines, taxi horns, the high-pitched bells of streetcars. Suddenly no one was left at the outdoor tables, as if, after hearing a crash, a flock of birds had quickly taken flight. There were chairs overturned, glasses of beer and untouched cups of coffee on the round marble tables, bottles of seltzer trapping light in the shade of the awnings, lit cigarettes in the ashtrays. Behind panes of glass and at the open windows of nearby buildings, people watched in silence. Lying across the sidewalk, a body still twitching, one hand extended as if clawing at the ground, one leg trembling. He looked like a rag doll or a mannequin, wearing an impeccable suit of light-colored, lightweight fabric, a good shoe on the trembling foot, a sock with a diamond pattern. Half of his head showed the straight part in pomaded hair; the other half was a pulp of blood and brain matter. Tossed to the ground, stained with blood, their pages blowing in the gentle, late afternoon breeze of early June, were the Falangist newspapers the young man had been hawking next to the café terrace when a car stopped beside him long enough for the window to be lowered and the barrels of two pistols to appear, according to one of the few witnesses, a man whose voice trembled between gulps of cognac, surrounded by waiters and patrons as he described the scene. "Today it was their turn," observed someone near Ignacio Abel, "and yesterday some young gentlemen from the Falange killed a man on the corner who was selling the Communist paper. One to one, like a soccer match. Tomorrow they'll break the tie." By then an ambulance had taken away the body and some municipal workers had cleaned the sidewalk with brooms and bursts of water from a hose, and a clerk from a hat shop passed a damp cloth over the shop window, supervised by a man in a pinstriped suit who smoked a cigar and bent toward the glass to be certain no trace of blood remained. A couple of Assault Guards in high boots and blue uniforms inspected the sidewalk where people were walking again, more numerous now and better dressed, on their way to movie theaters or coming out of them, beneath the light of the street lamps that had just been turned on, beneath the marquees with announcements of films, beside the recently lit shop windows. Ignacio Abel and Professor Rossman sat down again at their table next to the window. Under the electric light the professor seemed older, less well dressed in the same dark suit he'd worn in the winter, more singular in his misfortune, his exile, the torment of a clairvoyance that no one paid attention to and that never did him any good, never helped him avoid any error or prevent any future trouble. On the sidewalk, among the tables that were occupied again, young Falangists peddled their newspapers, some of them defiantly wielding pistols now that the Assault Guards had withdrawn, shouting slogans that erased traffic noise and that people sitting on the café terrace seemed not to hear, just as no one seemed to see the blue shirts and leather straps and the metallic gleam of weapons. On the corner of Calle de Alcalá and the Gran Vía, other Falangists watched the flow of people and traffic, on the alert to prevent another attack. Even from a distance, Ignacio Abel recognized Adela's brother.

Perhaps that was also the first time he heard shots so close by. And never before had he seen a dead body in the street, struck down unexpectedly, not stiff and solemn in a bed, dressed in mourning, lit by candles; not lying on the boards of a wagon, covered by empty sacks. Ignacio Abel paid for the coffees, Professor Rossman's two glasses of anise, the ham sandwich he'd devoured, sputtering bread and bits of food as he spoke; his former teacher was undergoing a deterioration that Igna-

236

cio Abel had observed at each stage with some physical revulsion as well as remorse, an oppressive sense of responsibility. An early summer heat made the signs worse (in Madrid, summer arrived abruptly, suffocatingly, at the beginning or in the middle of May, following the rain and cold of an unpleasant spring): his bald head, the odor of stale sweat and uric acid emanating from his clothes, the bitter coffee and sweet anise on his breath. Perhaps he really hadn't done anything to help Professor Rossman aside from listening to his ramblings; out of stinginess, distraction, or laziness, one doesn't do for a person in desperate need what wouldn't be difficult to do. They left the café, and in the air on the Gran Vía one could almost touch the silky quality of May twilights. "You Spaniards don't want to see what's happening in your country," Professor Rossman said, as indifferent as a prophet or a visionary to the sensual realities of the world, the sweetness of the air and the beauty of the women passing by, the calligraphy of neon lights, one after another, the name of a store, a brand of soap. He too had become accustomed to the normality of exile, to being a nobody after having had a respected name and an eminent position as a professor, to living with his daughter in a squalid pensión whose rent he couldn't always pay on time. "You Spaniards think things are solid, that what has endured until now will remain forever. You don't know that the world can collapse. We didn't know when the war began in '14, we were even blinder than you, stupefied and drunk with happiness, jubilantly invading the recruitment offices, marching in step behind military bands playing patriotic anthems, parading on the way to the slaughterhouse, parents pushing their sons to enlist, women throwing flowers at them from the windows. The most illustrious writers glorifying war in the newspapers, the great crusade of German culture!" He spoke in German, as if he were giving a speech, and some passersby stared at him: the bald oval head, the suit of anachronistic mourning, between formality and filth, his voice guttural and foreign, the black briefcase clutched in his arms as if it contained something valuable, his diplomas and certificates in Gothic characters, the letters of recommendation written in several languages, the obsolete passport with a seal stamped in red on the first page — *Juden–Juif* — the safe-conduct passes or letters of transit typed in Cyrillic characters, copies of visa applications, disheartening notices from the American embassy in Madrid, sheaves of international newspapers dismantled with scissors, full of underlinings, exclamation points, question marks, scribbled notes in the margins. Ignacio Abel regretted inviting him to have two drinks: he'd probably eaten little or nothing during the day aside from the ham sandwich. "You'd like not to see but you do see, my dear man. You pretend you don't hear, just like those people in the café when shots were fired. But you're an attentive person despite yourself. I talk and talk and the only person who pays any attention at all is you. I telephone and you're the only one who answers. When I go to an office it's always closed or about to close, and when I go to see someone, he can't see me, or if he makes an appointment it's for sometime in the future, and when I arrive they tell me he isn't in or there's been a misunderstanding and I have to come back a week later. Except for you, no one's at home or in the office when I call. They think I'll grow tired or won't come back or fall ill, but I always come back, on the day I was told and at the exact time, not because I'm obstinate but because I don't have anything else to do. You, my dear friend, are so busy you can't understand me. You don't know what it is to wake in the morning and have the whole day, your whole life, before you, with no occupation other than requesting things no one is obliged to give me, or seeking out people who don't wish to see me. Or worse, attempting to sell things no one wants to buy, except for you, my good friend, who out of pity bought I don't know how many of those fountain pens that scratch the paper and stain everything. At least my daughter has some German students now, also thanks to you and your wife, your delightful children, and your children's friends whom you and your wife have persuaded, I don't know how, to study German. I should give lessons too instead of going around trying to sell pens with fake brand names, visiting offices, requesting documents, but you were my student and know me, I don't have patience for something as slow as teaching a language. They seem a lie, those days at the School! You remember, first in Weimar, then in the new building, in Dessau. I didn't want to know what was happening outside those clean white walls, our beautiful world of large windows and right angles. The beauty of all useful things, do you remember? The integrity of the materials, the pure forms conceived to fulfill a specific task. I don't remember reading in the paper that Hitler had been named Reich Chancellor. Another government crisis, one of many, the same politicians going and coming, approximately the same names, and I didn't have the time or the desire to read newspapers or listen to speeches. There were more important things to do, practical, urgent things, classes, the administration of the School, technical problems that had to be resolved, my wife sick, my daughter causing me so much distress because she didn't dare speak to anyone or look anyone in the eye and then suddenly became a Communist, and I couldn't find out who infected her. People obsessed by politics seemed as incomprehensible to me as those obsessed by sports or horseracing. I thought my daughter was deranged, intoxicated by the books she was always reading, by Soviet films, by the eternal meetings often held in my house, hours and hours discussing, smoking, analyzing the articles in their newspapers after reading them aloud, her entire life from the time she woke up until she went to bed, growing paler, somnambulistic, looking at me as if I lived on another planet or were her class enemy, the Social-Fascist father more harmful than a Nazi, the hypocritical collaborator in the exploitation of the working class, the corrupt bourgeois advocating imperialist warfare. She inherited her mother's musical talent and voice. She left the conservatory and stopped singing because opera was elitist, decadent entertainment. That was my daughter. She stopped taking care of herself and became ugly. You've seen her: she's managed to be ugly and look much older than she is. Now she resembles the female guards in Soviet hotels and the typists at the Comintern. What can we do, my friend? How little is in our hands! Acting honestly, fulfilling our duty, doing our work well. And what good is it? Saying what our conscience orders us to say, though no one wants to listen and we earn the hatred not only of our enemies but also of those friends who prefer not to know the truth or see what's in front of them. My daughter didn't want to see what was in full view from the moment we reached Soviet customs. Neither did I, for her sake, because I saw it as being disloyal to her and to those people who offered us asylum when we had to leave Germany. And now I see the posters in Madrid and it frightens me, hammers and sickles and portraits, as if I were back in Moscow, or they'd come after us, looking for us. I saw the parade on May Day, the red shirts, the uniformed militias, the children marching in time, raising their fists, the portraits of Lenin and Stalin, that giant shield with the hammer and sickle high over the heads of people in the midst of red flags. Those people can't imagine what their lives would be like if they're ever unfortunate enough to have what they've been taught to dream of. I went there with my daughter and would have liked to leave as fast as I could, but she was hypnotized, you wouldn't have believed it if you had seen her, after everything they did to her in Moscow, she remained at my side, clutching my arm, her eyes filled with tears when the band playing 'The Internationale'— badly, of course — passed by, and she raised her fist, she whose Soviet comrades almost murdered her, the same ones who had welcomed her with a bouquet of red roses when we crossed the border. So there's no cure, no one's safe, no matter how far you think you've run. Listen to me, my friend, you have to escape from here as well. The blue shirts and the brown shirts and the black shirts and the red shirts are at the door, and it's only a matter of time before they've infected everything. Look at the map and see all the space they've occupied. There's no place for people like us. No one will defend us. Hitler has broken the Versailles Treaty and invaded the demilitarized zone with his armies, and the British and the French haven't confronted him. I'm expecting letters from the Americas — not from the United States, not yet, though Mies and Gropius are there, and Breuer too. I write to them and they take a long time to answer. They say they'll do what they can, but it's difficult, you know, because of my daughter's whim, because it's recorded in our passports that we traveled to the Soviet Union, and for that reason they don't trust us. Perhaps to Cuba or Mexico first, and from there it'll be easier to enter the United States. You think there's still time, don't try to fool me, you hear what I say and think I'm exaggerating or beginning to lose my mind. You feel safe because you're in your city and your country and at heart you think that I and others like me belong to another species, another race. But time's running out, my friend, it slips away from us more and more quickly, and from you too, from those like us . . ."

At times the noise drowned out Professor Rossman's voice: the traffic, the jovial conversations of people walking by, the music of a hurdy-gurdy or from the radio in a bar, an ambulance or police siren, the tremor in the pavement when a metro train passed, a man peddling cigarettes and neckties, the lazy rhythm of nightfall in the center of Madrid, when summer was announced by the scents in the air and the touch of a breeze, verbena dust, recently watered geraniums, push-carts selling ice cream cones and meringues. Above the street and the traffic, the windows open to the mild night air, the Telephone Company Building stood in triumph, crowned by the luminous sphere of a clock. The night, the vibration of the city intensified his longing for Judith Biely, who was traveling outside Madrid on one of her educational excursions with American students to Toledo or Ávila. Ignacio Abel wanted to listen to Professor Rossman and accompany him to his pensión, but what he felt deep inside was an unspeakable repugnance. What he really wanted was to be alone and let himself drift through the human anthill of the street, waiting for Judith to miraculously appear around a corner, looking for him, having returned early from her trip. But it was late: the scarlet light of the hands on the Telephone Company's clock pointed to eight. Now he remembered that he had promised Adela he'd be home not much after eight-thirty for a large family dinner, somebody's birthday or saint's day. In the elevator he smelled the heavy perfume of Adela's mother and the liniment her father applied in massive amounts to relieve his rheumatism. From the landing he heard the family voices, the collective pleasure of the Ponce-Cañizares Salcedo clan at coming together en masse. Before entering the living room, Ignacio Abel crossed the hall toward his bedroom, but he spotted the light in the children's room and went in to give them a kiss. It was then that for the first time he saw a pistol in his own house: his son held the butt in both hands, one eye closed, and aimed at the mirror, following the lighthearted instructions of his uncle Víctor, who wore the blue shirt and leather straps under his sports jacket.

15

UNCLE VÍCTOR STOOD behind him and grasped his wrists because the pistol was too heavy for the boy to hold level. With an instructor's brusqueness, he had Miguel spread his legs, explaining that he had to have a firm stance so the recoil from firing didn't throw him off balance, that he mustn't believe the foolishness in movies — you don't squeeze the trigger with the pistol next to your hip but keep it raised to eye level in order to aim, and you hold tight with both hands. Uncle Víctor, whom Miguel admired so much as he grew older and projected onto him a vaguely romantic masculinity — even more so now, since a change had recently become visible in Víctor that Ignacio Abel hadn't noticed because he paid no attention to his brother-in-law. A general vagueness always surrounded his changing aspirations, which had almost nothing in common except a lack of practical substance and the indulgent, wishful spirit with which Adela received them. He was too precocious, but sooner or later he'd find his way. He'd been sickly as a boy, with weak lungs, spending time in a sanatorium in the Sierra, which had affected his character and held him back in primary and secondary school. Wasn't it inevitable that his parents and older sister were sometimes more permissive or more protective than necessary? He studied law but apparently didn't complete the course of study or had to extend it longer than usual because he decided to complement it with studies in philosophy — more appropriate, according to his sister, to his literary or artistic temperament; he undoubtedly would finish his studies with brilliant grades and perhaps sit for a competitive examination for a government position, which would give him the free time needed to cultivate his artistic tastes without fear of poverty. Slim volumes of verse with the austere typography of *Índice* or the *Revista de Occidente* occupied more space in the literary, smoke-filled disorder of his room than the numerous legal texts he'd once consulted so often that his mother, Doña Cecilia, had feared that so much studying of thousands of pages of tiny print would weaken his health and ruin his eyes, just as she feared that his immoderate fondness for cigarettes would eventually damage his lungs, forcing him to return to the sanatorium. It seemed he'd begun to write verses, though he was shy and very much a perfectionist and decided not to show them even to his older sister. A poem of his was accepted, but it took so long to appear in print that Víctor became discouraged with poetry and acquired a passionate interest in the theater. He withdrew to the house in the Sierra for several weeks during the winter to write a drama somewhere between symbolist and social realist. He submitted the first draft for Adela's consideration, requesting two things: that she be sincere in her criticism and that she not show the writing to her husband, a man totally lacking in literary sensibility, and informing her in confidence of the possibility that Cipriano Rivas Cherif might offer to stage the work. The first draft wasn't detailed, and the storm of theatrical inspiration didn't last long, perhaps because the prospects for the drama's premiere soon became uncertain, given the crudeness of the public and the blindness of the producers, interested only in the risk-free money provided by renowned authors. Hadn't García Lorca made a fool of himself with that overly poetic work in which the actors came onstage dressed as butterflies, grasshoppers, and crickets, provoking the coarsest jokes in the parterre? Adela would look at her brother and wish she didn't notice what she was sure her husband saw, a certain weakness of character, the fascination he felt for things he'd just discovered and soon forgot, no tangible occupation or project ever solidifying for him. In that regard, Don Francisco de Asís recognized with genealogical regret that his only son had turned out more Salcedo than Ponce-Cañizares. When it seemed that in spite of everything he was about to complete his two courses of study at the same time, after a period of prodigious seclusion with his books, it turned out that he'd temporarily abandoned the study of law, so enthralled by philosophy he forgot to let the family know of his decision; above all else he had to start earning a living—he was almost thirty and didn't think it honorable to go on being supported by his father; he'd attend night classes while he worked in the patent company owned by a friend of his, owner or second in command, so close a friend he'd offered him, a newcomer, a high salary and a position of responsibility. At dinner, Ignacio Abel, his head lowered, listened to Adela's rendition of her brother's new prospects, and she, suddenly aware of Víctor's untenable vagueness, defended him all the more vigorously. "Is Uncle Víctor really going to be an inventor?" Miguel's innocent question provoked a subtle smile on his father's lips, and fear in Adela that any comment from Ignacio would make her brother look ridiculous in front of the children. "Not an inventor," Lita corrected him, intensifying without realizing it her mother's humiliation. "Since Uncle Víctor's almost a lawyer by now, he's going to help inventors so nobody cheats them and steals their discoveries."

The almost-lawyer had girlfriends to whom he nearly became engaged, and through one of them he had been working for a time or was about to work for the theater company La Barraca, its repertoire dominated by classical and poetic works, and for them his knowledge of staging and lighting was quite adequate; he'd acquired it by studying foreign theatrical magazines, written in languages Víctor seemed to have learned when taking informal lessons with native teachers—the lively spontaneity of conversation preferable to rote memorization or the dullness of grammar—overcoming the legendary slowness with languages that afflicted both sides of the family equally, as Don Francisco de Asís admitted openly. Busy as a set or lighting designer on tour with the company—his father wasn't aware of its political significance, in part because of ignorant innocence, in part because he took it for granted that a theater company devoted to honor dramas and mystery plays would be composed of people as solidly reactionary as he was—Víctor hadn't been able to appear for final examinations at one of the two schools where he was still matriculated, or perhaps at neither of them. But that didn't really matter, for once he began working it wouldn't be so urgent for him to obtain his degree to establish himself in a position. And in the unlikely event that the practically certain job in the patent office fell through—guided by his incorrigible good faith, Víctor sometimes trusted more than he should have in his friends' promises and came away bitterly offended—couldn't Ignacio Abel find something temporary for him in the offices of University City or the studio of one of his architect friends, or look into the matter with Dr. Juan Negrín or one of those high-ranking public officers whom he knew? Didn't everything in Spain now depend more on political influence than on personal merit, no matter how high that might be, especially if you came from a family of monarchist importance, with "profound Spanish and Catholic roots," as Don Francisco de Asís declaimed in his tremendous organ voice at the family table? But Adela knew her husband wouldn't lift a finger for her brother. She would have to overcome her pride and appeal on his behalf. Ignacio Abel understood what Adela was suggesting, but he wasn't about to give in, wasn't going to spare her a single step or the humiliation of begging. He'd make some mild, irrelevant remark that he'd have prepared ahead of time. If Víctor had mastered so many languages and possessed such varied talents, why hadn't he found any work, not even as a clerk? Couldn't Don Francisco de Asís place him as a page in some provincial delegation?

Ignacio Abel didn't see the changes, subtle at first, and not only in matters of wardrobe. His brother-in-law's explanations, vague as always, were beginning to have a political tinge, an element of hysteria. The same people controlled everything in Spain. To accomplish anything, one had to submit to the political directives of a few intellectuals who meddled in magazines, newspapers, and the theater, and the teaching in university lecture halls was so dominated by Soviet agitators that classes were not worth attending. And women were renouncing their femininity. Some went to the university in berets and mannish jackets, and argued louder than men, never taking the cigarette out of their mouth. How long would it be before they shouted, "Children yes, husbands no," the way they did in Russia? Once again, Víctor fell victim to his own idealism, unaware of the price he would have to pay if he fully embraced the ideas he was preaching, the doors that were already closing because of his life decisions. Disillusioned by the hostility he found in literary cliques, he'd stopped frequenting the gatherings in Altolaguirre's printing house or those refined Sunday teas at the home of María y Araceli Zambrano, increasingly attended by suspicious-looking people. Others wanted it both ways: he gave himself body and soul to what he believed, especially since going to the founding meeting of the Falange at the Teatro de la Comedia, overwhelmed by the eloquence and gallantry of José Antonio Primo de Rivera. That man didn't talk like a politician, he talked like a poet. Nations in their moments of crisis were moved not by political leaders but by poets and visionaries. That his brother-in-law sometimes appeared in a blue shirt seemed as inconsequential to Ignacio Abel as his former enthusiasms for the black cape and wild hair of a bohemian and the absurd workers' coveralls worn by the young university gentlemen of La Barraca. The political manifestoes he now left behind after his visits were as florid and vacuous as the literary magazines he'd read with the same devotion a few years back. He stopped wearing rings on his fingers and reclining on the sofa smoking cigarettes. Now he'd become expert in motorcycles — as soon as he had a steady job he'd begin saving to buy one — and he brought his nephew Miguel photographs of soccer players and cycling stars, talking to him of sports about which he suddenly knew everything. He walked now striking his heels harder on the floor and combed his hair straight back, revealing the bony structure of his skull and the progress of the hair loss he inherited from his mother's family, the bald Salcedo heads immortalized in oil portraits and daguerreotypes for over a century. He began to laugh in sonorous guffaws, to shake hands in a virile fashion, obliquely curving his palm downward. He sat at the table with his shirtsleeves rolled up, wielding his knife and fork with a soldier's severity, forearms darker now, tanned by outdoor exercise, by the marches and sham military maneuvers he attended on Sundays in the Sierra, to which he promised Miguel he'd take him sometime, without his father knowing, he said, lowering his voice in a conspiratorial tone. When he came in and walked along the hallway the others could hear the heels of his boots resounding and smell the oiled leather. The children got up from the table without asking permission to run to greet him, and Adela got up too and followed them, containing the joy awakened in her by the surprise appearance of her brother, overcoming the silent censure of Ignacio Abel, who remained alone at the dining room table with the dishes served and the soup growing cold. Among the privileges of a brother was appearing unannounced at his sister's house.

"Brother-in-law, you don't need to pretend. I know you don't like my ideas."

"What ideas? It's uniforms, isn't it? Uniforms are more important than ideas, considering the love all of you have for them."

"Who are 'all of you,' may I ask?"

"All of you. Red shirts, blue shirts, brown shirts, black shirts. Aren't there some in Cataluña who wear green shirts? The golden age of the tailoring industry. Did you people make a pact with the Communists so they'd wear the light blue shirts and you'd wear the darker ones? Not to mention the boots, the leather straps, the neckerchiefs, the parades marching in step, the flags."

"Papá, the uniforms are pretty."

"You be quiet, girl, when adults are speaking. Do you play at wearing uniforms now in the schoolyard? Do you play at singing anthems and attacking one another with clubs and sticks when you meet on the street?"

"Ignacio, that's no way to speak to your daughter."

"You have to be retarded to put on a uniform for fun, for theater. To play at armies."

"Brother-in-law, don't say that, we'll get angry."

"I've said it and don't take it back."

"I'll bet when you see the Socialist Pioneers marching down Calle de Argüelles on Sunday when you come back from the Sierra, you're not quite so irritated."

"I feel exactly the same shame. The same revulsion. Everyone the same, marching in time, clenching their fists, clenching their teeth. I don't care about the color of the shirt. I don't like children praying like parrots with their hands together, and I don't like raising fists and singing 'The Internationale' in the same tone you'd use for 'With Flowers for Mary.' Decent people don't hide behind a uniformed crowd."

"When you get like this, it's better to leave you alone."

Adela, who feared his silence so much, was more frightened now of his cold rage, spoken with a conscious effort not to raise his voice and not to look in anyone's eyes.

"I don't think that's a bad idea."

"It's a matter of generations, Adela." The esthete suddenly became philosophical, speaking with an unfamiliar tone of equanimity, repeating the verbal food that nourished him. "Your husband's a very intelligent man but he's from another day. I know that and pay no attention. You have to be young to keep up with a time that struggles to be young, as José Antonio always says. You're right about one thing, Ignacio, and it's that ideas change just like clothes. There are people who still wear an old-fashioned frock coat, a beard, high shoes, a pince-nez. They're still in the days of the horse and carriage and don't know we're in the age of the automobile and the airplane. I don't blame you, you're from a different time. We're in the twentieth century—"

"Extraordinary." Ignacio Abel stood, sending away with an authoritarian gesture the maid who was carrying in the dessert tray. "Now it'll turn out I'm old-fashioned and you're progressive. This is extraordinary."

"Old-fashioned or progressive, left or right, they're all anachronistic concepts, brother-in-law. You're either with youth or with age, with what's born or what dies, with strength or with weakness."

"Uniforms are a fairly old-fashioned style."

"What's old are uniforms with decorations and crests, the ones used to indicate the privileges of powerful men! Now our uniform stresses equality, over and above individualistic stupidities and effeminacies. The worker's shirt, the loose, practical clothing of the athlete, the pride of everyone beating with the same heart!"

"And the pistols?"

"To defend ourselves, brother-in-law, because we'd be peaceful people if they hadn't declared war on us. We salute with an open hand, not with a clenched fist. An open hand for everyone, because we don't believe in parties or classes. The boys who'd go out to sell our newspapers were shot down by the Communists until we learned to shoot too. This degenerate government attacks our headquarters and locks up Falangists while it lets the red militias do whatever they please."

"The government of the Republic obeys the law and puts criminals and killers in prison."

"The government of the Republic is a Marxist puppet."

Suddenly Ignacio Abel saw the inanity of the conversation in which he'd made himself an accessory with unnecessary vehemence. Just listening to the gibberish was degrading. He saw his brother-in-law not as a Fascist but as what he'd always seemed, an idiot. An idiot in a blue shirt, black leather straps, and absurd riding boots, besotted by cheap newspaper lyricism, impassioned barracks harangues, and pieces of poetic prose badly translated from German or Italian. An idiot who perhaps at heart wasn't a bad person, who felt real affection for his sister, his niece and nephew, for whom he always brought presents, comic books about war or cowboys for the boy, princesses for the girl, a ball, a doll that cried when you bent it, who'd sat them on his knees to tell them stories when they were little and been eager to help when one of them fell sick. Or perhaps he really was a thug, in which case Ignacio Abel made the mistake of not taking him seriously.

And now the great idiot or great thug was holding his son's arms from behind and teaching him to aim with a pistol, bigger and more obscene in his delicate hands, almost translucent like the skin at his temples, hands that didn't have the strength to hold a soccer ball or grasp the climbing rope in gym class, hands that when Miguel was born were as fragile and soft as a gecko's feet. Watching his weak chest rise and fall on feverish nights, he'd feared his son had pneumonia or tuberculosis. Stronger boys hit him in the schoolyard of the Institute School when his sister wasn't around to defend him. So awkward in sports, so likely to come home from excursions with sunstroke or bruises from falling, because he was clumsy or because other children pushed him and he didn't know how to defend himself; living in the clouds, so dependent on Lita, with whom he shared games and movie magazines when he should have been with boys his own age, too fond of spending time with the maids, listening to the plebeian songs they sang at top volume. He didn't acknowledge to himself the degree to which this disapproval tarnished his feelings for his son. He disliked the boy's weakness and at the same time felt an urgent need to protect him; he watched him on the sly, alarmed by something he couldn't define. Miguel felt his father's presence, and knowing he was being observed made him all the more insecure and awkward, or produced in him an outburst of audacity or capriciousness that seemed calculated to make his father lose patience. And so instead of lowering the pistol when he saw him appear in the mirror or handing it to his uncle to avoid disaster, Miguel aimed it at his father, and a moment later took a step back and cowered, trembling, closed his eyes, feeling the blow of the slap that hadn't yet struck his pale face, instantly red, burning as if in a sudden attack of fever.

Watching his son's face and his brother-in-law's so close together, Ignacio Abel saw a resemblance between them. Not just some features, sketched in the boy and crudely visible in the adult, but a deeper resemblance, perhaps the secret weakness that would explain their resentment of him, the demanding father and disdainful brother-in-law, mother's spouse, sister's spouse, an intruder who couldn't be trusted. He didn't want Miguel to grow up resembling his uncle, having the same aquiline curve in his nose, the same scant, curly down on his upper lip, the same stare between sly and myopic, as if a part of him had retreated deep inside. Víctor took the pistol from the boy and said to Ignacio Abel, "Come on, man, don't be like that, we were only playing." Ignacio felt the rage growing in him, uncontrolled and yet as cold as the palms of his hands. He was going to slap his son, and while part of him was ashamed, another part moved ahead, animated by the boy's fear, offended by his instinctive gesture of seeking refuge in his uncle, turning to Víctor to feel protected from his own father. He was aware of the physical impulse that sustained and propelled his rage but did nothing to contain it, and his son's evident weakness, the tremor of his wet lower lip, instead of dissuading him, angered him more. Miguel took a step or two back, looking at his uncle, who'd moved away after placing the pistol in his shoulder holster and buttoning his jacket, as if to make it more invisible, intimidated or perhaps sensing that the more the boy wanted to take refuge in him, the greater his father's rage would be. "Come on, man," he repeated, but with a curt gesture Ignacio Abel silenced him, and Víctor moved to one side, all his manliness gone, fearful, in spite of his boots and leather straps and the pistol in its leather holster, that the punishment would fall on him as well.

He looked Miguel in the eye as the boy backed into the closet mirror where a few seconds earlier he'd seen himself as a movie hero. At what moment does one reach the point of no return, the hateful thing that can no longer be erased? Towering over his son, he raised his right hand, thought about leaving the room, slamming the door, and joining the obnoxious family celebration, perhaps shouting at his brother-in-law, demanding that if he ever wanted to set foot in his house again it would have to be without a pistol and a blue shirt. But that's not what he did. He didn't spare himself the future shame or indignity of hiding from Judith Biely the kind of act she wouldn't have forgiven, that would have made her see in him the shadow of someone she didn't know. His hand came down, cutting through the air, open and violent, as heavy as a weapon, the palm much wider and harder than the boy's face. He hit him noticing the sting on his palm and the flush of heat on his face. His son's face turned to the wall. The boy's eyes filled with tears, looked up at him from below, as if from the interior of a burrow, fear replaced by resentment, his cheek scarlet, a trickle of urine rolling down one of his thin legs. As Ignacio Abel turned to leave the room, he saw his daughter standing motionless by the door where she kept her school notebooks. She had seen it all.

16

ISOLATED GUNFIRE ON a fresh morning in May, the air perfumed with mountain aromas: thyme, rosemary flowers, white petals with yellow pistils among the bright rockrose leaves. The forest cut down a few years earlier to level the ground for University City was coming back to life on the cleared land and inclines of unfinished construction sites, the open spaces that weren't playing fields yet. The whistles of bullets blended with the whistles of swallows; gunshots like hollow explosions of fireworks at a distant fair, beyond the clattering typewriters and open windows of the drafting office, where draftsmen and typists looked out with more curiosity than alarm, trying to determine where the shots were coming from. The air still clean, the ashtrays and wastebaskets empty, the secretaries' lips and nails bright red. He liked that time of morning, the entire day ahead, the impulse to work still not exhausted by fatigue or tedium. Perhaps the mail clerk had been distracted by the commotion and delivery would be late: he'd come at his slow pace, his expression both self-important and servile, holding the large tray, and when he entered the office, ceremoniously requesting permission to do so, perhaps Ignacio Abel would recognize among the official letters an envelope with Judith's handwriting. As soon as they parted they began writing to each other. They wanted to relieve with written words the emptiness of their time apart, prolong a conversation they never grew tired of. More gunfire now, not pistols but rifles. At what moment had his ear grown accustomed, begun to differentiate? Better to behave as if he'd heard nothing: not look up from the desk, the drawing board, keep busy each minute of the morning, dictating letters, receiving calls, insisting against all odds that construction would go on; he'd tell his secretary to return to her typewriter instead of spreading rumors about gunfire; he'd call the Assault Guard barracks and request that they send reinforcements, though it would be more practical to call Dr. Negrín, who'd bring to bear his political influence. Much more vigilance would be required night and day at the building sites now that the Anarchists of the National Confederation of Labor wanted to declare another construction strike.

He should have spoken to Negrín some time ago but always put it off. He should have told him he'd been invited to spend the next academic year in America and hadn't done so; he should have asked his opinion before accepting the invitation but said nothing to him; now he would have to tell him he'd accepted without requesting official permission. He hadn't said anything to Adela and his children either. The invitation from Burton College had arrived in a long, ivory-colored envelope, and when he saw it on the mail tray he quickly put it in his pocket, then in the locked drawer where he hid Judith's letters and photos. He responded with vague remarks when the children asked about the promised trip, the nocturnal journey in a sleeper car to Paris, the Atlantic crossing, the elevated trains and skyscrapers in New York, the Automats, which Lita had read about in encyclopedias and illustrated magazines. He put off the uncomfortable moment of reciting the explanation he'd elaborated, aware that he had put himself in the contemptible position of lying when he promised them, months earlier, something no one had asked for: it wasn't a good idea for the children to miss a year of school, he planned to say; the salary was lower than it had seemed at first; there was no guarantee he'd be commissioned to design the library building (a clearing in a forest on the other side of the ocean, a few lines sketched on the broad sheets of a notebook, barely the shadow of a form that perhaps would never exist, as uncertain as his future). He discovered that a lie was a loan for which usurious interest accumulated in a short time, and new lies extended the time at an even higher rate and left him at the mercy of increasingly impatient creditors. Construction was advancing much more slowly than anticipated (everything so difficult, so slow, applications paralyzed in offices, machinery scant and defective, the means of delivery and transport primitive, the men unwilling, working in the sun with knotted handkerchiefs on their heads, breathing heavily, saliva-soaked cigarette butts hanging from their mouths, looking around in fear of gunmen and assailants); even if the construction strike was not total, it was clear that University City would not be inaugurated in October. To leave before the end—wasn't that disloyal to Negrín? Besides, Judith Biely took it for granted he'd travel alone to America. Ignacio Abel wasn't lying when he told her he wanted that as much as she did, but he did lie when he led her to assume his wife and children knew about a decision that by now was irreversible. It wasn't a complete lie, perhaps merely a truth delayed. Sooner or later that difficult familial conversation would be inevitable; he imagined it so clearly, it was almost as if it had already taken place (Miguel's serious, aggrieved face, Adela's expression of confirmed disillusionment, his daughter's peeved but unshakable faith in him), as when the alarm clock rings and you dream that you've already gotten up and showered and the dream allows you a few more minutes of uneasy sleep.

The days and weeks were slipping away without his taking action or saying anything; summer was approaching and there was less and less time until his journey was a problem only because others would have to find out about it, like a bank teller who thinks his embezzlement is less of a crime because it hasn't been discovered yet. (It had been the same twelve years earlier, when he was going to leave for Germany: the boy sick, almost a newborn, Adela's collapse after the birth, and he, the letter confirming his trip in his pocket, saying nothing, waiting.) The appearance of normality was in and of itself a poor antidote to disaster. Working every day, presenting an irreproachable face to the world, confirming that the landscape of buildings and avenues on the other side of the picture windows increasingly resembled the great utopian model of University City, its abstract buildings surrounded by groves of trees and playing fields, its straight avenues and winding paths along which groups of students would walk someday, in spite of the slowness of the work, the scarcity of money, the stalled applications, the apocalyptic propagandists for the strike and the Anarchist revolution who appeared at work sites brandishing red-and-black flags and automatic pistols. Getting up each morning and having breakfast with Adela and the children, reading the paper, while through the open balconies the fresh morning air came in, perfumed by the blossoms of young acacias; while his desire for Judith throbbed in secret (he'd call her as soon as he left the house, from the first telephone booth; better yet, he'd close himself in his study right now and ask her in a low voice to meet him as soon as she could, wherever she liked, in the house of assignation, in a café, in the Retiro) and the weight of postponed decisions grew like a barely perceived tumor. The greater the upheaval, the more he was driven to give no sign, to not lose control of what others saw. Going out and not thinking about the possibility of a gunman waiting by the entrance. Staying in the office, so busy with a calculation or the correction of a drawing that not even gunfire could make him look up for more than a moment. Not going into the corridor to look for the clerk with the unctuous manner and the tray of mail. Not sitting and looking at the telephone, as if the simple effort of his attention might cause a ring that would be a call from Judith. He gathered the courage to call Dr. Negrín at the Congress of Deputies, and a secretary granted him the relief of telling him that Don Juan wasn't in but she'd give him the message. The gunfire had stopped; from a distance came the sound of an ambulance siren or an approaching Assault Guard van. His secretary entered his office without knocking, upset, speaking in a rush, almost not giving Ignacio Abel time to hide under a folder of documents the letter to Judith Biely he'd begun writing.

"The Anarchists, Don Ignacio, a picket line. They came in a car, as in the movies, to the Medical School and started shooting at the workers on the morning shift, calling them Fascists and traitors to the working class. But some boys from the Socialist militia on guard duty shot back from the windows."

"Where were the police?"

"Where do you think? They arrived after the gunmen had fled. You should've seen the militia boys, how they fought back. The car windows were shattered. And what a pool of blood when they drove away. One of them must've been hit."

They chatted about the gunfire the way they would talk on Monday mornings about the Sunday soccer games or a boxing match: only a minor injury among the workers in spite of the shooting and the broken glass, but one or two of the others must be in serious condition, judging by the blood that poured from the car they escaped in; the blood bright red, not the black liquid of the movies, but dark and quickly coagulated, absorbed by the earth, raked by laborers who covered it with sand before returning to their work, guarded by young militiamen whom they reverently called the Motorized, a fanciful name originating from the fact that in parades some of them patrolled on old motorcycles with sidecars. "At least one of them's dead, that's certain," said the mail clerk, the tray of letters abandoned on a table, among them perhaps one that Judith Biely had written and mailed the day before, only an hour after leaving him. "Two men carried him to the car and he couldn't stand up and his face and shirt were covered in blood." If he died, they'd bury him amid gales of banners, the coffin covered with a red-and-black flag, advancing above a mass of heads and hands anxious to touch it, to hold it high, carried like a boat on the current of a river that flooded the entire street. They'd sing anthems, shake clenched fists, shout promises of reparation and revenge, insults hurled at the closed balconies of bourgeois residences. But a shot or an explosion could provoke a wave of rage and panic in the crowd that would demolish it like a cyclone in a field of wheat: more shots, real ones now, the Assault Guard's horses neighing, broken glass, streetcars and automobiles overturned. Someone lay dead on the pavement, and the collective liturgy of death would be repeated a little more passionately: perhaps someone attending the funeral or a passerby walked in front of a bullet; a Falangist gunman who'd fired from a moving car, around which the swelling crowd soon closed. This dead man would have his funeral with an identical mob, with other anthems and other flags, with speeches in hoarse voices and "Long live"s and "Death to"s before an open grave. At the funerals of the leftist dead there were forests of red flags and raised fists and parades of young militiamen in uniform; at the other funerals the smoke of incense rose, dispensed by priests, along with a choir of voices reciting the rosary. So ironic that both sides seemed blind to the similarity between their funeral rites, their celebrations of courage and sacrifice, of martyrdom, the rejection of the material world in the name of paradise on earth or the kingdom of heaven, as if they wanted to fast-forward to Judgment Day and hated nonbelievers and agnostics much more than their professed enemies. After the funeral of Jiménez de Asúa's police escort, the crowd returning from the cemetery attacked a church that eventually was enveloped in flames; firemen who came to put out the fire were greeted by bullets. During those days in May, Madrid was a city of funerals and bullfights. Almost every afternoon, crowds walked along Calle de Alcalá to the bullfight arena or the East Cemetery.

"You can't go around unarmed, Don Ignacio," Eutimio said when, at the end of the day, he told him about that morning's gunfire at the Medical School construction site. Eutimio, his senior by only a few years, looked much older, though stronger as well, with his erect posture, large hands, and dark face crossed by horizontal lines like hatchet blows in a block of wood. "You take a big chance coming alone every morning in your car and leaving in the evening when nobody's around."

The pistol Eutimio showed him after closing the office door behind him was much larger than Negrín's, more primitive than the one Adela's brother had. It looked like a solid piece of iron hammered into summary form on an anvil. Eutimio remained standing, beret in hand. Ignacio Abel knew that asking him to sit down was useless. So he stood too, leaning against the window, uncomfortable in his own office, his custom-tailored clothes, the softness of his hands, before this man who'd known him when he was a boy and his father took him to work with his crew of masons on holidays and during school vacations. Eutimio, then an apprentice stucco worker, took care of Ignacio: he applied grease to his hands skinned raw by the work, burned by the plaster and lime, and he showed him how to hold his fingers together and blow on the tips to keep them warm in the winter dawns. Ignacio had the admiration for him a small child has for a boy who's a few years older and yet moves among adults and behaves like them. Eutimio had seen his father's face before it was covered with the sack.

"I'm nearsighted, Eutimio. I've never fired a gun in my life."

"But didn't you do your service in Morocco?"

"I was so useless they assigned me to an office."

"Not useless, Don Ignacio, well connected, if you'll allow me to speak frankly." Eutimio, the beret in his hand and his head slightly lowered, had in his lively eyes a gleam both affectionate and sarcastic. "The useless ones who didn't study and couldn't pull any strings were sent to the frontlines anyway and died before anybody else."

"If I had a pistol, I'd be a danger to everyone except the man who wanted to kill me."

"A pistol can save your life."

"Captain Faraudo had one in his pocket and they killed him all the same."

"The sons of bitches came up behind him. His wife was with him. He was holding her arm."

"It has to be the law that defends us, Eutimio."

"Don't tell me that an eye for an eye and a tooth for a tooth doesn't work. If they are out to kill us, we have to defend ourselves. One of them for each one of us. You know I'm not a violent man, but we have no choice."

"That's what the other side says."

"Forgive me for saying so, Don Ignacio, but you don't understand the class struggle."

"You haven't become a Leninist overnight, Eutimio, have you?"

"There are things you can't understand, with all due respect." Eutimio spoke slowly, distinctly. As a young man he'd listened to the speeches of Pablo Iglesias, and every day he read the lead articles in *El Socialista* aloud, in a clear voice. "You may have a Socialist Party card and one for the UGT, like your father, may he rest in peace, but what counts in the class struggle isn't what you've read but the shoes you wear or what your hands are like. Your father began as a bricklayer's helper, and when he had the accident he was a master builder, but we called him Señor Miguel, not Don Miguel. You, Don Ignacio, are a gentleman. Not a parasite and not an exploiter, because you earn your living with your work and your talent. But you wear shoes, not espadrilles, and if you had to use a shovel or a pick, in five minutes your hands would be covered with blisters, like when you were a little boy and your father would take you with us to the work site."

"But Eutimio, I thought the class struggle was between owners and workers, not between one group of workers and another. When all of you start shooting, why fire at men who wear espadrilles too?"

Eutimio stood looking at him with some surprise but also with a good deal of indulgence, as when he was an awkward, chubby little boy who had to be pushed to climb up to the first plank of a scaffold.

"Just what I said, Don Ignacio—you don't understand. Probably, when people get desperate, they stop acting rationally. I'm not much good at arguing, but with this in my hand, nobody's going to silence me."

"Not silence, Eutimio, but worse, kill you. Never mind the pistol you carry. The question is, do you have the reflexes to confront those gangsters? And if somebody's desperate because he doesn't have work or his children go hungry, I understand his holding up a store or robbing a bank, whatever. I understand those people who wait in the pine groves until nightfall to steal construction materials, or come here in the morning hoping we'll give them a day's work. It drives me crazy when the guards take them away in handcuffs, or when other workers chase them with rocks so they won't compete for the little they have. But you tell me what those gunmen wanted today, or the ones who'll probably come tomorrow to take revenge."

"They want the social revolution, Don Ignacio. Not for workers' wages to go up but for workers to be in charge. To finally turn the tables, as they say. No more exploiters and no more exploited."

Eutimio, who'd always had the sonorous, precise speech of Madrid's working-class neighborhoods, nourished by the quick wit of the street and by politically charged novels, expressed himself now as if he were reciting a propaganda pamphlet or a newspaper editorial. The secretary came in with a folder of papers to be signed, and the foreman looked down and adopted an instinctive attitude of docility, retreating toward the door, as if to clear away any suspicion of improper proximity to Ignacio Abel. "With your permission," he said, bowing, both hands holding his beret. Any indication of familiarity had disappeared from his face. In an instant he'd canceled any link he might have had with the director of the office, seemed to have erased from his memory the image of the boy whose hands, stiff with cold, chafed and raw, he rubbed with grease, in the distant time at the turn of the century, on very early mornings illuminated by gaslight.

From the car after he left work, Ignacio Abel saw him walking alone to the distant streetcar stop, his quick step, the bag with his lunch pail over his shoulder, hands in pockets, among the groups of workers who flowed from the buildings where only custodians and armed watchmen were left, the afternoon sun on the recently installed windowpanes, motionless machines, cranes oscillating in the air crossed by swallows and swifts. Assault Guards stood here and there asking for identification and searching those leaving the construction area.

"Get in, Eutimio, I'll take you home."

He slowed down to move alongside him, but the foreman resisted, barely turning his head, walking faster. Perhaps he didn't want other workers to see him getting into the car of the associate director of construction.

"I'll get dust all over the upholstery, Don Ignacio."

"Don't be silly. Weren't you saying I shouldn't be so overconfident? Well, I don't like to see you walking alone here either."

"Nothing to worry about, Don Ignacio, they won't interfere with me." He'd dropped into the passenger seat with the weariness of an old man and had the pistol in his hand, the black barrel pointing toward Ignacio Abel. "And if one of them doesn't know who I am, I have this to make the introductions."

"You'd better move the pistol away, otherwise you won't just get dust on my upholstery, you'll fire it by accident when we hit a pothole and blow my head off."

"What an idea, Don Ignacio. As you get older you're more and more like your late father. I always say, if there were more gentlemen like you, the world would be a different place."

"Aren't you getting tired of calling me a gentleman? Aren't I a worker? Remember what the constitution says: Spain is a republic of workers of every class."

"Sounds nice, if only it were true." Eutimio leaned back in the seat, caressed the leather upholstery appreciatively with his broad fingertips, brushing the instrument panel with them, the ivory buttons on the car radio, carefully, as if afraid of damaging them. "But you can't eat the constitution. You know what the landowners say who'd rather lose the harvest than pay decent wages to their workers."

"'Eat the Republic.'"

"Exactly. They step on people and are shocked when those they've stepped on turn around and bite them."

"But that wasn't what we were talking about."

"Now you're angry with me, Don Ignacio, because I called you a gentleman, but you shouldn't be. I haven't called you an exploiter, God forbid. You haven't robbed or deceived anybody, and you're as much a Socialist as I am, or at least as Don Julián Besteiro and Don Fernando de los Ríos are, and they don't have calluses on their hands either, as far as I know. The masses you gentlemen like best are the ones in the head, as Prieto says. But things are the way they are, and from what I understand, Karl Marx and Friedrich Engels taught us to see them as they are, without cobwebs over our eyes, according to the principles of materialism."

"Now you're the one who resembles Besteiro, with that talk."

"It's clear, if you'll forgive me, that you drive a car and I walk, or ride a streetcar at best. You wear a hat and I wear a beret, Don Ignacio, and if it rains you don't get wet, because along with driving in your car you wear new shoes with soles that don't get soaked with water, and your feet don't get cold like a man wearing old boots with holes in the bottoms. You work hard, of course you do, but under a roof, and with heat, and when it's hot you work in the shade, not in the sun. If one of your children gets sick, God forbid, you don't have to take him to the welfare hospital, where he'll get worse as soon as he breathes the air that smells of misery and death, and if he gets a little worse a good doctor comes right away and prescribes the medicines he needs and you can pay for, and if he needs it there'll be a place for him in a sanatorium where they heal lungs with good food and the Sierra air. That's the truth, Don Ignacio, and you know it. Would you like it if things were different? Of course you would. But it's a law of nature that you don't have the same desires or the same urgency as a workman. Sorry, as a *worker*, to use the correct term. And let's be clear: I have no quarrel with you and wouldn't permit anyone to speak ill of you in my presence. I've known you since you were a boy. I know how much you had to struggle to go on with your studies, when you and your mother were alone after your father's accident, may he rest in peace. There's your merit and talent, but there's your father's too. He sacrificed to give you school instead of having you work with him at the sites, which is what another, less enlightened father would've done, one less able to move ahead in his trade and earn a little money, and if what happened to him hadn't happened, I always say Señor Miguel would've ended up as one of the great builders in Madrid. Anyway, you're as good as gold, Don Ignacio, and you remember what it means to work with your hands, but you're on the side of the gentlemen and I'm on the side of the workers, as clear as the fact that you live in the Salamanca district and I'm in Cuatro Caminos. And let's be clear: I'm not like some others, you know me, I don't feel resentful toward anybody, and I don't think that to bring social justice we have to cut off heads like they do in Russia. I wish I'd had a father like yours and not a poor bricklayer who put me to work as an apprentice at the age of eight. I wish a child of mine had been born with the talent God or natural selection gave you — there's an opinion about everything. But the way I see Spain, really awful things can happen, and I often wonder which side you'll be on when the dike breaks."

"There's no reason it has to break, Eutimio."

"That's what you and I think, each from our place in life, because we're reasonable people, and forgive me for comparing myself to you. Though I have much less education than you do, I've learned something reading the papers and all the books I can, and studying people since I began to earn a living in your father's crew. But everybody isn't like us, Don Ignacio. Let's not kid ourselves, you live like what you are, like a bourgeois, and me, for better or worse, have my needs covered for now. We're both calm, it seems to me, but others who come pushing from behind have much more quarrelsome blood, and there's not a lot of good sense on your side or mine."

"Aren't we on the same side? Aren't we in the same party?"

"You see how they shoot each other inside the party. I open *El Socialista* or *Claridad* and I have to put it down right away so I won't read the terrible things some comrades write about others. If we use up so much anger fighting our own people, how much will be left to face the enemy? There's a lot of bad blood, Don Ignacio. The crops are rotting in the fields because this year it rained more than usual and the owners would rather lose the harvest than pay a pittance in wages. Some men are born vermin and others become that way because they're driven to get more or were treated like vermin from the time they were born."

As he spoke, Eutimio became more impassioned, breathing more deeply, not looking at Ignacio Abel, his eyes on the road. This man awakened in him a kind of tenderness he no longer felt for anyone, returned him to a time and a part of himself that were accessible only through the presence of Eutimio. His archaic oratory is what he'd listened to when men held meetings on Saturday nights in the small living room of the porter's lodging, filled with voices and tobacco smoke. Thanks to Eutimio, the thought of his father acquired an intensity and lucidity he rarely experienced anymore, or only in dreams — his father and the overprotected boy, the boy who was now older than his dead father. Eutimio belonged to that time (the very early mornings, the weariness at the end of the day, the rough solemnity of the Socialist meetings where men dressed in dark smocks addressed one another with the formal *usted* and raised a hand to speak), and when he relived it, somehow his place in the present was turned upside down, the stable, solid life that seemed inevitable and yet might not have happened because there wasn't any link between it and the life he'd led during that past time, whose only witness now was Eutimio. Nothing back then foretold the present. The boy, studying at the table with the built-in foot warmer in the light of an oil lamp when the wheels of a wagon stopped near the small street-level window, had nothing to do with the gray-haired man with confident gestures who now drove a car along the outer boulevards of Madrid toward Calle de Santa Engracia and the traffic circle of Cuatro Caminos. But Eutimio, sitting beside him, knew; capable of establishing connections with his clear memory and sharp intelligence, he could recognize in Ignacio Abel's serious profile traits from his childhood, as well as the faces of his parents slowly revealed by age; the only thing that remained of them was a blurred, solemn photograph of pale tinted faces, as primitive as their postures or her embroidered collar and topknot and his slicked-down hair divided by a center part, his mustache with waxed ends. "They're your paternal grandparents," he'd once explained to his children, who looked at the photo as surprised as if they had seen people not only from another century and social class but of another species. But memories were not all that Eutimio brought him. There were also physical sensations that invoked his father's presence: his hard hands, his gestures, the smell of corduroy trousers.

"You can drop me off here, Don Ignacio. You continue on your way home. I can take a streetcar from here."

"Door-to-door service," he said with a smile and shrugged, confounded by a feeling of shyness he wouldn't admit to anyone, not even Judith Biely. "Let's see if I can corrupt you with the comforts of bourgeois life."

"The people in the CNT are calling me a strikebreaker as it is."

"That can't be anything to worry about."

They went up Calle de Santa Engracia, past the magnificent Water Tower, rising above the city like a Persian funerary monument before the distant blue curtain of the Sierra. Ignacio Abel drove in silence, listening to Eutimio, observing out of the corner of his eye the change in the other man's posture as they approached his neighborhood: uncomfortably erect, knees together, unwilling to abandon himself to an intimacy as easily withdrawn as granted. Before it reached its limits, Madrid expanded into rural spaciousness, rows of low houses in front of which women embroidered in the sun, sitting on rush chairs in large lots surrounded by plank fences covered with faded election posters. A dusty, village light floated above the Cuatro Caminos traffic circle: ragpickers' wagons, herds of goats, cowbells and the bells of streetcars, circling a waterless fountain that looked like a stage set, a fountain dislodged from the bourgeois promenade for which it was built. The strongest notes of color were the green and red of geraniums on the balconies. A group of children kicking a ball made of rags in the middle of the street interrupted their game to run alongside the car. They winked and made mocking faces, almost pressing their noses to the windows. One ran with a crippled leg, leaning on a crutch; on the head of another a rash of ringworm was turning white.

"Be careful, Don Ignacio, these kids could throw themselves under the wheels."

Behind grilles, from balconies and the doorways of small workshops, taverns, and grocery stores, suspicious, attentive eyes observed the car's passing. Three men approached, dressed in white shirts and old jackets, caps above their faces, legs far apart. In the waistband of one of them was the black butt of a pistol. They stood motionless in front of the car in the middle of the street, looking at Ignacio Abel, who kept the engine running and, with instinctive caution, had both hands still and visible on the steering wheel, his eyes alert and at the same time avoiding their questioning, defiant stares.

"Don't worry, Don Ignacio, these are good boys."

"What do they want?"

"They're on watch."

Eutimio lowered his window and signaled to the one wearing a pistol, who examined the interior of the car, a contemptuous expression at the corner of his mouth where a cigarette burned. A boy's nose was flattened against each window, open mouths fogging the glass with their breath, their eyes looking inside as if into an aquarium.

"You can trust this gentleman, comrade," said Eutimio, avoiding the other man's eyes, which were close, the smoke of his cigarette in his face. "He's my boss at work and I'll answer for him."

The men spoke briefly among themselves, then moved aside to allow them to pass, coming together again to watch the car, like watching a train or ship move away. In his rearview mirror, Ignacio Abel saw the men recede and let out a sigh of relief not as inaudible as he imagined.

"They frightened you a little, Don Ignacio. Nothing to worry about. You have to understand that in this neighborhood, when you see a car like yours, it means something bad's going to happen."

"The Falangists?"

"Or the monarchists. Or the boys from Young Popular Action. They speed up Santa Engracia and run over whatever's in front of them. They shoot and don't care who they hit. Last week they killed a poor woman sweeping at her front door. The class struggle, Don Ignacio. They lean their heads out of car windows, stretch out their arms, and shout '*Arriba España!*' Then they turn into Cuatro Caminos and no-body can find them."

Now Ignacio Abel observed more attentively his expressions and glances, as well as the mixture of discomfort and confidence Eutimio felt when he was recognized close to home. The confined space of the car and their physical proximity had favored an ease of manner that would vanish as soon as Eutimio got out, with a gesture of farewell that would conceal the intention to shake hands instead of thanking him by bending his head slightly as he stood on the sidewalk, having removed his beret. A blind at a balcony moved to one side; a woman's hand shook a curtain of cheap cloth; some boys playing leapfrog interrupted their game, and one turned his head to look at the car with an expression at once serious and adult; the rope some girls were jumping, colored ribbons in their hair, remained motionless on the pounded earth; young men in shirtsleeves approached the door of a tavern.

"I'm inviting you to have a glass of wine and get the fear out of your body, Don Ignacio."

"Eutimio, come on, this wasn't anything to worry about." Having shown his alarm so obviously embarrassed Ignacio Abel. Affectionate, almost paternal, Eutimio still took some pleasure in the weakness of a superior, more evident because when he got out of the car, Ignacio Abel found himself without defenses in unfamiliar territory. "I'll have a glass if you let me invite you."

He had plenty of time: he didn't have an appointment with Judith Biely and had no desire to return home on a May evening that seemed to have halted in a luminosity not yet dimmed by twilight. When he returned home he'd permit himself the consolation of telling Adela the truth—this would soothe the conscience of a recent, still inexpert liar—but she'd probably think his conversation with a foreman in a tavern in Cuatro Caminos was a lie, one of many she didn't bother to pretend she believed. Distracted, happy, almost virtuous, as if today's truth somehow would compensate for deceit on so many other occasions, he wouldn't even notice Adela's incredulity.

"Don't worry about the car, Don Ignacio, you can trust us here. You don't have to lock it. We're poor but honest, like in the operettas."

The children not only looked at the car—the soft green paint, the butter-colored leather top, the crank handle, nickel-plated like the wheel spokes—they looked at him in particular, as if he were from another universe: white hands, made-to-measure suit, the peak of a handkerchief in his jacket pocket, the gleam of his silk tie, his two-toned shoes. The children's black eyes were a mirror that reflected a distorted version of himself, the tall, strange man they were seeing, the one who got out of the car, slamming the door and looking around with an expression of instinctive guardedness, like a colonial dignitary on an inspection tour, benevolent, perhaps, but always distant, possessing an arrogance that didn't need to be a personal attitude because it was engraved on the character of his caste. He thought of his own children as he looked at these faces, which had a radiant dignity in spite of the poverty. He saw not the man he was now but the boy who so many years ago, late in the afternoon, went out fearfully to play on another street much like this one, in his neighborhood at the other end of Madrid. For a few seconds the children's voices had echoed in a kind of concave eternity, in the realm outside time of games and street songs, the ones he'd listened to so often in the porter's lodging, coming through the window high above his head, at the level of the sidewalk. He hadn't been one of them, not even then. A pure moment recovered from that distant time made him stop in the doorway of the tavern, happy and lost, blinking as if the afternoon light had blinded him.

"The same thing happened when you were a boy," Eutimio was saying, his face close and slightly out of focus. "You'd stand there, thinking your thoughts, and your father, may he rest in peace, would say, 'This boy of mine looks like he's turning into a sleepwalker.'"

The tavern, more like a wine cellar, was dark and deep and smelled of sawdust and sour wine, casks and herring in brine. Entering felt like advancing through the half-light of the past: as a boy his father would send him to taverns like this one to buy a pint of wine or to take a message to one of the masons or artisans who worked for him. But here, soccer, bullfight, and boxing posters lined the whitewashed walls, and a large radio played behind the counter. On the gaudy print from an almanac, under a legend that proclaimed *Happy 1936!,* the Republic was a young woman with a Phrygian cap pulled to one side of her head, her body barely covered by the folds of a tricolor flag that molded her breasts and revealed the fleshy thigh of a chorus girl or dancer.

The men drinking at the zinc bar and at the tables greeted Eutimio and examined Ignacio Abel from head to toe. Their presence and voices filled the space, and they gave off a strong sensation of vigor and weariness after work. The new arrivals sat at an isolated table, and the tavernkeeper brought them a squared flask of red wine and two low, thick glasses, still wet from the rinse water. When Eutimio sat down, the pistol in the inside pocket of his jacket bulged visibly.

"It seems unbelievable, Don Ignacio, that you and I are sitting here at the same table, when at work I have to take off my cap to speak to you and it's not a good idea to look you in the eye."

"Don't exaggerate, Eutimio. Hasn't life changed at all since my father's time? And it'll change even more now with the Popular Front government."

"A government of fine bourgeois gentlemen, Don Ignacio, who ignore the workers' vote."

"Our party's to blame, yours and mine. The one that hasn't allowed a Socialist to be president. It was so difficult to bring in the Republic and now they don't want it anymore, they don't think it's enough. Now they want a Soviet revolution. You were at the May Day demonstration where the Socialists paraded, and it looked as if they were on Red Square in Moscow. Red flags with the hammer and sickle, portraits of Lenin and Stalin. Our people were different from the Communists only because they wore red shirts, not sky-blue ones. Not a single flag of the Republic, Eutimio, the Republic that came in because we Socialists wanted it, because the Republicans were nothing. But these May Day Socialists didn't cheer for the Republic, they cheered for the Red Army. To the great joy of the right, as you can imagine."

"I already told you, Don Ignacio, the Republic's pretty but it doesn't feed you."

"And do strikes with gun battles and burned churches feed you?"

"You don't have to say that to me, Don Ignacio. I'm an old man, you know, and I've seen all kinds of things, but until now life hasn't gone badly for me. I have a decent little house right near here and a small orchard in the village, and my wife and daughters sew on Singers and earn a wage that's no worse than mine. Since I know how to read and write and have a good head for numbers, I could be a foreman, and in my house we might have hard times but not poverty. My younger boy, thanks to you, has a job as a clerk in the waterworks office, and though he doesn't earn much, he's hard-working. At night he's studying to be a draftsman, and I hope he can find a job in the University City office someday soon, if you give him a hand. But other men are much worse off, Don Ignacio, and they don't have patience and good judgment, and if they do, they can lose them when there's no work and not much justice and they see their children die of hunger, or they lose their house because they can't pay for it and find themselves sleeping under bridges or spending the nights in doorways."

"It can't all be done at once, Eutimio." Now it was *his* voice that sounded false, even though he was saying something reasonable, perhaps as reasonable as it was sterile. "The Republic's only five years old. The Popular Front won only three months ago."

"And who are we to tell anybody to be patient? Or to wait a few months to give food to his children or take them to a doctor? Neither of us is going to bed without supper tonight, and excuse me for comparing myself to you."

"And is setting off bombs and killing people going to solve anything? Having an armed rebellion against the Republic as they did in

Asturias? Threatening every day to break the truce and establish the dictatorship of the proletariat?"

"The working class has to defend itself, Don Ignacio." Eutimio gestured for him to lower his voice. "If it weren't for those boys on watch outside, you and I probably couldn't have our quiet glass of wine."

"You people don't understand, Eutimio." As soon as he said it, he realized the plural was offensive, but he was becoming inflamed, and an unpleasant but strong feeling of superiority erupted in him. "There are laws that are above everybody. There are police, there are judges. We're not in the Wild West or Chicago, the way everybody seems to think. You don't take up arms against the legitimate government just because you don't like the election results. You don't go around with a pistol taking the law into your own hands."

"I'm not a fool, Don Ignacio." Eutimio had left his empty glass on the table and was looking at him seriously, offended, at the same time leaning his head forward to make sure no one heard him. "What you say about the law is fine, but at this point nobody believes it anymore. Tell it to the rebellious military who never stop conspiring and the judges who let the Falangist gunmen who kill workers go free."

"Then what should we do? Should we all arm ourselves? 'One man, one pistol' instead of 'One man, one vote'?"

"I don't know what we should do, Don Ignacio. Probably younger people whose ideals are stronger than ours will give us the solution. When I was a boy and heard Pablo Iglesias and the speakers back then talking about the classless society, tears came to my eyes. And now, instead of the classless society, what I dream about is my little orchard and not losing my wages. Maybe you didn't imagine either when you were a boy that you'd enjoy driving a car and living in a building with an elevator in the Salamanca district—"

"We're back to that again."

"Don't make me lose my patience, Don Ignacio. Or my respect either, if you'll permit me. And don't raise your voice—you'll probably say something other people won't like to hear. Young people have a spirit we don't understand anymore. Even my boy, who never broke a dish, who always went from home to work and work to home, joined the Communist Youth last year. Upsetting for a father, but now they've joined with our youth groups, which makes me feel calmer. You and I will be happy if this world we know gets a little better — after all, it's our world. But what they want is a different world. Haven't you seen the posters? 'We carry a new world in our hearts.'"

Literature again, he thought, but he didn't say it for fear of offending Eutimio. Cheap literature, newspaper trash, third-rate verses, sometimes sung in anthems for greater effect. An entire country, an entire continent infected by mediocre literature, drunk on shoddy music, operetta marches, and bullfight paso dobles. In this tavern, with its poor electric light and stink of bad wine, the floor littered with wet sawdust and cigarette butts, he realized that deep in his soul he didn't feel much sympathy for his fellow men, that he needed the vagueness and protection of a certain distance to get along with them, to become emotional over principles and words of liberation like the ones he'd heard as a boy at his father's meetings. He thought that what he really wanted was to leave Spain: with no preparation, notification, or remorse, to put distance between himself and his country, get on a night express next to Judith Biely and wake in a port city where he'd sail that same day on a ship for America, disappear without a trace, free of any connection, as separated from the outside world and all the anguished obligations in his life as when he embraced her after undressing her and buried his face in her neck, inhaling her smell, as if he were breathing in advance the air of another country and another life, his eyes closed while the curtains filtered the workday-morning light, and muffled sounds of the city reached the brief, hired intimacy that welcomed them in the house of Madame Mathilde.

The next morning, when he arrived at the office, Eutimio bowed his head slightly and made a gesture of greeting without looking him in the eye.

17

TIME ON OUR HANDS, said Judith before hanging up the phone, confirming the time they would meet, the start of the trip, an almost dreamed-of flight, so there would be no possible doubt or confusion, and he liked the poetry implicit in the common expression, as he did so often when he learned a new turn of phrase in English from Judith or explained a Spanish one to her. Time on our hands, for once overflowing cupped hands like cool water from a powerful tap where someone who can finally satisfy his thirst will joyfully plunge his face or wet his lips; whole days and nights exclusively theirs, not shared with anyone, not contaminated by the indignity of hiding, not measured out in minutes or hours, a treasure of time whose magnitude was difficult for them to imagine. But what they couldn't imagine at all was the two of them away from Madrid, in a setting other than the city that had brought them together and imprisoned them, subjecting them to the curse of secrecy, lies, and never enough time. *Time on our hands,* he recalls now, repeating it in a soft voice, looking at his hands inert on his thighs, on the raincoat he didn't take off when he boarded the train, hands good for nothing except patting his pockets in search of some document or rubbing his face each morning after shaving, clutching the sweat-darkened handle of his suitcase, fastening buttons or discovering that a button has fallen off and left only vestiges of thread, or his shoelaces are fraying, or the right pocket of his jacket is coming loose. At least we had that, he thinks, that gift, not the anticipation of something that would come later but almost a final favor before the inevitable occurred, four whole days, from Thursday to Sunday, the straight white highway unfurling before the car when they left Madrid for the south while dawn was breaking, and at the end of their journey the house on the sand escarpment, the smell of the Atlantic coming in as forcefully as the smell of the Hudson comes in now through the train window: hands filled with time, with the craving proximity of the other, undressing each other as soon as they took a few steps inside the dark of the house, not opening a window, not taking the bags out of the car, exhausted after so many hours on the road and still aching with desire, incapable of putting it off any longer. It wasn't the same as saying *tiempo de sobra:* no matter how much time they had, it would never be more than enough, not even by a minute, and in any case those words didn't express the physical sensation of an undeserved abundance that fills your hands, like the coins or diamonds of a fairy-tale treasure, *tiempo a manos llenas.* Hands full of time, but no matter how tightly you squeeze your fingers and press together your hands curved like a bowl, water will always escape, time trickling away second by second like tiny grains of sand, gleaming like crystals in the morning light on the beach they walked together, not seeing anyone for its entire length, sole survivors of a cataclysm that had left them alone in the world, fugitives from everything, from their lives and the names that identified them with those lives, renegades from any tie or loyalty — parents, children, spouses, friends, obligations, principles — other than the ones that joined the two of them, apostates from any belief.

If at least you'd had real courage, he thinks now, looking at his two empty hands, hands with sinuous veins and badly trimmed, slightly dirty nails, if you'd dared a real apostasy and not a semblance, a real flight and not a fiction. Even the four days now fading away into nothingness for the lovers who until then hadn't been able to spend more than a few hours together, hadn't known what it meant to open one's eyes at the first light of day and find each other, to be present at the other's contented sleep and waking. Always so little time, the hours numbered, falling away into the sand of fleeting minutes and seconds, the timepiece ticking, the noisy mechanism in the alarm clock on the night table or the subtler one on his wrist, attached to it as if it were a pillory, second by second, the tiny jaws undermining the houses of time where they hid to be together, their secret refuges almost always precarious, always in danger of being invaded, no matter how deep they wanted to hide, one beside the other and one in the other, canceling the outside world in the single-mindedness of an embrace with eyes closed. Footsteps in the hall of the house of assignation, doors that at any moment might open, voices on the other side of thin walls, the moans of other lovers, inhabitants like them of the secret city, the submerged, venal Madrid of reserved booths, rooms rented by the hour, parks at night, the sordid border territory where adultery and prostitution came together. They lived besieged by creditors, by thieves and beggars of time, by greedy moneylenders and shady traffickers in hours. Time phosphoresced on the hands of the alarm clock on the night table in the room at Madame Mathilde's, in the low light of curtains drawn in the middle of the morning. The ticktock sounded like a taxi meter: if they were late by only a few minutes in leaving the rented room, they'd hear footsteps in the hall and knocks on the door; if they wanted more time they'd have to buy it at a higher rate. Time fled in numerical spasms like distance on the car's odometer while they traveled south as if they never had to return. The time of each wait dilated and even halted because of uncertainty, anguish that the other wouldn't appear. The lightning flash of arrival abolished for a few minutes the passage of time, leaving it suspended in an illusion of abundance. Illicit time had to be purchased minute by minute, obtained like a dose of opium or morphine. The scant wealth of time was lost waiting for a taxi, traveling endlessly in a very slow streetcar, driving in traffic, dialing a number on the phone and waiting for the wheel to return to its point of departure in order to dial the next one: how much time wasted waiting for an answer, listening to a bell that rings on the other end in an empty room, growing impatient because an operator takes a long time to answer or transfer a call, fingers restless as they drum on a table, his eyes vigilant in case someone approaches from the end of the hall, a hemorrhaging of time, drop by drop or in a gush. It was Philip Van Doren who gave them the four days when he offered them the house he'd bought or was about to buy on the Cádiz coast without even seeing it, knowing it only from plans and photographs. He seemed to take pleasure in sheltering them, urging them toward each other from a benevolent distance, intervening in the name of chance, as he'd done when he left them alone in his study that October afternoon. The house of time Ignacio Abel wanted to build so that only Judith and he would live in it really existed for only four days, between Thursday afternoon and the small hours of Monday: white, with cubic volumes, outlined in a horizontal on an escarpment, its forms variable in the photos Van Doren spread before him on the tablecloth at the Ritz where he'd invited them to dinner, in a reserved booth, implicitly acknowledging the advantage to Ignacio Abel of not being seen in public with his lover, while from the street, from the Plaza de Neptuno, came the muffled sounds of a battle with stones and bullets between Assault Guards and striking construction workers — whistles, breaking glass, sirens. He'd pushed the cuffs of his sweater away from his wrists with impatient gestures and placed the photos on the table as in a card game, raising his depilated eyebrows, puffing with delight on a Havana cigar, a smile on his fleshy lips, his too-small mouth, incongruous with his heavy square jaw and hairy fingers. "My dear Professor Abel, don't feel obliged to say no. I'm not doing you a favor, I'm requesting your professional opinion, asking you for a report on a painting before I buy it. Look at the house and tell me its condition. Live in it for a few days. They assure me it's fully stocked, but I don't believe anyone's lived in it yet. A German acquaintance of mine, loaded with money, had it built, and now he's not sure it's a good idea for him to go on living and doing business in Spain. I presume to imagine that Judith wouldn't mind accompanying you. It'll be good for you to escape the heat in Madrid and the more suffocating political climate. Now that there's another strike, it won't be prudent for you to be seen arriving every morning at

University City. Do you believe the military will finally rebel, Professor Abel? Or that the left will move forward with a new dress rehearsal for a Bolshevik revolution? Or will everybody take a summer vacation and then nothing will happen, as the minister of communications told me just a few days ago?"

Give me time. If I had time. It's a question of time. We're still in time. We're out of time. In the reserved booth at the Ritz, Philip Van Doren looked at them with the magnanimity of a potentate, an oligarch of time, offering them the tempting and perhaps humiliating alms of what they most desired, so powerful he didn't ask anything in return, not even gratitude, perhaps only the spectacle of the penury he detected in them, the subtle way in which hidden sexual passion debased them, consumed them, like respectable people subject to a secret addiction, morphine or alcohol, reaching the point where their deterioration becomes visible. I need time. How much more time do you want me to give you? Time like a solid block of calendar pages, each day an imperceptible sheet of paper, a number in red or black, the name of a weekday. Judith Biely, foreign and distinctive, inexplicably his, searching for his foot under the table as she smiled, raising the glass of wine to her lips, *playing footsie,* she had taught him to say. Time slow, fossilized, bogged down, solemn in the pendulum clock at the end of the hall, the one Ignacio Abel sees as he stands waiting, clutching the telephone receiver, impatient, the clock that strikes the hours with bronze resonances in the midst of his insomnia, in the dark expanse of the apartment, when he thought an eternity had gone by and he counts the strokes and it's only two in the morning, his face against the pillow and the racing heartbeat, the rhythmic surges of blood in his temples, while Adela sleeps beside him, or is awake and pretends to be asleep just as he does, and also knows he's not sleeping, the two of them motionless, not touching, not saying anything, their two minds physically as close as their bodies yet remote from each other, hermetic, submerged in the same disquiet, the identical agony of time. Time that doesn't pass, as crushing as a burden, a trunk or a slab of stone. Time at dinner, when the four of them fall silent and hear only the sound of the spoon scraping against the china soup bowl and the noise Miguel makes eating it and the small thump of the heel of his shoe against the floor. The time I have left before the deadline for requesting a leave at University City or applying for a visa at the American embassy. The exquisite time Judith takes to come when he's known how to caress her, attentive to her with his five senses, Judith's half-open mouth, her eyes closed, breathing through her nose, her long naked body tensing, the palms of her hands on his thighs, her jaw tensing as she is about to climax. The time that always comes to an end, although the fervor of their meeting made it seem unlimited at first. Knotting his tie in front of the mirror, a quick comb through his hair, Judith sitting on the bed and pulling on her stockings, observing his hurry, his subtle gesture when he consults his watch. The time of returning in a taxi or Ignacio Abel's car, both of them suddenly silent, far apart in the silence, already fallen back into the distance that does not separate them yet, looking through the window at illuminated clocks against the night sky of Madrid that indicate an hour always too late for him (but he doesn't think about the other time waiting for her when she goes into her room at the pensión and looks at the typewriter where she hasn't written anything for so long, the letters from her mother that she answers only now and then, suppressing a part of her life in Madrid, inventing in order not to tell her she's become a married man's lover). The time it takes for the *sereno* to appear after the echoing claps that call him in the nocturnal silence of Calle Príncipe de Vergara, more and more distressing, like guilt nipping at his heels; the time that goes by until the elevator arrives and then ascends very slowly and he looks at his watch again and thinks with disbelief that by now Adela must be asleep and won't notice the smell of tobacco and another woman's perfume, the crude odor of sex; the time for getting out on the landing, trying to prevent his footsteps from sounding too loud on the marble in the corridor, looking for the key in his pocket and making it turn in the lock, hoping no light is on in the apartment except for the altar of Our Father Jesus of Medinaceli with its small eave and two tiny electric lamps. Time will tell. Time heals. The time has come to save Spain from her ancestral enemies. The time of glory will return. If the government really intended to do it, it would still have time to head off the military conspiracy. Victorious Banners will return. I truly hope time does not pass. The Time of Our Patience Has Run Out. It is no longer the Time for Compromises or Vagueness with the Enemies of Spain. The time I have lost doing nothing, leaving urgent decisions for another day or the next few hours, imagining that passivity will make time resolve matters on its own. The time left before Judith decides to return to America or receives a job offer or simply goes to another European city less provincial and more stable, where there's no shooting in the streets and the papers don't publish front-page articles on political crimes. The weeks, the days, perhaps, to wait before the explosion of the military uprising everyone talks about, with suicidal fatalism, with impatience for the disaster, the social revolution, the apocalypse, whatever it may be, to finally happen, anything but this time of waiting, seeing funerals go by with coffins draped in flags, carried on the shoulders of comrades with a praetorian air, in red shirts or navy-blue shirts and military leather straps, raising open hands or clenched fists, shouting slogans, "Long live"s and "Death to"s, taking hours to reach the cemetery. The time it takes a letter recently dropped in a box to be picked up and sorted, canceled, delivered to the address indicated on the envelope; the time it takes each morning for the slow, servile clerk to distribute the mail, moving among the typists' and draftsmen's tables with the tray in his hands, stopping with unacceptable indolence to chat with someone, accept a cigarette; the time it takes for his greedy fingers to tear the edge and extract the sheets, for his eyes to move quickly over each line, from left to right, then return to the beginning, like the carriage of a typewriter, like the shuttle of a loom, drinking in each word as quickly as the time it took to write it, soaking up in the trickles of ink the traits of a handwriting as desired and familiar as the lines on a face, as the hand that slid across the paper writing it. *You can't say no to me. Imagine the house and us in it, we can't turn down what Phil's offering us, I have a right to ask this of you, only a few days.*

He looks at his watch and realizes it's been a while since the last time he looked, like the smoker who begins to free himself of his addiction and discovers that more time than ever has gone by without the temptation to light a cigarette: a few minutes after their departure, when the train had just passed the George Washington Bridge. *Time on our hands.* He's heard Judith Biely's voice on the phone, clearly recognized those words, their temptation and promise, their warning, *We're running out of time.* How little time they had left, much less than he'd imagined, than fear had led him to predict: his hands suddenly empty of time, barren fingers curving to grasp air, intuiting at times, like a tactile memory of the body they haven't caressed for three long months, the empty duration of his time without her. Running without a pause, *running out of time,* she said too, and he didn't know how to understand the warning, didn't perceive the speed of the time already sweeping them away. How much time has it been that these hands haven't touched anyone, haven't curved adjusting to the delicate shape of Judith Biely's breast, haven't pressed to him his children, who run to embrace him down the hall of the apartment in Madrid or along the gravel path in the garden in the Sierra; this right hand that rose in a fit of anger and descended like a bolt of lightning on Miguel's face (if only it had been paralyzed in midair, pierced by pain; if only it had withered before hurting and shaming his son, who perhaps doesn't know now whether his father is alive or dead, who's probably already begun to forget him). His child's hands so easily hurt by the harsh scrape of materials, paralyzed by cold on early winter mornings and warmed by Eutimio, who pressed them between his, which were so rough, scorched by plaster. "It was sad to look at your hands, Don Ignacio. I rubbed them in mine to warm them and they were like two dead sparrows." With these hands he wouldn't have been able to hold the pistol Eutimio showed him that morning in his office, the same one Eutimio raised and pressed to the middle of the chest of one of the men who pushed Ignacio Abel against a brick wall behind the School of Philosophy. He remembers with displeasure the sweat on his palms, as debasing as wetness in the groin. Time on our hands: time's not used up slowly, like a great flow of water that turns into a trickle and then driblets before it's extinguished. Time that ends suddenly, from one moment to the next you may be dead, your face in the dirt, or after a meeting someone says goodbye, someone you will never see again. The time of an encounter that seemed like any other concludes and neither of the lovers knows or suspects it will be the last. Or one of them does know and says nothing, has come to a conclusion but keeps the decision a secret and is already calculating the words that will be written in a letter, words one doesn't dare say aloud.

He hung up the phone and the expression Judith Biely had used remained floating in his mind like the timbre of the voice that after a few hours he'll hear again, close to him now, brushing him with the breath that gave shape to her words, *Time on our hands,* for once not numbered hours, minutes dissolving like water or spilling like sand between his fingers, but days, four whole days with no goodbyes or postponed longings, secret or stolen time, unlimited, overflowing, receiving them with the clemency of a country of asylum whose border will open with just a single lie, a false passport of limited but instantaneous validity, a lie that's not even completely false: *Thursday I'm going to the province of Cádiz and I'll be back Monday morning.* The truth and the lie said with exactly the same words, as difficult to separate from one another as the chemical components of a liquid. *An American client is thinking about buying a house on the coast and asked me to go and see it before he makes his decision.* It was so easy and the reward so limitless that it produced an anticipatory feeling of intoxication, almost of vertigo during dinner in the lethargy of the family dining room, where time went by so slowly, time like lead on his shoulders, the funerary rhythm of the large standing clock, an ostentatious gift from Don Francisco de Asís and Doña Cecilia, with its bronze pendulum in the body as deep as a coffin and its legend in Gothic letters around the gilded face, *Tempus fugit.* "You're always complaining you don't have time," said Adela, barely looking at him, attentive instead to the plate in front of her, conscious of Miguel's anxious vigilance, of the knee moving nervously under the table, "and now you accept another commitment. You could have taken advantage of the strike to relax with us in the Sierra." "I can't say no," he improvised, encouraged by how easy it was, not lying completely, using provable facts like the malleable material used to mold the lie. "It's the entrepreneur who offered me the assignment in the United States." But somehow the dissimulation trapped him: when they heard him mention the United States, Miguel and Lita broke into the conversation, interrupting him to ask if all of them were going to America, when, in which of the ocean liners displayed in the windows of travel agencies on Calle de Alcalá and Calle Lista, detailed models where you could see the portholes and the lifeboats and the tennis courts drawn on deck, posters of ships with high, sharp prows cutting through the waves, columns of smoke rising from smokestacks painted red and white, beautiful international names inscribed on the black curve of the hull. Like his mother, Miguel noticed his vexed, almost agonized expression, the contretemps of not having an answer prepared when the lie had flowed so comfortably until then. But Miguel didn't know how to interpret the incessant data his attentiveness provided, transformed for him into a confused state of alarm, the intuition of a danger that was near though he couldn't identify it: like those adventure movies in Africa he liked so much, when an explorer wakes at night and leaves the tent and knows a wild animal or an enemy is circling the camp but can't detect anything except the usual jungle sounds, and the leopard treads silently and is near, brushing the tall grasses with his long, muscular body, or the treacherous painted warrior approaches, raising a spear, while Miguel trembles in his seat, pulls in his legs, almost shudders, bites his nails, squeezes Lita's arm until he hurts her. He observes the muscle that moves in his father's closely shaved jaw, a throbbing that reveals he's irritated. "Now isn't the time to bother Papá with those questions. He has enough trouble at work. Will you go by car? All I ask is that you call us when you arrive. You know by now that if you're on the road and don't call, I can't sleep."

• • •

Everything so easy again, after the minor setback, he felt almost grateful to Adela, and the anger toward his son dissolved, anger provoked by that anxious question, that excessive expectation he'd planted himself and didn't know how to encourage or impede. But if Miguel's expectation irritated him so much, now, after three months of distance and remorse, on the train that carries him farther away from his children, he understands the senseless hope condemned by its excess to disillusion, because it resembled his own too much, because the boy's weakness, his nervousness, presented him with a mirror he perhaps would have preferred not to look into. He too was tortured by impatience to conclude as soon as possible the impersonation of family life at dinner; he too lived perturbed by desires he didn't know how and didn't want to control, dazzled by expectations that were never satiated and never fulfilled, incapable of appreciating or even seeing what he had before him, restless to have the present end as soon as possible and the future arrive, whatever it might be, any of the futures he'd been pursuing like successive mirages throughout his life, without age or experience or the habit of disappointment dulling his longing or chipping its cutting edge. Let the formalities of dinner conclude immediately, the routine annoyance of sitting down to read the paper, barely glancing at the headlines, while Adela in the easy chair next to his put on the glasses that made her look older and read a magazine or a book while she listened to the nightly concert of classical music on Unión Radio, near the partially open balcony door through which a light breeze entered along with attenuated street noises. From that balcony, if they'd been listening, they could have heard the shots that ended the life of Captain Faraudo on May 7. Let the children come in to give each a goodnight kiss, Lita in her pajamas and slippers, her hair brushed smooth; Miguel secretly indignant at the unavoidable obligation of going to bed, observing with his useless sixth sense that his parents rarely looked each other in the eye when they spoke, knowing that in a while his mother would walk to the bedroom and his father to his study, with the plans and models that absorbed his life, with the letters he sometimes wrote or read and immediately put away in a drawer when interrupted, the drawer he never forgot to lock with a key, a tiny key he kept in a vest pocket. Because he liked movies about Arsène Lupin and Fantômas (in fact there wasn't any kind of movie he didn't like), Miguel fantasized about dedicating himself as an adult to a distinguished criminal career as a white-gloved thief, an expert in opening safes, bank vaults, drawers in desks identical to his father's that hid under lock and key what in movies and novels were called compromising documents, perhaps the stolen letters used by an unscrupulous blackmailer to extort money from a beautiful woman of high society. Instead of the books given to him at school, the Clásicos Castellanos whose dry backs stood in a row on Lita's shelf, Miguel read the illustrated stories in *Mundo Gráfico*. The heading of one story made him lose sleep now: Behind a Façade of Apparent Normality, Family Hid Shameful Secret. He reflected on this with the light off, tossing in bed, bothered by the heat, upset at not having done his homework or begun to study for the final examinations that were approaching at a terrifying speed. At least his father was leaving the next day on that trip to the province of Cádiz and wouldn't be back until Monday: the prospect of his absence filled Miguel with an unmanageable mixture of relief and uncertainty. His father wouldn't be at the table to draw attention to him when he made noise eating soup or jiggled his leg, wouldn't make his half-interested, half-sarcastic inquiries about homework or tests. What if he was killed in a car accident? What if behind his apparent façade of normality he was hiding a secret as shameful as the protagonist's in *Mundo Gráfico*? "Lita," he said, "Lita," hoping his sister was still awake, "do you think our family is hiding some shameful secret?" But Lita was asleep, so all he could do was resign himself to the immense tedium of darkness and heat on a June night, the slowness of time, the striking of the hours on the hall clock that his father would hear just as he did, with an impatience that lengthened the waiting time even more and mixed with the fear of falling asleep and not hearing the alarm clock. It would ring at five, and at six, a little before dawn, Judith Biely would be waiting for him in the Plaza de Santa Ana, by the entrance to her pensión, a small suitcase in one hand and in the other her portable typewriter, shivering, her jacket collar pulled up against the damp cold of night's end.

He recalled the click of the keys filtering into his dream, like a nearby noise of rain falling on tiles or hollow zinc gutters; he recalled dreaming he was in the office listening to the click-clacking of the secretaries' typewriters. He opened his eyes and it was day; Judith wasn't beside him in bed. Through the shutters came a ray of sunlight and the powerful sound of the ocean. He'd have preferred not to think so soon that it was the last day, Sunday, and that very early the next morning they had to return to Madrid. He noted his body aching from making love, areas where his flesh had swelled, the overly tender, damp skin becoming irritated and red. Electrical current reached the house irregularly. He recalled Judith's body gleaming with sweat in the light of an oil lamp resting on the floor, a lock of damp hair adhering to her face, her mouth half open, turning to look at him over her shoulder, knees and elbows resting on the unmade bed. They taught each other the names of things, the ordinary words that designated the most intimate acts and sensations of love, the most desired parts of the body. They pointed in order to find out, as if they had to name everything in the new world where they'd hidden, and the exploration by index finger turned into a caress. New words, never applied before to a body born and reared in another language, childish terms, vulgar, shameless, sweetly crude, with a subtlety of nuance that acquired the carnal dimension of what was being named. They exchanged words as if they were fluids and caresses; Spanish words he never imagined he'd be able to say aloud were transformed into immodest passwords; it was enough to say again in order to request what would have had another name, less precise and less brazenly sexual as well, what perhaps neither of them would have dared to say to someone brought up in their own language.

The sound of the typewriter woke him. He was naked and didn't have on his wristwatch. In the unfamiliar light, he couldn't imagine the time. Nine, midday, two in the afternoon. Since their arrival at the house, time had expanded before them as if encompassing the ocean's horizon and the length of beach whose two extremes couldn't be seen in the distance that vanished in violet mist beyond the escarpments, demarcated in the west at nightfall by the intermittent beam of a lighthouse. As they approached the house, they'd passed a fishing village as horizontal as the landscape. From a distance he'd pointed out to Judith the beauty of the architecture, the white houses like blocks of salt against the greenish blues and silvery glint of the sea. On the beach, the rust-colored cliffs rose like dunes partially toppled by the force of the waves. He could hear them now, assaulting, undermining the base of the escarpments as gulls screeched and the typewriter clicked in the next room, the living room, with a large, wide window divided in half by the line of the horizon, where they'd found when they arrived an inexplicable bouquet of fresh roses. The interior spaces of the house had a mixture of elemental primitivism and modern asceticism: red clay tiles, whitewashed walls, broad panes of glass, railings of nickel-plated steel pipes. Ignacio Abel relives the smell of the ocean and the sound of Judith Biely's typewriter, sees her in an involuntary, and for that reason true, flash of memory, absorbed in her writing, wrapped in a silk robe with broad drawings of flowers, her hair carelessly tied back with a blue ribbon to keep it away from her face. She types quickly, not looking at the keyboard and barely looking at the paper; the carriage reaches the end of the line, ringing a little bell, and she returns it to the beginning with an instinctive gesture. He looks at her more closely now that she isn't aware of his presence. Her absolute concentration, the speed with which she types, the expression of serene intelligence on her face, cause him to desire her even more. Hair uncombed, barefoot, her robe loose around her shoulders, yet she has put on lipstick, not for him but for herself, just as she probably washed her face in cold water to be completely clear-minded when she begins to write; she uses the calm of dawn and the clean light that fills the house where they've been living since the middle of Thursday afternoon as if on an island, an island in time surrounded by the flat horizon of entire days that for the first time they've been able to share, as spacious as the rooms they walk through without being entirely accustomed to the idea that there'll be no one else but them, no voices or footsteps or words but theirs, partially unrecognizable in a place where the echoes are very clear, the house where it doesn't seem anyone else has lived or can live, so instantly has it become their own, made for the two of them as much as each was made for the other, as this moment was made, when Judith Biely in profile types on her portable Smith-Corona before a bay window, for Ignacio Abel to see the scene in full detail, standing in the doorway, desiring her again, waiting for the gesture when Judith will raise her head and notice his presence, seeing the smile that will form on her lips, the gleam in her eyes. A whole day ahead of them, he recalls, calculating, a whole day and night, and beyond that what he didn't want to see, what's there on the other side of the fog and the horizon of salt marshes crossing the highway in a straight line, the penance of Monday morning and the drive back, the probable silence, he driving and Judith lost in her thoughts, looking out the open window, the wind in her face, the hermetic expression behind her sunglasses, the residue of used-up time trickling out of empty hands.

Judith looked up and burst into laughter when she saw him as probably no one had ever seen him, dazed with sleep, unshaven, his hair uncombed, the man who'd been so guarded the first few times he pulled back when she approached him, as naked now *as when his mother brought him into the world,* according to the incontrovertible Spanish expression that made her think of Adam. Ignacio was immodest and even a little arrogant, with a male bravura he hadn't known himself capable of, which had been awakened by Judith and wouldn't exist without her. Only now did she have the feeling she knew him, now that he'd been sleeping beside her for entire nights, arms around her, breathing heavily with his mouth open, sprawled on the bed, the only piece of furniture in the bedroom aside from a full-length mirror leaning against the wall. There was a provisional air in the house that made it more hospitable. Sometimes they'd looked at themselves in the mirror sideways, surprised at what they saw, not recognizing themselves, uncertain whether they were the man and woman intertwined, examining themselves, offering themselves, wiping the sweat on their faces or moving hair away from their eyes to see better so nothing would fail to be observed, the mirror like the deepest space they'd inhabited and where there was room only for the two of them, the most secret room in the labyrinth of the house, with no windows or decorations, nothing to distract them from themselves. For the first time love wasn't a parenthesis conditioned and frustrated by haste. When they lay exhausted and satisfied beside each other for the first time they'd granted themselves the privilege of falling asleep, wet, sticky, letting the light breeze from the balcony soothe their bodies, the open balcony they never stood on. The house was a desert island with abundant provisions for a long period of being stranded, like the novels about maritime adventures Ignacio Abel read in early adolescence. In the icebox in the kitchen two blocks of ice hadn't begun to melt yet, as if someone left them there just when they arrived, the same invisible visitor who left the bouquet of roses on the table where Judith had put her typewriter. They didn't see anyone during the four days. From time to time Ignacio Abel was troubled by an uneasy desire to go to the village and find a phone so he could call Madrid, but he was afraid his other life would irritate or dishearten Judith. In the shameless fervor of mutual surrender there was a seed of reserve, as there was a portion of exasperation in desire. Each revealed to the other what had never been shown to anyone else, and they did, or allowed to be done, what shame wouldn't have permitted them to conceive of, yet there were regrets or complaints or silent outbreaks of anguish they both concealed. On the second night Ignacio Abel woke and Judith was sitting up in bed, her back to him, erect, looking toward the window. He was going to say her name or extend his hand to her, but the suggestion of self-absorption emanating from her motionless body, from the breathing he couldn't hear, stopped him. What will happen when we go back? How much time do I have left? How would they let me know whether something happened, whether misfortune struck one of my children, a car out of control on the way to school, the horrible, always lurking dangers you don't want to think about, a sudden fever, a stray bullet in the tumult of a demonstration? Adela waiting for the requested and promised call, the one that wouldn't have been so difficult, the one he wasn't going to make. Four days and four nights that would last forever and crumble into nothingness. He was leaning on his elbows at the bedroom window, enjoying the coolness of the night after a long hot Sunday, looking at the full moon that had risen from the ocean like a great yellow balloon, when he realized he didn't hear the typewriter. He went out to the living room and saw with a start that Judith wasn't there. Insects flew around the lighted lamp on the table next to the typewriter and the handful of pages the breeze was disarranging. She was writing an article, she told him, about the things she'd seen on the drive from Madrid, the beauty that took her breath away and made her feel she was living in the fantastic landscapes of Washington Irving, John Dos Passos, romantic lithographs, and the miserable poverty it was impossible to look away from. Leaving Madrid for the south at first light had meant becoming lost in another world for which nothing had prepared her, though she recognized its literary lineage. The dry, treeless expanse of La Mancha in the June morning, cool at first and then burning hot, was identical to the descriptions of Azorín and Unamuno and the color illustrations in a 1905 *Quijote* she'd found in the public library when she was fifteen or sixteen: the images made more of an impression on her because she barely knew Spanish and had stared at them in order to understand something of the story. But he, driving without taking his eyes from the dusty road, attempted to dissuade her from those dreams: she should forget about the Castilian ecstasies of Azorín and Unamuno, Ortega's vague observations; there was nothing mystical, nothing beautiful in the bare plain those writers had celebrated, no mystery related to the essence of Spain; there was ignorance, senseless economic decisions, the cutting down of trees, the dominance of huge estates and great flocks of sheep owned

by feudal lords, grossly rich parasites dependent on the labor of peasants crushed by poverty, uneducated, malnourished, subjugated by
the superstitions of the Church. What she saw wasn't nature, he said,
taking one hand from the wheel, gesturing with an indignation that
by now was a character trait; the uninhabited wastelands, the expanses of wheat fields and vineyards, the barren horizons where a
bell tower rose above a cluster of squat, earth-colored houses, were
the consequence of fruitless labor and the exploitation of one man by
another that was blessed by the Church. The precipices of Despe-
ñaperros brought to Judith's mind the stagecoach journeys of romantic chroniclers and the fantastic lithographs of Gustave Doré; driving
slowly along the narrow, dangerous highway, car tires squealing on
gravel at the edges of ravines, Ignacio Abel spoke at length and in a
loud voice about the need for the Republic to favor literary verbiage
less and the engineering of roads, railways, canals, and ports more.
Out of the corner of his eye he saw her taking photographs with the
small Leica she wore around her neck. He attempted to dissuade her
from the deceitful seduction of the picturesque: that barefoot boy
wearing a straw hat who waved at them as he rode on a tiny donkey
was probably destined never to set foot in school; the slow multitude
of sheep that obliged them to stop and crossed the road enveloped in
a storm of dust might remind Judith of the adventure in which Don
Quijote, in his delirium, confuses flocks and armies, giving her the
idea of a country halted in time, where things written in a book more
than three centuries before continued to be real — shepherds whistling to their dogs, holding staffs from which bags of esparto grass
and water gourds hung, their helpers using slings and hurling stones
with the dexterity of Neolithic herders. Wouldn't it be better if that
fallow land the sheep passed over were plowed, cultivated with the
necessary technical skill, turned over with tractors and not hoes, distributed in sufficiently large parcels to those who cultivated it? No
doubt, when night fell, the shepherds would light fires and tell one
another primitive stories or sing ballads passed down from the Middle Ages for the satisfaction of Don Ramón Menéndez Pidal and the

scholars at the Center for Historical Studies whom Judith so admired. But rather than singing ballads, perhaps it would be better for them to listen to songs on the radio and have the opportunity to sleep in a bed and work six days a week for a reasonable wage.

Judith listened attentively. She had the gift of listening. She asked questions: she didn't want to lose the meaning of any word, just as she wrote down in a notebook the beautiful names, Arabic- or Roman-sounding, of the villages they drove past. The urgent need to write revived forcefully in her; the feeling of something that wouldn't resemble anything she'd done before, the attempts that almost never left her feeling satisfied but only regretful, because of her sense of fraudulence, of squandering for unknown reasons the impulse that had brought her to Europe, the goal of giving herself an education, of living up to her mother's gift. The physical exaltation of traveling in a car next to him and of having the days and nights before them was linked to the proximate writing of the book that had appeared to her so often as a dazzling intuition about to be revealed; the audacity of love would be with her when she placed a blank sheet of paper in front of her and touched the round polished keys of the typewriter, white letters on a black background, its body so light, its mechanism so fast: additional spurs to the speed her writing would have, touched with a transparent sharpness, a clarity like the one she noted in her own attentiveness and alert gaze during the trip. She would have to recount what she was seeing with a fluidity that would contain the passing images and sensations: the dry plain, the blue background of mountains it seemed they would never reach, the precipices where torrents resounded and great eagles flew in slow circles, the straight rows of olive trees undulating as if on a static sea of reddish hills until they vanished in another, bluer, still more distant horizon. She would have to mix into the flow of the account the austere splendor of the landscapes and the affront of backwardness and human poverty, the dignity of the lean, dry faces that remained fixed as the car passed, motionless in front of white walls, looking out of shadowy doorways. As they left a village that didn't seem to have a name, or trees, or almost any inhabitants, only dogs panting in the sun on a dusty street, Ignacio Abel abruptly put on the brakes, forcing her to look straight ahead. A hammer and sickle had been painted in large brushstrokes on the half-collapsed wall of a drinking trough. In front of the car a line of men obstructed the highway. They wore berets and straw hats against the sun, and espadrilles and corduroy trousers tied at the waist with straps or lengths of rope. One or two wore a red armband with political initials, perhaps UHP. Two of them, one at each end of the line, held, but didn't aim, hunting shotguns. Yet there was no hostility in their eyes; curiosity, perhaps, because of the rarity of the car model, its body painted brilliant green, the chrome fittings of the handles and headlights, the folded-down leather top, the men's curiosity intensified by Judith's visibly foreign air. And a gruff obstinacy as well, the instinctive offense at the polished car in the gritty desolation of the village outskirts, the rage of promises never kept, the messianic dreams of social revolution. "They won't do anything to us," said Ignacio Abel, looking into the eyes of the man who approached and holding Judith's hand that had reached toward the wheel, searching for his. She didn't understand what the man said; he spoke with a strange accent, in a hoarse voice, barely parting his lips. There was no work in the village, the man said. The bosses had refused to plant, and they had decided that the scant barley and wheat harvest would be left in the fields. We're not bandits, the man said, and not beggars either. So that their children wouldn't die of hunger, they were asking for a voluntary contribution. As the man talked to Ignacio Abel, the others looked at Judith. She would have to write about those black eyes in dark faces, their chins unshaven; the toothless smile of the man who had the fog of mental deficiency in his eyes; the harsh surface of everything under a vertical sun; the faces, the black cloth of the berets, their hands, the barrels and butts of the shotguns; the anticipation of a possible threat; the way all their eyes stared at Ignacio Abel's soft leather wallet and white city hands, the glitter of his gold watch. When Ignacio Abel handed over some bills, one of the men stepped forward and grasped his wrist, examining the watch. Alarmed, Abel sensed that the men's request for a contribution was the pretext for a holdup. He didn't do anything, didn't try to free himself from the man's grip. "We're revolutionaries, not bandits"—Judith understood the words of the man who'd first approached, the shotgun now resting on his shoulder, pulling at the other man so he'd release Ignacio Abel's wrist. He said it, she thought, in a joking tone, but not completely, a joke that didn't eliminate the threat. She'd have to write about her fear and also her remorse at feeling it; the uncomfortable awareness of her privileged status, offensive to those men, and with that her desire to get away. But how could she dare to write that her abstract love of justice was less powerful than the instinctive physical repugnance at those men, her relief that the car was accelerating and they were letting them pass, staying behind, in a cloud of dust, in their desert poverty?

Though he hadn't heard the typewriter for some time, he realized it only now. He called to her, her beautiful name echoing in the empty house. In the typewriter a blank sheet of paper moved almost imperceptibly in the air, fragrant with algae, that entered through the open balcony. The written pages on one side of the machine, the blank sheets on the other. He called her again and his voice sounded strange. The electricity had gone off. He looked for her in the house, holding the oil lamp, calling her again, noticing the seamless transition from surprise to anguish. She couldn't be far, nothing could have happened to her, but her absence suddenly turned everything unreal, the white walls and the staircase lit by the oil lamp, the loneliness of the house on the escarpment, the presence of the two of them in it, the noise of the ocean. He couldn't calculate how much time had passed since he last saw her, when he stopped hearing the typewriter as he leaned on his elbows at the window, looking at the white, sinuous line of the waves, the beam of the lighthouse in the western sky where red streaks were fading behind violet fog like embers under ash. He went through the rooms one by one and Judith wasn't in any of them. He walked silently, barefoot on the clay tiles. In the kitchen, on the wooden table, was a glass half full of water, a plate with a knife and the skin of a peach.

Through the window he could see the beach and ocean lit by the full moon, beyond the tall dry grass along the edge of the escarpment. Below, where the wooden stairs ended, he could make out, with great relief, the silhouette of Judith Biely's back, her clear shadow projected by the moon on the sand, smooth and shining as the tide withdrew. He called to her, leaving the house, the wooden stairs trembling and creaking under his weight. He wanted to reach her and, as if in dreams, had a sensation of impossible slowness that worsened when he touched the dry, sifting sand at the bottom. He barely moved forward. He called but could not hear his own voice, weakened by the heightened crashing of the sea. Judith turned slowly toward him, as if she'd known he was approaching. The wind blew the hair from her face, widening her forehead, fastening to her slim body the silk of her robe. In her welcoming smile was something both fragile and remote that hadn't been there an hour or two earlier, when she'd offered herself to him and claimed him with fierce determination: an air of resignation, as if that very moment already belonged to a distant past. Confused in his male way, Ignacio Abel stood in front of her, still breathing in relief at having found her. He dared to embrace her only when he saw she was shivering, the skin on her arms bristling in the damp chill of the wind. "Where will we be tomorrow night at this time?" Judith said, trembling even more when he hugged her, her face cold against his, her hips pressing against him. "Where will we be tomorrow and the next day and the day after that?" But if she'd said it in Spanish, the words wouldn't have had the same prison-sentence monotony: *tomorrow and the day after tomorrow and the day after the day after tomorrow.*

18

WHERE HAVE YOU BEEN? You look rested," said Negrín, laughing. "In the Madrid of consumptives, you look healthier than a mountain climber."

But it wasn't possible to look at someone in the same way when you knew he was carrying a pistol in a holster tight against his left side, glimpsed when his jacket opened after an abrupt gesture, or showing a bulge you might not have noticed if you weren't certain this well-dressed, ordinary man had a firearm, or held by his belt, crudely thrust between trousers and shirt, or as bulky as a stone in the right pocket of the foreman Eutimio Gómez, next to his tobacco pouch and tinder lighter, or recklessly kept anywhere, the way Dr. Juan Negrín patted his pockets and vest to show Ignacio Abel the small pistol after using a napkin to wipe his broad fingers stained with the juice of langostinos and prawns.

"It's Czech," Negrín said, producing a metallic crack as he adjusted something on it with an expert gesture, "the latest model."

Then he forgot about it, as if it were a cigarette lighter, leaving it on the wet marble table with the tray of shells, the steins of beer, the ashtray, the crumpled napkins; his bulk had quickly occupied all the space, as it did anywhere he happened to be, whether at an office desk or a laboratory counter. Dr. Juan Negrín lived in perpetual physical discord with a world whose meager dimensions didn't correspond to his formidable breadth, whose rhythms were always unacceptably slow in contrast to his tireless energy. In Negrín's presence Ignacio Abel always noticed errors of scale, as on a plan or drawing where the proportions of some element have been badly calculated. Enormous overcoats became skimpy if he put them on, well-cut suits were too tight for him, hats that seemed large enough in his hand or hanging on a rack became too small on his head. He stood to receive Ignacio Abel in a private dining room at the Café Lion, and the vaulted ceiling of the cellar became so low he had to stoop; beneath the marble table he had to keep his knees pressed together so his legs would fit. His voice thundered with rich acoustics that demanded more ample spaces. His fingers cracked the shells of prawns with ease. He crisscrossed Madrid — his old laboratory, the Café Lion, the Congress of Deputies, University City — turning vigorously against the reduced dimensions of things, against successive carapaces that limited his movement. He should have lived in a larger country with taller people, wider highways, faster trains, much shorter official ceremonies, more expeditious functionaries, fewer sluggish waiters. He traveled by air whenever he could, more often than not in the diminutive planes of the Spanish Postal Transport Airlines, which presented another challenge to his corpulence. He accumulated job titles and political responsibilities with the same Pantagruelian spirit he brought to ordering trays piled high with shellfish, plates of ham, bottles of wine, steins of beer running over with foam. He called the waiter with two resounding claps and ordered more beer for Ignacio Abel and himself and a platter of fried fish. When the waiter took away the tray of discarded shells and the empty steins, the pistol stood out more clearly on the table, as incongruous and toxic as a scorpion.

"So you want to go away to one of those opulent American universities," he said, avoiding preambles, the languid waste of time of Spanish circumlocution. "I won't be the one to stop you."

"It's only for a semester. And only with your authorization."

"You don't have to pretend with me, Abel. Don't talk as if you didn't think much of it. You want out, like anyone with a little common sense.

Leave this place for a while, see things from a distance, have your family safe. If only I could. Doing your work well, with the current in your favor instead of having to fight against it. All that, not to mention the small advantage of going outside and not being afraid some visionary will shoot you in the name of the social revolution or the Sacred Heart of Jesus, or that you'll get in the way of a bullet aimed at somebody else."

"Things will calm down, I imagine."

"Or not. Or they'll get worse. Did you hear Prieto's speech in Cuenca on May 1 on the radio?"

"I'm afraid not."

"Didn't you read it in the paper?" Negrín laughed out loud. "Abel, I'm afraid that even for an architect your stay in the ivory tower, or on the beach where you got that tan, has lasted too long. Are you sure you didn't go to Biarritz for a few days with some girlfriend? What Don Indalecio said, aside from many sensible and fairly sad things, is that a country can tolerate everything, including revolution, but not permanent, senseless disorder. Of course, to say this he had to go to Cuenca, and me with him, as if I were his squire, because here in Madrid, as you know, our beloved comrades in the Bolshevik wing of the party would have lynched him. Do you still have your Socialist Party card, Abel?"

"And my dues are paid."

"Aren't you tempted to tear it up?"

"And replace it with what?"

"At heart you're sentimental, just like me. Except you're much more intelligent and haven't allowed yourself to be dragged into the vortex where I find myself now and, frankly, don't know how to get out of. In fact, I don't know how I got into it. I'm even catching the oratorical fever, come to think of it. I've never said the word 'vortex' before."

"You have a political vocation, Don Juan."

"A political vocation? The only vocation I have is being a scientist, my dear friend. Politics, what they call politics, either exasperates me or bores me to death, no middle ground. Azaña has a political vocation, or Indalecio Prieto, or poor Don Niceto Alcalá-Zamora, whom we threw out of the presidency of the Republic with a kick that most certainly was indecorous. What I like is to see things accomplished — *to get things done,* as the Americans say, with that pragmatism they have. But here politics is nothing but words, forests of words, hectares of speeches with subordinate clauses. Have you seen how Azaña listens to himself, how he rounds off a paragraph as if he were making a long flourish of the cape in front of a bull? The only thing missing is that from the bleachers in Congress instead of 'Bravo' they shout 'Olé,' lengthening the vowels a good deal: *Oooooleeeeeé.* And even so, from time to time Azaña says things of some substance. But what did Don Niceto say in all his kilometric speeches, aside from quoting the classics with an Andalusian 's' instead of a Castilian lisp? And the illustrious Don José Ortega y Gasset, how many afternoons did he put us to sleep in Congress with his flowery prose? Ultimately he became disenchanted with the Republic as well and didn't offer his services as a deputy again, otherwise I'd have been tempted to go much farther away than you to avoid hearing him. Like Don Miguel de Unamuno, the worst defect Don José Ortega sees in the Republic is his not being named president for life. I watched him speaking in his seat as if he were explaining introductory philosophy to his students. Do you believe one should trust a philosopher who colors his gray hair with cheap dye and makes so great an effort to hide his baldness when he has no chance of success?"

"He also seems to wear lifts in his shoes."

"As an architect, you notice the structural details! I'll stay with the ornamentation."

Negrín could eat and speak at top speed and at the same time guffaw, or acquire a serious frown when he imagined a gloomy future. But that apprehension never discouraged his activism or diminished his energy; instead it excited them. Beside him, Ignacio Abel easily felt guilty of passivity, languor. This man who was an internationally eminent scientist, and at some point would inherit a fortune, had chosen to dedicate his life and talent and his astonishing reserves of energy to improving a harsh, impoverished country where he may never receive any recompense, any show of gratitude. His generosity was un-doubtedly mixed with a potent dose of pride, a kind of reagent without which he wouldn't have acted. As for the vigor of his character, perhaps it was as hereditary and removed from his will as his colossal physi-cal size or the unlimited sexual appetite about which rumors circu-lated throughout Madrid. Nevertheless, Ignacio Abel found in Negrín a moral conviction that he didn't possess, a capacity that occasionally struck him as histrionic but essentially seemed much healthier than his own tendency to dissimulate and be reserved, to observe in silence and nourish rancorous irony, with no risk of being refuted and no effect on the reality of things.

"Believe me, what I want is to lock myself away and do research fourteen hours a day in a good laboratory. At the Residence I can't get myself to go into my own lab for fear I'll just break down. Or when I go to University City and see you behind the glass door of your office, bending over the drawing board, so absorbed that when I knock on the glass to attract your attention you don't raise your head . . . How I envy you, my friend — what a privilege. To do one thing and do it well, with your five senses. Don Santiago Ramón y Cajal used to tell me, with that lugubrious face he had toward the end, shaking his skinny, dead man's finger as yellow as a wax candle: 'Negrín, you're involved in too many things. The man who embraces too much holds very little close.' He made me angry, of course, but he was absolutely right. Though I was involved in some of those things because of him!"

"But you'll return to research sooner or later. I don't think you'll stay in politics forever."

"A scientific researcher is like an athlete, Abel my friend. What's the point of kidding ourselves? He has a few truly splendid years and then nothing, routine. He stops keeping up with the latest publications for a time and he's out of the competition. Like the boxer who stops train-ing, the athlete who doesn't run. He gets a potbelly, just like the one I'm getting! Why don't you finish your beer and we'll order another round. Don't you have any vices? It seems Hitler has absolutely none. Did you know he's a vegetarian and it's forbidden to smoke in his presence? Here, a politician who doesn't smoke and have a rich deep cough is considered a fag. Speaking of Hitler, would you like to know the secret of his success, according to Madariaga, our only international expert? His secret is the airplane. Other candidates traveled by train, at most by car. The result was that in the election campaign they are nowhere to be seen. Hitler always traveled by plane, so he had time to be everywhere. The airplane, the radio, and the movie projector have achieved the miracle of omnipresence. Meanwhile our poor President Azaña turns pale and holds on to his seat if his official car goes faster than thirty kilometers an hour, and when he climbs the steps to an airplane, he begins to tremble so much his aide has to push him up. The speed of Spanish politics is that of a mule cart. So you tell me what's to be done. Extend electrification, as suggested by Comrade Lenin, so admired now in broad sectors of our party!"

"Do you think the Leninism of Largo Caballero and his people is serious?"

"Probably not, but it doesn't matter. The most frivolous, most absurd idea becomes real if a few fools believe it and are prepared to take action. Can anyone take seriously calling Largo Caballero the Spanish Lenin? He does. And the fifth-rate literati with sour café-con-leche breath who fill their heads with Marxist fantasies. And, of course, fearful Catholics who listen to the awful speeches he gives in bullrings about the impending proletarian revolution —"

"Written by individuals who are much more astute than he is."

"And more sinister too, don't forget. Think of the nonsense he said, or they had him say, during the campaign: if the right won, civil war would be inevitable . . . Largo has become a supporter of the dictatorship of the proletariat because they've made him believe that when it comes, he'll be the dictator. All empty talk, of course. But empty talk that in no way favors our cause and serves only to further inflame our enemies. Believe me, they live in a delusion, a world of fantasy. They go to the Sierra on Sundays to shoot a few bullets with old pistols and sing 'The Internationale,' and they imagine they've formed the Red Army, and whenever they feel like it they'll seize power by storm. The Winter

Palace. Or El Pardo Palace, where the president of the Republic hasn't had time to go for summer vacation, given how calm things are around here . . . They don't learn anything. They didn't learn anything from the disaster of the 1934 uprising. Their heads are filled with propaganda posters and Soviet films. And the few of us who dare contradict them and ask for a little good sense are viewed as worse than Fascists. Do you see this small pistol that inspires so little confidence? Last week I drove Prieto in my car to a meeting in Ecija. A horrible road, as you can imagine, African heat, lots of flies, Prieto and I so fat we barely fit in the car, and behind us an old bus with a gang of armed boys, just in case. The meeting began all right, but after a few minutes they were booing us."

"In the bullring?"

"Where else, Abel? You're a monomaniac about the bulls."

"Architecture determines people's moods, Don Juan. Look at those stadiums where Hitler gives his speeches. In a bullring the sun softens brains and the public develops its instinct for seeing blood and demanding that ears be cut off."

"I see you're a real determinist . . . The fact is, we had to stop the meeting and take refuge in the infirmary to keep our dear comrades from lynching us. When we were leaving, a mob with sticks and stones surrounded us, calling us all kinds of names and shouting 'Long live's for Russia and communism. A crowd of our young people mixed with members of the Communist Youth groups, whom they've joined now, to the great joy of the weakest minds in our party. Believe it or not, I had to fire into the air so our comrades would let us get away, fleeing for our lives along those roads. If the Civil Guard hadn't helped us, they'd have finished us off. No need to stress the historic irony."

Negrín drained his beer, wiping away the foam with a broad sweep of his arm, then banging the stein down on the marble tabletop, next to the tiny pistol. The mocking expression was still on his face when the look in his eyes changed abruptly, along with his conversation, or the thread of his monologue.

"They hate us, Abel my friend. I'm not surprised you want to leave.

They hate you and me. They hate us inside and outside the party. The reactionaries who can't get over losing the February elections hate us, and so do many we thought were our people because they supported the Popular Front. They hate those of us who don't believe that demolishing the current world will make a better one possible, or that destruction and assassination can bring justice. It isn't a question of ideas, as some think on our side and the other side. You and I know that abstract ideas don't amount to much in practical life. In each case we face specific problems, and we don't resolve them with fuzzy ideas but with knowledge and experience. I in my laboratory, you at your drawing board. If we come down from the stratosphere of ideas, things are fairly clear. What's needed to keep a building from falling down? What do our compatriots need? You don't have to do more than go out to the sidewalk and look at the people going by. They need to be better fed. They need better shoes. They need to drink more milk as children so they don't lose their teeth. They need better hygiene, and they need to bring fewer children into the world. They need good schools and jobs with decent pay, and affordable heat in winter. Would it be so difficult to achieve a rational organization of the country to facilitate all that? Once everybody eats every day, and there's electricity and clean running water, I say that would be the moment to begin talking about the classless society, or the glories of the Spanish race, or Esperanto, or eternal life, or whatever you like. Notice I'm not talking about socialism or emancipation or the end of man's exploitation of man. I make no professions of faith, and I don't believe you do either. I don't see much difference between making a pilgrimage to Moscow or Mecca or the Vatican or Lourdes. What bothers the religious believer most is not the believer in another religion, not the atheist, but someone worse, the skeptic, the person who's lukewarm. Have you noticed that in speeches and editorials, the word 'neutral' has been transformed into an insult? Well, of course I'm neutral, though from time to time the blood does rush to my head. I don't want to be burned, and I don't want anybody or anything burned either. We had enough bonfires with the Holy Inquisition. Now I see many people who say they've lost faith in the Republic. Faith in the Republic! As if they'd prayed to a saint or a virgin asking for a miracle that hasn't been granted. They pray to the Popular Front to bring not only amnesty but agrarian reform, communism, happiness on earth, and because a few months have passed since the elections and there's been no miracle, they lose faith and want to do away with the legality of the Republic, as if they wanted to throw the font at the saint who didn't bring them rain after their prayers. Not to mention those others who are involved in something more than prayers and uprisings. Praying to God, not sparing the rod. There they are, conspiring more brazenly than ever, in the view of everyone except the government, which acts as if it hasn't heard a thing. Rich young monarchists go to Rome for the pope's blessing, pay their respects to His Majesty Don Alfonso XIII, then cash the check Mussolini gives them to buy weapons. Ready for the reconquest of Spain, as they put it. Insane. Furious because the Republic has expropriated a couple of barren estates or doesn't let them preach in the public schools or permits a man and a woman who've spent their lives hating each other to go their separate ways. Enraged because this poor Republic that doesn't have enough to pay teachers' salaries has retired on full pay all the thousands of officers who lazed around their barracks and thought it a good idea to apply for a pension, and it asked for nothing in exchange, not even an oath of loyalty. Do you know why I had to buy this pistol and why that man you see there looking so bored and chewing on a toothpick has to accompany me? Let me guess what you're thinking. It isn't that the pistol and the bodyguard look as if they offer much security — why kid ourselves. Though Jiménez de Asúa's escort saved his life . . . But this is the country we have, my friend, and it doesn't give much of itself for good or for ill. Half of Spain hasn't gone past feudalism, and our comrades who write for *Claridad* want to do away with a bourgeoisie that barely exists. Even the conspiracies are of little account, my dear Abel; they're the hooliganism of rich boys who can't keep a secret. There's a girl, a student of mine, not brilliant but very diligent, who was doing research with me in the laboratory before I lost my head completely and left everything to get involved in politics. This girl, modern but a little awkward, had a fairly ordinary fiancé who came to pick her up every afternoon at the Residence and greeted me courteously, one of those men who aspire to being a registrar or a notary and out of sheer listlessness end up having to spend several years in a tuberculosis sanatorium in the Sierra. Nothing to object to. As soon as they were formally engaged, she left the laboratory because it wouldn't be proper if a señorita already spoken for, as they say in those families, were to continue working in a place filled with men. Instead of biochemistry, where she could have done something worthwhile over the years, she would no doubt dedicate her efforts to bearing children and saying rosaries in the stupor of the province where they'd send her husband when he finally regained enough strength to sit for his examinations. I saw her from time to time after that, and she never forgot to send a card for my saint's day or greetings at Christmas. *On this the day of your saint I wish you and your loved ones every happiness and include you in my prayers,* the poor thing wrote to me last year. But not long ago she called one night, her voice shaking as if she were afraid someone might hear her. I asked if anything was wrong and she said no, not with her, but she had to see me urgently and please don't tell anyone she'd called. She came to my house the next morning, Sunday, before Mass, with the little veil on her head, more awkward than when she wore the white coat in the laboratory, not daring to look me in the eye. I thought she must be pregnant and had come to ask for help in getting a secret abortion. And do you know what she wanted to tell me?"

Negrín took a long drink of beer, and this time he wiped away the foam with a handkerchief that he then passed over his broad, sweaty brow. The police escort, more erect now, nodded from a distance at his explanations, conscious of his role, chewing on the toothpick.

"That her fiancé, in addition to caring for his lungs and studying for the profession of notary or registrar, had formed a Falangist shock troop with some friends and they were planning to assassinate me. 'Everything anticipated,' the poor girl said to me with that thin little voice that barely left her body, like her voice when she had to answer a question on an examination: the day, the time, the place, the weapons they would use, the getaway car, just as they'd seen it in the movies. Political ideas are more dangerous when they're mixed up with the foolishness of movies. They planned to kill me right here, at the door of the café, on the sidewalk of Calle de Alcalá. Then this detail: they intended to let me eat supper first."

"Have they been arrested?"

"How could I accuse them without hurting her?" Negrín guffawed. "Perhaps they realized I carried a pistol or had begun to enjoy the company of this good friend who's now my guardian angel. Or maybe they got bored or were afraid to move from words to deeds."

"And what happened to your student?"

"You're not going to believe this. The next day she called again, speaking in a thread of a voice, in tears, 'torn between conflicting feelings,' as they say in the women's magazines. 'My dear Dr. Negrín, for the sake of what you hold dear, forget what I told you yesterday. They're nothing but boys' childish fantasies.' Her fiancé in reality was a good person, incapable of hurting a fly. He didn't even have a pistol, and besides, he was sick, because it seems the examinations are at the beginning of the summer, and with so much memorization of a gigantic list of topics, he didn't take care of himself and suffered a slight relapse, so he may have to go back to the sanatorium and not sit for examinations this year. A drama more Spanish than those of Calderón. Worse yet, than those of Don Jacinto Benavente."

"You're too trusting."

"What shall I do? Not leave the house? Stay shut away like Azaña since he's been president of the Republic, taking walks in the gardens of El Pardo and thinking about what he'll write in the journal they say he's keeping before he goes to bed? I need people and movement, my dear Abel. I need to walk to the café from the Congress, so I'm hungrier and thirstier and enjoy the food and beer all the more. I've already had another and you've barely tasted yours. Is it true you have no vices?"

Negrín leaned his elbows on the table, and extending the thick fingers of one hand, he counted with the index finger of the other, close to Ignacio Abel and looking at him with an ironic stare that made him uncomfortable.

"You don't smoke. That seems fine. As a cardiologist, I have no objection. You practically don't drink. You don't like bullfights. Good food is not your downfall, as it is mine. You don't look as if you ever go to whores ... Don't you have a voluptuous mistress hidden away somewhere?"

Perhaps Negrín did know, as irrepressibly fond of gossip about other people's vices as he was of food or women or great political operations. Perhaps he'd heard rumors and therefore from the beginning had worn a half-smile, suspecting that beneath his intention to go to a foreign university, Ignacio Abel was hiding not only the urgency of fleeing the disasters of Spain but a less admissible desire, a passion that gave the lie to his honorable air, his sober appearance of bourgeois, rather puritanical dignity. For a moment Ignacio Abel, examined so intently by Negrín's eyes, was afraid he'd blush, felt the heat rising from the base of his neck, oppressed by the knot in his tie. He imagined Negrín's sonorous laugh, his pleasure in a human weakness that would make his less exceptional. But fortunately Negrín had finished his beer and suddenly was in a hurry. He put the pistol in his pocket, wiped his forehead with a handkerchief, consulted his watch, and called the waiter with two loud claps.

"Count on me for whatever you need, Abel," he said as they were saying goodbye at the café entrance, and he looked up and down the street with rapid caution. "If you like, I'll make sure they give you the passport and your American visa right away. Leave as soon as you can, and don't hurry back."

He watched Negrín cross Calle de Alcalá, his broad shoulders standing out above the heads of other people, the light summer jacket tight at the sides, advancing with great strides through the traffic, not waiting for the officer's signal to pedestrians, walking so fast that his police escort was left behind.

19

H E'S ALWAYS BEEN about to leave. He doesn't know for how many years he's been a guest in his own life, the figure in a painting, the only one in a group to turn his eyes away from what holds the attention of the others, as if to say I'm not one of them; a dubious presence who appeared out of focus in photographs or simply was missing from them (mother, children, smiling grandparents, only the father invisible: distracted, perhaps using some pretext not to pose). *You must have thought no one would notice how you hid your disapproval, but I did. I know you better than anybody, though you don't think so.* In reality this written voice is the only one that has addressed him since he began his journey, the irate, accusing voice, no longer hurt, only filled with rage, a rage chilled by distance and the act of writing, and perhaps, too, by the awareness that the addressee might never receive the letter, that he was dead, that the mail service, in ruins like everything else, had lost it, left it undelivered in some mail sack—how many letters must have disappeared this way throughout Spain during these months, how many are still being written? *You always had to go somewhere, you said nothing and suddenly you'd tell me, at the last minute, I'm leaving tomorrow, or I won't be home for supper tonight, or that time you went to Barcelona for a whole week to see the International Exhibition—for work, you said, even though Miguel had been running*

*high fevers and seemed to have something wrong with his lungs. You left
me alone night after night, lying awake beside the boy who was delirious. Don't think I don't remember.* He could tear up the letter right now,
get rid of it as he'd done with so many things as he traveled, from the
time he closed the door of his apartment in Madrid and out of habit
was about to lock it but decided not to; he probably wouldn't go back
and a patrol of militiamen could smash the lock at any time, that very
night; he might have torn up the letter before leaving the hotel room,
or better yet, not opened it when the receptionist handed it to him and
after the initial surprise, then hope, and finally disillusionment he recognized the handwriting. It wasn't Judith's. *It was almost worse when
you stayed here and it felt as if you were gone because it seemed as if you
weren't in your own house but someone else's or in a waiting room or a
hotel especially when my parents or brother or someone from my family
came to visit. I wish you'd seen the face you put on for them.*

So many grievances, all of them cited in the letter as if on the densely
written pages of a formal indictment, bringing him Adela's exhausted,
offended voice, vibrating and never silent in the receiver of a phone
he didn't know how to move away from his ear. *Leaving or being left
alone, that was all you wanted and it's what you've accomplished.* The
man who'd been an intruder or a furtive guest in his own apartment
became for several months its only resident; from the Saturday in July
when he came back from the Sierra and searched for Judith in a Madrid inundated with crowds, lit by headlights and the sudden flare of
fires, to a midnight three months later when Madrid was already a city
of dark, empty streets, disciplined by fear and alarm sirens, seized by
terror at the steady approach of the war, like the inexorable arrival of
winter. Long before, at the end of July, in August, on hot nights when it
wasn't wise to be seen on the streets, Ignacio Abel wandered aimlessly
through the apartment, up and down the long hall, from one room to
another, opening the glass doors between rooms with high ceilings and
moldings of an opulence he disliked more and more. He wrote letters;

he imagined he was writing them; laboriously he composed aloud the phrases in English he'd say to Judith Biely if he saw her again; he wound the clock in the hall, and every time it took less time for it to stop; he didn't uncover most of the furniture and lamps draped in sheets, which looked abstract now; he observed with displeasure how quickly dirt took over in the bathroom with no one there to clean it; he ventured into the kitchen to prepare himself a simple supper, a hermit's meal, whatever the porter's wife had brought up for him or he had found at the less and less well-stocked stands at the nearby market or the corner grocery that until recently had displayed a full window, now almost empty, in part because of real shortages, in part because the owner preferred to hide the goods in the cellar for fear they would be requisitioned at gunpoint.

How strange that he'd found an apartment like this acceptable, resigned himself to it, allowed it to be filled with furnishings as presumptuous as the dimensions of the building itself, the marble balustrades on the balconies, the drapes and rugs, not to mention the testimonies to the terrible taste of Don Francisco de Asís and Doña Cecilia, their terrifying generosity and love of fake antiques, or authentically abominable antiques, carved Castilian credenzas, the pendulum clock with its Gothic inscription in Latin, the Christ of Medinaceli with its Morisco eave and tiny metal lights. *I'm an architect and I live in an apartment I think is someone else's; I'm forty-eight years old and suddenly seem to be living another man's life by mistake,* he'd written to Judith in one of his first letters, stupefied to discover that without difficulty and almost without intending to he could cross in a few minutes the invisible frontier to another identity and another life, his true life. But he didn't tell Judith or didn't want to remember the gratification he'd felt when he saw the place for the first time with Adela and the children, who were still very young, and learned the price and calculated that he could afford it: a recently completed building in the Salamanca district, close to the Retiro, with a marble entrance where two caryatids supported the great arch over curved steps leading to the elevator, and a porter in a uniform with braid and white gloves who removed his peaked cap when he greeted the ladies and gentlemen. "This is a building of true magnificence!" Don Francisco de Asís had declared, his booming voice rumbling in the marble-covered heights, and he had felt a certain pride, fortified by Adela's enthusiasm as she walked from one room to another, admiring the size, the moldings on the ceilings, incredulous that an apartment like this could be hers, almost intimidated, while the children got lost playing hide-and-seek in the back rooms, their footsteps and shrill voices echoing in the empty spaces. *You thought yourself so upright and my father so ridiculous, yet you didn't hesitate to take advantage of his friendship with the developer to get a good price on the apartment. You didn't bother to thank him even though you knew we only got this deal because of him.* On hot nights his solitude and confinement became as unbearable as the air. (The shutters had to be closed before turning on the lights, as a precaution against bombings, they said, out of fear above all of the vigilance patrols who shot at lit windows, no questions asked.) He'd hear gunfire, car motors, tires squealing around corners. He'd hear shouts sometimes when he was dozing on the sheets that nobody changed, in the bed he didn't know how to make, the large double bed with a baroque headboard, where it was strange not to find the weight and shadow, the breathing of Adela. *It seems incredible not that you've stopped loving me but that you've forgotten how much you used to love me.* He left the bedroom door partway open in case he heard footsteps at dawn on the landing or the stairs (no one had repaired the elevator since some strikers sabotaged it early in July). He heard footsteps or dreamed them and woke with a start, expecting fists or rifle butts banging on the door. He dreamed about Judith Biely, detailed erotic dreams, more like re-lived memories, in which she turned into a stranger, her cold stare plunging him into a deep sadness that was still there when he woke. He masturbated without pleasure, with a kind of nervous excitation, with a feeling of humiliation when he finished, unsatisfied, longing for her skilled, delicate hand. He washed, trying not to look at himself in the bathroom mirror, and dried his hands on a dirty towel.

In a drawer in the wardrobe he dug out albums of family photos he hadn't looked at in years, the ones Adela filled so faithfully, long hours sitting at her desk in the library with the large pages spread open, piles of photographs, glue, the scissors she used to cut small labels, the pen she used to write down dates, names, and places in the hand of a student at a nuns' academy, with a conviction that seemed intent not so much on preserving memories as on building on unimpeachable testimonies a solid structure of family life. The albums themselves were a more lasting foundation than the events reflected in the photos. Classifying them, observing the regularity with which weddings, baptisms, Communions, Christmas dinners, birthdays, saint's days, trips to the coast, and summers in the Sierra appeared in them, Adela precariously granted herself the comforting sensation of having the life she'd always wanted, the one she hadn't dared to want when she was young and began to suspect that perhaps she wouldn't find a man to marry, and her parents didn't have much hope that it would happen either. The prospect of remaining single made her sad, but the generally accepted notion that if a suitor didn't appear her life would be a failure seemed humiliating, an attack on her personal dignity. A man held his destiny in his own hands, while a woman didn't possess so much as half of hers; without a man's protection the only possible life open to her was to be a spinster or a nun, since Adela's social class wouldn't allow her to be a governess or teacher. Her tending so much to her younger brother gave her a maternal air: she saw herself in the role of proxy mother who hasn't known even the degree of personal autonomy that belongs to a wife. On both sides of her family there was a wide selection of unmarried women, affectionate aunts who were resigned and pious and soon showed themselves ready to welcome her into their sisterhood, rather faded but not completely melancholy. An ancient cloistered nun underscored the family tendency to female singleness. Adela resisted accepting so premature a fate, but she wouldn't have had the rare courage to displease her parents by telling them she wished to follow the eccentric example of those few young ladies from good families in Madrid who went to the university and endured the ignominy of sitting in lecture halls separated by a screen from their male classmates, subject less to scorn than to mockery, the whispered gossip about a kind of quirk that went beyond the simple whim of occupying male positions in life. Besides, what would she have studied? After so many years at the nuns' boarding school, the only pedagogical outcome was an exquisite though completely anachronistic handwriting and a few inadequate notions of needlework and French. During summers in the Sierra she'd become fond of long walks and reading, walks that she wasn't allowed to take by herself and books that had to be approved by her father or her uncle the priest. Adela felt deeply the humiliation of waiting and not doing anything, of seeing herself displayed on social calls and at family celebrations as a marriageable young woman whom no suitor approached, a parrot in a cage, a freak in a circus stall. But her feeling of personal affront was neutralized by love for her parents and a general benevolence or forbearance of character that made her go along with it all with little effort, preferring passive obedience to the discomfort of a scene that would end in tears and remorse and in any case wouldn't grant her any result. The resolve of her inner rebellion never provoked the slightest turbulence in the sweet, mild appearance she presented to others, interpreted as a symptom of Christian resignation to the solitary future that with the passage of time would cover her in ridicule. When she was twenty-one or twenty-two, the cabal of her aunts and mother had already determined she'd remain a spinster, and they devoted long, laborious analyses to an explanation of this inevitable fact, which was enigmatic because somehow all of them had deemed it a certainty almost from the time she left childhood behind, with no obvious reasons to support it: she wasn't at all ugly, or fat, or skinny either; she had pretty teeth; she was pleasant and considerate, though perhaps a little sad. She may have had a gravity that dampened her sparkle and made her seem older than she was, choosing dresses that weren't flattering or that exaggerated her small defects, analyzed by aunts and female cousins with subtleties worthy of a class in histology, a science made fashionable by Don Santiago Ramón y Cajal. Didn't she have a double chin from the time she was very young? Eyebrows that were too thick, a certain tendency to walk as if she had a weight on her shoulders which made her seem shorter? Among the girls of good family in her generation, she was one of the last to adopt the fashions that came from Europe after the Great War, and in this case not for fear of opposing her parents but because of something that might be interpreted as the negligence of a woman no longer interested in making herself attractive. In 1920 she was thirty-four years old and hadn't yet cut the long hair appropriate to a woman of another time, another age, or given up corsets, and so she seemed to belong more to the generation of maiden aunts than to her female cousins not destined for the hereditary female celibacy that in the Ponce-Cañizares and Salcedo family endangered the continuance of the line. Her adaptation to the new age was gradual, guided by the caution and timidity that were character traits. At a given moment the compassionate tone used to speak of her in the family took on a hint of misgiving; her shyness stopped being attributed to a mixture of humility and sweetness and was suspected of hiding an essential arrogance. Not long before, she'd apologized for not attending as frequently as she should the ladies' entertainments organized by the aunts, on account of her extreme social awkwardness and a propensity for solitude heavy with romanticism, and also — why not say it? — with sadness because of the love that didn't come and the youth that was passing. Now it was known that on more than one occasion she'd missed a novena or a charity raffle not because she was home attending to her parents or caring for her younger brother but because she'd gone to a lecture or a theatrical performance with suspect women friends. The rumor that she wore glasses at home and read newspapers and modern novels was true, and she didn't hide them from her uncle the priest, who was one of the first to make public her shocking heterodox traits: it wasn't true (and no one who really knew her and viewed her without malevolence would have believed it) that she'd angered her father by acquiring the habit of smoking ciga-

315

rettes. Nor was it true that because of modern influences her Catholic faith had weakened. She went to Mass every Sunday arm in arm with her mother, and accompanied her in prayers at the chapel of Jesus of Medinaceli, and confessed and took Communion with an inner devotion that filled her with serenity and had no hint of sanctimony.

Those glimpses of strangeness would have become the tolerable eccentricities of a woman trained for spinsterhood from the time she was young, but they were nothing compared to the seismic perplexity provoked by the great news of her engagement, which went against the laws not only of probability but also of nature. Who could have imagined that a fiancé would turn up when she was in her thirties? It would have been less unbelievable if she'd grown a beard, like those women in the circus to whom she compared herself in her younger years of meekness and humiliation. And not just any fiancé — though he wasn't entirely free of suspect attributes, beginning with origins that part of the family surmised were undesirable — but Don Francisco de Asís accepted him more willingly than anyone, not because by this time he was prepared to consider any candidate as suitable, but by virtue of a good-natured lack of practical prejudices that often did not correspond to the Paleolithic obstinacy of what he called his "body of principles." The suitor of the woman they still called "the girl" turned out to be an architect younger than she, without a personal inheritance but, according to Don Francisco de Asís, with a promising future, recently hired by the municipal government, the only child of a widowed mother, having lost his father at the age of fifteen.

The fact that the widowed mother had also been the porter in a working-class building and the father little more than a shrewd, ambitious bricklayer were additional merits, according to Don Francisco de Asís's point of view, or lamentable drawbacks according to other family members who had the opportunity to congratulate the newly engaged fiancée and her parents as if really offering condolences, alleviating the vexation of having to accept in their cousin and niece a happiness they hadn't counted on. It was a harsh obligation, from one day to the next, to envy someone who until then had been the recipient of their compassion, the drama of poor Adela who'd passed the age of thirty without waking the interest of any man. *I don't know how much you love that woman and I don't care either but I do remember how much you loved me and I've kept all the letters you wrote to me.* But there was no need to lose hope: the good news could still be undone; the fiancé might not be as honest as he seemed. Didn't they say he was a Republican? Even worse, a Socialist, or a Bolshevik, just like his father, the late bricklayer who rose to master builder, owing his position with the municipal government not to merit but to influence, the machinations of left-wing councilmen avid to place one of their own. But as it turned out, the possible reprobate or dowry hunter had excellent manners, learned no one knew where, and a strangely mild way of showing, or rather hiding, his leftist sympathies, because from the beginning he fulfilled to the satisfaction of the most punctilious observer each of the family's obligations and rituals, and didn't have the slightest objection to expressly accepting that his children, when they were born (but wasn't Adela too old to conceive, wasn't it possible for a woman past thirty whose health had never been outstanding to suffer a difficult delivery or give birth to some genetic aberration?), would be baptized with the required pomp by the uncle who was a priest, and brought up in the Catholic faith. And speaking of ideas, hadn't Jesus Christ been, as Don Francisco de Asís argued in a moment of polemical audacity, the first Socialist? Wasn't the evangelical message—properly understood and applied according to the Social Doctrine of the Church—the best antidote to godless revolution? Besides, the fiancé's parents were dead and he had no brothers or sisters, which spared everyone the embarrassing formality of having to deal with individuals of obvious social inferiority, whose presence, though picturesque, would have been offensive at an offer of marriage and more so at a wedding ceremony worthy of the family's position, which would probably merit an article in the society section of the *ABC*—a modest article, of course, certainly with no photo, but everyone knew that in the *ABC* the snobbery of noble

317

titles prevailed, especially since the founder had received one, though he'd begun his career as a soap manufacturer. Since when was soap nobler than cement and brick? Don Francisco de Asís asked in his stentorian voice. With no father or mother or close relatives, Ignacio Abel's origins lost much of their vulgarity and projected a certain shadow of mystery, a dark background against which his elegant figure stood out, veiled by a degree of reserve behind which he could hide the memory of the years of perseverance and sacrifice it had cost him to study for a career and learn manners that were irreproachable even to the most suspicious and demanding gaze. In the eyes of the family, Adela acquired a new and on occasion piercing luminosity; from the first days of her engagement she exhibited an almost indecent amount of happiness. She looked ten years younger. The aunts and cousins said she was as mad with love as the film stars who sighed with their eyes turned to heaven and their hands clasped, glimpsing in the clouds the face of their beloved, thanks to an optical effect that at the time was widely reproduced on postcards. *Think of how you called on me, the things you said to me, it isn't possible you were lying.* The languidly slow pace that had marked the progress of her spinsterhood gave way to a liveliness appropriate to the new age and the technical competence of the fiancé, who aside from his undemanding municipal occupation was beginning to receive substantial commissions, celebrated, not without some exaggeration, by Don Francisco de Asís, who at heart had always sinned on the side of naïveté and reckless enthusiasm. After less than a year's engagement the wedding date was agreed on, and this speed, which wouldn't have required an evil disposition to regard as haste, did not fail to raise suspicions, dissipated only when a careful accounting of the time passed between that date and the first birth revealed the undeniable legitimacy of the newborn. Adela, who seemed so sluggish, had been in a hurry for no reason other than to make up for lost time, with an impatience and a passion more suited to the heroine of a risqué novel than a woman of her years. But neither did she have any scruples about going to live with her husband in a small apartment in an unfashionable Madrid neighborhood where her only help was a maid. *I do remember how happy we were even though I had to climb four flights in all the heat that summer so pregnant with the girl it seemed impossible I could swell up any more.* Don Francisco de Asís let it be known admiringly that his son-in-law hadn't wanted to accept the help he offered to rent a house centrally located and in better condition: accustomed to earning his living by his own efforts, Ignacio Abel was grateful for any hand extended to him but preferred not to have recourse to it unless required by a critical situation that endangered the welfare of his wife or the heir Don Francisco de Asís soon was proud (and relieved) to announce. For her part, Doña Cecilia, more stubborn or less of a dreamer, would have preferred that between the wedding and the birth a period had gone by that wasn't more decent but certainly more dignified and leisurely and more suited to individuals who didn't give themselves over to their conjugal duty with more enthusiasm than required to fulfill the purpose of the sacrament. *I still remember, if you don't, how I trembled when I heard you run up the stairs.*

That a girl was the firstborn was a setback but not a disappointment. Don Francisco de Asís's male child was, after all, the one designated to assure the continuation of the family name, and the girl was born strong, big, and healthy in spite of a difficult labor: during two days of anguish the worst family predictions regarding Adela's advanced age seemed to be confirmed. But mother and daughter came through, and it soon was obvious that the rumors originating nobody knew where and spread by the malevolence of nobody knew who regarding the possible retardation of the newborn were without foundation, though the aunts on their visits looked at the cradle with an expression of condolence. The proud father, as they said in the birth announcements in the newspaper, asked Don Francisco de Asís to be godfather at the baptism of his first grandchild. Before the frantic scrutiny of the family, and the close vigilance of the uncle who was a priest and officiated at the sacrament, Ignacio Abel's behavior in church was as respectful toward the rite as it had been on his wedding day, when everyone had seen him take Communion with exemplary devotion and kneel with eyes closed and head bowed as the sacred wafer dissolved on his tongue (reviving a childhood memory when it stuck to the roof of his mouth, leaving the strange, forgotten taste of flour with no leavening on his palate). The girl would be named Adela, like her mother. *It was you who wanted her to have my name and whispered so in my ear.* That the boy, when he came, was named Miguel, for his dead paternal grandfather, and not Francisco de Asís, was a disappointment to his other grandfather, but like a gentleman he rose above it, taking refuge in the hope, by then somewhat faint, that any day now the grandson born to his male child would be the one to perpetuate not only his family name but his first name too, and in the rather more solid prospect of his son-in-law and Adela continuing to expand the family, and if they had another boy they'd undoubtedly call him Francisco de Asís. In certain cases he knew of, hadn't a change in the order of family names been authorized in the civil registry so as not to lose the memory of an illustrious lineage? In the photos of the baptism, he smiled as he held his grandson, though less broadly than at the girl's baptism because he was concerned by the baby's extreme fragility. How carefully Adela had classified them, album after album, from the formal studio photographs in the early years to the ones taken with the Leica she'd given her husband on one of his more recent birthdays, which he generally used to photograph works in progress. (It was the camera he took on his four-day trip south with Judith Biely, whose pictures he kept in the locked desk drawer.)

Perhaps Adela was slow to accept what Ignacio Abel now realized as he turned the album pages under the dim light of a lamp in the apartment where he was the sole inhabitant, and the figures in the photos took on a ghostly quality, as if they were people who had died long ago, so distant from the present, from Madrid in the shadow of nights of war (lit by the headlights of speeding, solitary cars that suddenly appeared at the end of a street, stopped with the motor running next to a doorway, where after a while a man would be seen coming out in an undershirt or pajamas, sometimes barefoot, dazed with sleep and panic, hands tied, moved along by kicks, guarded by pistols and rifles). Blinded by love, at first Adela wouldn't have noticed his expression in the photos, including the ones he'd sent her as mementos when they became engaged, or the ones from their wedding day, or the portraits they'd taken together on a whim of hers in a studio on the Gran Vía soon after they were married, each seated in an antique chair in front of a painted backdrop, he with his legs crossed, showing his high-top shoes, she holding a book in one hand, her chin resting on the back of the other, wearing an indolent smile in which he could detect what neither of them knew at the time, that she was pregnant. On his face was an expression of not being altogether present, his glance fixed on a point in the middle distance, a self-absorption tinged by ennui. But perhaps he was mistaken, looking at the photographs fifteen years later; perhaps, lacking the imagination to see himself in what to all intents and purposes was another life, he attributed to the younger man a reluctance that became more apparent as he turned the pages of the albums. His entire life, watched over by Adela, by her fondness for keeping everything in its place, not only photographs but letters as well, each one he wrote during their engagement and the ones he sent during his year in Germany, arranged chronologically and held together by rubber bands, which he didn't want to remove from their envelopes, to spare himself the humiliation of his own lies, the expressions of love in his own hand. *You no longer remember how you'd complain if a letter of mine was late.* He looked, hypnotized, at the photos, while outside he heard bursts of gunfire. He went through a series documenting his children's early years and the tedious family celebrations, the changes in the face and body of Adela, who'd been more slender than he recalled. (But who could trust memory? What would Judith Biely be thinking about him now, erasing him from her new life who knew where, with what younger men, in Paris or in America?) He didn't appear in many photographs (he must have been traveling, or working, or away on some pretext or other); in some he was present but wore an expression that separated him from the rest, resistant to the collective happiness, a celebration meant to bring them all together. In them Adela was almost always beside him, holding his arm or leaning against him a little, proud of his male presence, perhaps understanding later, when she put the photos in order and placed them in the album, or much later, when she went back to them to look for signs of what had always existed or to console herself for her loneliness and sense of deception and failure by reliving a time she remembered as happier: their early years together, the birth of Lita, the move to the new building on Calle Príncipe de Vergara, its balconies that opened on the unlimited expanse of Madrid—"Madrid modern and white," as Juan Ramón Jiménez wrote in one of her favorite poems. Her secret malaise might still be a response to her husband's work. He was so insistent on showing others his own worth, committing his very life to the completion of each assignment, perhaps uncertain about the position he'd achieved, wanting to prove that if he prospered it wasn't because of the influence of his wife's family, toward whom he displayed an increasingly dry coldness that hurt her deeply, especially because of the affection she had for her parents, her fear that her husband would hurt them with a defiant remark or sarcastic comment, or simply with the indifference that was apparent in reality and more so in photographs—even, she would realize much later, in the pictures from their wedding, and in those where Ignacio Abel held his newborn children or placed his hand on their shoulder on the day of their Communion. He raised a glass in a toast and looked away. But Adela hadn't failed to complete her albums, to make note of exact dates, circumstances, and places in handwriting that was always the same over the years, as regular as her own presence in the photos, a mixture of passivity and childish hope, as if in spite of everything promises might eventually be kept, as if the only condition for avoiding disaster and not suffering disillusionment and even a raw lie was to maintain a serene attitude, a slight smile, raising her chin and straightening her torso, pretending she was immune to the bite of his coldness, that suspicions didn't keep her awake, that rectitude was the best possible path. On the first page of each album Adela had written the dates it covered. The last one indicated only the beginning, September 1935. In the photos, Ignacio Abel saw not what was captured by the camera but what was already happening elsewhere and in secret: Adela, the girl, and himself on the evening of his talk at the Student Residence; the family party in the house in the Sierra on Don Francisco de Asís's saint's day. The first photograph had been taken a few minutes after he'd seen her at close range and heard for the first time the name of Judith Biely. In the second he searched for the traces of Judith's memory he invoked while someone snapped the picture: the long table filled with people and plates of food, the warm sun of an October afternoon, the already remote faces, the family life that seemed a life sentence then, and now had disappeared without a trace: Don Francisco de Asís, Doña Cecilia, the maiden aunts, smiling and faded, infantilized by spinsterhood and old age, the uncle who was a priest, stuffed inside his cassock (what had happened to him—he might have had time to hide if the outbreak of the war caught him in Madrid, or he might be lying in some ditch, rotting in the sun and covered with flies), his brother-in-law Víctor, his face clouded with grievance, his two children, Lita smiling happily at the camera and Miguel fragile and shy, and Adela, near them, a woman suddenly mature, older-looking and wider in that photo than in his memory, leaning toward him, her husband, an attitude that survives the irreversible changes in her state of mind, as if her body hadn't learned what her mind knew, that the physical support sought and seemingly found is by now illusory, that things have changed though appearances remain the same. And he, in a corner, smiling this time, not on guard or absent, as in most of the photographs, with an idle smile, visible despite the shadow that covers half his face, a little sleepy from the food and wine and the sweet autumn sun. Had Adela been able to see (when she looked at it slowly after pasting it in the album, smoothing it with the palm of her hand, writing the date and place on a tag beneath it) that in the photo her husband already wore the face of his deceit, that the ease and affection he displayed and she was so grateful for were symptoms not of the return of love but of its loss? There was another photograph in the album that wasn't pasted in and had no indication on the back of the day and place; it had been taken that same evening, beside the pond of the

323

abandoned irrigation ditch. Miguel and Adela had argued about the Leica, and it was Miguel who in the end prevailed, but Ignacio Abel didn't recall the moment the boy took the picture, hiding perhaps in the pines, pretending he was an international reporter, a blurred photo, perhaps because there wasn't enough light, or because Miguel didn't hold the camera steady: his parents sitting on the grass, close to the pond's edge, leaning toward each other, absorbed in a conversation Ignacio Abel doesn't remember, the two figures as calm as the water where they were partially reflected, obscured by the oblique shadow of the pines.

20

H E'D ALSO BEEN ORGANIZING an archive, almost from the time of their first meeting, collecting not only letters and photos but any physical object that alluded to Judith's presence in his life: the handbill announcing his talk at the Student Residence, the newspaper clipping with the date in a corner, a day like any other that still shone for them with a radiance invisible to others, a page of the calendar he would like to have rescued from the wastebasket in his office where he'd tossed it the following morning, not realizing yet what was happening to him. Every lover attempts to keep a genealogy of his love, afraid treasured memories will inevitably fade away. He wanted to keep everything, prevent one meeting from being confused with another, as he wanted not to forget any of the English words and expressions Judith had taught him. He wrote them down in a little oilskin notebook he kept in his jacket pocket, the same pocket where he kept the tiny key that locked the desk drawer. He could with no danger leave Judith's letters in his office, but that meant separating from them: letters and photographs, telegrams sent in moments of spontaneity or impatience, with their naughty expressions in English that the telegraph operator filled with errors, a telegram sent from Toledo one morning when she was visiting with a tour group of American students, or from the central mail and telegraph office on the Plaza de Cibeles that Judith had passed, unable to resist the temptation to send him an instant message: the marvel of electrical impulses along telegraph wires, the tiny strokes translated into words, printed on a blue sheet, delivered within an hour to the office where Ignacio Abel interrupted an important meeting because the unctuous clerk had opened the frosted-glass door, holding a telegram and wearing a somber expression, the face of someone perhaps delivering grave news — the clerk was young but already moved with the solemnity of many administrative years. But Ignacio already knew the telegram was from Judith. A busy man who had to attend to so many things at the same time, he made his excuses to the others, moved a short distance away, impatience in his fingertips. And the pleasure in finding her words was more intense because he was reading them in front of others, struggling to keep a smile from appearing on his face, to maintain a frown of concern, or at least of high responsibility. *I'll be waiting for you at Old Hag's 4 p.m. please don't let me down please.*

A short time before he wouldn't have known what *Old Hag* meant. Now it was written in a tiny hand in his notebook, a nuance of the language and also a password, because that's what Judith called the woman who said her name was Madame Mathilde, the owner or manager of the chalet at the back of a garden near the end of Calle O'Donnell, who always received them with a fiction of reserve and distinguished hospitality, as if instead of a house of assignation she managed a literary and artistic salon. In the notebook was the date and the place and in many cases the hour of each of the times he'd been with Judith, along with a key word that alluded to something specific about each meeting. On the same pages were notes of his work appointments, technical observations, sketches of architectural details he'd seen or imagined, but he distinguished among them, sole keeper of its secret code, tenacious archivist. *Leaving your little slips of paper everywhere and me finding them without wanting to when I went through the pockets of your trousers or jackets before sending them to the cleaner's.* Forgetting was wasteful, a luxury he couldn't allow himself. Forgetting was like not looking closely at Judith when he was with her, not making an effort to fix in his memory those details that inspired love in him and excited him so much and yet afterward he couldn't invoke, even with the help of photographs. What was the true color of her eyes, the exact shape of her chin, how did her voice sound, what were the two lines that formed at the sides of her mouth when she laughed? He didn't see her for a few days, and in spite of letters and phone calls the brief interval destroyed everything, so that seeing her again was always a revelation, and his expectation so filled with suspense, it didn't seem her real presence could live up to what he'd intensely desired. Seeing her naked took his breath away. Each time he kissed her open mouth, he was transfixed by the same lightning flash of desire and astonishment he'd felt on the first night in the bar at the Florida, her shameless tongue searching for his. But the thirsty man doesn't savor the first sips of water on dry lips, doesn't stop to appreciate the shape of the glass or how the light pierces it. He could be distracted by something, she might be nervous, badly affected by a sleepless night, dazed by the noise around them in a café, deeply affronted at having to meet her lover in a hired room, with a bidet half concealed behind a screen of faded vulgarity and an odor of disinfectant made worse by the rose perfume that attempted to disguise it. In Madame Mathilde's house you could hear the birds in the garden, the bells of streetcars, the sound or laugh or moan from an adjoining room. Other lovers must have looked into that slightly clouded mirror in the chipped gilt frame in front of the bed. The touch of the sheets on her naked skin produced an unpleasant sensation; the sheets were clean but rumpled, washed many times, dampened many times by sweat or bodily secretions identical to theirs in their anonymity.

Meetings reduced to cryptic scrawls — *M.Mat.Fr.7.6.30;* movie tickets kept between the pages of his notebook that alluded to a particular afternoon, Judith's delicate hand advancing toward his fly in the dark, Clark Gable in a sailboat on an ocean as fictitious as his sailor's undershirt; programs for films he didn't remember seeing; messages written on hotel letterheads, on paper from the Student Residence or the technical office of University City; the brief archeology of their common past, the chronological trail established by canceled postage stamps and the dates in headings of letters, the long winding river of words that was the reflection and prolongation of real conversations, the ones dissipated in air. The time of being together was always too short, too distressing for them to be fully aware of what they were experiencing; they restored it, gave it form, in memory and in letters. Narrow blue envelopes Judith had bought in a Paris stationery store; sheets of a fainter blue covered on both sides by handwriting roused by speed and a tendency to boldness, the lines curving like Chinese characters, preserving the impulse of the gesture that had traced them. A forthcoming letter had something of the magnetism of Judith's arrival, waiting for her with eyes fixed on the door of the café where her silhouette would appear, seeing her suddenly without having followed her approach on account of a blink, a momentary distraction. The fact that there was a new general strike when they returned from the coast of Cádiz, with vans of Assault Guards circulating on the empty streets, interfered with his receiving a letter from her. At the hour of the morning when he knew the clerk would be distributing mail, Ignacio Abel was alert, raising his eyes at times from the papers on his desk or drawing board, looking out at the corridor over the typewriters, the office of the utopian city, the large model of the future campus. How wonderful that among all the thousands of letters, Judith's wasn't lost but came to him hidden among the others, though visible to the eye skilled in distinguishing it, the blue edge, the clerk unaware of the precious gift he brought, holding the tray like a waiter at a banquet. If he was alone in his office, Ignacio Abel closed the frosted-glass door that only his secretary was authorized to open without knocking; if someone was with him or he had an urgent call, he put the letter in his pocket or in a desk drawer, saving it for later, having held it, felt its thickness, the pleasing touch of many folded sheets ceding to the pressure of his fingers with a promise of delight. The words they hadn't had time to say during their last conversation or the ones lost in the ephemeralness of voices on the phone he now possessed without uncertainty or haste, as he would have liked to be with her one day, taking pleasure in indolence, unbuttoning, untying, removing each article of her clothing just as he carefully opened the envelope and removed the folded sheets that smelled of her, not because she put a drop of her cologne on them but because the scent of that paper resembled no other and was associated only with her. But at times his impatience was too powerful: he ripped the envelope and then had to make an effort to repair it in order to keep that letter in it, which couldn't be in any other envelope and belonged to a specific day, visible in the cancellation stamp, to a certain hour, a particular state of mind that agitated or calmed the writing like a lively breeze on the surface of a lake. The minutes of their meeting passed, shortened by nervousness at the beginning, the speed with which the end imposed itself. But in a letter time was preserved; the phantom conversation of paper and ink evinced a tranquility that was the only sustenance for absence, an effective tranquilizer, when the letter had been read the first two times, folded and placed in the envelope so it would fit in the inside pocket of his jacket. The moment fled and was impossible to recover; the letter was always there, amenable to examination by his fingers, to the intensity of his eyes, capable of being committed to memory, with no effort, after a few readings. *I was going down the hall and without meaning to I saw the tip of the envelope peeking out of your jacket on the rack, how hard it must've been for you to leave her letters in the office if she sent them there. It was obvious you didn't want to be away from them even for a moment.* The sustenance was more like an addictive substance: ink like nicotine, words like opium, alcohol intoxicating slowly, dissolving the shapes of the external world. What would he do if the letters suddenly stopped? If Judith grew tired of what had taken both of them so long to find the courage to name (but it was she who had the courage, not he): being a married man's lover; if she found another man, younger and more accessible, with whom she wouldn't have to maintain a secrecy that Judith, at heart, thought shameful; if she decided it was time to return to America or to continue the European trip she hadn't completed, an education she hadn't thought included the skills needed to sustain a Spanish adulterous affair (but he never asked about her plans; it seemed he counted on her always being near, available, obliterating herself when away from him, existing again at the moment he walked in the door and found her there beside the bed, open, sensual as a magnificent flower).

From the time she was very young, her urge to express herself had been as powerful as her desire to learn. Writing letters was an exercise of talent that hadn't found its true channel until then, not in the literary attempts she showed no one, not in her journals, not in the articles she sent to the Brooklyn paper that asked her for more political analyses and fewer observations on the daily life of Spaniards. When she wrote letters she felt the new exaltation of having an interlocutor with whom there would be no misunderstandings, because his intelligence was a challenge and a complement to hers, and because basically they resembled each other a great deal, a fact they hadn't needed more than a few minutes to recognize. Everything was memorable and new and deserved to be celebrated; wandering through Madrid produced euphoria. Explaining in a letter to the man she hadn't known until a short time ago the most secret ambitions in her life and the nuances of the sexual passion it seemed they'd awakened to together was for her an unsurpassed experience: her hand flew over the paper, ink flowed from the pen, forming volutes of words in which her will almost didn't intervene, words erupting with the memory of something that had occurred barely a few hours earlier, desire reborn in its invocation as it was sometimes in a distracted caress that made them return unexpectedly from the edge of exhaustion. (The book was somehow also in those letters. The book was in everything she did, yet it slipped away when she began looking for it consciously, when she sat in front of the typewriter searching, hoping for a first word that would unleash everything.) They told each other what they'd done and what they'd felt, and anticipated what they'd do when they met again, all they hadn't dared to suggest or ask for aloud. A letter was a confession and an account of desire and also a brazen way of inciting passion in the other: as you're reading, do what I imagine doing to you, let your hand move, guided by mine; let it be my hand caressing you though you're not with me.

How strange that it took them so long to become aware of the danger, to discover there was a price and damage and no remedy for the affront once it was committed. Each word an injury, the thread of ink a trail of poison.

"Where do you keep the letters?"

"You've asked me that before. In a desk drawer."

"At home or in the office?"

"Where I have them closest to me."

"Your wife can find them."

"I always lock the drawer with a key."

"One day you'll forget."

"Adela never looks at my papers. She doesn't even come into my study."

"How strange that you've said her name."

"I didn't realize I hadn't said it."

"You don't realize a lot of things. Tell me your wife's name again."

"You're my wife."

"When you divorce and marry me. Meanwhile your wife's Adela."

"You never say her name either."

"Promise me something—burn my letters, or keep them in your office, in your safe. But please don't have them at home."

"Don't call it my home."

"There's nothing else to call it."

"I don't want to be away from your letters. I wouldn't burn a single one, or a postcard, or a movie ticket."

"You keep movie tickets too?"

"Finally I'm seeing you laugh this afternoon."

"I don't want her to read what I've written to you. It embarrasses me. It frightens me."

"I always have the key with me."

"When she suspects something, she'll break the lock. Or she won't have to. She'll pull the drawer and that day you'll have forgotten to lock it."

"I know her very well — she doesn't suspect anything."

"You don't know her. I ask you things about her and you can't answer. You become uncomfortable."

"She's in her world and we're in ours. We always said there was a barrier between the two."

"You're the one who said it."

"What we had was enough."

"Only for a while. Now it's enough for you."

"You know I want to live with you always."

"I know that's what you say. I also know what you don't do."

"I'm going to America with you after the summer."

"You've really told your wife and children?"

"You know I have."

"You've told me you have. What if you're lying?"

"You don't trust me anymore."

"I'm getting to know your voice, the way you look when something makes you uneasy. I see your face right now. I see you don't want to go on with this conversation."

"I'm going to America with you."

"What if I don't want to go back so soon? What if I'd rather stay in Spain a little longer?"

"Spain is becoming a very dangerous place."

"I still have some money left. I can keep traveling a while longer in Europe."

"You don't want to be with me anymore."

"And will you hide me when you're at Burton College too? Will I have to wait for you to come and see me in New York?"

"You wanted me to make that trip."

"And you didn't?"

"What I want is to be with you. I don't care where or how."

"But I do. I care where and how."

"You said you wouldn't ask me for anything."

"I've changed my mind."

"Your feelings have changed."

"I don't want to see you in secret. I don't want to share you with anybody else."

"You don't share me."

"You sleep with Adela every night, not with me."

"I can't remember the last time I touched her."

"It makes me ashamed. It makes me sad for her. Even if she doesn't know, the sadness I feel for your wife humiliates her."

"She doesn't know you exist."

"She looked at me that day at the Residence and realized something. As soon as she saw me, she didn't trust me."

"But we'd just met."

"It doesn't matter. A woman in love senses danger."

"You thought she was in love?"

"I saw how she looked at you while you were giving your talk. I was sitting next to her. I think about it now and can't believe it. Next to your wife and daughter."

"She's less suspicious than you imagine."

"She saw how you were looking at me. Don't keep the letters at home. Don't call me from there."

"You've called me."

"With a good deal of embarrassment, because I was frightened. Only once."

"You gave me life that night."

"But then you went back to your home. We were in bed in Madame Mathilde's house and I saw you in the mirror looking at your watch."

"You didn't say you wanted us to spend the whole night together."

"I didn't want you to say no."

"I wish you'd asked."

"She knows you're with me. She's watching you. Please, burn the letters, hide them somewhere else."

"I don't want to be away from them."

"And what will you do when you finish the semester in America? Will you go back to Madrid, and will I have to wait for you to write to me?"

"There's no reason to talk about what's so far away."

"I don't want my entire life to depend on you."

"You knew what mine was like when we met."

"I didn't know I'd fall so much in love."

But before the shame and guilt emerged they knew that paradise was lost, that they'd left it, or stopped deserving a state of grace as remote from their wills as a favorable wind that would have lifted them above the daily accidents and limitations of their lives and now, like wine, had come to an end. Their desire was no less intense but now it had an edge of exasperation. As soon as it was satisfied, it dissolved into solitude, not gratitude, infected not with reluctance but with a secret disappointment, a kind of disrepute. The house of assignation no longer offered its usual sanctuary: like a remembered affront, they saw the bordello extravagance of Madame Mathilde's room, the wounding vulgarity of the painted paper on the walls, the loose threads in the carpet; they smelled the cheap disinfectant, saw the unclean bathroom behind the Oriental screen partially covered by a manila shawl. They returned from the too-transient days in the house by the sea and Madrid's June heat was unbreathable, its dry air like the breath of an oven, the immense weariness on suffocating cloudy days, the hostility in the glances of people on the street, sullen bodies sweating inside streetcars. For the first time they both could imagine a future when love would no longer illuminate them. In fleeting moments of lucidity and remorse, they saw each other again as if they'd never met, secretly ashamed of themselves, exhausted by the dejection of excitement sustained without pause for too long. Perhaps they should give themselves breathing space, free themselves for a while from their unhealthy obsession with being together, with writing so many letters and constantly waiting for them to arrive.

The ring of the phone startled him one burning night in June at the end of a day when he'd been overcome by an uneasiness that in retrospect would take on the dubious value of a premonition. The word "accident" was used from the start, but with a strange inflection, something indeterminate it would have been preferable not to say, a suggestion of accusation, of a slightly troubling enigma. "Come right away, Adela's had an accident." It was the hostile voice of her ever-vigilant brother, self-appointed guardian of the family honor, endangered by an upstart intruder, the lamentable husband needed to continue the line but always dubious for his ideas and behavior. "She's out of danger, but it might've been very serious." He didn't say much more, at first not even what had happened or where he was being asked to go. What mattered was to suggest by his tone of voice and scant information that they, the family, had gathered to help their daughter and sister, and once again the husband not only was irrelevant but also suspect, and so it was advisable to tell him no more than the essentials. That Adela had tripped or slipped and might have died, and they'd taken her to the closest hospital, the tuberculosis sanatorium. The sanatorium where the sudden anguish, the guilt, the appearance of strength so precariously maintained, collapsed all at once because of the seismic jolt of fear. When the telephone rang Ignacio Abel was sitting in his study at the desk with the open drawers he'd forgotten to lock that morning before leaving for work, rushing because of an urgent call, the desk beside the balcony where not a hint of a breeze moved the curtains and through which heat unmoderated by nightfall entered in an unmoving gust. He arrived home when the street lamps were beginning to go on and his daughter, who got up from her desk to greet him when she heard his key in the lock, said she didn't know where her mother was, but neither of them was alarmed because she might have gone to Mass or to pay a visit or to a meeting of her readers' club. He went into the living room with Lita and she brought him the paper, which he'd have preferred not to read because of its daily dose of alarming headlines, and especially because of the blank spaces of censored information, the disastrous news, the incompetent opinions. The government denied that health clinics had experienced a rush of sick children, victims of poisoned candies that according to unfounded rumors nuns had been handing out at the doors of some churches in working-class neighborhoods. Men who wished to join construction crews could do so, but were advised that the authorities would not tolerate the slightest violation of the law on the part of armed elements. He took off his jacket and tie and unfastened his sticky shirt collar, reduced by heat and fatigue to an invincible ennui. The boy came from his room and kissed him with that touch of excessive formality he'd been acquiring recently as he grew away from childhood. Perhaps he still felt some rancor because of the slap after the incident with the pistol. He asked his father whether he could help him with his geometry homework. For Ignacio Abel it was a relief to assist his son in matters that involved no emotional tension, when he could be generous with no effort, when he didn't project too large a shadow over him. Miguel easily felt fearful, incompetent, inferior to his sister, who obtained with ease what was so difficult for him: excellent grades and her father's visible approval. He kissed the boy and passed a hand distractedly through his hair as he reluctantly opened the paper. "Give me a few minutes and then we'll look at the notebook in my study." The daily circle of habits, their comfortable, boring repetition, like the sight of the furniture in the living room, the pictures on the walls and the clock on the mantel; like the entrance of the maid, who came from the kitchen drying her hands on her apron to ask whether he wanted something to drink before supper, the greasy shine of sweat on her face. He'd never have told Judith Biely that in his heart of hearts the routine was not at all oppressive.

"Do you know where the señora has gone?"

"No, señor. She left and didn't say anything. I didn't even see her go out."

"Did she leave a while ago?"

"Yes. The children hadn't come back from school yet."

Concern for Adela's absence filtered weakly into his mind. He was tired, and in reality he was pleased she'd gone out because now he wouldn't have to make an effort to engage in conversation or watch her for possible signs of unhappiness or suspicion. Through the open balcony came steamy air, heavy with the smell of geraniums and acacia blossoms, along with sounds from the street several floors below, the voices of men in a tavern doorway, car engines and horns, music from a radio, the sonorous texture of Madrid that he liked so much though he rarely heard it, muffled in this neighborhood that was still new, still growing, with wide, straight streets and rows of young trees.

It was nine o'clock and Adela hadn't returned yet. His son was waiting with his geometry notebook, standing at the door, undecided about attracting his attention. On the way to his study he placed his hand on the boy's shoulder and realized how much he'd grown. He turned on the light and instantly understood why Adela had left without saying anything to anyone and was so late coming home. The desk drawer he usually locked was overturned on the floor. There were envelopes and letters scattered around it, blue sheets densely covered with Judith Biely's slanted handwriting, photographs, a handful of the most recent, the ones they'd taken of each other on the trip to Cádiz. Brusquely he told the boy to wait outside but noticed he'd seen the same thing his father had and probably understood, with his intuition for the dark areas of his parents' intimacy and his instinct for alarm and censure, which Ignacio Abel had seen so often in his eyes, attributing to him an astuteness a boy scarcely could possess and that was only a child's panic at the indecipherable disturbances of adults. He closed the door and examined the details of the disaster, overwhelmed by the eruption of the irreparable. The letters, all of them, from the first, dated last summer; the postcards; the trivial, obscene, equally accusatory details; the envelopes ripped by impatience, the sheets filled with writing and notes and exclamations in the margins, the greedy use of all the space on the paper. And the photos of Judith in Madrid and New York and leaning against a white railing on the deck of a ship: one, on the floor, stepped on, with the mark of a shoe clearly visible on it; another facedown on the desk, among the papers; another two on the floor, near the drawer, as if Adela hadn't seen them or didn't consider it necessary to look at them. On the floor, torn in two, was the letter he'd begun to write the night before and quickly put away when Adela came in to say good night. He looked at her standing there and felt embarrassed by his ardor: suddenly it seemed insincere, forced; writing love letters could also be a debilitating task.

He touched his face; he'd turned red. Sweat made his shirt stick to his back; his hands were disagreeably damp. He gathered together the letters and photographs in a haphazard way, returned the drawer to its place, and locked it. In a flash of belated and totally irrelevant lucidity he relived a moment that morning when, as he prepared the papers he had to carry in his briefcase, he'd looked at the drawer and told himself to be sure to lock it before he left and put the tiny key where he always put it, in the small inside pocket of his jacket where he didn't keep anything else. At times throughout the day he made certain he had the key by patting the lining with automatic caution. The telephone rang and he picked up the receiver with a start: it must be Adela, calling from her father's house, and he'd have to make the effort to improvise an unlikely explanation, which would worsen the indignity without resolving anything. Before speaking he recognized the voice of his brother-in-law, greeted by the girl on the other telephone, and he said nothing. The guardian brother, knight-errant of the family honor, must be calling to demand an explanation of the affront. His daughter knocked on the door of the study without opening it. "Papá, Uncle Víctor wants to talk to you."

21

S HE DID EVERYTHING carefully, not hurrying, as if putting into
effect a plan she'd conceived long before, the only sign of negligence the disorder of the letters and photographs thrown on the
floor and the toppled drawer with the little key in the lock, which Adela had noticed that morning, perhaps, as she supervised the cleaning
of the study. The maids tended to dust inefficiently and to move things,
and this irritated Ignacio Abel, who maintained in his workroom a peculiar equilibrium between discipline and disorder, frequently mislay-
ing loose papers or newspaper clippings or photos from international
magazines and later needing them urgently. She must have seen the
key earlier, when the maids were straightening the rooms and airing
the house, but it took her a long time to decide to open the drawer he
always kept locked, and in fact she might not have noticed the presence of the key, since it was so small, a glint of metal in the study with
its open balcony. She might not have felt the shock, or she might have
resisted the temptation, at first not powerful, at least not conscious, not
something that would have persisted like a thorn or a physical discomfort in the midst of the day's activities. But she didn't forget it, not even
when she was absorbed in other tasks: going over menus for the next
few days with the cook or talking on the phone with her mother — distraught, Doña Cecilia said, her body going to pieces, nothing but terrible news, decent people couldn't go out anymore, couldn't go to Mass

without being insulted, and now they were slandering the poor nuns with that lie about giving poisoned candies to children, shouting vile things at the sisters on the street and threatening to burn down their convents. She listened to the plaintive whine of her mother's voice on the phone but didn't forget about the key. She seemed to see it, tiny and hateful, shining in the gloom when she lay down in bed with the curtains closed and the shutters open, seeking to alleviate a headache that became more oppressive on hot, overcast days, the gray light disorienting her sense of time. How she longed for the few days before the children finished the school year to pass quickly so they could leave Madrid for the dearly loved house in the Sierra, the relief of twilights and a breeze that carried the scent of pine and rockrose and returned her unconditionally to the happiness of her childhood, made not of memories but instinctive sensations, the singing of crickets in the damp and dark of the garden beyond the terrace, where the dinner table hadn't been cleared yet, the creak of the swing where her children moved back and forth, bringing back to her, like an echo in time, that same creak and those other children's voices, similar but belonging to her and her brother, so many years ago.

She had to overcome her depression, made worse by physical lethargy, to organize as if for a military campaign the annual tasks involved in moving to the Sierra ("The sooner all of you leave Madrid, dear girl, the better. Your father says something very bad is going to happen, and I ask him to stop reading the paper to me because you know how I get—I hardly have enough time to rush to the bathroom"): picking up the carpets, laundering all the linens, arranging the closets, waxing the parquet floors and the furniture before covering everything with cloths to keep out the desert dust of Madrid summers. But where would she find the strength to give orders to the maids and maintain the necessary authority if she shuffled around the house in a robe and slippers at this hour, her hair uncombed, with no desire to look at herself, no energy to scold the cook for playing the radio so loud, those commercials and flamenco songs resonating in her skull. Like the throb of pain in her temples, the little key insinuated itself into her conversations and actions. There were moments when she made an effort to forget it, others when she lamented the accident of having seen it and at the same time reproached herself for her curiosity and cowardice, her impatience to examine the inside of the drawer, her fear at what she might find there. But there also might be nothing to justify so much anxiety, and the best thing would be to sit calmly at the desk in the study, turn the key, and one minute later be cured of uncertainty and even allow herself a little remorse for having succumbed to curiosity and invaded a private place that didn't belong to her.

She wasn't blind and she wasn't a fool; she couldn't help but suspect, not because of her distrust but his typically male negligence, his inattentiveness to what he revealed in his actions. If he wasn't there, Adela entered his study only to oversee the cleaning, moving with combined reverence and discretion in order not to disrupt anything, and at the same time act with invisible diligence to prevent the spread of disorder. She looked at things, examining a sheet on which something was drawn and putting it back in the same place, or perhaps imposing a certain geometric harmony on the objects and papers on the desk. (What envy she felt when Zenobia Camprubí told her she was Juan Ramón's right hand, secretary, typist, almost his editor, that he read everything to her and considered nothing definitive, wouldn't agree to have anything typed, until Zenobia had given her approval.) She put pencils and brushes in a jar, gathered together loose notes, visiting cards, pages torn out of a notebook, and placed them under a paperweight, not trying very hard to decipher the tiny handwriting he was well known for and that with the years had become less legible and closer to microscopic, though not more difficult for her to read. (It hurt even more to hear Zenobia talk about her exhausting duties—smiling, with her mixture of complaint and gratification, her light eyes brilliant, just like her light skin and American dentures—because Adela, too, had once enjoyed typing Abel's articles and class notes, happy to help him, to do something useful that actively connected her to his work.)

With caution, she preferred not to start reading, avoiding the possibility of learning something that might be painful; she checked the pockets of his jackets before sending them to the cleaner's, trying not to look at what he'd written on some forgotten piece of paper, not wondering why there were two movie tickets for a matinee showing on a workday, not finding out whose phone number was written in the margin of a newspaper. What you don't know can't hurt you — it may never have existed in the first place. Curiosity was capitulation in advance, a sign of danger, of panic. Adela had been brought up not to question or have doubts about men's behavior beyond the domestic sphere. You didn't subject the honor of individuals to overly stringent scrutiny. If you did, you allowed and even encouraged an eruption of the indecent and the unacceptable, and once such a thing came to light, you couldn't pretend you hadn't seen it. Now the indecent was always on view in Spain, with an offensive carnality, and no one cared. In the daily life of an intelligent, vigorous man who didn't intend to abandon other projects and was beginning to receive his first international commissions, a position with so much responsibility in the construction of University City demanded all his time. Since she had an honorable spirit and a passive character, Adela liked things to be what they seemed. Didn't her husband always say a building has to honorably show what it is, what it's made of, what it's good for, and for whom? Some mornings the disorder was greater because he'd stayed up working until dawn; in order not to wake her, he'd slept on the divan, usually stacked with books and files of plans. Over time it became more customary for him to sleep in his study. The divan was large and comfortable; she made certain a blanket and clean pillow were always in the closet. Sometimes she was ill, and it was uncomfortable for the two of them to sleep together. From time to time, above all during this past year, he was so burdened with work that he didn't get home until two or three in the morning. No matter how quietly he opened the door and moved down the hall, she heard him come in. She was awake, looking at the time on the luminous hands of the clock on the night table, or she'd dozed off and her sleep was so light the distant noise of the elevator woke her, or the friction of the key cautiously entering the lock. The footsteps approached; Adela closed her eyes and remained rigid in bed, attempting to give her breathing the regularity of sleep. He mustn't know she'd been awake, waiting, mustn't suspect he was being watched. But the footsteps didn't stop at the bedroom; they continued on to his study. How clearly she heard everything in the silence of the apartment, how detectable each familiar sound, catalogued in memory: the study door opening and closing, the click of the lamp he turned on, the tired weight of his body on the springs of the divan. So exhausted, so many hours of work without respite, so many days without a break, so submerged in his concerns and obsessions: deadlines approaching, countless details requiring his attention, accidents at the sites, scaffolds collapsing because they were put up hurriedly and negligently, strikes, lost days, threats on the phone, anonymous letters in the mail. *What else could I have wanted than to help you if you'd let me, if you had the confidence in me you had at the beginning and thought I was intelligent enough to understand what you told me.*

More and more, what kept her up at night was the fear that something had happened to him. In the mornings she'd go to the balcony to watch him leave the building and walk to the garage where he kept the car. Some gunmen had waited for an engineer on the Lozoya Canal at the entrance to his building, not far from theirs, right on Calle Príncipe de Vergara, and shot him at the streetcar stop, and when he fell to the ground they finished him off in front of the people who were waiting and looked away. Zenobia had told her she passed the corner of Lista and Calle Alcántara with Juan Ramón on the night Captain Faraudo was killed and saw the pool of blood no one had cleaned, and people were walking in it, paying no attention, leaving their tracks on the sidewalk. Adela preferred not to think about such things if she could avoid it. What you didn't think about didn't exist. But she feared for her husband, almost as much as she feared for her brother, especially since the great fool had been reckless enough to start dressing in uniform and carrying a pistol. The telephone rang in midmorning and her heart seemed to stop. She heard shots or shouts on the street and the maids ran to the balconies with the same curiosity they brought to watching a wedding or a funeral procession. The day the engineer was killed, the cook came back from the market insisting she'd seen the corpse on the sidewalk with her own eyes, which undoubtedly was the reason she'd been out for almost two hours. "His leg was twitching like a rabbit," she said. "Exactly like a rabbit." But it was better not to say anything to the maids, because they confronted her, muttering under their breath as they went down the hall toward the kitchen: what does she think, does she think she'll always be the señora and us the servants? People had no judgment. The maids and the building porter and the grocery clerk gathered on the corner and talked about people killed in an attack as if they were incidents at a soccer game. Ignacio Abel was late coming home at night and she thought about the daily radio reports of gunfire and assassinations, always incomplete because of censorship, which made them even more alarming. She was frightened by how casually her father and brother predicted that very soon something serious would happen; the country couldn't continue sliding down the same slope, and only after a great bloodbath would things begin to be rectified in Spain. Those words, repeated so often, made her shudder. "Bloodbath" wasn't abstract to her: she imagined the bathtub in her apartment filled with blood that overflowed and stained the white floor tiles. She asked Ignacio, timid about pestering him or saying something that might worsen his nervousness and fatigue, more visible as the months passed and summer approached, "What will happen?" "Nothing will happen, the same as always. Smoke and no fire," he replied without looking her in the eye. So tired that when he came home he fell asleep as he read the paper, waiting for supper. So overburdened that after supper he went into his study to work on the drawing board or write letters or talk on the phone. It took her a long time to suspect him. She never imagined he could deceive her or take a mistress, like so many men. What she'd liked about him from the very beginning was his not being like other men: he didn't smell of tobacco; he was always considerate with her, affectionate with the children, never raising his

344

voice to them, never raising his hand (except that time in May when he came out of their bedroom distraught and saw her in the hall and said nothing, and the boy's face was red and he was paralyzed, about to burst into tears, trembling, his mouth open as if gasping for air, just as when he was an infant and his crying stopped and his chest swelled and he seemed about to suffocate); when her father and brother, like almost everyone else, began to argue about politics, he kept his opinions to himself or expressed them in an ironic tone; he didn't go to cafés; his life was guided by a single purpose; when he concentrated so much on work that it seemed the people and things closest to him had become blurred, it was a consequence of his vocation, which Adela accepted with melancholy admiration. When he was close there was, increasingly, a degree of absence; that this absence surrounded a nucleus of coldness was a discovery Adela preferred not to make. Her inadequate education as a Spanish señorita had left her with a feeling of intellectual inferiority, made more pronounced because her sharp intelligence allowed her to understand the extent of what she hadn't learned. How could she assess the formidable energies deployed by a man of will and talent in the exercise of a profession as filled with difficulties and possible rewards as her husband's, so rich in different disciplines, with room for invention as well as mathematical rigor, for the secret, manual shaping of forms (the drawings on his desk each morning; the small models the children had once played with), and the courage to give orders and control machines and teams of workers. A man paid a price for the privilege of immersing himself in action, of visibly acting on the world. Perhaps her husband hadn't known at first how to calculate what he ought to be paid. He'd wanted so much to be named to this position. Perhaps only she, because she knew better than anyone the signs of what he struggled to hide, knew how much it mattered to him, though he feigned indifference; how impatiently he'd waited for calls that didn't come, letters with an official letterhead that took too long to arrive. It mattered to him to be chosen from among so many architects, to have the opportunity to work on a project of an originality and scale uncommon in Europe. But also, she knew, it mattered to him to rank higher than the others: those who'd enjoyed more opportunities than he had, those who had powerful family names and took advantage of influential connections. He also made use of his: at the same time that he asserted his Republican and Socialist credentials to Dr. Negrín, he didn't reject the help of his father-in-law's friends, well established and close to the last monarchist government. Perhaps, at that time, not even he had realized the intensity of his ambition. Men, Adela had observed, were not perceptive regarding their own weaknesses, least of all when they touched on a certain shamelessness in the temporary suspension of their principles. Her husband's principles mattered less to her than to him, so it was easy for her to observe his fondness for two or three decrepit members of the king's coterie who enjoyed honorary positions on the University City Construction Commission and were old acquaintances of Don Francisco de Asís. The benevolent father-in-law, well placed in the regime whose imminent collapse no one could imagine, wrote letters, arranged meetings, celebrated with verbose abundance the merits of his daughter's spouse. She observed her husband at close hand, saw what he himself wasn't aware of, the eager gleam in his eye, his growing capacity for sincere adulation, the longing that had always been in him and was the cause and not the consequence of frustrated desires not always formulated in his own mind, much less communicated to her. What could she have given him, what satisfaction, not to mention relief, had she not been educated to be an intellectually crippled creature, like one of those Chinese women whose feet were bound from the time they were little girls.

If she'd been able to study; if she'd enjoyed the advantages awaiting her own daughter, advantages already there at age fourteen; or if she'd had the courage to go back and forth selling and buying and furnishing and renting apartments, like Zenobia Camprubí, immune to the opinion of others or the censure of her own family. How many times had Zenobia asked for her help in her popular handicrafts shop? She'd earn some money and escape the tedium of housekeeping now that the children no longer needed her constant presence. Of course she would have liked to, but she'd never dare. Her son's not being brilliant or diligent didn't worry her. Men eventually found their place in life. But the girl, Lita, it was important for her to study, to be confident in public, never paralyzed by her mother's shyness, never submissive, not only to expressed orders or looks of censure but to the unformulated desires of others, the sickly need for gratitude through obedience, to know what other people thought of her. How she admired her husband's ability to listen to other people's opinions only to the extent it suited him. She'd seen him courting, flattering, at times humbling himself so much that it had been uncomfortable for her to watch. A man with so high an opinion of himself couldn't acknowledge he'd behaved hypocritically, and so he needed to believe his own lies while saying them and forget them as soon as they'd been said. She didn't judge him. If she detected these weaknesses, it was because she loved him. She consoled him in periods of uncertainty, she stayed awake beside him when he couldn't sleep, anxiety-ridden because of the wait for a decision that was taking too long to arrive. No one but she knew how shamelessly Ignacio Abel had longed for his appointment, yet in public he displayed an educated skepticism about it. But the thing most desired was transformed before long into a burden, the trap one willfully constructs and then falls into. A man had before him so great an abundance of possibilities that any goal he chose would be undermined by his awareness of the ones he'd discarded. He always had to be wanting something; his enthusiasm and his disappointment followed parallel courses. To work at University City, he'd suppressed his own artistic vision: the projects he didn't do or postponed were lost opportunities that fed his longing and didn't allow him to enjoy what he was actually doing. His good life, what he'd achieved with so much effort over so many years, was more than anything the tangible reverse side of other lives he might have known. Adela had always feared this, the temptation not of other women but of his longing for things he cared about — above all because he didn't have them or because others, no better than he, did — and his desire to visit places whose greatest attraction was his not having seen them. In magazines he looked at buildings his colleagues had designed and that he might have worked on had he not been mired in the endless construction of University City. He'd been invited to design a library in the United States, and not even that could please him; perhaps it wasn't an international commission as important as the ones Lacasa or Sánchez Arcas or Sert received, and they were younger than he was; perhaps the confirmation wouldn't arrive or the government wouldn't grant him permission to leave; perhaps he preferred not to take his family and still hadn't decided to say so, and therefore changed the topic when the children asked about the journey and evaded her eyes. But he always did. He didn't look her in the eye, and if he did, it was for an uncomfortable instant and he didn't really see her. She couldn't give him anything he was looking for. What she'd given him in the past he no longer remembered. Perhaps he was ashamed of having loved her once, or at least of having needed her. He wrote his notes in a tiny hand and kept them locked in a drawer, just as he guarded his thoughts when he was with her and the children and for a moment his gaze was lost, or he nodded at something they told him about school without paying any attention, or suddenly seemed to remember that he had to make an urgent phone call or attend an unexpected meeting.

Lying down in the dark bedroom, in the oppressive heat of a June morning, she listened to the maids coming and going in the house. They must be chattering about her, how lucky the señora is, she can go to bed in the middle of the day with a migraine, after a bad night. Wasn't it because her husband was giving her a lot of grief, and what else would he give her when she looked like his mother? Where would he look for what he clearly wasn't getting at home? Adela was afraid of them. She saw with closed eyes the little key in the lock and saw herself opening the drawer, and suddenly she saw something or imagined something even more painful than the possibility of having been deceived. Perhaps it was not that he no longer loved her but that he had never loved her, had approached her because no other woman of the type and class he found attractive would have accepted him, had courted her with the same calculation and the same appearance of sincerity with which, years later, he flattered those who could influence his appointment. Perhaps the aunts and cousins, disappointed by the failure of their predictions of her spinsterhood and astonished that a well-educated young man, though poor, wanted to marry her, had been correct in their initial suspicions, diluted as the years passed but never completely discarded. There was no middle ground in his ambition for respectability. He'd calculated everything since the time he was very young, when he discovered that his father's death wouldn't mean the end of his education, but also that nothing would be given to him but the small sum his father had saved, which would allow him to survive until the end of his course of study only if he lived with an austerity close to indigence. He hadn't allowed himself any weakness, any vice. His intelligence and tenacity brought him to a point where he had all the necessary qualifications but not the right to take another step toward the social position that mattered so much to him, even though he saw himself as a radical contemptuous of bourgeois formalities and had a wholesome resentment of a caste system he'd experienced first-hand, literally born and brought up on one of its lowest rungs, in a porter's basement lodging. How could she accept that their entire life had been a deception? Adela got out of bed and ate something light. The telephone rang and her heart seemed to stop. Something had happened to him, gunfire or a bomb at the construction site; someone had shot her brother. The maid answered the phone and left the receiver off the hook. She'd said she didn't know and would ask the señora. It couldn't be anything serious. "Doña Zenobia Camprubí wants to know if you can come to the phone." "Tell her I'm not in. Say I'll be back this afternoon and you'll give me the message." Her friends were puzzled that she no longer attended the lectures at the Lyceum Club, that she never had time to go with them to the theater or concerts or simply to have tea in the house of Señora Margarita Bonmatí, who lived only a few doors down, or at Zenobia's, which was closer, a step away almost, at the corner of Príncipe de Vergara and Padilla. But she went out less and less, and realized she was frightened of people, hostile people who shouted but also people she knew who were affectionate with her; she suddenly felt paralyzed, had a need not to be seen, not to look at herself in the mirror. All she wanted was to stay still, not see anyone, lie on her bed in the dark, but fear pursued her even in that refuge, her alarm at footsteps approaching or the telephone ringing, or her uneasiness that the children would be late coming home from school, or that night would fall and her husband wouldn't have returned yet, better to close her eyes and not listen to anything or feel anything, not die but be safe from any shock. Afterward the maids would say that in the morning they'd noticed the señora acting strange, seen that something was wrong. She got up from the table, unaware that her napkin had fallen to the floor, and the cook saw that instead of withdrawing to the room where she embroidered and read, she went into the señor's study, being careful to close the door behind her.

She left the house without saying she was leaving, without putting back the drawer that fell from her hands when she found the letters and photographs. Only a few letters were out of their envelopes, as if Adela hadn't been curious to read all of them, or had the sang-froid to refold them after she read them and put each one where it belonged. The drawer remained overturned on the floor, the tiny key still in the lock. What wounded her most deeply wasn't the young face and slender body of his foreign lover but his face in some of the photos, the open, cheerful smile she'd never received. Adela must have crossed the hall to her bedroom, where she dressed for the street, and left the house without being seen by the maids, who missed her only when the two children came home from school and didn't find her in the sewing room, where she sat each afternoon, looking out at the street because she liked to see them arrive and make certain they crossed properly. This is how she'd once waited for her husband to come home, when they were both younger and he worked in a municipal office and kept more regular hours (she'd watch him arrive from the balcony, and he'd jump off the streetcar on the corner and look up at her). She probably wanted to avoid the risk of running into her children and frustrating her plan, if she'd already formulated it when she left the house and knew where she was going. The doorman was the only one who saw her go out, and he said afterward that he thought Señora de Abel was more distracted than usual and didn't stop to exchange a few words with him, only nodding her head as if she were in a hurry to get somewhere, like when she'd rush out on Sundays for twelve o'clock Mass. The owner of the grocery on the corner saw her cross the street and wait for a taxi, raising her gloved hand slightly each time one came near, with the kind of distinguished timidity typical of her gestures, as if she were uncertain whether it was correct for a lady to be alone on the street and hold out her hand for a cab. She carried a handbag and wore a small hat with a short veil, a light dress, white shoes, short lace gloves. The heavy fog dimmed the shadows of things without blurring them completely: the shadows of trees on the sidewalk, her own preceding her. The store owner saw her get into the taxi, and after a while he saw her children coming home from school, pushing each other and arguing as they did so often. On a corner of Calle de Alcalá, at the gates of the Retiro, Adela asked the driver to stop. She gave him a bill and told him to keep the meter running, she'd be back in a few minutes. At the door of the small church where she often went, not to pray but to sit in silence, in the cool shade tinted by light coming through the stained-glass windows, there was always a blind violinist with a dog. When young girls passed, their high heels clicking rapidly, the blind man played tunes from operettas or the music hall; when he heard the slower steps of a mature woman and smelled her perfume, he put on an expression of religious ecstasy and lengthened the notes of Schubert's or Gounod's "Ave Maria," leaning forward, the dog between his legs as if guarding the cardboard box where he collected alms. Here he stood in spite of the hour, at the door of the church no one else would enter until much later. "Ave María purísima," he said to Adela, perhaps recognizing her footsteps or her perfume, and she replied, "Sin pecado concebido," frightened by the gesture with which he stretched out to her the arms that held his violin and bow, and made a parodic bow, but it didn't occur to her to give him a coin, she was so dazed, so impatient to enter the church and enjoy the benign sensation of coolness and shadow, of refuge, of quiet that for a few minutes wouldn't be disturbed. She'd become fond of visiting the church because she rarely saw anyone there and the priest didn't know her. The one in her parish called her Doña Adela or Señora de Abel and from time to time suggested she join groups of pious ladies in the distribution of clothes to the poor, or in novenas. In his homilies he thundered against the impiety of the times and demanded prayers for the salvation of an afflicted Spain. In February, on the Sunday before the elections, as Adela was leaving the church, the priest approached, holding envelopes in his hand. He knew she was an exemplary Catholic lady, he said, and that he could speak to her in confidence. It was necessary to render unto Caesar what was Caesar's and to God what was God's, that was the evangelical commandment, and the sole concern of the Church — the daughter of Christ — was to follow the doctrine without becoming involved in the business of this world. As he spoke, the hand holding the envelopes extended toward her, though not so much that Adela felt obliged to take them. But when the Church suffered persecution, wasn't it the task of good Catholics to do everything possible to come to her defense? Now Adela understood and kept smiling, nodding, still comforted by the Mass and Communion, the black embroidered veil on her head. She, like a good Catholic, surely would be able to follow her conscience when it was time to vote in the upcoming elections, but who could be sure her maids, young and uneducated, wouldn't succumb to demagogic propaganda, the charm of impious forces? Or simply, in their ignorance, in their innocence, they might not vote at all, depriving the defenders of the Church and her Social Doctrine of their humble but invaluable support. Adela extended her right hand, and the priest extended his, thinking she was going to take the envelopes with electoral ballots, but what Adela did was to gently push the hand offering them to her, barely touching it, leaning forward slightly, smiling before turning away, saying with all the good breeding her voice could hold, "Don't worry, Father. We'll all know how to vote the dictates of our conscience, with the help of God." What would her priest think if he knew she'd voted for a candidate of the Popular Front, and a Socialist besides, Julián Besteiro, not telling anyone, not her parents or her brother or Ignacio, who hadn't asked her; he probably considered it a foregone conclusion that she'd vote for the right. *You believe you're not as intransigent as others but you also think if a person has faith she has to be reactionary and even a little bit retarded.* Now she sat in a corner of the empty church, in the last row of pews, after dipping her fingers in the font of holy water—the stone so cold, oozing dampness—and kneeling briefly before the Blessed Sacrament as she made the sign of the cross. Her body felt heavy, weak from the heat, her swollen knees painful. The church was small, without much merit, vaguely Gothic, built at the end of the last century. The walls, painted pale blue, had sentimental images of Christ, the Virgin Mary, Saint Joseph with his staff of spikenard, his expression of kindhearted nullity, his curly beard, along with a saint dressed as a nun, her eyes turned toward heaven. The largest image was of Christ crucified, before which candles always burned. She liked his expression of noble human suffering, of acceptance of the pain and injustice driven into his mortal body. She liked the name written beneath the crucifix: *Most Holy Christ of Forgetting.* She could imagine her husband's sarcastic comments if he were to see the ogival chapels with their gold-tinted ceilings, the images. But she liked the floor tiles, like those in a middle-class living room, the combined smells of wax and incense in the air, the delicate shade that made the faces of the images paler and their ecstatic glass eyes more brilliant, the trembling of the lighted lamp in the main altar, above the probably false gold of the Eucharist. *Hail Mary, full of grace.* She prayed in a quiet voice, not asking for forgiveness but with the feeling she was wrapped in a melancholy mercy as soothing as the cool darkness. *Blessed art thou among women and blessed is the fruit of thy womb.* The evidence of her unbearable sorrow would be enough for forgiveness to be granted her. The only thing she wanted was for the calm and silence never to end, for the unrelenting sun not to wound her eyes, for the gleam of the tiny key to be erased from her mind, and for the radiance of that young foreign smile in the photos to disappear, along with the cheerful assurance of that handwriting, so different from hers, taught in the nuns' academy, in which she too had written love letters many years ago. Rest was all she asked for, to free herself of an exhaustion so profound she'd need years to notice some relief, to sink into the forgetting that the crucified Christ seemed to want for himself, the forgetting that was the only absolution for pain. The words of the prayers came effortlessly to her lips, just as her fingers had gone to the holy water and then to her forehead, chin, breast. *And forgive us our debts as we forgive our debtors.* But for now there was no rest. The taxi driver was growing impatient and blowing the horn. Each blast of the horn shook her like a scream. If he left, it wouldn't be easy for her to find another taxi at this hour of the afternoon. With infinite reluctance she stood and crossed herself again as she passed in front of the Blessed Sacrament. She lit a little oil lamp before the high plaster Virgin — it had a faint dab of color on cheeks as yellow as wax — and dropped a coin into the slot of the poor box. The metallic clink inside the tin box resounded in the silence. *Turn thine eyes of mercy toward us.* She had to ask forgiveness for something, but not the desire to dissolve into a sweet darkness without memory: she had to ask forgiveness for the rancor she'd nurtured toward her daughter because of the girl's unconditional devotion to her father, which had unjustly seemed an affront to Adela. To what extent had pain caused her to lose her dignity (it was a lie that pain ennobled)? To the extent of being jealous of her daughter, of feeling resentful when she saw her go out to meet her father every time his key sounded in the lock at the apartment in Madrid, or the rusted hinges of the gate creaked at the house in the Sierra. In her high-heeled shoes her swollen feet hurt. When he heard her leave the church, the blind man put out the cigarette he was smoking and stuck it behind his ear before beginning, somewhat tortuously, the "Ave Maria." The driver, his elbow leaning out the window, his peaked cap pushed back on his head, saw her approach with a look more of indulgent mockery than impatience. Let him not talk to her in such a loud voice when she gets back into the cab, let him not say anything at all on the way to the North Station. She was opening the back door when she realized she hadn't given anything to the blind violinist this time, either. She retraced her steps, opened her handbag, then her change purse, and chose a coin more generous than usual. The blind man doffed his cap when he distinguished the coin by its sound and made an exaggerated bow.

Two hours later, at about six, they saw her get off the train at the village station on the other side of the Sierra. The sky was as overcast as in Madrid, but the heat was not as overwhelming. The stationmaster, who'd known her since he was a little boy, was surprised to see her dressed in city clothes, and even more surprised to see her alone, without a suitcase, in high-heeled shoes that would make it difficult for her to take the shortcut from the station to the road to her house and then into pine groves after leaving the village. Some of the men playing cards and drinking wine in the tavern must have seen her too, the ones who fell silent and looked out the window each time a train pulled in. Though it was hot, the summer families hadn't begun to arrive. The men saw her walk away on the narrow path past rockrose bushes — they'd just bloomed, with yellow pistils among white petals and sticky, glistening leaves — maintaining with difficulty the regularity of her steps on the pebbled path. They must have assumed she'd come to inspect the house before the family moved in, but it was strange for her to come alone, without the maids, and dressed in that formal manner. She stopped for a moment at the fence and didn't go in. Or if she did go in, she came out again quickly, leaving everything the way it was, not even opening the shutters, as if she'd decided not to touch anything, not to disturb the tranquility of things kept in darkness all winter.

She continued along the dirt path, looking dignified in her city hat and the handbag held tightly in her hand, though it turned out that there was virtually nothing in it aside from the change purse, empty after she had given money to the blind man with the violin and paid the cab fare, and a one-way train ticket. The path climbed gently west, toward the slopes of pines and oaks and the pastures, separated from one another by low stone walls. It was the same path that led to the irrigation

355

pond they'd walked to since her children were small. In the mornings, after breakfast, or after their siesta as the heat began to ease, though at that height it was unusual for at least a little breeze not to blow. The children at first held by the hand, then, year after year, running ahead of them, impatient to reach the pond and jump into the clear icy water. How could she not have noticed how fast they were leaving childhood? And they, Ignacio Abel and Adela, watching them from a distance, sitting in the folding chairs on the shore, in the shade of the pines, conversing more impersonally as the years passed. Persevering in spite of the heat, as if she'd shaken off some of the weight that made her walk more slowly in recent years, Adela followed the path — which became less defined in the pines, the serene endurance of things indifferent to human presence — distracted and at the same time self-possessed, finally armed with a purpose, clutching the bag in which there was only a ticket stub and an empty change purse. The Sierra air plunged her into her most treasured memories, into the warm waves of summers that retreated past the childhood of her children into the distance of her own early years. She reached the pond, and its motionless depth made the silence more dense. The light gray sky beyond the somber arch of the tops of the pine trees was reflected in the pond's smooth surface. For a moment she thought she wasn't alone, but there was no one at the shutterless windows of the abandoned power station. To the south, beyond the foggy horizon, was Madrid. To the west, between rocks and oak groves, she could see the blurred silhouettes of the domes of El Escorial. Not a single detail had changed in the landscape of tenuous lines and faint smudges of color she'd been looking at since she was a girl. She took a few steps along the retaining wall and stood still at the edge of the water, looking at her own image, her thick knees and wide hips, the light dress she'd never known how to wear with elegance, her hat. She closed her eyes and stepped into the emptiness, clutching her bag in both hands, as if afraid she might lose it.

22

AS SOON AS HE SAW her sitting at the usual table in the back of the café, he realized her face was not the same face and her eyes would not look at him in the same way. It was she who suggested they meet in the café—that morning, the idea of going to Madame Mathilde's house produced a physical revulsion in her. She didn't look up, though she must have heard the glass door opening in the almost empty café. She wasn't reading the open book in her hand. She was smoking, unusual for her at that time of day. She hadn't touched the coffee in front of her. For one painful instant she was a stranger, a woman he wouldn't recognize when she raised her head and to whom he'd apologize for mistaking her for someone else. Ignacio Abel saw himself in the mirror behind the red divan where she was sitting. His face wasn't the same either, and not only because he hadn't slept the previous night, most of it spent in the sanatorium, sitting by a closed door behind which he couldn't make out a sound no matter how closely he listened. Sometimes the door to her room opened to let in a nurse, who closed it immediately, or the doctor with the somber expression, who at first gave him no hope and only later, at daybreak, told him the patient had responded to the treatment to revive her. Probably, though it was too soon to say so with any certainty, she'd recover with no aftereffects. The doctor never asked what had happened; he looked at Ignacio Abel with an air of reserve that perhaps hid an accusation, the same look as in the fatigued eyes of the nurse as she closed the door without letting him look in on Adela. In the silence Ignacio Abel thought he heard violent retching, guttural sounds that in the strangeness of the sleepless night seemed the product of his imagination. But after a few minutes the nurse came out carrying a pail, half filled with something that resembled dirty water and smelled of plumbing mains and vomit, and a clinical device ending in a black rubber tube.

"The doctor's given her a shot of a sedative. What she needs now is rest."

"When can I see her?"

"You'll have to ask the doctor."

Daylight was flooding the windows when they let him enter the room. Adela's brother was guarding the head of the bed, pale, eyes glassy, lids swollen, unshaven, staring straight into his eyes.

"You'll have to explain how you arranged for them to keep me out," Ignacio Abel said.

"You're the one who has some explaining to do."

Víctor pointed to his sister, who was sleeping, her broad face ashen against the white sheet. Her mouth was open and her lips had traces of lipstick. Her damp hair spread in a graying tangle on the pillow. Ignacio Abel remained silent, just as he had the night before on the phone when Víctor accused him of something unintelligible, not bothering to tell him what had happened to Adela or where she was.

"You're to blame for this. You don't fool me."

"Blame for what?"

"My sister almost drowned."

A chill ran through his body, a wave of nausea. He thought: he knows what happened, knows Adela found the letters and photos. But that was impossible, he quickly realized, when he learned she was unconscious in a room at the tuberculosis sanatorium. The caretaker at the abandoned power station, who made his rounds at about that time of day, heard what he thought was the sound of a body dropping into the water. He didn't see anyone at first, only the rings expanding on the surface that always was motionless. Someone or something, perhaps an animal leaning over to drink, had fallen into the deep water, but it was strange that it wasn't struggling to reach the surface. He ran down to the edge, to where a vertical string of bubbles had appeared. The late afternoon sun pierced the layers of water: he saw a woman sinking or, already having reached the bottom, beginning to rise, then suspended as if trapped in the underwater vegetation, her hair floating like a tangle of algae, her arms motionless at her sides. He leaped into the water, attempted to bring her to the surface, but she was heavy and seemed to be pulling him down and struggling not to lean against him. "We both could've drowned," he said afterward, in the tavern at the station, to the men who'd seen Adela walking along the platform at the hottest, emptiest hour of the afternoon, with her handbag and gloves, her small hat, her city clothes, advancing awkwardly on high heels. At first the caretaker didn't know who she was, didn't recognize the woman he'd known for many summers: the bluish face, the closed eyes, the flattened, streaming hair. He ran to the road and miraculously saw the forest warden's truck approaching. The only place nearby where she could be cared for was the sanatorium. A doctor recognized her when he saw the stretcher come in, the doctor who'd treated Víctor during one of his rest cures and was an acquaintance, perhaps a Falangist connection, Ignacio Abel thought, observing his rather flashy, defiant air, imagining a blue shirt beneath his white coat.

The night before, the telephone had rung on the desk in his study, where he stood looking at the open drawer and the papers and photos on the floor, not bending down to pick up anything. He let it ring, imagining in a cowardly way that Adela must be calling, perhaps from her parents' house, dignified, vengeful, her voice trembling, choking on her tears. It was Lita who picked up the phone in the hall, who opened the door (Miguel was there, holding his notebook) and saw her father standing, on his face a disconcerted expression, as if he'd discovered a robbery or a natural disaster. Wherever the guardian brother had called from that night, he reserved the right not to answer certain questions: where they'd found Adela, who'd found her, and why she was in the sanatorium. "She's between life and death. If anything happens to my sister, I hold you responsible. You'll have to answer to me." The letters and photos remained scattered on the floor, the drawer overturned, pouring out its content of sweet words suddenly transmuted into poison. The reality of a few minutes earlier now belonged to a remote time. Ignacio Abel clenched the receiver, repeating questions his brother-in-law didn't answer, and the sweat on his hand made it slip. From the street came a tune from a saint's day fair, one of many *verbenas* held at the beginning of summer in Madrid; Judith had become very fond of them. (Only a few days earlier he'd taken her to the *verbena* of San Antonio; he'd finally kept his promise to show her at close quarters the Goya frescoes inside the dome of the hermitage; he'd pressed her to him and kissed her, taking advantage of a stretch of shadow.) He looked up and Miguel and Lita were in the doorway of the study, watching their father with alarm and suspicion, as if they, too, accomplices in their uncle's vigilance, knew and accused, witnessing the disorder of papers and photos on the floor, each of those gifts transformed into part of a contagion that had already brought Adela down, he didn't know how or where, and perhaps would irreparably damage his life, bringing him face to face with the lethal consequences of his actions. "Where is she?" he repeated, afraid the children might find out something. "Where are you calling from?" The line seemed to have been cut, but Víctor was still there, silent, subjecting him to the uncertainty, a punishment that would undoubtedly fall on him more harshly because he hadn't anticipated it. He'd preferred to believe his impunity would be unlimited, that between the world in which he lived with Adela and his children and the one he shared with Judith there would always be a separation as radical as the one dividing parallel and simultaneous universes. Now, in astonishment, he was witnessing the magnitude of the disaster without wholly accepting it, like a flood or cave-in caused by an earthquake, a calamity no one can foresee.

"I told you so many times," said Judith, looking away after her eyes had met his for an instant. She no longer seemed the same behind the smoke of the cigarette she didn't bring to her lips, the cup of café con leche she hadn't touched. She seemed separated from him by an invisible wall she herself had raised. "I told you to tear up the letters or let me keep them. Not to keep them in your house. There was no need. It wasn't decent."

She too was accusing him. Cold, so close and yet beyond his reach, the house of time he'd built in his imagination for her, sitting in the same corner of the café where they'd met so often. Under the table they'd often searched for each other's hands, touched knees. They'd left substantial tips so the usual waiter would save that divan for them, the waiter who brought their coffees and didn't come back unless they called him, who was accustomed to dealing with other secret couples or at least very dubious ones, mature gentlemen with young girls they'd found through classified ads, aging engaged couples, lovers trapped in a routine as curdled as marriage who didn't have the money to rent a room for their assignations. One morning the same place changes abruptly; the lover's familiar face is the same but also a stranger's. Ignacio Abel had seen his in the mirror in the café, and it was the face of a bad night spent at the sanatorium and of shame and remorse; the face his children had seen the previous night, before focusing on the letters and photographs of someone they couldn't identify; the one his brother-in-law looked at in the sanatorium, identifying the stigma of disloyalty that finally had been exposed after so many years when he'd yielded in his vigilance or allowed himself to be deceived by an air of rectitude everyone else accepted and his own sister revered without question. Ignacio placed his hand on the marble tabletop, and Judith withdrew hers. She'd preferred not to look at him as he approached, or perhaps, absorbed in her own remorse, she hadn't seen him approaching, hadn't stood to press against him as if they hadn't seen each other for a long time. A kind of innocence had ended, and now they were beginning to wonder how it had lasted so long, and at what price: the face he'd seen for several months, as free of guilt as it was of any shadow from the world beyond the two of them; perhaps she wouldn't look at him again and her eyes would always have this new expression. In the same place where on other occasions they'd taken refuge as lovers, they now seemed to have the suspicious air of accomplices in a sordid crime, in that café far removed from the center of the city, in that shadowy corner badly lit by an electric lamp as weak and yellow as a gas flame. For Judith the shame was no less intense: her upbringing made the strictest moral demands. Now she was struck by her own inconsistency, her blindness sustained for so long without seeming to do her harm, without calling into question her own integrity, dispelling the mist and intoxication of words and desires that had enveloped her in recent months. In another country and another language, reality might have seemed subject to more benevolent rules; what she desired, what she dared to do, must have had a partly dreamy, partly conjectural element of fiction, as if she were just living the book she hadn't begun to write. She detected signs, warnings, but preferred not to see them. She'd accepted humiliating norms — secrecy, lies — and wrapped them in literature to make her capitulation acceptable. She'd effortlessly suspended her own principles, childishly imagining she was experiencing a novel-worthy love, sinking into a darkness as full of phantoms and echoes as a movie theater, and as removed from reality. The ceiling lights suddenly came on, making her blink in disbelief when she went out into the harsh light of the street; on this June morning, after hearing the news on the phone — from the time she'd lifted the receiver and heard his voice, she'd understood he was going to tell her something irreparable — she'd crossed Madrid in a taxi to reach this empty, gloomy café where confirmation of the anticipated awaited her, and with it the invalidation of the very things that had attracted her earlier, a stage set onto which the light of day was mistakenly projected, revealing false, carelessly painted arches, dusty wooden platforms, artificial plants, rumpled curtains. A woman lay in a coma in a sanatorium, and she,

Judith, had gently pushed her to the edge of the pond where she sank after offering no resistance. Judith remembered clearly the only time she'd seen her, focusing on her, observing that she looked older than her husband, that her figure and age didn't correspond to the lively daughter who ran to throw her arms around her father's waist when he came down from the platform where he'd given his lecture. Days so distant, the beginning of October, now enveloped in imprecision with which boundaries of time are remembered, when you're at the edge of something and don't know it yet, the first step past a threshold you didn't notice as you crossed it. There was something incongruent between that woman and man: his avid look made him seem younger, his look and the obvious care he took in his physical appearance, the alert, restless tension of someone not resigned to what he's achieved, who resists considering the shape of his life as final. That's where they did not fit: her fatalism, sweetened by placidity, nourished by melancholy; his not completely conscious vanity, his unstable blend of insecurity and arrogance, a man who still expected something or expected everything, who perched uncomfortably on what he'd already achieved and stood quickly like an uneasy guest waiting for something or someone, though he doesn't know what or who. And the daughter, almost a young woman, halfway between one life and another, embracing her father with the ease of a little girl, with a spontaneity and sensuality her mother would never have. Caressing his daughter's head, he searched for Judith with the caution of a man who prefers not to have the direction of his eyes followed: there was something brazen and furtive in them, a subtle yet complete examination she perceived as physically as if a hand or a breath had brushed her skin. Everything seemed inevitable even before it occurred, everything somehow unreal, part of the suspended life granted her by her status as a foreigner, absolved from the gravity of her own country, exalted by being submerged in a different language, so clear of memory that everything in it shone with excessive colors. Before writing a single word on the portable Smith-Corona, always on the table in her room at the pensión, she'd lived as if dreaming a novel in complete detail, a novel about the European journey of a Henry James heroine, the heroine she'd imagined she would be as she read novels in the public library. But unlike James's intelligent, generous women, she would travel alone without answering to anyone, earn her living, sit by herself in a café with no one to set limits for her. But what had she done with her hard-won freedom, with the fantasy delegated to her by her mother, with her European novel? That morning she saw them dissolve in a café on the outskirts of Madrid, its floor littered with sawdust and cigarette butts and a vague smell of urinals and sour milk, with worn plush divans and clouded mirrors, sitting across from a married man older than she was, with whom she'd sustained not the love of an intrepid Henry James heroine but a wretched adulterous affair. From the time she was a child she'd forged an idea of freedom that was the antithesis of her mother's bitterness: in recent months she'd taken part with no remorse in the deception of a woman in whom her mother would have recognized herself. Perhaps she had unconsciously noticed that similarity the one time she saw Adela behind her manners of an educated, bourgeois woman in Madrid, well along in years, older than she should have been according to her daughter's age and the worldly disposition of a husband to whom time was being kinder than to her.

She'd heard the trembling of the badly fitted glass in the café door and knew he was coming in but preferred not to raise her head, expecting she'd find in his eyes the remorse and fatigue of the previous night, and above all the refutation of a feeling that had begun to desert them in recent days, though neither had acknowledged it. Time had ended; it had collapsed for them like a tower or sandcastle since the last night they'd spent in the house by the sea. Fleeing from anguish to revived desire, from desire to insomnia, to waiting for dawn on a Monday when their parting would be crueler than on other occasions precisely because they'd been together a longer time. It was necessary to pay, but they didn't know the price; love was built on someone else's destruction. Sitting in the café, her eyes fixed on the round marble tabletop, smoke from her cigarette rising to one side of her face, Judith imagined the other woman's pain like a knife thrust with crude obstinacy into her abdomen. Ignacio Abel stood across from her, his tie crooked, hat in hand, as if he didn't dare sit down. What was gained in one dazzling minute is just as easily lost. The glitter of desire in a pair of eyes can be extinguished just as it illuminated them. After spending a sleepless night at the sanatorium in the Sierra, Ignacio Abel had driven back to Madrid and hadn't had time to shower or change. His hair was dirty, flat against his skull, his unshaven cheeks dark, the skin under his chin flabby, and his hat left a mark across the middle of his forehead, made tender by the heat.

"Have you been waiting a long time?"

"I don't know. I didn't look at my watch."

"I couldn't come any earlier."

"Shouldn't you have stayed with her?"

"She's out of danger. I'll go back this afternoon. She was still unconscious."

"We almost killed her, you and I. We pushed her over the edge."

"It's still not certain it wasn't an accident. No one saw her jump in the water. She was wearing high heels, and the stone at the edge was wet. She might have slipped."

"Do you really want to believe that?" Now Judith was looking at him, her light eyes dilated, a stranger to him, rejecting the lie, the attenuation of deserved shame. "Can you convince yourself, or are you only trying to convince me?"

Her voice was cold, sharp, with a sarcastic edge, a rigidity that denied him closeness. He had seen hints of this side of her before, heard this tone of voice, in passing, when she grew irritated and familiarity between the two of them seemed gone. Perhaps it wasn't fair, now that what he'd feared was happening, when he was beginning to lose her because of her guilt over Adela's unhappiness. Perhaps they'd begun to lose each other earlier, worn out by all the secrecy, by the simple movement and friction of things, unworthy of a love that abandoned them as gratuitously as a bird flying away one quiet afternoon, the same love that a few months ago had come to rest on them without their having sought it or done anything to deserve it. Suddenly it was intolerable to go on living, to leave the café like two strangers, face the inhospitable Madrid morning, turn a corner, and perhaps never see each other again.

"You're not to blame," he said.

"Of course I am, as much as you. More than you, because I'm a woman. She didn't do anything to me and I almost killed her."

"She was the one who chose to take the train and throw herself into the pond. It wasn't a sudden impulse. She had time to think. She changed her clothes. She put on her gloves and her pearl necklace. She put on lipstick."

"Would it have been less serious if she'd thrown herself off the balcony in a housedress?"

"She might have thought about her children."

"Did *you* think about them?"

"I didn't do anything to leave them without a father."

"Do they know anything?"

"Their grandparents came to stay with them last night. We told them their mother fainted in the street and they can't visit her right now because the doctors have her under observation."

"They're bright. They'll suspect something. What did you do with the letters?"

"There's no danger. I locked them up."

"That's what you said before."

"It won't happen again."

"I want you to burn them. I want you to promise me you'll burn them. The letters and the photographs."

"Then what would I have left of you?"

He heard his own voice: he was talking as if he'd already lost her. He extended his hand and Judith's hand drew back automatically. If she got up from the divan and he didn't hold her back, he'd lose her forever. He saw her glance at her watch, measuring the time she still had, calculating her flight. *Time on our hands.* In the next half hour he had to go to his house, call the office, talk to his children, subject himself to his in-laws' questions and affronted looks, take a shower, put on clean clothes, drive back to the Sierra, to the sanatorium where Adela perhaps was awake, her brother standing guard, filled with anger, he too looking at his watch, to measure the added insult.

"I have to go," she said. "My students are waiting for me. They're waiting for their final grades."

"Tell me when I'll see you again."

"You have to take care of your wife."

"Don't call her my wife."

"I'll call her that for as long as you're married to her."

"She wanted revenge. She wanted to hurt us."

"She's crazy about you. Can't you see? You said she didn't care about anything, just marriage and appearances. You don't notice anything."

"If you leave me, I'll die."

"Don't be childish."

She said *childish*: the thirty-two-year-old woman looked at the man of almost fifty with the ironic disbelief she'd have shown to the theatrical outburst of a student claiming to be in love with her. She repeated in her foreign voice, drawn back into her language, the other life in which he didn't exist: *I really have to go*, gathering up her things, as if she were no longer in Madrid but in New York, back home, accustomed to a faster rhythm, unhesitating, unceremonious, the dry, un-adorned frankness that was one of the many traits put on hold recently. He was losing her. Watching her stand up dissuaded him from trying to hold her, her hair on her cheeks as she moved her face away so he couldn't kiss her, as distant from him as from the gloomy setting of the café. She gave him a smile that was more wounding because only her lips were part of it, not her eyes, a smile that said it all.

"When will I see you again?"

"Leave me alone for a while. Don't call me. Don't follow me."

"I can't live without you."

"Don't say things that aren't true."

"Tell me what you want me to do."

"Go back to the sanatorium and take care of Adela."

The name, spoken aloud, accentuated the presence they could no longer pretend didn't exist. He watched Judith leave, her back very straight, her dress clinging to her slim figure, her head bent, the heels of her white-and-black shoes echoing on the dirty wooden floor. He didn't see her chin tremble or the hand brush hair away from her face, wincing on the street in the violent light of the summer morning, so close to the ending and the disaster, he thinks now on the train traveling up the Hudson, his face against the glass, so hopeless, neither of them knowing this unceremonious farewell would be their last.

23

PERHAPS WAITING and traveling will be his natural state from now on. He no longer has the feeling that his journey has been a phase, a more or less broken line between a place of departure and another of arrival, solidly there on the map despite the great distance separating them, Madrid and the small town that in less than an hour will cease to be merely a name, Rhineberg, where strangers will be waiting for him on the platform, prepared to welcome him, to return part of the identity that has been eroding as the days have passed, wearing away in its brush with inclement weather like poor-quality material. In one of the school atlases Lita liked so much, Ignacio Abel had traced for her and Miguel the itineraries they'd follow on the adventure he promised them for the following school year, knowing that if he went to America he'd do it alone and meet Judith Biely there, but still incapable of dispelling the deception he himself had fed. His two children leaned over him, in the living room with the balconies open to the twilight air, while his index finger ran in a straight line over the coated paper of the atlas, from Madrid to Paris, Paris to Saint-Nazaire or Bordeaux, the Atlantic ports from where ships sailed regularly for New York, ships whose names Lita and Miguel knew by heart after checking them in nearby travel agencies, the Cook agency on Calle de Alcalá, the other on Calle Lista at the corner of Alcántara: the *Île de France,* the SS *Normandie,* as alluring as the name of the train they'd take to Paris, its cars painted dark blue with gold letters, *L'Étoile du Sud,* the title of a Jules Verne novel, the headlight on its locomotive illuminating the night. In the window of the Cook agency, next to the color posters of coastal landscapes in the north of Spain and the Côte d'Azur, was a splendid model of an ocean liner, as detailed as those of University City, and Miguel and Lita looked at the details, pressing their faces to the glass: lifeboats, smokestacks, hammocks on the first-class deck, the swimming pool, the tennis courts with lines clearly marked on their green surfaces and tiny nets. Putting off the moment when he'd tell them the truth, Ignacio Abel fed to his children a dream that was a fraud and would end in a disappointment he couldn't confront. The tip of his index finger effortlessly crossed flat colored spaces, left behind borders that were lines of ink and cities reduced to a tiny circle and a name, navigated the luminous blue of the Atlantic Ocean. The outside world was a tempting geography of postcards with exotic stamps, and full-color posters of international railways and maritime crossings displayed in the shop window of a travel agency. Lita, always meticulous, an expert in adventure novels, took measurements with a ruler and calculated the real distances to scale, to the great annoyance of Miguel, who grew bored with the arithmetical deviation from the game and even more tired of his sister's permanent flaunting of her knowledge to their father. Now the awful grind was demonstrating that she excelled not only in language and history and literature but in mathematics too — what next?

Ignacio Abel has been traveling that distance on the maps for more than two weeks, assaulted by illusions, by his desire for the woman he looks for among the foreign faces and whom he may have lost, knowing he hadn't done everything possible to stay in touch with Adela and his children on the other side of the frontlines. He could have crossed them, at least in the early days when you could still move with relative ease from one zone to another, before the fronts were defined and the war became something more than terror, uncertainty, and confusion, when the word hadn't come up yet — war — with its strange, primitive obscenity. Wars, like misfortunes, happen to other people; wars are in history books or on the international pages of newspapers, not on the street you go down to every morning and where you can now find a corpse or a hole left by a bomb or the debris of a fire. He leans his face against the train window and spots in his eye sockets the fatigue of the countless landscapes he's seen slip by since leaving Madrid, all joined now in a single sequence, like a film of unimaginable length that keeps going. He's seeing the autumn woods Judith talked about so much, but he doesn't have the energy to focus on them: reds and yellows vibrating in the sun like flames, leaves raised by the rush of the locomotive floating in the air like crazy butterflies, flying into the glass, then disappearing; thickets of reeds emerging from the cobalt-colored water; flocks of aquatic birds rising with a metallic gleam of wings. He remembers what Judith had said to him the first afternoon they were together, drinking and talking in the bar of the Hotel Florida until they lost track of time: those colors were what she missed most about America in the Madrid autumn. Now that he finally sees them, they seem to form part of his personal catalogue of the things he's lost. Along the riverbank the woods extend to the horizon in waves of hills, and at their tops he can see a country house, isolated and solemn like an ancient temple in a painting by Poussin, the glass pierced by the gentle October sun. How would it have been to hide in a house like that with Judith Biely, not just four days but a lifetime; how will the library building at Burton College look from a distance if it ever comes into existence? (In the most recent letters and telegrams no one has mentioned the assignment. Perhaps he has traveled so far only to arrive at nothing, without so much as an excuse that might give a little dignity to his flight.) He'll reach his destination soon, and it becomes impossible for him to imagine his old life or remember with any certainty a time when he wasn't going from place to place, when his permanent state wasn't solitude, his natural environment wasn't trains, stations, border crossings, daybreak in odd cities, hotel rooms, life suspended each day. How strange it will be to have an office again, schedules, a studio, a drawing board. But even stranger to have been the man who returned home every day at roughly the same time and sat down to read the paper in the same chair molded by the shape and weight of his body and worn by the rubbing of his elbows; the man who one afternoon opened an atlas on his knees to imagine with his children the itinerary of a future trip, though a fictitious one, with an accurate timetable and a return date.

As disconcerting as how easily everything that seemed solid collapsed in Madrid in the course of two or three days in July was his own skill in adjusting without complaint or much hope to this transitional state. How quickly one becomes used to being a nobody and having nothing, reduced to the face and name on a passport and visa, to the few possessions that can fit into one's pockets and a suitcase, stuffed with papers and dirty clothes and his toiletries case, the only vestige of another existence, another way of traveling, restful and bourgeois, a comfortable parenthesis of movement between two fixed points. The leather case, a gift from Adela, matches the suitcase — made of hide, with chrome fittings and compartments where toiletry items fit, held in by straps: the badger-bristle shaving brush, the silver-plated bowl for lather, the razor with its ivory handle and a supply of rustproof steel blades, the flat flask for cologne, the comb, the shoehorn, the clothing brush. Each thing in its precise place, in its pocket or leather opening, the careful order of a former time, of a life fading in his memory.

So close to the end of his journey he feels not relief but fear, fear and weariness, as if the distance traveled in recent weeks, the bad nights, the vibration of the trains, the sound of the ship's turbines, nausea in a poorly ventilated cabin where hot air took on an oily consistency, the effort of dragging his suitcase from one place to another — all had suddenly fallen on his shoulders in a rush of weakness. Instead of impatience to arrive, he's overwhelmed by fear of the unknown, the need to adapt to new circumstances, hold tiresome conversations with strangers, feign interest, be grateful for the favor of precarious hospitality because he has no way to reciprocate. (Perhaps Van Doren doesn't have as much influence as he implied, perhaps the project will come to nothing because it was a pretext for offering him a temporary refuge, for influencing his life from a distance, controlling time like a benevolent deity, granting Judith and him the only four consecutive days they'd spent together.) It's the same fear he felt as the end of each stage of his trip approached, the reluctance of someone who comes out of sleep in an unwelcoming light and doesn't want to wake. The train approaching Paris at daybreak over the gray horizon of industrial suburbs and brick factories; his waking in a ship's cabin and realizing it was the silence of the engines after a week of nonstop motion that dragged him out of sleep; and before that, after the first night, the surprise of reaching Valencia, the blinding light of that spring morning, as removed from the order of time as it was from the brutal winter that was to accompany the war in Madrid.

In Valencia the cafés were filled with people and the streets with traffic; had it not been for the headlines the newsboys shouted, one might have thought the war was going on in another country or was just part of a nightmare, vanished at the first light of day. In Valencia he wrote the first postcard to his children: a view of the beach in pastel colors, with white houses and palm trees. He wrote the card while sitting in a café, drinking a cold beer in the shade of an awning, near the station where his train for Barcelona and the border would leave in a few hours. He put a stamp on it and dropped it in a mailbox, trying not to think that it probably wouldn't reach its destination and he wouldn't receive an answer. Red-and-black flags and vehement Anarchist posters hung in the station's waiting room and on platforms, but in the first-class carriages the conductors were as helpful and wore blue uniforms as neatly buttoned as if the war or the revolution didn't exist. Even the militiamen who demanded documents reflexively doffed their caps to well-dressed travelers, whom a moment later they might place under arrest or drive off the train with rifle butts. Unexpected areas of the old normality remained intact in the midst of the destruction, like the balcony he'd seen one morning as he passed a bombed-out building, a balcony suspended in air, held by an invisible bar to the only wall left standing, its wrought-iron filigree perfectly preserved, as were the pots of geraniums that hung from the railing. Didn't Negrín always say that in Spain people lacked the seriousness to make a revolution? That everything was done halfway, or carelessly, or badly, from the laying of railroad track to the shooting of some poor bastard? Now Ignacio Abel understands that on the first morning of his journey in Valencia he hadn't shed his old identity, preserved as astonishingly as the balcony with geraniums hanging from the only wall left standing after a house was bombed. He was still somebody, still wore polished shoes and kept the crease in his trousers, still spoke with a clear voice and instinctive authority to conductors, porters, and ticket clerks at the windows he'd soon approach as fearfully as he walked toward the checkpoints at border crossings. Inside the suitcase his clothes were clean and orderly. He hadn't yet developed the nervous gesture of repeatedly bringing his hand to the inside pocket of his jacket to confirm that his passport and wallet were still there; when he pressed his wallet he could still feel the comfortable thickness of banknotes recently withdrawn from his account, some of which he'd changed for francs and dollars in a bank on Calle de Alcalá, where he was recognized as soon as he walked in and treated with a certain reverence.

While he waited for the manager to return from the safe with his money discreetly placed in an envelope, Ignacio Abel thought, looking around him, of the primitive millenarianism of Spanish revolutions: so many churches had burned in Madrid and yet it hadn't occurred to anyone to burn or even attack any of the enormous banking headquarters along Calle de Alcalá, which plunged him into architectural despair. The bank entrance was protected by sandbags and the façade covered by crude revolutionary posters; trucks of militiamen passed along the street and wagons of refugees poured in from the villages to the south, recently conquered by enemy troops, but inside the bank the same, somewhat ecclesiastical half-light endured, and employees bent over their desks or murmured among themselves against a muffled background of typewriters. Indifferent to the careless dress that had become obligatory in Madrid, the manager wore his usual gray suit, black tie, and starched collar. "And so you're leaving us, Señor Abel.

Other highly valued clients have also left, as you know. We hope this doesn't last. And that your absence doesn't need to be prolonged." He smiled and rubbed his pale hands together. When he said "as you know" and "we hope this doesn't last," he'd looked at Ignacio Abel with caution, as if testing a possible complicity with the client who'd had a solid account for years and also wore a tie. "It won't last, you'll see," Ignacio Abel heard himself say with a conviction he didn't have, offended by the bank manager's insinuation, his hope that Franco's troops would soon enter Madrid. "The Republic will make short work of those rebels." The bank manager's half-smile remained frozen on his waxen face, as ecclesiastical as the light that filtered in the stained-glass windows in the ceiling. "Let's hope it is so. In any case, you know where we are." He accompanied him to the door, suspicious now but still deferential, satisfied with having proved his influence even in these new times when he handed over, with prudence and discretion, an amount of money much higher than the sum allowed out of the country in the exceptional circumstances of the war.

He took off his tie when he went out. There was no point in attracting attention and risking a search when he was carrying so much money in his briefcase, carrying his passport with the visa, the letter of invitation from Burton College, and hiding in his pocket the fragile credentials of a flight that seemed more unreal to him the closer it came. The approach of his departure made time go faster, made him look more intensely at the things he soon wouldn't see, the streets of Madrid, the entrance to his building where the elevator no longer worked. The porter had traded his old uniform with the gold buttons for a blue coverall, but he still bowed, obsequious and venal, waiting for a tip, perhaps studying the possibility of denouncing as an undercover agent or spy some resident against whom he harbored an old grudge. In each trivial detail, Ignacio Abel saw an indelible sign of the time that would pass before his return, of what he might never see again. He felt not exaltation or sadness but crushing physical distress, the pressure in his chest, the weight on his shoulders, the empty hole in his stomach, the weakness in his legs. He walked through his empty apartment like a ghost, as if he were seeing the rooms and furniture not in the present or in memory but in the future of his absence that would begin the moment he closed the door and inserted the key for the last time, in the tenacious endurance of what remains in shadow, what no one looks at. Before turning on the lights, he'd closed the shutters one by one. From his bedroom window he'd looked for the last time at the darkened outline of Madrid's rooftops, the streets submerged in an abyss of shadows where one could hear only the speeding cars of guard patrols and the distant bursts of gunfire, and toward midnight the engines of invisible enemy planes flying over a city with no searchlights or antiaircraft defenses. It had turned cold and the heat didn't work. The supply of electricity was so weak the bulbs gave off a yellowish light. On his last night in the apartment, where he'd been alone for so long, a dazed Ignacio Abel went from room to room, listening to his own footsteps, seeing his image in the clouded light of mirrors. His suitcase lay open on the bed he hadn't bothered to make in recent days (but he'd never made a bed before, just as he had only a vague idea of how one lit a burner on the gas range). His suits and Adela's dresses hanging in the deep closet were phantoms or incarnations of their previous life, recognizable in their forms but lacking their former substance and reality. Clumsily he folded clothes to pack in the suitcase. He selected notebooks of drawings, a book, a photograph of the children taken one or two summers earlier; he took his architect's diploma out of its frame, rolled it up, and placed it in a cardboard tube. He'd been advised not to carry too much luggage: documents and safe-conducts might not do any good, and he might have to cross the French border on foot along a secret pass. Nothing was certain anymore. Trains weren't running from the South Station, though this was said to be temporary (but the newspapers claimed the always victorious militias had foiled an enemy attempt to cut the rail line between Madrid and Levante); he'd have to travel by truck to Alcázar de San Juan, where at some point the Valencia express would pass by. He closed the suitcase, turned off the light, decided to lie down on the bed, just to rest with his eyes closed for a few minutes;

what with alarms and bombings, and his nervousness as the date of his departure approached, he hadn't slept for two or three nights. The moment he lay down on the rumpled bed, he sank into sleep like a stone in water. He knew he'd slept because the knocking on the door woke him, the voice saying his name.

Ignacio, for the sake of all you love best, open the door.

How much distance fit into the smooth tinted space of a map over which he slid his index finger: the cold in the back of the truck, the lapels of his raincoat raised and his hat pulled down on his head, the ailing engine, faces lit by the glow of a cigarette, and sometimes in the background the white patch of a village. At one point he heard plane engines, and the truck advanced slowly, its headlights turned off. But it took Ignacio Abel a long time to realize the true scale of the space, the expanse of the world he'd cross on his journey, made vaster because he lacked the reference points of Judith Biely and his children. He sensed it, perhaps, not with his intelligence but with his fear the night before he left, the last night, as he packed his suitcase, stood in a room or in the middle of the hall, not remembering where he was going in the large apartment he'd never really felt was his, checked his documents and money over and over again, deciding not to hide some of it in the lining of his coat or the double bottom of the suitcase; suddenly secretive, threatened, frightened, a deserter of his city and his country, a fugitive of the war in which others were fighting and dying for the same cause that nominally was his, though he no longer knew what name to give it without feeling that words were a fraud and he was being infected by the lie when he pronounced them, with or without capital letters — Republic, Democracy, Socialism, Anti-Fascist Resistance — everything out of focus unless he thought about the others, the enemy, those advancing toward Madrid from the south, the west, the north, not with flags and words and worn uniforms but with mercenary butchers determined to kill, military chaplains with pistols at their waists and crucifixes held high, well-oiled machine guns, the merciless discipline of machines; men who rode horses and hunted down peasants as if they were exterminating predatory animals; who raped women after shooting their husbands; who first bombed then attacked with bayonets the working-class outskirts of Granada and Sevilla; who from airplanes machine-gunned scores of terrified fugitives. The Madrid newspapers pushed the propaganda, and radio announcers hailed the boldness of the popular militias, as the other side continued to advance. He packed his shirts, ties, underwear, socks, the things that had always miraculously appeared folded and ironed in his drawers, in the suitcases used on trips he'd made in earlier times. He hadn't eaten supper and wasn't hungry. He took a sip of cognac and felt nauseated; in a few hours he'd have left this apartment perhaps forever. My love, my daughter, my son, my betrayed and humiliated wife, forgotten shades of my dead parents. The cognac in his empty stomach accelerated his vertigo. He lay down on the bed and slept for a few minutes, and what happened when the knocking at the door woke him had the quality of a bad dream he preferred not to remember, as the voice continued to resonate in his mind. *Ignacio, for the sake of all you love best, open the door.* At midnight the truck would be waiting at the Atocha Station. He knew it was foolish, yet he crossed Madrid on foot along secondary streets where patrol cars weren't likely to appear. When he was about to leave, the suitcase by the door, his coat and hat on, he went through all the rooms turning out the lights, making sure the faucets were closed, as if going on vacation. What seems to have lasted a lifetime and will last forever, so easily discontinued from one day to the next. In his children's room, on Lita's desk, was the atlas they'd flipped through together at the end of May or early in June, when Madrid was already hot and the balcony doors were opened wide to let the afternoon breeze in, carrying the sounds of traffic and the shrill voices of the newsboys, the whistle of swallows nesting under the eaves. In the wardrobe mirror he saw himself as an intruder and remembered with shame the time he'd slapped Miguel. My son, many regrets. Lita's books were arranged on a shelf over the desk; in the titles he could follow her apprenticeship as a reader in recent years, books about Celia, followed by Verne and Salgari, then *Jane Eyre* and *Wuthering Heights.* He touched the spines of the books, the wood of the twin desks. In Miguel's drawer the papers and notebooks were piled haphazardly, indications of the last-minute rush before leaving for the house in the Sierra, programs for movies and photographs of actors cut from film magazines, one of them the young Sabu with his torso bare and wearing a turban. SCANDALS IN THE MECCA OF CINEMA: EVERYTHING ABOUT THE MYSTERIOUS DEATH OF THELMA TODD. Reading programs for films his father hadn't given him permission to see was how Miguel must have spent many of the hours when he was told to stay in his room and study. He remembered walking in and seeing the boy quickly stuff something into a drawer or between the pages of a book. With what useless harshness he'd treated him, with what silent cruelty, especially in comparison to the girl, for whom he'd barely hidden his favoritism. But perhaps his son was already used to his absence, to the new school life he'd have on the other side of the war's border, enemy country where it was difficult to send letters and postcards. Perhaps the unfulfilled promise of a trip, false from the start, pained the father much more than it did his children, the victims of the deception.

He turned off the twin lamps on the two desks and left the room stealthily, as he had in the days when he'd hope they had fallen asleep. Suddenly he felt suffocated by all the absences that filled the apartment, at once expelling him and blocking his path. With the caution of a thief he walked out, uneasy at having forgotten something important, closing the door slowly, not locking it, going down the marble stairs in the dark, fearful he might run into someone or be seen by the porter, who'd be surprised to see him going out at this hour with a suitcase and perhaps would inform one of the patrols that came from time to time to search the apartments, looking for suspects and snipers in a bourgeois district where most of the residents had been lucky enough to be away on vacation when the revolution broke out.

A solitary figure walking close to the buildings, under the moonlight, in the city with closed windows and street lamps turned off, wearing his hat, his travel raincoat, suitcase in hand, his steps resolute and at the same time full of caution, alert to the strokes of the clock in a tower indicating he had more than enough time to reach the Atocha Station, where a safe-conduct signed by Dr. Juan Negrín would allow Ignacio Abel to occupy a place in a truck leaving for Valencia and carrying an unspecified cargo of official documents guarded by men in uniform. At first it was difficult for him to get used to the permanent uncertainty, the discomfort of trying to sleep bundled against the cold, resting his head on the suitcase, his body subjected to vibrations and braking, or lying on a wooden bench, or on cold marble in the waiting room of a station; to opening his eyes at dawn and not knowing where he was; to not knowing whether his documents would be approved by the guard or police officer or gendarme or border official or customs clerk who scrutinized them interminably. Each departure was a relief, the end of a wait; each arrival, each approach to a new destination brought an un-easiness that gradually turned to anguish. Patience was pure physical inertia: lines of people waiting for a window to open, for a traveler's interrogation to end, for a guard to examine each item of clothing and each toilet article and each trivial memory contained in a suitcase. In waiting rooms, at control barriers and border posts, Ignacio Abel had joined a new variety of the human species: passengers in transit, people carrying scuffed suitcases and dubious credentials, nomads in shoes with rundown heels whose documents had many stamps and an air of falsification. The train that had taken him from Barcelona to the sec-ond or third day of his journey stopped in Port Bou at nightfall; the passengers advanced in silence and formed a line in front of a sentry box at the border crossing. On the other side a French gendarme paced, protected from the drizzle by a short oilskin cape. A few steps from the French flag, on this side, was the flag not of the Spanish Republic but an enormous red-and-black banner with the Anarchist initials in the center. What would Negrín think if he saw that usurpation, if he had to submit his deputy's identity card and his diplomatic passport to two militiamen armed with Mauser rifles, pistols at their waists, cartridge belts across their chests, red-and-black handkerchiefs tied around their necks, wearing the sideburns of bandits in romantic lithographs and interrogating the passengers one by one. As a precaution, Ignacio Abel had removed his tie before getting off the train and put his hat in the suitcase. He wasn't yet proficient in the new trade of waiting and patience. He presented his passport opened to the page with the photograph, looking for a moment into the small red eyes of a militiaman who chewed on a cigarette butt, so bored or so tired he didn't bother to relight it. Sitting on a bench against the wall, a woman who'd been denied passage was crying under a poster portraying a foot in a peasant espadrille flattening a serpent with three heads: Hitler, Mussolini, and a bishop. The other travelers glanced at her with no trace of sympathy, looking away when the woman raised her head, as if not wanting to be contaminated by her misfortune. The weary militiaman spat out the butt and turned the pages of Ignacio Abel's passport, wetting his thumb with the tip of his tongue. He couldn't imagine how many similar inspections he'd have to undergo in the next few weeks, how many times an inquisitorial gaze would look up from the photo in the passport to search his face, as if it were necessary to establish the veracity of each feature to eliminate the possibility of an imposture, or perhaps merely to cause a delay, so the suspect foreigner would miss the next train or be late or more exhausted in his flight.

The impassive, aggressive harshness of the Spanish militiamen was less wounding than the coldness of the French gendarmes in neat uniforms, shouting obscenities at the Spanish peasant women who feared them so much and didn't understand their orders. Taller than the people around him, better dressed, able to answer the gendarmes in French, Ignacio Abel knew he was included in the same contempt, and that awareness gave him a feeling of fraternity. He too was a *sale espagnol;* the only difference was that he could understand the insults, and the greatest of them didn't need to be formulated because it became clear as soon as one crossed the border: the tidy station; the clean-shaven gendarmes in their impeccable hard collars, the glow of good food on their cheeks; the posters showing beaches along the Côte d'Azur and transatlantic cruises, not revolutionary slogans; the large window of a restaurant; the neon sign of a hotel. By crossing the border he discovered the weight of the Spanish disease he might escape, but for which perhaps there was no cure, though it was possible for him to hide the symptoms, to distance himself from his compatriots, who couldn't elude the hostile looks or hide the stigmata of their foreignness and poverty: berets, unshaven faces, black shawls, funereal underskirts, bundles of clothing on their backs, infants nursing at sagging breasts, Spanish refugees leaving third-class cars and camping like Gypsies on station platforms. But he'd traveled first class; he could go into a restaurant on the square and have supper at the window and drink a bottle of excellent wine; behind the restaurant's curtains he could while away the time until the Paris train, savoring a glass of cognac, looking at his compatriots crowding the station steps as they shared pieces of bacon, dark bread, cans of sardines. Over the years he'd lost his instinct for frugality and his fear of tomorrow, lost the ability to measure out his money or renounce the privileges that had made his life comfortable for so long. Social distance still protected him. He began to realize it had been stripped away that same night, on the express to Paris, where no first-class tickets were available and he had to sit without a reservation in a second-class seat from which he was turned out at the first stop, when an irritated traveler entered the compartment and claimed the seat that wasn't his, by the intangible right of a French citizen. The train's corridors were also filled with people, and it took several hours before he could find a place to sit on the floor and doze off on his suitcase. He woke up to an indifferent kick from the gendarme, which continued to hurt his pride for many days, perhaps the first lesson of his new life, when he had not yet learned how to accept humiliation and be grateful to those who could otherwise harm him.

Judith Biely suddenly leaped from the sadness of memory to the imminence of the future, the one unfolding before him as well as a phantom parallel future, the trip to America they'd planned together, suspended now between memory and imagination with the radiance of a timeless illusion. And the desire for her fed his jealousy: which men had she been with before meeting him, a young, free woman dazzled by Europe, as forgetful of her own attractiveness as she was ignorant of the ideas men could have about her when they took her American self-assurance for sexual availability; which men had she met now that she'd left Madrid, relieved not only of love but of the guilt and indignity of their deception? *If your wife had died, if she'd drowned in that pond because of us, I'd never have forgiven myself.*

In luminous, fitful dreams on the nights of his journey, Ignacio Abel was with her again in the innocence of their first times together. As he was losing everything, as his money ran out and his clothes deteriorated and he lost the most basic habits of hygiene, as he grew resigned to the idea that his journey would never end, Ignacio Abel recovered the phantom presence of Judith Biely with ever greater clarity. He'd wake from a few minutes of restless sleep in a station or in his berth on the ship with the gift of having heard her voice and touched her body; for a few seconds he saw her coming toward him, memory superimposed on the present like a double photographic plate. He woke one night certain he had been dreaming of her and didn't know where he was. The tenuous light from the porthole over his berth situated him in space but not in time. He could have awakened after several hours of sleep or dozed for just minutes. He wasn't sleepy and he wasn't tired. He put on his raincoat over his pajamas and went up on deck, following narrow, poorly lit corridors empty of people. A sensation of sharp lucidity and physical lightness was as intense as the dream-like air the silence and solitude imparted to things. He leaned on a railing and saw nothing except the strings of lights hung over the deck, dimmed in a thick fog, immobile in the windless night. From time to time he heard the faint splash of water against the hull, and in the distance the siren of another ship, revealing the breadth of invisible space. Close by, he also heard a sound identical to a church bell, a bell monotonously repeating a certain cadence, like the summons to Mass or the recitation of the rosary in the late afternoon in a Spanish provincial town. His ears were adjusting to distant sounds as his eyes adjusted to the slow arrival of the light. He heard nearby voices but couldn't see anyone. Then he began to distinguish forms leaning on the rail, overcoats thrown over nightgowns and pajamas, hands extended in a direction he couldn't make out. Gradually he became aware of a raucous sound that seemed to come from the deepest holds of the ship. But it faded and the silence returned, and with it voices and water lapping against the hull, the voices becoming clearer, like the faces illuminated by lighters that burned for an instant, familiar faces after a week at sea. On one side a long line of blinking lights, on the other a tall, compact shadow, like a basaltic cliff, barely visible in the fog, black against the dark gray into which it was dissolving, dotted now with constellations, as the sound became more powerful, gradually discordant. Those cliffs surging out of the water were the towers of a city; that sea of steel-colored water and shores lost in the distance was a river. He'd have to review his documents again, prepare for another examination, for scornful, hostile looks, for patience and indignity. In the faces ravaged by so short a night, Ignacio Abel recognized those who were now his brothers: the fugitives from Europe carrying suitcases bound with cords, nervously handling briefcases of documents. How did he distinguish them from the others, the travelers for pleasure and the businessmen, those who had solid passports, unquestionable credentials. Perhaps when you crossed the border with one group or the other it was no longer possible to return. Perhaps he himself, when he submitted his papers to the scrutiny of the American customs agents, would discover that during the time he'd been traveling the Spanish Republic had been defeated and he was, as a consequence, the citizen of a nonexistent country. He went down to his cabin to dress and pack his suitcase, and when he returned with it to the deck, the fog had lifted. He discovered the faint colors things were taking on, the bronzes of the cornices, the blues of the sky, the somber greens of the water at the docks, the reds and ochers of the bricks, the glossy tiles reflecting the first light of day from atop the tallest buildings, where sometimes he could also see green patches of trees, autumnal ivy in golds and scarlets. Judith Biely hadn't warned him and he hadn't been able to imagine that New York wasn't the black-and-white city of the movies.

24

THE CONDUCTOR IS announcing the name of the next station in a solemn, powerful voice that rises above the noise of the train. Other passengers are already standing, putting on hats, raincoats, light topcoats, looking out the windows with an air of fatigue, men tired after a full day's work who return home at nightfall, picking up briefcases, folding newspapers, looking at a landscape so familiar they barely notice it, the immense width of the river, the bank the train runs along, so close to the water that small waves break against the tracks' incline, the landscape of daily life that never seems to change, or only to the extent that the seasons change, night falls earlier or later, reds and yellows replace the bright greens in the treetops. There's an end to each journey and to each flight, but where does desertion end, and when? The river's current has an oily texture stained red in the declining light. You can keep running from misfortune and fear, but there is no hiding from remorse. The hills on the opposite bank acquire a darker and denser rust color, interrupted by white splashes of houses where lights are being turned on, though it's not dark yet. Perfect places to take refuge, for two lovers to meet, for someone to come back to, tired and at peace, and not lock the door or fear noises in the night. With briefcases or small suitcases in hand and overcoat lapels raised against the damp cold of the woods and the river, the passengers will walk home along gravel paths. He too had walked from the small station in the Sierra, one afternoon in late September or early October, the vivid memory of an autumn that had just begun: early nightfall, the aroma of damp earth and pines, the smoke of an oak log rising from the chimney against the still blue sky, the creak of the gate and the cold iron on his hands, while from the house, at the end of the garden, came his children's voices. Back then he didn't have a car. He'd have returned by train, enjoying the trip, going over papers or letting his eyes linger on the stands of oak that had a gleam of dusty gold in the afternoon sun, the silhouette of a deer among the oaks, or the flash of a hare. He would walk on fallen leaves covering the gravel path that led to the house; as he got closer, the children's faces became visible, pressed against a window, Adela standing behind them. The train whistle always alerted them of his arrival.

He prepares again for another arrival, his suitcase ready, his wallet in place, safe in his inside pocket, his passport in the other. Ignacio Abel touches the roughness of his beard, wondering about his appearance now that he'll be scrutinized by the eyes of strangers: his suit not cleaned and pressed, his raincoat wrinkled, his shirt stained with coffee, the shoes he should have had shined this morning. Some passengers are moving toward the exit at the back of the car, others remain seated. Sudden weariness in his shoulders and the back of his neck, in fingers that have to grasp the suitcase, in feet that after more than two hours on the train have swollen inside his worn shoes, discouragement on an arrival so long postponed, the end of his journey but perhaps not of his flight and certainly not of his desertion. So much impatience to arrive here, and now he'd like the trip to last longer, a few hours, perhaps all night, to avoid all movement, the need to speak, to reestablish human communication, become again the man he was, avoid the anguish of answering questions — how was your trip, you must be very tired, what was it like to live in Madrid, is this the first time you've visited the United States. He'd give anything for this not to be his station, to remain seated a little longer, his neck against the back of the seat, his face near the glass, watching the autumnal woods go by, and the river, nothing more than that, making out from time to time a light on a dock, in the window of a solitary house, a house where lovers can hide or a woman and her children can hear the train whistle and know the father will arrive in a few minutes along the path through the trees.

He can calculate how many days his trip has lasted, his flight. But he knows his desertion didn't begin three weeks ago in Madrid, when he closed the door of his apartment and didn't bother to insert the key — the key that jingles in his trouser pocket along with some Spanish, French, and American coins, the same pocket where he keeps the train ticket and the receipt from the cafeteria where he had a cup of coffee and a pastry this morning — but much earlier, more than two months earlier, on Sunday, July 19, to be precise, a few minutes before five in the afternoon, at the exact moment he closed the iron gate at the house in the Sierra and heard the train whistle nearby. Weak, almost a hiss, scaled to the Spanish penury in things, not like the deep vibration of a ship's siren with which this American train announces its approach, resounding in the river and the woods, the woods that just a step from the tracks have a jungle's untamable density. He looked at his watch, two minutes to five, for once the train would be on time. He began to walk quickly along the dirt path, past the adobe walls of other summer houses, beneath the vertical sun of the July siesta, even though he had more than enough time since the station was very close, the little station where two or three weeks earlier Adela had arrived at about the same time on the train from Madrid, when the men who played cards in the tavern were surprised to see her on the platform alone, wearing high-heeled shoes and a small-brimmed hat tilted over her face. The same men would stare at him when he arrived on the platform, deserted in the lethargy of noon. A couple of Civil Guards walked along the platform, their uniforms old, their primitive muskets on their shoulders, their dark features contracting in the heat beneath their three-cornered hats. One of them asked Ignacio Abel for his identity card and whether he was going to Madrid. Under the marquee the station clock had stopped, its glass broken. On the list of scheduled arrivals and departures, written in chalk on a blackboard, there were two or three spelling mistakes. The July heat crushed the will and made things unravel, anesthetizing consciousness under the blinding sunlight and the cicadas' chirping. The train pulled in and the coal locomotive filled the air with black smoke. Inside the carriage he trembled with impatience, with disbelief; he looked at his watch as he settled onto the hard wooden seat. For the first time in many days he'd meet Judith Biely not in a café, not at a park corner, but in the house of Madame Mathilde, in the rented bedroom where the curtains would be closed, where he'd see her naked, coming toward him, Judith recovered, offering herself again, resisting her own decision, tied to him by a need more powerful than remorse or decency. *In spite of it all you were dying to get back to Madrid. You couldn't care less about your children, and me even less. You were lucky to catch the last train to the city. You probably don't remember how the children liked to watch the trains go by, anticipating your arrival. So strange not to hear the trains come and go anymore. I don't have to tell you what would have happened to you had you stayed.*

He'd walked away from the house along the garden path, brushing against the rockrose, the overnight bag in his hand, resisting the temptation to look at his watch, to quicken his pace while still in sight of everyone, trying to control his impatience and haste, at least until he heard the gate close behind him. It was then that he took one last look at the house; the family had resumed their conversation in the shade of the grapevine, as if they had already forgotten his existence. The scene couldn't have been more distant or insular had he been looking at a photo of a stranger's family on their Sierra vacation. People were frozen in a casual manner while keeping their distance from each other: the older man in an undershirt, who at any moment will doze in his rocking chair, a straw hat down over his eyes; the white-haired woman in a dark apron, the matriarch of the house, sitting in a low chair, sewing or embroidering or holding in her hands what might be a rosary; the corpulent priest with his legs wide apart and the collar of his cassock unfastened; the frail unmarried ladies, their hair arranged in an outdated style; the other younger woman still attractive in spite of the gray streaks in her hair and the glasses on her broad, placid face which she wears to read a book, and who appears to be lost in her reading and not looking at the man in the light suit who walks down the path, his back to her, attempting not to quicken his pace in too obvious, too shameless a way; going to a place, a person, in spite of his awkward promises, his contrition that's false not because he's lying but because there is nothing to be done, because the irreparable has already taken place. As she watched him leave, she knew he'd turn when he reached the gate. Between shadow and light, the back of a figure holding a tray: for the person who sees the photograph after years have passed, that face will remain hidden; the young maid, a white apron over her dark dress and the cap the señora insists she wear even though they're in the Sierra, holding on the tray a large pitcher of fresh lemonade and some glasses: when she moves between shadow and light projected by the trellis, the sun shines for a few seconds on the yellow-green liquid, turning it golden. He should have had a glass of lemonade before he left; Adela offered it, looking at him out of the corner of her eye, but he couldn't take the risk. Now he was thirsty, and when he turned at the gate he felt that the soft collar of his summer shirt was too tight. In the photo, perhaps in a blur, the figure of his daughter, who, after accompanying her father halfway across the garden and giving him two kisses and telling him to come back soon, sat on the swing and began to sway back and forth, more childish in the house in the Sierra than in Madrid because she's closer to her little-girl memories, the treasured memory of so many identical summer vacations, the same garden and the same swing with its rusty hinges, her father walking away, his briefcase in his hand, the sleepy voices of the family gathering behind her as she begins to swing, the solemn voice of her grandfather, the chirping-bird titters of the maiden aunts. She'll call her brother to come and give her a push, now that they no longer fight as they did only a few years ago about who'd sit on the swing first, they won't count aloud the number of times each pushes the other, and it won't be necessary for their mother or father to come and order a rigorous taking of turns. In the photograph, in memory, the boy is a figure separate from the others, sitting on the highest step at the entrance to the house beside one of the squat granite columns that support the veranda on the upper floor, in front of the area of densest shade from the portico where flies buzz. The boy does nothing, he simply looks at his father, who's leaving; he is suddenly grown, taciturn, with a shadow of thin facial hair on his upper lip, having entered adolescence, aggrieved because his father's going to a life he doesn't know and his mother and sister don't share; watching him leave with the old rankling mixture of relief, resentment, and nostalgia, the son who hasn't stopped watching his mother since they brought her home from the hospital, where she spent a week after an accident no one explained and only he knows, imagines, has to do with his father, with his father's unfamiliar, terrified face on the night he saw him standing in the center of his study, in front of the overturned drawer, among disordered papers and photographs on the floor. There are things he sees so clearly yet others seem not to notice, and this disconcerts him and draws him into himself, something that is not obvious in photos from previous summers but is captured in this image, existing only in Ignacio Abel's mind, fixed there because of his own guilt. A child changes so rapidly at that age, he must already have pimples, his voice must be deepening, and if his father heard it now, after only three months, perhaps he wouldn't recognize it. What school would he be attending, if any schools are open on the other side, in the enemy zone, his son, so fond of movies and magazines, who failed half his exams in June, though his father and mother didn't pay much attention to a setback that in other circumstances would have angered them, his mother in the hospital and then convalescing in the bedroom where the curtains were always closed, his father so distracted by his work at University City, leaving the house at dawn and coming home in the middle of the night, picked up at the entrance to the building by a car in which someone he trusted traveled with him and, Miguel and Lita knew, carried a pistol, a bodyguard like the ones in movies, though he wore a mason's cap, not a gangster's hat, and had a cigarette in a corner of his mouth.

· · ·

What was it like to have experienced that Sunday, that entire week? How many people are left who still remember, who preserve a precious image like a fragile relic, one not added to in retrospect, not induced by knowledge of what was about to occur, what no one foresaw in its monstrous scale, its irrationality, lasting so long no one would remember normal life or have the strength to miss it, life already in hopeless disarray though there's not a single sign of change in the things Ignacio Abel saw when he left the house, after closing the squeaking gate and using a handkerchief to wipe the rust from his sweaty hand. I want to imagine, with the precision of lived experience, what happened twenty years before I was born and what no one will remember anymore in just a few years: the brightness of those few distant days in July and the darkness of time, that very afternoon, the days that preceded it; to do this I'd need an impossible sixth sense to perceive a past that precedes memory itself: I'd need to be innocent of the future, ignorant of what is imminent in the present, in each of these people's lives, their astonishing, uniform blindness, like one of those ancient epidemics that erased millions. But if I could reach out my hand across the frontier of time, touch things, not merely imagine them, not merely see them in museum display cases or by staring hard at the details in photographs: touch the cool surface of that pitcher of water a waiter has just left on the table in a café in Madrid; walk along the Gran Vía or the Calle de Alcalá and feel the bright sunlight vanish in the shade provided by striped awnings whose colors can't be distinguished in black-and-white photos; touch the fleshy geranium leaves seen around a window frame in the photograph of a station in the Sierra very similar to the one close to the house where Ignacio Abel's family spends the summers. The most trivial thing would be a treasure: getting into a taxi in Madrid on a July day in 1936, the odor of the worn, sweaty leather, of the hair pomade men used in those days, of the back seat, a smell of tobacco that must be very different from what can be breathed in now because everything's minutely specific and everything's disappeared, or almost everything, just as almost everything I could see looking out the window, if I were granted the gift of riding in that taxi, has disappeared except the topography of the streets and the architecture of a certain number of buildings — everything demolished by a great cataclysm, more efficient and more tenacious than war, one that occurs each minute and has carried away all the automobiles, all the streetcars with their advertisements faded by the weather, all the awnings and all the store signs, that has submerged paving stones in asphalt and before that torn up the tracks of the streetcars, the mannequins in the shop windows in their summer dresses and bathing costumes and the large smiling heads in the hat stores, all the posters pasted on façades, faded by the rain and sun, torn off in strips, posters for political meetings and bullfights and soccer games and boxing matches, posters for contests to choose the most beautiful señorita at the festival of Carmen, election posters from the February campaign that display categorical statements of victory by candidates who were then defeated. To see, touch, smell: one hazy morning late in May, as I pass by the fence of a country manor half in ruins, I smell the dense, delicate aroma of poplar blossoms from a gigantic tree that has prospered in abandonment and weeds, and the aroma is undoubtedly identical to what someone might have smelled when passing this same spot seventy-three years earlier. I touch the pages of a newspaper — a bound volume of the daily *Ahora* from July 1936 — and it seems I'm touching something that belongs to the substance of that time, but the paper leaves the feel of dust, like dry pollen, on my fingertips, and the pages break at the corners if I don't turn them with the necessary care. It isn't hard for me to conjecture that Ignacio Abel would read that Republican, politically moderate paper, with excellent graphics, an abundance of brief articles in tiny print that after three-quarters of a century continue to transmit, like the buzz of a honeycomb, a powerful, distant drone of lost words, voices extinguished long ago. He bought the paper on Sunday, July 12, when he got off the train in the station at nightfall, back from the Sierra, and probably glanced at it and put it in his pocket or left it in the taxi that took him to the center of the city, to the Plaza de Santa Ana, with the carelessness that characterizes how most ordinary things are handled and lost, things that are everywhere every day and yet disappear without a trace after a short time, or are preserved by pure chance because someone used the pages of that day's paper to line a drawer, or because the paper was left in a trunk no one opened again for seventy years, along with a little notebook that had a few dates written in it, a packet of postcards, a box of matches, a coaster from a cabaret on which a red owl is drawn, seeds of a time that will bear fruit in the imagination of someone not yet born. He was going to the Plaza de Santa Ana in the hope of seeing Judith. Three days earlier she'd agreed by phone to meet him when she returned from her trip to Granada, so frequently postponed, on condition he not look for her, not call her, not write to her. She didn't say when she'd go to Granada or when she'd return and had no reason to give him that information. She'd be waiting for him in Madame Mathilde's house on Sunday, the nineteenth, then perhaps she'd leave to take some literature courses at the International University of Santander. Ignacio Abel agreed with the urgency of an addict ready to lose everything in exchange for a single dose of guaranteed pleasure. He hung up the phone and began to count the days until he'd see her. On Saturday morning, the eleventh, he left the car at a repair shop on Calle Jorge Juan and went by train to the Sierra. He chatted with Don Francisco de Asís, the uncle who was a priest, the maiden aunts; he said the construction strike couldn't last much longer and it wasn't true that gangs of threatening strikers were breaking into grocery stores; he denied that he himself was in any danger; he'd received a few anonymous letters like everyone else, but the police assured him he had nothing to worry about, so he'd dispensed with the armed guard who came to pick him up each morning, to the disappointment of Miguel, who found it worthy of a novel that no one could tell the serious young man was carrying an automatic pistol under his jacket; his brother-in-law Víctor had told them it would be impossible for him to come to the family dinner that Sunday, and so Doña Cecilia's rice and chicken could be enjoyed without the uncertainties and surprises of almost every summer Sunday, though Doña Cecilia couldn't stop wondering where that boy would eat, in some inn or tavern or whatever, especially considering how much he liked her rice, which in the judgment of Don Francisco de Asís had no equal in the best restaurants in Madrid. Adela was present for everything, calm and withdrawn, a little drowsy because of the pills prescribed for her when she'd been discharged from the sanatorium. She accepted with a forced smile her husband's new deferential treatment; Miguel, observing her, was surprised the smile was so affected, that there was in her an even more meager sense of authenticity than in his father's conjugal attentions: adjusting the cushion at the back of her wicker chair, filling her glass with water. When he arrived on Saturday, Ignacio Abel had brought her a bouquet of flowers. Adela thanked him, saying they were pretty, but she didn't look at them once after she'd handed the bouquet to the maid to put in a vase. Beneath a façade of normality the family hid an unspeakable secret. After the rice, and coffee in the shade of the trellis, Ignacio Abel seemed to have dozed off for a while in the rocking chair, but the hands resting on the curved arms couldn't abandon themselves to rest. Miguel saw the tension in the knuckles beneath the skin, the movement of the eyeballs beneath the lids. Detectives at Scotland Yard solve seemingly unsolvable mysteries by studying the most insignificant details at the crime scene. It was enough for the sound of a train to approach for his father to open his eyes, to dissemble as he consulted his watch. It was amazing how little capacity for pretense adults had, so predictable and yet so pompous, so sure their actions would awaken no suspicions. A few minutes before the six o'clock train for Madrid arrived, Miguel saw his father cross the garden in his light suit and summer hat, his briefcase under his arm, walking to the gate where he'd turn to say goodbye before he disappeared for several days. He holds his briefcase tightly to let us know that what he carries inside is very important and he has to leave. He turns after he's opened the gate and doesn't wait to be lost from sight before erasing from his face any indication of still being here.

• • •

In the house in the Sierra, being deprived of Judith had been more tolerable because it fell into the order of things. As soon as he left the station and breathed the hot air of Madrid in the July twilight, he could no longer not look for her. He wouldn't have the patience to read the paper, thicker in its Sunday edition. He got out of the taxi at the corner of Calle del Prado and Plaza de Santa Ana with the premonition that one of the women with short hair and a print summer dress would be Judith, that he'd see her coming out the doorway of her pensión or behind the glass of the ice cream shop where she liked to have horchata and meringue ice cream, her two new Spanish passions. Searching for her was a way to invoke her presence. He could feel her in the sensual touch of warm air at nightfall, in the luminous blue sky over the fantastic tower of the Hotel Victoria, which she loved from the first morning she saw it above Madrid when she opened her window. But perhaps she was still in Granada, and the sense of imminence was an illusion, his search fruitless. Ignacio Abel walks along the Plaza de Santa Ana, filled with open-air cafés where people are having beers and soft drinks, grateful for the first signs of the night's cool breeze. At the open balconies you can see the lighted interiors of houses, family conversations and the clink of dishes blending with music from the radios: the broadcast of a concert by the Municipal Band of Madrid, conducted by Maestro Sorozábal. A bewildered imagination allies itself with knowledge of those mundane details and for a few seconds, like a hallucination, a night in July, a night seventy-three years ago, falls before one's eyes. The Municipal Band of Madrid is playing on the Paseo de Rosales, and the person listening will smell the recently watered grass in the Parque del Oeste. By consulting the newspaper program for Unión Radio on the night of Sunday, July 12, you can find out which piece of music is heard through the open balconies while Ignacio Abel sits down, disheartened, on a still warm stone bench on the Plaza de Santa Ana, the paper folded on his lap, the hand that had been holding it sticky with ink. In his house at 89 Calle Velázquez, Deputy José Calvo Sotelo, who's also spent the day in the Sierra, listens to the concert on the radio with his wife and children in a living room I imagine as pretentious, a room with old religious paintings and Spanish furniture, the kind Don Francisco de Asís likes. Lieutenant José Castillo walks along Calle de Augusto Figueroa, erect in his black Assault Guard uniform, swinging his arms, his right hand brushing the holster where he carries his pistol with instinctive caution, because in recent months, ever since he fired on the Fascists accompanying the coffin of Second Lieutenant Reyes on the Plaza de Manuel Becerra, he's received anonymous death threats. Calvo Sotelo is a man of solemn haughtiness, with a broad, fleshy face and the bearing of someone who has occupied with complete confidence his position of supremacy in the world; he speaks with a warm voice and a rhetoric somewhere between exalted and apocalyptic, which captivates the ladies and arouses the boundless admiration of Don Francisco de Asís when he reads Calvo Sotelo's parliamentary speeches aloud to Doña Cecilia. Lieutenant Castillo is slim, short, erect, almost rigid when in uniform, with round glasses and thinning hair plastered to his skull. He's said goodbye to his wife at the entrance to the house on Augusto Figueroa where they live with her parents — the young, recently married couple can't afford their own place yet. Only in the middle of the festive Sunday night crowd on the Plaza de Santa Ana does Ignacio Abel capitulate and decide he'll return to his house on Príncipe de Vergara, taking a long walk across Madrid; he'll sleep better if he's tired; he'll eat something standing up in the kitchen, and on his way to the bedroom he'll pass through the rooms in the dark where the furniture and lamps have been covered with white cloths since the family moved to the Sierra at the beginning of July. As Ignacio Abel walks down Calle de Alcalá on his way to Cibeles, Lieutenant Castillo crosses Augusto Figueroa toward Fuencarral and looks at his wristwatch to make sure he will report for duty punctually at the Assault Guard barracks behind the Ministry of the Interior. He'll cross the Puerta del Sol, and on the large ministry clock it's a few minutes before ten, still enough time. In Calvo Sotelo's house, someone has turned off the lights in the living room to lessen the heat and make it more pleasant to listen to the concert by the Municipal Band in the Parque del Oeste. In the shadowy living room the radio dial shines brightly, illuminating the heavy-lidded, strong face of Calvo Sotelo. Lieutenant Castillo is crossing the street when suddenly there's a commotion, and in the midst of the confusion his heart contracts in his chest and his right hand holds on to his pistol without taking it out of the holster. Lieutenant Castillo is stunned by the mass of human shapes and the hollow sound of shots, so close they don't seem like gunfire, and when he opens his eyes he sees only blurry forms that quickly slip away because he's lost his glasses and is bleeding, the smell of gasoline makes him dizzy, he's in a taxi on its way to the emergency room. By the time the audience applauds at the end of the Municipal Band's concert and the musicians pack up their scores and instruments, Lieutenant José Castillo is dead. José Calvo Sotelo has never crossed paths with him and will never know he's been killed or that because of the crime he'll die in just a few hours. Before lying down, Calvo Sotelo kneels in his pajamas before a large crucifix hanging above his bed. It's no more than a fifteen-minute walk from Calvo Sotelo's house on Calle Velázquez, corner of Maldonado, to Ignacio Abel's on Príncipe de Vergara. At two in the morning, Ignacio Abel tosses in his bed, unable to sleep, listening through the open balcony to the sound of cars in the empty city, thinking of Judith Biely and counting the days until he can see her, only a week. "It's better if we stay silent for a while. We've said too much and written too much." In the middle of the night, in the great sound of the city that stretches beyond the half-closed shutters through which an occasional breath of wind comes in, each life seems lodged in the orbit of a solar system, distant from all the rest. José Calvo Sotelo slept so soundly in his conjugal bed beneath the large crucifix that he didn't hear the violent pounding of gun butts right away, the voices ordering him to open the door. On Tuesday morning, the fourteenth, Ignacio Abel buys the daily *Ahora* and the face of José Calvo Sotelo fills the front page, the broad, solemn face that now belongs to a dead man. Day after day that week he buys newspapers, listens to heated conversations in the cafés and unsubstantiated news on the radio, and calculates the time remaining until he can see Judith Biely. In history books names have a crushing finality, and events follow one another like necessary links in a chain of cause and effect. In the infinite present that one would like to imagine in its entirety, in the innermost throbbing of time, every detail entangled, voices upon voices, page after page in newspapers half read, waves of words breaking against the unknown of the day, against what tomorrow will bring and what no one can foresee.

Two atrocious crimes in the space of a few hours. An Assault Guard lieutenant and Señor Calvo Sotelo assassinated in Madrid. Lieutenant Castillo waylaid and shot when he left his house shortly before ten o'clock on Sunday night. The head of Spanish Renewal abducted in the small hours, shot dead, his body dumped in the municipal cemetery. The corpse of Lieutenant Castillo moved to Security Headquarters. Señor Calvo Sotelo's family says he was tricked into leaving his home; he'd spent Sunday in Galapagar, just outside Madrid. Minutes before he was killed, Lieutenant Castillo said goodbye to his young wife at their front door. Many German tourists visit Ceuta and Tetouan, in Morocco. An automobile collides with a motorcycle, and the cyclist and his companion are seriously injured. In Michigan, the morgues are filling up with the dead, victims of a heat wave afflicting the United States, and doctors claim they have never seen so many die from heat stroke. In Murcia, numerous people with right-wing affiliations are arrested. Fire destroys a shack, and the ragpicker who lived there is hurt. A man dives from a board into a pond and smashes his face against a rock. Rafael Díaz Rivera, thirteen years of age, desperate at having gambled and lost 90 céntimos given to him for an errand, commits suicide in Priego by hanging himself from a tree. Hundreds of athletes representing twenty-two countries will gather in Barcelona next Sunday, July 19, to celebrate the great People's Olympiad. One eleven-year-old boy stabs another and leaves him gravely wounded. The ghost some residents of Tarragona believed they saw was actually an old, mentally disturbed woman. Four armed men attack a radio station in Valencia and gag the announcer in order to give a Fascist-leaning speech in which they proclaim that the hour is near and the redemptive movement will come soon. Gypsies shoot and seriously wound a farmer, intending to rob him. At the monument to the dead at Verdun, German veterans fraternize with French in a homage that evokes deep emotion. A truck runs over a child, and the boy's father attacks one of the drivers of the vehicle. The German-Austrian peace pact can lead the way to an alliance among Germany, Austria, and Italy. Mussolini says the accord should be greeted with satisfaction by lovers of peace. To celebrate the fifth anniversary of the founding of the Swim Club of Sevilla, a comedy festival was held in which participants wore grotesque bathing costumes. Last Sunday a dinner was held at the Brazilian embassy in honor of the president of the Republic and Señora de Azaña, attended by members of the government, eminent diplomats, and other prominent figures. The public lines up at the door to Security Headquarters to view the body of Lieutenant Castillo. At the yearling bullfight held in Madrid to benefit the Railroad Workers' Widows and Orphans Fund, the bull-fighter Señorita Julita Alocén made her debut. All the parliamentary minorities in the Popular Front condemn the murders of Señores Castillo and Calvo Sotelo and confirm their loyalty and support for the Republican government. Three people attack a peasant and extract his blood after anesthetizing him. In honor of his birthday Commissar Maxim Litvinov has been awarded the Order of Lenin. Señorita Lidia Margarita Corbette, of Swiss nationality, attempted to end her life by shooting herself with a pistol. The president of the Republic will spend his summer vacation in Santander. It is believed Il Duce has the peaceful goal of unifying Europe. Four cars of a train out of Bilbao careen over an embankment, killing four people and injuring sixty. Barcelona police raid a secret meeting of affiliates of the Spanish Falange. Soviet expedition lost in Kazakhstan desert. The director general of security announces his deep involvement in efforts to discover those responsible for the murders of Lieutenant Castillo and Señor Calvo Sotelo. An intoxicated motorist driving his car at top speed crashes into a wall. The blacksmith of Coria del Río, José Palma León, called Oselito, will run from Sevilla to Barcelona inside a wagon wheel to participate in the People's Olympiad. To perform the autopsy on the body of Señor

Calvo Sotelo, the occipital region was shaved, revealing two entry wounds made by bullets fired at close range. In honor of the feast of the Virgin of Carmen, lively celebrations, including a bullfight, have been held in the picturesque village of Santurce. The body of Don José Calvo Sotelo, dressed in a Franciscan habit and holding a crucifix, lay in state in a mahogany coffin with silver fittings. In London, a thirty-three-year-old mother of five is executed for poisoning her husband. The hippopotamus at the Barcelona Zoo has successfully given birth to a robust offspring. The permanent delegation of the Cortes prolongs the state of emergency. The terrace of the Hotel Nacional was the site of a banquet in honor of Dr. Guillermo Angulo, a pediatrician, for his recent appointment to the competitive position of director of children's services in the National Institute of Social Welfare. The file on the death of Lieutenant Castillo has been given to a special judge, Señor Fernández Orbeta, who is proceeding with great diligence. A farm worker climbs through the window of a room where a young woman is sleeping and she shoots him to death. Señor Calvo Sotelo's abductors cut the phone lines to prevent anyone from calling for help. Medieval festivities in Hitler's Germany a great success. City in Anatolia is fuel to flames. Beginning next week, audiences at the National Palace are suspended until after the summer vacation of his excellency the president. The family of Señor Calvo Sotelo says he was taken from his home on the pretext of an official investigation. The eminent astronomer Señor Comas y Solá warns of the possibility of great electromagnetic disturbances in 1938. The director general of security congratulates the Murcia police on the capture of a dangerous Fascist who escaped prison. Lieutenant Castillo and his young wife married in Madrid last May. The eminent Spanish professor Señor García y Marín delivers the inaugural address at the formal opening session of the International Congress of Administrative Sciences in Warsaw. The military commander of Las Palmas, General Balmes, was examining a jammed automatic pistol when the weapon discharged and the bullet entered his stomach and exited his back. A Catalán engineer discovers a wine-based fuel to profitably replace gasoline. The efforts of the special tribunal successfully identify the leader of the abductors who entered the home of Señor Calvo Sotelo last Sunday. A young woman aboard a Spanish yacht anchored in Gibraltar accidentally shoots herself with the revolver she was handling and is seriously injured. When the British sovereign was on his way to Hyde Park to present new flags to a regiment of guards, a man broke through the police cordon and rushed at the monarch, revolver in hand. Those responsible for the death of Captain Faraudo have not surfaced, and the prosecutor demands seven years of imprisonment for the detained accomplices. The eminent Dr. Marañón and his family have left in the Madrid-to-Lisbon mail plane for the capital of the neighboring republic. The man responsible for the attack on King Edward VIII is a social reformer who has taken part in campaigns against the death penalty. A man who killed his mother and aunt in Barcelona has been sentenced to sixty years in prison. The widow of Señor Calvo Sotelo arrived in Lisbon yesterday and intends to spend the summer vacation with her family in Estoril. An army unit that represents Spain in Morocco has rebelled, turning on its own country and committing shameful acts against the nation. The heat wave in the United States has claimed the lives of 4,600 people. At this time, air, sea, and land forces, with the sad exception previously indicated, remain loyal to their duty and have turned against seditious elements to bring down this senseless, shameful movement. The Republican government is in control of the situation and states that in a matter of hours it will report to the nation.

"I'll be back Thursday night, Friday morning at the latest," he said to Adela, who hadn't looked him in the eye or registered his presence since she came home from the hospital, and when she did talk to him, it was in a neutral, unemotional tone. Only he was aware, and perhaps his sensitive son too, of that indifference, that subtle retaliation, a wound inflicted with a blade that left no trace, discrediting anything he might do or say, the adulterous husband whose betrayal only she knew of, the man overwhelmed by a guilt she alone administered, for it wasn't dispensed in public or through familial vilification. Adela, contrary to what Ignacio Abel in his cowardice expected, said nothing to anyone, sought no refuge in her parents or her brother, who questioned her solicitously, certain that the reason she'd attempted to take her own life was the infidelity of her husband, whom he'd never trusted. Not even to Víctor did she acknowledge that this had been her intention. She regained consciousness in the hospital bed and at first didn't remember anything or know where she was. As she gradually recalled in disconnected flashes the letters and photographs, the key in the drawer lock, walking in high heels on the path soft with pine needles, the water entering her nose, she decided she would explain nothing, at first because of fatigue and then so as not to allow anyone to join in a resentment she preferred to discharge whole on the person who had humiliated her; it would belong to her marital intimacy as much as her love of earlier times. She wouldn't raise her voice. She wouldn't make any accusation or cause a scene. She wouldn't lower herself to that level, despite the injury that the man she'd trusted for sixteen years had inflicted on her. She wouldn't give anyone, least of all him, the opportunity to feel sorry for her, and she wouldn't offer him the spectacle of a hysteria that would allow him to feel justified in his impulse to run away from a suffocating situation. She wouldn't grant him the benefit of rejecting and then gradually accepting the false explanations, the promises to change inspired only by male cowardice and a transitory remorse. All she did was agree distractedly if he spoke to her, or look away, or imply with a subtle gesture she no longer believed anything that came out of his mouth, reducing his status from an adulterous husband to a mediocre impostor, a contemptible hypocrite. On Sunday morning, when the table was already set and lunch delayed because she and her parents still hoped Víctor would come from Madrid, she saw Ignacio Abel approach her and the children and understood he was going to tell them he'd go back to Madrid after lunch and not that night, or the next morning, as he had assured them on Saturday morning when he arrived. (The car was in the shop for repairs; the mechanic told him he could pick it up on Monday or Tuesday; one constantly makes plans in life, taking the immediate future for granted.) She saw that he was approaching but didn't have the courage. Almost with pity (he was so impaired, so anxious in recent days), Adela noted his nervousness, she knew him so well, better than anyone, the way his gestures betrayed him, too awkward to lie, too lacking in courage to know what he wanted. She acted as if she were devoting all her attention to how the always negligent maids had arranged the silverware and napkins on the table under the trellis, on the north side of the garden, where it wasn't so hot, where a stream that flowed over mossy rocks highlighted the sensation of coolness. When they were alone the fiction they usually performed in front of others was more uncomfortable. Without witnesses, they didn't know how to speak. He delayed the moment of saying he'd leave after lunch; Adela guessed how disconcerting the continuing postponement of lunch was for him; time stood still and at the same time it was fleeing; the train's departure was approaching without the meal arriving, without his saying anything. It was a relief for Ignacio Abel when Don Francisco de Asís came out to the garden holding his pocket watch. He too was waiting, wondering why his reckless fool of a son was so late in coming from Madrid. "And he knows how his mother worries," said Don Francisco de Asís, with no theatrics now, looking older, his shirt without a collar, his suspenders hanging beside his trousers. "It's nothing. He's always late. We shouldn't make others wait. Let's eat." Adela spoke to her father, but Ignacio Abel knew it was him she was addressing, letting him know she was aware of his impatience and couldn't care less whether he went back to Madrid that afternoon.

"How annoying. And to think how much he likes my rice and chicken. Something must have happened to him."

"I demanded his word of honor as my son and a gentleman that he wouldn't attend Calvo Sotelo's funeral."

"God rest his soul."

"And the poor Assault Guard lieutenant too."

"I feel sorry for his widow, so young, she wasn't to blame for anything."

"They say she was pregnant."

"What a feat for whoever committed the crime, making an orphan of a baby who hasn't been born yet."

"He promised me he'd come today. Something's happened to the boy."

"What happened to him is what happens every Sunday, Mamá. He gets distracted in Madrid and always arrives late."

"Or with all this upset the trains aren't running."

"Of course they're running. I've heard them go by on time all morning."

"A sign that nothing serious has happened and you don't have to worry."

"We should have waited a little longer to put in the rice. There was no hurry."

"But Mamá, we're all famished."

"That boy doesn't eat right when he's alone in Madrid. At least if I see him eating well on Sunday, I rest a little easier."

"Keep a plate covered for him, and when he comes you'll see how hungry he is when he eats."

"But Adela, you know that if the rice sits too long it's no good and the taste is ruined."

"Your chicken and rice is a classic, Mamá. It gets better with time."

"What ideas you have, Papá."

Don Francisco de Asís and Doña Cecilia called each other Papá and Mamá. Ignacio Abel listened to the conversation and could predict the exchange almost word for word, just as he predicted the saffron-heavy taste of Doña Cecilia's rice casserole and the sucking sounds of the diners, including the paterfamilias, as Don Francisco de Asís called himself. So many Sundays, one after the other, exactly the same, so many summers around this same table, the present identical to the past and undoubtedly to the future. Víctor would arrive at the last moment and Doña Cecilia would urge the maid to serve him his plate of rice, lamenting that its time was past, it's a shame but rice can't wait. Víctor would devour it, denying with a full mouth his mother's protestations because the rice was delicious, he liked it better this way. But this Sunday lunch ended and Víctor hadn't arrived, and Doña Cecilia, as she had so often, ordered the maid to keep the señorito's plate of rice covered in the pantry, listening for a car coming down the road or a whistle announcing the arrival of a train.

He remembers the torpor into which the heat of a July afternoon and Doña Cecilia's rice-and-chicken casserole immersed the people in the house after Sunday dinners. "If it's so hot here," someone would say, about to succumb to sleep, "I don't want to think what they're suffering in Madrid." "There's a difference of only three degrees centigrade." The day before, on Saturday, he'd bought the paper before boarding the train, and a report on the Council of Ministers said nothing about the rumors of a military coup. "Everybody envies the noble Spanish institution of the siesta." "I can't get over how upset I am about that boy not tasting the rice today." He couldn't imagine that in a few hours he'd be with Judith, hearing her voice. "He still might come and have it for tea." Impatient, he'd ring the bell at Madame Mathilde's, which would emit a sound of chimes. "It's not good anymore." He'd cross the hot, dark house smelling of perfume and disinfectant, push the door open. "Your rice is incomparable, Mamá." The sound of their voices was as lethargic as the cicadas at that hour of high heat. Ignacio Abel went into the cool, shadowy bedroom, put on a clean shirt and tie, and washed his hands with lavender soap. He looked at his watch over and over again with a reflexive gesture. Through the open window came the sound of the rusted swing his children were sitting on. Had he heard the train whistle? Impossible — it wasn't due for another half hour. He'd have time to wait, alone, on a bench on the platform. Nothing mattered to him now. Only the expectation of his encounter with Judith, more and more real as the minutes brought it closer. He'd arrive in Madrid and the suffocating tension of Friday night would have dissipated, erased by the heat and the invincible normality. He'd take a taxi and ride through the empty city on a summer Sunday to the chalet of Madame Mathilde.

Someone entered the bedroom and he turned, thinking he'd see Adela's face. But it was Don Francisco de Asís in his collarless shirt and house slippers, his face that of a helpless old man.

"Ignacio, you shouldn't go to Madrid this afternoon. My daughter should have told you this, but I'll say it. Don't go. Wait a few days."

"I have to work tomorrow, early. You know I can't stay."

"Nobody knows what will happen tomorrow."

Ignacio Abel closed his overnight bag, which was on the bed. He put his wallet and the keys to his apartment in a trouser pocket. He couldn't waste a minute. Time on our hands. Don Francisco de Asís blocked the door, not a trace of farce on his slack features, shorter than he was; the image of the man he'd had for so many years had suddenly disappeared, and in his place was an old man dying of fear, his voice turned into the sound of entreaty.

"You'll know how to take care of yourself, but my son won't. My son will look for misfortune — if something hasn't happened to him already and that's why he didn't come today. You have good judgment and he doesn't, you know that. Promise me if something happens to him you'll help him. You're my son, just as he is. You've been like my own son since the day you walked into my house. What each of us thought or didn't think doesn't matter. You're a good man. You know as well as I do that shooting down people as if they were animals doesn't solve problems. All I'm asking is that when you're in Madrid, if you find out my son's involved in something idiotic, you'll help him out. When will you be back?"

"Thursday night. Friday at the latest."

"You're a good man. Bring him back with you. My son's almost forty years old and he is worse than a child — no sense. Why deceive ourselves? He'll never get anything right. But I don't want him in trouble. I don't want him killed. Or doing something stupid. Don't let him."

"What can I do?"

"Please give me your word, Ignacio. I'm not asking for more. Give me your word and I'll be reassured and able to reassure his mother."

"You have my word."

Ignacio Abel made a move to walk out of the room with his bag in one hand and his hat in the other, but Don Francisco de Asís didn't move. He grabbed his son-in-law by the neck with both hands, embraced him, and gave him two kisses.

25

H E'D NEVER SEE HER AGAIN. He knew it with the dizzying sensation of not finding a step in the dark, or when on the verge of sleep one's heart stops for a second. He knew it when his longing turned to uncertainty as the train pulled into Madrid and he got off and made his way through the crowd on the platform, looking for the closest exit and a taxi. Judith had promised him a meeting, and he didn't know whether it was to be a parting or a reconciliation. It hadn't occurred to him that she might not show up. He desired her so much he couldn't accept the idea of not seeing her after waiting so many days, after so many futile phone calls and letters. The Sunday afternoon crowd filled the station, young men and women wearing neckerchiefs and vaguely military shirts with large circles of sweat under their arms, feeding off one another's energy, both sexual and revolutionary, chanting slogans, directing defiant looks at his tie and shoes, his obvious bourgeois status. His age, too, would have made him suspect. How distant he felt from those people who had invaded the train at each of the stops in the Sierra — distant not from their arrogance or political extremism but from their youth. He heard vendors' shouts, train whistles, anthems, fragments of conversations as he walked past. Everything less insistent than the stabbing pain in his stomach, the pressure in his temples, the sweat soaking his shirt, the knot of his tie squeezing his neck. Boys in caps and beggars' rags hawking the afternoon papers, waving the wide, recently printed sheets, black ink running in enormous headlines. Announcements of departing trains blaring over loudspeakers. Groups of police and armed civilians in the station lobbies. If they stopped him to demand his papers or ask him a question, he'd surely miss the chance of finding a taxi. Taxis are the first to disappear when there's a disturbance. So many armed men, yet so few in uniform, rifles in their hands and pistols on the slant in their belts, red or red-and-black kerchiefs tied around their necks. The train was slow, it was already after seven, Judith must be growing impatient. With luck, if he found a taxi, he could get to Madame Mathilde's before seven-thirty. Perhaps he ought to call from a booth or use the telephone in the station café to let her know he'd be late but was on his way. He patted his wallet, looked for loose coins in his pockets as he continued walking toward the exit. But if he stopped to call and the phone was in use or didn't work, he'd lose crucial time for nothing. A corpulent, well-dressed man walking ahead of him, who'd ridden in the same car of the train, had been stopped and roughed up as they searched his clothing. A wallet and a handful of coins and keys fell to the floor, and a swarm of urchins began to fight over them while the armed men guffawed. The police, close by, watched and did nothing. "This is an outrage," the man repeated, his face red, as Ignacio Abel walked past, trying not to meet anyone's eyes. "An unspeakable outrage." He walked faster, his heart pounding. If they stopped him, if he didn't find a taxi, he'd lose her forever. Your whole life can depend on one minute. From a delivery truck that braked abruptly, fast-moving newsboys unloaded large bundles of papers. He bought one and glanced at it as he hurried out. The government of the Republic is in control of the situation, and in a few hours it will inform the nation that the situation is under control. For the moment it seemed it wasn't in control of syntax. But perhaps Judith hadn't arrived on time either. She'd be lost, like him, at the other end of the city, without streetcars or taxis, her walk interrupted by one of those armed groups, frightened perhaps. SECURITY FORCES AND CIVIL GUARDS CHEERED ON THE STREETS OF MADRID. But she wasn't afraid of anything and was a foreigner besides. She'd want to witness everything and write an article about it. Or perhaps she'd left Madrid. Her friends at the embassy had told her that for a time it would be dangerous to remain in Spain. Philip Van Doren had invited her to join him in Biarritz at the end of July. *How I wished we could have left together but I can't go on wanting things I can't have.* Van Doren smiled and with a contemptuous movement of his hand dispelled any serious danger, as if waving away a cloud of tobacco smoke. "As long as they take turns killing one another nothing will happen. A Communist, a Falangist, a factory worker, a business owner. Catholic countries have a talent for eloquent funerals, the Anarchists imitate Catholic pageantry when they bury one of their own, and don't they all talk about martyrs, Professor Abel? A well-administered bloodbath guarantees social peace." He remembered the blood shed by the Falangist or Communist selling papers one May afternoon on Calle de Alcalá: the puddle, bright red under the sun, gushing out of a black hole. The blood of martyrs. To the last drop. The blood that will wash away injustice. He left the station, eyes lowered, his briefcase held tightly under his arm, the newspaper in his sweaty hands. No one had stopped him. General Queipo de Llano has declared a state of war in Sevilla. But there was no taxi at the stand. At dawn vigorous action will be taken against all rebellious centers. Time slipping away minute by minute, she sitting in the armchair in the bedroom, not on the bed, fully dressed, unlike other times. He'd never see her undressed again. The thought pained him. How was he going to find her—Judith's blond hair backlit against a window, her figure in the large mirror in front of the bed, her legs crossed, ill humored because of the heat, tired of waiting. She must be looking impatiently at her watch, sorry she agreed to a meeting she perhaps didn't want. On the esplanade in front of the station, where the afternoon sun beat down, there was a loud noise of bombs and someone shouted at Ignacio Abel, gesturing at him from a doorway. He dropped to the ground, not letting go of his briefcase, his body flattened against the burning-hot edges of paving stones, in his chest the vibration of an underground train. A little farther away, in the shade of a café awning, several people sought protection behind a man in an undershirt who aimed a rifle at the terraces across the way. They looked around as if they'd taken shelter in a sudden downpour and were searching the sky for signs of clearing. Isolated shots became bursts of fire, followed by silence. As if obeying an order, Ignacio Abel and the man on the ground in front of him stood, brushing off their clothes, the people protected by the café awning dispersed, abandoning the man who pointed the rifle, now in another direction. Cars moved again. A woman didn't get up. She lay not face-down but on her side, as if she'd stretched out for a short nap in the middle of the esplanade. The man who'd been searched by the patrol in the station, standing next to the fallen woman, took out a white handkerchief and waved it at the cars driving by. His eyes met Ignacio Abel's: recognizing him from the train, the man imagined he must be on his side because he also wore a suit and tie and was more or less the same age, and thought he could count on his help. But Ignacio Abel looked away, stopped an approaching taxi that had suddenly appeared, and urged the driver on. He saw the eyes watching him in the rearview mirror. He felt his face and found a little blood on his fingers, the sting of a scrape on his cheek. He'd hurt himself when he pressed his face against the paving stones. If he wasn't careful he'd stain his shirt, the light linen of his summer jacket. He had his briefcase but had lost his hat and the newspaper. "If you hadn't been right in front of me, I wouldn't have stopped," the cab driver said. "I'm doing you a service and getting myself away from the trouble. The way things are, they'd either shoot me or steal the car, and you can't say which is worse. But I saw that you're a respectable person in a fix and I wasn't going to run you down . . ." For Ignacio Abel, the driver's words evaporated into air like the images on the other side of the window, or the sensation of gunfire and lying vulnerable on the ground in a large open space. ". . . the same in '32, with Sanjurjo, and in '34, in Asturias. Things seem to blow up every two years . . ." The driver didn't give up, looking in the rearview mirror at the face of his silent passenger, so well dressed he probably sympathized with the rebels and that's why he didn't say anything. ". . . around O'Donnell things'll be calmer, but you never know. Just in case, I'm going up to my cabin and tomorrow, God only knows, probably tomorrow it'll all be over, though to me this looks blacker than a storm cloud, what do you think? . . ." Words dissolving as Ignacio Abel looked again and again at his watch and was alarmed each time the taxi braked and seemed about to be trapped, surrounded by clusters of people. The driver sounded the horn and blows fell on the car; an open truck full of men waving flags blocked their way. He'd never get out of the center of town and reach the clear spaces of the Salamanca district, beyond the Retiro, the small hotels with gardens on Calle O'Donnell, which since last fall had been the prelude to his meetings with Judith Biely, the sparsely built frontier territory at the edge of Madrid where it was unlikely anyone would catch them going into Madame Mathilde's house or leaving it, discreetly, separately, burning with desire, Judith's eyes adjusting to the daylight after one or two hours in the dark.

The closer he came, the more afraid he was. He wanted to move time ahead and leaned forward in his seat, his right leg moving rhythmically, feeling on his face the warm air that came in the window when they began to drive faster. He searched for signs of what was going to happen to him in a few minutes, prophecies of the immediate future, possible outcomes. He enters the house and Judith has just left. He walks behind the silent maid down the dimly lit corridor, opens the door to the room, and sees Judith sitting on the bed, wearing her high-heeled shoes and street dress, as if she's just arrived. He gets out of the taxi, pushes the gate, and finds it locked. He rings the bell, whose faint echo reaches him from inside the house, and the sound that had so often announced a meeting with Judith is now a warning. The maid opens the door, and before she has time to say anything, he understands that Judith hasn't come. Panic seized him. A young woman, alone, whom he saw through the window as the taxi slowed down, was, for a moment, Judith leaving Madame Mathilde's house after waiting for an hour. Her features dissolved as rapidly as the driver's chatter or the blurred spectacle of a street disturbance in the center of the city. He paid quickly with a wrinkled bill and got out. At the end of Calle O'Donnell, wide and unobstructed, with an open horizon where the rows of trees and streetcar tracks and electric wires disappeared, Madrid was once again the deserted city of Sunday afternoons in the summer, paralyzed by a dusty heat that the rows of too-young trees didn't alleviate, submerged in a silence of closed balconies. Without a hat he felt insecure and unprotected on the street. He passed his hand over his hair, adjusted his tie, brushed off his trousers. Madame Mathilde's maid sees him with his head uncovered and a bruise on his face, shakes her head in disapproval, and opens the door. Each step he took was bringing him closer to the undeniable; whatever it was, it would abolish the torment of uncertainty. The gate opened without resistance. In the garden stood a fountain with a basin but no water, topped by a small statue of a nymph. As soon as he climbed a few steps and pressed the bell that triggered a muffled sound of chimes, he'd know what his ultimate fate would be. He wasn't asking for a lasting future without distress, only a moment to look at her, hear her voice. He wouldn't even try to embrace her; it would be enough for him to be at her side and tell her what he needed to say and hadn't said clearly before. He pressed the bell. No one came to the door. The house wasn't empty; he could hear echoes of a radio broadcast. He rang again and the maid's suspicious face appeared in an opening between the frame and the door, narrower than on previous occasions. If she said nothing and led him to the usual room, it meant Judith was waiting for him. The servant wore a black dress and cap, and on Madame Mathilde's specific instructions had no makeup on her eyes or lips. She closed the door and with the same faint smile and silent docility she'd displayed at other times indicated that he should follow her. He didn't ask whether Judith had come; saying something would have risked frightening away a fragile hope. At the door the servant lowered her head and moved to one side. When he didn't dare to look inside, the maid's voice confirmed his fear. "If the señor wishes, I can serve you a drink while you're waiting for the señorita to arrive."

The ice had dissolved in the glass of whiskey when steps that weren't Judith's approached the door and someone knocked. He'd been sitting in the red easy chair by the window, not moving, or moving just enough to take an occasional sip, noting the gradual warming of the drink and the aftertaste of alcohol, watching the progress of nightfall. Like the ice in the glass, his anxiety had gradually dissolved into despair, into the simple inertia not of waiting but of maintaining the immobility of the wait, because of fatalism or reluctance or the inability to make a decision or do anything other than continue to sit, glass in hand, submerging himself in the growing darkness, occasionally seeing himself from the side in the mirror when he turned his head. He could have pressed the bell on the night table to request more ice or ask if there was a call, a message from Judith. But he did nothing. He simply prolonged the wait, putting off the acceptance of what in reality he'd known, surmised not with his intelligence but with the ache in his stomach, the pressure of sorrow in his throat and chest, the warning of the unacceptable. He continued to wait as if the force of his obstinacy would influence Judith's actions and will. Unmoving and alert, he listened for sounds in the house, the silence of an abandoned place that didn't resemble the habitual hideout of adulterous plans and sexual appointments of specified duration. He didn't hear muffled bells, brief rings, footsteps near the door or above him. From the adjoining rooms came no heavy breathing, bursts of laughter, disconnected words, stifled shouts. Only the radio somewhere, broadcasting misled voices and music, announcements. And in the background the remote sounds of Madrid, beyond the sonorous birds in the garden, coming in through the shutters along with a breeze, a hot breath released by the soil and pavement upon the arrival of nightfall. Embers of light remained on the venal red of the bedspread, in the mirror, on the porcelain of the bidet and sink. In memory Judith's body had the same spectral quality as that dissolving light. How wretched to have brought her so often to a place like this, not to have paid attention to the vileness of almost every object in the room, the vulgarity, the depraved taste of a bourgeois bedroom from the turn of the century replicated in a brothel. Her young skin had touched those shiny, threadbare fabrics impregnated with the smell of tobacco and cheap cologne; her bare feet had stepped on the rug with a worn pastoral scene; when she leaned back, her tousled head had rested on that wall with drawings of flowers and a dark trail of grease. He saw her astride him, her hair over her face and her torso brilliant with sweat in the reddish light of a lamp that transformed the working hours of a Monday morning into night. He saw her kneeling, still dressed, removing his shoes while he sat in that same chair on one of the days when he arrived exhausted from work. Judith untying his shoelaces, taking off his socks, caressing his feet. She raised one of his feet and rested it on her breasts, leaning over to kiss it. He was going to say something and Judith put her index finger to his lips.

The approaching footsteps made him wake from his self-absorption. How long had he been in the dark? He turned on a light and stood, attempting to straighten his tie and shirt collar. After a few short knocks on the door, the old painted face of Madame Mathilde appeared, an envelope in her hand. His sentence would be on the sheet of paper inside, held by wrinkled hands wearing bracelets and rings. *No matter how much I want to, I can't be your docile lover, the mistress you keep at a distance while you go on living with your family. It's better if I go and try my best to forget you.* Madame Mathilde inspected the room with an expert glance and immediately put on her affable face of discreet complicity, saddened now, the bearer, perhaps, and an unwilling one, of bad news. "Forgive the young lady's confusion, she's a beginner." Madame Mathilde spoke as if she managed a respectable household with servants, and a good deal of protocol, a boarding school or strict social club where few first names and no last names were spoken. "I told the girl to let me know when you arrived so you wouldn't have to wait for no reason. The señorita came this afternoon and gave me this letter for you, asked me to say she was very sorry she couldn't come back later, as she wanted to, because it was urgent that she leave Madrid. Which doesn't surprise me at all, considering how things are going, if you don't mind my saying so." Ignacio Abel looked at her in bewilderment, nodding, as Madame Mathilde handed him the letter. He read it sitting on the bed, in the dim light of the lamp on the night table, drinking a whiskey he didn't remember ordering, facing the mirror where he'd so often seen Judith Biely naked on the red bedspread. *If we can't have each other without hiding and if I have to share you with a woman you don't love but whom we made suffer and almost die, I'd rather be alone.* Shouts and car horns sounded in the distance, military marches and announcements from a radio playing in the house, something he didn't recall ever occurring before. The night air no longer moved past the shutters. Sweat dampened the edge of his shirt collar, tight against his skin, and instead of relaxing him the whiskey had left a throbbing pain in his temples. *What good is it for you to say you were thinking of me if last night you slept with her in the same bed and this afternoon you kissed her goodbye when you left and took the train to come be with me.*

She'd leave Madrid by train that night, he thought with painful clarity. While he waited for her, filled with impatience and desire, in Madame Mathilde's house, Judith Biely would board a train at the South or North Station, on her way to La Coruña or Cádiz, because those were the two ports where ships for America could sail from, unless she traveled to Irún, on the border, to take a ship from the coast of France. Madame Mathilde had held on to the letter intentionally; she had let him wait to cover Judith's flight, so he wouldn't have time to go and search for her. *I can't keep writing in Spanish, so I'll do it faster and clearer in English.* She'd written quickly, knowing she was leaving, coldly resolved to carry out a plan perhaps made some time ago. *I'll miss you but eventually I'll get over it, provided I don't see you again.* He folded the letter care-lessly, put it in a jacket pocket — not ringing the bell that indicated his intention to leave the room, which guaranteed he wouldn't cross paths with any other of Madame Mathilde's clients — and went into the hall, where the old woman appeared before him, emerging from a shadowy corner as if she'd been waiting for him. "The drinks are on the house, don't worry. I always like to keep a real gentleman happy. There are so few left and there'll be even fewer if this business isn't straightened out soon — didn't you hear the radio?" Ignacio Abel almost pushed the obsequious madam out of the way as he handed her a few bills. "No, the señorita didn't give me any other message, didn't say anything to me, though come to think of it she was dressed for a trip." She pressed his hand as she took the bills, understanding, almost maternal, bringing her painted face close to his as she spoke in a low voice. "And permit me to say something in complete confidence. If, as it seems, the señorita will be away for some time, and you want to fill her place, as it were, with discretion and hygiene, you only have to say so, because I can introduce you to a clean, good-looking girl prepared to accept the friendship of a gentleman of your distinction. It goes without saying that in this house the doors are wide open to you." Ignacio Abel went out to the street, still carrying Judith's letter in his hand. He saw before him the smile that twisted Madame Mathilde's mouth slightly and the gleam at the back of her small, astute eyes beneath painted lids. Suddenly he knew. He remembered hearing the doorbell as he waited in the room, allowing himself to sink slowly into the darkness, into memories and lethargy: it was Judith who had rung and entered the house knowing he was in the room. Standing in the vestibule from where she could see at the end of the hall the door behind which he was waiting, Judith had handed Madame Mathilde the letter, speaking to her in a low voice, and then had gone, so close to him and yet resolved to disappear into a distance where he feels he'll never find her, though he's come to her country not to flee Spain or build a library close to the great river, but to look for her.

26

H E WENT OUT AND suddenly felt it wasn't the city he'd arrived in a few hours earlier on a Sunday afternoon. If Judith had been so near less than an hour ago, he still had time to find her and keep her from leaving. It was night now, and the streets that went down to Cibeles and the Paseo del Prado were filled with cars and people. Windows were open and houses lit, revealing bedrooms and dining rooms from which came a magnified, discordant cacophony of radios, and silhouettes at the balconies. Suspicion turned into certainty, an accusation; a resentful lover's rancor gave tangible reality to his suppositions: Judith had gone to Madame Mathilde's house knowing he was waiting for her, had the self-possession to drop off the letter and leave, and the astuteness to speak in a low voice and perhaps ensure the old woman's complicity with some money; in the pocket of the widow's gown the bills he'd just given her were next to Judith's. On Calle de Alcalá a crowd somewhere between boisterous and surly shoved him and shook raised fists and placards, waved red and red-and-black flags. In the background, toward the domes of the Gran Vía, a shifting light rose that had the drama of a red twilight. It smelled of smoke and burned gasoline, and ashes rained down on bare heads. Perhaps Judith had asked the taxi driver who took her to Madame Mathilde's to wait for her by the gate, she wouldn't be more than a moment; now Ignacio Abel thought he remembered hearing the sound of the waiting car's

engine, sure he'd heard the startling noise of a door opening and closing; when he went out to the vestibule, hadn't he detected a faint trace
of Judith's scent? He examined the immediate past because he was
obsessed with confirming he'd had her within reach, as if that might
somehow alleviate the reality of her disappearance. Without a hat,
briefcase in hand, I see him from the other side of the street as he walks
quickly down Calle de Alcalá, paying no attention to the window of the
travel agency that displays the scale model of an ocean liner his children always look at, as if he had an urgent appointment, reviewing the
possible routes Judith might have taken just a few minutes earlier because by now he's convinced she'd been very close by, and if he hurries
and acts intelligently, he can find her. She had reached and was inside
the Atocha or North Station or perhaps had returned to the pensión on
the Plaza de Santa Ana and was closing her suitcases, the taxi, its motor
running, at the entrance, the balconies lit around the plaza, the taverns
full. Any possibility he chose would eliminate the others. If he had his
car, if a taxi came along, if traffic weren't so tied up, if so many people
weren't crowding the sidewalks, getting in his way, overflowing into the
street. Without taxis or streetcars the distances in Madrid expanded.
In twenty or twenty-five minutes he could reach the Atocha Station. In
anticipation he saw the iron vault, the glass illuminating the plaza like
a great globe of light. Tied to the ground as in dreams by the slowness
of his steps, he saw himself running through the waiting room to a
Judith dressed for travel and about to get on the train. But most likely
he'd make the wrong decision and race between stations, exhausting
himself and missing Judith's departure. On the terrace of the Café Lion
they'd brought out loudspeakers, and people gathered around them
and climbed up on the iron chairs and tables to listen to proclamations
repeated by a metallic-sounding voice, the optimism of official communiqués. The government can count on sufficient resources to crush
the criminal attack that enemies of the regime and the working class
have undertaken. He looked inside the café, imagining that Negrín
would be there, but a sense of urgency he couldn't control kept pushing
him forward. A feverish public drank steins of beer and smoked and

ate plates of seafood while sweating waiters plowed their way through, trays raised above their heads. Forces loyal to the Republic are fighting boldly to quash the insurrectionists once and for all. The announcer's voice vibrated with the emphatic timbre of a sports rebroadcast. A column of heroic Asturian miners is approaching Madrid to offer their assistance to the people of the capital. So it was true they were going to revolt, he thought coldly, almost with relief, with an indifference born of unreality and distance to the voices he was hearing, the mob of bodies he had to pass to continue moving forward. After the official communiqué the "Himno de Riego" was played, followed by a piercing female voice singing "Échale guindas al pavo." Repeated reports of the defeat of the uprising or of fanciful military exploits were shouted, mixing with the patrons' hoarse voices ordering more rounds of beer and plates of grilled shrimp or fried squid. The felon Queipo de Llano is fleeing in fear from the enraged people of Sevilla, and soldiers deserting the rebel ranks are cheering the Republic. Again the sinister Spanish farce, he thought, the barracks interjection and bugle call, military parades to the rhythm of a paso doble, the eternal filth of the national fiesta. Trucks filled with armed peasants circled the crowd in a slow eddy around the fountain at Cibeles, then moved like a tide up the other section of Alcalá toward the Puerta del Sol. Through the trees in the garden the large windows of the Ministry of War were lit up as on the night of an official dance. At the entrance gates a small tank with a laughable cannon kept guard. The soldiers on duty came to attention every time an official car went in or came out. Rockets or gunfire exploded and the crowd swayed like a wheat field in the wind. Above the buildings on the Gran Vía, Ignacio Abel could see the dome of a church enveloped in flames. Red cinders fell on roofs with the splendor of fireworks. He turned toward the Paseo del Prado at the corner of Correos, where a parked truck was filled with Assault Guards, impassive under their service-cap visors that gleamed like patent leather in the low light. At the edge of the sidewalk a car brushed by him like a strong gust, and from it came warning shouts and the guffaws of young men who pointed rifles and pistols out the windows, a red-and-black flag flapping in the air like a boat's slack sail. Each car, each truck bris-tling with flags and upraised fists and rifles. Each human group seemed to advance in one direction, but each group's direction was different from all the others, and the general effect was of several parades com-ing together at a traffic barrier, a band competition. From the great whirlpool of Cibeles rose a discord of motors and horns, bursts of an-thems, catcalls, rage. There was light in all the balconies of the Bank of Spain. Something was about to happen and nobody knew what, something must have occurred already and was irreparable, something desired and something feared. Judith Biely had disappeared forever or could appear in the crowd around any corner; enthusiasm and panic vibrated like simultaneous waves in the nocturnal heat, a fever rising, a carnival, a catastrophe.

But the Paseo del Prado was dark and silent; coming upon it, with its enormous somber trees and classical façades of large columns and granite cornices, was like arriving in another city and another time, a city indifferent to the upheavals of a distant, plebeian future. Igna-cio Abel went down the central walk, always alert, looking for a street-car or taxi. Judith might be in the Atocha Station, in which case he'd have lost any chance of finding her. She also could have left by car. He paused for a moment: perhaps Judith had sought refuge in Philip Van Doren's house; wouldn't it be better to retrace his steps and set out for the Gran Vía? Or look for her at the pensión on the Plaza de Santa Ana? The map of Madrid expanded into a labyrinth of possible routes, points of departure. Cars filled with suitcases, their curtains drawn, were leaving on the La Coruña highway and on the road to Burgos, carrying those traveling to their long seigniorial summers in the north, fleeing the city and the nation, many of them knowing with absolute certainty what everyone else was whispering and fearing: something was going to happen, the storm that will make the air crackle with ex-plosions, and no one will know how to predict the moment the deluge will come and sink everything. But no one can imagine what will come or predict the scale of the disaster, not even those who helped unleash it. Now Ignacio Abel was walking toward Atocha, carried along by the inertia of his baseless decision — the express about to leave, the whistle and steam of the locomotive, Judith Biely beautiful and tall on the step in her hat and dress, jumping to the platform as the train starts to move and falling into his arms. His perturbed mind became agitated in a discord of impulses and imaginings: Judith fleeing him and Madrid on this night of brilliant fires and agitated crowds, Adela and his children isolated in the summer house, searching for news in a village where the electricity went off at eleven, radio signals didn't come in clearly, and the only telephone was in the station; and he clutched Judith's farewell letter in his trouser pocket, hurrying among the cars driving at top speed through the Plaza de Neptuno, blowing their horns to the rhythm of the shouts of excited people jammed into the Carrera de San Jerónimo in front of the Congress of Deputies, where all the windows were open and lit though the great door remained locked. He didn't understand what they were shouting, the word every throat repeated. What could be the physical principle that ruled the movements of the crowd, regulated its powerful currents, the overflowing energy of the flood? A group of boys splashed in the water of the Neptune fountain as they climbed the statue to hang a red flag from the trident. Reality broke into implausible images that suddenly became commonplace. Where had the weapons come from that everyone seemed to be brandishing now with an air more festive than war-like, or the luxury automobiles with labor union slogans painted on the sides, driven not by solemn chauffeurs in service caps and uniforms but by young men in unbuttoned shirts or proletarian coveralls, chewing on cigarettes and shouting as they stepped on the accelerator like horsemen launching into a gallop? But walking down the Paseo del Prado was enough to enter darkness and silence again; the faint light of the street lamps revealed the large mass and columns of the museum. He'd walked in this same spot with Judith, among the myrtle hedges and flowerbeds on the lawn, under the gigantic cedars; he'd introduced her to the Botanical Garden, sunk into a darkness fragrant with fertile soil and vegetation behind the high locked gates. Among the gardens on the paseo he saw shadows moving, lit ends of cigarettes. Bargain-priced prostitutes and poor clients looked for corners favorable to the night's lechery. The wide ogival vault of the station emerged at the end of a dusty esplanade where the unoccupied carousel of a deserted festival turned. Lanterns and little tricolor paper flags, huts with barbaric drawings in strong colors, shooting galleries with girls who looked sadly into the emptiness or applied lipstick to pursed lips, loudspeakers over which bullfight paso dobles and hurdy-gurdy tunes played for no one. A poster announced the wonder of Siamese twins joined at the head and a turtle woman who had hands and feet but no arms or legs. Under the awning of a stand selling drinks, scowling men smoked as they grouped around a radio that broadcast military marches and dance music. The iron-and-glass façade of the station shone like a beacon on the border of the night, and beyond it extended the empty lots and last suburbs of Madrid, the faint lines of lights on the nearby rural horizon. With all their windows lit, the buildings were sheets of black cardboard outlined against the intense navy blue of a night in July.

A streetcar on fire came down Calle de Atocha, trailing a wake of black smoke above the curls of flames and flashes of blue sparks in the electric cables. Another bonfire rose above some houses, a column of smoke lit from inside by the flames devouring the roof of a church. If Judith was taking the train, he couldn't stop her now: at the top of the station a clock showed ten minutes after ten. But perhaps no trains would leave tonight, or would leave late, trapped by the upheaval in the city. Shouldn't he take a train too, go back to the village where Adela and his children were waiting, isolated from everything, in the house where the electricity would be turned off soon and candles and kerosene lamps lighted? Too many desires, too many loyalties and urgencies, the disassociated thought of his actions, his consciousness breaking apart like shards of a broken mirror crumbling as he crossed the waiting rooms and walked up and down platforms in the station that didn't seem affected by the disturbance and disorder in the streets, where the night express trains were moving as indifferently as the carousel's horses and carriages would go around at the next festival. Well-dressed people looked out the windows of the blue sleeping cars, uniformed employees pushed carts with opulent suitcases, trunks with metal-reinforced corners and stickers from international hotels. The best families in Madrid took the night express to Lisbon. He searched among the people: one by one he looked at the faces at the windows, the ones he saw walking along the illuminated passageways, those he saw through the window of the bar; from a distance he made out a figure with her back turned who for a moment was Judith, and then was a stranger who looked nothing like her. "She hasn't left yet," he told himself. "She hasn't had time, she lost her courage, she hasn't found a train ticket, if I go home now I'll find a message from her, the phone will ring and it will be her, daring to call me because she knows I'm alone." Three men in civilian clothes and armed with rifles came toward him. The metal of a bolt grated and the cold mouth of a barrel pressed against his chest. One of the men wore a military cap pulled down over his forehead. The one whose rifle jabbed at him had a cigarette in his mouth and blinked to keep the smoke out of his eyes. The third had a pistol in the belt worn over a threadbare jacket.

"Come on, papers."

At first Ignacio Abel didn't understand: who were these armed men without uniforms, why did they demand his documents so peremptorily? As it happened, he had his national identity card and his UGT card in his wallet.

"A gent with a union card." They looked at the identification in the light of a lamp: the man holding the rifle kept prodding him with it. Up close, the weapon was an enormous thing, crude, heavy, a log with hardware. It might go off in the hands of this nervous young man, who obviously didn't handle it with much skill, and the bullet would shatter his chest. He might die right now, without warning, on this summer night, a step away from the well-dressed travelers who looked at their watches, impatient for the train to leave for Lisbon, in an act completely disconnected from the sequence of his life, on a platform in the Atocha Station. He heard shouts and shots nearby; bullets resounded against the metal rafters and a shower of pulverized glass fell from the vault. Called by someone, the three men lost all interest in Ignacio Abel and ran out with the dramatic gestures of film characters, crouching, looking from one side to the other, their weapons in their hands.

He walked out of the station. The taxi stand was deserted. His legs trembled and his heartbeat accelerated. Perhaps right now the phone was ringing in his dark empty apartment and it was Judith calling him — knowing that only he would answer — perhaps regretful, perhaps frightened and seeking refuge. *Too many times I lacked the strength to do what I should have done and leave you.* He'd open the door as quickly as he could because he'd heard the phone from the landing, and when he finally picked up the receiver, breathless, the voice he'd hear would be Adela's, calling from the bar at the station in the Sierra, distressed at not having heard from him. The burning streetcar had overturned at the end of Calle de Atocha and continued to burn close to the carousel and stalls of the festival, surrounded by a group of children who threw things onto the flames, jumping just as they did around the bonfires on the night of San Juan. On a shack a canvas sign lit by a border of lightbulbs announced in large red letters the spectacle of the Spider Woman and the Alligator Man. Now he saw Judith phoning, persisting, the bell ringing for no one in the shadowy hall of his apartment. He saw what wasn't before him, the faces lit by flames from the streetcar on the sidewalk of Atocha Square, and behind the glass doors of bars, and in the gloomy depths of drunkards' taverns, and on the sidewalks where neighbors argued loudly, raising their voices above the discordant sounds of horns and radios — their faces blurred, spectral. He saw as in a revelation, as a certainty, that Judith was phoning not from her pensión on the Plaza de Santa Ana or a booth at the back of a café but from Van Doren's house, beside the large windows that overlooked the horizon of roofs and fires in Madrid. She must be there, no doubt about it. He saw everything: Van Doren preparing for the journey she'd decided to join, the luxury trunks ready in the middle of the living room, the servants taking care of final details, and Judith deciding to call to ask him to come with them, out of love and the fear that something might happen to him. *It will hurt as much as if a part of me had been torn out* — and then in English — *but this is the only decent sensible thing for me to do.* The handwriting was almost illegible, it had been written so quickly, perhaps not because she was in a hurry to take a trip but because she wanted to finish a painful task as fast as she could. Roaring motorcycles of the Assault Guards went up Calle de Atocha in formation, making way for a fire truck, its bell sounding frantically and all its lights on. The more Ignacio Abel walked, the more suffocating the dense smoke and the smell of gasoline and burning wood became. Groups of children ran around as excited as on a festival night when they've been allowed to stay out late. Going up Atocha, he'd cross the heart of Madrid on a diagonal to reach the Gran Vía and the tower of the Palace of the Press, where he'd seen Judith for the second time and fallen in love with her. But he found himself trapped, pushed against a wall on the sidewalk when the fire truck tried to turn onto a narrower street and couldn't get through, because there were too many people or because they stood in front of the truck to block its way. On a balcony a man in an undershirt and pajama bottoms smoked a cigarette and fanned himself with a newspaper as he leaned on the railing. Women's screams mixed with the revving of the fire truck's engine and the useless ringing of its bell. A young man carrying a wooden shotgun or a broomstick climbed onto the running board and began breaking windows, shattered glass falling to the street. The truck moved forward with a jerk and the young man fell to the ground on his back. The sound of the engine and the bell drowned out voices: Ignacio Abel saw open mouths moving in the nearby glare of the burning church. If he didn't move away soon he'd be crushed by the torrent of people between the wall and the fire truck. He swallowed saliva that tasted of gasoline and ash and felt the glow of flames on his skin. But he could move only in the direction of the fire. *If I died tonight, if I never saw you again.* He moved ahead of the truck that was still blocked and the Assault Guards who'd dismounted their motorcycles and were waving their arms, blowing whistles or shouting orders no one paid attention to. Lightheaded from the smoke, he didn't realize at first where he was. In a sudden break he went back in time to a vision from his childhood: in the church enveloped in flames he'd made his First Communion; in its gloomy nave, under candlelight, his father's coffin had rested. Adjacent to the church was the secondary school he'd attended, with its corridors he'd walked so many times on his way to the classrooms or the church or the playgrounds, the favored student, the widow's son. From attic windows, on balconies looking over the plaza, the fire's brilliance turned transfixed faces red and gave them an enchanted air. The flames climbed up the church's dome. Torrents of melted lead ran like lava onto the roofs. A woman in a housedress lay on a corner of the plaza, covering her face with bloody hands. From the fire truck came a stream of water that turned into steam on the church's façade. "They fired from the bell tower," someone said near the injured woman, who was leaning now against the wall, wiping blood on her apron. "They should all be killed." From a balcony several armed men fired at the church tower. The flames shot out of the highest windows of the school after an explosion of glass. The dusty baroque altarpieces would be burning, and the painted plaster statues of saints, the confessionals with their sinister latticework where Ignacio Abel had kneeled so often, so long ago; the library would burn, the benches in the classrooms, the long tables in the laboratory, the oilcloth map of the world; the glass beakers and test tubes would shatter. (Once when he'd been in the plaza with Judith on a sunny winter morning, he'd pointed out the classroom windows, the ones from which he used to look out; they stood in silence for a moment and heard the sounds of children at recess, as distant as if they echoed from the far end of time.) The houses in the neighborhood were so close together that if a single spark leaped too far or a little wind came up, it would set fire to the frames of old beams and wattles. But people clustered around the fire truck to keep it from approaching the church, and with sticks and stones broke the windows of the cab and climbed onto the back to cut the hoses with knives. On the roof of the cab a little boy pretended to march with a broom on his shoulder, wearing a fireman's helmet in which his head disappeared. Beside their overturned motorcycles the Assault Guards, much taller and huskier than those harassing them, vainly shook the nightsticks and pistols that people leaped to grab.

But in memory, places and times are confused, that night's faces, discontinuous images in the surreal city where he keeps looking for Judith as in a dream. Blazing fires and empty streets, tunnels of darkness, sirens and gunfire one after the other, the bells of emergency vehicles, radio loudspeakers hanging in the doorways of cafés broadcasting urgent, triumphant government communiqués or tirelessly repeating "Échale guindas al pavo" and the simple tunes of the flamenco-style band in "Mi jaca." My pony gallops and cuts the wind when it passes through the port on the way to Jerez. All labor union members must report immediately to the headquarters of their organizations. He'd gallop if he could. He quickened his pace but didn't want to walk too fast for fear of arousing suspicion, a man so well dressed didn't belong in this neighborhood. He managed to leave the plaza where the church was burning, covering his nose and mouth with a handkerchief, and found himself, faint and lost, in alleyways he couldn't recognize. He has searched for Judith Biely in dreams resembling this night, passing through urban labyrinths at once familiar and impenetrable. On a deserted street a blind man came toward him guided by a dog, tapping the wall with a stick that turned out to be a violin bow. There was a sputtering of gunfire and the dog arched its back and howled in fear, tightening the cord that held him around the neck like a noose. From the Plaza de Jacinto Benavente he could see above the roofs the illuminated clock at the top of the Telephone Company tower. A squad of Civil Guards on horseback rode down Calle Carretas at a trot, hooves rumbling on the paving stones in an unexpected parenthesis of solitude and silence, and beyond that rose an uproar that undoubtedly came from the Puerta del Sol. The display window of a shop that sold religious books and objects was smashed. Books, illustrations of saints, and plaster figures were being gathered up by a man and woman with an air of mourning who turned in fright when they heard him approach. The sidewalks along

Calle Carretas were crowded with people heading for the Puerta del Sol, looking as if they'd just arrived in Madrid from much poorer and hotter regions, inhabitants of the outermost suburbs, huts and caves next to garbage dumps and rivers of fetid water, pits of poverty, advancing in great tribal clans toward the center of a city to which they'd never been admitted, dirty berets, scabby heads, toothless mouths, feet bare or wrapped in rags, a crude humanity that preceded politics. The metal shutters on bullfighter and flamenco taverns were battened down as they passed. Young men hanging in clusters from the trucks that passed with a squeal of brakes as they swerved back and forth on the curves greeted the destitute crowd by waving flags and raising fists, but these people looked in astonishment and didn't respond, alien to any indoctrination, observing with distrust the puerile habits of the civilized. They'd climbed out of their ravines of caves and hovels as if responding to a collective, archaic impulse awakened by the fire. They came with their nomads' provisions and rags, their packs of dogs, women with children on their backs or hanging from their breasts. Never until tonight had they dared to invade in large groups the streets forbidden to them. At the corner of Calle Cádiz a sudden stampede dragged Ignacio Abel along with it. Disheveled women and a swarm of children stormed an open grocery store. A tall case filled with glass jars and tin cans of food fell against the counter. The women put handfuls of lentils and garbanzos in their pockets, ran out with armfuls of loaves of bread and strings of sausages. Someone knocked the scale to the floor with the swipe of a hand. A knife slit open a sack of flour and the children scattered it in the air, rolling in it, their eyes big in their whitened faces. A hand entered Ignacio Abel's trouser pocket; others tugged at his briefcase. At the bottom of the stairs the store's owner appeared, shouting curses, waving his fists in the air. The barrel of a shotgun was pressed against his chest. The store opened onto a narrow alley that smelled of urine and fried food. There, Ignacio Abel was brushing the flour from his clothes when a voice spoke to him.

"Brother-in-law, good to see you."

Adela's brother took him by the arm and led him, almost by touch, up a dimly lit narrow staircase. At the top, off a corridor, was a room from which came a greenish light and the dry click of billiard balls. Someone appeared in the doorway when he heard approaching footsteps, a man much younger than Víctor who held a pistol, shiny with oil, in one hand and in the other a rag he'd been cleaning it with.

"Ignacio, what are you doing out on the street, and on this night?"

"Your parents and sister expected you today for lunch."

"What a way to talk to me. As if I were a kid."

"Who's this, comrade?"

"My brother-in-law. No danger. Come in and have a drink with us, Ignacio. This isn't a night to be wandering around."

"I'm in a hurry. You ought to go to the Sierra, be with the family. Enough now of fantasies and pistols. This afternoon your father asked me to look out for you."

They spoke quietly, close together in the corridor, near the half-open door through which came, along with the clicks of billiard balls, the sound of a radio program. The station wasn't in Madrid but Sevilla. In the crackle of static a bugle sounded and then a barracks voice. Ignacio Abel was going to say something but Víctor indicated silence with his index finger. Ignacio couldn't make out the words.

"That's a soldier with both balls, brother-in-law. This'll be over in two days. The best are with us. Look at the rabble that came out to defend your republic. To defend your republic by burning churches and breaking into stores."

"If they catch you listening to that station, you'll be in big trouble. You and your friends."

"How you talk to me, brother-in-law, I can't believe it, as if I were a kid."

"They'll kill you if they find that pistol on you."

"What pistol?"

"The one you're carrying in your jacket pocket. Are you carrying your Falange card too?"

"So many questions and you don't say anything."

"Go back to the Sierra tonight. Stay there with the family until this business calms down."

"This isn't going to calm down, brother-in-law. No going back now. Haven't you heard Queipo on the radio? In two days there'll be two columns of legionnaires cleaning up Madrid, the way they cleaned up Asturias in '34. There won't be enough street lamps to string up all the bastards. Blood will flow like water in the Manzanares. Remember what I'm telling you. Spain can be cleansed only with a torrent of blood."

"Is that phrase yours?"

"If it weren't for the situation, I'd shoot you right now."

"Don't deny yourself."

The same young man appeared in the corridor, still holding the pistol and rag. He wore military boots under his civilian trousers.

"Anything going on, comrade?"

"Nothing, comrade. We're just talking."

"Well, make it quick, there's a lot to do."

"Do you think because you're my sister's husband and the father of my niece and nephew that I'll always put up with your ridiculing me?"

"Get out of my way. I have to go."

"Go where? To cheat on my sister?"

"If you need anything, come to the apartment. You'll be safe there."

"You mean if I'm afraid, I can hide at your place?"

"If it were only mine, but no, it's also Adela's."

"Look, you're the one who ought to ask me for a place to hide."

"Not very likely. Your side surrendered in Barcelona."

"Do you still believe what the government says?"

"It's the legitimate government. It'll always be more trustworthy than a lying military gang."

"A legitimate government doesn't distribute weapons to criminals or open the jails to let out all the murderers. Look what your friends from the Popular Front are doing. Killing people like dogs in the street. Burning churches. Taking advantage of the confusion to commit armed robbery."

"I have to go, Víctor."

"If I were you, I wouldn't be out on the street tonight. Don't think you're safe because you're a Socialist. They're destroying Socialists like you. Even your own people are calling you traitors."

"Traitors are the ones who swear loyalty to the Republic and then rise up against it."

"Go home and stay there. This little party by your revolutionary friends will end right now. The Civil Guard is with us. The best of the army. Before midnight every garrison in Madrid will be on the streets."

"Aren't you running off at the mouth?"

Víctor, his thin hair flat against his skull, blocked his way in the corridor. He was breathing with a disturbing sound in his weak lungs. The pistol bulged on one side of his chest, under his summer jacket. He made a gesture of moving his hand toward it, perhaps to refute the sarcasm of his sister's husband with visible proof of his manhood. Ignacio Abel brushed him aside and looked for an exit in the dark. At his back he heard the snap of a pistol's hammer and resisted the temptation to turn around. He felt his way down the stairs, and when he reached the doorway he stepped on spilled garbanzos or lentils or grains of rice, the glass of broken bottles, of jars that gave off a strong smell of vinegar. The metal shutters of the grocery store were down and the looters had disappeared. He went to the street and walked to the Puerta del Sol. He should have retraced his steps or taken a side street, but by now it was impossible. He wasn't walking, he was pushed, dragged in the direction of the great uproar that rose from the square, not of human voices but the prolonged boom of a storm, an avalanche plunging down a slope, leveling everything, joined by car horns, the sirens of ambulances or fire trucks or Assault Guard vans. His sense of time was completely off. Running into Adela's brother, their absurd conversation in the dark. He counted the strokes of the clock at the nearby Ministry of the Interior: it was only eleven. In ten minutes at most he could cross the Puerta del Sol, go up Calle del Carmen or Calle de Preciados to Callao, reach Van Doren's house — he wouldn't wait for the elevator, he'd run up the stairs and go straight across the hall, where he'd heard the music that once led him to Judith. With the determination of a sleepwalker he gave himself until midnight to find her. If he persisted, he might still get her back. If he could manage to make his way through the multitude of bodies, heads, faces contorted by screaming mouths, fists shaking in the air, keeping time with syllables repeated like percussive blows against the concave line of buildings in the square, violent sound waves breaking against the cubic mass of the Ministry of the Interior, where the balconies were wide open, revealing interiors with large crystal chandeliers and salons upholstered in red. *Wea-pons, wea-pons, wea-pons, wea-pons, wea-pons, wea-pons.* The headlights of cars and trucks surrounded by the crowd illuminated their faces dramatically; drivers blew their horns, unable to get through the mob. *Wea-pons, wea-pons, wea-pons, wea-pons, wea-pons.* People were climbing up on the roofs of halted streetcars and the plinths of street lamps, to the barred windows of the ground floor of the ministry, as if trying to escape a rising flood. Above the roofs neon signs blinked for Anís del Mono and Tío Pepe — *The Sun of Andalucía in a Bottle* — the bottle of fino sherry topped by a broad-brimmed hat and dressed in the short jacket of a picador or a flamenco dancer. A single shout rose as one, the rhythm marked by feet stamping on the ground and fists shaken in unison, some holding pistols, rifles, sticks, shotguns, swords. *Wea-pons,* they shouted, separating the syllables, exaggerating them in a hoarse pulsation that made the air vibrate like the passage of trains beneath the pavement. The word sounded like a demand and also an invocation. *Wea-pons, wea-pons, wea-pons, wea-pons,* like a furious stampede, one syllable after the other, drowning out with their volume speeches that indistinct figures shouted into microphones from the balconies of the ministry. In his light suit and with his briefcase firmly held to his chest, I lose sight of Ignacio Abel in the sea of heads and raised fists that fills the Puerta del Sol, submerged at times in shadow, then illuminated by the blue light of street lamps or the headlights of cars trying to move forward. Like the voices, faces become confused. He pushes from the side, manages to move forward a few steps, and the flow of a human current makes him retreat again, as if losing strength as he swims toward a shore that seems constantly to recede, the corner of Calle del Carmen, though now there's a whirlpool that drags him toward it, while a storm of applause shakes the entire plaza, perhaps because on the balcony of the ministry another figure has appeared and cries out and gesticulates just like the previous one. The applause is transformed into a vibration of clapping, and above that another shout ascends, not two syllables but three, *UHP*, rumbling in the concavity of one's stomach like the bumping of a train's wheels beneath a great iron vault: *Yew, Aitch, Pee*. But perhaps what they are cheering isn't the figure gesturing wildly on the balcony but some Assault Guards who've been raised onto shoulders and sit erect above the heads with unstable gestures of triumph, like bullfighters who a little while earlier had been knocked down in the ring, caps to one side, tunics open over sweat-stained undershirts, shouting things no one can hear, and a moment later they've been taken down or have fallen in a sudden undulation of the shoulders that supported them. Just then the whirlpool carrying Ignacio Abel opens an empty space in its center, where a wardrobe or dresser thrown down from a balcony has broken into fragments, so close to the corner that if he boldly pushes a little more he'll be able to touch it. The crash of the furniture against the paving stones widens the circular space, where things continue falling, each collision received with shouts of rejoicing and a round of applause. From a balcony on the second floor, men wearing blue coveralls and peaked military caps, cartridge belts and rifles strapped diagonally across their backs, throw into the square a large desk that several of them have lifted over the railing, and from it comes a gale of papers that for a time fly over the heads of the crowd; they toss down chairs, coat racks, an overly large sofa that at first is stuck on the balcony and finally is pushed over, to shouts of encouragement; a militiaman appears holding a huge portrait of Alejandro Lerroux, and the people in the square receive it with shouts of *Fascist!* and *Traitor!* and when it falls to the ground they fight to trample on it. Ignacio Abel has reached the corner by now and breathes a sigh of relief when he's blinded by the headlights of a truck that has braked in front of him. With a roar the truck goes into reverse and turns, and people surround it, blocking Ignacio Abel's way again. In the truck bed a canvas tarp is raised and a group of men in civilian clothes, wearing military caps and helmets, begin to pry open long boxes. Now Ignacio Abel is pushed against the truck, and when he tries to move away, eager faces and extended hands prevent him. *Weapons,* they say, not shouting now. The word multiplies, extends, and each time someone says it, the group becomes denser and the shoving stronger. He'll have to move away if he doesn't want to be flattened against the back of the truck. He hears the creak of the boards as nails are pulled out, someone's voice shouting with an accent of command, *We don't give anything to anybody without a union card.* The man who seemed to be speaking with the certainty of being obeyed now stumbles and almost falls, holding a helmet too big for him down on his head. The people climb onto the truck, pull the lids off the boxes, take out rifles, pistols, and grenades, and the truck seems to move, to shift a little under the pressure of the bodies leaning against it, the hands and shoulders pushing, trying to get through, trying to reach the boxes, which are overturned now, spilling weapons with a crash of metal, pistols and rifle bolts and trampled boards, small boxes of bullets that roll to the ground and are grabbed by the handful. Ignacio Abel has stepped on something that crunches under his shoe but doesn't turn to see what it is, perhaps someone's hand, but he's managed to get free. He leaves the truck behind and finds himself looking at a suddenly empty Calle del Carmen.

He'll never get there. At the Carmen Church, beside its open doors, armed militiamen are putting up a barricade or roadblock of long benches and kneeling stools. Several are attempting to pull a confessional down the steps, shouting encouragement to one another. It may not be a barricade; they may simply be piling up benches and the gilded panels of altarpieces to light a bonfire. "Where are you going so fast? Papers, comrade." It seems that rigorous rules have been established overnight, which didn't exist yesterday and today are obeyed by everyone without question. Again the card hurriedly looked for in his pockets, his controlled impatience, his fear of rifle barrels held by inexpert hands, of sideways glances. If they let him go, in less than five minutes he could be ringing the bell at Van Doren's house. The one who's looking at the union card in the light of a street lamp doesn't know how to read and isn't used to handling papers. Perhaps he recognizes the seal, the initials in red ink, UGT. A small woman dressed in a blue coverall, from which a cartridge belt is hanging, asks him to open his briefcase: documents, plans. "I'm an architect," says Ignacio Abel, looking into her eyes, not too long, afraid of provoking her. "I work at University City." How little is needed for dignity to be wiped out, for you to move your head and smile and melt inside with gratitude toward someone who could arrest or execute you but instead returns your identification, gestures with a hand, and lets you pass. In the Plaza de Callao there are trucks with their motors running, their sides armored with metal sheets held on somehow, and mattresses tied to the roofs with rope. At the Cine Callao the blinking sign announces the premiere of *The Mystery of Edwin Drood*, 6:45 and 10:45, numbered seats. A triumph! At the door of the Hotel Florida a couple, foreign tourists, watch with placid curiosity the goings and comings of the militiamen, the parade of automobiles driving at top speed toward the Plaza de España, sinking into the darkness of the last stretch of the Gran Vía, where spectral buildings are under construction and wide empty lots are enclosed by board fences covered by political posters. Waves of people holding flags and walking toward the Puerta del Sol singing anthems in fatigued voices meet, but don't mix, with the slightly dazed people who are leaving the last show at the Cine de la Prensa. Air-cooled, 14 weeks!! *Morena Clara,* with Imperio Argentina and Miguel Ligero. On the sidewalk in front of Van Doren's building, two cars form a corridor to the curb where a truck is waiting, its back doors open. On the hood of each of the cars is an American flag. The automobiles and small flags delimit a parenthesis of stillness no one interrupts. Between the truck and the building entrance, Philip Van Doren's maids in caps and butlers in uniform come and go, carrying bundles, boxes, and trunks, holding crates of paintings in gloved hands, not hurrying, as if they were preparing their employer for a journey to the door of a country house. Inside the entrance, on each side of the elevator, stand two martial-looking young American men dressed in civilian clothes, their arms crossed, legs slightly apart. They inspect Ignacio Abel from head to toe and indicate with a gesture that he may take the elevator; another young American, his hair short, operates it. The elevator operators' strike has no effect here either. He once rode up in this same elevator not knowing he was going to meet her, walked along this hall listening to the clarinet and piano music from a distance. Butlers and maids come and go in methodical silence, carrying carefully packed objects, paintings, sculptures, lamps, all of the servants so sure of their assignments you barely hear anyone giving orders. An American flag is fastened above the door of the apartment. Ignacio Abel goes in without anyone stopping him or seeming to notice him. The almost empty space is larger and whiter than he remembered. Before that window Judith had stood, a shiny record in her hands. The gramophone has been packed, and a maid, kneeling on the rug, has just placed a pile of records into a made-to-measure box. A man in a mechanic's coverall is taking apart a complicated floor lamp with chrome tubing and a spherical globe of white glass. The windows are open but the street noises filter in like distant waves. Judith can appear right now in any doorway. Ignacio Abel sees himself in one of the tall mirrors and doesn't recognize himself: the sweaty face, the loosened tie, the briefcase pressed against his chest. At the end of the room, next to a window through which the Capitol Building's tower — as slender as a prow, crossed by the bright Paramount Pictures sign — seems close, Philip Van Doren is looking through binoculars and speaking on the phone in English, dressed in a short-sleeve shirt, light trousers, and white sport shoes, his shaved head gleaming under the ceiling lights. He's seen Ignacio Abel reflected in the glass and turns toward him, smiling, when he hangs up the phone. He smells of soap and fresh cologne, a recent shower. He doesn't know where Judith is, or if he does know, he won't say, because he's promised her not to tell him. On Ignacio Abel's face — the unfamiliar face Abel saw a moment ago in the mirror — Van Doren sees signs of a disappointment that suddenly makes Abel's fatigue worse. Van

Doren's Spanish has become even more precise and flexible in recent months.

"Professor Abel, you've arrived at an opportune time. Come with me. I'm leaving for France in half an hour. Unfortunately we'll have to take the long way, on the Valencia highway, because by now we might not be able to get out going north—the rebels will come in that way. The question is whether the government can count on a sufficient number of loyal units to defend the Guadarrama passes. Did you come in this afternoon from the Sierra, as you do every Sunday? Were the trains still running?"

Without waiting for a reply, he turned toward the window, gesturing to Ignacio Abel to approach. Implicit in the question about the Sierra was an allusion to possible confidences from Judith, perhaps to the double adulterous life he'd no longer take part in as an accessory, knowing she'd ended it. The vanity of showing or suggesting he knew things about others without revealing the source of his knowledge provided Van Doren with an intense satisfaction. He looked through the binoculars, pointing toward the long, almost dark tunnel of the end of the Gran Vía, down which came flashes of headlights. In the background, beyond the vague, barely lit rectangle of the Plaza de España, the Mountain Garrison was a great block of shadows dotted with small windows. Van Doren handed the binoculars to Ignacio Abel. Far away, at a distance the tiny size of the figures made remote, armed men stood guard at the corners, behind the street lamps, watching at their posts with the immobility of lead soldiers.

"The other question is why the rebel military didn't come out of the Mountain Garrison when there was still time to take the city. Now it's too late. Have you seen the cannon at the corner, on the right? They'll make sure no one comes out, and as soon as it's light they'll fire. *It'll be like shooting trout in a barrel.* But I'm sure our Judith would have found a better expression in Spanish."

Her name spoken aloud made Ignacio Abel's heart pound. He'd gone to Van Doren's house looking for Judith and now he didn't have the courage to ask about her.

"You speak as if you're sorry the uprising has failed."

"And what makes you think that? Do you believe those militiamen armed with old shotguns will defeat the army? As you can see, they've begun to devote themselves to the revolution. The strange thing is that they're putting so much effort into burning the churches in Madrid, so unfortunate from an architectural point of view. The military will win, but they're very dim and will wait too long, and in the meantime there's nothing for people like you or me to do here. I at least can count on the protection of my embassy. But you, Professor Abel — what are you going to do? Is there still time for you to go back to the Sierra with your family? It's better if you come with me until the danger's past. You know you're not safe in Madrid. It was enough to look at your face when you came in to realize you know it. From Biarritz we can make arrangements with the embassy and Burton College for your trip to America. You just have to tell us who'll be traveling with you."

The telephone rang in the empty room, where workers had just finished rolling up the calfskin and zebra rugs. Beyond the windows a horizon of fires shone above the roofs. A maid brought the phone to Van Doren, who moved away from Ignacio Abel, listening with his head lowered, responding with monosyllables in English. It must be Judith calling, and he'd hide it from him, warn her not to come, to wait for him somewhere. Van Doren hung up and looked at his wristwatch, making the automatic gesture of pushing up his sleeves as if to get to work.

"Things no one has seen are going to happen here, Professor. Now it's the turn of those who control Madrid, but then the others will come, and I'm not referring to the old soldiers who haven't dared to leave their garrisons and are waiting to be killed. I'm referring to the Army of Africa, Professor Abel. You and I, if we're still alive when they come in, will not want to see what they do in Madrid. They'll descend like the Italian legionnaires in Abyssinia. They'll have even less pity, except they know how to kill. They know how, and they like it."

"The Army of Africa can't leave Morocco. The navy hasn't joined the uprising. What ships will they use to cross the strait?"

Standing in the middle of the empty room, Philip Van Doren looked at Ignacio Abel as if pitying him for his incurable innocence, his inability to understand the things that mattered, which he discovered thanks to sources he wasn't going to reveal. In all the empty space, the only thing left was the telephone on the floor. A servant closed the windows and took down the blinds, and when he finished, he approached Van Doren and said something in his ear, looking at Ignacio Abel out of the corner of his eye.

"For the last time, Professor, come with me. Why stay here? You have no one left in Madrid."

27

WHAT HE REMEMBERS about those days was the permanent sense of suspended reality and frustration: Madrid a turbulent glass bubble of shouted or printed words and music and dry bursts of gunfire, a clouded bubble that didn't let you see what lay beyond it, what had become inaccessible, a conjectural country of cities subdued by rebels, reconquered by loyal forces, then lost again but about to fall before the advance of our heroic militias; and he, from one day to the next, torn by blows, Adela and his children in the Sierra, Judith he didn't know where, construction at University City suspended and the offices empty, the wind blowing through the windows shattered by explosions and gunfire, covering the desks with dust, scattering blueprints and documents across the floor. Córdoba controlled by loyal militias. The surrender of Sevilla is imminent. Having quashed the uprising in Barcelona, loyal regiments from Cataluña are in sight of Zaragoza. He wrote letters he didn't mail because he didn't know where to send them or had discovered that the postal service no longer functioned. Government forces surround Córdoba, surrender of rebel forces expected. He turned on the radio, turned it off again, not a single piece of real information in the tidal wave of headlines, interrupted from time to time by announcements and military marches, that then inundated all the front pages. The government has imposed its authority on the entire peninsula except for a few cities where the rebels are still resisting, and confirms that the uprising has been defeated. The window of the store that carried stationery and stamps had been broken and the store sacked; in a shop a few blocks away, a bald, unctuous clerk, crouching behind the counter, waited on him as if nothing was going on, though he did say the supply of stamps had been interrupted, and if the Canary Islands were once again under the control of the government, why weren't they sending any tobacco? The government confirms that the insurrection in Cataluña was suppressed soon after it began. The topography of "daily life" was partly in ruins and partly undamaged, just as the geography of the country had become capricious, with entire regions as inaccessible as if suddenly swallowed by the sea, and borders so malleable no one knew where they were. The people's justice, implacable and powerful, will fall on the ringleaders of this heinous, ill-advised attack that is doomed to failure. On a corner of Calle de Alcalá, the small church where a blind man always played the violin was in flames. The impression steadily grows stronger that the dramatic episode we've gone through since last Sunday is coming to an end. He dialed a number, and the ring was repeated endlessly with no answer; he picked up the receiver again a little while later and there was no dial tone. Radio Sevilla is transmitting the latest proclamations from the insurgents, filled with lies and intended to raise the sinking spirits of those who have taken up arms against the people and their legitimate government. Several regiments of loyal forces and militias are advancing against the rebels in Sevilla, where insurgent soldiers are beginning to desert. He scrutinized the newspaper reports on fighting in the Sierra for the name of the village and didn't see it mentioned. The attack by Republican militias on Córdoba is imminent. Just as the censors left entire columns blank, there were cities and provinces erased from the map, their names not spoken or written. Several units from Cataluña have reached Zaragoza, where the rebel situation is critical. He stayed in his apartment, larger now because he lived in it alone, feeling remorseful for not doing anything, for not joining his children, for not looking with more determination for Judith. The heroic regiment of the glorious Colonel Mangada has overrun the enemy on the peaks of the Sierra de Guadarrama and with implacable force has advanced toward Ávila. He'd go out with no real purpose and feared that in his absence the telephone would ring and he would miss an urgent message. According to reports that reached our editorial offices yesterday afternoon, the forces of Colonel Mangada are at the gates of Burgos, ready for the final attack against the insurrectionists. Sitting on a bench in the shade of the acacias on the central walk of Calle Príncipe de Vergara, Professor Rossman perspired on the July afternoon and searched in his briefcase for news clippings. "I didn't wish to bother you, my dear Professor Abel, but I wanted to be certain you were all right and had returned in time from the Sierra. How do you explain that according to yesterday's report Colonel Mangada's unit was advancing toward Ávila and in today's paper they say he's at the gates of Burgos?" Armored combat vehicles are prepared to take the Alcázar de Toledo, which is in flames. Ignacio Abel called the station to ask whether the trains were running, and no one answered the phone. Government troops surround Córdoba, assuring the quick surrender of demoralized rebel forces. The station's number kept ringing when he dialed it, or else there was no sound at all. In Madrid numerous arrests are being made of Fascist elements, clergy and army officers, all traitors to the Republic. He wanted to send a telegram but the post office was closed. Even if he'd been able to send it, how could he know it would reach its destination? *Dear Judith, I don't know where you are but I can't stop writing to you. I can't live without you.* On the Aragón front the insurgents, in their disorderly flight, have left numerous dead and wounded on the field, along with trucks, machine guns, and rifles. In the extreme confusion of the Cibeles Palace, where a militia recruiting center had been improvised on the main floor, no one was at the telegraph windows, and no one answered the ringing phones. Zaragoza is beginning to feel the hardships of the siege imposed by loyal forces. He managed to speak to a clerk and learned that all service to the far side of the Sierra had been suspended indefinitely, and that the map of Spain, filled with sudden blank spaces it was forbidden or impossible to establish communication with, changed every day and almost every hour according to the rumors and embellished reports of offensives and victories. A group of friars armed with knives assaults militiamen preparing to carry out a search. *Dear Adela, tell your parents I saw your brother a few days ago and thought he looked fine.* The status of the rebellion in Sevilla is so desperate that the traitorous general Queipo de Llano is preparing to flee to Portugal. Ignacio Abel got up before dawn to go to the American embassy, and though it was still dark, the sidewalk was lined with refugees, trying to hide their social status: upperclass ladies without watches or jewels, men without ties or wearing a cap or beret and an old jacket. To obtain a visa he first had to present the letter of invitation and the contract from Burton College, but international mails weren't working, or the mail carriers had enlisted in the militias and replacements hadn't been found. The troops of the Republic have occupied the outskirts of Huesca and cut off electricity in Zaragoza, where the rebellion is in dire straits. *Dear Mr. President, Burton College, Rhineberg, N.Y.,* he wrote in English, *it is an honor for me to accept your kind invitation, and as soon as current circumstances improve in Spain I will send you the documents you have requested.* The troops from Cataluña, their morale high, continue their victorious march through the lands of Aragón, advancing toward Zaragoza, bombed again by our air force. He wanted to be far away, to leave and never come back, to sink into a silence where day after day there would be no sound, not just of gunfire and explosions but of words, words repeated, obtuse and triumphal, vengeful and toxic, almost as frightening as actions. The Carlist beasts march like packs of hyenas, accompanied by the ever more ferocious and terrifying cassocks of the priests. The same words in a constant barrage, on loyal radio stations and on the enemy's, in newspapers and on postered walls, immune to the evidence of the lie, imposed through the brute force of repetition. Day by day, enthusiasm grows among the fighters defending the cause of the Republic and freedom on the frontlines, rendering the rebels' desperate efforts useless. How could he not listen to them, not be infected by them, the drunken binges of words supporting the collective hallucination? Each morning and afternoon he waited for the mailman, who on many days didn't come. He waited with the same painful intensity for a letter from Judith, from his children, from Burton College, from the American embassy. A large number of militias from Lérida paraded through the city to wild cheers before reconquering Zaragoza. He went down to ask the doorman if any mail had arrived for him and saw that he'd traded his blue livery with gold braid for a coverall over his undershirt, and had stopped shaving. The surrender of the insurgents in the Alcázar de Toledo is imminent. On the advice of a driver in the neighborhood, the doorman had joined the CNT, and though he continued to wear the peaked cap that made him so proud because it gave him the look of an Assault Guard, he now tied a red-and-black handkerchief around his neck and wore a pistol on the right side of his belt, as bulky as the key ring that had always hung on the left. Loyal forces marching toward Zaragoza encounter no resistance. He said he'd been given the pistol in a distribution of weapons taken from the Fascist military defeated by the people in their assault on the Mountain Garrison. Tanks of loyal forces are leaving Guadalajara for Zaragoza to protect the infantry's advance. The doorman polished his pistol with the same concentration he'd once brought to polishing the shoes of some affluent resident, but he hadn't managed to obtain ammunition, and he asked his friend the Anarchist driver for some, assuring him that, after all, he was an official too, and kept a sharp eye out for possible ambushes or saboteurs hidden in the building. Five by five, their arms raised high, the rebels defending the Alcázar de Toledo abandoned it. Ignacio Abel went out in the morning and the doorman, in his proletarian coverall and with the pistol at his waist, opened the door for him and bowed as he removed his cap and discreetly held out his hand to receive a tip. "You don't have to worry about anything, Don Ignacio. In this neighborhood the working people know you, and if it comes to that, I'd put my hand in the fire for you." Granada is about to surrender to government forces, and according to reliable reports, soldiers are deserting or rebelling against the insurgent leaders who have brought them to dishonor and defeat. He called the pensión on the Plaza de Santa Ana in the insane hope that Judith hadn't left, and an irate voice shouted that there wasn't any guest there by that name. The squadron of airplanes that left Barcelona this morning is reconnoitering the terrain and protecting the advance of the loyal troops that will take Zaragoza and have almost reached the city. Please check — Judith Biely, with a *b*, a foreign señorita, American. He took a streetcar up Calle de Alcalá on the way to the Plaza de Sevilla, where a large red flag waved over the tower of the Círculo de Bellas Artes and the bronze Minerva. On the outskirts of Córdoba our troops are waiting for the decisive moment to launch an attack. When he was closer, if not to Judith, at least to the house and room where she'd lived, it became impossible to go on: at the corner of Calle del Príncipe gunfire broke out as suddenly as a summer storm; he left the doorway where he'd taken refuge, and in the sunlight coming from the Plaza de Santa Ana, he thought he saw Judith crossing the street. All drivers of vehicles confiscated from the enemy are strongly urged to respect traffic signals placed on public thoroughfares in Madrid to avoid accidents.

He remembers his stubborn insistence on remaining skeptical at first, as if he'd touched something familiar that instantly disintegrated into sand. On Monday, July 20, the day following his failed appointment with Judith, Ignacio Abel went out at eight-thirty in the morning convinced that if he followed the routines of any other Monday, some semblance of normality would be reestablished. To the west he heard the rumble of distant cannon fire. A small plane flew back and forth over the city with the persistence and lack of purpose of a blowfly. There was a thread of hysteria in the triumphant announcement on the radio, interspersed haphazardly with threats. With the blood of heroic militiamen and armed forces loyal to the Republic, with the courage and sacrifice of all anti-Fascists and the enthusiastic collaboration of our valiant aviators, the most glorious pages in the history of our people are being written. He walked outside, where it was a little cooler. There was a certain reluctance in the widely spaced firing of the cannon, as if any one of the shots might be the last. It had been like this in 1932, in 1934. Gunfire and empty streets and stores with metal shutters closed, people who raised their arms as a precaution when they turned a corner, then nothing. From every town in Spain, with unanimous Republican fervor, come long lines of volunteers to combat the insurgents. Cool, showered, slightly dazed by a sleepless night, without breakfast, remembering with the strangeness of a dream his long walks through Madrid the night before, Ignacio Abel clutched the handle of his briefcase as he crossed Príncipe de Vergara on his way to the repair shop where they'd promised his car would be ready first thing that morning. The owner of the dairy store on the corner of Don Ramón de la Cruz gave him a friendly wave from behind the counter (perhaps he'd go back there to have breakfast after he picked up the car); an ice seller passed by, dozing in the driver's seat of a wagon pulled by a skinny horse, leaving a trail of water on the paving stones. The rout of rebels in the Sierra de Guadarrama confirms the imminent victory won by the blood and daring of the people's militias. If you followed your old routine, the life that had always been connected to that routine would automatically resume. If you dressed and combed your hair before the mirror and adjusted the knot in your tie and didn't turn on the radio and descended the echoing marble stairs at the usual clip, things might return to normal. The only extraordinary, though irrelevant, thing was the distant, grudging cannon fire and the flight of the old-fashioned small airplane, gleaming in the distance as the morning sun shone on it, producing the iridescent effects of an insect wing. In the victorious assault by popular forces on the Mountain Garrison, where cowardly conspirators attempted to barricade themselves, the Republican air force has again written a glorious page. "They're defeated," said the doorman, opening the door and speaking with no danger of being overheard by residents who in that bourgeois district might favor the rebels. "In Barcelona they had to surrender. In Madrid you can see they haven't even dared to come out on the street. But you take care, Don Ignacio, they say Fascists are shooting from the terraces, the miserable bastards." Like a detail remembered from the previous night's bad dream, he saw his brother-in-law Víctor's face in the light of a passageway where the sound of conspiring armed men came from a room at the end of the hall. In a radio address the popular Communist Party deputy Dolores Ibárruri gave an impassioned speech to the working people of Madrid, telling them to pursue without mercy the reactionary jackals who shoot like cowards from balconies and bell towers at the working-class forces. He'd left his house with determination but in reality had no idea where he'd go once he had the car. To University City, to the Plaza de Santa Ana — or to the La Coruña highway, if it was true that a heroic squadron of loyal airplanes from the Cuatro Vientos base repelled the insurgents advancing from the north in a doomed attempt to take control of the peaks and passes of the Sierra. But only a few minutes before leaving the house he'd managed to reach the Civil Guard barracks in the village, and a voice responded with the Fascist slogan — "*Arriba España!*" — before slamming down the phone. Hour after hour there is confirmation of the imminent reestablishment of Republican order throughout the nation and the defeat of the insurgents who at this point can expect no mercy. On his way to the repair shop in the Jorge Juan alleyway he passed the Hotel Wellington, where a doorman of imposing stature and livery scrutinized the end of the street with a whistle in his mouth, hailing a taxi for a foreign couple dressed for travel who waited under the awning next to a pile of trunks, suitcases, and hatboxes. Forty rebel officers, faced with inevitable defeat, commit suicide in Burgos. As he crossed under the double row of trees on the central walk of Calle Velázquez, he heard a flock of birds and felt a breeze as cool as at dawn in the shade of the acacias. Turning at the corner of Jorge Juan toward Alcalá, a line of cars, the faces of young men at the windows, appeared so unexpectedly that Ignacio Abel jumped back onto the sidewalk to avoid being run down. The last of the cars, its top down, was a green Fiat identical to his own. It was almost nine, and most of the stores on Jorge Juan were still closed — the dairies, the charcoal store, the bakery — but the metal shutters of the car repair shop were raised. Cannons rumbled again in the distance, followed by what sounded like a series of fireworks. Next to the shop entrance, the owner's son, a boy of fourteen or fifteen dressed in a coverall, sat on the ground, his back against the wall, his head between his knees. When he got closer he saw that the boy's knees were knocking against each other and his head, covered by his hands, shook convulsively. Spittle hung from the boy's chin, and a puddle of vomit lay between his legs. In the vast space of the shop, lit by a skylight, a strong odor of gasoline mixed with the stench of vomit, but not a single car was there. Lying face-up on the cement floor, his legs spread and his arms outstretched, was the shop owner, blood on his mouth and in the middle of his chest, and a piece of cardboard propped on his coverall: *For being a Fascist.* "He didn't want them to take the cars," said the boy, standing now, sobs breaking his voice. "He told them they weren't his cars — what would he say to his customers?"

He remembers the primal fear, the one that returns at night, the darkness deeper and full of danger. Retiring when it was still daylight, checking the bolts and locks, hiding like a child under the blankets, closing his eyes tight and covering his ears, as if seeing or hearing were enough to attract misfortune. *Serenos* and porters of urban properties are instructed that law enforcement officers and militias are authorized to carry out residential searches only when they have been officially charged with that mission and must always show their credentials. One night he watched through the peephole as armed men took away his neighbor on the other side of the landing. The Ministry of the Interior reminds you that only the police, the Assault Guard, and the Civil Guard may make arrests. His neighbor was in pajamas and offered no resistance. They'd almost never exchanged more than a gesture of greeting. He didn't feel compassion but rather relief. A few days later, the man's wife appeared, dressed in black. Life in Madrid goes on, the spirit of the people heightened by reports of daily advances by the Republican forces and defeats of the insurgents. In streets empty of people after nightfall, you could hear the approach of any vehicle before you saw it. He was in his study reviewing some blueprints when a car stopped at the entrance to his building. Those who take advantage of temporarily chaotic circumstances to carry out acts against another person's life or property will be considered rebels, and the maximum penalty established by law will be imposed. He left the pencil on the wide sheet of blue paper and took off his reading glasses. He made certain the shutters were closed, according to official instructions. He walked into the hall, feeling under his feet the familiar vibration of the street door closing. There were very few occupied apartments left in the building, according to the doorman. He went to stand in the middle of the spacious living room. The footsteps might remain on a lower floor or reach his landing, then continue up the stairs, perhaps because the militiamen wanted to make sure that residents followed orders to keep their terraces locked, to prevent the enemy from shooting from them. There might be shouts, pleas, sobs, and blows with rifle butts echoing up and down the marble-lined staircase. But this time he heard only footsteps, and he waited, almost with serenity, his Socialist Party and union identification ready, the framed photos of him with Fernando de los Ríos, with President Azaña, with Don Juan Negrín in full view on the table in the living room, along with his and Adela's wedding picture, in a silver frame, and those of Miguel and Lita in their First Communion outfits. In the children's room hung a painting of the Holy Spirit, a gift from Don Francisco de Asís and Doña Cecilia. Negligence, not dignity, was why he hadn't bothered to remove religious ornaments from the house. Now it would be dangerous to try to hide them. Ignacio Abel waited by the door, beneath the chandelier wrapped in white cloth, oddly calm, listening to the muffled voices. He assumed they'd pound on the door with their fists and rifle butts, but they rang the bell, with some urgency though not too much, like an impatient deliveryman. He preferred to wait a little before responding. Better if they didn't think he'd been standing by the door or had a reason to believe they'd come for him as soon as the car engine stopped on the street, in the strange silence of a summer night. But there was no reason to make them impatient: why let them think he was playing for time to burn or hide things, trying to flee to the attic or roof through the service door. After the second ring, longer and more insistent than the first, he opened the door and decided he wouldn't ask for identification. It was just three men, aside from the doorman, young, carrying muskets and pistols. Ignacio Abel immediately identified who was in command: the shortest one, wearing round glasses and a clean shirt, the only one not carrying a musket, only a pistol, the one who smoked. The second had a remote expression and wore a military cap with a red tassel dangling over his forehead, and the third, who looked familiar, had the large face of someone he knew, someone he'd seen often but couldn't place, a man young yet slow and flabby who walked almost without lifting his feet off the ground. Now he remembered, didn't know whether it was cause for relief or alarm: it was one of the clerks at his office, the one who every morning delivered the tray of mail. So they know who I am, whose house they'll be searching. The clerk now had long sideburns, his chubby cheeks darkened by a beard, and he wore a military tunic, unbuttoned, with the insignia of the infantry at the cuff. The doorman, lagging behind them, greeted him with equivocal effusiveness.

"Don Ignacio, these comrades, they've come for a routine search."

The man in charge looked askance at him.

"Papers," he said.

"I told you the señor is trustworthy," the doorman said.

"Haven't you heard? There are no more señores here."

As if they'd entered a church, the militiamen looked at the size of the rooms, the soaring door frames, the high ceilings with wreathed moldings, the polished parquet floors, though weeks had passed since the maids waxed them. The clerk made a slight gesture of recognition toward Ignacio Abel and nearly bowed his head, as he did when he left the mail on his desk and asked if he desired anything else. The one who seemed most directly under the command of the patrol leader took off his tasseled cap to wipe away sweat. Ignacio Abel saw that on his closely shaved nape he'd left in stubble the initials FAI. In the men's presence he saw his own house with discomfort, irritation, almost with fear, the unnecessary spaciousness of a reception room where no reception had ever been held, the rich folds of curtains that fell luxuriously to the floor, the rooms that followed one after the other through double-paned glass doors. But they didn't seem to search with much zeal or be in a hurry to find something compromising.

"You stay here," the leader told the doorman, who, like an uncomfortable visitor, didn't move from the entrance hall, while Ignacio Abel showed the militiamen each of the rooms, opening closets whose farthest corners, behind the hanging clothes, they examined with flashlights.

"So large an apartment just for you?"

"I don't live alone. My wife and children are on vacation in the Sierra."

"On our side or theirs?"

"On theirs, I think."

"Well, don't worry, you can join them before long."

"That's what I'm hoping."

"You're not hoping their side wins."

"You've seen my identification."

"These days anybody can arrange to get a union card, but not an apartment like this."

The short one spoke, the one with the round glasses and clean shirt; the others watched and nodded. Ignacio Abel tried to make eye contact with the ex-clerk but didn't, wanted to remember his name but couldn't. Their witnessing the disorder in the kitchen, the dishes piled up in the sink, upset him. They searched the maids' room, the leader supervising from the doorway, directing them to lift up the mattresses and open a trunk against the wall. He didn't recall ever having looked in the room. When one of the men turned on the bare lightbulb hanging from the ceiling, he was surprised the room was so narrow: two bunk beds, the trunk, a shelf lined with newspaper, a tiny window with a flowered curtain, photos of movie stars tacked to the wall, an old night table that must have been discarded many years ago by Don Francisco de Asís and Doña Cecilia, and on it a small copper Virgin. He felt embarrassment rather than remorse, but he understood he wouldn't have felt this way if he hadn't been afraid. The patrol leader looked around, said nothing. Ignacio Abel led them to his office and stood to one side after turning on the light.

"And whose room is this?"

"My office."

"It looks like the office of a minister."

"I work here. It's my study."

"You can call anything work."

"And these two in the picture? Old servants?"

"They're my parents."

"Are they in the Sierra with the insurgents too?"

"They died many years ago."

"And all these maps? Maybe you use them to find out if the enemy's nearby."

"They're not maps. They're plans. I work at University City. You know that."

"Don't use formal address with us — we're all friends."

It was hot in the house with all the shutters closed. The former clerk, with calculated impertinence, looked through papers on the desk and let them fall to the floor; he averted his eyes when Ignacio Abel looked at him and exchanged a glance with the other man. Then he opened the drawers one by one and let them fall to the floor. When he found the last one locked, he signaled to the leader.

"Why do you keep that one locked?"

"No particular reason. Here's the key."

"Are you getting nervous?"

"I have no reason to."

"Smoke?"

"No, thank you."

"You're used to better tobacco?"

"No, it's just that I don't smoke."

"Okay, we're going."

For a moment he felt relief, a weakness in the muscles more revelatory than his dignity would allow him to recognize. Then he saw the eyes of the patrol leader and the smile of the former clerk and understood that the plural included him. Okay, we're going. The one in the tasseled cap stepped on something and Ignacio Abel heard glass breaking and wood cracking. The framed photo of Lita and Miguel on the swing was no longer on his desk.

"Just a moment," he said, noticing the difference fear had made in the sound of his voice. "There must be some misunderstanding."

"No misunderstanding," said the leader, the cigarette in his left hand, on his wrist an expensive watch that Ignacio Abel hadn't spotted before. "Don't think you fooled us with all your cards and your photographs with Republican reactionaries. Nobody gives us orders. To us you're nobody, worse than nobody. The comrades in construction remember you well. You hired strikebreakers and invited the Assault Guards every time a strike was called. Now you're going to pay."

The clerk took him by the left arm and the one in the tasseled cap by the right; in the grip of their large hands his own weak muscles embarrassed him. Without pushing or pulling him they led him across the hall, and they passed the doorman, still standing like a humble visitor. He thought of Calvo Sotelo on the night just a few weeks earlier when they'd come for him: how they said in surprise that he didn't resist, didn't assert his immunity as a deputy to those arresting him. He remembered the neighbor from the apartment across the landing, tiny in the peephole in his pajamas, and the woman on her knees clutching awkwardly at the trousers of the man taking him away. He was still in his building and also far away. As they reached the landing on a lower floor he heard a door closing and understood that a neighbor must be peering through the peephole, grateful not to be the one arrested. The black vehicle that would take him away started up as soon as the entrance door opened. It was a rather small van, on its roof a panel with a drawing of a bar of soap from which bubbles rose. LÓPEZ SOAPS. The clerk, forcing him to bend to get into the van, squeezed his head hard, pressing his fingers into his skull. *Dear Miguel and Lita, dear Judith, dear Adela.* With the street lamps out and the windows shuttered, Calle Príncipe de Vergara was a tunnel of darkness opening before the van's headlights. He was in the back seat. Nobody would shoot him in the back of the head without his realizing it, without his knowing he'd die, the way Calvo Sotelo had been shot, twice. He asked where they were taking him. He asked in a voice so low the sound of the engine erased it, and he had to swallow and clear his throat to repeat the question.

"Weren't you really proud of your job? Weren't you in a hurry to finish the construction? Where better than your University City?"

He was crowded in the back seat between the two militiamen, the clerk to his left, smiling with his fleshy mouth, and the tassel on the cap of the one to his right swinging back and forth. After a ride through darkened streets and lots whose duration he couldn't measure, he recognized beyond the illumination of the headlights the shapes of the first buildings in University City. There was a checkpoint before they reached it. Militiamen with flashlights and rifles signaled for them to stop.

"Who are these guys?" said the clerk.

"The UGT, judging by their look, the brand-new rifles," Ignacio Abel said.

"Shut your mouth."

Long classroom benches blocked the dirt road. He recognized the benches from the Philosophy Building. The patrol leader took out identification, and a guard used his flashlight to study it. Ignacio Abel wanted to ask for help but his jaws were locked, his legs paralyzed, his hands cold on his thighs. The beam from a flashlight shone full in his face, forcing him to close his eyes. That he was about to die was inconceivable. Much more humiliating was the possibility of pissing in front of those who'd arrested him, or worse, shitting and having them smell it, bursting into laughter, making gestures of disgust.

"And who's that with you?"

"A Fascist," said the driver. "It's our business."

The guards hesitated. Finally the one with the flashlight signaled and other militiamen pulled away the benches to let the vehicle through, raising a cloud of dust that shimmered in the beam of the headlights. The van came to an abrupt stop and Ignacio Abel felt a sharp pain in his right knee as it banged into a metal edge. He was limping when they took him out. He wanted to walk but his legs gave way. They pushed him against a wall, and he recognized it as a wall of the Philosophy

Building, the rows of brick peppered with bullet holes and spatters of blood. They hadn't handcuffed him. He thought that the next morning, when he was found by the magistrate and the officer responsible for collecting the corpses before the municipal garbage trucks passed, they'd have no difficulty identifying him, because as a precaution he carried in his pocket his UGT and Socialist Party cards. Then another car arrived with even brighter headlights, forcing him to cover his eyes. He heard heated arguments around him but didn't understand a word. He slid to the ground when a rough hand pried his hands away from his face, and in the confusion of the moving shadows and headlights he recognized the voice of Eutimio Gómez, the lean figure bending over him.

"It's okay, Don Ignacio, it's okay now."

28

BEFORE THE TRAIN emerges from a meander in the river, the signal is heard, solemn as a ship's foghorn, and the electric cables and iron columns of the elevated platform vibrate. The nervous traveler will see the station in the distance like an Alpine castle crowning a wall of bare rock. Rhineberg: someone must have thought of the wooded cliffs above the Rhine when the name was chosen, and the nostalgia endured in the peaked towers of the station. A long metal staircase and the elevated passage that crosses the tracks like a covered bridge join the main building and the platforms. A man looks at his watch when he hears the train approaching and raises his eyes to a glass door. In the setting sun, the yellows and reds of the trees radiate embers of light; a wind from the river brings a wintry cold to an afternoon that had been mild, and moves waves of dry leaves across the platforms and tracks. The ground trembles beneath his feet when the train appears, its headlight shining, and stops with a screech of brakes. For a few long seconds it is quiet, hermetic, filling the entire platform with a suggestion of suspended energy. The only passenger to get off wears a raincoat of European cut and carries a suitcase too small for someone who's come a long way. He stands in some bewilderment as the train begins to move, his suitcase in one hand, his hat in the other, disconcerted at not seeing anyone, afraid he got off at the wrong station, enveloped by the solitude of the riverbank, the silence of the woods. At his back he hears a voice saying his name and is afraid he's imagining it. Behind the glass of the elevated passage, Philip Van Doren smiles when he recognizes him, watches him turn to the other man, Professor Stevens, chair of the Department of Architecture and Fine Arts (they met briefly in Madrid the previous year), and welcomes him, shaking his hand vigorously, the first person with whom he's spoken in many days, the first time anyone's welcomed him, granting him full existence, in any of the places he's passed through in recent weeks. Two figures seen from a distance, from above, in a secondary station on the bank of the Hudson River, one October afternoon seventy-three years ago.

He gets ready as soon as the train leaves the previous station. One by one he goes through all his pockets, neurotically checking their contents, his passport and wallet with documents and photographs, Judith Biely's last letter, Adela's letter, *I don't know where you are or what you're doing right now though I can imagine. Just know that if you want to come back to me and your children when this is all over, because someday it will be, the door is open.* He went to the toilet and managed to wash his face, comb his hair, straighten his tie, brush fallen hairs and dandruff flakes from his lapels, rinse his mouth for fear that whoever came to meet him might smell his breath, and examine his nails, which should have been trimmed. He's seen the bags under his eyes, the loose flesh under his chin and jaw. He remembered shaving in front of a mirror and seeing beside his reflection Judith's much younger face, her hair brushing his cheeks while her naked body pressed delicately against his back. They were in the house facing the sea, the house where they woke up next to each other for the first time, the smell of the Atlantic coming in the window. A flash of memory so fleeting it's extinguished without bitterness, without wakening a real connection between past and present. The conductor has passed, calling out the name of the station and gesturing to confirm that this time he does have to get off. Through the window, as the train begins to lose speed, Ignacio Abel sees the name in large black letters: RHINEBERG.

He doesn't see anyone at first. He gets off and finds himself at the end

458

of a long platform facing the great river, a row of tall iron columns and arches supporting what seems to be a covered passage where someone's looking down and perhaps signaling to him. The smells of the river and the leaves and damp earth from the woods fill his lungs as he feels a silence descend in which the distant clatter of the train and the echo of the locomotive's whistle fade away. Then someone says his name but he almost doesn't acknowledge it, almost fears a trick of the imagination, his first and last name pronounced with improbable fluency and a certain reverence. *Professor Ignacio Abel, it's great to have you here with us at long last.* He nods awkwardly, instinctively reticent, adapting himself with difficulty to being near another human and trying to catch words in English that are spoken too fast, his hand caught in the warm handshake of Professor Stevens, who, with the same determination, has taken hold of his suitcase: tall, a bit awkward, his arms and legs long, a lock of hair over his forehead, his face no longer young, his skin, a reddish brick color, covered with fine wrinkles, his eyes light blue behind his glasses. Stevens confuses him with his excessive energy, the speed of his praise, his questions, his request to be forgiven for delays and misunderstandings whose explanations Ignacio Abel can't understand (secretaries, offices, telegrams, inexcusable slip-ups); what an incredible honor finally to have you with us after so many difficulties, how was the train trip, you must be very tired after crossing from Europe. He can't see in himself the person to whom Stevens's signs of esteem and excuses are directed, as if they had mistaken him for someone else, and he lacked the necessary command of the language to correct the mistake or the strength to rise above the display of fresh enthusiasm by the head of the department, with his checkered sweater under his jacket and his green polka-dot bow tie, his long-fingered hand that refuses to return the suitcase, *don't mention it,* pulling at it vigorously as he leads the way to the elevated passage, the iron steps vibrating under the tread of his large shoes. Following him up the stairs, facing the broad Hudson stained with reddish glints of the setting sun, Ignacio Abel feels a weariness he doesn't remember having experienced before, all the more evident in the presence of someone younger (but he didn't feel the age difference when he was with Judith; how strange to have lived so long in a state of total unawareness, to have thought himself immune to the years, to weakness, to death). Leaning against the glass door that leads to the tracks, his arms crossed, the same expression on his face as on the night three months earlier when he stood by the window on a top floor in Madrid, Philip Van Doren looks him up and down with a serene smile before approaching him, as if observing signs of the accelerated passage of time, the result of an experiment. But then he changes in an instant, moves away from the glass door, and for an uncomfortable moment Ignacio Abel thinks Van Doren will embrace him, but he is observing everything, perhaps controlling his surprise, not wanting to reveal that he's noticed the state of Ignacio Abel's shoes or shirt or tie, the difference between the face he sees now and the face of the man he met in Madrid a little more than a year ago, the man he saw walk away along the Gran Vía one midnight three months ago. He doesn't embrace Ignacio Abel but extends his hands, clasps both of his, he, too, subtly changed in this place where he's not a foreigner, where his figure doesn't stand out against an alien background, perhaps stockier, fleshier, the same gleam on his shaved head and his chin lifted above a high collar. "Dear Ignacio, what a pleasure to see you," he says in Spanish, stressing with a smile the complete correctness of the expression *dichosos los ojos,* his vanity at knowing how to use it, he who was always asking for Judith's help in finding equivalents of English phrases. "You have so much to tell me. I telegraphed the embassy in Madrid every day. I called. I tried to call your apartment, but it was impossible to get through. Dear Ignacio. Dear Professor. Welcome, at last. Stevens will take care of everything. He's impressed at having you here. He can't believe it. He knows your work, your writings. He was the first person who talked to me about you." He gives orders, just as he did in Madrid. Brief signs, glances. Stevens walks ahead carrying Ignacio Abel's suitcase, opening doors for them, standing to one side, remaining behind, obedient, conscious of his position. Van Doren gives him instructions, and Stevens listens and nods, taking care of everything. The back seat is spacious and has a subtle smell of leather. Abel sits uncomfortably, rigidly, not leaning back, his knees together, hat in his lap. He has lost the habit of comfort as well as the habit of flattery. Van Doren takes out a cigarette, and Stevens, who'd started the engine, turns it off to look for a lighter and give him a light. Van Doren leans back, barely moving his right hand to wave away the smoke or to indicate to Stevens with some impatience that he should get started at long last. "You'll spend the first few days in the university guesthouse, if you don't mind. In a week at most you'll have your own place, in a convenient location near campus and the library site. Within walking distance. How do you say that in Spanish? Wait, don't tell me. A stone's throw? Our dear Judith wouldn't have hesitated for a second. Though perhaps *sitio* isn't the correct translation for *site* . . ." How little time it took him to say her name, invoke her presence; observing Ignacio Abel's face, looking for signs of surprise, the name spoken aloud to him for the first time in so long. He must be waiting for Abel to summon the courage to ask whether he knows anything of her, as he did that night in Madrid at the window where the light of the fires was reflected; planning his little experiment, saying a name as if pouring a drop of some substance into a beaker. But now he looks out the car window, leaning back in the leather seat. He takes a breath, perhaps he's going to say something, that he knows where Judith is. "I imagine you haven't had time to hear the latest news from Spain. Their army took Navalcarnero yesterday. I don't think it'll be in tomorrow's papers. How beautiful the names of Spanish towns are, and how difficult to pronounce. I look at the map and read them aloud. The most difficult thing is knowing where the accent goes in such long words. I see the names and miss the car trips along those highways. They took Illescas only three days ago. How far is Navalcarnero from Madrid? Fifteen miles, twenty? How long do you think it'll take them to reach Madrid?"

The car advances along a narrow road flanked by enormous trees, and beyond them he watches autumnal woods glide past, meadows where horses graze, isolated farms, fences painted white that gleam in the declining afternoon light. On the rolling fields the oblique light reveals a faint mist rising from soil dampened and enriched by the rain and covered by the mantle of autumn leaves that will slowly rot until they turn into fertilizer. He recalls his first trips through the fertile, rain-soaked plains of Europe, misty dawns beyond a train window, daylight revealing straight lines of trees along sumptuous riverbanks, cultivated fields. What an injustice to come from the Spanish barrens, the bone-dry plains and mountains of bare rock inhabited by goats and human beings who lived in caves, who had, men and women both, skin as dark and harsh as the landscape where they barely survived by scratching at the earth, their faces deformed by goiters, injustice bending them like a curse without remedy. "No reason to despair, Abel my friend, like those ashen gentlemen of the Generation of '98 — Unamuno, Baroja, all the rest," Negrín would say, laughing. "Two generations will be enough to improve the race without eugenics or five-year plans. Agrarian reform and healthy food. Fresh milk, white bread, oranges, running water, clean underwear. If they only give us the time, the other side and our own people . . ."

But they didn't. Perhaps there never was any time to give, the real possibility of avoiding disaster never existed, and the future that the year 1931 seemed to open before us was a fantasy as foolish as our illusion of rationality. In the ditches along the recently paved avenues of University City, there are now piles of corpses; in the classrooms we hurried to have ready for the beginning of the school year, no one's come to study; everything prepared, new benches and blackboards, echoing corridors where some of the windows have probably shattered, where cannon fire will roar very soon, and as happens now, between midnight and dawn, rifles firing at bodies against the walls. Tomorrow, within a few hours, as soon as it dawns over the plain, they'll continue to approach, heading for Madrid as they have throughout the summer, coming up from the south along desolate straight highways like a pernicious epidemic against which there's no antidote, no possible resistance, only immolation or flight, bewildered, poorly armed militiamen throwing themselves unprotected against canister shot or fleeing cross-country and tossing aside their rifles to run faster without even seeing the enemy, terrified by the shadows of riders on horseback or by the shouts of others as lost as they. With the pink manicured nail of an index finger — the finger that now distractedly taps the cigarette to shake off the ash while through the car window a landscape of meadows, white houses and fences, red, ocher, and yellow splashes of woods that follow one another in orderly succession — Philip Van Doren has followed on a map the line drawn by the names he read in the papers, or in who knows what reports, which reach him even before they're published: sonorous, abstract names, Badajoz, Talavera de la Reina, Torrijos, Illescas, as conspicuous with their hard consonants and bright vowels in the music of the English language as their exotic spellings in news columns and headlines. But what does Van Doren know of what lies behind those names? And what can Professor Stevens imagine when he reads the paper or listens to the radio while he eats breakfast next to one of those large windows without shutters or curtains, before these landscapes free of sharp edges, the signs of poverty, drought, or scars of dry streams, bathed in a soft light that seems to touch things ever so delicately while the afternoon fades slowly, enduring in the clear blue of the sky and distant mountains, the dusty gold of hills covered with maples and oaks, the west sides of houses painted white? Names he remembers, places he passed on a trip, villages where he stopped to study a church tower or take photographs of a mill, a washing site, a structure devoted to labor — not even that, a stone wall crowned with tiles, the arch of a bridge over a stream. Day after day, beginning at dawn, in the terrible heat of summer afternoons, in the more temperate twilights, the armed invaders have continued to advance through those landscapes stripped of trees where no one can hide, attacking villages, each a name quickly eliminated from maps, leaving behind a harvest of corpses, a horizon of burned houses along the white strip of highway, the lines of telegraph poles and wires. They advance in military trucks, in requisitioned cars, in cavalry squads that terrorize unarmed fugitives with raised swords and shouts of primitive fury. Turbans and scimitars mixed with machine guns; trophies of cut-off hands and ears, and range finders for the artillery that demolishes with cannon fire a church tower where peasants armed with old shotguns have taken refuge, resolved to die; barbaric acts executed with the kind of precision all of you wanted to realize in the University City project, says Philip Van Doren, uncertain about the verb he's used — it's either too inaccurate or too vague. "How do you say *to carry out* in Spanish?" he asks, not looking at Ignacio Abel, or looking at him obliquely to let him know that the person who could give him the answer is not there. Both of them are thinking about her. "*Llevar a cabo,*" he says, satisfied now, relieved, Judith's shadow invoked between them, as present as the war that's invoked in the names of the towns the enemy continues to take, the ones that will fall tomorrow, within a few hours, when it's still dark here but dawn in Spain: motors starting up; horses neighing; the deafening noise of weapons, of military boots on gravel (but they don't wear boots either, or only the officers do; they wear espadrilles, just like our men, united in penury, in their destiny as cannon fodder); slaughter as an exhausting but intoxicating task, like a human hunt where without effort the astonishing number of retrieved prey multiplies, all uniform in the terror of their flight and their helplessness. The beautiful names on maps now designate cemeteries. The other country, occupied now and an enemy, spreads like a stain as the troops advance, reinforced by a retinue of blue-shirted butchers who go through villages with typed lists of those condemned, leaving behind a trail of corpses. While he waited and did nothing in Madrid, they continued to approach, while he traveled by train to Paris, dissembling in his flight, and boarded the ship and was hypnotized looking at the ocean as gray as a steel plate, writing postcards that wouldn't reach their destinations, imagining letters he'd never write. From Navalcarnero the highway runs almost in a straight line to the outskirts of Madrid. Long before they arrive, the invaders will see in the distance the white patch of the National Palace on the cliffs of the Manzanares; they'll see the red outline of its roofs, interrupted by the Telephone Company tower beneath the immense sky of Castilla.

"The president of the Republic has left Madrid, as you probably know," says Van Doren, observing Ignacio Abel to be certain of what he suspects, that Abel didn't know.

"Probably the government will leave too, if it hasn't already done so, in secret. Your family is safe, far from Madrid? I seem to remember that the last time we saw each other you said you'd left them in the Sierra. If you'd like, perhaps we can arrange for them to join you here after a time. Other professors we've brought over from Europe, from Germany especially, are in a similar situation. And of course, what happened to your friend Professor Rossman?"

When he hears the name, Stevens turns his head toward them for a moment, his face red.

"Professor Karl Ludwig Rossman? He's a friend of yours, Professor Abel?"

"He was," he says, in a voice so low Stevens doesn't hear him over the noise of the engine, but Van Doren does and immediately is on the scent, excited by the possibility of finding out, uncovering something.

"Did he die? Recently? I didn't know he was ill."

"Here we admire him as much as Breuer or Mies van der Rohe." Stevens nervously takes his eyes off the road, turning his head toward Ignacio Abel with a bird's rapid twist. "Did you really work with him? How exciting. In Weimar, in Dessau? His writings from that time are incomparable. His analyses of objects, his drawings. Come to think of it, Professor Abel, with all due respect, in some of your projects one can see Rossman's influence."

Van Doren pays no attention to Stevens; he looks at Ignacio Abel, his head slightly bent, raising a match, the cigarette between straight fingers.

"He was killed? In Madrid?"

Reluctantly Ignacio Abel understands that it would be useless to tell what happened; recently arrived at his destination, not settled yet in the provisional refuge where he'll spend at least a few months, the precarious portion of the future covered by his visa, he feels the futility of trying to explain what he's seen, what his awkward English vocabulary won't convey, much less the articles published in newspapers, the photographs in which almost everything is remote and abstract. What can Stevens understand, with his young heart, quick to admire? How to explain to him or Van Doren the fear of dying that makes you wet your trousers or the nausea of seeing for the first time a corpse with bulging eyes and a swollen black tongue jutting out between its teeth? Having seen or not having seen is the difference: to leave and go on seeing; to squeeze your eyes shut and not have it matter; to go on seeing with closed eyes the face of a dead stranger that gradually is transformed into the face of Professor Rossman, so that it's easier to identify him by the collar partially detached from his shirt or the insignia of his cavalry regiment in his lapel than by the blurred features, disfigured and subject to fantastic distortions. "It was probably a mistake," he says. "They must have confused him with someone else." Professor Rossman was in the morgue, reeking of formaldehyde and decomposing in the heat of early September, a piece of cardboard with a number hanging around his neck like a crude scapular; not on one of the marble tables overflowing with bodies, rigid arms and legs projecting like bare branches, but on the floor, in a back room where flies buzzed and ants swarmed. He sees him now, and the stench invoked by memory is more intense than the smell of autumnal soil and fallen leaves that comes in the window and combines with the sweetish smoke from Van Doren's cigarette. What he sees with half-closed eyes is more real than this moment, this car trip through fields and woods; so close to Professor Stevens and Philip Van Doren in the confined space of the car, a frontier separates him from them, an invisible trench that words can't remedy. Suddenly he feels he's lived in unreality since the night he left Madrid. The world the others inhabit is for him an illusion; what he still sees, though he's left, is what turns him into a foreigner — not the data printed in a passport issued by a republic that from one day to the next may cease to exist, not the photograph taken several months earlier of the man he no longer is. He sees what they'll never be able to imagine: the gray faces of the dead in the empty lots and cleared sites of University City, beside the adobe walls of the Museum of Natu-

466

ral Sciences, on the sidewalk of Calle Príncipe de Vergara, next to the entrance to his apartment house, beneath the same grove of trees in the Botanical Garden where not long ago he'd met Judith Biely, in any ditch on the outskirts of Madrid; the dead as diverse and singular as the living, frozen in a final gesture like the one caught by the flash of a photograph and yet gradually stripped of their individuality, preserving only their generic condition, old or young, men or women, adults or children, fat or thin, office workers or bourgeois or simple unfortunates, wearing shoes or espadrilles, with the gaps of lost teeth or gold teeth pulled by the thieves who come out early to plunder the bodies, some of the dead still wearing their eyeglasses, their hands tied or their hands and arms open and dislocated like those of a doll, with a cigarette in the corner of their mouth, with a *churro* that some wit had put between their teeth, hair standing straight up or disheveled as if just out of bed or flattened with brilliantine; dead bodies in pajamas, dead bodies in undershirts, dead bodies in ties and hard collars, dead bodies with eyelids squeezed tight or eyes wide open, some with jaws distended as if laughing out loud, others with a kind of somnambulistic smile, dead bodies on their backs or with their faces pushed into the ground or leaning to one side with their legs bent, a single hole in the back of the neck or a thorax ripped open by bullets, dead bodies in a puddle of blood or felled neatly as if a bolt of lightning or a heart attack had killed them, dead bodies with their bellies as swollen as the cadavers of donkeys or mules, dead bodies alone or piled on top of one another, dead bodies irreproachably clean or with their trousers stained by piss or shit, vomit on their shirts, all alike in the opaque grayness of their skin; unknown dead bodies, photographed from the front and side, classified in the records of the Ministry of National Security, where a photographer and his assistant came every afternoon to attach to large sheets of smooth cardboard the recently developed photographs they'd been taking since dawn in the empty lots of Madrid. With scissors and a pot of glue the assistant cut out the photographs and attached them to the cardboard pages of albums, above a panel that had at the bottom blank spaces indicated by dotted lines that were never filled in: name, address, cause of death. Fearful people huddled over the albums, looking at photographs, turning pages, elbowing their way into a room that was too small and badly ventilated, filled with smoke, the floor littered with cigarette butts. After a while their eyes grew weary and the faces in the photographs began to look identical, such generic black-and-white portraits that it was difficult to identify anyone. There was whispering, the sound of footsteps, from time to time a scream.

He was out the entire day and at ten that night still hadn't learned anything regarding Professor Rossman's whereabouts. Since his car had been confiscated and streetcars ran erratically, he walked all over Madrid under the summer sun or rode in the suffocating metro, looking for him. Señorita Rossman was waiting in front of his building, she'd appeared early, before eight o'clock. "You have to help me, Professor Abel. Some men took my father away yesterday afternoon, told me he'd return as soon as he answered some questions, but wouldn't tell me where they were taking him. You know so many people in Madrid, surely you can find out what happened to my father. You know how he is—he says whatever's on his mind. He'd go down to that café next to the pensión, tell everybody that war isn't a fiesta and unless there's more discipline and fewer speeches and parades the Fascists would take Madrid before the summer was over. You know him, heard him say the same things a thousand times. Those people had no idea what he was saying, all that talk about Marcus Aurelius and the barbarians, the foreign barbarians and the domestic barbarians. He argued with the landlady at the pensión, whose son is an Anarchist. Perhaps because of his accent someone decided he was a spy." But she was afraid for herself too, afraid the men who'd come for her father would come back to take her away. She'd spent a sleepless night. It was hot, her father had unbuttoned his hard shirt collar and was dozing in a rocking chair by the balcony that faced Calle de la Luna, where there was a militia barracks or an Anarchist headquarters. They came for him, and the only thing he asked them was to let him button his collar and put on his jacket and tie, take off his slippers, put on high shoes. But they took him away with his shirt open and no jacket, in his old cloth slippers. He did have time to put on the glasses he'd placed on a small table beside the rocking chair before he fell asleep. They were three well-mannered men armed with pistols, behaving with the neutrality of the police. Nothing had alerted her or her father to the danger because they hadn't heard the usual heavy steps on the staircase or violent pounding on the pensión door while ringing the bell. At first she didn't understand what was happening. She remembered that her father had sat motionless in the rocking chair, blinking because of the light that flooded the room when one of the men opened the curtains to begin the search. The three men filled the reduced space where Señorita Rossman and her father had moved cautiously to take advantage of every inch: the two identical beds with iron frames, the sink with its oval mirror, the wardrobe, the small bookcase with the few volumes they'd been able to save after years of travel, the mantel where they took turns writing letters and filling out forms, and where Señorita Rossman prepared her German lessons. Within minutes the beds were unmade, the mattresses overturned, the books strewn across the floor, along with valuable documents, forms, Professor Rossman's diplomas, the contents of his bottomless briefcase, the clothing they kept in the wardrobe. Señorita Rossman sat in a chair, her bony knees and large feet close together, her elbows on her thighs, her skinny face resting on both hands, shaking just as she had a few times in her room in the Hotel Lux in Moscow, when no one would visit her and her father and they didn't know whether they'd be allowed to leave the USSR. When they took him away, he said something to her in German, and one of them put a pistol to his side. "Be careful about passing messages we can't understand."

"He told me to come and see you, that you'd help us, just as you've always helped us. I don't know anyone else." Señorita Rossman fixed her colorless eyes on Ignacio Abel from behind her glasses, which she wiped with a handkerchief that she returned each time to her sleeve with a kind of obstinate, automatic correctness. There was in her something resistant to attractiveness, a kind of helplessness doomed to awaken discomfort, not sympathy. He asked her to come in. She sat on one of the chairs, covered for the summer, in the dining room he rarely entered and where the disorder wasn't so apparent. She had to catch her breath after having climbed five flights of stairs. Ignacio Abel brought her a glass of water, and she placed it carefully on the edge of the table, avoiding his inquisitive glance when their eyes met. Overwhelmed not only by her father's arrest but by remorse at having dragged him to the Soviet Union when they had to leave Germany, she was ultimately responsible for Professor Rossman's being denied what he most desired, a visa for the United States, where he might have continued his career like so many other colleagues from the Bauhaus, expatriates like him who were welcomed into universities and architects' studios while he wandered Madrid, where his reputation was nonexistent and his credentials were worth nothing, selling fountain pens on commission in cafés, sitting in the waiting rooms of offices that never opened for him, devising new plans that would lead nowhere: a trip to Lisbon, where he'd been told that visas for America were less difficult to obtain, or where he and his daughter could board a ship that would carry them to an intermediate South American port, to Rio de Janeiro, Santo Domingo, or Havana, where someone would be careless or corrupt enough not to see the stamps with the hammer and sickle in his stateless person's passport, almost as useless as the expired German passport that had red letters across the page with the photograph: *Juden–Juif.*

He'd seen Professor Rossman from a distance on Calle Bravo Murillo, and as on many other occasions he'd been tempted to cross to the other side of the street or pass by without attracting his attention. Professor Rossman probably wouldn't see him anyway, so myopic, so distracted in the crowd on the sidewalk in front of the Cine Europa, beneath large red-and-black flags and posters with bright colors and enormous figures in heroic poses, though they no longer displayed only advertisements for films but also battalions of muscular militia-men, workers carrying hammers and rifles, peasants shaking sickles against a red sky where squadrons of airplanes were flying. THE LIB-ERTARIAN REVOLUTION WILL CRUSH THE HYDRA OF FASCISM! AIR-COOLED, HIT PREMIERES. VISIT OUR SELECT REFRESHMENT COUNTER. Militiamen with rifles on their shoulders, tanned by the Si-erra sun, drank steins of beer in the shade of a café's striped awning. They talked in noisy groups, some in blue coveralls open to the waist, in odd tunics and trousers of uniforms, in military caps pushed to the back of their heads, almost all of them young, dark-skinned, with long sideburns and kerchiefs around their necks, emboldened when a girl passed near them, intoxicated by the feeling of omnipotence granted them by the collapse of the old order, their possession of weapons, the war, carnival and slaughterhouse all in one. For more than four hours the Popular Front Youth marched through Madrid in an impressive demonstration, cheered enthusiastically by an immense crowd. The war seemed to be simply this rough, nervous joviality, the general un-tidiness and indolent air of people on a hot August morning, the epic character of those gigantic figures outlined on placards covering the theater's façade, which no one seemed to notice. On the sharp peaks of the Sierra de Córdoba our troops are preparing their assault on the City of the Mosque, waiting impatiently for the order to advance. The war was triumphalist lying newspaper headlines, funerals with fists in the air, somber marches in which death was always something abstract and glorious, parades with large banners and no one keeping time, preceded, as in the now abolished religious processions, by costumed crowds of children marching with wooden shotguns. The unstoppable advance of our troops continues over the rugged terrain of the Sierra de Guadarrama, where day after day enemy forces are being pushed from their positions.

"My friend, my dear Professor Abel, how happy I am to see you." Professor Rossman, his black briefcase pressed to his chest, wiped his hand on the skirt of his jacket before shaking Abel's; he seemed to be in a great hurry and at the same time not to know where he was going, jumping from one topic to another. "Have you read today's papers? The enemy is retreating on all fronts, but the lines defended by our glorious militias are closer and closer to Madrid. Believe me, I know, I spent four years studying maps of positions on the western front. Have you noticed that the reports deal not with what's already happened but what's about to happen? Granada on the point of surrendering to loyal troops, the fall of the Alcázar de Toledo is expected at any moment, the imminent capture of Oviedo or Córdoba is announced. And what about Zaragoza? How many weeks is it that troops have been advancing and putting the enemy to flight or meeting no resistance, and yet they never reach the city? I spend the day looking at the map and the Spanish-German dictionary. I have to look up Spanish words I thought I already knew. Are you well, still working? Your wife and children? You're not accustomed to living alone, you look thinner. Would you like a drink, a stein of beer? The revolution is now a reality, yet the cafés are still open. It was the same in Berlin when the war was over. This time it's on me. We have to celebrate my daughter's excellent new job . . ."

They looked for a table inside a café. As he sat down, Professor Rossman opened his briefcase and began to take out sections of newspapers and clippings, maps of the kind published every day, with modifications in rebel-occupied territory that according to all the reports kept shrinking, though some rebel positions were close to Madrid. The overwhelming advance of Republican troops along the Aragón front is seen as an imminent threat to the rebels of Zaragoza. Loyal forces are six kilometers from Teruel and continue to hold advantageous positions. Regiments under the command of the heroic Captain Bayo continue their advance toward the reconquest of Mallorca. The rebels of Huesca are in a desperate situation.

Ignacio Abel looked around uncomfortably, afraid someone would overhear what Professor Rossman was saying, be suspicious of his foreign air and war maps.

"Be more careful, Professor," he said in a quiet voice. "People are denounced on the slightest suspicion."

"And you ought to take better care of yourself, my dear friend. You don't look well, if you don't mind my saying so. Do you have something to occupy your time? Is it true construction at University City is temporarily suspended? I hear the insurgents plan to attack Madrid on that flank, which makes sense, militarily speaking. Don't look at me that way, don't be afraid. Personally I'm not afraid. I'm an old man and a refugee from Hitler's Germany. Those who expelled me from my country are the ones helping the rebels with armaments and airplanes. What interest can I have in being on their side? Where can I go if they enter Madrid? But as I was saying, there's good news for us, for my daughter above all, excellent news."

"Did they finally give you visas for America?"

"Who can think now about visas? We'll have to wait for all this to be over in Spain. Not before the end of the summer, if you'll permit my pessimism, no matter what the newspapers say. Will the British and French pressure Hitler and Mussolini not to aid Franco? I don't think so. Your government wants to tell the world it's facing a barbarian invasion on its own, but newspapers throughout Europe are filled with photographs of burned churches and murdered priests and monks. You say the other barbarians kill more? Probably, but that's not held against them by Mussolini or Hitler. And how are you going to explain yourselves if no one in the government speaks foreign languages? I'm not complaining — thanks to that, my daughter's finally found an excellent job now that the children to whom she gave German lessons are all away for the summer. And better paid. She's been hired as a translator in the censorship service for foreign correspondents. She speaks English and Russian almost as well as German, as you know, and her Spanish is excellent, much better than mine will ever be. She works near the pensión, in an office in the Telephone Building, and has a safe-conduct and food coupons. I help her in whatever way I can, as you see. I look for newspaper articles for her, take her to the Telephone Building and pick her up. My poor child's never known how to look after herself, not even when she became a fanatical Communist. She'd go to endless meetings, and her mother would fall asleep — she was already ill at the time and taking strong pain medicines—but I'd stay awake until she returned. My poor child, in love with Lenin and Stalin, just as she'd once been in love with Douglas Fairbanks and Rudolph Valentino. Now, if you will excuse me, I have to go home to review today's press with her before she goes to the office. My daughter thinks she's a Communist, but basically she's a romantic señorita from my grandparents' generation. Instead of reading Heine, she took to reading Karl Marx. Do you know what I'm afraid of? That she'll fall in love with one of those American correspondents who arrive each day in Madrid to see the war at first hand. My daughter's destiny is to suffer for love. For love of a man who ignores her or uses her and deceives her with another woman, or for love of a cause that promises her a total explanation of the world and heaven on earth. The worst has been when the two loves were combined. Do you know why she wanted to go to Russia when we could no longer live in Germany? I followed her, alarmed at her living alone in that frightening country. She wanted to go to Russia to see for herself the homeland of the proletariat and to follow like a dog the leader of the German Communist Party, with whom she fell in love and who took her to bed on a whim even though he was married and had children. Revolutionary morality. They gave my daughter a job as a typist in an office of the Comintern, and from time to time the heroic comrade visited our room in the Hotel Lux and I had to go out for several hours. There are no cafés like this one in Moscow, my friend, no waiters in short white jackets who go on serving you as they did before the revolution. Suddenly the comrade stopped coming, and my daughter spent her nights crying. The new Soviet woman weeping like a señorita of the last century because her beloved no longer visits her as he once did. But the hero also stopped going to the office, where my daughter helped him body and soul in the propaganda struggle that would soon overthrow Hitler, casting an international spotlight on his crimes. He hadn't gone off with another typist or secretary. He hadn't gone back to his wife, about whom nothing was known. One day we learned he'd been arrested. They accused him of complicity with the assassins of Kirov in Leningrad. But he'd never gone to Leningrad and wasn't even in the USSR when Kirov was killed! The other girls in the office stopped speaking to her, and after a few weeks they didn't even look at her. Not at her and not at me. We were like two phantoms in the halls of the Hotel Lux. But we didn't talk to each other when we were alone in our room either. She didn't tell me, but I knew what she was thinking as she sat by the telephone. Her lover had done something worse than betray her — he'd betrayed the revolution or the party or the proletariat. Why would they accuse him if he wasn't guilty? And what if he'd been arrested because of her, because of some indiscretion she'd committed without realizing it? My daughter always burdens herself with the guilt of the world. She still hopes he'll appear, the misunderstanding will vanish, and his good name will be rehabilitated. Day after day no one spoke to us, but she wasn't fired, and we weren't thrown out of the hotel or arrested. But like most people in our situation, we kept a packed suitcase under the bed in the event the police came to take us in the middle of the night. Then one day they came for us. Not in the middle of the night but at eight o'clock in the evening, a short time after my daughter had come home from the office. We heard their footsteps on the stairs, then in the corridor, they knocked on the door, my daughter remained seated, trembling. I felt a certain relief, to tell you the truth. If it was going to happen, better for it to happen sooner rather than later. Young men, polite, in clean uniforms and shining boots, told us to accompany them, and as we walked along the hall I thought, how strange that they've come so early, that they are taking us through the hotel in sight of everyone, not after midnight. They had us climb into a black van — clearly we weren't going to Lubyanka Prison, which wasn't far from the hotel. The van stopped at the railroad station. They almost dragged us along the platform, pushed us into a car, and handed us an envelope with our passports. They could've killed us or sent us to Siberia, but they expelled us, I still don't understand why, why they let us live . . ."

Professor Rossman must have seen it all happening again, this time with the certainty that there was no way out: the footsteps on the stairs, the pounding on the door, his daughter shaking, the same suitcase that had been packed in Moscow ready under the bed. But it wasn't his daughter who'd been chosen by misfortune, as he'd always feared. It was him. Sitting in a rocking chair in the heat of an August afternoon, Professor Rossman slowly realized that these methodical men who didn't raise their voices and weren't wearing the coveralls of militiamen or carrying rifles were probably going to kill him.

"Of course you did everything you could to save him," said Van Doren. "Perhaps you even put your own life in danger."

"Is Rossman dead?" Stevens looked at them in the rearview mirror, not quite following the conversation in Spanish. "In Madrid? I didn't see anything in the paper."

"I didn't have to risk anything. He was dead and I kept looking for him."

29

H<small>E WAS DEAD</small>, and for several days early in September Ignacio Abel searched for him in vain, wandering from one end of Madrid to the other, looking suspicious in his light suit and tie and neatly folded handkerchief in the breast pocket of his jacket among the men with unshaven faces in unbuttoned shirts and blue coveralls who filled the streets and café terraces, the young men who carried rifles over their shoulders and wore pistols and cartridge belts around their waists, demanding papers or ordering passersby to put up their hands. That morning he told Señorita Rossman to wait until he returned, and if he learned anything he'd telephone her; he showed her where the kitchen was in case she wanted something to eat, though there was little food left in the cupboard or refrigerator. Throughout the day he thought of her, imagining her in the same position in which he'd left her, sitting at the dining room table in front of the glass of water, waiting for his return or a telephone call, crushed by a grief that when transmitted to him changed into guilt, a bottomless remorse for not having helped her and Professor Rossman as much as he should have, helped them with true conviction and not out of pity, perhaps turning in a timely way to influential friends. Señorita Rossman's desperate overconfidence in coming to him for help led him to an unrealistic sense of resolve. He leafed through his pocket diary for names, addresses, and telephone numbers; with her present he made calls that weren't answered (the telephone lines weren't working or phones rang in empty houses or abandoned offices). With a decisive air he put on his jacket and tie and placed his wallet and keys in his pocket but didn't know where to go, whom to ask for help. Since the hot July night when he'd looked for Judith Biely in a Madrid that had become alien to him, he'd lived in a state of lethargy, a sort of convalescence, in the empty apartment, going every day to his office in University City, now deserted except for patrols of militiamen, or people who stole building materials, or groups, almost always women, who walked the empty lots at first light to search among the previous night's dead. Toward the middle of August, large families who'd fled to Madrid before the advancing enemy army camped in some of the unfinished buildings: waves of refugees with wooden-wheeled carts and donkeys and mules, bent under the weight of possessions they'd attempted to save: mattresses, furniture, metal bed frames, cages of chickens. They lit their fires and cooked their pots of food in the half-completed lobbies, just as they did in public gardens in the heart of Madrid or under the arches of metro stations. Their goats and sheep grazed on the weeds of future sports fields where corpses would randomly appear, hands tied behind their backs. Packs of boys with shaved heads chased one another up and down the staircases and abandoned scaffolding until they bumped into a corpse, the boldest boys daring to go through the pockets or remove an article of clothing in good condition. As on so many mornings when he left for his office, with purposeless obstinacy that at least allowed him the deception of a certain degree of normality, Ignacio Abel told Señorita Rossman not to worry. The porter, now in a proletarian coverall and beret, greeted him as unctuously as when he wore blue livery and a visored cap. "Still no news about the señora and your children, Don Ignacio? I wouldn't worry. As I say, things are calmer in the Sierra, even if they're on the other side, and it's healthier for the children. And a summer away from Madrid is sure to do the señora good." The porter said this knowingly: he'd learned the reason Adela spent the last two weeks of June in a sanatorium — she didn't have weak lungs. He smiled, leaning forward and perhaps calculating the possibility of denouncing him now, since he knew that Ignacio Abel, though he'd saved himself once, wasn't invulnerable. "I see the señor has had a visitor," said the porter. "The foreign señorita asked for you and I let her up because I remembered seeing her when she came to give your children lessons. The truth is she looked like someone who's had some sorrow, but these days who doesn't have troubles?" He proffered the insinuation along with a cautious hand: he'd close his hand around the offered coin just as he'd clutch at a confidence that might be of benefit to him and perhaps harmful to the one who'd formulated it, his old status as gossip elevated in the new era to that of expert informer.

He looked for Negrín in the Café Lion and was told he should look for him at the Workers' Cooperative on Calle Piamonte, or at the War Ministry. His usual activity accelerated by the war, Negrín had always just left the place where Abel had almost found him. "Don Juan comes and goes all day," said the man who shined shoes at the café and had an undying devotion to Negrín. "If he isn't on his way up to the Sierra with his car full of bread and canned food for the boys in the militias, then he's at a field hospital telling the nurses how to bandage wounds. You know how he is — that man never stops. And when he does have some free time, he comes here for me to shine his shoes and to drink down a mug of beer in one gulp. Too bad we don't get the fresh prawns anymore that he likes so much. What a man. Things would've gone better for us if he'd been president when the insurgents rebelled. Though now you hear rumors that they're going to name him to something big, a minister at least. What an honor. I tell him I'd like to be twenty years younger so I could go to the front and fight, and he tells me, 'Agapito, if what you know how to do well is clean shoes, then clean shoes, it's a noble trade. Things would be better for us Spaniards if instead of all of us talking so much, we worked harder at our trades.' Would you like me to give him a message?" the shoeshine man asked Ignacio Abel. Hanging on the post office was an enormous half-torn poster of militiamen advancing, brandishing rifles with bayonets against a horizon of burned houses. The revolution was an apotheosis of typographies in strong colors, the war a catalogue of victories announced or predicted by newspapers in headlines that ended in exclamation points, and illustrated with pictures in photogravure of groups of ever-victorious volunteers raising rifles at the top of rugged crags or towers in towns just taken from the enemy. Ignacio Abel crossed the Castellana, which reeked of manure fermenting in the summer heat. Under the trees along the central paths, evacuees from the villages had hung their canvas tarps and made their fires, their donkeys tied to the trees. Where will they go when the cold weather begins and all of this isn't over? How will it be possible to house and feed them if they keep arriving in increasing numbers, fleeing the enemy no one is stopping except in the fantasy of newspaper headlines and radio news reports? Where will the blankets come from, the winter uniforms, the boots to equip the militias who are now fighting bare-chested? He was stupefied to discover that without the links provided by his marriage to Adela and his affair with Judith Biely, he was almost totally lacking in social connections, a hermit who suddenly leaves his enclosure and knows nothing of the outside world. The relationships he'd established at work didn't extend beyond the office, hadn't evolved into friendships. Except for Judith, he didn't recall ever having an intimate conversation with anyone. The cordiality he shared with Moreno Villa and Negrín was characterized by a strict reserve. A mixture of personal arrogance and keen class insecurity had always kept him at a distance from most of his fellow architects. Going around Madrid in search of Professor Rossman, stripped of the confidence his work, his family, even his lost lover had given him, he experienced his isolation as impotence, a lack of an anchor that had moved him away from things long before the city — the entire country — was set adrift by the upheaval of the military insurgency and a war. How solitary his life had been, an only child, then an orphan, entrusted to shadowy guardians, protected not so much by his intellectual abilities and determination to study as by the foresight of his father, who knew he was sick and saved money and took the steps necessary to continue protecting his son when he was no longer there, so he wouldn't have to leave secondary school, so he could support himself at the university, watched over by his parents in the fulfillment of a destiny they had apportioned to him with their sacrifice. "My son, you'll be so alone," his mother said, touching his face with a hand deformed by work, in the provincial hospital bed where she lay dying. Her hand in his, grasping it, and one by one he had to loosen her fingers before letting it rest on the bed sheet. Only now did Ignacio Abel relive in memory the afternoon more than thirty years earlier when he'd walked from the East Cemetery to the dark porter's lodging on Calle Toledo after burying his mother.

If he hurried, if he was lucky, perhaps he could still save Professor Rossman. He knocked on the doors of quasi-official agencies and elegant houses that had been seized and, he'd been told, were now secret prisons. In the courtyards, car engines roared and men in civilian clothes armed with rifles and large pistols tucked diagonally between the shirt and waistband of their trousers blocked his path and subjected him to interrogations that didn't always end when he opened his wallet to show his credentials: his Socialist Party and General Union of Workers membership cards, the safe-conduct issued to him so he could continue visiting the suspended construction sites at University City. He said Professor Rossman's name, explained his status as an eminent foreign anti-Fascist refugee in Spain, and showed the photograph his daughter had given him. He caught looks of possible recognition, gestures of complicity. He put the photo away after receiving a negative reply and continued searching: perhaps he ought to ask at the Academy of Fine Arts, at the State Security Office, at the police station on Calle Fomento. "This guy has the face of a dead man," someone said to him, laughing. "You should look for him in the morgue, or on the San Isidro meadow. They have a picnic there every night." He knocked on the doors of palaces decorated now by red or red-and-black flags, their façades covered with layer upon layer of propaganda posters. He made his way along narrow corridors filled with tobacco smoke, saw fatigued, garrulous, unshaven men talking on the phone, dictating lists of names to secretaries, all of them pulled along by a nervous urgency in which the presence of Ignacio Abel was an inconvenience: his insistence on making inquiries regarding someone no one knew anything about, repeating a name he had to spell over and over again, showing a photo that elicited an automatic negative response. In a salon with large balconies overlooking the Paseo de la Castellana, he approached with instinctive meekness a table with legs carved into lion's claws, where a harried group of men, some wearing a suit and tie and with an official air and flanked by stenographers, judged or heard cases and examined papers. They passed around the photograph of Professor Rossman as if doubting its authenticity. One of them handed it back, shook his head, and gestured to an armed man in plain clothes sitting on a balcony. The guard seized Ignacio Abel's arm and forced him out of the hall. "If I were you, I'd stop asking so many questions. Maybe this friend of yours turns out to be an insurgent and gets you in trouble." As he walked down the staircase, he passed a group of militiamen pushing a man in handcuffs up the stairs, hitting him. For a moment their eyes met. In the man's eyes was a plea for help; Ignacio Abel looked away.

He returned to the Workers' Cooperative, and the sentry at the door told him Negrín had just left but had gone to a place nearby, the Socialist commissary on Calle Gravina. Negrín was loading cardboard boxes filled with foodstuffs and beverages into his car, wiping away sweat with a handkerchief, which he then stuffed into the breast pocket of his jacket.

"Help me, Abel, don't just stand there," he said with a peremptory gesture, not surprised to see him.

The two of them filled the trunk with canned food, sausages, sacks of potatoes. On the back seat were cases of beer and demijohns of wine wrapped in blankets.

"Don't think badly of me, Ignacio. I'm not seizing all this food, and I won't pay the comrades in the commissary with IOUs, like our heroic revolutionary patrols."

The manager handed Negrín a long bill, and Negrín went over it with the point of a tiny pencil held between his large fingers. From a wallet held together by a rubber band he took out a handful of banknotes and paid the manager. He was already in the car and had started the motor when he told Ignacio Abel to get in and said good-bye to the commissary manager by holding his arm out the window with his fist clenched, in the same efficient way he'd extend it to signal a turn.

"Do you want me to drop you somewhere, Abel? I'm off to the Sierra to bring some food to the boys in the regiment my son Rómulo enlisted in. It's a disgrace — there are no regular supplies of anything. They send those brave kids to the front and then don't remember to bring them ammunition or food or blankets. If they don't have enough trucks for food and ammunition, how come they're still parading them through Madrid?" Boxed into a space that was too small, Negrín gestured over the wheel as he drove with abrupt accelerations and stops on the narrow streets, carried along by a mixture of indignation and enthusiasm. "So instead of despairing and wasting time by calling and asking the authorities to do something, I decided to take drastic action and do it myself. It's not much, but it's better than nothing, and besides, it keeps me busy. Come to think of it, how about helping me with your car?"

"It was requisitioned, Don Juan. I left it at the mechanic's a few days before all this began and haven't seen it since."

"You've used precisely the right phrase: 'all this.' What are we living through? A war, a revolution, sheer absurdity, a variation on traditional Spanish summer fiestas? 'All this.' We don't even know what name to give it. Did you hear what Juan Ramón Jiménez called it? When he was safe and sound in America, of course. A 'mad tragic fiesta,' that's what Juan Ramón called it. The people's great triumph. But he and Zenobia, just in case, rushed to put some distance between themselves and 'all this.' Do you know they were about to take him for a ride, as we say now? It's a shame how things like this enter our vocabulary."

"They were going to kill Juan Ramón Jiménez? What could they have suspected him of?"

"Suspected? Nothing. He had the same name as somebody else they were looking for, or he resembled him. His good teeth saved him."

"So he bit his way out of it? He's quick-tempered."

"It's no joke. The militiamen were sure of only one detail about the man they were looking for: he had false teeth. When Juan Ramón insisted they had the wrong man, they began to have their doubts. One of them figured they could just pull on his teeth and find out. Now you know that Juan Ramón has the best teeth in all of Madrid. A patrol almost arrested Don Antonio Machado because they thought he looked like a priest. But tell me, how long ago did they arrest your friend? It would be an international disgrace for us if anything happened to him. Yet another one."

"I don't know where to begin looking for him."

"You don't and neither does anybody else. It seemed we were going to abolish the bourgeois state, and now each party and union has its own jail and police force in addition to its own militias. What a great step forward. I suppose our enemies are delighted with us. In the Anarchist militias they vote on whether it's a good idea to attack the enemy, in ours they shoot the few military commanders we have left for sabotage if an offensive fails. The miracle is that in the Sierra we've been able to contain the insurgents, and from the south they haven't reached Madrid yet. And what about the Aragón front? If the brave columns of Catalán Anarchists keep breaking through and crushing the enemy's defenses, how come they never reach Zaragoza? And if every day we're about to take the Alcázar de Toledo, why haven't we taken it yet? From what you tell me, I assume the people who picked up your friend were Communists. They wouldn't have killed him right away, they would've wanted to interrogate him. Didn't he live for a time in the Soviet Union? Go talk to Bergamín, at the Alliance of Anti-Fascist Intellectuals. You know that one way or another he's connected to everybody. Leave me a message at home if you find out anything. As soon as I get back from the Sierra tonight, I'll look with you."

"And where's this Alliance?"

Negrín burst into laughter and made a sharp turn at the corner of the Plaza de Santa Bárbara to head west along the avenues.

"For God's sake, Abel, you don't know anything! The cream of the anti-Fascist intelligentsia has installed itself in the palace of the marquises of Heredia Spinola, one of the best in Madrid. They make war by editing a little newspaper with revolutionary poems, and to rest from their labors they give masquerade balls using the wardrobe of the marquises, who may have fled or died, I don't know which . . . Forgive me for not taking you there, but I'm pulled in the opposite direction, and I would like to reach the Sierra in time for supper."

He hadn't walked so much in Madrid in a long time, not since he was young and conscientiously saved the few céntimos of carfare. Perhaps that was why he remembered the long walk he took from the cemetery after his mother's funeral on what had then been the uninhabited edge of the city; one step after another, just like now, head down, with the solitary determination to get somewhere and be somebody. He'd felt fatigue but also energy, the mad euphoria of oxygen pumped into his brain by the muscular effort and rhythm of his steps; the sensation of being a transient stripped of any resemblance to the people who passed by and never saw him, alone in the world, as he'd been then, walking through a city that was his own but also alien to him, just as he had passed the windows of toy stores or bookstores or clothing stores and stared at things inaccessible to him. As a child he looked with horror at the world around him, a world of death and hunger, the curse of poverty, bare feet in winter, bare heads white with ringworm, bodies crippled, deformed, as if they belonged to another species yet living a few minutes away from his home. With a childish sense of empathy, but also relief, he was just as aware of his similarity to those unfortunate boys at the margins of society as he was of the privilege that saved him from sharing their fate. But he was not aware of how different he was from the others, those who received electric trains, regiments of lead soldiers in brilliantly colored uniforms, toy theaters, magic lanterns: those children he saw playing, watched over by uniformed maids, in the gardens of the Eastern Palace or riding in a cart pulled by a goat wearing a bridle with bells; those who looked at him with a smile of curiosity or disdain when he shared a classroom with them in the Piarist Academy, whispering behind his back that he was a porter's son. Some, in time, he met again in the School of Architecture, and the smile hadn't changed, or it appeared when someone new got wind of the gossip: his mother had been a porter—or even worse, a washer-woman—in the Manzanares (she did that when she was young, long before he was born), his father a construction foreman or a mason or one of those mule drivers who transported rubble from demolitions to garbage dumps. One of Adela's relatives had called him a fugitive from the scaffolding. A fugitive now from he didn't know what or whom, on the sidewalk of the Glorieta de Bilbao where Negrín had dropped him, carried along by circumstances, like so many people in Madrid and in all of Spain, from one side to the other of fractured battlefronts, as unpredictable as chasms in an earthquake, carried down the stairs to the tunnels of the metro by the crowd, rushing to the doors that opened when the train arrived, bodies too close repelled him, jammed together in a hostile silence, everyone afraid, resistant to propaganda, even less believable in this subterranean world than in the open air and light of day. Carried along by forces beyond his control, he still didn't feel that he had any excuse or that his powerlessness gave him an alibi. Always a fugitive deep down, but now more than ever: eager to recover his children even if he had to cross the lines to the other side (the children he'd abandoned on the afternoon of July 19); eager to leave Spain and escape the general disaster or at least the ultimate fate of so many others—Professor Rossman, perhaps, if he didn't find him—as if they were in a sinister lottery. His mind whirled in a monologue accelerated by a sense of feverishness; he was wearing himself out circling around Madrid. He emerged from the metro on the corner of the Bank of Spain, which he'd passed only an hour earlier, the great granite edifice covered up past the gratings by a flood of posters. JOIN THE PEOPLE'S GLORIOUS AND INVINCIBLE BATALLION AND IT WILL CARRY YOU TO VICTORY! Silhouettes of tall Soviet blast furnaces, hammers and sickles, a fist crushing a plane adorned with a swastika, an army officer wearing gold braid, a Falangist with the mouth of an ogre. WORKER! BY JOINING THE COLUMN OF IRON YOU STRENGTHEN THE REVO-LUTION. Around the entrance to the metro swarmed a crowd of beg-gars, peddlers of lottery tickets and cigarettes and lighter flints, of revo-lutionary color pictures mixed with the old religious ones, of postcards and rumpled pornographic magazines, barefoot boys hawking the first afternoon papers with the usual report of the imminent capture of the Alcázar de Toledo. TO ATTACK IS TO CONQUER! EVERYONE TO THE ATTACK LIKE A SINGLE BODY! WITH OUR BLOOD WE WILL WRITE THE MOST SUBLIME PAGE IN THE GLORIOUS HISTORY OF MA-DRID! Among the people strolling that afternoon through the gardens and sitting at café tables beneath the plantain trees, he recognized the proud back and neck of his brother-in-law Víctor. Instead of crossing the street where Negrín had told him he'd find the Alliance of Anti-Fascist Intellectuals, he rushed to catch up with Víctor, who had turned his head to one side, as if he'd sensed someone following him. With his skin tanned and a beard of several days, Víctor was hard to recognize.

"You gave me a fright, brother-in-law. Keep walking. What's going on?"

"What are you still doing in Madrid?"

"What about you?"

"I'm looking for a friend."

"Walk faster. Aren't you going to denounce me?"

"I thought you would have left."

"It's not worth it anymore. Our forces will be here soon. And those of us still here have a great deal to do."

"What a fool you are. You could hide."

"It's what I'm doing right now, if you don't get in the way. In the light of day and among people, I'm in no danger. You wouldn't want me to hide like a rabbit in his burrow, waiting for them to hunt me down."

"Do you have any news of the family?"

"Don't stop, damn it, keep walking! Don't look to the side. A patrol is on the corner asking for papers."

"Do you have any?"

"I'm sure you do, now that your side's in charge."

Out of the corner of his eye Ignacio Abel saw the militiamen at the end of the path. Turning around now would be dangerous for Víctor. Perhaps if they continued walking and he showed his credentials, they wouldn't suspect his companion. A rowdy group of children surrounded a peanut vendor's cart pulled by a little donkey. From a small brass pipe wafted the delicious aroma of freshly roasted peanuts. The vendor advertised his merchandise by singing outlandish rhymes as he mixed the contents of the portable oven with a small scoop or filled narrow cones of wrapping paper. One of the militiamen held a rifle horizontally. The other examined the documents of a couple with their arms entwined. The smoke from the peanut cart drifted into Ignacio Abel's face when he took out his wallet. He closed his eyes, and when he opened them Víctor was no longer beside him.

"The revolution is a necessary surgery," Bergamín said to him, his palms held together before his lean, closely shaven face, in a gloomy office with collections of weapons and leather-bound books on shelves of dark wood, where, when the door was closed, you could barely hear the noise of typewriters and voices in other offices and the constant rhythm of the printing presses.

I see the address on a map and walk up a narrow street behind Cibeles, Marqués de Duero, until I find number 7: a gate, a brick building with a Mudéjar-style roof, an iron-and-glass marquee over the entrance stairway, where Ignacio Abel walked in and saw, in the midst of a throng of busy people loading bundles of newspapers onto a truck, a fair-haired, smiling man with a fleshy face that looked familiar, though he couldn't quite identify it, perhaps because he was dressed as a militiaman, in a spotless blue coverall and gleaming leather straps, a camera hanging from his shoulder instead of a rifle. When he got closer he realized it was the poet Alberti, whose eyes rested for a moment on him, alternately acute and absent, perhaps because Alberti knew vaguely who he was but didn't consider it essential to greet him. He asked for Bergamín, saying he'd come on behalf of Bergamín's brother the architect, and a short female secretary wearing a belt with a pistol in a leather holster led him to an office. Bergamín did remember him: in recent years he'd published some of Ignacio Abel's articles in *Cruz y Raya*. I can almost see him, as if I myself had sat down in front of him and cleared my throat and swallowed before I stated, assessing the right tone, the reason for my visit: the methodical men who took away Professor Rossman after searching his room. Bergamín is thinner, more emaciated than ever, his nose more pointed, the tip damp and red from a cold that forced him to blow it from time to time, his eyes smaller beneath thick eyebrows, his voice weak, nasal, his black hair straight, parted down the middle.

". . . the cut, of necessity, has to be bloody," he says and inhales, "but what counts is not the spilled blood in and of itself but the smoothness of the operation. There is always more than enough blood, as our enemies take care to remind us, and they have no misgivings about spilling it. You've heard about the rivers of blood flowing where they've won—in Sevilla, in Granada, in Badajoz. The moral scruples that paralyze us don't exist for them. So what should concern us at this glorious and tragic moment is not the volume of blood being spilled on account of the revolution but its success, and on this point it definitely is possible to have doubts. The Spanish people are behaving with an instinct for justice appropriate to the spirit of the race, but also with an anarchy that is equally atavistic and can turn against itself if we don't channel it. What a talent for improvisation, a superior instinct, even in the language. Suddenly there are new words and expressions that seem to have always been there. What genius of farce thought up that verbal marvel of 'taking for a ride'? Or 'to lance someone'—the bottomless quarry of bullfighting speech that's at the very heart of what is irreducibly Spanish. Don't make a face. I lament the excesses as much as you do, but how trivial they are compared to the great good sense of the people's instinctive heroism, and in any case we weren't the ones who started this war, it's just that the weight of the blood falls on the accomplices of those who provoked it. Don't be shocked at the blood or the flames. It was necessary. Obligatory. Defense, not injury, on our part. I remember the article in which you celebrated the marvelous capacity of popular Spanish architecture to adapt. Isn't the same thing happening now? The Spanish people, accustomed to scarcity, make do with what's at hand. The disloyal army rebels? The people rise up in militias and guerrilla groups, just as they did in 1808 against the French, with the same instinct that had been dormant for more than a century, and they take what they find at hand, make the most ordinary thing epic, the proletarian blue coverall transformed into a new uniform, one without the negative connotation of a military uniform. That's why I wanted to name our magazine *The Blue Coverall.* Isn't that better than the name Neruda gave his, *Green Horse*? A green horse, if you stop to think about it, is foolishness. The blue coverall is serious. It would be a good idea, come to think of it, if you'd write something for us. It isn't a good idea to go around asking about a suspect when you're not adding anything to the cause, you know, when it isn't obvious you're as committed to the struggle. The time of pure intellectuals has passed, if in fact it ever existed. Look at the public shame of Ortega, of Marañón, of Baroja, of the miserable felon that Don Miguel de Unamuno turned out to be. I suppose you've heard what they did to poor Lorca in Granada."

"I heard but couldn't believe it. You hear so many things that sound true and then turn out to be rumors."

"I see you still have doubts. You suspect our propaganda is overdone and our enemies not as savage as we claim. You retain the humanist scruple about not drawing a definitive line between them and us. You don't accept that we're right and all the savagery is theirs. The man who seemed to be above it all howls in Salamanca against the Republic as he licks the spurs of the military and the rings of the bishops, who for him are now the defenders of Christian civilization. Look at what they do when they enter towns in Extremadura, how they behave. The servants of the nation hunt down their compatriots the way the Italians hunted down Negroes in Abyssinia. They're not after military victory but extermination. And we're to be remorseful because the people, in their own defense, take justice into their own hands?"

"My friend hasn't done anything. They took him away because they can take anybody away. I don't think that's justice."

"If he's innocent, and for me your word is guarantee, you can be sure they'll release him."

"Do you know where I can find him?"

Bergamín remained pensive, his elbows on the large mahogany desk, his eyes half closed.

"Are you absolutely sure your friend hasn't called attention to himself in any way? Is it possible he had contact with the German embassy?"

"He had to leave the country when Hitler came to power. If they didn't put him in prison, it was because he had earned the Iron Cross in the war."

"He was a man of clear anti-Fascist sympathies?"

"Why do you say 'was'?"

"A manner of speaking. Anything specific about the car they took him away in?"

"Nothing. They didn't show his daughter any credentials, either."

"In these times, who thinks about credentials? You don't realize the urgency of the struggle. We can't allow our enemies to escape us in the name of some outdated legality."

"Professor Rossman isn't an enemy."

"If he isn't, why have they detained him?"

Ignacio Abel swallowed, shifted uncomfortably in the chair with its faux-medieval filigree, in the office of noble woods and weapons displays that would have impressed his father-in-law.

"Because they detain anybody. They go around in requisitioned cars, imagining they're gangsters in a movie, and the names they've given themselves—Eagles of the Republic, Dawn Patrol, Red Justice. Don't tell me that's any way to do things, Bergamín. No police, no Assault Guards? They stop you on the street, they put a rifle to your chest, and sometimes they can't even read the name on the card."

"Do you consider yourself superior to a soldier of the people because you had the privilege of being taught to read and write? It's the people who impose their law now, and we, people like you and me, have the option of joining them or disappearing along with the class into which we were born. The people are so generous in their victory that they are giving us a possibility of redemption as radical as the one Jesus Christ brought in his day."

"What victory? Each day that passes, the enemy is closer to Madrid."

He wanted to add: I wasn't born into the same class as you; your father was a minister in King Alfonso XIII's court and mine a construction foreman; you were born in a big house on the Plaza de la Independencia and I in a porter's apartment on Calle Toledo. But he said nothing. He swallowed again, sat erect in the carved chair, the knot of his tie pressing against his neck. Bergamín wiped his nose, rubbed his hands together gently, looked at Ignacio Abel for a moment over the baroque expanse of his desk, with its leather cover and pseudo-antique writing materials—false inkwells and silver pens and letter openers shaped like Toledan daggers—and piles of proofs under the title *The Blue Coverall*. He spoke as if he were reciting one of the lead articles he dictated each day to a secretary, pacing from one side of the office to the other, pleased by the creak of his leather boots, sometimes pausing, lost in thought, beside the leaded-glass window that overlooked the palace courtyard.

"I respect you, Abel. I like the articles you've written for us, and my brother has spoken highly of your work and assured me you're an absolute Republican. But don't place your trust in that. Nowadays there's no room for the niceties and finickiness of the old bourgeois politics with its tepidities and legalisms. It wasn't the people who set the bonfire in which all of Spain is burning today, but it will be the people who emerge triumphant from this battle and will dictate the terms of victory. There's no place for defeatists, no coddling of the lukewarm. Are errors and excesses committed? Of course. They're inevitable.

They were committed in the French Revolution and in the Russian. When a great river overflows its banks, it carries away everything in its path. Those great canals and hydroelectric plants being built right now in the Soviet Union can't be made without destroying something. And what sacrifices won't be necessary to complete the collectivization of agriculture, which we can't dare to imagine here yet. The Republic attempted a modest agrarian reform and look at how the landowners were up in arms about it, along with their usual servants, the military and the priests. It was the blindness of their own egoism that unleashed their ruin. They began to spill blood, and now blood is falling on them. Think of the passage in the Bible: 'His blood be on us, and on our children.'"

"But you don't achieve justice by killing innocents."

"You're speaking to me about a legalistic justice of individual innocence and blame. But the forces of history act on a much larger scale, that of the great class struggle. In nature, individuals don't count, only species. You or I are nothing in isolation, and our personal destiny signifies little unless we join one of the great currents colliding now in Spain. What were we all doing before April of '31, each absorbed in his own affairs, elaborating chimeras, imagining we were conspiring against the king? Added to the force of the people on April 14, we became part of the flood that overthrew the monarchy. We're either the people or we're nothing, the remains of a species destined to perish . . ."

The telephone rang. Bergamín turned to answer it, nodding as he listened, covering his mouth when he spoke. He hung up and seemed to have difficulty remembering who was sitting across from him. He stood, thin, awkward in an aviator's leather jacket, incongruous in the office in the late August heat.

"Will you help me find Professor Rossman?"

"Don't worry. If your friend hasn't done anything wrong, he'll show up eventually. I'm not the one to do it, but I give you my word."

Bergamín must have rung a bell under his desk, because the uniformed secretary with the pistol at her waist appeared at the door.

"Abel," said Bergamín, not raising his voice, still standing, his thin hands resting on the desk. "Come back soon. We can't do without men like you. You must help us save the artistic patrimony of the Spanish people. Those savages are destroying it ruthlessly. Besides, the way things are right now, it would be to your advantage to make it obvious where your loyalties lie."

30

PERHAPS HE WAS ALREADY dead while I was listening to Bergamín, he thinks now, remembering the somewhat high-pitched, monotonous voice in a half-light of leaded glass, remembering the long clammy hand, the hand of a man susceptible to the cold, awkward in his aviator's leather jacket, who looked into his eyes for a moment and then lowered his gaze to continue talking while his thin fingers played with a letter opener shaped like a Toledan sword which must have been expropriated from the evicted owners of the palace. Perhaps Professor Rossman was already dead or waiting to be killed in a basement or the damp wine cellar of one of those palaces converted into prisons or barracks for the militias, or into places of execution, and I might have arrived in time to save him if I'd been more astute or more aggressive or hadn't been discouraged from continuing the search or trusted so uselessly in Bergamín's help or had been more insistent with Negrín, who managed to save so many people, including his own brother, a friar he helped escape to France—"and not without difficulty," Negrín had told him, "as if the poor man were a conspirator or a fifth columnist, my brother, who hadn't left his convent in twenty years." He had to wait, Bergamín said to Ignacio Abel, looking into his eyes for a moment from the cavern of his own, shadowed by heavy eyebrows, but he didn't accompany him to the door of the pseudo-Gothic, pseudo-Mudéjar office; he had to have confidence, not believe the lies of enemy propaganda that had filled foreign newspapers with reports of crimes and excesses committed in our territory, with doctored photographs of churches being desecrated and militiamen pointing their rifles at innocent priests, as if they were the martyrs of a new persecution of Christianity, they who'd been the first to betray the evangelical message and encourage and bless the spilling of innocent blood, said Bergamín. He raised his voice slightly, but not too much because he was hoarse, to give instructions to his secretary: "Mariana, take Comrade Abel's address and phone number, and connect me right away with the director general of security." He smiled a feeble smile from the other side of the enormous desk, carved, Abel noticed, with the depraved self-indulgence of rich Spaniards, with the brutal Spanish display of money, then raised his handkerchief again to his nose, as thin as a bird's beak, sneezing behind the closed door while Ignacio Abel gave his phone number and address to the secretary, an attractive young woman possessed of a severe beauty, light eyes, and short hair combed back with a part. Perhaps he'd met her before and didn't remember; perhaps her militiawoman's trousers and shirt and the pistol at her waist made her a stranger to him. "Ask for me when you call. Mariana Ríos. I'll write down my number for you. Though you know you can't always get a connection." He must have taken a wrong turn when he looked for the exit and found himself crossing a large hall with aristocratic coats of arms and standards on the walls, an enormous fireplace with medieval pretensions, probably authentic suits of armor in the corners, some with militiamen's caps placed at a slant over the helmets. On a long dining table pushed against the wall and transformed into a stage, a small band rehearsed a burlesque waltz with syncopated trills on the saxophone and trumpet and rolls on the drum. Young workers carried in large trunks and left them open on the parquet floor, exchanging jokes and cigarettes with the girls kneeling in front of them, who with preening gestures pulled out evening gowns, old dress uniforms, tailcoats, hats with ostrich feathers. A militiaman marched up and down carrying a halberd on his shoulder and wearing a diplomat's three-cornered hat pulled down to his eyebrows, a lit cigarette in his mouth. The band began to play a foxtrot, and two of the girls went up onstage, keeping time with a loud stamping of their heels that resonated in the coffered ceiling, one of them wearing a tiara of feathers and fake diamonds above her small round face. A clatter of typewriters came from somewhere, a powerful cadence of Linotypes working. The smell of ink mixed with the odor of camphor and dust from the clothing recently exhumed from the large trunks, which had gilt fittings and labels from international hotels and ocean liners. The hall was cluttered with mountains of books, paintings leaning against the walls, piles of recently printed newspapers and posters. With a hammer and chisel a militiaman forced open the doors of an armoire, and out tumbled an avalanche of footwear, men's, women's, patent leather, satin, shoes, boots, mules, everything in perfect condition, spilling onto the floor covered with dust and papers and cigarette butts. In the palace courtyard, in front of the entrance stairway, the poet Alberti pointed his small camera at a group of dignitaries with a foreign air — round glasses, carefully trimmed goatees, looks of irritation or impatience. He asked them to stand closer together, gesturing a great deal, giving instructions in precarious French.

He returned home at dusk after looking in vain for Negrín at the Workers' Cooperative and the Café Lion (where they told him he hadn't come back from the Sierra; someone repeated the rumor that there'd be a new government and Negrín would be appointed minister of something). He opened the door, exhausted, and Señorita Rossman was waiting, as if she hadn't moved since he left her in the morning, sitting on the edge of the chair, the glass of water before her untouched, her hands in her lap, staring into the fading light of the empty dining room, the sounds of the street and the whistles of martins and the crackle of distant gunfire filling the air. He invented hope, vague measures taken in administrative offices that would undoubtedly have a favorable outcome. He offered to accompany Señorita Rossman to the pensión, unless she preferred to spend the night in his apartment, where there were more than enough bedrooms. Señorita Rossman blushed slightly when she said no: thanks to her job, she had a safe-conduct to move freely around Madrid, and there was time to get back before dark.

"Don't worry," said Ignacio Abel, hearing the lack of conviction in his own voice. "It doesn't look like anything serious."

"But do you know where they're holding him?"

He looked at her before responding, seeking the right tone so his negative reply wouldn't sound completely discouraging.

"You know the situation we're in, things are complicated. But your father is not in irresponsible hands. Influential people have assured me that everything possible's being done to find him. Remember—your father has an international reputation."

"So did García Lorca."

"But the other side killed García Lorca. There's a difference."

Señorita Rossman looked at him, offered her strong hand, her rough palm. She left with her head down, took the stairs, passed through the front door, went out to the street, and only then looked up, suspecting she was being followed, hoping to find a streetcar that would take her to the center of the city, a woman alone, a foreigner, conspicuous despite her efforts to keep invisible. And as Ignacio Abel saw her walk away, watching from a balcony (the plants withered, the soil hard in the pots Adela tended so carefully), Professor Rossman perhaps was already dead, on the cement floor of a basement or in a ditch or ravine or beside a wall on the outskirts of Madrid, dead and nameless, with no identification documents in his pockets, only things no one would bother to steal from a corpse: the torn half of a movie ticket, a copper coin caught in an almost inaccessible fold, a book of matches, a small red-and-blue pencil, sharpened at both ends, a stub but still serviceable, the kind used to underline—any of the trivial objects that continued to fascinate Professor Rossman with the humble mystery of their usefulness and form. But he, whose fingers had always been busy, examining by touch what his myopic eyes couldn't, automatically playing with anything on the table or in his pocket, died with his hands tied behind his back with a coarse piece of twine that sank into his swollen, violet-colored skin. How strange to have come to a country to die like this, he must have thought, with the gentle fatalism of those who let themselves be pushed into the back of a truck, then get out on their own and follow their executioners to a wall peppered with bullet holes and bloodstains or to the edge of a ravine, their eyes squinting to avoid the glare of headlights, the faint silhouettes readying their weapons. What must he have seen in those last few seconds: the shadows of the pines in the Casa de Campo, perhaps, the sky covered in stars, a blue-black night in early September, a cool night.

"If your friend hasn't done anything wrong, he'll show up eventually," Bergamín had said in his high-pitched, composed voice. As he rubbed his hands together when he rose to his feet behind the desk in his office, perhaps Professor Rossman had already been dead for several hours. Or was still alive and was killed on the night his daughter arrived at the pensión and locked herself in the room no one had straightened in her absence, and Ignacio Abel closed the balcony door after watching her walk to the corner of Calle O'Donnell. He realized he hadn't eaten anything all day, just a cone of roasted peanuts he'd bought from the vendor on the Paseo de Recoletos after leaving the Alliance of Anti-Fascist Intellectuals. Suddenly he was ravenously hungry. In the kitchen he found a can of sardines in oil and ate them sitting at the table, placing a double sheet of newspaper under the can, dipping pieces of hard bread into the thick oil, scraping the bottom of the can with his fork. There was something primitive in the act of eating alone, in his reluctance to lay a tablecloth and look for a napkin. He wiped his fingers on the stained sheet of newspaper, and on it he left the empty can and the fork with brilliant drops of oil. He paid attention only to his clothes, which the doorman's wife washed and ironed for him once a week. The porter had suggested that once in a while his wife could clean the house, until the situation had been resolved, though it didn't seem as if all this could last much longer, two or three weeks and it would be over, and the señora and the children and the two maids would be back from the other side of the Sierra. But he didn't like the idea of the two of them spying on him, or was simply too embarrassed to let them see the disrepair, the dust, the newspapers strewn everywhere, the dirty sheets on the bed he never made, the bad smell and grime in the kitchen and bathroom. He tried to telephone Negrín, the phone rang and rang, but no one answered. He dialed the number Bergamín's secretary had given him, and when he was about to hang up he heard a woman's voice asking, in a loud voice, who was calling, a clamor of voices and music in the background. Mariana Ríos wasn't there, neither was Comrade Bergamín, best to call again first thing tomorrow morning. He thought about Judith Biely as he sat by his desk, imagining the letters he could write but wouldn't know where to send. Resentful, he sees himself fading from her memory on the very night that Professor Rossman waits in a dark basement or lies dead, anonymous, his body unclaimed. He turned on the radio and an announcer with a sonorous voice proclaimed yet again the reconquest of Aragón and the unstoppable advance of the people's militias toward Zaragoza. He turned down the volume to look for one of the enemy's stations, and on Radio Sevilla a similar though more distant voice, besieged by whistles, announced the heroic resistance of the Alcázar de Toledo against whose Numantian fortress the waves of Marxist hordes shattered in vain. When all this was over, not only rubble and dead bodies will have to be cleared away, but words as well, a rigorous national abstention from adjectives: unstoppable, uncontainable, imperishable, unpardonable, unavoidable, inflammatory, frenzied, heroic. He heard footsteps and turned off the radio, then the light. Standing motionless in the dark, he heard voices, among them the doorman's. They knocked at a door on the other side of the landing. He tiptoed down the long hallway. The wall clock had stopped, he hadn't wound it in a long time. He reached the door and pressed his face to the peephole but saw no light on the landing, heard nothing. Beyond the shutters, Calle Príncipe de Vergara and Madrid's roofed horizon were an impenetrable darkness, full of terrors, like the forests in the stories he read to his children when they were little. Flashes of headlights, sirens. In the silence, someone's footsteps, a conversation, the click of a cigarette lighter. He threw himself onto the unmade bed without taking off his clothes or shoes, fell asleep, then woke with a filthy aftertaste of sardines in oil, his heart pounding in his chest. The bed, the lamp on the night table, the entire house shook, and for a moment he had no idea where that prolonged crash of thunder came from. Then, the sirens: enemy planes flying low and leisurely bombing targets in a city with no antiaircraft defenses except for rifles and pistols firing from rooftops at the German Junkers. Motionless, on his back, with lethargy stronger than fear, he felt the ground vibrate less and less as the sound of the planes' engines faded away. They bomb poor neighborhoods, not this one. They know many people here are on their side. And what an air force we have, only some French discards from the Great War, no powerful alarms that can actually shake the air but pitiful sirens, which some Assault Guards have mounted on their motorcycles and turn with one hand while they hold on to the handlebars with the other. The whistle and roar of the bombs, a long silence, broken by ambulance sirens and fire engine bells. When he's still half asleep, an unexpected and vivid memory of Judith begins to take shape, her body tensing, her eyes closed, her heels rubbing against the sheet, her hands guiding his fingers, making him slow down, she moans softly in his ear. In the darkness of the conjugal bedroom, on wrinkled, dirty sheets where there was no trace of Adela's scent, he tried to imagine that it was Judith's hand touching him, that when he masturbated with a brusque, mechanical urge he was invoking her delicate body. But it was useless, a spasm and it was over, leaving him with only a rankling, sterile longing, a feeling of absurdity, almost embarrassment, a fifty-year-old man jerking off in the insomnia of war. It was growing light when he fell asleep, a cold, wet drop on his stomach, filled with remorse for not having gone out in search of Professor Rossman.

He woke thinking it was late, but it was not yet eight o'clock. He took a shower, brushed his teeth, shaved the gray and white stubble of his beard, avoiding his eyes in the mirror. At least there was still running water and he still had clean and pressed clothes in the closet. He'd go back to see Bergamín. He'd ask again at the offices and requisitioned

501

palaces and militia barracks he'd visited the previous day. He'd go to the State Security Office, the Workers' Cooperative, the Academy of Fine Arts, the Europa movie house, the Beatriz movie house—he'd been told that since the basements were full, they held some prisoners, their hands tied, in theaters. He was adjusting his tie in front of the mirror in the entrance hall when the telephone rang. It was Señorita Rossman, begging his pardon for calling so early, silent for a moment when he told her he still had no information, but she shouldn't worry, he was about to leave the house to continue the search. He called the number for Bergamín's secretary, but no one answered. The urgency of war didn't change office hours. He remembered a poster in the metro: EVERYONE TO THE FRONT! DEATH BEFORE RETREAT! THE RED BULLETS REGIMENT CALLS ON YOU! (*Registration from 9 to 1 and from 4 to 7.*) Not even for Death Before Retreat were administrative hours expanded. He went for breakfast to a nearby dairy store on Calle Don Ramón de la Cruz. It looked closed. He knocked on the metal blinds and the owner, who knew him, let him in, looking up and down the street, then closing the blinds again. In his old life, the owner would come up the service stairs early each morning carrying the milk and butter his children liked best, and in the summer he sold delicious meringue ice cream. The counter and walls preserved their usual white brilliance, but a calendar with the Virgin of Almudena, and a framed print of the Christ of Medinaceli, had disappeared from the walls. "I open up for you because I know and trust you, Don Ignacio, but tell me what I should do if one of those patrols with muskets shows up and requisitions several days' worth of stock. They take a hundred-liter can of milk they say is for militiamen at the front or for orphaned children and pay me with a voucher on a scrap of paper, and you tell me what good that is to me, or they raise their fists and boom: *UHP! Unite, brothers of the proletariat!* They say they're all proletarian brothers, and what am I, a bourgeois? Haven't I been getting up at four in the morning every day since before my head reached the counter? He who doesn't work doesn't eat, they always say. And if they take what's mine away from me, what am I to eat while I work myself to death? And what work are they doing if they are not at the front? What committee or what International Red Aid will feed my children if I have to close the store because they steal everything from me, or if it occurs to them one morning to collectivize my business, or pronounce me an insurgent, and I end up filled with bullets at a cemetery wall in Almudena or on the San Isidro meadow or wherever it is they kill people? Excuse me for letting off steam, Don Ignacio, but you're a decent man, and if I stay here all day without talking to anybody, I think my head will explode. How much longer do you think all this can go on? Because if things don't get better soon, in a few days I won't have any milk or coffee left, and the reserves of sugar are running out. Wouldn't you like another coffee, on the house?" The shop owner was a fat, gentle man with a soft double chin, as if nourished by the same excellent butter and thick cream he was proud to sell to his distinguished clientele, almost all gone now, fled or in hiding, and some turned out of their houses after midnight and executed not far away, on some empty lot. He spoke to Ignacio Abel and at the same time was attentive to the cup of coffee and the expression with which this rare patron, who hadn't left Madrid and didn't seem frightened, sipped it, and every few seconds his restless eyes went to the partly open door when he heard footsteps or the sound of a car engine on the street. The jolly merchant who ceremoniously greeted the señoras of the neighborhood and knew the names of all the maids now crouched in the store he had refused to abandon or close, the redoubt with the white counter and tiles into which he'd put the effort of a lifetime, the inhuman small hours of the morning, the céntimo-by-céntimo saving, the servility toward ladies and gentlemen who insisted on being called Don or Doña or Señora de and Señora Marquesa and yet sometimes didn't pay their dairy bills; and now, without understanding why, he who'd never been political had to live in fear, he said, lowering his voice, in fear that somebody would come and take away his life's work or shoot him. Then his eyes filled with fear as it dawned on him that his trust in Ignacio Abel was without foundation. Well-known, respectable-looking neighbors were not above accusing others if it meant saving themselves or staying in the good graces of a gang of killers. Besides, how could a man of his rank still live so comfortably in this neighborhood without being in cahoots with those killers? The same affable expression was on his face but now doubt had passed like a shadow across his eyes, and they became evasive as he charged Ignacio Abel for the coffee and thanked him for the tip. One had to look closely to read fear, because everyone knew that showing it openly could be interpreted as a sign as clear as buying batteries of a certain size to tune in enemy stations, or slipping, early on a Sunday morning, into the side door of a church, not yet converted into a garage or warehouse, where Masses were still being said.

But fear also had a subtle hue on the faces of those who felt relatively safe: the doorman, for instance, proud in his blue coverall and leather straps and raising his fist when parades passed by, remembered defending, among a group of deliverymen and maids from the neighborhood, what he called the forces of order and celebrating the Foreign Legion's victory against the rebellious Asturian miners in 1934. Somebody else might also remember. Ignacio Abel saw a familiar face approaching (perhaps a neighbor, making a clumsy attempt to hide his bourgeois status, unshaven, without a tie, wearing a beret instead of a hat), saw the fear in those eyes as they evaded him. He couldn't see it in his own face but felt its effect and imagined that same look, unfamiliar and frightened, persisting in an impossible pretense when an armed patrol came toward him, or a car stopped abruptly beside him, or at night when footsteps raced up the marble stairs of his overly opulent building. But who would acknowledge the terror, even in secret, deep down inside, each with his share of the great universal, unnamed fear one learned to hide in the light of day but unraveled when night fell and the streets emptied.

He walked along the street on the second day of his search for Professor Rossman, and in every face he recognized a different gradation of fear, more obvious the more it was hidden, the more it was wrapped in euphoria, lightheartedness, or feigned indifference. He saw fear in the families of fleeing campesinos who walked along Calle Toledo; he saw it in people coming out of the metro, getting off a streetcar at the last stop, at the empty lots where he began to look that morning for Professor Rossman among the corpses; on the faces of the dead fear had dissolved or hardened into a grotesque grimace. But fear was also in those who went there for the pleasure of walking among the bodies and pointing at postures they found comic or ridiculous, and with a foot turning up a face that had fallen into the dirt. There was fear in their laughter as well as in their silence, in the fatigued indifference of municipal workers who loaded corpses into trucks, and in the meticulousness of the court officials who prepared death certificates and consulted their watches to make a note of the time the bodies were found. *Unidentified male, bullet wounds in the head and chest, perpetrator or perpetrators unknown.* He went to see Bergamín again, but he was not in his office yet, and the secretary, not the one he had met before, knew nothing about measures taken to resolve the disappearance of Professor Rossman, but she made a note just in case, along with Ignacio Abel's address and telephone number. He climbed on a moving streetcar going up the Castellana and got off at the Museum of Natural Sciences and the road to the Student Residence. Was it Negrín who'd told him that the bodies of the executed appeared there too, every morning? "On our playing fields, my dear Abel, against the museum walls, steps from my laboratory, which has been closed for who knows how long."

"I hear them every night from here, close by," said Moreno Villa, aged, thinner, unshaven, looking like a beggar or a martyr in a painting by Ribera.

The Residence was now a barracks for militiamen and Assault Guards. Next to the reception desk was the guardroom, a mass of armed men who came and went with rifles on their shoulders, straw mattresses spread on the floor, smelling like a pigsty, tobacco smoke everywhere, the walls full of posters covered with handwritten slogans, the floor littered with cigarette butts. In the corridor leading to Moreno Villa's room were hospital beds occupied by wounded militiamen; the air reeked of disinfectant and blood. Yellowish, badly shaven faces turned incuriously as he passed, eyes possessed by a kind of fear unlike any other, the somber, hermetic fear of those who have seen death.

"I hear a car driving up the hill, the doors opening and closing, orders, sometimes laughter, as if it were a party. Then bursts of gunfire. By counting them I know how many they've killed. Sometimes they're sloppy or drunk, then it takes longer."

Moreno Villa in his large, ascetic room, the cell of the anchorite he'd become after not seeing anyone for so long or not venturing out for days, not even to the garden at the Residence's entrance, now occupied by Assault Guard trucks and motorcycles. He went out only to go to work at the archives of the National Palace, with the punctuality of a dutiful official who didn't have to be asked. The president of the Republic, who had his office near Moreno Villa's, had suggested that he sleep at the palace. But he preferred to return every evening to the Residence, as incongruous among militiamen and the wounded as he would have been anywhere else in Madrid, in his old-fashioned suit, high shoes, and the bow tie he'd been in the habit of wearing since he came back from the United States, the trip he'd written about in a short, heartfelt book, as all of his were, a book by an author who enjoys some prestige but whom no one reads. He was just as Ignacio Abel had seen him a year earlier, surrounded by books, sitting near the window in front of a small, unfinished still life, perhaps the same one he'd started in late September, in the remote past of less than a year ago.

"By this time they've already taken away the bodies. A municipal crew comes in a slow garbage truck. I recognize it by the sound of the engine. They arrive a little after dawn. If your friend was here last night, he must be in the morgue by now. Rossman was his name, wasn't it? Or still is, poor man, who knows. I remember chatting with him once."

"Last year, in October, he came to my lecture."

"It's strange, isn't it? Remembering anything that happened before all this began. Things happen and they seem inevitable, as if anyone could have predicted them. But who could have told us our Residence would be turned into a barracks? A barracks and also a hospital, a few days ago. Now, aside from the shots at night we have to listen to the moans of those poor boys. You have no idea how they scream, Abel. No medicine, no sedatives, no anesthesia, no nothing. Not even good gauze to control hemorrhages. I leave my room and find puddles of blood on the floor. We didn't know how sticky blood is, how shocking it is, the quantity of blood a human body holds. We thought we were men with experience and judgment, but we were nothing and knew nothing. And the little we knew is ridiculous and serves no purpose. Don José Ortega stayed for a few weeks before he left Spain, like so many others. He was ill. It was painful to see him sitting in a hammock in the sun, an old man, his mouth hanging open, yellow, with that lock of hair he always carefully combed to hide his bald spot. Our great philosopher, the man who had an opinion on everything, silent, looking into the void, dying of fear, just like all of us, or more so, because he was afraid his fame would work against him and he would not be allowed to leave Spain. I don't know if you know that some people came to ask him to sign the manifesto of intellectuals in favor of the Republic. Bergamín, Alberti, someone else, all of them with boots and leather straps, with pistols. But Don José didn't sign. As sick as he was, feverish, scared. They left and he was much worse. I approached him to ask after his health, and he didn't answer."

"And they didn't ask you to sign the manifesto?"

"I'm not famous enough. It's the advantage of being invisible."

"Poor Lorca didn't have it."

"He left Madrid because he was frightened. He took the express after they killed Lieutenant Castillo and Calvo Sotelo, July 13. I spoke with him a few days earlier. He was very frightened."

"I saw him from a taxi. He was sitting on the terrace of a café on Recoletos, in a light suit, smoking a cigarette, as if waiting for someone. I waved to him but I don't think he saw me."

"Now we spend our lives trying to remember the last time we did something or saw a friend. It frightens us to think it was the last time. Before, we would say goodbye as if we were going to live forever. How many times have you and I said goodbye, Abel my friend, or passed each other if we were in a hurry with no more than a tip of the hat. When we say goodbye this time, it's not unlikely we won't ever see each other again."

"It's dangerous for you to be living here alone, so removed from everything. Come to my apartment. I'm there alone. One of the maids stayed with my family in the Sierra and the other disappeared. You'll be safer and we can keep each other company."

"Don't worry about me, Abel my friend. Who'll want to do anything to an old man?"

"You're not that old and you aren't safe. No one is. I saved myself at the last moment almost by accident."

What would happen to Moreno Villa, sedentary and stubborn, determined to live as if the world hadn't collapsed around him, alone in the Residence, wandering the hallways and classrooms where the foreign students who'd left toward the end of July wouldn't return, where the beautiful exotic voices he loved no longer sounded? He spent sleepless nights in the dark, listening to the gunfire, the car engines, the shouting, the laughter.

"Do you know what I've been thinking about a good deal lately, Moreno? An article you published last year about the desire everyone seemed to have to kill his adversary. I thought you were exaggerating."

"I've been thinking about it too. 'I Was Killing Them All' was the title. Then I saw it in *El Sol* and was almost ashamed to have used those words, though it was meant to be ironic. Some words shouldn't be written or pronounced. You say something without conviction or thinking, and once you've said it, it begins to be true."

They said nothing else, uncomfortable in a silence they couldn't break. A bugle sounded from the garden in front of the Residence. On the athletic fields groups of militiamen were training to the beat of a drum.

"And you, Abel, do you plan to leave?"

He took a while to answer. How could Moreno Villa believe that if he was leaving, or trying to, it was because he'd planned the trip long before the war started, because in that earlier time, already as distant as a dream, he'd been invited to spend an academic year at an American university, to give classes and perhaps design a library? Others had already left, taking advantage of privileges, inventing international missions, diseases that required treatment abroad. There were rumors that Ortega himself hadn't really been gravely ill when he left, that at heart he sympathized with the Fascists or was in some way involved with them and feared reprisals. Ignacio Abel's words told the truth but sounded false, even to his own ears; they sounded like the lie of someone who's going to desert and repeats an explanation, an honorable alibi, especially when he heard himself saying that worst of all was not hearing anything from his wife and children on the other side of the front, so close and yet in another country, another world, the antithesis of this one but just as delirious. "I expected to take them with me," he said, knowing it wasn't quite true, knowing the lie contaminated his sorrow over the absence of his children, imagining that perhaps Moreno Villa suspected other reasons, not just his possible cowardice and intention to flee Spain, but also what he'd probably learned or been told in a Madrid so rarefied and filled with gossip, especially because he lived in the Residence and had met Judith, witnessed with the astute eyes of an easily infatuated bachelor the first meetings between her and Ignacio Abel. Out of vanity or lack of imagination, you convince yourself that others pay attention to every little thing you do. Moreno Villa's sad, questioning eyes troubled Ignacio Abel, they probed his conscience, but as he spoke he noticed in his own voice a tone of imposture or guilt. Moreno Villa was thinking about something else, as much a prisoner of his ruminations and uncertainties as Abel was, just as perturbed by the eruption of all this madness, this bloody world he didn't understand and couldn't escape and couldn't ignore.

He said goodbye, promising he'd come back, and on the shaded side of the hill where the Residence stood like a tower keeping watch over the outskirts of Madrid, he looked for corpses, looked for Dr. Karl Ludwig Rossman. The scent of rockrose, thyme, and rosemary made him think of his children, the garden of the house in the Sierra, the path to the pond. He felt surrounded by death, days and nights haunted by an emptiness more powerful than the proximity of real people. Adela and his two children, their absence more real than his presence in the shadows of the house. And the thought of Judith Biely, invoked by his footsteps on dry grass, Judith coming toward him at nightfall through the grove of trees lit by paper lanterns while dance music from a radio played nearby, Judith still recently and secretly his, Judith seated with a group of foreign students, talking, looking at him with a complicity only he noticed. Behind the solitary dome of the Museum of Natural Sciences ran the irrigation ditch called the Canalillo. When the good weather came, metal tables and chairs were set up there, garlands of café lights hung among the tree branches. On the wall of the café kiosk, the whitewash was chipped by bullets and stained with blood. There were shoes in the summer's dry undergrowth, widowed shoes that had lost their mates, some women's, some men's, some worn down, and others still with the gleam of a recent shoeshine. He stepped on things that crunched: a shotgun cartridge, eyeglass lenses. He examined the frames but none resembled Professor Rossman's. In that cool morning at the end of August, the cicadas' chirping merged with the sound of running water in the irrigation ditch. Beyond the shade of the Lombardy poplars, the great expanse of Madrid, a city calmed by summer. From the hill of the Residence, not a trace of smoke, not a sign of war.

31

FROM TIME TO TIME he dreams a phone is ringing and he wakes too slowly, misses the call by a few seconds. The rings continue, each one more shrill than the last, and because he doesn't answer it, he won't know who's calling to ask for help, or to warn him of danger, or if it's Judith Biely, and, receiving no answer, she'll assume he's no longer in Madrid and they won't meet again, all because of a few moments' delay. In the dream he wakes: one ring, then another, and his body unresponsive to his will, wood or tiles or a rug under his bare feet, his bewilderment at not remembering where the phone is, then a rush to reach it, his hand stretching out and touching the receiver at the instant the vibration of the final ring dies down. Though her image now escapes his dreams, Judith Biely hovers over them like an oppressive absence, an unconquered void, a knife's edge present in the open wound, a footprint in damp sand. But if he had wakened more quickly and run unhesitatingly to the phone, she would have been there. If his fatigue hadn't been so profound, he'd have reached the phone in time to hear the voice of one of his children: a voice distant, altered by interference but recognizable, a little strange after not hearing it for so long.

In reality the phone call in his dream and the one when he is awake coincided only once. He opened his eyes knowing it had rung many times, and he was lying in the large, unmade bed. His body was heavy, slow, as in the dream. Light filtered through the closed shutters, but the house was so dark it was impossible to estimate the time. The hall seemed to lengthen as he walked down it. He brought the receiver to his ear and asked who was calling. At first he didn't recognize Bergamín's voice, weak and harsh at the same time, nasal.

"Abel, what took you so long? Come to the Alliance as fast as you can. I didn't wake you, did I?"

"Do you know where Professor Rossman is?"

"Come right away. I'm leaving town very soon."

He understands now that there had been fear in Bergamín's voice, hidden behind the urgency, just as it was there later in his small eyes, tearing because of the cold that wet the tip of his nose, irritated by so much wiping with the wrinkled handkerchief he returned to his pocket as if hiding something indecent. Or perhaps not fear exactly but an uneasiness he wouldn't acknowledge, a disquiet because of a danger too varied or subtle to contemplate: the enemy might be advancing toward Madrid more quickly than anyone had foreseen; someone might doubt his orthodox loyalty to the cause in spite of his dedicated work at the Alliance and the articles he wrote blazing with a rage for justice; he might be compromised by having been seen with Ignacio Abel that morning in the courtyard of the Alliance, or making inquiries regarding the whereabouts of his German friend; he might be too late to board the plane at Barajas Airport that would take him to Paris and then on to Geneva to participate in the International Congress for Peace as a representative of Spanish intellectuals. He came out to the staircase of the Heredia Spinola Palace wearing a vaguely English formal suit for travel instead of the open shirt and aviator's leather jacket, and the morning sun made him blink, his eyes sunken beneath his eyebrows, not used to the light, fatigued by so much work in the gloomy office where he spent nights on end writing articles or ballads in his tiny, meticulous hand, correcting galleys of *The Blue Coverall*. After calling Ignacio Abel, he'd sat with both hands in front of his face, his thin fingertips brushing his damp nose. He'd consulted his watch, confirming that the large baroque clock hanging on the wall with the weapons of the marquises of

Heredia Spinola was running slow—weapons repeated in all the palace's decorations, on the backs of chairs and fake-Renaissance carved credenzas, on ceiling frescoes and the chimneys of fireplaces. The plane to Paris was supposed to depart at eleven in the morning; it had the French flag clearly painted on the fuselage, so there was no danger of its being pursued by the enemy. He checked with his secretary that the car to the airport was ready in the courtyard and his briefcase with his passports, visas, and safe-conducts was already inside. With distracted pleasure he looked over the day's newspapers spread out on the enormous desk in his office, with their usual news that at no moment relieved the uneasiness, the disquiet that he shouldn't show even to himself, the fear that insinuated itself in his eyes, the drumming of fingers that reached for a cigarette or a match or counted the syllables of verses. He looked at the clock again and put on the tweed jacket suitable for travel, gathered up papers and put them in his portfolio and his pen in the breast pocket of his jacket, impatient, restless, irritated with Ignacio Abel, who sounded sleepy on the phone, who still hadn't arrived though he'd told him to hurry. "Mariana, I'm leaving. When the architect Abel arrives give him the instructions, tell him how important it is for him to complete the mission he's been entrusted with." In a nearby hall the band was rehearsing for the masquerade ball the poet Alberti and his wife had been organizing for several days to honor the French writers visiting Madrid, taking advantage of the abundance of dress uniforms and carnival outfits in the wardrobes and trunks of the fugitive marquises. Bergamín was happy to miss the party. He avoided the collective festivities that Alberti and María Teresa León enjoyed so much, just as they relished poetry readings and speeches at the end of banquets honoring someone or other. Alberti had the slick profile of a film star; his wife, blond and buxom, her lips painted bright red, would put her hands on her hips and sway beside him, as if at any moment she might begin to sing a *jota* instead of reading a proclamation or reciting a war ballad. He heard her now, speaking loudly over the discord of the rehearsing instruments, giving instructions. When Bergamín spoke in public, he placed his lips too close to the microphone and hunched his shoulders instead of thrusting out his chest and lifting his chin; when anthems were sung and he raised his fist, he did so as if contracting rather than clenching it; and he was conscious of his own posture as well as his weak voice when singing "The Internationale." He probably looked ridiculous now as he stepped out onto the palace stairs, his eyes squinting, frail among the militiamen and drivers going back and forth in the courtyard among the trucks that came and went, the workers gingerly moving paintings, sculptures, boxes of books, so many valuable objects rescued from churches in danger of being burned or palaces abandoned, subject to looting after the owners had been detained or executed. *The implacable surgery of the people's justice.* He'd written the sentence himself in his beautiful hand, so tiny it damaged his eyes. He thought of the line when he saw Ignacio Abel coming through the entrance gate, agitated, for once not wearing a tie, afraid Bergamín had left. He'd have preferred not to see Abel. One minute more and he'd have watched him through the window of the car now waiting for him at the foot of the stairs, a gleaming Hispano-Suiza that perhaps had also belonged to the owners of the palace, on which there were no painted slogans but a modern, discreet sign on the doors: ALLIANCE OF ANTI-FASCIST INTELLECTUALS — PRESIDENT'S OFFICE. Ignacio Abel had already seen him. Bergamín signaled that he should follow him into the vestibule, where the leaded stained glass diffused an opalescent light tinted with bright reds, yellows, blues.

"Do you know where they're holding Professor Rossman?"

"Not so loud, Abel, slow down. Slow and steady wins the race, says the Spanish proverb. You're compromising yourself and compromising me as well. It's imprudent to go around asking about someone who sounds a little shady. I have some information, not much. It's not a good idea for either you or your friend to make too much noise about this case."

"They detained him by mistake, I'm sure."

"You can't be sure of anything these days. Our Soviet friends were sure of Bukharin and Kamenev and Zinoviev, and look at the monstrous conspiracies they were plotting and eventually confessed to.

We're facing an enemy without compassion who unfortunately isn't just on the other side of the frontlines. They're active here in Madrid as well. You know what General Varela says on insurgent radio: he has four columns ready to attack Madrid, and a fifth that will conquer the city from within. They're among us and with impunity take advantage of the confusion they themselves created when they rebelled, and the moral scruples and bureaucracy that paralyze us —"

"What are you talking about, Bergamín? A few minutes ago, on my way here, I saw several bodies along the fences of the Retiro. They're loaded into garbage trucks like trash, and people laugh."

"Don't you wonder what they might have done to end up like that? Don't you read the papers, don't you listen to the radio? They believe their people are about to arrive, and they want to make the conquest easier. They shoot from terraces and the bell towers of churches. They speed past barracks in cars and machine-gun the militiamen on duty and whoever is in front. Their planes bomb working-class neighborhoods, and they have no misgivings about women and children dying. I told you the other day and I'll say it again: it wasn't the people who began this war. We can't allow ourselves any weakness or carelessness. We can't trust our own shadows. Do me a favor and do the same. I don't have time to explain too much because I have to be at the airport in half an hour. Risking a great deal and out of consideration for you, I've made inquiries and can assure you your friend is in no imminent danger."

"Tell me where he is, what he's accused of."

"You're asking too much. I don't know."

"At least tell me who's holding him. Is he in a Communist *cheka*?"

"Be careful what you say, Abel. I've been assured he was detained because of an accusation that seemed well founded but turned out to be not too serious. The normal thing would be for them to let him go tomorrow or the day after. Maybe today, who knows? Our side doesn't act as blindly as you imagine, man of little faith."

"Tell me where to go and I'll make a statement in his favor. Negrín is also prepared to answer for him."

"Negrín has just been named minister in the new government . . . Didn't you listen to the radio this morning?"

"I'll call Professor Rossman's daughter. She hasn't slept in two nights."

"You're not going anywhere, Abel, only where I tell you to. They called me this morning from the Committee for the Restoration of the Artistic Patrimony asking for a favor, and I thought of you. They're swamped with work, as you can imagine."

"They wouldn't be if they hadn't burned so many churches."

"You always blame everything on our side, Abel. You see only our errors."

"The entire world sees them."

"The entire world sees what it wants to see!" Bergamín's voice grew shrill. "They have eyes and do not see, ears and do not hear, says Scripture. The entire world refuses to acknowledge that it was the insurgent planes that bombed the palace of the duke of Alba, and the people's militias who risked their lives rushing into the fire and rubble to save artistic treasures that a family of landowning parasites has been usurping for centuries."

Bergamín looked at his watch. He was uncomfortable and in a hurry. His pale face tinged by the colors of the stained glass, he watched the flow of people between the great staircase and the courtyard and grew uneasy when he saw André Malraux, who would accompany him on his flight.

"Speaking of treasures, you've probably heard about the retable on the main altar of the Capilla de la Caridad in Illescas. It has no less than four paintings by El Greco. The Committee asked for our help in rescuing it."

"The enemy has already reached Illescas?"

"Don't be alarmed, Abel. Someone will hear you and think you're a defeatist."

"If it's not one thing it's another. It's obvious I don't strike you the right way, Bergamín."

"Don't get angry. I'm alarmed by your political naïveté and would like to make you more aware or at least protect you. As you know, the militias are forcing the enemy to retreat on all fronts, including Talavera. If the Fascists haven't been able to take Talavera with forces much larger and better armed than ours, how will they approach Illescas, which is much closer to Madrid? This is a different problem. We've been told that in Illescas those rather wild-eyed boys from the Iberian Anarchist Federation have seized power and decided to proclaim Anarchist communism. For the moment they've eliminated private property and money and converted the Capilla de la Caridad into a warehouse for collectivized foodstuffs. A Socialist councilman managed to call the Committee for the Patrimony yesterday from the only phone in the village. In the commune they're debating what to do with the altarpiece — sell it and collect funds to buy weapons, which is the position of the more moderate members, or burn it in a bonfire in the middle of the town square. Don't look at me like that, Abel. We can't reproach the people for not appreciating what they haven't been taught to appreciate. With the help of our friends in the Fifth Regiment, we've prepared a small rescue expedition. Discreet but effective. A few well-armed militiamen were provided with a decree from the National Directorate for Fine Arts authorizing them to remove the El Greco paintings from the retable and store them temporarily in the basement of the Bank of Spain, which is what we've been doing with many other endangered works of art. You're the person chosen to direct the operation. Don't protest. I've told you on various occasions: make yourself visible, make yourself useful. Make your loyalty to the Republic known with actions and not just words. Though words are also a good idea. Why didn't you sign the intellectuals' manifesto of loyalty to the regime?"

"No one asked me to."

"Everything has a solution. Write something for the next issue of *The Blue Coverall*. A few pages on whatever subject you like, architecture in the new society, or something along the lines of what you gave me for *Cruz y Raya* that everybody liked so much. The masters of popular architecture, as anonymous as the authors of the old ballads. And please leave right away for Illescas, an Alliance truck will be waiting at the corner of Recoletos. Time is of the essence, Abel."

"Give me your word that nothing will happen to Professor Rossman."

"I can't promise anything. I'm not in charge. Do as I advise and no promise will be needed. If you hurry, you can be back with the paintings this afternoon. Ask Mariana. She is in charge. She'll have a message for you."

This time Bergamín didn't offer his hand when he said goodbye. He saw a tall man with an arrogant profile going down the stairs in a leather jacket, breeches, and riding boots, and in a hurry to meet him Bergamín forgot about Ignacio Abel, but not without first telling him who the man was.

"There's Malraux."

Why had he foolishly allowed himself to be persuaded, taking Bergamín at his word? Why, instead of climbing into the truck that would take him to an uncertain and probably dangerous destination, didn't he leave the Alliance and keep looking for Professor Rossman, who might still have been alive that morning? The militiamen taking the sun at the entrance, sitting in wing chairs removed from the palace — smoking, chatting on the sunny sidewalk, their rifles across their laps — wouldn't have done anything to stop him. Problems have a solution for a certain period of time, almost always brief, and then they are irreparable. He went into the courtyard and a militiaman told him the truck was ready, its motor running, the men prepared. Bergamín's secretary came down the marble staircase, heels clicking, to give him a folder with documents whose contents she reviewed quickly with him, not giving him time to ask questions. How strange to have lost so easily the almost arrogant feeling of control that had become a character trait when he made decisions and gave orders at the construction sites in University City. The band was playing somewhere, he could hear the Linotype machines at work, orders and shouts around him, raucous engines and horns in the courtyard, boot heels pounding, weapons firing. In the rooms where only two months earlier liveried servants and maids in black uniforms and white caps went about their work, a disorderly crowd swarmed: unshaven men in blue coveralls, rifles over their shoulders, and women in militia caps, pistols at their waists. The war was a state of improvisation and urgency, a reckless, convulsive theatricality in which he was caught up, knowing that he shouldn't allow himself to be persuaded, that he lacked the courage or simple adroitness to resist. He remained motionless, like an animal caught in the headlights. When he did nothing, the danger increased; if he did something, it was futile, wrong, and he knew it, but he couldn't overcome his own incompetence. In one of the improvised jails in Madrid, in a dark basement where prisoners crammed together could barely see one another's faces, Professor Rossman might be waiting for a door to open and someone to say his name, aware that in all of Madrid Ignacio Abel was the only one who could save him. That morning he should have turned again to Negrín, even more influential and activist, just named a minister. Through large open doors came the sound of the bugle that announced war dispatches on the radio, and people came from all directions to gather around a radio as ostentatious as the palace's carved doors, desks, and credenzas. Militiamen, clerks, workers, musicians who interrupted their rehearsal, girls dressed in eighteenth-century ball gowns and wigs. Beside Ignacio Abel stood Bergamín's attentive secretary. The first solemn, blaring measures of the Republican anthem sounded, and the voice of the announcer declaimed: "Attention, Spaniards! The victory government has been formed!" Applause rang out each time the name of one of the new ministers, Socialists and Communists now, was announced, but almost none when the name of Juan Negrín López, minister of finance, came up. Silence was restored with difficulty, and the rhetorical voice announced a speech from the new prime minister, Don Francisco Largo Caballero. As had happened so often in his life, Ignacio Abel found himself surrounded by a fervor he would have liked to share, yet it merely accentuated his feeling of distance, his sense of being an outsider. How strange that on those young faces, Largo Caballero's unpolished oratory, his way of speaking in front of a microphone — an old man, disconcerted by modern inventions—should awaken unanimous attention and enthusiasm. The unbreakable unity of all the organizations in the Popular Front guaranteed the imminent defeat of the Fascist aggressors. The enemy retreated on all fronts, desperately trying to resist fierce attacks by the workers' heroic militias. The Spanish people would expel the Moorish mercenaries and the invaders sent by German Nazis and Italian Fascists, just as it had expelled Napoleon's armies in the War of Independence. To each "*Viva*" pronounced by Largo Caballero, the people grouped around the radio responded with a "*Viva*" that resounded in the hall. They stood up and raised their fists and sang "The Internationale," played by the band. Ignacio Abel raised his fist too, with an involuntary yet true emotion awakened by the music and the beautiful words learned as a child at the Socialist meetings his father took him to: *Arise, you prisoners of starvation! Arise, you wretched of the earth!* They think the revolution is now reality, that they've triumphed just because they occupy the palaces of Madrid and march in parades with bands and red flags. They're intoxicated by words and anthems, as if they were breathing air too rich in oxygen and didn't know it. But perhaps it was he who was mistaken, his lack of fervor proof not of lucidity but the mean-spirited hardening of age, favored by privilege and his fear of losing it.

He left the Alliance, obeying the militiaman's brusque orders when he should have gone to find Negrín, who must have been in the office of the prime minister at the foot of the Castellana, so close he could have walked there in less than fifteen minutes. Nothing could shock Negrín. In exceptional circumstances he unleashed, knowledgeably and without hesitation, his formidable capacity for action. Too late now: they were beside the small truck, its motor running, and the militiaman who'd accompanied him jumped in the back where his comrades were, sitting in the shade of the canvas, laughing as they passed around a *bota* of wine, perched on gasoline drums and lighting cigarettes. War was a job for the young. Older people who took part did so with the cold sordidness of propagandists, or were themselves caught up in a delirium of imbecilic rhetoric and monstrous vanity. The driver waited in front, younger than the rest, bareheaded, with an overgrown boy's round face, round glasses, and curly hair flattened by combing it back with pomade. The war was an obscene slaughterhouse of defenseless people and very young men. Dressed in bizarre military fashion — officer's shoes, worker's trousers, peasant's jacket, leather straps, a pistol — the driver seemed a recruit destined for the battalion of the dimwitted.

"Don Ignacio, don't you remember me?"

In the young face he could see enduring signs of a childhood that had been familiar to him. The driver blushed as he smiled.

"Miguel Gómez, Don Ignacio. Eutimio's son, the foreman at the School of Medicine . . ."

"The Communist?"

"Did my father tell you that? With the Unified Young Socialists, for now."

"Miguelito . . ."

Ignacio Abel put both hands on his shoulders, resisting the temptation to pull him close, as he would have done not many years before. He must be twenty-one now, twenty-two at most, but he was still chubby and hadn't grown much. Only his eyes had the intensity of an adult, anguished life, fevers fed by reading until the small hours of the morning, debilitating arguments about philosophy and politics. "My kid's turned out to be a reader on me, like you turned out on your father, may he rest in peace," Eutimio once told him. That the boy had the same name as his own father and son caused a rush of tenderness in Ignacio Abel: he'd been the boy's godfather, and Eutimio had asked his permission to name him after the elder Miguel. He recognized him fully when he saw him climb awkwardly into the driver's seat, the pistol's holster catching on the door handle. This Miguel had been a late child, the last of Eutimio's five or six, weak when he was little, and several times it seemed he might die of a fever or develop lung disease. He started driving the truck with an abrupt acceleration that provoked laughter and falls in the rear, intimidated perhaps by Ignacio Abel, who'd been a mysterious presence in his childhood, the godfather he was sometimes taken to visit in a building with an elevator and marble stairs that seemed immense to him, though he and his father didn't walk on them or take the elevator, they climbed up the narrow, dark service staircase; the distant protector from whom came toys and books on his saint's day; the man who'd intervened when he was a little older so that instead of going to work as an apprentice in construction like his other brothers, he could study for his high school diploma (perhaps Ignacio Abel had used his influence to get the boy enrolled in a good school free of charge, or had taken on the payments without telling anyone). A maid would open the door for Eutimio and Miguel and show them to a room that had a window overlooking an interior courtyard. They waited in silence, Eutimio stiff in a chair, uncomfortable in the boots he seldom wore and that squeaked when he walked and pinched his feet; Miguel's chair was so high his feet barely touched the floor. Just as when he was a child, it was difficult for Miguel to look into his godfather's eyes and speak to him. "Thank Don Ignacio," his father would say. "Nice and loud, we can hardly hear you." He was a careful driver, conscious of Ignacio Abel's presence, afraid of seeming clumsy or making a mistake, his chest over the wheel, his glasses sliding down his nose at each jolt of the truck. The former child was now a man with the beginnings of a beard and had a pistol at his waist and his own convictions. Ignacio Abel liked saying the name aloud, Miguel, like my father who died so many years ago, like my son, whom I don't know when I'll see again, and if I do see him, he'll already have made a huge stride in time that will take him out of childhood and away from me, even more irreversibly than physical distance.

"Your Miguelito must be a man by now."

"He's twelve."

"Hard to believe! You'd bring him and the girl to University City and my father would bring me so I could watch them and play with them. How they fought. Scratching like cats."

"Your father used to take care of me when he worked on my father's crew."

They'd crossed the Toledo Bridge and were driving up the dusty slope of Carabanchel. When they saw the red banner of the Fifth Regiment flying from the cab, the militiamen at the checkpoints moved to one side to let them pass, raising their fists. Groups of men with an air of city people unaccustomed to such tasks were digging trenches that were more like shallow ditches at the sides of the road, their barracks caps pushed back.

"Is it true your father was one of the founders of the Socialist Party?"

"I don't think so. But he joined when he was very young, and the union too. Pablo Iglesias liked him a lot. He once asked him to do a small job in his house."

"My father told me he was at your father's funeral. Do you remember?"

"Pablo Iglesias? Your father has a good imagination. What he did was send my mother a letter that a comrade from the union read aloud at the cemetery. Calle Toledo was filled with people, construction workers from Madrid grouped by trade, directed by the UGT. Neighborhood women gossiping because it was a secular burial. My mother was very religious, but when the priest from San Isidro arrived, she thanked him and said there was no need for him to stay. She'd go alone to pray afterward, but her husband would be buried in the way he would have wanted."

They were silent, hypnotized by the straight highway, the flat, dry landscape, dazed by the rumble of the engine and the jolting of the truck. They passed farmhouses with large corrals that seemed abandoned, beside wheat fields that had been cut down and fallow fields where autumn plowing hadn't begun yet. Along the low, whitewashed wall of a cemetery a sign in large red brushstrokes stood out in the sun: LONG LIV RUSIA UHP. They approached a checkpoint at a turnoff to a dirt road that probably led to a village not visible from the highway, watched over by two campesinos in straw hats with shotguns and cartridge belts crossed over their chests. They'd blocked the road with a cart and on each side had placed, like two scarecrows, a crucified Christ with a long head of natural hair blowing in the wind, and a Virgin in elaborate petticoats and skirts. From a distance her crystal tears and silver heart shone in the sun. But the impression of a desert didn't last long: a large truck and a bus filled with militiamen on the way to Toledo pulled ahead of them with a great roar of horns, shouts, and shots in the air, enveloping them in a dense cloud of dust. A little farther on they left behind a slow line of old military vehicles, cars with mattresses tied to the roofs, trucks protected by makeshift sheets of armor. "By the time they get to Toledo, the Alcázar will already have surrendered out of boredom," said Miguel Gómez, not smiling. In the silence the estrangement between them had grown, the distance of the years and of political suspicion; Miguel's concern for his own circumstances, his instinctive gratitude but also resentment toward the man who'd paid for his secondary education and even would have helped him establish a career, if his desire not to go on being grateful hadn't been stronger than his ambition to move up socially. Yet he hadn't escaped a debt he could never repay: studying at night, he became a draftsman and passed his examinations without much effort, but the position he obtained in the drafting office of the Lozoya Canal wouldn't have been his, in spite of his outstanding record, if not for the discreet help of his godfather, whom he hadn't seen for many years. It was his father who provided the rationale: "If rich men's sons get their positions through connections, why shouldn't we let Don Ignacio give you a hand when you're worth more than all of them put together?" Now Miguel was gnawed by the fear that Ignacio Abel might think he'd found easy work on the Committee for the Restoration of the Artistic Patrimony to avoid going to the front, that like so many others he showed off his leather straps and a pistol to disguise a comfortable job behind the lines. "If they'd only let me go to fight," he said, indicating with a motion of his head the convoy they'd left behind. "Not your fault you're nearsighted," said Ignacio Abel. "Your father always attributed it to your love of books." "And besides, I have flat feet," Miguel Gómez muttered, less with resignation than self-mockery, as he tightened his grip on the wheel to take a curve around a bare limestone hill cut by erosion. At least he knew how to drive, he thought as he moved his body forward over the wheel as if to see the road better. He smelled something burning, smoke. Maybe the engine was overheating, the truck was old and had been badly mistreated recently, or he drove erratically, with abrupt braking and acceleration. The smell was not just gasoline; as they passed the hill, the air filled with light mist and the flat landscape spread out before them. Miguel Gómez felt a rumbling, as if deep beneath the earth, like thunder or an underground train, like a mallet hitting an immense drum, very distant and very close, under them and the wheels of the truck, and also vibrating in the air, something neither of them had ever heard before, the booming mixed with the stillness of the countryside and the smell of smoke whose origin they didn't know, gasoline and something else, denser and more oppressive, hot metal, burning tires. One of the militiamen riding in the back of the truck banged on the glass at the back of the cab, saying something they couldn't hear. "We can't be close to the front," said Miguel Gómez, the sweat making his hands slip on the wheel, wetting his back. "They can't have advanced this far." "Could we have taken the wrong road?" asked Ignacio Abel, looking for traffic signs, some indication of the distance that separated them from Toledo, but they saw nothing ahead, no houses, no village. They continued moving, their eyes fixed on the highway that was rising now, limiting their field of vision. The militiaman knocked on the glass with the barrel of his rifle and gestured, but Miguel Gómez didn't turn around, incapable of making a decision, stepping on the accelerator to get up the slope because the motor didn't have much more to give and was overheating. Now the smoke was visible and the smell unmistakable: burned tires and burned flesh.

At the top of the hill the smoke blinded them. Ignacio Abel shouted at Miguel Gómez to stop and lunged toward the wheel to turn the truck. The desert had suddenly been transformed into complete chaos. In front of them was a blaze and a pile of scrap metal, the remains of the bus that had passed them less than an hour before, overturned and on fire in the middle of the highway. Burning bodies jutted out of the windows, contorted faces, their features like melted rubber. Coming toward them through clouds of black smoke, a confusion of human figures overflowed the highway: they gesticulated and opened their mouths but their voices couldn't be heard, drowned out by the explosions and the horns of motorcycles, cars, and trucks bogged down in the multitude of people, halted by the burning bus. "Go back, turn around," said Ignacio Abel while the militiamen continued to bang on the glass, pressing their faces against it, twisted by horror. But the engine stalled and Miguel Gómez couldn't start it again, kept turning the ignition key, couldn't tell whether he was stepping on the brake or the accelerator. Now the long whistles of mortars, and a few seconds later the earth rose in the fields along the highway like streams of lava in an erupting volcano. They could make out the faces approaching them, militiamen tossing their weapons in order to run more quickly, old campesinos, women with children in their arms, animals weighed down by mattresses, heaps of sacks and suitcases, chairs, sewing machines, the mules' big eyes even larger with terror, open mouths searching for air, bodies trampling one another, while at the edge of the highway, between a line of trees, red flashes and columns of smoke rose. The morning light had the opacity of an eclipse. The truck started up again with a shudder, but instead of shifting into reverse, Miguel Gómez stepped on the gas pedal, riding in a straight line toward the burning bus and the turmoil of vehicles and militiamen and animals and fleeing campesinos. On one side of the highway, his legs wide apart, the heels of his boots deep in the dust, his head bare, an army officer flailed his arms and shouted, brandishing a pistol, threatening the militiamen who ran, throwing down not only their weapons but also the French steel helmets from the Great War, canteens, cartridge belts with ammunition, jumping over corpses and smashed suitcases, hopping over the dry furrows of a plowed field, throwing themselves to the ground with heads pulled in when they heard the whistle of an incoming mortar. We're going to run over someone and not know it; people desperate to flee will grab onto the sides of the truck and overturn it and we'll never get out of here; at any moment the invisible enemy on the other side of that row of trees will come at us and we'll be spellbound by the approach of the horsemen, the Moorish mercenaries who raise their sabers and shriek in the intoxication of a gallop carrying them to slaughter or their own deaths, the legionnaires who know how to advance with bayonets fixed or wait on a rise, their machine guns ready, and effortlessly mow down bewildered, foolhardy militiamen who don't know what war is, who imagine war is a parade through Madrid where they mark time in an unmartial way with a rifle at their shoulder and a fist at their temple. Ignacio Abel saw the intermittent shreds of images unfolding before him, submerging him in an unreality that erased fear and suspended time. Beside him, Miguel Gómez drove the truck, turning the wheel, accelerating and braking, wiping the sweat from his forehead and eyes, his thick fingers under his lenses. A campesino's mule cart came toward them, with suitcases and furniture falling off the sides, a pack of dogs chasing it. Beyond the trees and the smoke, the silhouettes of horses appearing by the score. "To the right!" he heard himself shout, turning the wheel with a blow of his hand. "Accelerate, don't stop now!" On the right side of the highway was a burned house and in front of it a horse with its belly gaping open, its guts spilling out, and beyond that, visible for a moment and then erased by smoke, the start of a road, almost perpendicular to the highway. The truck leaned when it took the turn, barely avoiding a ditch, leaving the war behind as it drove on, the trembling of the earth easing, the mortars' whistles fading. On the curve of a nearby hill, a line of dun-colored houses and a church tower emerged. A column of smoke rose from the hood of the dilapidated truck.

"We'll have to stop, Don Ignacio. We have to put water in the radiator. The motor's burning out."

"Do you have any idea where we are?"

"I'm a disaster. I'm lost."

"Don't worry. We'll ask in the village. We'll find a road back to Madrid around here."

"But we have to go to Illescas, Don Ignacio. They entrusted us with a mission."

"Our mission right now is to not get killed."

"Did you see the Fascists? Did you see the Moors' sabers shining?"

"Slow down. The village seems empty."

"They must've evacuated it."

Never having learned the name of the village, Ignacio Abel remembered it as a phantom site. There was a fountain with several spouts at the entrance, and Miguel Gómez stopped the truck beside it. The three militiamen jumped down from the back, shaking their legs, telling jokes. Whose idea was it to send them for paintings, as if they worked for a moving company instead of killing Fascists? They were young; the evidence of danger and the spectacle of death were lost on them. "What do we do now, comrade? Go to Madrid without the paintings and not take any insurgents back with us?" Past the fountain, the only street in the village curved toward a small, arcaded square where the church stood. Not a single tree, no shade. Ignacio Abel washed his face in the fountain, drying it with the handkerchief he hadn't forgotten to fold that morning into the breast pocket of his jacket. Miguel Gómez had unscrewed the radiator cap and was letting the engine cool before putting in water. The militiamen had taken out lunch pails and a *bota* of wine. They left their rifles leaning against the fountain wall and sat down in the sun to eat. Ignacio Abel moved away from the group, impatient to be alone, to find someone who'd tell him where they were and what would be the best way back to Madrid. He walked down the middle of the street. A little farther on a woman's shawl, an open suitcase filled with tableware, folders of what seemed to be legal documents. He saw a door ajar and, after knocking on it a few times, pushed it open. He entered a kitchen, its walls curved like a cave and black with soot, where embers smoldered in a stove and a cooking pot sat nearby. The air held a residual odor of boiled garbanzos and rancid bacon. Something moving at the edge of his field of vision caused a rush of alarm: a canary in a cage, fluttering about, bumping into the wire sides. Back on the street, the vertical sun hit his eyes. Ignacio Abel was about to go back when he saw something projecting from the next corner: a shoe, the bottom edge of corduroy trousers, a man against the wall covered with bulletholes and spattered blood, in the middle of his chest a black hole of torn flesh and coagulated blood. He was lying face-up, but next to him was another man with his face to the ground, and a little beyond them two or three more piled up, and a barefoot woman with broad white thighs, her dress soaked in blood. Flies buzzed around their wounds, mouths, eyes. The air smelled of excrement and intestines. A vertical swaying shadow was projected onto the whitewashed wall: in a hayloft a man had been hanged from a hook on a pulley. His eyes were bulging, his swollen tongue sticking out of his mouth. At his feet a puddle of urine, both of his ears cut off.

He tested his back against the wall, close to the legs of the hanged man. He felt rough wood: a door. He slipped inside. It was a stable. He stepped in manure. A hen looked at him with a severe air as she sat on a straw nest on top of a sack of wheat. *We're lost on the other side of the lines,* he thought. No sign, no border. Madrid suddenly a place as unreachable as America. They kill as they advance, methodically eradicating with a pitiless efficiency no one can stop. They'll discover the truck and in a few seconds they'll have machine-gunned those three boys playing at war and poor Miguel Gómez, who won't be able to get his hand on his pistol. An oblique thread of sun traversed the ground in the stable; a shadow crossed it, and then another. Ignacio heard with absolute clarity the metallic sound of a rifle on a shoulder. Then an engine starting up, the neighing of a horse, the sound of hooves, first on paving stones, then on the ground. In the silence, the minutes had the inconsistency of time in dreams. He was struck by fear that the engine he'd heard was the truck's. *But Miguel would never leave without me.* He went out to the street, staying close to the wall, and when he reached the corner, he heard at his back the mechanism of a rifle bolt and a gruff voice ordering him to halt. Fear was a stab wound in the middle of his spine. He turned his head slowly and the person aiming at him was one of the three militiamen, pale in the wounding light of midday and as frightened as he was, and just as much a stranger. "Don Ignacio," said Miguel Gómez, "where have you been?"

They advanced along stray highways, unsure whether they were approaching the enemy or had already met him on the other side of the shifting frontline, whether at any moment they would fall into an ambush. The empty fields were a threat. No signs at the crossroads. They tried to be guided by the position of the sun and head north, but the roads seemed to go only west and south; in that direction lay Talavera de la Reina, and there the enemy certainly was advancing. But then where had they been when they came to that nameless village? Had they come across a regiment or just a scouting party? "They cut off her nose and ears," said Miguel Gómez. Before or after raping her. Ignacio Abel was driving now. Miguel had agreed with no resistance, relieved really, leaning against the seat, holding on to the door handle, unable to forget the woman's face, the enormous purple feet of the hanged man. The motor vibrated and roared beneath the sole of the foot stepping on the accelerator. Soon it would begin smoking again. A little faster, taking maximum advantage of the truck's scant power and crude machinery. A little faster, but where? Along the harsh plain where they didn't cross paths with anyone, a country uninhabited as if after a plague, barren fields and solitary houses, their roofs fallen in, vineyards disappearing into the distance on the reddish earth.

"It was a miracle they didn't see us. And those three idiots joking and making noise as if nothing was going on."

"Or maybe they thought there were more of us and ran away."

"How scared I was not to see you, Don Ignacio. How could I face my father if anything happened to you?"

A sign carved into a boundary stone finally indicated the road: TO MADRID, 10 LEAGUES. They want Anarchist communism and we haven't gotten as far as the decimal metric system. The road led to the national highway, and the slow river of refugees moving toward Madrid forced them to slow down. The multitude looked at the red banner with the emblem of the Fifth Regiment, didn't move out of the way when the horn sounded. They had the air of fatigued, solemn poverty, of a primitive exodus, a universal migration leaving deserted lands behind. The mules, the donkeys, the carts with crude wooden wheels, the old men, fathers with children on their shoulders, women in black skirts and shawls, herds of goats, the cry of a newborn searching for its mother's dry breast, the dust and silence enveloping everything, the unanimity of the flight, the urgency lessened by the exhaustion of walking since before dawn, leaving everything or almost everything behind, dropping on the road what became too heavy or unnecessary, like a trash heap the length of the highway, traces of shipwrecks in the dirty foam left by the sea when it recedes. They flee from an army of legionnaires, Moors, and Falangists who've been advancing toward Madrid since the end of July, fatigued from their killing spree. Now they lift their eyes and see Madrid for the first time, in the distance, as fantastic as the shapes of clouds, the formidable buildings, the terrifyingly wide streets they won't dare cross for fear of the cars, the great yellow Telephone Company tower that Ignacio Abel and Miguel Gómez were grateful to see, shining in the sun above the rooftops.

Night was falling when they entered the city, and under the trees along the Prado and Recoletos the café tables were full. A heavy rain had fallen; the air was clean and the leaves on the trees glistened. On the wet paving stones streetcar rails gleamed. The setting sun illuminated the width of Calle de Alcalá with a dusty light, gold and violet, striking the glass in the high windows of the buildings. Ignacio Abel took his leave of Miguel Gómez in the courtyard of the Alliance without saying much. He was dying of hunger, weariness, thirst, but he climbed the stairs of the palace two by two in search of Bergamín's secretary. From the large hall came the sound of an energetic paso doble. He was in the doorway of Bergamín's office when the poet Alberti appeared, dressed as a lion tamer in a red jacket with gold braid, white trousers, high boots, carrying a folder of printer's proofs. He looked at Ignacio Abel and made a distracted gesture of greeting or recognition. In the waiting room Mariana Ríos was taking dictation at her typewriter from a tall man who was standing behind her, his hand resting on the back of her chair. The secretary stopped typing, opened a drawer, and handed Ignacio Abel a sealed envelope. She told him he'd find Professor Rossman in the morgue of the National Security Agency, on Calle de Víctor Hugo. He walked out of the Heredia Spinola Palace, leaving behind the lit balconies and dance music, tearing open the envelope to read its contents in the light of a street lamp: a judicial document written in an ornate hand and detailing the discovery of a man *killed by bullet wounds caused by an unknown perpetrator or perpetrators, the sole identity document on his person a card issued by the National Library in the name of Don Carlos Luís Rossman.* On the table at the morgue, Professor Rossman wasn't wearing his glasses but he did have on one of his felt slippers, held by a rubber band around the instep of his right foot. He had one eye open and the other almost closed, his face turned to one side, his upper lip drawn back and showing his gums with a few uneven teeth, his expression a frozen smile or one of surprise. Hunger and exhaustion, the growing unreality of it all, sank Ignacio Abel into a daze. In the labyrinth of narrow streets around the National Security Agency he walked to the Gran Vía to find the pensión where Señorita Rossman must have spent another day waiting for his call. The globes of the street lamps, painted blue as a precaution against night bombing raids, lit the corners with the sickly light of a theater set. Some militiamen asked for his papers in the Plaza de Vázquez de Mella, and he saw only the metal of their pistols and the lighted ends of their cigarettes. From a door came a reddish light, the noise of loud laughter, the music of a barrel organ, a brothel smell of disinfectant and perfume. What would he say to Señorita Rossman? What could he do but stand silent in the doorway of her room, so narrow her father would go out to a café to allow his daughter a few hours' privacy. But Señorita Rossman wasn't in the pensión, and the landlady told him she hadn't appeared for several days; they'd come to ask for her from the office where she worked in the Telephone Company, and she, the landlady, had told them she didn't know anything, she had enough troubles of her own — probably the German had left to avoid paying her monthly rent, and if she didn't show up in another two or three days, she would have to collect the debt by taking anything of theirs that had value, even if it was only the suitcase on top of the wardrobe.

From time to time Ignacio Abel thinks of Señorita Rossman; the phone rings and he thinks she must be calling, and before the ringing stops he knows he's been dreaming. Before he left Madrid, he called the press censorship office in the Telephone Company Building several times, and was told that Señorita Rossman was out sick or had left for unknown reasons, and finally that no one by that name worked there. He didn't call again.

32

S TANDING NEAR THE window, Ignacio Abel watches the taillights of the car that brought him to the guesthouse move down
the path through the trees. The sound of the engine gradually
dissolves in the silence of the woods, where he can hear the dry rapping of a woodpecker. Above the dense treetops a pale blue light remains in the sky, where he can just make out the evening star. The trees
are evergreens, pines standing high above the house. He sees no other
building, and he doesn't recall ever being submerged in so profound
a silence. Stupefied, relieved, exhausted, hypnotized, he stays in front
of the window, his coat still on, holding his hat, in his left hand the
pain of having clutched the handle of the suitcase for so long, a gesture
as instinctive now as patting his pockets to search for his passport or
turning around thinking someone has called his name.

He isn't accustomed to the idea of having reached his destination. He
can't calculate the exact number of days that have passed since he left
Madrid. And he doesn't remember the day of the week or today's date,
just that it's near the end of October. Trains, hotels, a ship's cabin, border crossings, names of stations are confused in his memory, a continuous yet disconnected sequence of places, sensations, faces, days
and nights. He isn't who he was when he started this journey. What
for so long had been the sound of a name and a black dot on a map

is now what his eyes have seen since he reached the station, what he looks at as he stands at the window: fields where horses or cows graze, wooden houses and fences painted white, barns, narrow roads, autumnal woods where light continues to vibrate in spite of dusk. There will be no ragged refugees fleeing along these roads, no dead horses in the ditches with swollen bellies, no black smoke on the horizon, suitcases tossed beside the highway, their contents plundered or scattered by passing vehicles, the trampling of animals, the flood of refugees. Rhineberg was a promise, an enigma, a place difficult to imagine in Madrid, and now it's the house in a clearing in the forest with a porch and wooden columns, large rectangular windows without curtains or grilles, built perhaps at the turn of the century by a tycoon whose taste was more neoclassical than Victorian. He'd touched one of the columns when he got out of the car—Professor Stevens had hurried to open the rear doors, first for him, then for Van Doren. The smooth paint and solid wood were soothing to the touch. Like someone who's just disembarked after a long sea voyage, he feels the firm floorboards vibrating beneath his swollen feet. His body has become accustomed to constant movement: train wheels, iron bridges, turbine pistons continue to buzz in his ears. How distant now the night he left Madrid in the back of a truck, driving along the Valencia highway with its headlights off, surrounded by men who smoked in the darkness or slept leaning on bundles, covering themselves with old blankets and overcoats, clutching the handles of their suitcases. In the passageway of the crowded night train that carried him to Paris, he slept sitting on the floor; a plainclothes policeman woke him with a kick because he was blocking the way, and with ill humor demanded his papers. He got to his feet, fatigued and half asleep, numb with cold. At first he couldn't find his passport in any of the pockets he patted with increasing alarm. The rough voice repeated, "*Papiers, papiers,*" and then the policeman thrust his flashlight close to Ignacio Abel's face to compare it with the passport photograph, his hair smelling of pomade, his breath of tobacco.

• • •

Things that just happened, unhinged from the present, plunge into a distant past: his final hours in the apartment he was about to abandon, his departure from Madrid, his journey through France at night, the ocean horizon unchanging for six days, the four days of anxious waiting in New York, the two hours on a train this afternoon along the banks of the Hudson. Instinctively he pats his passport in the inside pocket of his raincoat, as if listening to his heart. No one's going to ask him for it now, tonight. No one will ask for his papers in America, Van Doren told him when they entered the foyer of the house and he took out his passport. He can empty his pockets and put his things in the desk drawers or the night table with no fear. He can hang his spare suit in the closet so it won't be too wrinkled when he puts it on tomorrow to go to his first, and dreaded, social engagement, after sinking into a bathtub full of hot water for the first time in he doesn't remember how long and shaving and combing his hair at the mirror above the sink, respectable again, an architect, a *visiting professor*. But he doesn't do anything yet: physically he's reached his destination, but his body holds the tension of the journey, the instinct to distrust, to keep vigilant. Standing at the window, Ignacio Abel drinks in the novelty of stillness and silence while the car's taillights glow like two live coals in the growing darkness of the trees. He's safe from immediate uncertainties. No urgent deadline, no train to catch. He won't hear footsteps tonight on the wooden steps that go up to the bedroom, and when he falls asleep no one will wake him by pounding on the door. The house has welcomed him with cordial austerity: the amplitude of the spaces, the bareness of the walls painted a light cream color, the suggestion of strength in the materials transmitted by touch to his hands when they brush the banister, to his body through his soles resting on wooden boards. Solid beams and powerful columns made of large tree trunks; stone foundations sunk into the fertile dark earth to the depths of living rock. From the car he observed the outcroppings of that rock and liked the variations in color, not as dark as the schist in Central Park: a greenish gray like patinaed bronze that corresponds subtly to the colors of the trees. In his legs there's a trace of vibration, in his temples the buzz of electric cables. "The entire house is for you," Philip Van Doren told him before he left, with a proprietary expression (he's probably the owner, or was: someone in his family gave the building to the college). "I've made certain there'll be no other guests in the next few days. Light the fire, use the library, play the piano, cook your supper. There's more than enough food in the refrigerator and pantry. There's stationery, and ink in the inkwells. There's a typewriter, and a good record player in the library, and a collection of records. Rubinstein played that piano only a few months ago. You must have the impression that at Burton College we live like pioneers in the middle of these woods, but you'll see how many eminent guests visit. There's a good radio, though I'm afraid not good enough to pick up Spanish broadcasts . . ."

In the distance he hears the noise of a train that takes a long time to pass, coming up the bank of the Hudson emitting the sound of a ship's siren. He can't believe he's not riding in that train, that he doesn't have before him the urgency and uncertainty of another trip, doesn't have to anticipate any sudden fright, or find he's lost, or know he's anonymous. In the car, to flatter him, Stevens cited his articles in international architectural magazines, and Ignacio Abel had the feeling he was hearing about someone else. So many years of study, work, ambition, and vanity dissolve into empty hands, hands with dirty nails protruding from the worn cuffs of a shirt he hasn't changed in several days. One morning, his feet aching from walking around New York, he sat down on a sunny bench in Union Square and thought no one could distinguish him from the other solitary, honorably poor men who read the help-wanted pages in the newspapers or pawed through trash baskets. He looked up and a banner hanging between two lampposts trembled in the gentle October breeze: SUPPORT THE STRUGGLE OF THE SPAN-ISH PEOPLE AGAINST FASCIST AGGRESSION.

It's a relief to be left alone in the house and not have any engagements scheduled for tonight. The banner in Union Square announced a meeting that evening in support of the Spanish Republic. If Judith was in New York, she'd probably attend. Tomorrow morning Stevens will take him around the campus and show him, if he's not too tired, the hill and the clearing in the woods where, in not too long a time, everyone in the college hopes, the new Van Doren Library will be built (perhaps not white after all, too visible; perhaps the color of the rocks that peek out of cultivated land, or of the stone walls in the woods that marked old farm boundaries). In the evening the college president will give a dinner in his honor for a select group of guests (Stevens smiles, as if uncertain whether he's among them). In a few days he'll be assigned convenient housing for the entire year, closer to campus. But today he doesn't have to worry about anything, Stevens said, turning to him as he drove with one hand along those country roads he knows by heart; just rest up after the long journey. (Stevens looks at him and speaks to him as if he were ill, he thinks, uncertain of the tone he should use with a man who's just left a country at war, a distant European suffering that for him must have something exotic about it.) And he shouldn't be frightened if he hears strange noises at night, his host says afterward, as they're saying goodbye, and Ignacio Abel understands that Stevens has repeated the identical joke to other guests: the house is old, and at night the wooden structure tends to creak, but he can be sure it isn't bewitched, *It's not a haunted house as far as we know,* though it's possible some forest animal may approach, a ferret, a deer. On winter nights, bears and wolves are on the prowl. What a relief to hear the outside door close and the car drive away as the taillights begin to fade. He remains still, the weariness of the past few hours and so many days dissolving into a muscular weakness, his eyes charmed by the landscape at the window, the forest of tall conifers where night has fallen beyond the clearing in which the house stands, the sky of gradually darkening blue, and against it the treetops outlined with precision, the branches curved upward like the roofs of pagodas. Ignacio Abel has never experienced a silence like this. The silence is a crystal bell, a vault under which the most cautious footstep, the lightest touch, would have resonated. His hotel room in New York faced a gloomy courtyard where machinery rumbled night and day, and at regular intervals the walls and floor shook because an elevated train passed nearby. (In his sleeplessness he'd count the days he had to wait, the amount of money he'd spent since leaving Madrid, how much he had left.) The silence has a depth, an oceanic extension as limitless as these woods, which must extend, he imagines, to the cold of the Arctic Circle, to the Great Lakes and Niagara Falls, to the shores where at this moment the Atlantic is pounding. The silence weighs so powerfully it muffles the voices that haven't stopped sounding in his memory in recent days. Before leaving, Stevens turns on the lamp on the night table like a bellboy presenting the room to a recently arrived guest: he shows him the bathroom, how the hot and cold water faucets work. When the stream of water hits the bathtub it gives off steam. He opens a closet that emits a scent of varnish and pine. Stevens moves with agility, a hysterical touch of speed, like a dancer dressed in street clothes in a movie musical. His red face, his blue eyes behind gold wire-frame glasses, he is always conscious of the ironic or censorious or simply disdainful presence of Philip Van Doren, before whom he acts as if he were constantly being subjected to an aptitude test for which he's not prepared; more anxious when Van Doren is silent, when without saying a word he makes his displeasure or approval known with a fleeting expression the inexpert observer may not perceive. In the kitchen Professor Stevens explains how the coffeepot and toaster work while Ignacio Abel absent-mindedly nods without understanding very much, impatient to be alone, his feet hurting under the weight of his body. After so many days without a real conversation, it's difficult for him to pay attention to Stevens's chatter or Van Doren's comments and to respond coherently in English.

He inspects the bedroom, slowly becomes conscious of every detail, the high bed with its plain wooden headboard, plump white pillows, a white quilt on which he left his unopened suitcase. Pressing on the soft quilt is like submerging his hand in deep, warm, still water. He regains the pleasure of starched bed linen, fragrant sheets, the warm shelter of domestic comfort. How would it be to have Judith Biely with him in this room — Judith who perhaps right now is somewhere on this continent of dark forests undulating beyond the window. How would his children have explored the house, Miguel and Lita chasing each other on the stairs, going out into the woods to imagine they were living in a novel by James Fenimore Cooper, a film about soldiers in long jackets and three-cornered hats and Indians with tomahawks and stiff crests of hair and painted faces. There's a wide, solid desk of varnished wood in front of the window. When he turns on the brass lamp with a green shade that stands on it, the darkness of the landscape becomes a mirror in which he sees his face, partially in shadow, against the background of the room. Who has seen you and who sees you? Who would recognize you now? His face with the rough shadow of a beard, an edge of grime on his shirt collar, his tie carelessly knotted. The face Van Doren and Stevens have seen, which he has detected behind their courtesy. From a distance comes the sound of a train that takes a long time to pass: lit windows through the trees, reflected in the ocean-like current of the river. In Madrid night fell hours ago and it's still a long time until daybreak. The tremor of battle goes on in the distance and darkness, just like the sound of the train. REBEL FORCES EXPECTED TO FURTHER TIGHTEN THEIR GRIP ON LOYALIST CAPITAL, a newspaper headline said yesterday or the day before. Standing in front of the window, Ignacio Abel empties his pockets onto the desk: train tickets, hotel bills, French and Spanish coins, American pennies, receipts from Automats in New York, pencil stubs, the telegram from Stevens that reached the hotel after three days, when he thought he'd be thrown out for lack of payment, loose one-franc bills, a wrinkled five-peseta note, the few dollars to which his entire capital has been reduced. Forgotten things, like archeological remains of a lost time: the keys to his apartment in Madrid, two movie tickets from an afternoon in early June, the letter he decided several times to tear up and yet has kept, *Dear Ignacio, allow me to call you that, despite everything. I'm your wife and have the right and still love you.* Adela's letter and Judith's, his wallet swollen and misshapen by use, Judith's photo next to one of his children, his Socialist Party card, the General Union of Workers card, his identity document, his notebook with the first sketches for the library, lines and pencil smudges, uncertain attempts at forms that have become irrelevant in the context of the power and scale of this landscape: what can he design that won't be trivial and ridiculous, his Spanish imagination nullified here, just as it is in New York City, by the excessive size conspicuous both in human works and in nature, requiring an energy, a spirit, a lack of restraint for which he isn't prepared. He's been alone in the room for a while and still isn't calmed by its spaciousness or its silence. He sees himself as a foreign body, potentially infectious, propagating disorder, smells that have clung to his clothing during his journey, dirty clothes now turned out of the open suitcase on the bed and things spilling out of his pockets onto the desk, the silence oppressing him, the external darkness increasing the dimensions of distance.

A metallic noise wakes him, blows from a hammer or monkey wrench, steam whistles. In fractions of a second his mind, alert but still disoriented, eliminates a succession of places: his bedroom in Madrid, the tiny cabin on the ship, the hotel room in New York, the one in Paris. With the sudden shock of antiquated pipes, the heat has come on. He remembers dreaming about voices that dissolve before he can identify them. One said his name amid the noise of a crowd, murmured it in his ear; another begged for his help on the other side of a closed door. *Ignacio, for the sake of all you love best, open the door.* What he has no memory of is lying down on top of the quilt, not taking off his shoes, covering himself with his raincoat, as if he'd gone to sleep on a bench in a waiting room. He is aware of his body but sees it from the outside. He knows that if he so decides, he can lift the hand resting on his chest or open his eyelids a little more or close them again or bend a leg, but he does nothing, and in this inaction is a kind of indifference or physical distance, as if the neural connections between brain and muscles had temporarily been suspended. It isn't that he's lost feeling, as when a limb goes numb in a cramped position. He notes the pressure of his body on the quilt and the heat of his hands, one on the other, notes the thin weight of his lids on his eyeballs. His body is heavy and at the same time it floats on the quilt that's both dense and light. His body is heavy but not his thoughts, not the flow of consciousness or his perception of things. At some point as he slept and the night thickened, the woodpecker's beak stopped striking the tree trunk, but the owl's call or hoot did not; it returned, identical, after longer intervals of silence. Is this how it is to be dead, when the heart has stopped but there remains, so they say, a final glimmer of lucidity in the brain, when the bullet's just torn open the chest or the severed head's fallen into the guillotine basket? If only Professor Rossman had known a last moment of pity like this one, lying face-up on the ground, his lifeless body resting on the great breadth of the earth, beyond fear and pain, beneath a summer sky at dawn. Inside his shoes, Ignacio Abel's feet are swollen now and more painful, as if each foot weighs the millions of steps taken on his journey. The air enters his nostrils and leaves an instant later, warmer, the temperature of breath. In a rhythm just as involuntary, his heart contracts and expands in his chest, the waves of blood in his ears, the pulsation in his temples, a pressure in his skull that isn't quite a headache.

Who has seen you and who sees you? Who are you tonight, suspended in a place too strange and distant to be grasped in this large empty house, in this ocean of silence, this dark forest where the light from your windows travels to the highway? In his sleep he heard trains passing, as they'd passed during siestas and on summer nights in the Sierra, going to and coming from Madrid, the express trains heading north at midnight and those approaching the capital close to dawn after a night in transit. And the slow, short-distance trains too, that didn't go beyond Segovia and Ávila, the ones the fathers took during the summer to go to work in Madrid and return to the Sierra on Saturday afternoon, so recognizable, in their light suits and straw hats and briefcases under their arm, among travelers from the villages, dark unshaven faces, women with black scarves and kerchiefs on their heads, rustic wares of traveling vendors, containers of honey they'd peddle on the streets of Madrid, canvas sacks filled with cheeses, cages of hens, recently weaned piglets. It seemed that everything had lasted forever and would always be that way, the passage and whistle of trains as regular as the course of the sun or the bells in the village church. Now trains don't pass close to the house, shaking the pavement and the windows every hour. Now the old, slow trains that summer people and campesinos rode leave Madrid crowded with noisy militiamen, slogans painted on the cars and banners hanging from the locomotives, and they travel only half their route, to the last stations on this side of the Sierra, almost at the front. It's only October and the militiamen are already shivering with cold when night falls. Not enough blankets, said Negrín, no wool clothing, or hats, or boots, not enough trucks to keep the front supplied with food and ammunition, and no guaranteed relief forces. The heavy pain of Spanish poverty: in the photos of staged heroism published in the newspapers, the men advance or drop to the ground, dressed in old jackets or helmets that seem the castoffs of different armies. They shiver at night in the shelter of shepherds' huts, in the hollows between large granite crags. How will it be if the war hasn't ended when winter comes? They don't light fires so as not to give their positions away to the enemy. They hear noise, and fire into the darkness, wasting scant ammunition; for no reason, the shooting spreads up and down the frontline. On the other side his children must hear it, the house is close to the lines, to the names of towns now the lexicon of war. No doubt the family has gone to Segovia: suddenly almost another country, an inverted image of the Bolshevik and Anarchist Madrid that sprang up overnight late in July; military men and priests on the streets, processions of saints, not parades with red flags, the open hands of the Fascist salute instead of clenched fists, the ecclesiastical severity of the Spanish provinces in the previous century. My children in that world, unavoidably swallowed up by a clerical darkness from which I won't be able to rescue them, by candles, novenas, scapulars, and cassocks into which their mother's family submerged them as soon as I became careless, or as soon as I desisted, too weak, lacking the necessary intransigence, compelled by Adela, by her obedience to her people, unless in her heart she shares it too and hasn't shown it openly in order not to oppose me, not to emphasize the abyss that separated us from the start, the misunderstanding that neither of us wanted to look at, two strangers who have children in common and share nothing but a bed, a resignation indistinguishable from boredom. *It's never mattered to you that I love you, and you've never shown gratitude for the affection my parents gave you and have felt only contempt for them* — the letter also on the desk now, within reach, almost memorized, hidden inside the envelope and distilling from so great a distance its constant complaint. In Segovia Don Francisco de Asís owns a house with a coat of arms carved in stone above the lintel of the street door; he calls it "my ancestral home," though in reality it isn't very old and came into his possession many years ago at an auction, and the stone coat of arms with a shield crowned by a helmet and a cross of Santiago he bought at a demolition site. You leave and it's useless, you wear out the soles of your shoes walking through city after city, you spend a week nauseated in a cramped cabin on a ship that crosses the Atlantic, and it's as if you had lost your strength in one of those revolving tunnels at a carnival, the tube of laughter, you never manage to move from the same spot. You go away and one part of you remains torn by separation and guilt, and the other part suffers the oppression of not being able to leave, to create distance. Continents and oceans can't loosen the knots of captivity. *Because you must know that whatever you do you're still my husband and the father of your children. Those ties can never be broken. Not even animals abandon their young.* From so far away he sees them, like the photographs in which he never appears though he's hovering nearby, conferring in the familial circle around a table with built-in foot warmers in the house in Segovia, with gloomy paintings of saints on the walls, Don Francisco de Asís and Doña Cecilia and Adela and his two children and perhaps the uncle who is a priest, and who gives religious pictures to the children and suggests they pray at night and go to Confession and take Communion, if only to make their dear grandparents happy. He sees them like a ghost, a soul in purgatory in whom Doña Cecilia says she believes and to whom she lights little oil lamps that according to her go out when touched by the passage of a soul, the wing of an angel. *The most sacred thing of all isn't the sacraments, but the love you and I have had, our children are the proof.* They all pray the rosary, murmuring, their heads lowered, Miguel and

Lita kicking each other, Don Francisco de Asís and Doña Cecilia and Adela offering fervent prayers for their son and brother, not knowing whether he's alive or dead, and perhaps also for him, the son-in-law, who disappeared on July 19, though with some misgivings, because it disconcerts them or they think it's unsuitable to pray for someone who has no faith, but they must set an example for the children, they who are severe in their mourning for the two who are absent and about whom they've heard nothing for months, the son and brother, the husband and son-in-law to whom Adela wrote the letter, run through with rancor, that's taken so long to reach its destination and yet hits its target with the accuracy of a poisoned arrow. *Why is it bad for your children, who are just as much mine as yours, or even more mine because I gave birth to them, I brought them up and have been there for them every day, every night when they were burning up with fever, what harm can it do them to be brought up in the Catholic faith?* Her family will indoctrinate the children, they'll fall again into the hands of priests and nuns, they'll be forced to confess and take Communion on Sundays and perhaps they'll be pointed at in the school where they've begun the new year as secular children, offspring of an enemy, who don't know how to chant prayers or sing church hymns, not to mention the Fascist anthems.

Ignacio Abel lies in bed, exhausted, silent, as memory acquires clarity in the midst of his loneliness and guilt. He travels with the lightness of dreams to the house in the Sierra, past which the trains no longer run and from which perhaps the gunfire on the front can be heard. Perhaps it's been abandoned or converted into a barracks, like the Student Residence, a barracks for the others, for that abstract and not completely human species the newspapers call the Enemy, a word, he realizes now, of theological inspiration. In his old school, transformed into a lot with burned ruins, the priests called the devil the Enemy and warned that the word must always be written with a capital letter. Now the Enemy must occupy the neglected garden that for his children was a forest where they staged adventures copied from novels and collected insects and plants for their biology classes; the garden with the rusted swing on which they were swinging on that Sunday three months ago when he saw them for the last time, though they were both too old for it. Lita with her well-formed chest, Miguel in short pants he won't wear again after this summer. He's changing so quickly that when I see him again I won't recognize him. He'll have the shadow of a mustache, he'll part his hair and brush back the bangs that would fall over his eyes, an adolescent who'll look more like his uncle Víctor, his features usurped along with his soul, distancing him from me into an adulthood in which perhaps I, his father, won't exist. If I haven't already ceased to exist, erased by distance, lack of news, the likely absence of the postcards I've been sending them since I left Madrid, just as when they were younger and I took trips: the Plaza de la República in Valencia, the beach at Malvarrosa, the Eiffel Tower, the recently inaugurated Trocadero, Notre-Dame from a bridge over the Seine, the Boulevard de Saint-Nazaire that ends at the port, the SS *Manhattan* sailing at night on the high seas with the portholes illuminated and garlands of bulbs over the deck, the Statue of Liberty, the arcades at Pennsylvania Station, the hotel in New York where I stayed, its vertical sign running along the side of the building and a small pencil mark over a window on the fourteenth floor, *this is my room,* the Empire State Building crowned by a dirigible (but he never managed to mail that postcard: he stamped it and forgot about it in his concern not to miss the train). Lita has a tin box filled with postcards and letters arranged by date. At the beginning of her vacation she took it to the Sierra along with her books and journals. Miguel brought with him the textbooks for the classes he'd failed in June and the notebooks with assignments he'd done at the last minute, covered with the teacher's red-pencil markings, his spelling mistakes underlined, his inkblots. But he couldn't have taken his examinations in September. In that regard the war has been a respite for him. He'll have to repeat the year, and Lita will too if the war doesn't end soon.

It's no longer possible to avoid the word: he saw it in the French papers, obscene in the red and black ink of the headlines: GUERRE EN ESPAGNE. He's seen it in the New York papers he sometimes worriedly looked for — and other times tried to avoid — at the stand outside his hotel: LATEST NEWS ON THE WAR IN SPAIN. Like a congenital illness he can't be cured of, and those who printed and delivered the papers were immune to, like our poverty and picturesque backwardness, our baroque Virgins with glass tears and silver hearts pierced by daggers, and that colorful, savage slaughterhouse that is our national pastime. KILLINGS AT THE BULLFIGHT RING IN BADAJOZ. Our names, so sonorous and exotic, standing out among the words of another language, thatched walls in ruins, barren lands, photographs of our poor people's war, our women with black shawls and bundles on their heads fleeing along roads, crossing the plains, shoved with rifle butts at the frontier by French gendarmes while I looked away and did nothing and felt the cruel privilege of my formal dress and my papers in order. That still didn't exempt me from the Spanish disease: the customs officials searched my suitcase with calculated rudeness, took their time examining my drawings and sketches, the passport they'd already gone over once, the photograph I was beginning not to resemble, the page with the U.S. visa. Who'd accept without suspicion that title, *Spanish Republic,* inscribed in gold letters on the cover above the shield with its mural crown, if at any moment that republic might cease to exist, and if a few steps away, on the Spanish side of the border, there were no uniformed guards and clerks but militiamen who'd hauled down the tricolor and hoisted a red-and-black banner on the flagpole. In spite of everything, while he waited, dignified and upright, for the gendarmes to return his passport and permit him to close his suitcase, there was his pride at being a citizen of the Spanish Republic and rage at the indifference of the French and British who watched it turn, awkward and defenseless, to face its attackers, but also the feeling of inferiority for belonging to such a country, and the desire to escape it, and guilt for having run away, for not having known how to be useful, for not having remedied anything.

He remembers being on the Plaza de Oriente one morning, the last one, when his escape was assured and he went to say goodbye to Moreno Villa. Lashed by wind and rain, the plaza looked larger, the National

Palace more gray than white against the background of dark storm clouds coming out of the west over the sharp greens of the Campo del Moro, with the Casa de Campo dissolving in the fog. In the French gardens an encampment of refugees protected themselves from the rain under their carts or canvas cloths stretched between the hedges and trees. In the middle of October, winter announced its arrival in Madrid, as if brought there by the gradually approaching war along the southwest highway, the one to Extremadura. How strange to imagine with such clarity what I haven't lived, what happened more than seventy years ago, the plaza with the encampment of tarpaulins and shanties among the hedges, around the equestrian statue of Felipe IV supported only by the hind legs, delicate against the gray sky and the rain, wielding a sodden red flag; Ignacio Abel walking by it, a solitary bourgeois silhouette under an umbrella, approaching the guardpost where soldiers in the impeccable uniforms of the presidential battalion — steel helmets, leather straps, shining boots, well-shaven faces — will let him pass with no more formality than checking his name on a typed list. Footsteps and orders echoed in the granite cavities of the foyer. In a porter's lodge behind a small glass door, one could hear a radio and a typewriter and smell the aroma of food. He climbed broad staircases of granite and then of marble that had no carpeting to muffle his steps. He crossed halls with tapestries and clocks and swirling mythological scenes painted on the ceilings, and bare corridors that led to courtyards with stone arches covered by glass domes on which the rain drummed. Moreno Villa was in an office behind a paneled door with a low lintel, a tiny office overrun by books and file folders in the middle of a magnificence of empty spaces. Ignacio Abel thought that throughout his life Moreno Villa had maintained an invariable model of a workroom, identical in the National Palace and the Student Residence, in any place where chance might lead him in a future that had suddenly become uncertain. The cold was insidious, slowly overpowering you, first your fingertips and the end of your nose, then the soles of your feet. In a corner of the office was a small electric heater. But the current was weak and the glow of the element as sickly as in the lamp on the desk where Moreno worked, absorbed in his files, his investigations into the buffoons and madmen who served the kings in the time of Velázquez. His white beard had grown pointed, like a figure by El Greco. He was thinner than in the summer, and wore reading glasses that made him look older.

"You're finally leaving, Abel. You must find it hard to believe you have all your papers in order. It's obvious you're a man who wants to leave, who knows how to leave, if you'll allow me to say so."

"Are you still sleeping in the Residence?"

"And where would I sleep if I didn't sleep there, Abel? It's my home. My provisional home, but I've lived there so many years I can't imagine myself anywhere else. The garrison is gone and now they've set up a field hospital. How those poor boys scream. The horrible wounds. You think you know war's dreadful but have no idea of anything until you see it. Imagination is useless, impotent, cowardly. We see soldiers fall in films and believe that's how it is, that everything's over quickly, a bloodstain on the chest. But there are things worse than dying. Tell me what kind of insanity that is — what's the good of such suffering? You look away, because when you look, you'll retch. And the smell, my God! The smell of gangrene and excrement from burst intestines. The smell of blood when the nurses cover them with newspapers or sawdust. Sometimes I tell myself I'll have to draw these things, but I don't know how, it makes me ashamed to attempt it. I think no one has done it, no one has dared, not the Germans in the Great War, and not Goya. Goya got closer, but even he lacked the courage. I think of the caption he put on one of the prints in *Disasters of War*: 'One cannot look.' You won't have to any longer."

He didn't need to go on waiting. He was there saying goodbye to Moreno Villa and it was as if he'd already begun the journey, postponed so many times because of tortuous procedures, papers or stamps or signatures, promised letters, delayed or lost in the mail. Before going to see Moreno Villa he'd picked up the final document and carried it like a fragile treasure in the inside pocket of his jacket, a safe-conduct on the letterhead of the Ministry of Finance, signed by Negrín in his new position as minister, authorizing the trip to Valencia and from there to France and suggesting a vague official mission—in case new difficulties arose and his passport with the American visa and the French transit visa wasn't enough when he reached the border. "We're a government that almost doesn't exist," Negrín told him in his large office in the Ministry of Finance. He finally had a space that corresponded to his physical size, with an enormous desk, a large window facing Calle de Alcalá, a thick rug into which footsteps sank silently. "We give orders to an army of phantom divisions in which a handful of officers still loyal to the Republic have no troops to command. They've made poor Prieto minister of the navy, but the few old warships the Republic has are lost, and we don't know where they are because the sailors killed the officers and threw them in the ocean and didn't leave anyone who knows how to read a nautical chart or set a course. We write decrees that no one obeys. We're unable to control the borders of our own country. Governments that should be our allies want nothing to do with us. We send telegrams to our embassies or set up conference calls, and the ambassadors and secretaries have gone over to the enemy. We're the legitimate government of a member of the League of Nations, and even our French comrades from the Popular Front treat us as if we had the plague. They don't want their excellent relations with Mussolini and Hitler ruined on our account, not to mention the British, who for some reason despise us more than they do the insurgents. They don't want to sell us weapons. We have no planes, no tanks, no artillery, and barely a fraction of the materiel left over from the Great War that those thieving French didn't want and were selling to us until a few months ago. And now not even that, no helmets from 1914 or muskets from the Franco-Prussian War . . ."

But strangely, Negrín's lucidity before the magnitude of the catastrophe didn't dishearten him. When Abel entered his office, he found him dictating a letter in French at top speed to a secretary, walking back and forth, his hands behind his back. He paused to make a call, grew impatient that it took so long to be connected, slammed down the receiver. "Even so, we won't surrender," he said, stopping in front of Abel. "We'll rebuild the army from the bottom up, an effective and well-equipped army, with discipline and muscle, an army of the people and the Republic. We'll end this madness—reality is the best antidote to mental derangement. We know why the enemy's fighting and why the military rebelled, but what we don't know is why *we're* fighting. Or if there is a *we* that we fit into, all of us who'll end up shot or exiled if the other side wins. Each madman has his mania. Don Manuel Azaña wants the French Third Republic. You and I and a few others like us would settle for a Social Democratic republic like Weimar. But our coreligionist and now president of the government says he wants a Union of Iberian Soviet Republics, and Don Lluís Companys a Catalán republic, and the Anarchists forget we're at war and facing a bloodthirsty enemy and in this chaos experiment with the abolition of the state. And to put into practice its own particular delirium, the first thing each party and union does is invent its own police, its own prisons, and its own executioners. But I refuse to believe all is lost. Our currency has fallen internationally, but we have more than enough gold and can pay cash for the best weapons. Our sister democracies, as they say in speeches, don't want to sell them to us? We'll buy them from the Soviets, or international traffickers, whoever." The telephone rang: the connection he'd asked for was possible now. He requested something in a categorical way but with the greatest courtesy, and since the secretary who'd been typing the letter took her time removing the paper from the typewriter, Negrín pulled it out himself with a precise gesture and checked the spelling by pushing up his glasses and bringing the letter close to his eyes. "And that's not all, Abel my friend. Those photographs our militiamen take of themselves dressed like priests in the ruins of burned churches and that do us so much good in the eyes of the world when the newspapers publish them? Those same papers refuse to publish the photographs we send them of children blown to pieces by German planes because they say they're propaganda. We have no people who speak foreign languages. We send loyal Republicans and Social-

551

ists abroad to fill diplomatic posts and explain our cause, but how are they going to explain it if in the best case they never went beyond first-year French in a priests' academy. This good-looking girl who works with me here is a treasure, she speaks French. But letters in English or German I have to write myself, and if foreign emissaries or journalists come to interview someone in the government, I act as interpreter." A functionary came in with a document in a folder, which he presented ceremoniously to Negrín, calling him "Señor Minister." Negrín looked it over quickly before signing it with a flourish and passed it to Ignacio Abel. "If they don't let you cross with this, I can think of only one measure," he said, laughing. "You carry a pistol too, just in case, and shoot your way out." Ignacio Abel carefully folded the safe-conduct and put it in an inside pocket. He remembers now that when he left Negrín's office, his relief was stronger than his remorse or his gratitude. In the waiting room stood officials, militiamen, and uniformed carabineers. The carabineers came to attention when they saw the minister, who took Ignacio Abel's arm and accompanied him to the exit. He's going to ask me not to leave, Abel thought, suddenly frightened, feeling on his arm the pressure of Negrín's enormous hand; he's going to remind me that I can speak foreign languages and should offer my services to the Republic just as he's doing, sacrificing a career far more brilliant than mine, that if he wanted to, he could obtain an appointment at any university outside Spain. But Negrín didn't ask anything. He ignored Abel's extended hand, gave him a hug, and told him, laughing, not to take too long with that building in America, come back soon and finish University City once and for all. So many ruins will have to be razed, he said, you architects will turn into gold. He stood for a moment on the threshold of a door with elaborate gilding, then turned and disappeared.

Lying in bed, he relives the sensation of cold drops on his cheeks, on a morning in October that felt like December. He thought of Negrín turning to go back to his office, thought that perhaps he too had been infected by a form of madness. The rain streamed down the tall gray façades on Calle de Alcalá, soaking the torn posters, shreds of wet paper breaking up the slogans in red letters and the figures of heroic militiamen in boots trampling swastikas, bishops' miters, bourgeois top hats, shirt fronts with medals, workers breaking chains and advancing toward brilliant horizons of factory smokestacks. The peddlers, shoeshine boys, and habitual idlers in the Puerta del Sol took shelter from the rain under the awnings of shops and in the doorways of buildings. The city had become sullen and wintry, and smelled of wet soot, garbanzo and cabbage stew, and overheated air from the metro tunnels. He took refuge in a nearly empty café, waiting behind a window clouded with steam for the rain to let up. The odor of sawdust reminded him of another café several months earlier, equally gloomy at that same hour of the morning, of Judith Biely, who didn't lift her head as he approached and didn't get up when he stood beside her, her face transformed into that of a woman who didn't know him. He couldn't risk the safe-conduct recently signed by Negrín getting wet. How a life can depend on a sheet of paper, an official letterhead, an ink signature so easily dissolved by a few drops of water. As if they were hidden treasure, he thought of all the papers he already had in his desk drawer, the same locked drawer where he kept Judith's letters: the documents he's brought with him and had to present so often during his trip, obtained one by one after exhausting transactions and weeks of waiting, interrogations, lengthy inspections of each document, each stamp and signature on each letter. To apply for the transit visa through France, he had to present his American visa and ticket for the ship as well as a certificate of financial solvency. The letter of invitation from Burton College, which he needed to apply for the American visa, took months to arrive. Most of the personnel at the embassies had left the country; the few officials left were irritated, overwhelmed by applications, insolent with the growing crowd of those who came early every morning and waited for hours in front of the closed doors, each with a briefcase or folder of documents held close to the chest, longing to escape, or at least find refuge in the embassies, looking out of the corner of their eye each time a car with rifle barrels at the windows or a truckload of militiamen went by. He recognized some of the regulars on the lines and in the offices: in a hallway at the French consulate he passed an architect he knew was a rightist, and neither greeted the other; a Russian woman he'd seen several times showed him her worn czarist passport and a diploma in Cyrillic characters issued, she said, by the Imperial Conservatory of Moscow. A contract for teaching piano was waiting for her at the Juilliard School. Couldn't he, since he looked like a gentleman, help her with a small amount, since she had all the necessary emigration documents and needed only the cost of a third-class passage?

Moreno Villa's bony hand was cold when he shook it. "You make me envious, Abel, leaving for America, disembarking in New York. I went so many years ago, and it's as if I had been there yesterday. When you called to say you were coming to say goodbye, I took the liberty of bringing you a present." He had a book on the desk, and before giving it to him he wrote a dedication on the title page. That copy must be somewhere, on a shelf in a library or a used-book store, the paper brittle after so many years, slightly more valuable because it has a dedication in the cautious hand of Moreno Villa, so similar to the line in his drawings, under the red letters of the title, *Proofs of New York:* "For Ignacio Abel, in the hope it will be of some help as a guide on his journey, Madrid, October 1936, from his friend J. Moreno Villa." "It's one of those books one publishes that no one will read," he said, as if apologizing. "The advantage is that it's short. I wrote it on my return trip. You can read it on your trip out. You don't know the envy I feel." And like Negrín that morning, Moreno Villa accompanied him to the door, leading him along bare halls and rooms of rococo opulence where at times the strokes of pendulum clocks echoed. They passed several footmen in knee breeches and long coats carrying boxes of papers, followed by a soldier in uniform pushing a large trunk with wheels.

"The president is leaving," said Moreno Villa. "He says it's against his will."

"He's leaving Madrid? The situation's that bad?"

"It seems the government doesn't want to take any risks. But Don Manuel is suspicious and thinks they want him out of the way."

"They've always said he was a fearful man."

"I don't think he's afraid this time. He gives the impression of simply being tired. Sometimes he passes me and doesn't see me. He pays no attention to what's said to him. Not because he doesn't care about the course of the war but because he doesn't expect anyone to tell him the truth. Do you know his aide, Colonel Hernández Sarabia? A civilized man, fairly well read. He told me the president can barely sleep at night. The gunfire and shouting at the executions in the Casa de Campo keep him awake, just as they kept me awake at the Residence. Hernández Sarabia says that when it's silent and the wind comes from that direction, you can hear the death throes of those who take a long time to die. In the summer, when the gunfire stopped, the frogs in the lake croaked again."

At the end of a corridor, outlined against the tall windows of a balcony facing west, I see a motionless figure, enveloped in the gray light of a rainy morning that resembles an old black-and-white photograph. At that distance the first thing Ignacio Abel saw was the gesture of the hand that held a cigarette, while the other was bent behind the man's body, a fleshy hand against the black cloth of a jacket. The president had walked out of his office, where he spent hours writing, to stretch his legs and smoke a cigarette while looking through the large windows toward the horizon of oak groves and the Sierra de Guadarrama, invisible now under the clouds, his manner the same as on another occasion, not long ago, when he looked into the crowd that filled the Plaza de Oriente to cheer him, shouting in chorus the syllables of his last name on the day in May when he was elected to the presidency. He'd stood at the marble balustrade, looking out at the sea of heads in the plaza, his expression a cross between remoteness and mourning. He turned his head slowly when he heard Ignacio Abel's and Moreno Villa's footsteps.

"Let's greet the president."

"Let's not, Moreno. I don't want to bother him."

"He'll ask me who you are and will be annoyed and think I brought you in behind his back and am scheming."

President Azaña exhaled smoke, his bulbous face swelling slightly.

"Don Manuel," said Moreno, "I'm sure you remember Ignacio Abel."

"I once drove you in my car to inspect the construction at University City," Abel said. "And another time I was with you at the Ritz, at the dinner for the opening of the Philosophy Building."

"With Negrín, wasn't it? The two of you wanted to convince me that razing those magnificent pine groves at Moncloa had been worth it."

Azaña's eyes were a light, watery gray. He extended his right hand and held it almost inert while Ignacio Abel shook it. It was a soft hand, colder than Moreno Villa's. Seen up close, the president looked older than he did just a few months earlier, and somewhat unkempt, with dandruff and white hairs on the wide lapels of a funereal jacket that had the shine of wear. An air of lethargy and extreme exhaustion slackened his features, made his skin colorless.

"How's your University City coming along? Have you completed the building we inaugurated with so much fanfare more than three years ago?"

"For the moment everything has been suspended, I'm afraid, Don Manuel."

"An elegant way to say it. Negrín and the architect López Otero and the minister of education insisted on telling me that by October of this year they'd take me to the dedication of the completed site. But that was before the construction strike and all this began."

"Dr. Negrín has always been an optimist."

"I imagine by now he's found reasons not to be. Though I couldn't say. He doesn't come to see me anymore. He's probably busy, being a minister . . ."

"Señor Abel leaves tomorrow for the United States. He came to say goodbye to me and pay his respects to you."

Azaña looked at Abel from behind his glasses, on his face an expression of subtle sarcasm.

"On another of those official missions we sponsor so our most distinguished intellectuals can hurry out of Spain without losing their self-respect? The minute they cross the border and feel safe, they say bad things about the Republic."

"Señor Abel has been commissioned to design a building at a university in the United States," said Moreno Villa, as if improvising an excuse. "A great library."

Azaña looked at the two of them but no longer seemed to see them, or didn't trust them. The nail on his left index finger was yellow with nicotine; the tip of his right had an ink stain.

"If you think I can do something when I'm there, let me know."

"No one can do anything. We're our own worst enemies. Have a good trip."

The president bent his head slightly and without shaking hands returned to his office, to the notebook where he wrote in a tiny, regular script, in the light of a lamp even during the day, an artificial glow he liked to be enveloped in as if it were a refuge.

About the rest of that day he remembers almost nothing, only the unreality in which everything seemed to sink in the face of his imminent journey, as if all the actions, once completed, were done for the last time. He'd have liked not to recall the solitude of the apartment on that final night, the hours approaching his departure, the electric light weakened by the damage of a recent bombing raid, the unpleasant taste of the cognac he drank to calm himself as he lay down on the bed, fully dressed, his suitcase on the floor, the documents in a folder on the night table. He took off his shoes, turned out the light, closed his eyes to rest for a few minutes. He woke with the anguished feeling that it was late and the truck would have left by the time he reached the station. But the clock on the night table told him that only a few minutes had passed. In the darkness a voice repeated his name from the end of the hall, on the other side of the closed door, secured on the inside with a double lock and bolt. A hand knocked gently to call him without raising an alarm, someone repeated his name, the mouth at the space between the door and the frame, breathing, pronouncing the name as if the sound would be enough to overcome the resistance of the wood, the thickness and weight of oak, the firmness of the steel lock and bolts. "Ignacio," it said, "Ignacio, open the door." This time violent steps on the staircase didn't wake him, or the car coming to a stop on the sidewalk in the silence of four in the morning, or the glare of headlights shining through the shutters into the dark bedroom. It was a slow, familiar voice, which he identified as soon as the daze of sleep vanished. He sat on the edge of the bed. Had he dreamed the voice? He sat a while longer, alert now, his back straight, his hands on his knees, wanting to believe he wouldn't hear that voice calling him again, the knocking on the door wouldn't be repeated. If the silence hadn't been so profound, Víctor's voice wouldn't have penetrated so clearly the closed doors and the space of empty rooms. He stood, trying to make no noise; he didn't turn on the lamp for fear the click of the switch would betray him. He moved cautiously, one step and then another, pausing after each movement, advancing in the darkness from one room to another, catching glimpses of the white sheets covering the furniture. Before he reached the door, he froze when he heard the voice again, identified it without the slightest uncertainty, recognizing its impatience, the anger mixed with fear, the hoarseness of someone who hasn't spoken aloud for a long time, perhaps hasn't had water to drink, has a fever, is wounded. "Ignacio, for the sake of all you love best, open the door, I know you're there, I hear you breathing." But it was impossible for Víctor to detect his presence if Ignacio himself was barely aware of the silent breath in his nostrils, so still he could feel his heartbeat in his temples and in his chest. "Ignacio, they're after me, I have no place to hide, let me in. I promise you I'll leave before daybreak. No one saw me come in. I won't compromise you, Ignacio, no one will see me leave, for the sake of all you love best." Ignacio stretched out his arm until he touched the door. With extreme care he lifted the thin metal cover of the peephole. He peered out quickly, as if he might be observed from the outside. But he saw nothing. The landing was in darkness. The bulb in the ceiling light had blown out a while ago and the porter hadn't changed it. He heard the brush of Víctor's body against the door, adhering to it, his agitated breathing, the click of his tongue in a mouth with no saliva. His palm hit the door repeatedly but cautiously. The panting was interrupted by the voice repeating his name: "Ignacio, Ignacio, for God's sake, open the door, if you don't hide me they'll kill me, I know you're there, I hear you, even though you don't want me to, I saw you come in and I know you haven't left." Now he closed his fist and hit the door with his knuckles, and with his other hand he turned the bronze doorknob as if trying out the possibility that it would not resist, that the door would open, allowing him to step into the safety of the other side. He stopped knocking for a while. Though Ignacio heard no footsteps, it was hard to tell whether he'd left. On the other side of the peephole, nothing but concave darkness. But he was still there, only he'd leaned his back against the door and slid down to the floor. And if he never left, if he passed out, if he stayed much longer, by the time Ignacio had to leave, it would be too late for the truck to Valencia. Perhaps he'd been wounded and was bleeding to death. Perhaps he'd spent many nights without sleep, fleeing from one hiding place to another, and was asleep at the door. But the voice sounded again, closer, hoarser, his lips against the edge of the door. "Ignacio, I swear I haven't killed anybody, I haven't harmed any of your people. Ignacio, open the door. What will your children think when they find out you let them kill me?" He could almost feel Víctor's breath on his face, that other body glued to his, the sour smell of his fear. He listened for footsteps but didn't hear any. The seconds ticked on his watch. A door suddenly opened then closed, keys and bolts turning after the rumble of the heavy wood door. Motionless, cold on his face, on the soles of his feet, Ignacio knew the voice spoke to him from farther away, perhaps only a few centimeters but already beyond this world. "Damn you, Ignacio. Damn you. You never had a heart. Not to be a red or to be a man. I know you're there, Ignacio."

33

HE LEFT THE FACULTY CLUB after lunch, relieved to be alone after spending the morning subjected to Stevens's chatter, his inexhaustible enthusiasm, his condescending smile as if addressing an invalid. Stevens had said he'd come for him at nine that morning, and at five to nine he heard the car stopping in front of the house, and the horn. Ignacio Abel had been waiting for some time, reading, sitting beside the window, observing the treetops that disappeared into the distance, listening to the birds in the forest and those that flew by in high triangular formations across the clear sky, making loud cawing noises that raised distant echoes. He woke early, aware of having slept deeply, with no dreams of voices saying his name or phones ringing. He stayed in bed for a while, barely moving, content in the warm softness of the quilt and pillow, the clean sheets, their whiteness growing purer as the first light of day entered the room, a little before the sun appeared above the conical treetops. He saw his raincoat tossed at the foot of the bed, his shoes and socks on the floor, his trousers and shirt hanging over the chair, like the traces of someone else's presence; weariness and the smell of cheap food and hotel rooms still clung to them. He took a long bath in hot water, submerged in the tub that had the spacious proportions of everything else in the house, and when he closed his eyes and lowered his head beneath the water, holding his breath, he felt himself dissolving in the weightlessness of rest, protected, absolved, his skin soothed by the touch of soap and sponge, his sex revived like an underwater plant or animal, bringing with no effort of memory the recollection of Judith's body — no, not the recollection, the physical sensation, intense and fleeting, like having her close in a dream and losing her as he woke, as the water in the tub began to cool, his phantom lover accompanying him to places he'd never been with her. When he wiped the steam from the mirror he saw the exhausted face of his journey, the restless eyes of someone who hasn't yet reached his destination. He soaped his face slowly, making a good deal of lather with the badger-hair brush, part of the pigskin case stamped with his initials, a gift from Adela on his last saint's day, when they were still planning the entire family's move to America. The razor slid gently over his skin, softened by the heat of the bath. He shaved as meticulously as in his bathroom in Madrid, though without the rush that tended to rule him then, the rush to get to the office right away or to meet Judith Biely early in the morning, the most gratifying secret encounter because it occurred at the busiest time of day. Today he was early and had time for everything. In the guesthouse time was as plentiful as space. The loose skin on his neck made shaving more difficult. The line of his jaw was no longer as clear as it had been. Age, which he'd rarely paid attention to — out of distraction, pride, the flattery of Judith's love — had begun to slacken muscles that once were firm, softening his face, almost erasing in his dewlap the shape of his chin. But carefully shaven and combed, a straight part in the center of his hair, his sideburns cut cleanly at a suitable length, he looked younger and more respectable, not a dubious refugee or an upright pauper, one of those who read newspaper want ads at cafeteria counters or on park benches, or those fugitives from Hitler who'd begun to arrive in Madrid from Germany a few years earlier. How grateful Professor Rossman would have been for a room like this, a slow bath and clean clothes, a tranquility that didn't alleviate uncertainty but left it suspended. Now he could finally put on the clothes he'd set aside with great care for this day: the white shirt, the cuffs and collar not worn, the spare suit he'd hung in the closet before going to sleep, the vest, the tie pin, the cuff links. He polished his shoes as well as he could, but there was no way to hide the cracks or worn soles, and one of the laces had to be tied gently because it was frayed and could break at any moment. I learn most from observing how everyday things wear out, the engineer Torroja had told him in Madrid: how they deteriorate, how time and use give them their true form and then destroy them. The soles of these shoes, cut and sewn by hand and now unrecognizable, the laces rubbing against the eyelets, subject to wear that in Torroja's scientific mind was similar to that of the ropes on a ship or the steel cables of a bridge. He could toss his dirty clothes into a wicker basket in the bathroom, which Stevens had pointed out to him; the smell of them embarrassed him, signs of the lack of hygiene to which he'd gradually surrendered in recent months. On the closet door was a full-length mirror where he examined himself, brushed his suit and hat and tried to give the brim the proper tilt. Too formal, perhaps, but maybe that was the effect of not having really dressed with care ever since being well dressed in Madrid had become strange and dangerous. He saw in the mirror not so much the person he was at this moment but the memory of the man he'd been a year ago, in this same suit, on the day in early October when he dressed to give his talk at the Student Residence, the first image of him that Judith Biely would remember, if she still remembered him.

Too formal: the suit cut by a modern tailor in Madrid is, here at Burton College, suddenly old-fashioned, almost antiquated, compared with the students' casual clothing and the flannels and checked jackets of the professors, who project an air of rural English gentry in harmony with the vague medieval mimesis of the architecture. That's why it's so easy to distinguish Ignacio Abel when he leaves the Faculty Club and walks along a path in the central quadrangle of the campus. He's more formal and moves more slowly than the rest, more leisurely with his hands in his pockets and his excessive Spanish pallor, enjoying the early afternoon sun without his raincoat or a suitcase in hand, passing groups of young men and women carrying books and briefcases and hurrying to their classes or the library, where there is no more room for books, a pseudo-Gothic building that will be abandoned as soon as the new library is built, the one that exists only as an imaginative conjecture sketched in a notebook he carries in his pocket. He observes supple bodies and healthy faces that seem never to have been brushed by the shadow of fear or distorted by cruelty or anger. The girls in light dresses on the warm October morning, in flat shoes and white socks, and the boys in brightly colored sweaters, almost all of them bareheaded, mixing in a seemingly effortless camaraderie. The quality of their teeth allows their laughter: he recalls Negrín's judgment when he observed people's faces in Madrid with the eyes of a physician and saw the sad signs of malnutrition and lack of hygiene. Pasteurized milk and cod liver oil, abundant calcium for rotten teeth, would be the remedies for Spain's backwardness! He has time; they won't be picking him up for the dinner the president of the college is giving in his honor until six. Hours seemed to sprout within hours: he finished dressing this morning and still had time to eat breakfast, write a letter, and examine the solitude of the guesthouse. In the hallways hung oil portraits of men in colonial dress or nineteenth-century frock coats, landscapes of the banks of the Hudson with blue mountains in the background and hills covered by autumnal forests, and watercolor renderings of projected college buildings. On one crudely executed, vividly detailed picture, a label with the inscription *Burton College, 1823* floated above a view of a large, fortified, Gothic-looking tower rising from a clearing, as meticulous as a medieval illuminated manuscript. Like an intruder or a phantom he walked down the oak steps of the staircase that led to the foyer. In the light of day everything was different from what he'd seen the evening before. He crossed a large library with half-empty shelves, a grand piano in the center, folding chairs propped against one wall. He crossed a sitting room that overlooked a garden and had a hearth where a fire of fragrant wood crackled, and deep leather armchairs beside which hung newspapers on frames. It seemed as if someone diligent and invisible had been waiting for him to wake. He heard the sounds of plates and flatware. At the end of a long dining room table was a breakfast service. A stout black woman said a jovial good morning and asked a series of questions he understood only gradually, deciphering the obvious sounds with some delay. He agreed to everything: he wanted coffee, he wanted sugar and milk, he wanted orange juice, butter and marmalade, rye bread. The woman was at once majestic and accommodating: she said things to him that were indecipherable when he thought he was on the point of understanding them, and she observed with indulgent patience as he attempted to say something and suddenly a trivial word would escape him. She watched him eat, respectful and affable, served him more milk and more coffee and slices of dark, porous bread, and indicated with gestures that he should spread on more butter and try each of the pots of marmalade arranged on the table. She quickly gathered the breakfast things and told him with exaggerated hand movements not to worry about anything, she'd come back later to clean the house. Her expression was sad as she watched him eat and said something about the Great War and the lack of food then, and that her husband (or her son) had fought in Europe and come back sickened by poison gas. There was something wholesome in everything around him, in the construction of the house and the thickness of the slices of bread, the rich density of the milk and the heavy china of the cup, a kind of robust cordiality that was also in the woman's presence and the size of her hands, with their pink nails and white palms.

When he was alone again the dimensions and silence of the house seemed to multiply. A murky touch of unreality was in the presence of things, the sharpness of his perceptions. Comforted by breakfast, he again crossed spaces that seemed conceived for him alone to inhabit, distant from his life and yet as hospitable as if he'd lived in them a long time and had returned now, this morning, to the rooms flooded with sun, the fire lit, the day's newspapers on the racks next to the leather armchairs. He opened one with the fear he had felt so often, the simultaneous longing for and revulsion at finding news about Spain. It was a two-week-old *New York Times,* and he was about to put it back but anxiety drew him to its wide pages and tiny print. And there it was, on an inside page, the eternal curse of the bullfight's language and cruelty: DEATH IN THE AFTERNOON — AND AT DAWN. He saw those words and knew they referred to Spain. They had to be there, "death" and "the afternoon," as if it were an article about a bullfight and not a war, and the word "sun," the white-hot brilliance exaggerating the colors of the national fiesta to the delight of tourists: DEATH UNDER THE SPANISH SUN — MURDER STALKS BEHIND THE FIGHTING LINES — BOTH SIDES RUTHLESS IN SPAIN. For them, both sides are the same in their exoticism and taste for blood: *Elimination of Enemies by Execution Is the Rule.* Who could have read the paper two weeks earlier, leaning back in the chair with broad, worn arms, the leather as noble as the logs burning in the fireplace or the marble mantel, who could have been interested in the news about executions in those arid landscapes punished by the sun while on the other side of the large window that faced the garden, a gentle, early autumn breeze would have been stirring the leaves and bringing the smell of soil and rain. What was a country at war like for someone reading the paper after breakfast: remote, cruel, doomed to misfortune, prompting perhaps a virtuous sympathy that costs nothing and strengthens the comfortable feeling of being safe, protected by distance and the civilization that permits you to take as a given the pleasures of the morning, bathing after a night of sleep, the abundance of breakfast in a spacious room illuminated by the clean light of day, the smell of coffee and of ink on the newspaper, of toasted bread and fresh butter gently melting on it. That's how he'd read the news about Abyssinia not many months before, looked at the photographs in *Ahora* and *Mundo Gráfico* of defenseless Ethiopians with their spears and tribal robes, insolent Italian legionnaires in their epic colonial uniforms copied from bad adventure movies, their Fiat planes armed with machine guns and incendiary bombs. Now the Abyssinians are us: we are the victims of merciless invaders and those entrusted with the most rudimentary part of slaughter.

Murder Stalks Behind Fighting Lines. He put down the paper without having read the whole article and left the guesthouse, inhaling the fresh air that held the dew's moisture and a smell of earth and fallen leaves, resin and the sap of the tall cedars or firs that edged the clearing, their tips moving gently in the breeze. A woodpecker's rapping resonated, as powerful and clear as the knocking on a door or the echo of steps beneath a dome, the entire trunk vibrating, the wood strong and fresh. The ground covered with leaves gave gently under his feet, and the dew on the grass wet his shoes and the bottoms of his trousers. On one side the road disappeared into the woods. On the other, the side of the house struck by the sun, lay a rolling landscape of pastures and cultivated fields interrupted by white fences and farmhouses and tall barns painted vivid colors. He would have liked to follow either of those roads. But he was afraid he might get lost or be late, and he went back to the guesthouse, not only as a precaution but also because he saw himself as incongruous in his European city suit and shoes. From the outside, measuring it against the scale of the trees, he admired the shape of the building, the suggestion of deep roots in the way it rested in the clearing, solid and closed in to resist the cold of winters, a structure beautifully integrated into the countryside, yet singular, the balustrade of the terrace above the columns of the portico, the large windows facing all the cardinal points, the woods, the cultivated fields, the river, and beyond, the elevated line of blue mountains. He went back to his room to polish his shoes again and the bed was already made, the fold of the sheet straight, the pillows plumped up. Sitting by the window, his back erect in the solid chair, his hand resting on the desk, on the folder of drawings and watercolors he'd brought from Madrid, he imagined letters to his children and Judith Biely, calculated the time in Spain, listened to the sound of Stevens's car slowly approaching.

Stevens was flushed, recently showered, resplendent, as if not only the gold frame and lenses of his glasses had been polished but also his light blue eyes, his nails, his teeth, his shoes of creaking leather that transported him from the car at almost the same speed as he'd been driving. He smelled of cologne and mint toothpaste. When Ignacio Abel sat down beside him, Stevens started the car and looked at his watch, impatient to make use of his time, to complete each of the tasks he'd planned for the morning, jumping arbitrarily from English to a Spanish so heavily accented it was unintelligible, gesturing to show him the points of interest around the campus, more at ease this morning, more sure of himself because he wasn't subjected to the intimidating presence of Philip Van Doren. They stopped at buildings that had an air between Gothic and rural and contained overheated offices. The secretaries or typists smiled when they shook Ignacio Abel's hand and paid close attention to hear his foreign name clearly, demonstrating by their high-pitched voices the enthusiasm they felt at meeting him, especially when Stevens listed his accomplishments, then showing a pained compassion when Stevens mentioned the war in Spain and the difficulties Professor Abel had to overcome to leave the country. He had to fill out forms, show documents, answer questions, nod even if he was confused, didn't understand what he'd been asked, couldn't find his passport or the document he'd put in a pocket moments before in another office. He had to get in the car again and continue the rest of the tour: meadows, patches of forest, rural paths, churches, classroom buildings, dormitories, athletic fields, more overheated offices and introductions, then again the fresh air with the smell of forest and lawn, the car backing up abruptly and Stevens looking at his watch, the labyrinth of goings and comings shrinking, reassuringly, to one scenario, the irregular quadrangle around which the principal buildings of the campus were organized: another University City, not half in the planning stage and left hanging and abandoned before it had come into existence, not erected on a tabula rasa of desert-like fields and eradicated pine groves, but having grown gradually, first as pioneer settlements in clearings in those forests long ago, then taking on a form both haphazard and organic, with visual similarities to British universities: Gothic towers, expanses of lawn, ivy-covered walls, and always—it seemed to Ignacio Abel, a newly arrived guest to this peculiar slowness of time, a convalescent from Spanish cataclysms—a serenity that corresponded to the immemorial cycles of the world, the passing of the seasons and the course of the river close by, gradual building rather than fits of rapture as sudden as disasters. At one of their stops, Stevens opened a door, preceded him up a spiral staircase, crossed a corridor with a low ceiling and stone ribs, opened a door that led to a small, comfortable room, and said, to Abel's surprise, that this would be his office. In another room he was introduced to a group that welcomed him eagerly, it is so exciting to finally have you here as part of our faculty, and a moment later Stevens unceremoniously tugged on his sleeve and took him downstairs to a windowless room that was a photography studio. In the few minutes before the next undertaking, he ought to have his picture taken for his college identity card. The photographer had him sit on a stool before a black curtain and worked hard to get him into the correct position, making jokes Ignacio Abel didn't understand but that provoked in the photographer hilarity not shared with Stevens, who kept glancing at his watch because soon they were to have lunch with a group of professors at the Faculty Club, and before that, a visit to the site of the future library. It was Mr. Van Doren's special wish, he'd told him that very morning, that Professor Abel see the spot and make his preliminary notes on the terrain. That photograph must be somewhere in the archives of Burton College, the file card with his name typed in, faded because of the passage of time, the corners worn or folded, the attempt at a smile by an overly serious man who that morning looked older than his age, his face baffled, worried, unfamiliar, his lips curving rigidly at the corners.

Now he doesn't have to smile, or nod, or make an effort to understand what's said to him, or follow Stevens's hurried steps. Stevens begged his pardon for leaving him, he had to teach a class. Would Ignacio Abel manage on his own for the next few hours? Would he like a student to accompany him or drive him back to the guesthouse? But nothing appeals to Ignacio Abel more than being alone with his thoughts. He's discovered that in reality everything is close: the car made distances seem longer. He knows now that it takes less than fifteen minutes to walk to the guesthouse that seemed so deep in the woods. This morning the tree branches hit the windows of Stevens's car when it ascended the narrow road that led to the clearing of the first excavation for the future library, abandoned years earlier. Such a long trip to reach this destination: a hole in the ground half covered by weeds, fallen trunks, and dry leaves over several autumns, the edges raked by the teeth of steam shovels. After imagining it so often, Ignacio Abel hadn't been able to look fully at what he at last had before his eyes. To really see something, he's always needed to be alone. Only Judith's presence expanded his capacity for seeing, opened his eyes to things he wouldn't have noticed without her. Madrid was a different city because he discovered it through her eyes. Stevens was beside him, and even when he was quiet, his mere presence distracted and irritated him. The excavation extended from the top of the hill to the middle of a slope. To one side were the campus buildings at the end of the road, grouped against the landscape extending to the horizon, and at the same time spaced out, with a haphazard appearance that when closely observed revealed an axis, an organizing principle, around the quadrangle Stevens called *the Commons.* To the west, beyond the red and ocher and yellow undulation of the treetops, the river was a broad metal plate attenuated by blue mist where the sun reverberated, the white sails of boats suspended in it like butterflies. Stevens pointed out mountains or buildings in the distance, mentioned their names, cited dates of construction and the exact dimensions of the plot on which the library would be built. "And the river view," he said, like a guide longing to persuade a group of tourists of the value of the place he's sharing with them. He looked at his watch, impatient for the visit to fit into the amount of time allotted it, unable to be still and silent. It was twelve-fifteen, he said; at twelve-thirty they had a table reserved at the Faculty Club.

Now he follows the road up the slope, in the enormous shade of the trees, maples and oaks, which he thinks he recognizes, and others whose names he doesn't know in Spanish or in English, and he thinks of the labels on the trees in the Botanical Garden in Madrid, and of Judith Biely's surprise when she recognized some, like friends you meet unexpectedly in a foreign country, their sumptuous autumn colors standing out even more in a city of earth tones and dusty greens. But here they're much taller in this dark soil, fed by the rain, covered by fallen leaves, then snow during the long winters, infused by slim, secret threads of water when the thaw begins. He thinks with nostalgia, with melancholy, of the young trees planted along the avenues in University City, so fragile in Madrid's extreme temperatures, always threatened by the cold that comes down from the snow-covered peaks of the Guadarrama or by the heat of summer, their trunks almost as slender as those on the wire trees he sometimes put on maquettes, cutting foliage for them out of green-colored cardboard. Some mornings, when he drove to the office to check on the progress of construction, he found the trees broken, knocked down by vandals, the rancor against trees of people from dry, barren lands who fear the roots will rob them of already scarce water. But now he knows that the mere weakness of something encourages its destruction, and perhaps for that reason he's even more astonished that these trees have grown for several centuries, older than the buildings that can be glimpsed through the groves, perhaps more enduring than the future library, with branches so long they intersect over his head like the ribs of a vault that barely filters the sun's rays and sheds, at the least breath of wind, a cloud of leaves; branches that no one prunes, at least not with the rage he's seen so often in the axes wielded against the trees in Madrid. But I didn't care either, when construction of University City began, that the trees of Moncloa would be cut down, the pines with long trunks and rounded tops that succumbed to axes and power saws, roots like heads of hair torn out by steam shovels, streams buried with dirt then rerouted. We leveled everything to start as if on a blank page, on the flattened scars of what had existed before. Walking up the road between trees that gleam with flaming reds and yellows when the sun shines on them, Ignacio Abel remembers Manuel Azaña's face, not on the recent day when he said goodbye to him, but on an afternoon no more than four years ago. A cold, cloudy afternoon in November, the Sierra submerged in a gray-blue fog of rain. Azaña was prime minister then and had come almost on the spur of the moment to view the construction, probably urged to do so by Negrín, who brought him in his own car. Ignacio Abel waited for them with the director of University City, the architect López Otero, who'd been a friend of Alfonso XIII and didn't much like the Republic, not to mention the prime minister. "Don't leave this afternoon, Abel," Negrín had said, "we have an important official visit." But the visitors, whom they received at the temporary construction management office, arrived late in a small yellow car that pulled up with a screech of brakes. Negrín got out first on the driver's side and walked around to open the other door, holding it like a chauffeur, hat in hand, as the prime minister emerged from the car, awkwardly and slowly, his normally colorless face red with the effort, encased in an ostentatious overcoat, so heavy he couldn't detach himself without help from the low seat. Supporting himself on Negrín's strong hand, finally on his feet, Azaña ran his fingers through his thin, disheveled hair before putting on his hat, recovering his ministerial dignity, extending his hand — indifferent and fleshy, slightly damp — for them to shake. The group walked for a while among the skeletons of buildings, observed at a distance by some straggling laborers. While López Otero and Negrín acted as guides, moving their arms to conjure completed installations that would rise one day in that immense space still bare of recognizable forms, Ignacio Abel observed Azaña's expression, a mixture of boredom and affront, his watery eyes following the procedure without much interest, then fading, or meeting his, perhaps seeking assurance that nothing was expected of him. Azaña stopped, looked around, and the others stopped too, close to the foundation of what would be the Philosophy Building. "What did you do with all the pine groves that grew here? Half of Spain is desert. Why did you have to build your University City on the spot where there were woods?" López Otero cleared his throat and swallowed. "Your Excellency will remember that it was His Majesty Don Alfonso XIII who ceded at no charge the property that belonged to the crown." Ignacio Abel noticed the tension in Negrín, the vibration in the clenched jaw. Beneath the eyelids that partially veiled his eyes, perhaps Azaña assessed the unseemliness of López Otero's words, the possible lack of respect. Why "His Majesty" and not "Alfonso XIII" without the ceremonious "Don," or simply "the king," or "the former king"? "We'll have a campus like those at American universities, Don Manuel. People will come to stroll here as they strolled in the Moncloa pine groves. There'll be better groves." Azaña had a way of staring as he listened and at the same time remaining distant, as if he saw his interlocutor only vaguely. "I repeat my observation, Don Juan, and believe me, I'm as determined as you to complete University City. The fact that it began as a whim of Alfonso XIII — 'His Majesty,' as Señor López Otero calls him — doesn't detract from its merit. But why cut down the best trees in Madrid to plant new ones? It may be egotism on my part. No matter how quickly they grow, I won't be here to see them."

How difficult the first step in the conception of what doesn't exist yet: the line of a sketch that might contain in germ the final work, an angle that will engender the complete drawing, not obeying any external purpose but guided by an impulse toward organic growth. Where there's nothing, there has to be something. From a blank page the first form of a library must emerge. From a hole dug into the side of a hill and quickly covered by vegetation that replaces what was gutted or cut down, walls will rise, staircases, balustrades, windows. The form sketched in the notebook will be glimpsed through the groves of trees and may be seen from sailboats or barges with blunt prows and rusted hulls that pass along the river. Ignacio Abel has the notebook open on his knees and a pencil in his hand but hasn't drawn anything yet. He is seated on the partially hollow trunk of a tree that fell perhaps many years ago, its roots in the air, the surface burrowed by insects that in some areas have reduced the wood to soft powder. He hears cracking noises, the sounds of animals he can't see, the flapping of birds over his head that stir brief eddies of fallen leaves. This area of the woods hasn't been cleared out in a long time. Fragments of trunks, packed-down dry branches, and sheets of bark mix together on the ground under a carpet of many autumns' leaves, the oldest the color of the earth and in part blended with it, crumbled by insects juxtaposing their shapes and colors like disordered pieces in a mosaic, with a variety of ribs and symmetries he would have liked to decipher by drawing them in the notebook, or better still, picking them up and pressing them between its pages. From the river comes the muffled noise of a train, the sound of a foghorn he heard in his dreams last night. The fallen trunks, covered with lichen, remind him of the ruins in the Roman Forum: grass and wild mustard, broken columns, the marble on the capitals so eroded and porous it has become pure debris and turned a calcareous white like animal bones. He understands that the sketches he's made are useless. The building can't have existed in his imagination with that diamond-like perfection he's admired so much when he saw Mies van der Rohe's pavilion in Barcelona — admired with envy of something he knew he wouldn't be capable of achieving, feeling mediocre, limited, provincial. How would a prism of steel and glass look, surging before the eyes of someone coming up the road between the trees, or seen from other buildings on the campus when night fell, shining in the distance like an illuminated lighthouse. The imminence of work generates in him both excitement and dejection: sloth, almost panic, the vertigo of a void he isn't sure he'll know how to confront. A squirrel with a rounded body and lustrous fur approaches with a succession of brief movements and picks up an acorn, examines it, suspended between its front paws. He doesn't move, so as not to frighten it, and the squirrel turns its back, brushing one of his shoes with a tail as soft and full as a shaving brush, moves away in silent leaps, divested of weight, making a sound in the leaves as faint as the damp breeze that makes them tremble. The sky has clouded over, the air is cooler, and the leaves are falling in more frequent gusts of wind. A round drop dampens the middle of the page in the notebook where he hasn't drawn anything. He raises his head and Philip Van Doren looks at him, smiling, his arms crossed, leaning against a tree.

"I see you managed to free yourself from Stevens. But you should be careful in these woods, Ignacio. As a city dweller, you don't know its dangers."

"Are there wild animals?"

"Something worse, that I don't believe you have in Spain. Poison ivy."

"*Hiedra venenosa?*"

"Right now you're sitting close to it. You can't imagine the itching. But it's fantastic to see you wearing your suit from Madrid in our *American wilderness.* I wish Judith could see you."

They look at each other across the clearing, not saying anything now that the name's been spoken. A light rain has begun to fall. From an athletic field comes a burst of scattered applause and the sharp repeated sound of a whistle. Ignacio Abel has closed the notebook and put it in a jacket pocket, expectant for no reason, alarmed because he's heard Judith's name, the evidence of her objective existence.

"You want to ask me whether I know anything about Judith, but you can't bring yourself to. Like that night in Madrid, don't you remember? The city was burning and all you could think of was finding her. You're reserved, something I approve of. Given my Lutheran upbringing, so am I. But I don't like your distrust of me. I've given you proof of my loyalty. It wasn't easy getting you out of Spain and arranging for you to come to America, to Burton College."

"I regret not having thanked you."

"I'm not asking you to."

Now the sky was a darker gray that accentuated the shadows deep in the forest. Ignacio Abel swallowed.

"Were you her lover when you lived in Paris?"

"Splendid Spanish jealousy." Van Doren looked at him, smiling fondly, almost indulgently. "I imagined you took it for granted I don't find women attractive."

"Probably only Judith attracted you."

"Don't say it in the past tense. I find Judith very attractive. More than any other woman and more than a lot of men. I was drawn to her from the moment I saw her, on the deck of the ship that had just taken off from America. In that regard you and I are alike. We both saw in her a desire to experience everything, to enjoy everything, without irony, like a model student, which is what she should have been. You need a good deal of nobility to feel real enthusiasm. Judith's doctorate was Europe. Everything in Europe — architecture, museums, paintings. I don't think anyone has spent more time or been happier at the Louvre, or the Jeu de Paume, or the Uffizi, or the Prado. She felt the same rapture sitting in a café and writing a card or a letter and putting Paris in the return address. The letters she wrote to her mother, do you remember? Pages and pages, telling her everything, like class exercises where she demonstrated how much she'd learned. The Americans who come to Paris settle into a café on Saint-Germain-des-Prés as soon as they can and put on a weary look that says they've already seen it all and don't have to go on playing the tourist. Being a tourist is a humiliating condition. But Judith didn't have those reservations. She wanted to climb the Eiffel Tower and attend a Gregorian Mass in Notre-Dame and ride at night in a Bateau Mouche along the Seine. She also wanted to go to Shakespeare and Company and spend hours looking at the books she longed to read and standing watch in case James Joyce or Hemingway put in an appearance. Judith is the great American enthusiast. Even more American because her parents are Russian Jews who speak English with a terrible accent. Her mother, as you know, sacrificed everything so she could make this trip, and Judith had to show her that she was taking advantage of every penny. One invests hard-earned money and expects a profit. *To squeeze every penny of it dry.* She'd be offended if she heard me say it, but it's a very Jewish idea of return on your money. Very Jewish and very American. Money doesn't provoke in us the modesty you have in Europe, especially in Spain. Every cent her mother kept in a tin box, hiding it in the kitchen, was a small act of prowess when you think what the past few years have been like in my country for people of the class Judith belongs to. Penny by penny, the sound of copper in the tin box, the worn dollar bills. But your life wasn't very different when you were young, if I'm not mistaken. I have a gift for imagining what other people are living or have lived through.

That's my only talent. Just as you have a gift for seeing what doesn't exist yet."

"You haven't answered my question."

"Lovers, Judith and I? If it were true, you wouldn't need to ask. Judith would have told you. American honesty. *Full disclosure*, we say. *Just to set the record straight.* In Paris what I liked most about her was not so much Judith herself as the enthusiasm she radiated, the light that was in her. She'd go into a café filled with smoke on one of those horrible black rainy afternoons, and it seemed she was followed by the spotlight in a theater. But I fell more in love in Madrid. Not with Judith but with your love for her, what you were seeing when you looked at her and what she saw in you. I wanted to be you when I saw her looking at you. I remember it all so well. I saw how you came into my apartment in Madrid and almost blushed when you discovered Judith among my guests that afternoon. A *coup de foudre* if I've ever seen one. You probably assume it's inevitable that I like opera, with all its falseness that's truer the more exaggerated and unbelievable it is. You were Tristan the moment he takes the cup away from his lips and looks at Isolde. Operas should be performed in street clothes and ordinary places, Tristan and Isolde or Pelléas and Mélisande meeting in a café after walking through a revolving door. Drinking an icy martini instead of a medieval cup of poison. But I'll understand if you've grown to hate Wagner. Perhaps Debussy is more tolerable. I was in Bayreuth two years ago and saw *Tristan*. When everybody was seated, waiting for the curtain to rise, there was a rush of uniforms and evening clothes because Chancellor Hitler had just entered the box of honor, but I didn't come to see him. It doesn't matter. I lack the ability to tell something in a straight line. You don't discipline yourself as a narrator if your entire life is spent surrounded by people who have to listen to you. You and Judith didn't know it yet, but the moment you saw each other the two of you were lost. I was dying of envy. The magnetic current between you passed through me, crossed the air in my house. I wanted to be each of you. Few things that have happened to me have shaken me as much. Nothing, in fact. The world seems to me a very expensive theatrical production mounted exclusively for me. All alone in a box in an enormous empty theater, like Ludwig of Bavaria attending the premiere of an opera by Wagner. He couldn't permit himself that, and ended up bankrupt. But I can. And what I like is not to watch a performance but real life. Actors are vain and venal, and if you approach them, you see the unpleasant makeup that melts on their faces under the heat of the lights and their sweat. I do no harm by observing real lives. I don't stoop to paying for others to pretend to love me. I prefer to see other people's genuine love, or any passion that ennobles them. Judith in Paris, looking at Manet's *Olympia* up close, or in Madrid when she went to one of those tiresome flamenco dance performances, or when she once showed me that empty museum you'd taken her to, the Academy of San Fernando, happy to show me something that was almost a secret and not those rooms in the Prado filled with foreigners. Or you a moment ago, so deep in your notebook you didn't hear me arrive. I've never learned how to do anything. My passion is observing the passions of others. If they consent, or if they don't know, who gets hurt?"

"You spied on us in the house on the beach. You offered it so you could follow us."

"Don't give me so little credit, Ignacio. I wasn't drooling in the next room, watching through a crack. It was enough for me to imagine you on those days. To see you from a certain distance. A telescope is the most useful of inventions."

It has started to rain. Tiny drops gleam on Van Doren's shaved head and he continues to stare at Ignacio Abel, his gestures passing from irony to the appearance of affection or complicity or sadness.

"I hope you're not offended. Judith didn't ask me to, but I did everything I could to bring you here. Not that it was difficult. Your name carries weight, even this deep in the woods. I needed to find a solution, if only a provisional one, a breather for you both. I knew your work and that's why I invited you, but then it was no more than a project, like so many others that go nowhere. As for Judith, she couldn't go on

577

postponing her return to America. Her mother's savings weren't going to last forever. I had to bring both of you here."

"To continue to spy on us?"

"So you'd have a part of the life you both deserved. So that thanks to your talent, Burton College will have a beautiful, modern library, and something I can do will objectively benefit the order of the world."

Van Doren turns when he hears a car coming up the muddy road. Stevens puts his head out the window, looking distressed, blows the horn with triumphant vehemence, as if he were sounding trumpets. He'd been looking for them for he doesn't know how long, he says, getting out of the car with an umbrella; he's been everywhere, afraid something had happened, that Professor Abel was lost. First he escorts Van Doren, opens the back door for him, comes back to Ignacio Abel, reminds him that in less than an hour they must be at the college president's house, and under no circumstances can they be late. The rain lashes the windshield when Stevens turns the car to go back to the campus, fat drops drumming on the leather top. Ignacio Abel looks at Van Doren—who's wiping his head and face with a handkerchief and looking out at the woods—as if he didn't remember his presence. But he has to decide, in spite of his cowardice, his fear of not knowing and his fear of knowing.

"Do you know where Judith is now?"

"Finally you ask me. You're a proud man."

"I'll ask it as a favor if you like."

"I heard her mother died of cancer this summer. Then I was told she found a job as an assistant professor at Wellesley College. Not far from here, a trip of a few hours. I wrote to tell her you were coming, but she hasn't answered my letter. She's like you. Too full of pride."

34

HE'LL REMEMBER THIS NIGHT'S storm, the rain pounding against the windshield and drumming on the roof of the car when Stevens took him back to the guesthouse after the dinner with the president of Burton College. He had too much to drink; he was nervous and didn't know what to say, what to do with his hands; he drank to give himself the courage to speak English and confront strangers. He'll remember the dizziness he felt on the curves, the windshield wipers moving at top speed in a back-and-forth fan, and on both sides of the road, large tree branches flung about by the wind. Stevens drove cautiously: from time to time a gust of wind shook the car as if to overturn it, and he clutched the steering wheel tighter and leaned forward. But now he remembered having seen him drinking before dinner no less avidly than he, and guzzling glasses of wine at the table. Perhaps Stevens was nervous too, doubly insecure in the presence not only of Van Doren but of the other authority figure before whom he bowed with such assiduous courtesy. Stevens was a man who seemed destined to serve, who suffered the anguish of not knowing to what extent his actions merited the inscrutable benevolence of his superiors. *Take it from me,* he told Ignacio Abel when they were walking to the car and he obsequiously held the umbrella over him, *you've made quite an impression on the president,* identifying with Ignacio in the precariousness of a position that depended on the favor of omnipotent men.

Ignacio grew lightheaded in the car simply by remembering the conversations, the dishes with French names pronounced with punctilious correctness by the president's wife to whose right he was seated at the table, the strangers coming up to him, the names he heard and forgot or couldn't decipher. The president's sumptuous name was Jonathan Joseph Almeida, but he asked to be called Jon, shaking his hand and placing his other hand on top as if to confirm his welcome, his admiration for Abel's work, perhaps also sympathy for the afflictions of the Spanish Republic, which had, according to another dinner guest, a professor of medieval English literature, not much more than forty-eight hours left. He'd heard on the radio or read in the paper something he repeated as if he'd memorized a headline: "The rebels appear to be less than a day's march from Madrid." As he said it, he stared at Ignacio Abel as if doubting he was who he said he was, or curious to see the face of someone who before long wouldn't have a country to go back to. Through cigarette smoke and his growing alcoholic haze, faces approached Ignacio Abel and receded, or rather faded away, like the names and cordial phrases expressed and the visiting cards offered that he looked at appreciatively then put in his pocket, apologizing for not being able to reciprocate. He'd left his cards in Spain, was his excuse, but as he said it, he imagined he wouldn't be believed, and that no one, not only the funereal medievalist, took seriously the role he had to play that night, incompetently, or the awkward English that alcohol made even harder to understand. Across the table, with his partially protective, partially ironic air, Van Doren observed him, intervening at times to help him out of a linguistic difficulty, repeating Ignacio Abel's credentials as if to confirm his identity: Professor Abel, Van Doren explained, spent years directing the most ambitious university construction project in Europe, and had studied with Bruno Taut and Walter Gropius in Germany. And though what he said was approximately true, the portion of calculated exaggeration made it suspect, at least to the vigilant ears of Abel himself, more alert and insecure because he was engaged in several conversations at the same time and felt himself observed by pairs of eyes on whose scrutiny his future depended, above all the eyes of President Almeida, forceful behind round tortoise-shell glasses, his gaze arrogant and cool, as solidly protected against uncertainty as his large healthy body and his house, with its stone foundation and solid walls, were protected against the storm. He remembered an expression Judith Biely had taught him: *walking on thin ice.* He was feeling his way and walking on very thin ice. Observed by others, he was afraid they might discover his inner lack of substance, detect the discomfort behind his smile or the fear that had gradually become his natural state. The sullen professor of medieval English and a pastor or chaplain in a black suit and clerical collar looked at him as if suspecting a character flaw or secret vice or some kind of complicity in the burning of churches and killing of priests in the early days of the war, about which they seemed to have unlimited information. The president's wife sighed as she lifted her hand to her bosom, recalling the photographs of children in Madrid after bombing raids. He had to smile at the excessive gestures, keep himself upright to give the impression of personal integrity, accept pity as charity, knowing that at some point gratitude might be inseparable from humiliation. (Where would he go when the school year ended if it was true that Madrid was on the verge of falling?) He had to search in vain for clear, strong words to explain to the red-faced pastor in the black suit and clerical collar that the Republican government did not persecute priests, and though there were several Communist ministers, they were not planning to collectivize agriculture. He spoke, the heat rising in his face, the anxiety of the impostor who at any moment may be discovered; he swallowed and reached for his glass. A waitress approached from behind and filled it with wine. Over the noise of the general conversation, President Almeida asked him a question in his well-modulated voice, as if subjecting him to an examination: if Hitler and Mussolini were helping the rebels so shamelessly, did he believe the democracies would intervene at the last minute to save the Republic, or at least guarantee an armistice? "But there's no more time," the medieval scholar said, not without satisfaction, shaking his napkin, "they're lost." He leaned across the table to look at Ignacio Abel more closely and observe the effect of his question: "Do you see yourself being allowed to return to Spain any time soon, Professor?"

Meanwhile, at the back of his mind throbbed the name Van Doren had mentioned, Judith's name and the name of the place he could reach in a few hours by train. And another face and identity acquired a precise contour in spite of his confusion, exacerbated by his not being accustomed to drinking alcohol, a woman who looked American and spoke Spanish with a strange accent but who was a Spaniard: Miss Santos, the always useful Stevens told him, and then corrected himself, *Doctor* Santos, the head of the Department of Romance Languages, who was happy to greet a compatriot, she said, though she had been in America for so many years she was no longer sure where she came from. Van Doren had mentioned Judith Biely's name and the name of Wellesley College, then remained silent and devoted himself to observing the effect of his confidence, studying Ignacio Abel from his corner of the dinner table where Ignacio had Dr. Santos on his right, more aseptic and American in her gestures, taking small sips of water, never wine. It was she who named the place, not because Ignacio Abel had asked but because someone spoke of the many European professors, Germans in particular, coming to American universities. They spoke of Einstein at Princeton, of Thomas Mann settling in California, and Dr. Santos said to Ignacio Abel, assuming no one else would recognize the name, "I'm not sure you're aware that Pedro Salinas is at Wellesley College. Do you know him personally?"

The names, pronounced innocently, had a chemical effect. Everything became more unreal, as if out of focus, the dining room lit by a large chandelier, the faces, the voices, and the storm that rattled the windows. He reacts suddenly, shaken to his nerve endings not by the imminent expectation of satisfaction but only by the enunciation of its possibility: Judith Biely doesn't belong to the irretrievable past; she's not an invention; she has a life apart from him, she's returned to America, she perhaps was at her dying mother's bedside; she might be attending a dinner like this one, with its tedium of courtesies; she's in a place he could travel to by train or car in a few hours; she's on the same plane of existence as the poet Salinas, whom Dr. Santos has mentioned so casually, not knowing that by doing so she has extended another thread to Judith, Salinas's student last year at the School of Philosophy. Judith had a book of his poems he'd signed; sometimes she asked Ignacio Abel to read verses aloud so she could hear the intonation and asked him the meaning of difficult words. (How strange to read those poems and think they could have been inspired by Señora de Salinas, one of Adela's good friends, though somewhat older, as fond as Adela of English-style teas and lectures for ladies at the Lyceum Club; even stranger to recall the Lyceum Club and think it had ever existed, not in the remote past but a year ago, not even that, in the city that Hitler's and Mussolini's planes are flying over tonight, *Franco's rebel troops tightening their grip around three sides of Madrid,* said the newspaper Ignacio Abel leafed through nervously this very morning at the Faculty Club, providing no details, dryly enunciating the course of destiny.) "My wife and his are good friends," he said, returning to the conversation, conscious of the inattentiveness Dr. Santos would have noticed, and to compensate he forced himself to continue talking, relieved he could rest from English. From the window in his office at University City he'd watch Professor Salinas drive by every morning on the way to the Philosophy Building, and more than once they'd run into each other in the hallway. Dr. Santos listened, leaning forward with her pale Spanish face and American gestures, not suspecting that Ignacio Abel wasn't speaking to her but to himself, Judith's name now almost on his lips, because when he told her about running into Pedro Salinas in the Philosophy Building, he was invoking Judith without naming her, thinking about one of those times when resignation and decency and the normal order of life were overturned, as in the middle of some task when the phone rang and it was Judith calling him. As she left one of Salinas's seminars, she saw the row of telephone booths recently installed in the lobby and couldn't resist the temptation. He said he'd meet her right away and hung up so quickly he forgot to ask where she'd be waiting. He put on his jacket and crossed the office, eluding those who approached to consult with him. What excuse would he invent if he ran into someone he knew? He'd see Judith in a lobby filled with people or in the cafeteria and have to control himself so as not to embrace her. The impulse that guided his feet down the stairs had nothing to do with his will. In a few minutes he drove the distance between his office and the Philosophy Building, and as he climbed the staircase he saw in the distance the dean, García Morente, with his owl's glasses and absurd sideburns, and he looked away so he wouldn't have to stop and greet him. In the high, translucent stained-glass windows, the morning sun was transformed into a silvery brilliance that filled the lobby, reflecting the beautiful polished surfaces, the tiles on the walls and the banisters, the marble flagstones on which students' footsteps resonated, the hammering of workmen, the din of voices. After looking for Judith in the cafeteria, he went back to the lobby and in a flash of inspiration jumped on one of the automatic elevators. He found her on the terrace, leaning against the railing, her hair pushed back and her face turned toward the gentle March sun, her back to a Guadarrama horizon exaggerated by the distance, the peaks still covered with snow, her legs bare in short white socks. *I like that you look for me without knowing whether you'll find me.*

He could get up right now from the table, fold his napkin, and go out to look for her, without hope or dignity, not encouraged by any promise but only by the words that have continued acting on him like the drops of a drug entering his bloodstream and going straight to his brain. From across the table Philip Van Doren observes him, smoking, hardly having tasted the dinner, watching and watching over him, intrigued by the consequences of his words, the dosage of information he'd administered just a few hours before, impatient to know what the president's wife could be saying to Ignacio Abel, who's turned toward her after conversing with Dr. Santos. He could get up without remorse, leaving her in midsentence, and go look for Judith, as shameless as on other occasions when he left a meeting in the office or a family dinner:

though Judith hasn't called him or may not wish to see him, he is summoned not by her desire but by the fact of her existence. *If you were to call me,* she read aloud from the book, with its austere cover, signed by Salinas, in which she'd underlined the many words she didn't know and made notes in the margins. But Ignacio Abel didn't believe those lines, in part because of his general indifference to poetry and because he didn't associate those ecstasies of love with Señora Bonmati de Salinas. Too much the professor, he told Judith, lowering the level of his skepticism so as not to annoy her; too self-involved to lose his head over a woman and too busy with all those official tasks he was involved in. *I would leave it all, throw it all away.* And she said, "If you're so sure Salinas is lying, it's because you're just like him"— suddenly irritated in Madame Mathilde's house one very hot morning at the end of May, close to the end, turning her back to him, her skin glowing with sweat. Now he has nothing, nothing he'd need to leave behind to go away with her. The president's wife compassionately inquires about his wife and children, doesn't he know anything about them, are they in danger. He nods and puts on the required expression of sorrow, and at the same time feels in the beating of his heart, in the pit of his stomach, that he was ready to leave right away and drive for hours to look for Judith or sit on a bench in the station waiting for a train that would take him to Wellesley College. Without hope, almost without purpose, simply letting himself be carried along, seized by the undeniable fact of Judith Biely's presence in the world. "I'm sure we can find a way for them to join you soon. I can imagine how you must feel after so much time away from your children, your wife." Alcohol made self-pity easy, the imposture Van Doren didn't fail to notice, catching loose threads of the conversation, willfully joining in, pulling his shirt cuffs back from his hairy wrists, his neck muscles constrained by his tie; he'd need to use his influence with the International Red Cross, he said, looking Ignacio Abel in the eye, enthusiastically seconded by Stevens, who if necessary would appeal to his contacts in the State Department. And as Van Doren spoke, he was silently asking Ignacio Abel whether he really wanted to reunite with his wife and children or was he capable of acknowledging to himself that the only thing he wanted was to see Judith Biely again.

The clink of a fork on President Almeida's cut-crystal wineglass roused him from his self-absorption. Van Doren made a wry face, raising an eyebrow, with the benevolent look of someone attending a long theatrical performance, interested but always at the edge of boredom — here comes the inevitable speech, the toast. Gradually the voices died down along with the sounds of silverware and glasses, and for a moment all you could hear was the wind in the chimney. The glass of wine in his right hand, the president raised it toward Ignacio Abel. He had thin blond hair, almost white, a face crisscrossed with fine red veins radiating abundant health, like the table covered with food no one had finished, and the house filled with colonial furniture, shelves with valuable leather-bound editions, paintings and lamps and rugs, photographs on the sideboards and the mantel in which President Almeida posed with eminent public figures, smiling into the camera as he shook their hands (among them, the First Lady and President Roosevelt on one of his visits, not at all unusual, to Burton College, so close to his family home in Hyde Park). An oil portrait of President Almeida presided over the dining room. In the hall, among old landscapes in oil of the banks of the Hudson, was a drawing, clearly a sketch for the oil portrait. You had to listen to the speech with the proper expression of agreement, interest, satisfaction, your laugh ready for the jokes the president interjected and must have repeated at many similar dinners, and the seriousness when he enunciated the dim prospects of Europe and mentioned the college's tradition of hospitality, identical to the nation's, for three centuries a land of refuge for dissidents, molded by them, made great by spirits who had outgrown the borders of the old countries. Looking around him at this very table — he did so, turning his head slowly, his eyes enlarged behind his glasses — what did he see, he said, but the children or grandchildren or great-grandchildren of immigrants, with family names that declared so many diverse origins:

Dutch, Scots, Huguenots, Portuguese, like his own Almeida forebears. And Spaniards, he said, looking first at Dr. Santos, and now it was time for a well-bred joke, let's hope Dr. Santos isn't descended from a grand inquisitor, provoking a chorus of laughter and an uncomfortable blush on the face of the woman. And finally, closing the circle of glances and allusions, President Almeida spoke to Ignacio Abel, not without demonstrating that he knew how his last name was pronounced and on which syllable the stress fell: the red face, the glass of wine raised a little higher, the brilliance of the fire and the large crystal chandelier reflecting on his smooth skin, his shirt front stretched by the size of his shoulders and chest muscles. He thinks he's immortal, Abel thought as he smiled and waited for the end of the speech to give his thanks and dare a few sentences he'd been turning over in his mind for some time; he thinks he'll never grow old, that no misfortune will ever befall him, that his house will never be burned, that he won't be awakened at midnight and taken away in his pajamas to an empty lot and killed in front of headlights. President Almeida was now calling him *our new colleague, distinguished guest, outstanding, leading, accomplished,* but he looked sideways at Van Doren and Stevens as if asking for confirmation that the descriptions they'd put in his mouth were trustworthy. After the toast, the brief applause, the guest stood, dizzy from drink, a beginner again at his age, a guest of rather dubious standing, thinking of Judith Biely's voice, his desire for her as immediate and physical as a pain in the joints, a desire he was conscious of as he prepared to say something, his mouth dry, *walking on thin ice.*

He'll remember that as they came out of a curve, the windshield was clear for a few seconds and the headlights illuminated a house in front of which a recently fallen tree had crushed a car: a group of people lashed by the wind looked at it with an astonished air under the revolving lights of an ambulance. Without taking his eyes off the highway, Stevens spoke optimistically so as not to alarm him or to dispel his own fear: he'd heard President Almeida, he had to begin his classes and start work on the library project, in a few days his house would be ready and he'd have an office and a studio, work was the best remedy for discouragement. The way you speak to a sick man without giving him hope of a cure. Assuring him up to a certain point, don't forget your real condition, the distance that separates you from the healthy, they will be the first to point it out (as if certain of their immunity, certain they will never die). They arrived at the guesthouse, and when Ignacio Abel got out of the car the rain had stopped. The wind, calmer now, rustled in the treetops. Helpful, implacable, ridiculous, Stevens said goodbye and reminded him that he'd come for him at nine in the morning, *blowing my bugle right under your window,* immune to fatigue and the predictable hangover.

He'll remember entering the foyer and being enveloped by a darkness without limits, a total silence. He felt for the porcelain light switch, and when he finally found it he realized the power was out. The wind that an hour earlier had torn up trees by the roots must have knocked down utility poles. The house was much larger when you had to feel your way through it. Like moving through the apartment in Madrid on the nights of bombing raids. His hands brushing against the walls, his footsteps uncertain, his eyes slowly becoming used to the dark. Prudent, attentive to any eventuality, on the previous afternoon Stevens had shown him the closet next to the kitchen where brooms and defunct appliances were kept, along with an oil lamp and a supply of matches and candles. Touching the walls and bookshelves, Ignacio Abel crossed the library, reached the kitchen, tried to remember where the broom closet was. He lights the oil lamp almost by touch. The storm whistles in the distance, beyond the wooded hills and the river. He walks through the library again and catches a glimpse of himself in the mirror over the mantel, a gray-haired man, his features exaggerated by the contrast of shadows and oily light. The grand piano, the books on the shelves, the chairs folded against the wall, the morning newspaper on the arm of an easy chair, formulate the limits of an expectation, tense in their immobility, like the face in the mirror. I've come so far to walk around a house at night as deserted and dark as the one I left in Madrid, empty now, perhaps, accumulating dust, abandoned to the mysterious decrepitude of places where no one lives, or destroyed by a bomb, obscenely exposed to light from the street in the half-ruined building. One night he was standing in the dark hall, and suddenly someone knocked at the door. Lost in time, in the tunnel of shadows the lamp has cast in the mirror, he slowly realizes he is hearing it not in his head, not in the past, not in Madrid, but now. Silence shattered, his heart racing, overcome with the certainty that Judith Biely stands at the door, calling him, not in a dream, not in a delirium of desire, but just a few steps away.

35

S HE STANDS BEFORE HIM, lit by the lamp he holds. At the open door, the damp breeze from the woods blows in his face, his eyes blinded by the headlights of a car parked in front of the house, its motor running. He looks at her and doesn't say anything, neither one says anything, while the burbling of the motor continues and the windshield wipers click. The light strikes her face at an angle, her eyes, her damp hair now stylishly cut, shorter and not combed back but with a part and a lock of hair on one side that she brushes off her face with a gesture familiar and at the same time foreign, sudden, different. They look at each other without moving, his left hand holding the lamp, his right still on the doorknob. He looks at the car, its motor running and headlights on, in which he instantly fears there's someone, a man, who's come with her and at any moment will reclaim her by blowing the horn. "I thought nobody was in, I didn't see a light," she says in Spanish. Her voice, darker than he remembered it, has a more pronounced American accent. *Pensé que no había nadie:* so much time longing for this voice, the lips that form the words, not knowing how to invoke it, believing at times he'd heard it saying his name in the commotion of a street, a station, whispering close to his ear moments before waking. He takes a step toward her, or only takes his hand off the doorknob, as Judith draws back in an almost invisible gesture. He's afraid if he moves or says anything, he'll lose her; he's afraid she'll turn on her heels and get back in the car or vanish into the woods just as she's emerged from them. Judith starts to move as if to turn but remains still, looking at him, a corner of her mouth curving into the beginning of a smile. In the faint, close light of the lamp her face is less familiar because the short hair exaggerates her features: her large mouth, the triangle of her cheekbones and chin, the line of her jaw. Ignacio Abel doesn't move the hand that would have liked to caress her, but his eyes transmit to his fingers the sensation of touching her skin. Judith points at the car and says, now in English, *"I'd better turn it off."*

What surprised her most about Ignacio Abel was his dark suit, so European and old-fashioned, and how thin he was, his eyes sunk into their sockets. An attempt to bridge the distance between them causes an imperceptible retreat. Not a step back but a subtle gesture, little more than the dilation of a pupil, the bat of an eyelid. How strange to have once been so intimate with this middle-aged stranger whom she might now pass on any street without turning her head. They don't know how to act, what to say. Nothing dissolves as swiftly as physical intimacy. The gulf between them at the café in Madrid where they met for the last time is now in the doorway of this house, the slash of a knife in the space between their two bodies.

"I'd better turn it off": Ignacio Abel deciphered the words only once he sees them demonstrated by her actions. As Judith turns her back and walks to the car, he recognizes the self-confidence, the movement of her shoulders, her hands. He registers her face and presence as slowly as the words. The pride in her shoulders, the slight inclination of her head, her hips hugged by trousers. Her haircut modifies her face as it did when he'd see her wearing it pulled back, and she was more herself and at the same time another Judith, whom he desired even more because she was unexpected. She returns from the car, and as she climbs the stone steps, she reenters the circle of light from the lamp. Now she almost smiles at him when she says something he translates after hearing it: *"Aren't you going to ask me in?"* He looks at her as if gradually

recognizing the features he'd touched in the dark, when he breathed in the smell of her skin and hair with his eyes closed. She smells of herself and her old cologne and fatigue and the tension of many hours' traveling. She smells of the lipstick she put on a few minutes ago. Ignacio Abel looks at her face, at the details memory did not preserve and that were not reflected in the partial lie of photographs. Under her blouse and the wide-bottom trousers that narrow to encircle her waist, her beautiful tired body, so close to him, inaccessible now to his hands and eyes. The opened button on her blouse, the décolletage in shadow, the quiver of her breathing, red lips, gleaming in the light, the fatigued face she observed in the rearview mirror before getting out of the car, still motionless behind the wheel. A feeling of pity for him has taken her by surprise, lowered her guard. A troubling pity that would offend him if he ever suspected it, and a beginning of tenderness that doesn't resemble what she felt in the old days, the inexplicable past of only a few months ago. Then, Ignacio Abel looked no more than forty. When he opened the door, and even more so when she came back from the car, she saw a man much older, awkward, as if frightened, staring at her as he rigidly held up the oil lamp. The dark pinstriped suit, the double-breasted jacket with the wide lapels — wasn't it the one he wore the day of his talk at the Residence, and again at Van Doren's house? — now looks secondhand. The loosened tie encircles a neck that is almost an old man's. She sees his awkwardness, his alarm, not the yearning for closeness he had then, the physical affirmation of male desire, the instinctive arrogance. He looks shorter, but it's because now, unlike then, his shoulders are slightly rounded and his posture diminished and no doubt exaggerated by how loose his suit is. She wants to tell him not to hunch over, to straighten his shoulders. She could extend her hand and touch his face, noting the rough stubble of beard that was there by the time they'd meet in the late afternoon. She recovers the sensation of burying her fingertips in his thick hair, now grayer and lacking the sheen it had when he wore it combed back. "*Me dejarás entrar?*" she says, changing to Spanish, and the open smile on her face is a truce, almost a welcome to the side of the world where they find themselves now. "I'm dying to use the bathroom."

He hears her footsteps upstairs. He pays attention: he hears her urinate, then the water in the pipes, the sink faucet. Lying in bed, he'd listen to her wash in the wretched bathroom in Madame Mathilde's house, then turn his face to see her appear naked in the doorway, smelling of the soap and cologne she'd brought in her toiletries bag. She closed the door and turned on the faucet before sitting down to urinate: she told him it embarrassed her to have him hear her. Sexual excitement returns like a surprise, retrieved by memory and by Judith's presence on the floor above in this large house where only a few minutes ago no human closeness seemed possible, only the creaking and chafing of the wood floors, the gurgle of steam in the heating pipes. She told him she was cold and hungry. While he listens to her in the bathroom, he has stirred up the fire in the library and looked for something to eat in the pantry and refrigerator. The flames fill the library with a red glow where shadows oscillate like plants under water. The windowpanes are mirrors where Ignacio Abel moves accompanied by his shadow, looking for things with a male lack of confidence: sliced salami, rye bread, an apple, the tablecloth the maid spread out for his breakfast, a fork and a knife, a glass of water. He finds a beer in the refrigerator and nervously looks through drawers for an opener. Doing something has calmed him, given him a sense of reality as he waits for Judith to come down from the second floor and listens to her footsteps: the water in the sink is turned off and the door to the bathroom is closed; she walks slowly along the hall, her way lit by a small candle; she descends the stairs. She sees him standing by the fire and would like to shake him, wake him up, if only to see the man she had left with so great an effort of courage and pride, the man who told her lies or half-truths she chose to believe, closing her eyes as deliberately as she let herself be driven by him in his car, her self-respect suspended, just like so many undertakings in her life, her body abandoned in the seat as his right hand searched for hers or caressed her between her thighs while music played on the radio. Her anger with him gave her a confidence she misses now. If there's no trace of danger in him, the responsibility and remorse for her own past actions, for what almost happened, are hers alone: the woman with wide hips and gray in her hair who tried to drown, the humiliation of discovering a deception that she, Judith, was complicit in, for she had acceded to a lie no love could shroud. When she saw them together that time at the Residence, she thought Ignacio Abel was younger than Adela. Now in the library she sees him in the light of the fire and thinks that by some strange shortcut in time he's reached his wife's age and belongs to the same world, the bureaucratic Catholic middle class of Madrid she'd seen leaving churches on Sunday mornings, going to tearooms on the Carrera de San Jerónimo, the married couples so serious, men and women in dark clothing, the women wearing veils. She wants to shake him, to feel the danger again and be capable of rejecting it, or to spare herself the pity she feels for him, the self-pity she sees in him, the humiliation of having lost her and not being desired by her; the precarious thread from which hung the fiction of his masculinity, further undermined by the fear and suffering of war. It's also the war she sees in his eyes, she thinks, in the weakening of his shoulders and arms, the loose skin under his chin.

"I look at you and I can't believe you're here."

"I'll leave soon."

"Then why did you come?"

"It was on my way. A detour."

"You'll stay the night. There are plenty of rooms."

"And what would your colleagues think if they saw me leave here in the morning? You don't know what these places are like. Wellesley's the same way. They know everything and gossip. Like a novel by Galdós, but with professors as protagonists."

"Then you shouldn't have come."

"I'll go as soon as I've eaten something and rested a bit. I can be in New York in two hours."

"Don't you have to teach class tomorrow?"

"I've left that job."

"But I thought they just hired you."

"Philip tells you everything."

"Is it true you're working with Salinas?"

"Worked. I know you don't like him, but he does remind me of you."

"Will his wife and children be joining him soon?"

"He doesn't know. He doesn't know whether his contract will be renewed for next year. He's discouraged when he doesn't get letters or news from Spain, and even more discouraged when he does. It's easy in these places to become isolated."

"I just arrived yesterday and already it seems I've been here a long time."

"Poor Professor Salinas tells me he misses Madrid a great deal. Whenever he can he escapes to New York for the weekend. But he says the hardest thing for him is getting used to eating without wine."

"Does he have any hope of going back to Spain?"

"What about you? You left not long ago. You're better informed than he is."

"I read the papers here and listen to the radio and everybody seems convinced that Franco's about to enter Madrid."

"He hasn't entered yet. With a little luck he never will."

"And what do you know? How can you be so sure?"

"Because I don't believe the American newspapers or radio networks are telling the truth. They belong to the big corporations, and their owners have supported Franco from day one, just like the Catholic Church."

"This doesn't sound like you. More like the talk at a meeting the other day in New York."

"Were you there? Last Saturday? In Union Square?"

"I looked at the faces of all the women, hoping to see yours."

"The last thing I'd have expected would've been to run into you."

"I've been hoping to run into you since the day you walked out of the café."

"It was moving, all those people filling the square. Some climbed the trees and the statue of George Washington. I saw the Republican flag and heard the 'Himno de Riego' and 'The Internationale' and couldn't stop crying."

"Good intentions, but no one's helping. They look at us as if we had the plague, as if we were lepers. In a hotel in Paris they didn't want to give me a room when they saw my Spanish passport. They probably thought I'd fill the bed with lice. Civilized opinion seems to be that it's a good idea to leave us alone so we can keep killing one another until we grow tired of it. They look at us like those tourists who go to bullfights, ready to be excited or horrified, to enjoy being horrified in order to feel more civilized than us. And the fact is, they're not altogether wrong, given the spectacle we're offering them."

"It isn't right for you to say that. The military and the Falangists rebelled against the Republic. They haven't been defeated yet only because they have the help of Mussolini and Hitler."

"You're talking again as if you were at a meeting."

"Aren't I speaking the truth?"

"The truth is so complicated nobody wants to hear it."

"If you know it, explain it to me."

"I probably left so I wouldn't see it. Truth seen up close is an ugly thing."

"I don't think you can live with your eyes closed."

"And why not? Most people do and it's not hard. I'm not talking about people outside Spain, who after all may not know about the war, or read about it in the paper and care less than they do about a soccer game. Even in Madrid I know many people who've managed not to know what's happening or at least act as if they didn't. They lead perfectly normal lives, believe it or not. They adopt the new style and the new vocabulary. But I imagine I'd get used to it if I had stayed, at least if I was lucky and they didn't kill me."

"Why would they kill you?"

"For any reason. On a whim, or by mistake, or for no reason, by chance. Killing an unarmed, peaceful person is the easiest thing in the world. You don't know how easy — like putting out a candle. Unless the executioner is clumsy or gets nervous or doesn't know how to handle a rifle. Then it can seem endless. Like bullfights when the butchers miss with the sword or dagger."

"The newspapers here publish terrible lies about what's going on in Madrid."

"Some of those lies are true. The worst ones."

"The others commit worse crimes. They started it. They're to blame."

"Reason and justice are on your side."

"I don't like such abstractions. You didn't use them before."

"You did. That afternoon we talked for hours in the bar at the Hotel Florida. I was struck by how seriously you took it. It annoyed you when Philip Van Doren spoke contemptuously about the Republic and praised the Soviet Union and Germany in his snobbish way. You said you were Republican because you believed in reason and justice. I liked your passion."

"I didn't remember our talking about those things."

"Don't you think the same way anymore?"

"What I think is that killing doesn't bring about reason and justice."

"If someone attacks you, you have the right to defend yourself."

"And do you have the right to kill innocents?"

"I was afraid something might've happened to you."

"Then you didn't think everything they were saying was a lie."

"And you came close?"

"You could've written and asked."

"I'm asking now."

"I was saved by accident, at the last moment. You'll understand if I don't really feel like going back."

They have to learn to speak to each other again, to adjust the tone of their voices, to smooth away the strangeness, to move close to each other gradually, naturally, slowly, the way one learns to walk again after recovering from an accident, when you discover that it took no time for your legs to lose their muscle tone and the habit of taking steps.

Evasive eyes no longer know how to hold a stare; with greater difficulty mouths form words in another language that were once habitual. Perhaps it's not that they have become strangers in so short a time, but that they see each other for the first time in a light not clouded by desire. It's not the changes that have occurred during their separation but the reality not seen when it was there every day. They felt their way at first, asking neutral questions. I see you've had a haircut; this morning, before I left on the trip, do you like it? Of course I do; you don't like it; I have to get used to it; you always wore it longer and curlier; I didn't have time to go to a hairdresser. Neither one has said the other's name yet. Silence follows each question; they almost count the seconds it takes for words to arrive again, as if they didn't depend on the will of either one. A nuance, a barely suggested tone of intimacy miscarries. An isolated phrase sounds as if it had been memorized for a performance, an overly literal exercise in good manners in a language class. "May I use the bathroom?" she said when she finally came in, when he closed the door and they found themselves alone in the house. While she ate, he observed her in silence as he sat on the other side of the table in the library, in the somewhat incongruous formality of his dark suit and tie, relieved she wasn't looking at him, a healthy young woman unhurriedly satisfying her hunger after having driven for several hours, drinking from the bottle of beer, more American than he remembered now that he sees her in her own country. She's put salami between two slices of bread and eats it in vigorous mouthfuls. His desire for her is more of a pain than pure sexual appetite. It's the pain in his joints, the pit of his stomach. Since he hasn't set out napkins, Judith wipes her mouth with the back of her hand. What he finds unfamiliar and distant in her must have to do with the presence of another man. Jealousy is a physical snakebite, a toxic substance circulating in his blood. In photographs, in memories, Judith's beauty had a blurred quality, as if he were looking at her through a faint gauze filter. The word "beautiful" can't exactly be applied to the woman Ignacio Abel sees before him, with her short hair and simple shirt, her ringless hands that hold the sandwich of rye bread and salami and open the bottle of beer with such ease.

There's something more carnal, raw, excessive in the peremptoriness of her features: her nose, large mouth, pronounced chin, the hard shape of bone beneath the skin. He likes her even more, and more than ever. He especially likes what's taken him by surprise because he didn't see it before and sees it now. Lack of hope and the certainty he'd lost her allow him to enjoy a painful objectivity. Her existence is enough: the unexpected gift of having her near.

"Don't look at me that way."

"How am I looking at you?"

"As if I were a ghost."

"I'm looking at you because I never tire of looking at you. Because I've missed you so much I can't believe you're here."

"I'm not sure you see me when you look at me. I've never been sure. You would stare at me but seem to be elsewhere, lost in your world, probably thinking about your work, or wondering whether your son or daughter had a fever, or your wife, or what lie you'd tell when you got home, or the remorse you felt deceiving her. You'd look at me and then look away, though only for a second. We were kissing in that room at Madame Mathilde's, and I saw you in the mirror across from the bed looking at the clock on the night table. Just a glance, but I noticed it. I believe in the man you are, not the one I might have dreamed you were. And when I read your letters I felt like running out and getting into bed with you, felt as dizzy as when we had those cold beers in cafés. But then, reading them again, I felt the same doubt as when I just saw you looking at me. I wasn't sure it was me you were writing to. The letters were so vague. You talked about what you felt for me and our love as if we were living in an abstract world in which there was nothing else and no one else but us. You filled two pages telling me about the house you wanted to build for us, and I asked myself where, when. Promise me you won't get angry with me for what I'm saying."

"I promise."

"You'll get angry. Sometimes I thought you wrote to me reluctantly, because you felt obliged to, because I was asking you to. You made fun of those wordy articles intellectuals published in *El Sol,* but there was something in your letters that reminded me of them. You told me what you felt about me but didn't answer the question I'd asked. I thought of an expression you taught me: *dar largas*. You were putting me off so you'd never have to address our real lives, yours and mine. And the truth was that though we spoke so much and wrote to each other so much we never spoke about anything specific. Only about the two of us, floating in space, floating in time. Never about the future, and after a while almost never about the past. You said you were in love with me but became distracted whenever I brought up my life. And if I mentioned my ex-husband, you changed the subject."

"It makes me jealous to think you've been with other men."

"You'd be less jealous if you'd let me tell you that my husband and those others never mattered to me half as much as you."

"There were more men."

"Of course there were. Did you think I was in a convent waiting for you to appear?"

"I couldn't stand the thought of you with someone else. I can't now, either."

"I had to stand not the thought but the reality that after being with me you could dissimulate with no difficulty and get into bed with your wife."

"We hadn't touched each other for a long time."

"But you were with her, not me. In the same room and the same bed. While I went back alone to my room in the pensión and couldn't sleep, and if I turned on the light I couldn't read, and I sat in front of my typewriter and couldn't write, not even a letter. And if I wrote to my mother, I couldn't tell her that her sacrifice had allowed a married Spaniard to have a younger American lover."

"Van Doren told me your mother died."

"How strange for you to ask about her."

"I always wanted to hear about your family."

"But you became distracted the minute I started talking about them. You didn't realize it, and you don't remember, but you were an impatient man. You were always in a hurry for one reason or another. You were nervous. You were anxious. You'd throw yourself on me in bed sometimes, and it seemed you'd forgotten you were with me. You'd open your eyes after you came and look at me as if you just awoke."

"Is that all you remember?"

"No. At other times you could be very sweet. Other men don't even make the effort."

"I was crazy about you."

"Or about someone you imagined. I reread your letters and thought they could just as easily have been written to another woman. I was flattered at the time to be the one who inspired those words in you, but sometimes I didn't believe them. You'd look at me and I didn't know if it was me you were looking at."

"Who else would it be?"

"A foreigner, an American. Like those women in the movies and the advertisements you said you'd always liked. You enjoyed looking at me. It always seemed you could have done without the talking. You were more expressive in letters."

"Am I looking at you now the way I did then?"

"Now your eyes have changed. When you opened the door I didn't recognize you. Now I'm recognizing you again, slowly, but not completely. I don't see you sneaking a glance at your watch."

"Why are you going to New York?"

"The Spanish man, asking his questions."

"Are you going to see your lover?"

"Don't talk to me that way."

"You used to say you couldn't imagine yourself going to bed with another man."

"If I were to remind you of all the things you said to me."

"I wasn't the one who disappeared. I wasn't the one who promised to keep an appointment and then didn't show up."

"Do you really want to talk about that now? I didn't disappear. I left you a letter explaining how I felt, what I thought. Why I couldn't see you again. I didn't hide anything from you. I didn't tell you any lies."

"You left the letter knowing I was waiting for you in the room."

"That doesn't matter now."

"You could have stayed with me at least that afternoon. You knew I was waiting for you. You must have spoken softly so I wouldn't hear you. I'm sure you gave Madame Mathilde a good tip."

"If I'd gone into the room, I probably wouldn't have had the strength to leave."

"If I'd seen you that afternoon, I'd have left everything to go with you."

"As in that poem you couldn't take seriously? Don't tell me things that aren't true. That was what offended me about you. That you told me lies. That you said yes to something when both of us knew it was no. There's no reason to lie anymore. We're alone in this house and I'll be leaving soon."

"Did you leave Madrid that same night? Were you at Van Doren's house?"

"I was frightened. They stopped me at every corner to ask for my papers and I didn't have my passport with me, why would I? I don't know how I managed to get on a streetcar, on the running board, hanging on. I wanted to leave and I wanted to find you so you could protect me. See what happened to my decision to leave you and my yen for adventure? I reached the pensión and tried to call Phil or the embassy but the phones weren't working, or sometimes they did and other times they didn't. I called your house several times but you never answered."

"I was looking all over Madrid for you."

"It was better for me you didn't find me."

"Would you really have stayed with me?"

"You're yourself again. You want me to flatter you and say yes."

"Now you don't want to tell me why you're going to New York."

"I'm leaving on a trip."

"You're going to meet another man."

"Is that the only thing you can imagine in my life? Aren't you curious to know anything else about me?"

"And your job at the college?"

"I left it."

"To go where?"
"To Spain."

She answered so quickly it surprised her to hear the words she didn't intend to say, hasn't said to anyone yet. The immediate silence has another quality, of resonance, expectation, vigilance, while their eyes remain fixed, locked, each detecting the slightest movements in the other's face, both aware of the silence and the sounds behind it, the crackle of the fire in the hearth, the first sporadic drops of a light rain that will last all night, their breathing, each waiting for a sign the other will speak. They've been lowering their voices as they remained motionless, Judith sitting upright now that she's said what perhaps she shouldn't have said, Ignacio Abel serious, one hand resting on the other on the edge of the table, the bony hands that now seem as stripped of sensuality as his diminished, rigid body, his general mood of dignified capitulation. A passenger on the train they hear passing now will see in the distance, through the successive shadows of the forest, a wide lit window but won't be able to distinguish the two silhouettes. Someone approaching in the light rain would see two motionless figures on either side of a large table, leaning slightly toward each other, as if about to tell or hear a secret. He'd enter the house and advance silently along the dark hall, and though he came close to the open door of the library, through which come the light from the fire and a current of warm air, he'd hear nothing, perhaps indistinct voices, interrupted by silences, then superimposed, isolated words in Spanish or English, the secret of their two lives, protected by the walls of the house, the isolation of the forest, the darkness of the night, the intimacy in which there's room only for two lovers and where they've returned without knowing it yet, though they don't touch, and when they look into each other's eyes they sense a guarded secrecy not even the most shameless confession could break. They circle each other with looks and words, laying siege, testing the boundaries of their silence. Between the sound of lips separating, the first word is the emptiness of expectation. The next steps of your life, your entire future, will depend on what is said or left unsaid

603

in an instant. Judith has taken a deep breath and closed her eyes for a moment, as if to give herself courage, to store up the air she will need if she wants her words to sound as clear and confident as they do in her mind.

"I should've guessed."

"Don't try to talk me out of it. Don't. Any reason you can give me for not going I've already thought of myself and heard many times. I'm not going to change my mind. As soon as you start telling me what I already know you're going to say, I'll get up and go back the way I came. You have to live according to your principles. I can't ease my conscience by occasionally attending an event in favor of the Spanish Republic or going out to the street with a money box to collect donations. I don't want to think one thing and do another. I don't want to read the paper or listen to the radio or see a newsreel and die of rage seeing what the Fascists are doing in Spain, and then go on living as if nothing were happening. It's that simple."

"And what will you do? Madrid's about to fall."

"Why are you so sure? So you'll feel less remorse because you left? The Soviet Union's begun to send aid. Just this morning I heard on the radio that the French are going to open the border to let armaments through. There are things the newspapers don't publish. There are thousands and thousands of volunteers traveling to Spain right now."

"And what will they do when they arrive? You don't know what it's like. My country is nothing but an insane asylum, a slaughterhouse. We don't have an army, or discipline. And almost no government."

"I never heard you use the first person plural when talking politics."

"I didn't realize I was doing it. I must've got into the habit when I left Spain."

"Not everything is lost."

"You don't know what war is like."

"Stop telling me the things I don't know. I'm going so I'll find out."

"Do you plan to join the militias?"

"Don't talk to me in that tone."

"What tone?"

"As if I understood nothing. As if I were acting on a whim. I know very well what I'm going to do."

"Nobody knows. In a war nobody understands anything. The ones who seem to understand are the biggest charlatans of all, or the most demented, or the most dangerous. I've seen war. Nobody told me about it. I saw it in Morocco when I was young and now I've seen it again in Madrid, and it's the same thing, nothing to do with two armies and a battle with advances and retreats and then a bugle blows and everything's over and you collect the dead. In a war nobody knows what's going on. The professional military pretend they know, but it's not true. At best the only thing they've learned is to dissimulate or push others in front of them. A bomb explodes and you're dead or bleeding to death and holding your insides in your hands, or you're left blind or missing your legs or half your face. And you don't even have to go to the front. You go to a café or a movie theater on the Gran Vía and when you leave a mortar shell or an incendiary bomb falls and if you're lucky you don't know you're going to die. Or someone denounces you because he doesn't like you, or because he thinks he saw you coming out of Mass once or reading the *ABC*, and they take you in a car to the Casa de Campo and the next morning the kids have fun with your body, putting a lit cigar in your mouth, calling you an idiot. That's war. Or revolution, if you think that word's more appropriate. Everything else they're telling you is a lie. All those parades that look so good in films and illustrated magazines, the posters, the slogans — They Shall Not Pass. Brave, honorable men climb into an old truck to go to the front and the other side mows them down with machine guns, and they don't even have time to aim the rifles that in most cases they haven't learned to handle properly, or they have very little ammunition, or it's not the right kind. In half an hour they can be dead or lose both arms or both legs. The ones who seem the fiercest and most revolutionary stay behind the lines and use their rifles and clenched fists to get free service in bars or whorehouses. The Fascists have machine guns mounted on their planes and amuse themselves by firing on the lines of campesinos and militiamen fleeing toward Madrid. The militiamen waste ammunition firing at the planes because, even if they know how to aim, they don't know their guns aren't powerful enough to reach the planes. The pilot is annoyed, and instead of continuing on his way he turns around and machine-guns them in an open field as if they were ants. The only ones who end up on the frontlines, where death is almost certain, can't help it because they were dragged there or because they believed the propaganda and got drunk on banners and anthems. Every man who can, escapes, except the innocent and the deluded, and they're the first to die or be mutilated or disfigured. Not on the first day but in the first minute. Some don't even carry weapons. They think that going to war means lining up and keeping time while you follow a band playing 'The Internationale' or 'To the Barricades.' They see the enemy coming and can't run because their legs are trembling and they shit themselves in fear. It's not a figure of speech. Extreme fear causes diarrhea. The other side hunts them down with no difficulty. Just like hunting rabbits. Do you know what they enjoy? They get bored when it's so easy to kill, and they look for entertainment. You can imagine what they do to women. With men they often cut off noses and ears and then slit their throats. They cut off their testicles and stuff them in their mouths. They put a head with the ears and nose cut off on a broomstick and carry it in a parade. But our men do that too sometimes. Don't look at me like that. It's not enemy propaganda. I saw the decapitated head of General López Ochoa marched around Madrid. The leftist parties and the unions hated him because he led the troops in Asturias in '34. On July 18 he was in the military hospital at Carabanchel because he'd had an operation, and some brave man got the idea of killing him right there. They dragged the body through the streets and cut off his head, ears, and testicles. It was like a procession, a carnival, with a swarm of children running behind. You're going to tell me the other side is worse. I don't doubt that at all. I've also seen what they do. They rebelled, and it's their fault the slaughter began. They deserve to lose, but we've done so many savage and stupid things, we don't deserve to win."

"And you're above it all?"

"I've gone as far as I've been pushed. They could have killed me in Madrid — the other side surely would have killed me if I'd stayed with my children that Sunday in the Sierra. I'm not a brave man. I'm not a passionate man. I've almost never had strong emotions, except for you, or sometimes for my work, imagining it. I'm not a revolutionary. I don't believe history has a direction or that you can build heaven on earth. And even if you could, if the price is an endless bloodbath and tyranny, I don't think it's worth paying. But if I'm wrong, and revolution and slaughter are necessary to bring about justice, I prefer to step aside if I have the chance, at least to save my life. It's the only one I have. I'm not a man of action like my friend Dr. Negrín. I learned it these past few months, spending so much time alone. I hardly spoke to anyone and often couldn't sleep and thought about what I really like, what I need. I need to do something well that is also useful and lasting and solid. People obsessed by political passions frighten me, or seem ridiculous, like those who turn red shouting at a soccer game, or the racetrack, or a bullfight. Now they also disgust me. I think there are many more despicable people than I ever imagined. The old intoxicate the young to take revenge on their youth and send them to slaughter. Many people who seem normal become savages when they see and smell blood. They see a neighbor shot who until yesterday had greeted them every morning, and if they can, they steal his wallet or his shoes. My poor friend Professor Rossman was a saint. He never hurt anyone. He'd get on a streetcar and take off his hat if there was a woman in front of him. He made his bed every morning at the pensión to save the maid work. He'd been eminent in Germany, and in Spain he earned a poor living selling pens in cafés, but I never heard him complain about the country or lose his patience. You met him. Well, they killed him like an animal because some cretin must have thought he was a spy because he spoke with a German accent or carried a briefcase filled with newspaper clippings and maps of the front. Before they killed him, they beat his face to a pulp. And I didn't see his daughter again, either. They didn't know anything about her at the pensión or the office where she worked. As if the earth had swallowed her. I couldn't help either one of them. I probably didn't have any luck or was afraid to insist too much and put myself in danger. That's the truth. My wife's brother came one night to ask me to hide him because they were looking for him. I didn't open the door. If I'd let him in, I probably couldn't have left, or I'd have had to postpone the trip again, or they'd have locked me up for helping him. Maybe they killed him that same night. He was a Falangist and a fool, but nobody deserves to go around hiding in doorways like an animal. And that's not all. He really loved my children, and they loved him, the boy especially. He loved his uncle so much it made me jealous. And if in spite of everything he managed to escape and get to the other side, he'll be so full of rancor he'll become a butcher. It's possible he goes to see my children, and they admire him all the more seeing him turned into a war hero, and he tells them their father betrayed him. I could have told him to stay and denounced him. I would have done my duty, since my brother-in-law was in one of those Falangist groups that shoot militiamen from roofs or drive in a car at top speed machine-gunning people who line up for bread or charcoal. A traitor. A saboteur. But it's not that I felt compassion for him. I didn't want my trip ruined because of him."

He speaks without moving and without taking his eyes off Judith. Words leave his mouth, though he barely separates his lips. He speaks and doesn't think about what he's going to say next, the sound of his own voice spurs him on. The fury is in the words, not in him. He maintains a monotonous neutrality, as if testifying at a trial or making a statement, being careful not to speak too quickly for the typist who's transcribing it. Speaking alleviates and exalts him. It returns shame and lucidity to him in waves, and restores an abused but not abolished shadow of personal integrity. He can't be the only one who's fled, who hides behind a submissive courtesy, who before speaking must be certain not to offend or annoy anyone. His hands still rest on the table, one on top of the other, and the muscles in his face don't move either, though the unequal light from the fire and oil lamp modifies the shadows. But he's become more confident as he speaks, raising his voice a little or perhaps pronouncing words with more precision and a different kind of energy, just as he hasn't once lowered his eyes or stopped speaking when Judith looked as if she were about to say something. He's been silent for so long that even if he wanted to, he couldn't stop talking. It's now, stimulated by his own words, that he begins to realize how long his silence has lasted, the huge volume of what he's kept silent, its monstrous proliferation, silence a habit and a refuge and a way of accommodating to the world, then transformed into the very space around him, the cell and bell jar where he's lived in recent months. The silence in his apartment on sleepless nights, the silence in his office at University City; looking and keeping silent, looking away, not saying anything, traveling in silence on trains, alone in hotel rooms, in a cabin on the ship that crossed the Atlantic, in New York cafeterias where he sat by the window to look at the street and the signs painted in bright colors. He's been silent for so long, and now words come easily to him, the images of what he's seen and what he'd like to describe to Judith with absolute accuracy, though he suspects he won't succeed. No explanation can convey the experience, the terror, the absurd truth that only someone who's lived it can understand, though he tries in vain to turn it into words and moves his lips as if gasping for air, not looking away from Judith's eyes; looking at her now with an openness he didn't have before, slowly taking pleasure in her reclaimed features, her proximity, the marvel of her existence now that he has no hope, and desire is stunted by her physical reticence, by the inertia of a bitter male capitulation, wounded vanity, and sexual humiliation. But it's this lack of hope that allows him to see Judith more clearly than ever, his attention for the first time free of the urgency of a desire that in its former fulfillment was always undermined by the fear of evanescence and loss. Now he sees Judith exactly as she is. Her voice reaches him as precisely as the brush of a hand on his eyelids.

"If you know so much, tell me the honorable way to act. Tell me whether you think there's a just way to behave."

"I don't know anything. I don't know whether I'm as much of a clown as the rest. Each person justifies his shameful behavior the best he can. Only the murdered are without guilt, and you don't want to be one of them. Professor Rossman, or Lorca."

"I couldn't believe it when I read it in the paper. Professor Salinas was distraught. I wanted to think it was a rumor, a false report. Why would they have killed him?"

"For no reason, Judith. He was innocent. Do you think that's a small crime? Innocents are not wanted anywhere."

"You finally said my name."

"You haven't said mine yet."

"'Living in pronouns.' Do you remember? I didn't really understand the meaning of that poem. You explained it to me. The lovers can call each other only 'you' and 'I' so they won't be found out."

"Don't go. Stay with me."

"I already have the ticket. The ship sails tomorrow from New York. Three hundred of us are going. And many more will go soon. In small groups, to keep a low profile. Some will go to France first, others to England."

"The borders will be closed."

"We'll cross where the smugglers do."

"This is not a novel, Judith."

"Don't talk to me again in that mocking tone."

"I don't want you to be killed."

"I asked you to tell me what can be done, and you haven't answered."

"There's nothing you can or should do. You're lucky, it's not your country. Forget about it because you can. Many more people were killed in Abyssinia than in Spain and neither of us lost any sleep over it. And neither did the democracies or the League of Nations. Hitler wants to expel all the Jews from Germany, and he's put the Social Democrats and Communists in camps, and there hasn't been a single international protest. Will anyone be shocked to learn that he's helping Franco? In Russia they die of hunger by the millions and nobody cares, but all the generous lovers of justice are moved by Soviet propaganda. With some exceptions, this whole world is a horrifying place. Don't they lynch Negroes in the south of your country? How many were killed three or four years ago in Paraguay, in the Chaco War? Hundreds of thousands. You may not have heard of it. Do you really believe that your actions, just or unjust, can make any difference? If you want to ease your conscience, join a committee of solidarity with the Spanish Republic. Ask for money in the street, collect warm clothing. The militiamen need it now in the Sierra. If you send them a sweater or a blanket, you'll have been more useful than letting yourself be killed. If you collect just one can of condensed milk or a pack of cigarettes for them."

"I hear you speak and I don't know you."

"I'm not here to tell you what you want to hear."

"I shouldn't have come. I could have been in New York by now."

"Go on, then. Maybe by the time you get to Spain the Republic won't have collapsed yet. They'll welcome you with placards and bands. They'll take you on a tour of some peaceful front. In Madrid they'll give a dinner dance in your honor at the palace of the Alliance of Anti-Fascist Intellectuals. The meal they'll serve will be much better and more abundant than the food they give the soldiers at the front — that is, if there are trucks to bring the food, or gasoline for the trucks, maybe there isn't any, or it's being used for parades or for taking people to slaughter. Alberti and his gang of poets in nicely pressed blue coveralls will recite yards of verses for you. They'll take you to a bullfight and a flamenco performance. They'll take pictures of you and you'll be in the papers. They'll present you as further confirmation that all over the world sympathy is growing for the struggle of the Spanish people against fascism. Then they'll take you to the border and you'll all go back to your countries with a clear conscience and the joy of having had a dangerous, exotic adventure. You'll even go back with a tan."

"I'm leaving. I don't have to listen to this. I'm ashamed of you."

She stood up and now looks at him from above, as if challenging him to try to block her way. His two hands are separated, parallel on the table, but that's the only movement he's made. He raises his eyes to her, then looks at the fire, then at the spot where Judith had been only a moment before. She'll leave, and each step she takes will be a definitive parting. He thinks of Moreno Villa this summer, in his room at the Residence: now we've learned that in these times a casual departure may be forever. She'll cross the darkened library, the foyer. He'll hear the door shut, then wait for the car engine to start. Angry and nervous, Judith won't begin to drive right away. The sound of the engine will become steady. Sitting still, his eyes on the fire, he'll hear the sound fading until it's gone, the red taillights dimming like embers at the end of the road, the tunnel of entwined tree branches. In the silence the patter of the rain will return, the crackle of the fire, a brief burst of logs burning. After a while no sign that Judith has been here, only the plate with her unfinished supper, the half-consumed bottle of beer. He'll go up to bed, lighting his way with the oil lamp, and search for Judith's scent on a towel. He'll look in the mirror to brush his teeth, half his face erased by darkness, his own eyes eluding him. He makes no move to stop her, now that he still has her within reach. Judith speaks, framed by the door she's just opened and at any moment will cross. She is calm.

"You think you know everything, but you don't know anything. The volunteers I know don't go to Spain to be tourists, I can assure you. Many are already there receiving military training to join the Republican army. Many more will arrive from America and half the world. If there were so few differences between the two sides, and it all amounts to nothing more than savagery and senselessness, there wouldn't be so many intelligent and brave people prepared to risk their lives in Spain. You know I'm not a fanatic. I don't feel much sympathy for the Communists. But they're organizing recruitment, and I'll go to Spain with them and many others who aren't Communists. If I hadn't fallen in love with you, I probably wouldn't have fallen in love with Spain. But by now it's my other country, and what's happening there breaks my heart. Just reading the names of the towns in the paper or hearing them pronounced on the radio. When they say 'Madrid,' it's my city because you showed it to me. I lived two years in London and Paris and never stopped feeling like a foreigner. A foreigner who visited extraordinary museums with a guilty conscience because I got bored too soon and wasn't European. I went to Madrid, and as soon as I took my first walk around the Plaza de Santa Ana, between the shoeshine boy and the grocery, it was as if I were back in New York. I like the Spanish. *Me caen bien,* as you say. I like the slow, shabby streetcars and the pots of red geraniums on the balconies. I like the Rastro as much as the Prado. But it isn't the romanticism of an American, though you may think so. It's political common sense. I was moved by the poor lining up with so much dignity to vote on the day of the last elections. I liked to go through your neighborhood and see people entering and leaving the new modern market you designed, with the flag on the façade. If Hitler and Mussolini help the military win in Spain, what will happen next in the world? I don't want those people to enter Madrid."

"And what will you do to prevent it?"

"Anything. Whatever I can. I can drive an ambulance and help in a hospital. I speak French, Yiddish, and a fair amount of Russian, aside from English and Spanish. I can act as an interpreter. Someone will have to help all those people who are arriving to communicate with the Spaniards. You say you're not brave and not a revolutionary, and neither am I. You say what you like is to do something well, and that's what I want. I don't plan to argue politics. Ever since I was married I've had a horror of the aggressive arguments about Stalin and Trotsky, kulaks, five-year plans, world revolution, socialism. I want to work for the Spanish Republic. I want to be in Madrid, just as I was this time last year."

"That Madrid no longer exists."

"It can't have disappeared in so short a time."

"You won't recognize it."

"I prefer to find that out for myself."

"Stay with me. If you go now, I know I'll never see you again."

"You didn't count on seeing me now anyway. Nothing will happen to me in Spain."

"Even if nothing happens to you, if you go now you won't come back.

613

Think of how big the world is, how complicated it is for two people to meet. We've been lucky twice — there won't be another time. When you came tonight, it was for a reason."

"I came to say goodbye."

"You didn't have to."

"It was on my way."

"That's not true."

"I have to go now."

"Just stay the night. I'm not asking for anything else."

"I'm not your lover anymore."

"I'm not asking you to go to bed with me. The only thing I'm asking you is not to leave tonight. You'll have to sleep somewhere."

"What do you want from me?"

"I want us to go on talking. I'm here with you and I can't believe it's true. So many times I imagined that I'd see you again and that we would talk and talk, without getting tired, without falling silent. I never stopped imagining what I'd say to you when I saw you again, all that I'd tell you. Thinking was talking to you. I don't know how many letters I wrote to you in my head those three months in Madrid and while I was traveling. Crossing the ocean, when we reached New York. A lot of people were waiting at the gangplank, and I thought I saw your face, heard your voice calling me."

She's gone out to the car to fetch her suitcase, which seems too light for the long trip she's about to take. In her absence Ignacio Abel has remained attentive, afraid to hear the sound of the engine. He's heard only the rain on the windows, the tin gutters, the slate eaves, the glass roof of an abandoned conservatory behind the house. Judith sits behind the wheel and watches the drops on the windshield, clouding the sight of the porch and the door she left ajar when she went out. She has both hands on the wheel and the nape of her neck rests against the back of the seat. She knows that he's waiting inside the large, darkened house, perhaps still motionless at the table in the library, the candle almost extinguished, his thin face illuminated by the light of the fire. She knows him too well. She sees his long hands on the table, the prominent knuckles, hands that made no move toward her, no attempt to touch her. She thinks if she stays now, it's because she doesn't have the energy to face two more hours on the road, or the idea of arriving very late in New York and having to find a room in a cheap hotel. He'll think that she's taking too long, but he won't move, fatalistic and alert, sitting at the table in the library, reduced inside the jacket whose shoulders are too wide. He does and doesn't wait for her. The restlessness of another time is now a self-absorption that has a touch of physical neglect. When he saw her move toward the door, he felt a mixture of anguish and acceptance. Then something happens. The foyer and several windows in the house fill with light. Judith returns holding her suitcase, drops of rain wetting her face and hair. She knows he's heard her steps and the door close. The electric light shines on the waxed wooden floor, but the hall that leads to the library is still in shadow. Judith pushes the door, hearing fragments of music and voices on the radio. Ignacio Abel is in front of the radio, his face lit by a candle. Judith puts down the suitcase and walks toward him. He looks at her and discovers in her eyes something that wasn't there before, an unexpected gleam, a trace of another time. It frightens him suddenly to desire her so much, to be so hopelessly drawn to her, now that he can't or isn't allowed to touch her. She left a few minutes ago and now she's back, a second chance, as if she's returned from Madrid and not the distant past when she was his and he was hers.

36

H E CLIMBS THE STEPS deliberately, pausing on each one, sliding his right hand along the banister that follows the staircase
conceived for the flair of evening gowns in another century.
Amplified by the strange acoustical laws of the house, he hears water filling a bathtub. He is as conscious of this sound as he is of each
step he takes, each heartbeat rebounding inside his chest, the air that
doesn't quite fill his lungs, makes him feel that he is beginning to suffocate, the feeling as powerful as the emptiness in his stomach. In his
mind he sees Judith undress, behind the closed bathroom door perhaps, extending her hand to test the water temperature. It seems as if
the dead of another time are watching him from the penumbra of the
oil portraits, the solemn dead above him reproachfully examining an
intruder, a thief whom they can't expel. Time expands on this night
so dense with words, and what happened a while ago already has the
hazy quality of memory. Judith returned to the library with raindrops
shining on her face and hair, and remained standing in the doorway,
not recognizing the place she'd left just a few minutes earlier, which
seemed so long a time to him. The ceiling-high shelves, grand piano,
long table, and large globe of the world constituted the inhospitable
stage set. He turned the porcelain switch, and they again found themselves in the space their words and presence had shaped as much as
the flames in the fireplace and the candlelight, the dark room mirrored

in the windowpanes, and the cold damp night. She asked him not to turn off the radio now that he'd found a station broadcasting the distant pulse of a song marked by clarinet solos and a woman's melodious, high-pitched voice. Behind their conversation, the music and voices on the radio have continued to play, though they've barely heard them, just as they've heard the rain only intermittently, when they were silent for a moment, close to each other, the invisible gulf not abolished but at least no longer the hostile frontier across which they looked at each other, their words forming like ice crystals in no man's land, the space between those who no longer touch. Judith shivered a little when she entered the library, the light damp cloth of her shirt rubbing against her skin. At other times, on spring nights in Madrid that suddenly turned cold, she'd taken shelter in his arms as they walked after leaving a booth in a café or in the rain along the banks of the Manzanares. He'd put his jacket over her shoulders. Now he saw that slight trembling in her and did nothing, sitting beside the fire, near the radio she'd asked him to leave on and to which she paid no attention, his hands resting on the worn leather of the armchair, incapable of moving toward her as if he'd lost the use of his legs, as impotent as when he heard her go out and thought she wouldn't come back. She put some wood on the fire and sat on the floor, her legs crossed casually, looking at the flames as she hugged herself to take away the cold, looking at him, as formal and solemn in the armchair as the ghost of one of the former inhabitants of the house. Judith took off her shoes and wet socks. He would have liked so much to warm her feet. Her strong heel, the faint pulse in the modeling of her ankle, her long instep with sinuous blue veins, her toes with painted nails. He opened his mouth to say something, wanting to shorten the silence, but Judith interrupted him.

"Why are we talking as if we didn't know each other?" said Judith. "I hear your voice but it doesn't sound like your voice. And I recognize mine even less. I've thought a great deal about the things I'd say to you if I saw you again, but now I don't like having said any of it. We talk and words betray us. You think of them and when you say them out loud they mean something else. What the words say has nothing to do with us. They become harsher, less true. Even though they tell the truth, it would be better not to have said them. You know who I am and I know who you are. We talk as if we didn't know each other, but what we've experienced together can't be gone, so there must be a lie in what we've said."

"But you've decided to break with me."

"I haven't decided it. I've looked squarely at the facts. I was prepared to live with you. The only thing you had to do not to lose me was act according to the feelings you said you had for me. But I'm not reproaching you. I think I know you well enough and can see things through your eyes. Do you remember Salinas's poem? I don't know how long it took me to decipher the syntax. *Que hay otro ser por el que miro el mundo . . .*"

"*. . . porque me está queriendo con sus ojos . . .*"

"It's the first time I've heard you recite a poem."

"Only those lines. I learned them listening to you."

"I asked you to read them for me to be sure of the accents. Do you remember?"

"I remember everything. I have all the times we were together marked down in a notebook. The day, the place, the time."

"I understand the love you feel for your children and the difficulty in leaving them. But in your country there's a divorce law. People who are in love, and certain of their love, marry. And to do it, sometimes they have to get divorced first. It's painful but fair. To win something, you have to lose something. The harm you might have done by staying can be greater than the harm you've done by leaving. I don't want to think about the person I would have become if I hadn't divorced, the poison I'd have inside me. I don't want to think and feel one way and act in another. I liked going to bed with you, but I would have liked it much more if afterward I could have walked quietly in Madrid holding your arm or stopped for you at your office. You thought our meeting secretly was romantic. You say you're not interested in literature, but in this you were much more literary than I was. It struck me that what we were doing is called 'having an adventure' in Spanish. I didn't like hiding. I didn't see any adventure in going to that house of assignation or those sad, empty cafés you took me to where nobody would know you. I only did it because I was so in love."

"You were in love."

"I still am. More than I thought. If I'd known how vulnerable I was, I wouldn't have come. You see, I'm not hiding anything from you. But it'll pass in time, when I leave here and have no expectation of seeing you."

"So you can think and feel one way and act another."

"What I think and feel is that I don't want to have an adventure with a married man even if I'm in love with him. But I also don't want to spoil the memory of what I've experienced. I can't reproach you for anything. You didn't force me to do anything I didn't want to do. If we'd continued as lovers for a little longer, everything would have been debased. It was already beginning, and you and I knew it. Think of that morning in that awful café when you came from the hospital and your wife was still in a coma. We were no longer worthy of what we'd been. We were like those seedy couples we saw at other tables. Old men with young girls. Lovers who looked as embittered and bored as married couples. We looked at each other for a while, not recognizing each other, reproaching ourselves. It was dirtier than making love in a bed that belonged to Madame Mathilde. If I couldn't have you for myself, the best thing was for me to leave, and then at least the memory would remain intact."

He understood with a strange sense of relief, looking into her eyes, that Judith was absolutely right: there was no longer any reason, any excuse, for not telling the truth. By examining the past with clarity, what they were doing was restoring it, seeking shelter in it. What they didn't say now they probably would never say. They would have to be careful that their true words didn't mean something unintended or acquire on their own an edge of resentment or injury. Her suitcase was by the library door. Tomorrow it would be as easy for her to put it in the back seat of the car as it had been for her to bring it in. With an ease he'd never have if he sat on the floor, Judith hugged her knees and leaned her chin on them, her feet, projecting from her wide trousers, close together. He hasn't known anyone who looks and listens so attentively, with such longing to learn, as alert to words as to silences and subtle gestures, exercising with the same passionate intensity both her intuition and her reason, asking, guessing, examining herself with a lucidity as incorruptible as her curiosity. But now her gaze, her questions, didn't frighten him. An advantage of having lost everything was that there no longer was anything to lose. Just as it had once been, their conversation wasn't composed only of words: their eyes were a part of it, the proximity of their bodies, pure physical presence their magnet, the timbre of their voices and the darkness around them, the movements of Judith's lips, the corners of her mouth, the faint music on the radio and the rain on the windowpanes, the night that was advancing and yet seemed halted, begun long ago and without a visible ending, without a dawn.

He told her that throughout the summer in Madrid his longing for her had been much more intolerable than for his children; that he recalled each meeting in the tiny notes coded to seem like work-related appointments and went back to the places where they'd been together as humiliated as a dog searching for a lost trail; that in everything and in spite of his guilt it had been a relief not to have to face Adela's permanent expression of sacrifice and affront; that in the disorder and irresponsibility of the war he'd found a kind of unspeakable liberation; that he masturbated almost every night in the large double bed with the dirty sheets thinking of her, looking at her photographs, reading her letters. He told her that when the militiamen stopped him in University City and took him to a wall of the Philosophy Building to shoot him, they had to lift him because his legs didn't hold him and he pissed down his trousers and the urine soaked one of his shoes, and as he walked he heard the liquid squishing at each step he took; and when he got home he took a shower and no matter how much he soaped himself he still smelled of urine and fear; and while they searched his briefcase filled with plans and technical reports and asked if they weren't maps of the front meant to guide the enemy in their advance toward Madrid, what he feared was that they'd discover her letters and photos and take them; he didn't feel terror at dying but passive indifference, an acceptance disturbed only by the sorrow of thinking he wouldn't see her again, wouldn't see his children become adults. Judith looked at him, against the fire, her eyes bright, the changing light of the flames molding the delicate bones beneath her skin, and he swallowed and kept talking. Behind him dance music played on the radio as if from a distant, large, empty ballroom, the band playing and the filigrees of the clarinet followed by the singer's guileless, high-pitched voice, scattered applause, and the announcer's excessive enthusiasm as he recited song titles and commercials. He told her he'd taken it for granted that the sexual upheaval he experienced for the first time with his Hungarian lover in Weimar when he was in his thirties would never be repeated. The women who'd offered themselves in Madrid, painted and livid beneath the gaslights in certain alleys when he was young, had excited him and at the same time produced panic in him, and a revulsion not so much toward them as toward himself, toward his instinctual desire for them and the shame that made him blush and walk faster if they called to him. He hadn't believed a woman could really feel pleasure with him. Adela would ask him to turn off the light and she'd remain motionless, perhaps moan faintly in the heavy darkness of their bedroom; his Hungarian lover squeezed her eyelids shut and rhythmically stroked herself while he labored on top of her, as irrelevant as the insect that pollinates a flower, joined to each other and both self-absorbed and busy with their own lust. He told Judith that the first time he touched her he'd noticed a vibration both delicate and powerful that he didn't know existed. He found her hand and instead of moving it away she pressed his, and it was as if they were embracing (they both remembered: in the car, driving up the Castellana, the radio playing, his left hand on the wheel, the right caressing Judith's thighs, the headlights illuminating groves of trees and fences and the façades of palaces); as he discovered her, he'd been discovering himself, being touched, kissed, nibbled, explored, guided by her. He'd never had friends, he told her, or real conversations with anyone, least of all sexual conversations, which, he observed, other men were so fond of. Only when he met her did he realize the solitary life he'd always led, from the time he was a child and his parents didn't let him leave the porter's quarters except to go to school, for fear he'd get lost in the hustle of the neighborhood, or the violent boys from the outskirts would hit him, or he'd catch a disease. The only child of parents who were too old; his father dead when he was thirteen; keeping vigil over his dead mother when he was twenty-one and returning on foot to the empty apartment on Calle Toledo from the distant East Cemetery, his feet aching in tight boots, enveloped in the derby hat and black cape that had belonged to his father; so young and a figure from the last century, with a burden of excessive responsibilities that would never be alleviated; his course of study, the inhuman privations to finish it, using up his father's legacy; then examinations, the weight of his engagement, the new burden quickly made heavier by children. Strange, but now was the first time he felt something resembling relief, though it was inseparable from the feeling of dispossession. He wouldn't hold anything back, he told Judith, sitting across from her, sunk like an invalid into the leather armchair, his palms rubbing the worn part of the upholstery. Only with her had he discovered and now regained what he'd never known could be so pleasurable, the habit of conversing, explaining himself to himself, confirming immediate affinities in what until then he'd thought of as solitary sensations and thoughts. Always his fear of inconveniencing, his slowness in finding the exact words and the courage to say them, always the temptation of silence and conformity, the permanent frustration of feeling like a guest in his own house and in a life that was the only one he had and yet had never belonged to him. Because Judith listened, he'd learned to explain himself to another person. When she disappeared, as oppressive as her absence was the great bell jar of silence falling over him again when he'd already lost the habit of living inside it, of looking at everything from behind the glass of indifference, distance, and bitterness. But now he'd lost even the more or less unconscious scrupulousness about saying things she'd like to hear, that would make her fall in love. With no hope of seducing her again, almost convinced not only of the uselessness but also the moral baseness of attempting to, he said what he thought, what he was, and what he often didn't acknowledge even to himself. Remorse for having left wasn't strong enough to provoke in him a real longing for Spain, he told her. The weight of responsibility had for too many years been as oppressive as the burden of his ambition, including his dark, unconfessed vanity, and at that moment, he told her, on that night, he felt relieved of all three — vanity, responsibility, ambition — though he didn't know for how long or when guilt or nostalgia would overpower him and make him distort both memories and desires. He didn't want to cause grief. He didn't want to pretend he'd have preferred to be in Madrid now, impotently witnessing the destruction of his city, the disaster of a delirious revolution that burned churches and left banks intact, the carnival of parades and murders, the cold villainy and the squandered heroism. He didn't believe that Salinas, in his comfortable position as a visiting professor at Wellesley College, felt as much anguish as he showed when he talked to her, basically flattered by the cordiality of so young and attractive a woman who spoke Spanish with that clear accent between American and Madrilenian, and who flattered him with an admiration that must act like a balm to his professor's vanity, a shell of his former brilliance. Of course he'd like the Republic to win, he told her, but he wasn't sure what kind of republic there'd be in Spain when the war was over, or whether he'd be permitted to return, or whether he wanted to. Everything destroyed with so much fury had to be rebuilt; the trees uprooted by bombs or cut down for firewood replanted; systems of pipes that had been blown up and railroad tracks twisted in the air above mountains of paving stones relaid; bridges dynamited by retreating armies reconstructed; telephone posts and lines that had cost so much to install raised again. But who would resuscitate the dead or return arms or legs to the mutilated, paint the lost canvases or print the unique books burned in bonfires, palliate mourning or hatred, reconstruct the libraries and churches and laboratories and apartment buildings so difficult to build and demolished in the course of an afternoon, a single night. And how could Spain be governed by the same fools, criminals, and misguided men who'd dragged her to disaster, each with his degree of irresponsibility and irrationality, all, with few exceptions, immune to remorse and the bitter wisdom of those who've learned from experience. There was something his work had taught him: it takes a long time to bring a building to completion, because no matter how much effort you put into it, things grow with organic slowness; but the instantaneousness of destruction is resplendent, the spurt of gasoline and the flame that rises devouring everything, the shot that fells a man as strong as a tree. He told her that what astonished him most was to have been so wrong about everything, especially the things he was surest of; to have trusted the solidity of everything that collapsed overnight, without drama, almost effortlessly; to have been so wrong about himself, believing he was a rationalist, a pragmatist, a sarcastic witness to the ideological ravings of those who predicted with all seriousness the coming of the dictatorship of the proletariat or Libertarian Communism, those convinced that by abolishing money and taking up nudism or Esperanto or free love, paradise would be established on earth, the idolaters of Stalin or Mussolini, those who roared with a clenched fist or an open hand; believing himself to be a skeptic, he'd been more deluded than any of them, imagining he was concerned only with what could be calculated and measured, what produced a modest but indisputable benefit, some progress. But progress was precisely what was being denied in Spain: not the abolition of property and money, apparently advanced successfully in certain towns in Aragón, not the great Soviet theater of giant posters of Lenin and Stalin hanging in the streets and proletarian battalions parading with arrogant, unanimous discipline, but tangible progress, the methodical, gradual development of technical inventions, everything that to him had seemed earthbound and undeniable, far from the verbose nonsense of visionaries, what he'd discussed so often with Negrín — good nutrition, daily milk in schools to strengthen the bones of poor children, spacious, airy housing, and health education so women would not be encumbered by unwanted children. No other dream had turned out to be more foolish; common sense was the most discredited of the utopias. But how was it possible not to have believed in progress, believed the present and future were the luminous country where one belonged, unlike the sad inhabitants of the past, confined to a decrepit realm he knew well because he'd spent the first part of his life there. You don't know what I remember, he told her: the Madrid of the last century, women in black shawls and men with beards and large mustaches and capes covering their mouths in winter, streetcars pulled by mules, and carts with creaking wooden wheels slowly climbing the slope of Calle Toledo. Progress hadn't been an illusion of brains overheated by verbal vapors: he'd witnessed the explosion of electric streetcars and automobiles, telephones and movie projectors, all the things that disconcerted or terrified his parents, who, after all, were inhabitants of the somber country of the past, his mother especially, who'd lived a few years longer, who at the end of her life didn't dare cross the street for fear of speeding vehicles, who was frightened each time the phone that had been installed in the porter's lodging rang, who didn't venture beyond the Plaza Mayor for fear of everything, even the glare of illuminated signs that made her dizzy, who never got in a car or took an elevator. Progress had the inevitability of a river's abundant current. Buildings were taller, and because of electric lights, night didn't plunge the city into darkness. Progress was more undeniable because he'd seen it with his own eyes when he traveled in Europe. What already existed in Paris or Berlin wouldn't take long to reach Madrid. He'd disbelieved the political and visionary fervor of some of his teachers in Weimar, but not the luminous reality of the architectures and forms he learned from them. Human intelligence exploded in the austere model of a house, or in one of those ordinary objects whose internal laws Professor Rossman demonstrated to them, or in the drawings as faint as dreams in appearance and yet as precise as the typographies Paul Klee designed in his classes. My children were going to have a life better than mine, just as I'd had a life better than my parents', he told her. The Republic had come thanks not to any conspiracy but to the natural im-

pulse of things, by virtue of which the monarchy was an antique as decrepit as silent movies or the mule drivers' carts swept off the Cava Baja
by the eruption of trucks and buses. But now, when night fell, Madrid
was darker and more dangerous and emptier than a medieval forest,
and human beings behaved like jackals, like primitive hordes armed
not with sticks or axes or stones but with rifles. He told her about the
sensation of emerging onto the Gran Vía from a metro station after a
bombing and finding himself lost between two narrow passes of darkness, treading on broken glass, tripping over rubble, among frightened
shadows in doorways, and with ordinary people transformed into fugitive beasts or hunters and executioners. He'd been wrong about everything, but especially about himself, his place in time. All his life thinking he belonged to the present and the future, and now beginning to
grasp that he felt so out of place because his country was the past.

He remembered something, staring fixedly into Judith's very wide eyes
where the fire was reflected: in the doorway of a church in the Salamanca district, across from the Retiro, which he passed almost every
morning, a blind man with a dog played the violin, always Schubert's
or Gounod's "Ave Maria" or the "Hymn to the Sacred Heart of Jesus," a
cap at his feet into which devout women dropped their alms, watched
over by the dog, which wagged its tail at the sound of the coins. One
day the church was burned and all that remained were the walls. The
blind man disappeared, and he thought he wouldn't see him again, but
one morning, before he reached the ruins of the church, he heard the
pious scraping of the violin: the blind man at the door of the ruined
church, as if he hadn't noticed its destruction or didn't care. Now between one "Ave Maria" and another, he attacked "The Internationale"
with the same mixture of sweetness and dissonance, or the "Himno
de Riego," or "To the Barricades." One day as he was walking down
the street, approaching the blind man on the sidewalk across from the
church, a speeding car pulled ahead of him, an old luxury car with an
open driver's seat, a silvery shine on the spokes of the tires, heads and
rifles protruding from the windows. He tried to go on, walking natu-

rally, even when the car went into reverse, the tires squealing on the paving stones, the engine forced by an inexperienced driver; the rifle barrel aimed at the spot where the blind man stood; a burst of gunfire and laughter, the dog blown to pieces, transformed into bloody tatters. With his violin in one hand and the bow in the other, the blind man trembled, understood nothing; he kneeled hesitantly and with extended fingers felt the puddle of blood. But I'm not telling you this to discourage you, he told her. You'll do what you have to do. I'm telling you this so you'll have an idea of how things are. It was true: he didn't want to dissuade her; what excited him most about Judith at this moment was what he'd seen glowing in her that disconcerted him so much and frightened him at times when he first knew her, a beautiful woman, independent, confident, smart, like the solitary women he'd seen crossing the avenues or sitting in the cafés of Berlin in their short skirts and high heels, laughing out loud, smoking, removing a shred of tobacco from their red-painted lips. The strong will that separates her from him is what makes him love her more. Judith speaks now, and for the first time she smiles.

"I told my mother about you, in the hospital, a few days before she died. There was no way to deceive my mother. When I was writing less and my letters had a different tone, she knew that something was going on. Your letters were travel guides, she said. But this time she didn't want to ask, didn't want to give any sign of being concerned about me, afraid that any kind of censure would make me behave more foolishly. I talked to her about you, I even brought a photograph of you. I was showing it to her as if I'd just become engaged, as if you'd given me a ring. She put on her glasses to see you better. *I'm glad to tell you this one is far more handsome than your former husband. He looks like a true gentleman to me,* she said, and I felt proud and was annoyed with myself and turned red when she took off her glasses and asked what I knew she was going to ask, what she had guessed from the moment she saw the photo, or long before that, when my letters to her became infrequent. *Is he married?* But instead of scolding me when I told her yes, she moved her head and began to laugh but couldn't; a cough came out instead, and she choked, so small in her nightdress, like a bird, just skin and bones, and her hands that had been so pretty and that she was so proud of as dry as a corpse's. What's the word in Spanish? Like *sarmientos,* like shoots on a vine. But it was clear she liked you, and I thought you would've liked her. *A good man is hard to find,* she said, and I was amazed she hadn't been angry with me. *A good man is hard to find but it can get even harder once you've found him.* She asked me where you were, whether you planned to join me in America or was I thinking about going back to Spain, in spite of what the papers and the radio said was happening there. I'd been so afraid she'd find out about your existence, and now she only regretted not being able to meet you. So much fear and remorse for nothing."

He goes to the kitchen for a glass of water and to leave the tray with the remains of Judith's supper. When he returns to the library, he doesn't see her. Her shoes and socks are in the same place, in front of the fireplace, but the suitcase she'd put by the door is no longer there. A candle burning weakly on the table, wax dripping down the candlestick. The flame inside the oil lamp is a dull blue tongue. The music still plays on the radio, but is more distant, with whistles of interference. If Judith is upstairs now, she's barefoot and he won't hear her footsteps. He turns off the radio and hears the wind in the trees, and a short while later the gush of water filling a bathtub. Now he's reached the second floor, and since he no longer hears the sound of water, he's guided only by the line of light under a door at the end of the hall where his room is. His right hand trembles slightly as he feels his way along the walls. His fingertips are cold. He swallows a great deal of saliva, and a moment later his mouth is dry again, his tongue as rough as his lips. Each time he pushes a door, he's afraid he'll find it locked. He goes into the bedroom and sees Judith's suitcase open on the floor, next to the night table, where a lamp is lit beneath a corolla of blue glass. Behind the bathroom door he hears the sound of a body moving in water. He'll probably find it locked if he pushes it. He'll try to turn the porcelain handle and it won't move. The door is only half closed; he pushes it and hot steam comes out. With her wet hair lying straight back, Judith's forehead is larger and the shape of her face changed. He sees her body submerged in water and foam but doesn't dare lower his eyes. He sees her shoulders jutting out, her knees shiny and together. Her clothes are on the damp tile floor. "Hand me the towel," says Judith, and he looks around and doesn't understand. "It's behind you, hanging on the door."

He has left the bathroom without closing the door all the way and is sitting on the bed, his back to the window where the shadows of the trees oscillate, and in the distance a train's straight line of lights becomes visible. He's heard her sink all the way into the water, emerge again, the foam perhaps spilling out of the tub, her eyes closed, her body brilliant when she stands, feeling for a towel. Then the rub of thick cloth against her reddened skin. He sees what he hears, his eyes fixed on the bathroom door where Judith will appear at any moment. He's still wearing his jacket and tie. From an iron radiator with curved feet comes heat, but the cold he had felt before only in his fingertips has spread to his hands. He shivers. If he tried to stand up, he'd feel vertigo, be afraid of vanishing, of waking. No matter how much he tries to take a deep breath, the air doesn't fill his lungs. He hears a knock against the glass shelf, the porcelain sink. Judith has been combing her hair and brushing her teeth. A faucet stops running. But no sound of the door opening. He looks up and Judith is in front of him, her shoulders bare, the towel knotted under her armpits. *Long time no see:* how long has it been since he's heard that expression, which she'd say ironically and sweetly every time they were naked in front of each other. He makes an awkward effort to stand, but she dissuades him with another familiar gesture. She kneels in front of him and begins to untie his shoelaces. She removes a shoe, and when she lets it drop it bounces on the wooden floor. In the light of the lamp he sees her solid, lightly freckled shoulders, her face leaning forward, her collarbone, her breasts encircled by the towel.

She removes the other shoe, letting it drop, and then his socks. She caresses his foot between her hands, and as she does so the towel loosens. Her slim body emerges and she doesn't attempt to cover herself. She looks up, searching for his eyes, and holding his foot between both hands, she presses the broad, rough sole against her breasts. As much as the touch of her flesh, the intimacy of this act, no longer a figment of memory, moves him. She stands, he is about to say something, but she covers his lips with her index finger. We've talked enough. Everything is the same as before and much better than in memory. He tries to take off his clothes, but she doesn't let him. She arouses him and at the same time controls his urgency. *There's time, plenty of it. We're not in a hurry, not anymore.* Aloud she recalls: *Time on our hands.* Her hands tousle his hair, loosen his tie, pull it off, unbutton his shirt down to his belt. A train passes with a long, distant whistle, and he wonders how long ago he entered the house, returning from that dinner lost now in time, his intoxication and dizziness in Stevens's car and the rain lashing the roof and windshield; how long since he heard the knocking and walked to the door. *Time on our hands:* his hands hold her breasts still damp from the bath, and Judith's hands caress his face as if to recognize it, feeling the hard stubble of his beard. But now he's not afraid and not dizzy and his hands aren't cold. His heartbeats are just as strong but not rushed. She must be aware of them when she kisses his chest, pressing her lips softly. Judith pulls the blanket and lies down, the towel on the floor with his clothes and shoes, and remains motionless, covered up to her chin. He lies down on his side next to her, not completely eluding embarrassment at his own nakedness, and a moment before embracing her can't remember or predict the exact sensation of her body, revealed simultaneously from the taste of her mouth to the softness of her abdomen and hips and knees and heels and the tips of her toes, from the hardness of a nipple to the scant, somewhat coarse hair on her pubis, coarse in contrast to her skin. He raises the blanket to see her in the light of the lamp. Judith's knees and feet are cold, her eyes closed, her lips parted and sensuous, with a taste as singular as her eyes or her voice. Still awkward, he takes her in his arms, and after a few minutes she's stopped shivering but continues to press against him, entwined in his legs. When his hand goes down to her stomach, she brings her thighs together and holds his wrist. There's no hurry, she says in his ear, my whole body is here for you to caress.

37

I N THE DARK, JUDITH'S voice spoke his name so close to his ear
he felt the brush of her breath and lips. But he was half asleep and
didn't really understand what the voice was saying: the three syllables of a declaration of love in Spanish or English or only the three of
his name, pronounced like the key to a secret, with an inflection that
makes the vowels slightly different, less rounded than in Spanish, with
a short pause between them, each demanding a different position of the
tongue and lips. For a moment the voice, both a call and a caress, has
been the only thing that existed in the dark; he doesn't know whether
it's in his wakefulness or his sleep, on one side or the other of waking,
or when, or where. Around him night is an expanse of blackness with
no shores or visual or auditory points of reference, just the voice in his
ear pronouncing the name or the phrase with three syllables stressed
the same in Spanish and in English. Perhaps he's just fallen asleep and
has dreamed with sweet exactitude the same thing that was happening
to him. His consciousness and his sensations — the delicious fatigue,
the naked body clinging to his, the damp skin — are as delicate a part
of this darkness as the sound of the voice, forming and dissolving, slow
undulations in the air, stripped of volume, as much a part of nature
as the sound of rain and wind in the woods or the nearby squeak of a
bat. The clothes on the floor, the open suitcases, the wallet in a pocket
of his raincoat, the sketchbook, the pages of drawings left on the table

by the window, the passport, restaurant receipts, hotel bills with dates and stamps and handwritten columns of numbers, the postcard for his children he forgot to mail in Pennsylvania Station because he thought he'd miss the train and still doesn't remember, though he'll be surprised to find it tomorrow when he feels in his jacket pockets, looking for a pencil. He's shed everything temporarily in this suspension of time that isn't going to last more than a few minutes, absolved of the past as well as the future, like a swimmer floating on his back in a lake, in the deepest part of a night without lights, holding Judith, who's called him by name to find out if he's awake or asleep, or simply to confirm their presence, his and her own, the name that is an invocation and a recognition, an incantation, air coming out of her mouth and floating and dissolving in the dark, both names, written by hand on an envelope, Ignacio Abel, Judith Biely, typed in the blank space above the dotted line on an official document, on a carbon copy, the letters gradually fading with the passage of the years, as this night in late October of 1936 remains in an increasingly distant past. But it grew dark hours ago — the light faded this evening and he continued to draw beside the great pit filled with underbrush and fallen leaves on whose walls the vertical striations of the steam shovel were visible — and though his eyes are now wide open he detects no sign of the inhospitable dawn, and what's happened and is happening to him tonight has a simultaneous quality of memory and dream. Judith's lips that have just curved to say his name now brush against his neck, and the hand that had grasped his now guides it along her torso, squeezing it lightly just as she parts her thighs, her index finger on his middle finger, the tip wet now and entering very carefully, as cautiously as her other hand searches for him, recognizes, almost squeezing, demanding again, reviving him in spite of his exhaustion with an intensity close to physical pain; again the two of them pressing together, ecstatic, Judith wide open and embracing him with her legs and digging her heels into his back as if she could receive him even deeper, covering with a hand the open mouth that moans above her face, saying things into his ear, words in Spanish and in English they taught each other and only now say into the other's

633

ear, Judith's body shining with sweat in the dark as his shadow grows gigantic over her, his breathing violent in his nostrils, the rasping of a fallen animal, then collapses beside her, not all at once but slowly, tumbling, swooning, and kissing her eyelids, her temples, her cheeks, her lips.

He'll fall asleep, and when he wakes with the sensation of emerging from a very deep sleep — and with a brief shock of cold and alarm — it will already have begun very faintly to grow light and Judith won't be beside him in bed. He'll want to know the time, but last night, when Judith undressed him, she also took off his watch, and now it must be down among the clothes on the floor, probably stopped. He'll notice his aching bones, his muscles without strength, the chilled odor of their bodies strong in the air, on the sheets. He'll be afraid that Judith has left while he slept and he'll listen, the silence of the house increasing his alarm, the rain as steady on waking as when it filtered into his sleep or they heard it in the background last night as they talked, the unceasing American rain that feeds the oceanic breadth of these rivers and makes these forests of trees grow like cathedrals. Because of that first gray light weakened by a mist that floats above the treetops, the night that remains in the hollows of the room will still be the previous night. He'll get out of bed and go to the window, afraid Judith's car won't be in front of the house. On the fogged glass, isolated drops trace twisting paths. But he'll confirm that the car is still there, black and compact, shiny in the rain. Then, still standing naked by the window, touching the cold glass made more opaque by his warm breath, he'll hear like a confirmation that Judith hasn't left, a sound of plates and cups in the kitchen, and smell the aroma of coffee and toasted bread. Waking up beside Judith and sharing breakfast are gifts he's known very few times, a domestic expanse of love he tasted only during those four days in the house by the ocean, the anguished eve of their return to Madrid, to the heat and rage of the beginning of summer, to the discovery of the open drawer and photographs and letters thrown to the floor in his study and the ringing of the phone. Before dressing and going down to the kitchen, he'll wash his face before the mirror in the bathroom where Judith showered this morning without waking him. He ought to shave: last night she passed her hands over his rough face and told him to be careful not to scratch her. But he'll only run his fingers through his hair and go down, still unsure he'll find her, and when he sees her in the kitchen, Judith will turn toward him smiling, already dressed for her trip, with a rested, serene expression and full of energy though she won't have slept at all. He'll remember to respect the condition she imposed last night for staying: not to ask her not to leave. He'll have seen her packed suitcase in the foyer beside the door. He'll think, as Judith sets out the plates for breakfast and the cups of coffee and divides the toast and scrambled eggs, that he has needed each of the days he has known her and all the time of their separation and the fear of never seeing her again and the certainty that now she's about to leave without his being able to stop her, to appreciate the truth of this simple moment. Everything will have been a meticulous apprenticeship that began for him not when Moreno Villa introduced them at the Residence a year ago but a little earlier, the day he saw her from the back as she sat at the piano and then turned toward him, showing him her profile for a moment. As patiently as she'd repeated for him intimate words and turns of phrase in English, Judith had taught him how he had to kiss her on the mouth or caress her, holding his hand, pressing on his fingers, restraining his wrists, showing him the necessary precision for each caress, the rhythms of her desire. But she'd also taught him to converse passionately and to notice things with the esthetic intention, both premeditated and intuitive, that she brought to the way she dressed, chose shoes, a hat, a flower for a dress, and to the way she arranged the table now for breakfast, the plates and cups symmetrical, the knife, the fork, the coffee spoon, the pots of marmalade she found in the cupboards. Always fast and at the same time conscientious. Unhurriedly, she recalled her days in Madrid, her love for Spanish sayings. About to separate and not knowing whether they'll meet again, they'll resist the temptation to say definitive things, to show grief as minute by minute the line in time approaches, the irredeemable frontier of their parting.

Their confessions will have remained in the sealed chamber of the previous night, in the wakeful light of the fire, when they still didn't dare touch each other, not even take a step or stretch out a hand so that each would stay within the physical space of solitude that surrounded the other. Now, as they have breakfast, they'll exchange pleasantries, not wanting to reduce with words the memory of what happened to them in the bedroom in complete darkness where gradually the window's rectangle of attenuated luminescence grew more precise, barely letting them see each other, conjured up in shadow as in silence, repeating each other's name. They'll ask each other how they've slept, ask for the sugar or milk, offer a little more coffee. He'll want to know how long it will take her to drive to New York and what time the ship sails and to which French port and in how many days the voyage will end. Judith will tell him that while he slept she's looked at his sketches for the library, the drawings he did yesterday afternoon on the slope overlooking the river. He'll tell her the building has to be visible from a distance but a surprise when entering its periphery: it must be seen from the river or from a passing train, but someone walking toward it will lose sight of it as he advances along a road through the trees, not only in summer when the trees are thick with leaves but in winter as well, because its exterior walls will be made of the local stone, whose color is between rusted iron and bronze, a tonality similar to bare trunks and the trunks covered with lichen. If anyone hears them, if anyone passing along the road sees them through the kitchen window, he'll think they were up early to enjoy peacefully a shared breakfast, that a long day of work and a tired, contented return home at nightfall awaits them, that they must have had many days like the one just beginning in this house or in another, accustomed to a passion that time and experience will have tempered to comradeship but that continues to join them in an intimate sexual fever they don't display before the eyes of anyone but that's revealed in their every gesture. Knowing each other so well, there's no part of the body of one that the other hasn't explored and enjoyed, no appetite they can't guess instantly; gradually noticing as the day brightens and the minutes pass that though they don't want it

636

to, their separation weighs on them, as if the ground beneath their feet is shrinking or becoming more fragile, as if gravity were becoming more emphatic and it was difficult for them to raise the hand that holds a fork, bring the cup to their lips, then take the few steps on the brittle floor, *walking on thin ice,* toward the foyer, toward the solid wooden door. With her back to him at the large kitchen window, facing a neglected, shaded garden where shreds of fog are slowly lifting, Judith will watch the progress of the light revealing muffled colors, fallen leaves, red, yellow, and ocher, whirled around by the storm at the beginning of the night and shining now in the rain, wooden eaves rotted by the damp, dripping branches, corners of gleaming ferns, a toolshed, its roof caving in, a low wall covered by the wine-colored leaves of a Virginia creeper. Ignacio Abel will embrace her from behind and she'll shudder at his touch because she hasn't heard him approach. He'll kiss the back of her neck, bury his face in her hair, touch her lips, but he won't ask her to stay, not even a few hours more, or to write to him when she reaches Spain, or long before that. If only it's all over before she arrives, no matter who wins, he'll think, ashamed of himself, a venal lover who'd accept any price as long as Judith's in no danger and returns definitively settled, ready to stay in a place he knows she won't move away from, where she has work she likes that gives her enough time to discover what she was seeking when she left for Europe almost three years ago, the shape of her destiny, what she felt as imminent, about to happen when she sat in front of the typewriter, and then slipped out of her hands. He hopes the French gendarmes stop her when she tries to cross the border, and deport her as they have so many others, fulfilling the democratic watchword that the Spaniards have to be left alone to go on killing one another until they're sick and tired of their own blood, spilled with the help of the centurions of Mussolini and Hitler, German incendiary bombs and Italian machine guns that have already annihilated so successfully the people of Abyssinia. He'll attempt to drive away those negative thoughts, more disloyal because, while he harbors the hope that Judith won't accomplish her purpose of arriving in Spain and throwing herself into a war she can't imagine, he'll embrace her and delay releasing her when she wants to break free. Even if she doesn't come back to me, even if in New York or on the ship or on the clandestine trek through France she meets the other, younger man I've always been afraid will take her away from me. Judith will move his hands away from her waist, saying she really does have to leave, looking at her watch with a spontaneity that suddenly wounds him, as if she were leaving only to run an errand or spend the day in New York and return at nightfall. In the foyer she'll pick up the suitcase and he'll be the one who makes the effort to unbolt the lock. When she goes to the car the grass will wet her shoes, though it'll have been a while since it stopped raining. Now she will leave. Though she hasn't climbed into the car yet or started the engine, Ignacio Abel's already living in the country of daylight and obligations where Judith is not and where he is probably going to spend the rest of his life. I see the silent scene so clearly, the gray, damp start of the morning, Ignacio Abel — unshaven, in his white shirt, wearing shoes without socks — standing on the porch, dwarfed by the height of the columns, and Judith placing the suitcase in the back seat, not turning toward him, aware of his gaze, then opening the door on the driver's side as if ready to get in and drive away. But she closes it, like someone who realizes at the last moment that she's forgotten something, turns to him, and climbs the steps to the entrance. She'll take his face in her hands that are cold and give him a long kiss, putting her tongue in his mouth, greedily searching for his. He puts out his hand but doesn't touch her. If he did he wouldn't be able to avoid the instinctive gesture of holding on to her. He'll see the car drive away on the road through the woods. He'll notice the deep, damp cold that comes up from the earth but will lack the courage to enter the house and face the rooms made gigantic by the loneliness and strangeness that will envelop him as he closes the door, bringing the avalanche of obligations, the normality it will be so difficult for him to become accustomed to, though gradually he'll be drawn in by it, subjected to its charm, used to its daily doses of delay, expectation, and routine, one among so many displaced professors from Europe, speaking English with a heavy accent, timid and rather stiff, excessively ceremonious, eager to please, to gain a certain confidence that compensates for what they've lost, dressing with a formality impervious to the easy clothing of America, waiting for letters from relatives scattered around the world or disappeared without a trace, beyond the reach of any inquiry.

But that moment hasn't arrived yet, it belongs to a time that doesn't yet exist, the future of a few hours away. In the dark where Judith has brought her lips to his ear to whisper the syllables of his name, Ignacio Abel can't estimate the time, how long before the night ends. There are no pendulum clocks in the house, and no matter how attentive he is, he doesn't hear church bells. He dreamed about them in the unusual silence of the ship's cabin, and what he heard was the bell of a buoy. When he was a child he'd have sleepless nights, and at each hour he'd hear the metal of different bells in the churches of Madrid, and knew dawn was approaching when he heard on the paving stones the echoing hooves of the horses and mules on Calle Toledo, pulling carts loaded with produce. Under the blankets in his room, so small he could touch the cold stone ceiling with his hand, he'd hear his father, who got up long before dawn to go to construction sites. Wrapped in his cape, his cap pulled down over his face, a cigarette in his mouth, happy his son could stay in bed until daybreak, preparing his books and notebooks before leaving for school, dressed and combed like a rich man's son, his boy who wouldn't have to work as hard as he did or live when he was an adult in the unhealthy rooms of a porter's lodging. Miguel, when he was little, was frightened of the dark. So frightened he continued to wet the bed until he was six or seven years old, when he would stretch out his hand looking for Lita's and grasp it as he did in the first days of his life. His fever would shoot up, his scant hair glued to his forehead, and his chest, weak and convulsive, as agitated as a bird's, his ribs visible beneath his helpless flesh. How far away everything was, and how near. When Ignacio was a boy, he was afraid to go down to the cellar with the low vaulted ceiling in his apartment building on Calle Toledo. He'd open the door and from the first stone step begin the descent into a dense, damp darkness where he could hear the rats' scratching. On this night the building residents have gone down to take shelter in the cellar he hasn't visited for more than thirty years, and when the bombs fell close by, the floor and walls would reverberate and the dirty bulb hanging from the ceiling, its light reduced to the red glow of the filament, would tremble like a candle and go out, dissolving into darkness the silhouettes huddled together, whispering, moaning. The night is a bottomless well where everything seems lost and everything continues to live and endure, at least for a certain time, as long as the memory remains clear and the mind lucid in the person lying with eyes open, attentive to the sounds taking shape in what seemed to be silence, trying to guess by the breathing if the other person's still awake or has been carried away by the somnolence of satisfied desire. In the hospital room, beside her mother's bed, Judith would doze in spite of the uncomfortable chair, and at the very moment she fell asleep she would wake with a start, hearing slurred speech or a moan caused by the gradual tapering off of the effect of morphine, or worse, alarmed by the silence, missing her mother's ragged breathing, fearing she'd died alone while Judith was sleeping, that her mother had called or moaned and she hadn't awakened. The dead haven't yet left the house where they lived, and their slow disappearance into the dark has already begun; they're already strangers. Ignacio Abel approached the open coffin his father lay in, and when he looked he no longer knew him. In the light of the candles, his father's face was yellow and swollen, as if his mouth and nose had been lightly flattened under glass; the hands that emerged from the cuffs of his shirt and were crossed on his chest were those of another man: bloodless, an old man's hands, the nails prominent and the fingers curved and thin, the opposite of his father's hands, broad, blunt, solid, dark, his father who hasn't appeared in his dreams for many years, so distant, like the gas lamps that lit Calle Toledo and like the Madrid Ignacio Abel doesn't want to think about now and Judith won't recognize when she returns and finds no lights, all of Madrid in darkness and silence like the bottom of the sea, perhaps crossed by headlights and flashlights that pierce the thick blackness like divers' lamps. In the New York night, neon signs floated in the dark, pink or yellow or blue silhouettes of steaming cups of coffee, or spirals of cigarette smoke, or bubbles ascending from glasses of champagne. Between sleep and consciousness images dissolve without becoming completely formed, and the border between memory and imagination is as fluid as the one that joins and separates bodies wrapped in an embrace composed equally of weariness and desire. Judith's voice that said his name so clearly in his ear might also have sounded in a half-sleep or a dream, at the exact moment Ignacio Abel has fallen asleep, as if floating in the serene immobility of time. It's Judith who remains awake, watching over him, the man who's become more attentive and more fragile, who was almost murdered without her knowing it. I see her in profile, more clearly as dawn breaks, sitting against the back of the bed, restless now, fearful, anxious, impatient, resolved, as clearheaded as if she'd never feel the need to sleep, listening to the freight trains, the masculine breathing beside her, the wind in the trees, the call of a bird, discovering the first, still uncertain signs of dawn, the first gray light of the first day of her journey, of a tomorrow she can't make out and I can't imagine, her future unknown and lost in the great night of time.